The Legend of the First Super Speedway

The Battle for the Soul of American Auto Racing

By Mark G. Dill

ISBN: 978-1-09833-516-8

Front cover image by Daiv Barrios
Interior book design by Esther Rodriguez Dill

Printed and bound in the United States of America
First edition November 2020

Published by Bookbaby.com

Visit www.firstsuperspeedway.com

This book is based on actual events.

Dedication

This book is dedicated to my wife, Esther Rodriguez Dill. I needed the emotional support and encouragement she provided to keep me believing *The Legend of the First Superspeedway* is an important story that must be told.

Contents

Foreword by Willy T. Ribbs

When Mark Dill asked me to write the foreword to his book, *The Legend of the First Super Speedway,* I agreed without giving it a second thought. I've known Mark for several years now, and we have become tight friends. We share a lot of values and interests, not the least of which is the sport of auto racing and especially the Indianapolis 500, where I became the first black driver to qualify in 1991 and then again in 1993. That was racing history that maybe even I did not fully appreciate until the release of "UPPITY," the 2020 Netflix documentary that chronicles my career.

I think that experience piqued my curiosity about the broader context of the history of my sport, dating back to its early days. As my friendship with Mark grew, I came to realize not only his knowledge of early days racing but his passion for the topic as well. His attention to detail and concern for accuracy is the same as mine was in winning races and championships. That's professionalism.

I say with total confidence that Mark is the perfect person to tell this previously untold tale. He brings to the surface the true-life characters that created American auto racing. There's no sugar coating on this one. What you'll find is not only an entertaining and revealing story of how American racing was born but the larger, sometimes ugly context that admits but does not dwell on racism and gender roles in early 20th Century America. The story is cast in reality that never apologizes for the faults and foibles of the men who made what seemed impossible happen. They shaped both a sport and so much of the technology we take for granted today.

Introduction By Al Unser, Jr.

Coming from the Unser family, I knew from the earliest days of my life that I wanted to be a race car driver. Most importantly, my goal was to get into the Indianapolis 500. While I am grateful for every opportunity that was ever provided to me, winning at Milwaukee or Michigan or any of the well-known tracks that were on the Indy circuit was not what fueled my passion. My victories at places like Daytona, Long Beach, and in IROC are treasured memories. Still, the place that ignited the fire in my belly was the Indianapolis Motor Speedway and the Indianapolis 500 in particular.

Several years ago, I was asked to drive Wilbur Shaw's famous Boyle Maserati that he raced to victory in the 1939 and 1940 Indianapolis 500s in some exhibition laps at the Speedway. When I climbed out of the car afterward, some of the media asked me about my impressions. It was simple. I said, "That was when men were men."

The Legend of the First Super Speedway dates back to an even earlier time to the first decade of the twentieth century and the dawn of American auto racing. Still, I think of my experience with the Boyle Maserati because it drove home to me how hard and dangerous it must have been for those men (only with rare exceptions were there women racing then) to push equipment with such imprecise handling to the limit.

These were machines drivers had to physically wrestle with for car control. You were so exposed, and there was no safety gear, including helmets in those early days. Tires were primitive by today's standards, with rubber that frequently blew out with no warning. They were affixed to wheels of artillery-grade wood. Racing is and always will be a risky business, but those drivers were a different breed. Consider the Marmon Wasp in the Indianapolis Speedway Museum – forget seat belts, roll hoops, fuel bladders, or Nomex.

This book entertainingly chronicles those early days. The story is told from the point of view of two of racing's most influential pioneers, Barney Oldfield and Carl Fisher. Those men were indispensable in creating the sport we love today. Mark Dill's narrative doesn't allow them to come off as cartoon characters. They were rugged and determined men, with a high tolerance of risk, and would be anything but politically correct in today's society. Historians and aficionados of the Indianapolis 500 will recognize their names, but this book reveals their complex personalities – the good and the less savory.

Like my opening comments here, this is a journey to the Indianapolis Motor Speedway, from the dirt horse tracks, the Vanderbilt Cup, and the track's crazy and deadly first races. It takes you to the creation of the Brickyard and how that beautiful facility I love defined American auto racing. When I won my first of two Indy 500s in 1992 and Jack Arute asked me how I felt in the victory circle, I said, "You just don't know what Indy means." *The Legend of the First Super Speedway* captures the essence of what Indy means from a unique angle and in a creative fashion.

Preface by Tony Parella

I have relied on Mark Dill as a highly-skilled and talented communication professional since we met after I purchased the Sportscar Vintage Racing Association (SVRA) in 2012. His knowledge of the history of auto racing has been invaluable to me in creating meaningful events for my racing series – and marketing them. I know he has been laboring away on the book you are about to read since well before we met, and that was eight years ago as I write these words.

Admittedly, as time passed, I had my doubts about whether he would get to where he is now with a thoroughly enjoyable and entertaining book. At the same time, I was aware of his commitment to his family, his physical fitness, and, frankly, assisting me to succeed as SVRA President and CEO. Squeezing in the time to craft what I see as a massively informative history book that reads as an engaging novel is a wonderful lifetime accomplishment.

As Mark neared the point of completing his draft manuscript, he was quite excited to talk to me because he was proud of his work – and he should be. He explained that what he has pulled together is best described as a fact-based novel and that the primary characters were historical figures. Something he said really struck me.

"Tony, I've read so much about these guys I really feel I can get into their heads."

That rang so true to me from my personal experience with Mark in crafting SVRA news releases and other public statements. I found he has an uncanny ability to extract thoughts from my head and capture them in text with my authentic voice. In fact, I have told him several times that he expresses what I am thinking even better than I can myself. I have absolute confidence that if his two main characters, Barney Oldfield and Carl Fisher, could sit with us today, they would say much the same thing. I am confident what you will read is as if Mark channeled their spirits. Maybe he did.

The Legend of the First Super Speedway touches my heart in that Fisher and Oldfield were entrepreneurs, and that is how I have led my life. Like me, they were built to carve their own way. This is the story of how they took a lot of craziness and imperfection to create something amazing from scratch. It is no exaggeration to say our world would not be the same today but for their contributions. This is a remarkable story.

Chapter 1 – "Like the Battle of Santiago"

(Detroit, Thursday, October 23, 1902)

Thunderous blasts echoed off the walls of the brick warehouses along the docks of the Detroit River. Barney Oldfield reveled in the sensation of power of his giant engine as explosions from its cylinders rattled the windows in the buildings that towered as much as five stories over him.

Oldfield's imagination failed him as he scanned the startled faces of workers behind the vibrating glass, and considered the miserable toil disrupted in the rooms hidden from daylight. To his left, a horse pulling a loading cart along the wharf cried and kicked at the air. Restraining the smile at the corner of his mouth, Oldfield flicked the throttle linkage with his grime-coated hand to make the animal jump again.

Warm oil droplets flecked off valve rockers to pelt Oldfield's big, round face and cling to two days growth of beard as he adjusted fuel flow through the mixer bowl. Shouting faces and shaking fists loomed steadily larger as he peered over the top of the big, cast-iron block. Only rich men could afford automobiles, and he hoped the angry dockworkers were envious.

The blood flow at Oldfield's right bicep was pinched to a stop by the tourniquet grip of a beefy hand reaching out from a man that stormed at him from behind. His curled mustache was so stiff with wax Oldfield wanted to fill both his hands with each side and yank the face. The fat man's torso grounded him like a fence post, and when he jerked, Oldfield had to shuffle his feet to avoid falling. Unlike most men, this fat one was plenty tall enough to lock eyes with him.

"Shut it down! Shut it down!"

Oldfield wanted to clobber the man's face. Nobody orders Barney Oldfield around.

He scanned the countless figures about him and then nodded at his partner, Spider Huff, who obediently shut the engine off. The clamping pressure on Oldfield's arm relaxed.

"Damnation, boy! What the hell are you doing? This contraption sounds like the Battle of Santiago! You've spooked every horse for miles. You ain't got the sense God gave a goose."

His temples pulsating, Oldfield fought an impulse to hit the man, to punch his superior tone back into his face. Where was the response that would protect his pride?

"Listen, old man. I do what I do. I got a right to make my way in the world."

"Keel-haul the fucker," came an anonymous shout, the originator lost in a blur of faces. Somewhere deep in Oldfield's gut, a jolt set his jaw and clenched his fists as he braced himself more in fear than rage. Deceived by the boxer in him, he had misjudged impossible situations and taken beatings in the past. Taunting, sour faces of a dozen or so men surrounded him. Mercifully, the big, waxy mustache shifted its position on the fat face to accommodate a smile.

"Aw, Hell, boy, you better come with me. There ain't no advantage I can see from you losing your teeth. You, other men, get on back to whatever you do."

With an undercurrent of indistinguishable groans, the group melted away. Some men pointed at the car, some at Oldfield. They talked, or worse, laughed, as they walked back to loading docks. The fat man looked to the other side of the car at skinny Spider Huff, whose head was consumed by a gray felt cap and a wild mustache that obfuscated his mouth and reminded Oldfield of the hand brush he used to clean his workbench.

"That your partner?"

Oldfield glanced over his shoulder to the always-quiet Spider.

"Yeah. Good man. Hell of a mechanic."

The wooden cart not two hundred feet from the car grew larger as Oldfield followed the fat man. He introduced himself as "Red Hot" John, the owner of the lunch wagon some workers relied on for all their meals. A large glass jar packed with hardboiled eggs in green-tinted pickle juice made clear John's intentions to feed the working men in Detroit until they stopped coming. Beside the cart were a grill and a tray of sausages.

"Shit," John muttered, looking down at his dirty leather boots. He scraped his left sole against the street gravel to clear off horse manure.

"You want a red hot?"

"No money."

"That ain't no never mind. I'll make you one, and one for your friend, too. You just tell me about that horseless carriage. That's the funniest looking one I've ever seen. Bigger than all get out."

Oldfield studied John as he pivoted more like a ballerina than a fat man. With the quick precision of a surgeon, he sliced a couple of small loaves of bread with a knife, then stabbed two red sausages and inserted them. Like a machine stamping metal, it was fluid motion. The gravel street crunching under his filthy boots, he stepped around the side of his cart. In greasy hands that had tiny black lines under each fingernail, he extended the food.

Oldfield grabbed the meal from John's hands, and hungrily took big bites of sausage that steamed in the morning air. While Oldfield ate, John served several other young men. He didn't breathe as he clamped down on the sandwich before chewing the previous bite. Quiet Spider smacked his lips as crumbs lodged in his mustache.

"Jesus Christ! You boys eat in the last week or so?"

Like a rodent, Oldfield shifted a wad of wet bread and chewed sausage to the inside of his cheek. Caught forgetting himself, he felt naked. He never liked people seeing him, really seeing him. A weak smile stretched his face.

"So, what the hell kind of horseless carriage is that, anyway? It looks like it ought to be on rails."

"It's a race car. Just came over the lake from Cleveland. We're taking her over to Grosse Point for the meet. I'm going to whip Alexander Winton."

"Winton, huh? How old are you, boy?"

Oldfield ran his fingers through his thick brown hair now matted down with machine oil.

"Twenty-four."

"Well, shit-fire, you ought to be old enough to know better. Son, do you know who Alexander Winton is?"

"Does he know who Barney Oldfield is?"

"That's easy. Of course, he doesn't. You're a nobody."

"Look, mister, maybe we ought to just start hitting each other right now, because it seems like it was meant to be, don't it?"

John stared down at his grill and flipped a couple of sausages. He smiled and shook his head.

"Alexander Winton is the most famous automobile man in America. I know that, and I don't give a crap about those races. Everybody knows Winton has those Bullet cars. They are fast as blazes, and the newspapers call him the world champion. What makes some farm hand like you think he can whip a millionaire with nothing but a wagon with an engine on it?"

Oldfield's eyes traced the Ashwood frame of his blazing red race car, with matching metal spoke wheels, four inches wide, and nearly three feet in diameter.

"That motor is twice as big as Winton's. You're looking at seventy horsepower right there."

John paused, and Oldfield marveled at how stupid he looked as his mouth unconsciously dropped open, and the point of his first chin disappeared into the fatty layer of his second. The obese man studied the red-painted wood car.

"Well, son, you damn sure have all the gumption it takes. Now how are you going to get that crate out to the horse track?"

"I was trying to drive it when you got all riled up."

"You need to get a horse."

"Now, how am I going to get a horse when I told you I couldn't even buy a red hot?"

"See that nag over there?"

A dumb-looking brown mare, with its tongue hanging out and a sagging spine, cast a blank stare at the telegraph pole it was roped to.

"That's my horse. You hitch her to your machine and have her pull you out to East Jefferson Highway and then turn her loose. She knows the way back. Your contraption won't bother anybody out there."

Oldfield cocked his head, squinting more than the rising sun required.

"Why are you doing this big man?"

"Look around this wharf, son. These are my boys. Most of 'em will be working all their lives just to get by. You, you're different. Different can be good, or you might just be a loon. I'm going to be watching you. In a couple of days, all I have to do is read the papers to know if Barney Oldfield is just another tough guy shooting his mouth off, or maybe something special. And if you are a big deal like you say you are, you remember "Red Hot" John, you hear?"

Oldfield nodded. Surveying the dock, he saw a handful of men beside his car talking to Spider. His head pivoted ninety degrees to a crane lifting a crate onto a barge. Just beyond the crane, men rolled barrels along a loading ramp. Soot from the steamboats of the Detroit River wafted through the air like dirty snowflakes and a pungent confluence of rotting fish heads and horse manure mingled with the faint scent of John's lunch wagon. A breeze swirled the world into an Earthy mixture that Oldfield wished he could swallow and feel in an instant.

Chapter 2 – The Champion of the World

(Grosse Point, Michigan, Friday, October 24, 1902)

Barney Oldfield studied the man holding a revolver and wearing a straw hat with "Event Referee" in black letters spelled on it. A loud crack immediately preceded a spark at the tip of the gun barrel, and then smoke floated from the chamber to dissipate in the Michigan sun of a bright, unseasonably pleasant October afternoon. Driver J.J. Miller's tiny eight-horsepower Elmore rolled away from the start line below the judges' stand at the Grosse Point horse track.

Oldfield, with friend Tom Cooper, leaned on the white wood fence at the inside of the track. He always respected Cooper's toughness since seven years back when they raced bicycles against each other on the wood ovals.

The chattering din of thousands of voices triggered a memory of when they were first drawn together at a board velodrome in Toledo. Oldfield thought about how he and Cooper tangled handlebars on a banked turn and thudded onto the rough planks. They scooped up their bikes, hopped on again, and hustled back into the contest. When Cooper pulled in front, a spray of blood sprinkled back onto Oldfield's legs and arms. Later, Cooper showed him a pocketknife-sized sliver of wood lodged in his thigh, causing blood to stream onto his rear wheel and spray a warm scarlet rooster tail backward onto Oldfield. With cuts and tiny splinters in his legs, Oldfield figured that their blood mixed that day, and they were brothers.

Oldfield liked that kind of toughness. He loved walking into saloons with his friend because they were both tall and muscled, and people got out of their way when they wanted a seat at the bar.

And Cooper always had ideas. Not necessarily good ones - like the time he bought the rights to a gold mine in Colorado and offered to work it with Oldfield. That was the meanest summer of Oldfield's life. Hand blistering, gut-busting shoveling, and not a damn thing came of it. Cooper was always good for an adventure.

And he had something Oldfield envied. Women noticed the healthy rose color of his smooth cheeks, which were always freshly shaved. Just the right amount of tonic to hold his coal-black hair in place, Oldfield thought Cooper could pass for a Broadway actor – even though he had never been to New York.

It was even okay with Oldfield that Cooper wasn't much for fighting. He knew the compliments his friend got from women were too precious to him to risk a flat nose or missing teeth. His looks gave him confidence with the ladies, and that made him a great partner to chase skirts.

Cooper hadn't been the same man the last month or so. A couple of weeks earlier, when they were drinking, he pulled up his shirt and showed Oldfield the jagged scar from when a doctor damn near killed him carving his appendix out. He was slower to leap from his seat or jump the final three steps of stairs in the last few weeks. Oldfield knew that was why Cooper asked him to drive one of his race cars.

Cooper's latest venture was a pair of race machines he purchased from an engineer named Henry Ford. After the gold mine, Oldfield went back to racing bicycles and motor bicycles but was tired of fighting teenagers that hadn't figured out how hard the boards were.

One of Cooper's cars, the bright red "Nine-Ninety-Nine," was parked at the gate behind them. The schedule called for them to give the crowd an exhibition run with the big Ford, as soon as a ten-mile handicap event ended.

Oldfield studied a group of Winton Motor Carriage Company employees on the other side of the fence as they stood beside the famous Bullet racer. The even more famous Alexander Winton sat up top, gripping the steering wheel, and then adjusting his goggles.

Oldfield wondered what it would be like to have Winton, a distinguished man he guessed was in his forties, be his father. Appearing groomed and perfect, the millionaire presented a neatly trimmed, thick handlebar mustache to the world. Winton dressed immaculately in a white shirt, black tie, tweed suit, and matching sports cap.

The Bullet was polished and metallic and as perfect as its owner. Flat and sleek, the car reminded Oldfield of a river raft with a dining table chair sitting on top of it.

Cooper's voice brought Oldfield's mind back to their side of the fence. "That Bullet's racing engine has four in-line cylinders with just over five hundred cubic inches of displacement," Cooper said. "I know a lot about them, but I don't know that they know much about us. It's only half the size of the Nine-Ninety-Nine's engine and has about half as much horsepower. They look all fancy with that metal, but it's just a thin sheet of light armor wrapped around a wood frame like ours."

Oldfield wondered about the handicap race. Race officials gave slower cars head starts, based on the judges' discretion. Winton, the fastest, was forced to start last. Oldfield asked

Cooper if he thought Winton could win.

"Dunno. It's gonna take that little Elmore better than two minutes to do a mile, and they only give him seven minutes on Winton, so he won't have a prayer. But that Oldsmobile can get under two by a fair piece, so that's where I'd put my money."

"They look pretty sure of themselves."

"Winton? Yeah. They call him the champion of the world. A million dollars can make a man plenty sure of himself."

The gunpowder in the starter's pistol exploded again, and Oldfield, impatient for action, screamed an animal-like noise. Joe McNamara, on one of the small, spindly Oldsmobile cars, leaped forward and headed down the front stretch, thirty seconds after Miller, the first starter.

Oldfield thought the Oldsmobile looked like a contorted bicycle, its frame made of brazed metal pipe with a small, twenty-horsepower engine driving the rear wheels. Its narrow bicycle spoke wheels kicked up a puny puff of dust. Two cylindrical fuel tanks with cones at the front made the car look propelled by giant firecrackers. It just seemed too slow, and Oldfield shook his head in disgust as he expelled air from between his teeth.

One by one, cars responded to the starter's gun. The two steamers, driven by Windsor White and W.C. Bucknam, were the only two to leave the line together. On the second mile, McNamara's Oldsmobile, after closing steadily, easily slid by Miller's Elmore in the second turn. As he completed his third lap, John Maxwell, in the slightly more powerful Northern, was closing on the skeletal Olds.

Oldfield squinted and zeroed in on Winton, who tapped his fingers on his steering wheel as first the Olds, then the Elmore sped past the judges' stand. Harry Harkness, another millionaire in his Mercedes, spun his wheels briefly as he powered from the starting line.

The starter nodded at Winton, who jumped the gun by a fraction of a second. Oldfield gripped the wooden fence with both hands and stood on his toes. Finally, something exciting was going to happen.

"This ought to be good."

Oldfield carefully traced the red Bullet as it entered the corner wide, and then pinched down on the pole at the center of the turn. The red car continually picked up speed. A dust cloud steadily expanded as Winton increased the red car's momentum. Cooper pulled out his stopwatch.

Oldfield didn't need a watch to see Winton was the fastest car on the track. The millionaire quickly passed one car after another but was more than a lap down to everyone. Winton leaned to the left of his steering wheel and peered around it as he slid through the corners. At the front, safely two-and-a-half miles ahead of the Bullet, Maxwell in the tiny Northern passed McNamara in the Oldsmobile for the lead.

On the front stretch, Winton inexorably reeled in the two steamers as they ran just a few yards apart. Oldfield tapped Cooper on the shoulder and pointed. The Bullet bore down on the steam cars. Winton cut left, then right, as he split the distance between the two bulky racers.

To Oldfield, the ordinary sounds of voices transformed into one giant eerie gasp as if the thousands of people in the grandstands were struggling to fight off suffocation all at once. The vapor puffing from the steamers made the Bullet look like a red rocket poking through thin clouds.

Oldfield turned toward his friend. Cooper knew what he wanted before he could say a word.

"He's doing maybe a minute-five," Cooper reported.

Turning his attention back out to the track, Oldfield saw Winton begin to close on the leader, Maxwell. Still a lap down, Winton was running out of time. He had to make up more than a minute. Winton entered turn one wide, while Maxwell in the Northern hugged the inside fence. Winton passed him in the corner, but inexplicably, the Northern continued to go straight. Oldfield stepped up on the lower rail of the fence to try to get a clear view.

"Whoa Nellie," he shouted as the cars collided.

The Northern's right front wheel touched the Bullet's left rear, and the Northern turned violently, tipping onto two wheels. In an instant driver Maxwell was face down in the loose dirt kicked up from the wheels that churned it all day long. A wave of shrieks rolled across the grandstand. Oldfield, with the only exciting aspect of the race ruined before his eyes, shook his head.

Behind him, a man shouted, "It's a *kill!*"

Annoyed by the man's stupid comment, Oldfield watched Maxwell's head lift from the ground as if he were in a foxhole ducking for cover. Winton's Bullet skidded sideways twenty yards farther down the track. Uninjured, Maxwell ran to the outside fence as McNamara and his Oldsmobile made its way through the turn and entered the backstretch.

"No record," said Cooper. "Let's get our boat ready to sail."

"Ready?" Spider Huff shouted. Oldfield nodded and reached down to the right of the seat to flick the Nine-Ninety-Nine's spark lever to the "on" position. Spider's head bobbed up and then down and out of sight behind the huge radiator at the front of the car as he cycled the big engine's crank handle.

Skinny little Spider didn't say much, but he was smart about cars and worked harder than two men. As Spider cranked, Oldfield reached to his left and adjusted the gas flow with a thumbscrew. Spider's head disappeared and reappeared behind the massive, rectangular radiator once, twice, three times until the engine erupted in its relentless battle cannon blasts. He jumped back to release the crank handle.

Both men stopped for an instant, wary of some impending catastrophe. Spider screamed an instruction, but Oldfield couldn't make it out and didn't bother to try.

Spider pointed at the gate from the paddock to the track, which was now open. Unlike Winton's Bullet, the Nine-Ninety-Nine steered with a tiller bar, not a wheel, and Oldfield filled his left hand with one of the handles. Gripping the clutch lever with his right hand, he slipped it to engage engine and gear gradually. Tentatively, the wheels began to turn, like they were timid of what might happen if they surrendered to the engine too quickly. The beastly machine rolled forward.

Cooper stood at the paddock gate, and Oldfield caught his eyes. Part of him wanted to ask his friend to get in the car with him or just ask him one more time how close to the pole he should drive. He wondered if Cooper could see any jitters in his eyes.

Oldfield entered the track, building up speed slowly to make a flying start on the clock the next time around. Oil droplets felt like a light sprinkle of warm rain on his face and arms as they flicked off the exposed cylinder valves. The faster Oldfield went, the more the wind felt like pinpricks to his skin, and his thick brown hair blew back. Smoothly sliding through the corners, he entered the front stretch faster than he had ever driven before.

The thunder of seventy horses wanted to explode from the big iron cylinders that contained them, but he could still hear, or maybe just *feel* his heart beating his eardrums. Squeezing the tiller bar handles hard, Oldfield noticed a shakiness in his arms. *Damn, let's just get this damn thing started!*

Oldfield approached the start line running as fast as he could urge the Nine-Ninety-Nine on. The starter appeared tentative like he was in a bullfight and trying to figure where the animal might lunge next. The blurry figure unfurled a big red flag to signify the start of a timed run.

Oldfield pressed the accelerator pedal, not backing off the power nearly as much as the previous lap. Scenery melted into a stream of colors, and the outside fence rushed toward him. As he entered the first turn, the car's rear tires wanted to slide around like they could catch up with the front wheels. The nerves he felt before he got started had vanished as his eyes and his mind locked on the road.

Every muscle from Oldfield's hands to his biceps hardened like the statue of David, and his chest tightened. Familiar feelings of his bicycle-racing days flooded back into him. Instead of backing off, he let his rear wheel slide almost imperceptibly, countering that movement with the slightest adjustment of pointing the handlebar into the skid.

Oldfield's teeth clenched together like opposite sides of a vice, and he held his breath as he drifted out to the fence and began to turn the tiller bar left. Nine-Ninety-Nine responded, and turned down across the track, toward the inside fence. As the rear wheels started to slide, Oldfield cocked the tiller bar in the direction of the skid. Dirt spewed from under his tires.

Nine-Ninety-Nine slid toward the fence as Oldfield guided her out of the turn toward the front stretch. The rear wheels were no longer trying to pass the front, but even Oldfield's massive arms couldn't turn the big machine. He cringed and shifted sideways in the driver's seat as if by re-positioning his entire body, he could *will* the car to move itself a few feet further from the fence. For a second, he thought about how he could explain wrecking Nine-Ninety-Nine to Cooper. Then he closed his eyes and braced himself for the crash.

Dust swirled around the Nine-Ninety-Nine, and Oldfield could not see. Suddenly, he emerged from the cloud and thrill electrified his spine — he had *not* hit the fence! The beautiful brown carpet of the backstretch extended out before him like the path out of a burning barn!

Oldfield again took his broad approach to the second turn, skating out to the fence and nearly clipping a post. He almost laughed at the sight of seven or eight men at the edge of the track, scrambling like rats when a feed bin's door opened. He cocked the tiller bar, and dirt showered them, knocking one man's bowler off his head.

Nine-Ninety-Nine darted to the pole and continued its controlled slide, churning dirt every inch of the way. Oldfield heard roars from the grandstand as he exited the corner and brushed the fence with his right rear tire. The tiny man with the straw hat and flag looked uncertain as he ventured out on the track to signal the end of Oldfield's run. The image of the men brushing dirt off their suits flashed in his mind, and he erupted into a belly laugh so spontaneous it seemed odd even to him. It felt good. *He was in command.*

Oldfield guided the Nine-Ninety-Nine through the open gate into the infield. Cooper strode along behind it. Confident he had broken the mile-a-minute barrier Oldfield shut down the engine and sprang up from his seat.

"How'd I do? How'd I do?"

Cooper nonchalantly fished around in his pants pocket like he was searching for coins. Oldfield impatiently shifted his feet and put his arms on his hips as he watched his friend pick at the lint and wax paper that stuck to the piece of black licorice he had finally located. Cooper popped it in his mouth.

The lump of licorice bulged his left cheek as he furrowed his brow and looked thoughtful. He squinted in the bright sun, lower in the sky as the day stretched into the afternoon, and spat specks of wax paper from between his teeth.

"Do you brake?"

Oldfield shoved his goggles high on his forehead and felt them push his hair back like a cowlick. In just two laps, the oil and dust had started to coat his exposed skin. Oldfield thought about the question. Cooper worked on the car for months. Now he was asking Oldfield how he was handling the car. His friend spat out another speck of wax paper. Oldfield lifted his hands to his side and cocked his head.

"Why the hell would I brake, Tom?"

"Just curious. You did a minute six and some."

"Damn!"

Remembering Winton's minute-five mile in the handicap, Oldfield was pissed off. How could that be? He even felt angry with Cooper for telling him. He believed he was faster than any man alive.

"Barney, he was building cars and driving them when we were racing bicycles. You've run about twenty miles in your whole, damn, miserable life. What we gotta do is get ready for the Manufacturer's Challenge Cup tomorrow. That's what we gotta do."

Lots of times, Oldfield believed Cooper knew what he was thinking.

(Grosse Point, Michigan, Saturday, October 25, 1902)

Cold rain pelted the canvas draped over Nine Ninety-Nine. Oldfield and Cooper sat on old army blankets underneath the cover just behind the car's left front wheel. Spider was wrapped in two other blankets, asleep under the car. Oldfield listened to the faint taps of the tiny droplets on the opposite side of the cloth. The water ran off the edge and dripped into the wet grass at his feet. The ground grew ever moist, and he felt the cold and damp seep through his underwear. Cooper opened a can of beans, and he and Oldfield each had tablespoons, scooping the food out and munching thoughtfully.

"You know, I been watching both you and Winton," Cooper said. "I think I got something for you. When you go into the corner, try going in just a little lower, and don't dive down so close to the pole. Slide that thing sideways, right down the middle. The way I figure it, you won't come out of the corner so close to the fence. I think you could pick up some time."

"It *sounds* easy, but that big old engine winds up. Sometimes I feel like I'm just hanging on."

"I know, I know. And I have to hand it to you, Barney, you're doing a great job. I'm trying to help. Maybe even if you back off just a second, she'll be easier to handle in the corner. If you can get those turns smoother, like what Winton does, I think you got him beat."

A roar of laughter came from under a big, white tent that the Winton Motor Carriage Company had erected. The Winton Team was yelling and laughing so loud Oldfield thought they might be drinking. Just before the rain, Charlie Shanks, Winton's right-hand man, won an open ten-mile handicap in the Winton "Pup," a smaller version of the Bullet. He held off Harry Harkness and his Mercedes that started a minute and a quarter behind him. Alexander Winton had not started the race due to a faulty radiator. Shanks drove tough, passing five cars that started in front of him, including Windsor White's White Steamer.

Through the opening into the Winton tent, Oldfield saw Shanks prancing like a Russian Cossack dancer, his arms crossed as he kicked his legs high in the air. He stumbled, and there was another round of laughter. Oldfield glanced over his shoulder at Spider, asleep under the car. He jabbed Cooper's arm.

"Want to see something funny? Let's fire up the engine and see ole Spider jump."

Spider stirred and rolled over, facing his friends. "Grow up, boys. I'm tired, not stupid."

"Oh, man, Spider, you're always spoiling my fun."

The soaked canvas leaked water, but the rain soon stopped. Throughout the paddock, teams uncovered cars and prepared for the Manufacturer's Challenge Cup, a five-lap, five-mile event, with five cars entered. Winton and Shanks were in their Winton entries, White in the White steamer, Bucknam in the Geneva steamer, and Oldfield in Nine-Ninety-Nine.

Under the car at the back, Spider packed grinding compound into the crown and pinion gears that delivered power to the rear axle. On his back at the front of the car, Oldfield lubricated the crankshaft. When he looked up, he saw Henry Ford's scowling face staring down at him.

A tall man, thin but sturdy, Ford had sharp features and deep black eyes that never blinked. His bowler was a size too small, and his well-worn wool overcoat was so thick it would have suffocated him in the heat of the day before.

Oldfield remembered the story Cooper told him about how he and Ford had worked together since Henry left the Henry Ford Company in March. The Red Devil and the Arrow, two identical cars completed in August, were nothing but trouble, inexplicably stalling. In a fit of frustration, Ford told Cooper he wanted to dissolve the team. Led by industrialist Alex Malcomson, Ford had the backing of some investors and wanted to get back into passenger car manufacturing. Oldfield heard Ford ask Cooper if he had licked the engine problems.

"Sure thing. Barney figured it out. We were in Dayton, in the races Carl Fisher was promoting. We kept working with both the cars, but nothing. Then Barney figured it was fuel flow to the mixer."

Cooper laughed.

"You should have seen us, Hank. Barney cut a hole in the tank and jammed a rubber tube in there and taped it up. He got on the back of the car and started blowing up a storm. I drove, and Spider was clinging on the side, squirting oil at the feeder sites. We did a couple of exhibition laps with all three of us hanging on for dear life."

Cooper continued laughing, but Ford grimaced.

"You can't run in a race like that. Haven't you done anything to fix the mixer?"

"Yeah, yeah. C'mon, Hank, I'm not stupid!"

Oldfield heard the anger in Cooper's voice.

"We cooked up a new mixing pot with a coppersmith. She runs real good now. She's fast, Hank. Barney's been running about a minute-six."

Ford was silent. A relentless stare that withered others didn't bother Cooper.

"Relax, Hank. We won't make you look stupid. We won't mess up your business."

Ford wasn't through with his challenges.

"Oldfield? Since when did he start driving the car?"

Ford pivoted and directed his attention to Oldfield.

"You're serious about running in the Challenge Cup?"

Oldfield felt a surge through his body as his heartbeat quickened. He didn't like his abilities questioned, and that's how he felt about Ford's comment.

"I'm serious about making money. I can drive this here car faster than any man alive, and I intend to prove it. And I'm going to make as much money as I can."

Ford shook his head like he was listening to one of the patients at the insane asylum where Oldfield's father used to work.

"You're going to have to go some to run with the likes of Winton. I know; I raced him last year," Ford said. "He had me licked by better than half a mile until he broke. You shouldn't try to keep up with him."

"You watch me. I'm not afraid of Winton. I'm not afraid of anybody. Winton ought to be afraid of me."

"You're liable to be killed."

"I might as well be dead as dead broke."

Oldfield was intent on his work and studied the engine as he spoke. Averting Ford's stare, he wiped his hands on a rag. He saw Ford scrutinizing the back of the seat where the numbers "999" painted in white against black leather appeared.

"What's this Nine-Ninety-Nine business? I thought this was the Red Devil?"

"That was Carl Fisher's idea when he promoted us at Dayton. He named it after that New York locomotive that goes over a hundred miles an hour. I like it," Cooper said.

Ford shook his head in a dismissive, disgusted manner, mumbling "Carl Fisher" as if he just heard a juvenile joke.

A Detroit Auto Club worker strolled by with a megaphone, barking to the teams of the Challenge Cup to assemble on the track. Oldfield didn't feel as nervous as he did the previous day, partly because the official's announcement was a great excuse to get away from that pain-in-the-ass Ford.

Cooper, Spider, and Oldfield joined the crews of the other five cars as they rolled onto the dirt running surface, about an eighth of a mile from the starting line. The same tiny man wearing a straw hat stood at the edge of the track with his pistol and a flag. The drivers knew he was to fire the gun as the signal for the cars to roll, staying even until the little man waved his big red flag at the starting line.

Oldfield's heart began to pump like a fire engine. Beside him was the huge Geneva steamer. The hot vapor felt good as it puffed from the ugly machine's stovepipe stack, and wafted over Oldfield before dissipating.

Alexander Winton claimed the inside of the track in the repaired Bullet, and Shanks in the "Pup" was beside him. Between Shanks and Oldfield were the two steamers of White and Bucknam. A mechanic rode with Bucknam, and he appeared busy adjusting valves.

Oldfield nervously fidgeted with the thumbscrew that regulated fuel flow at the bottom of his seat. Spider gripped the crank handle and began to turn. The Wintons started, but when Nine-Ninety-Nine exploded, nothing else was audible.

His heart pounding a drumbeat in his ears, Oldfield pivoted his head to take a panoramic view of the other drivers and their cars. The steamers quietly puffed water vapor while the other three belched smoke and angrily detonated gasoline.

Winton smiled and gestured to one of the officials in the manner of a private joke. Oldfield could barely stand waiting for another second, but Winton acted like he was driving to the general store.

Oldfield slipped his goggles over his eyes. His hands were shaking, strangely acting without consulting him. Focusing his eyes on the starter, he took a deep breath.

The man in the straw hat raised his gun. With the relentless drumming in his ears, Oldfield began to release his clutch lever. The Ford racer rolled forward before the others, and then the gun fired. Oldfield made a fast start and was a car length ahead of everyone as they reached the starting line.

Detroit Auto Club officials ran to the edge of the track, frantically flailing their arms, but Oldfield was confused and wondered *what the hell they were doing.* Frantically, the starter fired three more shots in rapid succession, waving his flag vigorously.

The Wintons and the steamers slowed, but Oldfield refused to give an inch. Hitting the accelerator, he stormed into the first turn with Nine-Ninety-Nine sliding and kicking up dirt. Charging down the backstretch, he saw everyone stopped on the other side of the track. As warm blood flushed his cheeks, part of him wanted to bust through the fence and keep going. Lifting his foot, he shrank inside as quickly as the sound of the engine quieted.

Oldfield slowed Nine-Ninety-Nine to cruising speed and then brought it back into the row with the other cars. The starter pointed at him and motioned to slow down with his hands.

The other cars moved away in formation, leaving Oldfield behind. The sensation in his stomach was like the nervous-sick feeling he got as a boy when his father told him they were moving to the city to get jobs. Smiling Winton would get to the starting line first, and the starter would send the others away without him. Shanks' victory dance in the tent flashed vividly in his mind.

To hurry to the starting line, Oldfield pushed the accelerator, and Nine-Ninety-Nine leaped forward. Picking up speed over the next eighth of a mile, he quickly closed in on the other cars.

The starter suddenly fired his pistol before Oldfield could get to the line. Expecting to finish last, he wondered if all the others had broken down as Nine-Ninety-Nine swept by them and into the lead! Without planning it, by faltering with the clutch, and then panicking to catch up, he got a run on the others when they came to the line. Easily in the lead, Oldfield cut across in front of the others as everyone approached the first corner.

Taking the middle of the track, Oldfield slid the car broadside through the turn to muscle aside everyone. He'd do anything to block those bastards. But nobody was close. Nine-Ninety-Nine roared down the backstretch with Winton lurking in the background.

Oldfield remembered what Cooper said about not entering the corner as wide and coming down to the middle of the track, not as close to the pole. But as he went into the corner, Nine-Ninety-Nine fought him for control, and he skidded toward the outside fence. He dodged the barrier by inches, and men standing there turned and darted aside.

"Shit!" he screamed, feeling like he didn't know what he was doing, feeling out of control.

Screams from thousands of people, most of them under the giant awning that protected their grandstand seats from weather, eclipsed even his engine's constant explosions as Oldfield soared by, leading the first lap. The rain had changed the track. Muddy now, Nine-Ninety-Nine's wheels slid like they were lard.

With no dust, there was a stark clarity to the vibrating, jerking images that unfolded before Oldfield. Peering over his shoulder, he caught a glimpse of the vivid, bright, colorful cars kicking up clods of wet clay and slithering like giant snakes.

Oldfield gunned the Ford engine down the homestretch and into the first corner. He cocked the tiller bar, and the rear wheels abruptly jerked to the right and toward the fence. His stomach suddenly dropped to his shoes, and Oldfield was sure he would lose control.

Delicately, like he was sneaking past a graveyard, Oldfield lifted his foot from the accelerator, and then abruptly re-applied the gas. The tires found traction. Oldfield powered the car around the corner, continually working the tiller bar to correct for a skid, and then adjust the counter swing.

Clearing the fence by several feet as he entered the backstretch, Oldfield checked over his shoulder again. The creamy red Bullet was halfway through the corner. Winton, hunched over the steering wheel, appeared to make his correction to a slide. The millionaire was gaining ground.

Nine-Ninety-Nine surged down the backstretch, at one point hitting a bump and leaping like an equestrian. When it landed, the stiff wooden frame bounced like a trunk rolling down a hill. Oldfield involuntarily jumped too, up and out of his seat, but he instantly thrust his leg forward to keep the accelerator mashed wide open.

His butt slammed back down, but Oldfield never flinched. Instead, he gripped harder on the tiller bar handles and stared over the massive block of iron in front of him. The railing on either side of the track blurred into two white lines, and the brown dirt track flowed like a river rushing at him.

Oldfield's run down the backstretch pulled him further ahead of Winton. He entered the second corner a few feet off the outside fence and kept his foot on the accelerator. As he turned left, the car started to slide around, and Oldfield corrected as he had every lap before.

The tall, skinny wheels kicked up mud and spun off some of their energy. Nine-Ninety-

Nine was in a broad-slide, and Oldfield kept the power full on. Drifting up in the corner, he saw the fence loom larger in the corner of his right eye.

Again, he gritted his teeth in anticipation of a crash - he cleared the fence, but just barely. Nine-Ninety-Nine straightened and felt five hundred pounds lighter to Oldfield as it leaped forward. Another stolen glimpse over his left shoulder only served to piss him off. Winton was closer still. Nine-Ninety-Nine was faster on the straightaway, but Winton was driving those corners.

Oldfield barreled into the first corner with the determination that no hunk of iron and wood could resist him. Success was all about mastering this car in this corner - now. Oldfield entered the turn a shade lower than the other laps. This time, he was gentler with the tiller bar, allowing the car to travel just a few feet more before throwing it into a slide.

The rear wheels churned and glided through the mud, and Oldfield cranked the tiller bar hard. Almost perpendicular to the two fences, Nine-Ninety-Nine was like a bridge between them that fell short on either end.

Finally, the slide was smooth and flawless, and the driver's constant inputs at the tiller bar kept the car on a consistent arc, instead of like ragged saw teeth. He wasn't out of the corner yet when the car shot forward in a straight line, starting his trip down the backstretch sooner than ever before – like a longer straightaway and a shorter corner! *Damn, that felt good!* The Bullet had grown smaller behind him.

"Yeah! Okay! Take that, you, gink!"

The track, the fence, the infield grass, and the leafless gray-stick trees lost all their details, like an Impressionist painting. Hunching over the tiller bar, Oldfield wiggled in his seat and screamed.

"Yeah! Yeah!"

Oldfield couldn't wait to get to the next corner. He wanted to slice through the turn again and leave Winton further behind. Following the same pattern as the corner before, everything was smooth until he hit a bump on the track that was unnoticed earlier.

Nine-Ninety-Nine, sideways in the corner, almost stumbled, and Oldfield slid to the right in his seat. His foot briefly slipped off the accelerator. Quickly back on it, he straightened the car to hit the front stretch.

White's steamer was in front of Oldfield, a little over halfway down the home stretch. Behind him, something was wrong with Winton; the Bullet slowed. Blue smoke streamed from the exhaust pipe.

Oldfield was thrilled at the notion of lapping the steamer. Charging into the first corner, he again slid through smoothly and came off the turn directly behind White. He quickly passed the lumbering, puffing machine on the backstretch.

Next, Bucknam and Shanks came into view. Shanks had pulled four car lengths ahead of the other steam car. Steadily, Oldfield reeled in the two machines. Catching the steamer on the backstretch, he made the pass. Nine-Ninety-Nine closed on the Pup as they entered the second corner for the last time.

Shanks held a low line near the pole, and Oldfield glided on the mud through the middle of the track. He came out of the corner high, and Shanks was at the inside fence. The two red cars bore down on the finish line, Shanks a lap behind.

Just before the tape, Oldfield edged by Shanks to lap everyone. Punching at the air with one hand, he screamed. The moment was surreal like he was hearing somebody else. A rolling wave of a roar erupted from the grandstand. Still, Oldfield slid his big machine at top speed through the first corner.

He screamed wild animal noises. When he came back around to the home stretch, Cooper, Ford, and Spider ran out onto the track. Police blew whistles and extended their arms in the air, but no one paid attention.

Hundreds of people poured from the stands and paddock onto the track. Six Detroit Auto Club officials cleared a path and directed Oldfield down the middle of the track in front of the judges' stand where he came to a stop. Surrounded, Oldfield scanned the crowd and thought of the loading dock the previous Thursday -- all the ugly, shouting faces and "Red Hot" John.

Cooper jumped on Nine-Ninety-Nine, grabbed Oldfield's hand, and raised it above his head like a victorious prizefighter. They stood high atop their car; it was their pedestal above the rest of the world.

Oldfield's head bobbed back, and he felt the leather strap of his goggles drag over his hair as Cooper pulled them off his head. Slimy motor oil was on his lips, and he knew it coated his face. Running his fingers through his greasy hair, Oldfield felt it matted to his head. Ford stood immediately below them. The grumpy engineer cupped his hands around his mouth and yelled up to the driver.

"I'll build another car for you, Barney, and we will challenge the world with it."

Oldfield nodded; and then cast his eyes past Ford to the broken Bullet parked fifty yards away, near the inside fence. Winton solemnly strolled away from it, moving toward Nine-Ninety-Nine as he pulled off his gloves. Oldfield watched him and then scanned the crowd. People swarmed Nine-Ninety-Nine, touching it and reaching out to touch him.

Oldfield spotted an attractive young woman at the periphery of the crowd and blew her a kiss. A man stepped in front of her, frowning and blocking his view. The driver flashed a smile and saluted the man. The man's countenance remained grim for a second, but he melted, smiled, and tipped his bowler.

Cooper moved to the other side of the car and helped Spider up to the top of Nine-Ninety-Nine as well, and into the car's seat. Cooper lifted his hands in the air and shouted Oldfield's name, but people were having a hard time hearing him.

Alexander Winton strode alongside Henry Ford, shaking hands. The millionaire fixed his eyes on Oldfield and extended his hand. The driver squatted and leaned his head down, so his ear was close to Winton's mouth.

"You drove a fine race, young man — a fine race. I hear you just set the track record of a minute-four and a fifth. The best man won today."

Turning to Ford, he added, "And the best car."

Oldfield thanked Winton, and the most famous race driver in America disappeared into the crowd.

Cooper began to lead them in a chant.

"Barney! Barney! Barney!"

The sound was surreal. Oldfield felt like they were talking about someone else. Reveling in their attention, he shook hands and made funny faces. He wanted everything to go on and on forever. A feeling that the moment may never happen again scared him. Worse, would everyone suddenly see who he was?

"You know me? You know me, I'm Barney Oldfield!" he shouted.

Chapter 3 – Son of the Horseless Age

(Toledo, Ohio, June 5, 1903)

The warped, loose boards of Toledo, Ohio's Air Line Junction station platform rattled like a wagonload of lumber as Barney Oldfield bounded from a passenger car with a duffel bag slung over his arm. His eyes scanned the people milling around and then locked on the slim profile of his father, some twenty feet away, hands in his pockets and leaning against the station office wall.

"Pa!"

Not quite sixty, deep furrows crossed Hank Oldfield's sun-leathered face and neck, and combined with his unkempt grey beard, Barney thought his father appeared old, disheveled, and lost. His faded eyes were obscured by the shadow cast by a wide-brimmed and well-worn black felt hat, eyes the son once feared as too stern to stare into, eyes he had come to see as weak and unsure.

Barney noticed the old man's threadbare coat and white shirt frayed at the collar and cuffs and thought about his father failing to get the things other men had. A strange sensation of pride over his new cotton shirt, polished shoes, and jacket filled the son.

"Pa, look what I got! You know what this is?"

Appearing confused, the withered man shook his head.

"It's six-hundred and fifty dollars, Pa, that's what it is! Enough to pay off the mortgage on your house! And you know who gets every penny of it?"

The elder Oldfield muttered, "No," and shook his head.

"You and Ma, Pa! You and Ma! You'll never have to worry about the house again because you own it!"

An uncertain vagueness nagged Barney; he knew his feelings were something less than genuine. Unsure what he felt, he knew his gift was not enough, no matter how many mortgages he could settle.

Barney started to tell his father about how he had ridden the big express from New York by way of Cleveland. He wanted to explain how he and the Nine-Ninety-Nine had just put a whooping on Charles Wridgeway, who drove an eighty-horsepower Peerless against him at the Empire City track in Yonkers on May 30. Barney wanted his father to know how important he was and how he netted one thousand, three hundred dollars, or twenty-five percent of the gate receipts for his win in New York.

As Barney studied his father, he noticed old Hank Oldfield's eyes swell with tears. As far as Barney knew, his father, his father's father, and another generation back to eighteenth-century England were all poor farmers who labored until they died.

The old man worked a farm since returning to Ohio after the Civil War. Then they moved to the city like everyone else seemed to be doing.

Barney thought back when his father became a janitor in an insane asylum in old Toledo. Barney worked there too for a while and watched his father mop up vomit, diarrhea, and urine. The old man saved his money until he could purchase an ice cream parlor on Main Street.

So cautious, so inarticulate, he sniffled and fumbled in front of his son.

They shuffled down the back steps of the station to a hitching post where a panting, ancient horse awaited them. The horse was a sure sign to Barney that time had passed. His father was a little older, but the horse was ready for pasture. Air Line Junction was little more than a mile from his parents' house, so Barney figured even the broken animal the family had owned since the farming days could find the strength for the trip.

From the front bench of the slow-moving wagon, Barney breathed in the putrid odor of horse manure and sweat. Hank Oldfield stared straight ahead, expressionless in a manner that used to intimidate Barney, but now just made him bored and disgusted with his father's dullness. As the horse plodded, Barney tried to remember if things had always been this annoying, even when he was a boy. Wanting to hop on his bicycle and beat his father home, the son gritted his teeth.

He had plenty of time to think about where they were going. The Oldfield house, at 1325 South Street, was in a sparsely developed neighborhood surrounded by railroad tracks. The house was only one-half block down from tracks that crossed South Street, and Barney remembered how the window panes rattled when the heavy iron steam locomotives lumbered by, spreading a haze of soot. As a kid, he just accepted it. Now, Barney thought about what a crappy deal it was. Barney had lived there with his parents and older sister Bertha since he was eleven years old.

Hank Oldfield directed the wagon down an alley behind the house, to a shed for the horse. His son jumped from the bench before the carriage stopped. He had to break the monotony of the ride and his father's life to tell his mother exciting news. Sprinting to the back door of the house, Barney yelled like he had done a thousand times before as a child.

"Ma! Ma! Guess what I brought ya!"

The son liked how his mother yelped when she heard the news. He put her in a bear hug, lifted her feet off the ground and twirled her until he stumbled.

By evening Barney felt like he could go to sleep and wake up thinking Nine-Ninety-Nine, his records and racing could all be a dream. Familiar feelings and sensations came back to him.

Ma's dinner of boiled chicken, white flour and butter dumplings, and dandelion greens was the same as always. The tiny kitchen, with its cast-iron wood-burning stove, was as miserably hot in the summer as it had ever been. Pa sat at the same nicked and scuffed wobbly table. Barney and his father sat stripped to their sleeveless undershirts with beads of sweat dotting their foreheads.

Recognizing some of the scratches on the table that had been there since he was eleven, Barney's mind drifted, first to a scratch, and then to nothing. Stirred back to the moment by flies and coal soot that seemed more plentiful than he remembered, the son fanned them away from the white dumplings with a folded piece of paper. The chicken and dumplings were good, even though Barney had grown accustomed to steaks and potatoes.

"Have you been reading about me, Ma? Did you see my track record at Empire City?"

Horseless Age, the authoritative trade publication, arrived regularly at the Oldfield home – the son had seen to that.

"Sonny, I sure do try. I see some things, but my lands, I'm never quite sure of everything they are saying. But I see the pictures of those big, new-fangled machines, and I pray for you."

"Now, don't you worry about me; I can handle these carriages. I know what I'm doing."

"They look dangerous. I can't believe those horseless carriage companies make machines that go so fast. It is a new day."

"Damned, if that don't beat all," his father inserted. "New York, you say? You driving them contraptions in New York?"

"Did you read about me? I'm the world champion, you know."

"Well, you are still my little boy," his mother scolded playfully. "So, I want you to be careful, and always find time to say a prayer every day."

Barney leaned back on the hind legs of his chair, with a toothpick in his mouth. Studying his parents, he wondered when they had gotten so old. Time was running out, and even after paying off their mortgage, he felt hopeless at the thought of ever catching up.

"The next thing I need to buy you folks is a car so that you can retire that old horse."

"That beast and I are retiring together," his father said. "Hell, I might have him buried with me alongside your Ma. What you say, Sarah?"

Sarah Oldfield frowned at the suggestion.

"I don't need no horseless carriage, son," Hank Oldfield said, "That's for the young people of this newfangled century – like you."

Barney excused himself and walked out to the backyard shed. He was curious about his old bicycle. The aging horse shook his head and blubbered his lips as if greeting the young racer. The dim light of dusk was enough for Barney to find the tattered, dirty blanket over his bicycle and air pump, which leaned against the inner wall.

"Bicycle champion of Ohio," he said to no one.

Out in the alley, he hopped on it. Barney felt the tires grind the gravel as he pumped his way down the lane toward Hiett Street to turn left to South Street. Turning left again, Barney headed west, stopping in front of his parent's home. Amazing how tiny the wooden bungalow had become, he thought.

The lot to the east was empty, but the house on the other side was so close Barney always imagined reaching out to their window and shaking hands with the kid next door. The window provides just a glimpse into the tiny room that had been his as a boy. Inside was the partition his father had built across the room to give his sister Bertha privacy.

Barney thought about how a week earlier, when Tom Cooper and he were in New York, they toured Fifth Avenue and saw the mansions of the Vanderbilts, Goulds, Brokaws, and Carnegies. Some day he might just buy himself one of those big houses. Smiling, he thought that when asked for an address, he still said, "1325 South Street, Toldeo, Ohio." Now, the place seemed more like home when he was away than when he confronted it.

Riding his bicycle another half block, Barney stopped when he saw a train coming toward the intersection with South Street. The setting sun made it almost impossible to see across the tracks. Shielding his eyes with one hand, Barney surveyed the opposite side. The train approached, sounding its whistle, with a blast of vapor that only briefly lightened the filthy black coal exhaust to a shade of gray.

Barney reached inside his coat pocket, extracted a short rope of chaw, and bit off a piece. Then, with the train barreling toward him, he pulled up on the bike handlebars to clear the first big rail and bounced across the tracks toward the big glowing sun.

Chapter 4 – "A Mile a Minute!"

(Indianapolis, Indiana State Fairgrounds, June 20, 1903)

The goddamn blazing sun! As if these goddamn, shitty eyes weren't bad enough! Carl Fisher cupped his hands like binoculars and wished they had lens so he could goddamn see. To get a pair of spectacles would admit to everyone he was weak-eyed, and he didn't want any part of that.

Even though his astigmatic eyes melted the people in the stands into a contiguous blur of random, inconsistent color, Fisher knew there were five thousand people in those stands. Just like he could tell the number of bees in the hive at his car dealership. Guess the number of bees and the Fisher Automobile Company will give you a free test drive in a new Maxwell runabout and a ticket to the next race he promoted at the Indiana State Fairgrounds. Farmers and city folk alike swarmed to see daredevils break world records and spit in the grim reaper's eye. Yes sir, ladies and gentlemen, yes sir - just like Fisher told them in hundreds of broadsides and newspaper ads.

Fisher stormed the paddock yelling greetings while his kinetic brain flashed pictures on a screen in some corner of his mind. He knew everyone and shook the hands of those he couldn't remember even more vigorously than of those he did.

The lip of his wide-brim white felt hat folded back in the breeze and then dropped forward, lightly tapping his forehead as he charged about. Tugging the brim down, Fisher made sure the cap obfuscated his decimated hairline. Without that goddamn hat, he looked older than his goddamn twenty-nine years.

The sun to his back, Fisher's shadow playfully ran just ahead of him, keeping pace with his spirit who reveled to see his latest grand scheme unfold. Rushing, as one of his familiar starbursts, erupted inside him and exploded through his limbs like the energy could escape through his toenails. He would grab the automobile industry by its goddamn throat and shake it, that's what he would do.

This ain't no saddle and packhorse world! Wake up! It makes *no goddamn sense* to live any other way when you can harness the power of dozens of horses in one carriage and put miles and miles of distance behind you in mere hours. *By God, what's wrong with people?* Look at how fast you go! By God, people will have to get new goddamn watches to keep up with the way things are going to change around here. Around everywhere – *just imagine!*

"I feel a hen coming on," Fisher announced as Barney Oldfield, Tom Cooper, and Spider Huff, who were working on their identical cars, the red Nine-Ninety-Nine, and the yellow Arrow, finally came into the range of his feeble eyes. "I've been looking for some ripe fools! And by God, the first thing I see is you three!"

It was just a matter of time before somebody somewhere covers a track mile in a minute. So, it needed to be at a Carl Fisher show. Best of all, it was going to happen in Indianapolis, the home of Fisher Automobile Company right downtown at 112 North Pennsylvania Street.

Fisher saw the North Penn sidewalk clustered with people. Insatiably filling their eyes with the window display of his brassy Stoddard-Daytons, Maxwells, and Nationals, their voices swirled into a low hum about Oldfield and that mile-a-minute. They gasped and imagined themselves in one of the cars – like Oldfield.

Oldfield was one of those guys Fisher got madder than Hell at when they were racing bicycles in the nineties. That son-of-a-bitch would fall, and then goddamn it if he wasn't elbowing at you a couple of laps later. *Hell, cuts and splinters were no big deal,* especially if you never gave up, and you always remembered what you wanted.

"Barney, can I see you for a second?"

Fisher studied Oldfield as he stepped around Nine Ninety-Nine. *Yes, this was the man who could break a mile a minute – he's got plenty to prove.* They walked a few paces as Cooper and Spider remained in the background, finishing the inspection of their cars.

"Barney, looks to me you have Nine Ninety-Nine in a hell of a lot better shape than the deal you guys handed me in Dayton. I'll bet you've hopped that old wagon up since Grosse Pointe, huh?"

"That's a hell of a jacket, Carl. You look like a goddamn canary. The only yellow jacket in the place."

"It's a polo coat."

"Polo? I thought we were here to race cars."

Struggling to control the situation, Fisher stopped and put each of his hands into a firm, friendly grip on the driver's biceps. Then he turned his head and spat tobacco juice downwind. Reaching into his breast pocket, Fisher revealed a tin and flipped it open with a beefy thumb.

"Pinch?"

Oldfield extracted a wad between his thumb and index finger and inserted it between his cheek and gum.

"Moist."

Fisher impatiently shrugged his shoulders and nodded his head back toward the car.

"Okay, Carl, we did a lot of work on her. The big problem in Dayton was the mixer. We made it better for Grosse Pointe, but we came up with something even better in March. Just between us girls, we stole the idea from Cadillac. We did away with the suction intake valves completely and put on valves that work mechanically. It's a lot more dependable."

"So, you drive the valves from some gears?"

"Yup. We hooked up two sets of bevel gears, with one set driven by the crankshaft. Then we ran a shaft up to the top of the motor that connects to another set of gears attached to an overhead camshaft. Now the inlet valves open or close according to the speed we want. It's a lot smoother. She's definitely got more hop."

"Good, good," Fisher said thoughtfully.

"What do you want, Carl? We aren't just passing the time."

"Barney, you and Cooper are doing the big five-mile match race this afternoon. Why don't you try to bust a world's record right here in Indianapolis? We have record corn and wheat crops and record everything else. I don't see why you can't give us a dirt-track record."

"Well, Carl, I like to make records. You like to have records right here in Indianapolis. You sell a lot of cars here, don't you?"

Fisher knew Oldfield and that no extra effort would come free.

"There's two hundred and fifty dollars in it for you if you circle this track in less than a minute. Hell, tell Cooper that I'll give another two hundred and fifty dollars to the winner as long he beats down that mile-a-minute. Okay? Maybe a little rivalry for you, boys."

"Just bag that cash and hang it on the fence right down past the finish wire, and I'll grab it on my way by," Oldfield said.

Fisher squirted another stream of brown saliva. Reaching upward, he placed his hands on the driver's broad shoulders and shook him playfully – it was a deal.

A step back and then two, Fisher accelerated away, still in eye contact with Oldfield even as the driver's features melted into a murky blur. Fisher ran rapidly backward with determination, consciously showing off a style he developed at picnics as a kid when he outraced other normal, forward-running boys. You have to encourage these daredevils, Fisher thought, shouting a final message.

"Barney Oldfield, the first man in history to go a mile a minute. Right here in Indiana! It's going to be great! Barney, people are going to go crazy for it. You're gonna be the hero, Oldfield!"

"You better watch where you're going, Fisher, I don't want nothing to happen to you until I get my money," Oldfield shouted.

"Hell, I can't see any better when I'm turned around, so what difference does it make?"

After feeling sure he had demonstrated his talent to Oldfield and others around them, Fisher turned and continued his walk through the infield, headed to the judges' section in the grandstand. Squinting to make sense of his edgeless, watercolor world, he pondered hues and shapes until he moved to within just a few feet of them.

"Goddamn it," he muttered.

As the roped off judge's area came into focus, Fisher bounded into the stands, taking steps three at a time, and leaping over two rows of benches to his seat next to opera singer Gertrud Hassler. Since he couldn't see her from a distance, he took in a moment to let his eyes silently drink in her curvy shape and large, comfortable breasts. She smiled at him, and he smiled back, mostly in amusement that she was probably oblivious to the fact that he was thinking about her breasts.

Beside Gertrud was his friend Arthur C. Newby, the man who financed the old high-banked Newby Oval bike track. Fisher always thought Newby's sour face, thin body, and wire spectacles gave him the look of a schoolteacher.

Fisher was eager to tell Newby of his scheme with Oldfield. He knew Newby, who only recently started the National Automobile Company in Indianapolis and sold his cars at the Fisher Automobile dealership, would jump on it.

"Art! I've got some action for you. I challenged Oldfield and Cooper to take a run at the mile-a-minute. I told them there's two-hundred-and-fifty-dollars in it for the guy who turns the trick. I'll have my brother Rolla make a book on it, and we get it going by putting down one hundred each on Oldfield. It'll make things more sporting."

"I enjoy sport," Newby said flatly.

Fisher liked Art because he did enjoy the sport. Newby wasn't much of a drinker, didn't smoke, and never seemed to be all that interested in women. Still, he was always game if he could see a business angle, and Fisher loved that.

Turning his attention to Gertrude again, Fisher smiled. He squeezed her knee.

"How you doing, little honey?"

Without waiting for an answer, he leaned forward to the next row of bench seats to speak into the ear of Arthur Pardington, the presiding American Automobile Association officer for the meet.

"Art – Oldfield, and Cooper are going to gun for the record. We've got to make sure everything with the timers is perfect, and we alert the press. This needs to be a pursuit race, so they don't get in each other's way. We'll start Oldfield right out here in front of the grandstands, Cooper on the backstretch. We're going to put Indiana on the map today."

Fisher's eyes darted to Indianapolis Mayor Charles Bookwalter, who sat in the judge's section as the official timing officer to ensure everything was on the up and up. The popping blasts of the big Ford engines turned Fisher's attention to the track.

The race was an Australian pursuit where cars start at opposite sides of the track. The contest was to see who gained the most on the other guy. Fisher knew Cooper was on the backstretch, but his eyes couldn't make out exactly where the yellow Arrow was. Oldfield, in the red Nine-Ninety-Nine, was more visible because he was directly in front of Fisher's seat in the judges' stand. The cars rolled away and began to circle the track. The first one, then the other roared by.

Fisher nervously chewed his cigar and finally bit the end of it off in frustration as the wheels of both Nine-Ninety-Nine and Tom Cooper's Ford Arrow spun and broke traction on the muddy turns. After completing their five-mile heat, both drivers coasted back to their starting positions.

Fisher hung his head. *Goddamn it to Hell!*

Gertrude's soft hand touched his shoulder. Suddenly, he stood up and shouted, "Let's go!" Fisher heard people around him laughing, but he didn't give a damn. He was talking to himself, shouting doubts out of his brain. Purposefully, he turned to Mayor Bookwalter.

"Okay, your honor, keep a sharp eye. These boys are warming up, just getting comfortable. This second heat is the big one. They're going to bust it wide open this time."

Fisher studied the officials and had a senseless urge to scurry around them, doing their jobs for them to make sure everything was under control. The judges and official timers sat in the comfortable shade of the grandstand cover. Art Pardington confirmed all the timers had reset the clocks, and the Mayor and the press had a good view. The Indianapolis News, The Automobile, The Horseless Age, and Motor Age all had newspapermen present.

Fisher was conscious of the sounds of thousands of voices. They were there because of him, and the sounds they made projected a sense of importance and anticipation to the moment he had created. Fisher felt everyone in the place was on edge and speculating on the outcome – and he loved it.

The red Nine-Ninety-Nine and the yellow Arrow were bright and vital colors to the near-sighted Carl Fisher as he strained to follow their progress around the mile track. The bright colors of their cars helped Fisher see Oldfield as he started his run just below the judges' section, and Cooper, on the yellow Arrow, on the backstretch. The Australian pursuit format let the two drivers have a clear track – but it was soon apparent even to Fisher's blurry eyes that Oldfield was gaining ground when he came out of the second corner and onto the homestretch before Tom got out of the first turn.

Fisher delighted in the sound of the crowd roaring as Oldfield rocketed by. He reveled to hear gasps as the driver held his right hand up in the air, steering with one arm.

"Barney's perfect!" Fisher screamed to himself. In his head, he designed posters showing Oldfield driving one-handed like a rodeo cowboy.

As if he could drive the car for him from the stands, Fisher twisted his body as Oldfield slid the big Ford's rear out to the edge of the track. A cloud of smoke billowed from Nine-

Ninety-Nine's cylinders and Oldfield slithered the wooden carriage onto the backstretch. Fisher turned to Gertrude.

"Did he hit the goddamn fence?"

Gertrude shook her head.

Fisher squinted to see the red blur as Oldfield surged into the second corner, again frightfully close to the fence. Gertrude stood up and grabbed at Fisher's arm. Irritated at the distraction in this critical moment, he grabbed her and pulled her into him, not in affection, but just to hold her still.

Fisher's heart was in his throat as he watched Oldfield glide through the corner in an expert slice that scooted out to the edge of the fence and no further. The big block of iron and wood pushed its way through the atmosphere, and people screamed as he crossed the finish line. Mayor Bookwalter blinked at the electric timer and then shouted, "He did it! He did it!"

Fisher squinted, discarding Gertrude and leaping over an aisle of seats in the judges' stand. He still couldn't read the *goddamn clock*. Pardington leaned over one of the timers and then looked at another clock to corroborate.

"Oldfield – Fifty-nine and three-fifths seconds!"

"Yeah!" Fisher yelled, crumpling an Oldsmobile handbill he had rolled up in his hand. He threw his hat in the air. "A world's record in Indiana!"

To Fisher's delight, the newspapermen scribbled down the time in their notebooks, and the news expanded like a wave across the grandstands. Barkers with megaphones walked the aisles in front of the grandstand, announcing the time. People cheered, and men waved their hats, many throwing them in the air.

Hundreds of spectators climbed over the bench seats instead of filing into the aisles. They rushed the track, and Fisher screamed, urging them on as if they were doing his bidding. The big red car coasted to a stop in front of the judge's stand. Fisher spied a dark figure he knew to be Oldfield standing up on his seat and waving to the crowd swelling around him.

Fisher felt Gertrude clutching his arm as she jumped up and down, the ringlets of her auburn hair protruding beyond her flowered hat. He liked that she was excited, evidenced by apple redness interrupting the light complexion of her youthful, pretty face. Newby slapped Fisher on the back, and Pardington looked over his shoulder and winked. Earle Fisher rushed up the aisle against the tide of people with a burlap bag stencil-painted with dollar signs and stuffed full of dollar bills.

"For the show," he shouted to his brother. "Just like you ordered, big brother."

Fisher yelled at the newspapermen in the area to get their cameras ready because he was going to give the new world record holder a big fat bonus. He hoisted the burlap sack above his head and bounded down the steps. Walking onto the dirt track, people cleared a path for him, some slapping him on the back. Fisher lifted the bag to Oldfield, who stood on his driver's seat.

"Here's your dough," Fisher yelled. "Indiana has a world's record, and you have your money! The new world's record is fifty-nine and three-fifths seconds!"

The crowd screamed Oldfield's name, and Fisher loved it. Oldfield was perfect. Oldfield meant crowds. Fisher studied the driver's oily, dusty face with raccoon eyes outlined by his goggles. Oldfield stirred the crowd by lifting the bag as high as he could and then jumping up and down on Nine-Ninety-Nine. Everyone cheered again.

"You know me, I'm Barney Oldfield!"

(Indianapolis, June 20, 1903)

The water hit Barney Oldfield's face full-on, rushing into his nose and coursing into his sinus cavities. Water filled his mouth too, and some of it found its way into his lungs. Drowning, he was helpless and weak when his father reached down from his rowboat and pulled him by his arm to the surface. Oldfield gasped and flicked his eyelids as he glided through space. Clumsily scrambling his feet to gain control, Oldfield had a surreal sense of two men grabbing each of his arms.

Suddenly, Oldfield was on his knees, his legs skinned by gravel. He ran his fingers through his wet hair, slicking most of it back out of his face. He felt several thick strands still matted down against his left cheek, but his head was pulsating, and hair grooming was unimportant. A hitching post supporting Tom Cooper came into focus. Cooper was gasping like he was out of breath.

"What did you hit him for, Barney?"

Oldfield's shirtsleeve soaked up the blood dripping from his left nostril. His white shirt provided a stark backdrop for a scarlet stain. Stunned, he searched his mind to determine where he was and why he had thought it a good idea to go to the "Germanic," an old Meridian Street pool hall, just a few blocks south of Indianapolis' Soldiers and Sailors Monument Circle.

An electric jolt shot through his body, and he bolted to his feet, patting his shirt and pants pockets, his heart racing. Shocking delight as his fingertips brushed a wad of greenbacks in his right pants pocket! Still panicked, he fanned the bills to see that more than half of his two-hundred-and-fifty-dollar bonus remained intact. Exalting as if it were a new discovery, he clinched the wad in his right hand, dabbing at his nose again with his left shirtsleeve as he turned to Tom.

"Is it broken?"

Oldfield was conscious of how thick a dozen whiskey shots had made his tongue.

"Hell, I don't know, I'm no doctor. It doesn't matter, you can't get any uglier."

Oldfield clumsily tried to groom himself by tucking in his bloody shirt. Realizing it was soaked, he surmised it was probably from a pale of water the bartender must have thrown on him. Dried blood crusted to his swollen lip, and fresh droplets still leaked out his nostrils.

"Let's go get us some women."

The incredulous look that overwhelmed Cooper's face made Oldfield laugh. Cooper started to laugh but then yelped in pain.

"Oh, Christ, Barney, you're killing me. I think they cracked a rib. You got to stop acting so damn dumb. I'm dying."

Oldfield felt the pain of the split in his nostrils, stretching apart as he smiled.

"Come on, Tom, we still got a good amount of dough left. I hear there are some pretty little painted ladies over near Pennsylvania and Washington."

"Champion of the world! What a big deal you are! What the Hell, it's too damn early to go to sleep. You know they'll make you pay extra, don't you?"

"If she lets me be mean to her, I'll give her an extra tip."

As they walked to the corner of Washington Street, events of the night filtered their way back into Oldfield's consciousness, but he wasn't sure about the order. After buying a round of drinks for the house, Oldfield later hit a man with a pool cue for saying he was no big deal because Carl Fisher had the fix in on the mile-a-minute just to sell cars. As they walked, Oldfield felt Cooper grab his arm to steady him when he stumbled on an interurban rail buried in the dirt and gravel street.

BARNEY OLDFIELD ON THE BULLET

Chapter 5 – Triumph and Suicide

(Cleveland, Glenville Horse Track, Thursday, September 3, 1903)

The sun disappeared behind the giant grandstands as Barney Oldfield hustled Alexander Winton's newly designed red Bullet No. 2 onto the front stretch of Cleveland's Glenville horse track. Instantaneously, he felt the coolness of the shade and relief from the strain of squinting.

Ear-thumping blasts from the big engine overwhelmed every other sound as he gunned past the thousand or so fans that came to watch him, the world champion, drive on a Thursday afternoon. Called the "preliminary races," this practice session was pure fun for Oldfield, and he loved going faster as he prepared for the race meet on Friday and Saturday. Since he accepted Alexander Winton's offer in August of a twenty-five-hundred-dollar annual salary, the chance to keep all his track winnings, his transportation expenses covered, and a mechanic provided, Oldfield drove his new racecar at every possible opportunity.

With one-thousand-ninety cubic inches delivering eighty horsepower, Oldfield thought he might have the best car in the world. He saw the Winton mechanic at the edge of the track flash a chalkboard at the end of his first flying start lap.

Just under fifty-nine seconds! Better than a mile a minute!

On the home stretch, a glance backward revealed the Winton sucking dust and dirt out of the Earth and spewing a house-size cloud in its wake. Gliding the red machine through the first corner, the big Bullet straightened and lined up for a trip down the backstretch.

Bam!

What the Hell was that?

The Winton engine exploded. As his heart swelled to fill the back of his throat, Oldfield tried to make sense of what was happening.

The big Winton suddenly looped around. Oldfield, sitting high on the flat car, felt curiously light like God had reached down and pulled him up into the air, his collar pinched between a giant index finger and thumb.

In an instant, Oldfield was flicked to the Earth and felt a dull thud as he bounced once, then landed on his left side with his face in the dirt. Strangely numb, Oldfield had the sensation of watching the accident happen to someone else.

The driverless Winton spun crazily down the stretch, grinding to a halt. Left some fifty yards behind, Oldfield slowly rolled over, just like he did after sleeping off a drunk.

Flat on his back, Oldfield opened his eyes to the absurd perspective of a cloudless, sunny sky from the middle of the track. Slowly, a thousand pins began pricking him, growing in intensity. Especially on his left cheek, where warm blood leaking from his pores combined with dirt to create a pasty concoction, he felt coating his face.

Grit crunched between his teeth and melted into a dusty brown solution he spat out. Thicker than tears were the sensation of scarlet lines streaming down his face. Instinctively, Oldfield rubbed the back of his hand against the wound and saw a smudge of wet redness extending back from his knuckles to his wrist. His left shoulder ached, so he leaned on his right elbow to lift himself.

No big deal. The beating at the Germanic was worse.

Down the track, the Winton billowed smoke from under its bonnet.

"Shit."

(Cleveland, Glenville Horse Track, Friday, September 4, 1903)

The promoters told Barney Oldfield that the stands at Glenville held over six-thousand spectators, and he saw that every seat was filled. A cacophony of energetic shouts overcame the roar of the Winton Pup's engine when he soared down the front stretch. A thousand or more people, many sitting or standing in hundreds of topless touring cars lined both sides of the track.

The track was very different than the day before. Most of the front stretch was a corridor of people, restricted only by a white wood rail. Many leaned forwards, extending their arms as if to pat him on the back as he passed.

Oldfield thought of how engineer Charles Schmidt, in the Packard Company's first car designed for racing, the Gray Wolf, had crashed through the fence the day before when there was no crowd. Now he could grab the hats off hundreds of people's heads.

With two other competitors in close pursuit, Oldfield pushed the Pup's accelerator pedal as hard as he could down the front stretch. The promoter offered a one-hundred-twenty-five-dollar silver cup for the five-mile race for cars less than eighteen-hundred pounds, and that sounded like a pretty damn good award. For this race, it didn't matter the Bullet had a broken crankshaft; the Pup, at seventeen-hundred-fifty pounds and forty horsepower, was a perfect fit.

The Pup felt a lot different from the Bullet. With half the horsepower, Oldfield found the car too easy to drive. A boring pattern of cocking the steering wheel in a corner, and straightening the car for the stretches emerged, and he stopped slowing for turns. Anxiously, he bounced on his seat as if he could spur the vehicle like a horse.

Dan Wurgis, on a "Pirate" Oldsmobile, clung tenaciously in Oldfield's background. But the Winton pulled steadily away and ended the five miles eighteen seconds ahead of the ten-horsepower, ninety-pound racer.

Oldfield stopped in front of the judges' stand, pushing his goggles down past chin like a necklace. Conscious of the film of dust on his face, he waited anxiously for the timer's report. The judges flipped big, white signs over the side of their box to post his winning time: five minutes, forty - four seconds. An aide to Alexander Winton, John Jack, ran to the Pup as a Triple-A official presented the large silver cup to Oldfield.

Jack extended his hand, and Oldfield, energized in victory, gave it a vigorous shake. His cheek burnt as he felt the big, crusty scab on the side of his face crack as he grinned.

The Winton executive returned a bland smile. He was a tall, thin man, with a peculiarly long, narrow face that reminded Oldfield of an odd pumpkin that once grew on his father's farm when he was a kid.

Oldfield thought Jack believed he was a bigger deal than he was. Jack always talked about being Winton's riding mechanic in the 1903 James Gordon Bennett Cup race in Ireland. What was the big deal? They didn't do worth a crap. The Europeans were laughing harder at the Americans after they went over there.

A crowd began to surround the Pup, jostling Jack and shouting congratulations to Oldfield. Acknowledging people in a general way, the driver smiled and nodded and even pointed at one man he thought looked goofy. Jumping from the Pup, he put his arm around Jack and lifted the trophy.

"How are you doing, Barney? That cheek looks like it hurts."

"At least it was my face and not my dick," Oldfield shouted into John's ear and then roared with laughter.

Jack looked solemnly at Oldfield, shaking his head. Nodding in the direction of the infield, Jack nudged Oldfield as if to tell him to walk with him.

"Barney, I don't believe you know this, but Mrs. Winton passed away August 28. Mr. Winton planned to be here this weekend, but I suspect that will not be possible now. Mr. Shanks is here, and you should know he found the body. Please refrain from making off-color remarks around him."

Oldfield didn't like the sound of Jack's comment because it was like he was telling him he was stupid and how to behave.

"I'm sorry to hear that. How did Mrs. Winton die?"

"From a fall off a cliff into Lake Erie at their Rosemont estate on Lake Avenue. It happened in the middle of the night. She has not been well for some time."

Oldfield pondered why a sick woman would be outside near a cliff at night, but couldn't assemble the right question, so he turned his attention to photographer Ed Spooner with a big, boxy camera. The photo was taken, Oldfield reversed his direction, awkwardly skipping until he jumped up on the Pup and faced the grandstand again.

Raising the loving cup trophy above his head, it was Oldfield's signal to the grandstand crowd to yell for him – and they roared. He thought about how nobody in the stands gave a crap about John Jack.

Pivoting, Oldfield spotted Charlie Shanks as he emerged from a huddle of men in the paddock. Oldfield thought he was another serious character but not in the same way John was.

The truth was that Oldfield was envious of Shanks. Somehow, Shanks knew what to say to the big-shot millionaires, and they even laughed at his jokes. Oldfield wanted to believe it was because Shanks was, at thirty-one, a few years older and a little more experienced, but somehow, he knew it was more than that.

The story Oldfield heard was that Shanks started as Winton's publicity man, and became one of his top executives after they drove to New York from Cleveland in forty-seven hours back in 1899. Everybody said Shanks was a damn fine newspaperman and he had generated national publicity by telegraphing reports to something like thirty newspapers at every stop. Winton and his motor carriage made several front pages and created a national sensation.

Shanks looked like he could be fierce in a fight. He was built low to the ground, but sturdy and thick with a vice-grip handshake. A white felt hat, a light suit, and a white shirt with blue stripes and detachable collar and cuffs made Shanks look like some kind of Dandy. He clipped his shirtsleeves tight with a pair of glittering silver and diamond cufflinks. Oldfield thought about the clothes he would buy to prove his place in the world. Shanks approached him.

"A fine drive, Barney, a fine drive. You show our Winton motor carriages well."

"You ain't seen nothing, Charlie. If I had the Bullet, I'd be busting world records."

"We'll get the Bullet back to the factory and get a new engine just as soon as possible. But thank God you're okay, Barney. I hope you're not too sore. I understand Charles Schmidt broke two ribs and is on bed rest at the Hotel Hollenden under the care of a nurse."

"Well, if the nurse hops in there with him, he'll be in better shape than me!" Oldfield joked.

Shanks raised one eyebrow and nodded.

"Ahh…yes, now we do have to get back to it, don't we, Barney? We have to make a good showing in the manufacturer's cup. This one is ten miles; I'm sure you know. And Barney, I was just saying to Mr. Jack that you should join us for dinner tonight at the hotel. Given the circumstances, I think Mr. Winton would want us to have a controlled celebration of our team's triumphs today, don't you?"

Oldfield studied the little boulder of a man. He knew Shanks thought he was smarter than him.

"I'm always in control, Charlie, and don't you forget it. Yeah, sure, I'll let you buy me a steak. We'll see you at the hotel."

Charlie Shanks rose from his seat and greeted Oldfield as he arrived at their dining room table at the Hotel Hollenden. The driver still felt a little out of place in fancy hotels.

The splendor of the dining room would have overwhelmed his father. Tall, thin windows smothered in rich blue drapery that was so long, an extra three feet of material lay gathered on the thick carpeting. The red print design on the drapery matched the crimson color of the wallpaper. Several crystal chandeliers with honest-to-God electric lighting hung above.

Dozens of potted palm trees lined the walls and flanked doorways leading to the kitchen, a public restroom, and two hallways. Elegant silk rope portiere hung in every door, and giant paintings of wildlife and hunting scenes adorned the walls. Oldfield still thought it was a big deal to be in such a place, but he didn't want Shanks or Jack to know.

Oldfield was in the same suit he wore to accept the job offer from Winton the previous month. A fresh shave and bath made him feel like a new man, but he was conscious of the scab on his face.

"You're looking dapper tonight, Mr. Oldfield," Shanks said.

"The same back to you," Oldfield said.

Shanks and Jack shook hands with the driver, and he took a seat at the table. Jack offered him a choice of red or white wine.

"Wine? No thanks. I need a good, stiff belt of whiskey. I'm so damn sore I feel like I just went twenty-five rounds with Jim Jeffries himself."

Shanks interceded, saying, "Barney, how about we save the hard stuff for the banquet tomorrow night? It'll be in the adjoining private room, right here. We can have a special celebration after the race weekend."

"Let me ask you fellas something," Oldfield said. "You plan on coming to all my races? Because, if you are, you're going to have to get used to some of my ways. I drive hard, and I sometimes drink hard to relax. I'll have your highfalutin wine tonight because we're just getting to know one another. But when I catch up with my old buddy Tom Cooper, well, me and Tom are going to have some catching up to do, if you know what I mean."

"Now, Barney, we all like to have fun. I enjoy a twelve-year-old single-malt Scotch now and then. But consider you are an employee of Mr. Winton now. The Winton Motor Carriage Company has a reputation to maintain."

"You know, Chuck."

Oldfield figured calling Shanks "Chuck" would put him in his place.

"That twelve-year-old single-malt stuff is the kind of crap that bothers me about you two. You think your shit doesn't stink. When are you just regular fellas?"

Shanks, stone silent, stared into his glass like he thought he could change the color of the wine by concentrating on it. Oldfield sensed that the Winton executive was losing his patience, but he was determined not to give any indication he was intimidated or willing to back down. Jack broke the awkward silence.

"We had a very successful day. Barney, you won the five-mile manufacturer's cup, and if we hadn't lost a spark plug wire in the final handicap, we would have won that, too."

Oldfield decided not to challenge Jack's use of the word "we." He was the one risking his neck, to hell with anyone else that claimed any credit.

"I should have had four cups instead of only three," Oldfield said. "Hell, if I could have run the Bullet, I'd have some new records."

"We'll get the Bullet fixed as soon as possible," Jack said. He paused, extending his glass into the air. "To success."

Oldfield watched Shanks silently tilt his glass in Jack's direction. With no enthusiasm, he decided to raise his glass as well.

A waiter greeted the three men, explaining the special of the day, and making recommendations from the menu. Without opening the menu, Oldfield blurted out, "You got any catfish?"

The waiter explained that catfish was not on the menu. Shanks ordered Cornish game hen, and Jack requested a steak.

"A steak! Now that's the ticket! I want one of those New York-cut steaks," Oldfield said. "And make mine rare. Blood rare."

The waiter disappeared, and Oldfield's active mind fired a random thought. The moment he spoke, he regretted opening his mouth, but the words came out of him like it was someone else talking.

"So, why did Jean Winton kill herself?"

Jack frowned at Oldfield and then asked Shanks if he was comfortable talking about the circumstances of Mrs. Winton's death. Oldfield felt stupid and wanted to shout at the men to show him respect.

"Yeah, yeah. I am okay," Shanks said. "Maybe too, okay. I guess I keep expecting to feel something more profound than numbness. When I first saw her from the top of the cliff, in her nightgown, all I could see was her upper back. She just looked like a white sack somebody had thrown overboard. When I got to her, she had lost all her color. Somehow, even though I knew it was Jean, I had a hard time believing it was her body. Her death crushed Mr. Winton."

The men fell silent. Oldfield regretted asking the question and thought a fresh bottle of wine might help. He called the waiter over and started to place another order. Shanks interrupted him and told the waiter that there would be no more wine for the evening.

"You guys need to learn how to have some fun," Oldfield said.

"Barney, let's be sharp tomorrow. Whether Mr. Winton comes to see the races or not, let's show him our best performance."

"What do you mean, 'let's,' Charlie? Last time I checked, it's Barney Oldfield driving these cars. And you are damn right I'm going to be sharp, but it doesn't have anything to do with you telling me what to do. Now, I'm going to see what kind of whiskey they have around here and if anybody likes a good card game. But there is one thing I'm going to say to you before I go."

Shanks and Jack, apparently stunned, sat at the table in silence.

"Mr. Winton hired me to drive, not you. And he hired me to run his race team, and that's what I'm going to do. And both you boys better get used to it, because that's the way it is, and that's the way it's going to be. You're welcome to come to the races and help out. But you aren't telling me what to do. Only Barney Oldfield tells Barney Oldfield what to do. Thanks for dinner, Chuck."

Oldfield rose from his seat and walked toward the hallway that led to the hotel bar. In his heart, he didn't know if he felt right about what he had said. But he didn't know anything else he could have said or done.

Chapter 6 – Man About Town

(Grosse Point Horse Track, Michigan, Monday, September 7, 1903)

Thick grayness drained the color out of the world as a dreary, persistent mist melted the earth and washed away the day's racing at the Grosse Point, Michigan track. Bored, Barney Oldfield drove his Winton touring car the ten miles out to the loading docks along the Detroit River. He wanted those same guys who saw him a year earlier to see what the world champion race driver looked like in person. Combing the area for the old lunch wagon, he wondered if "Red Hot" John had stuck out the crappy weather or went home.

Oldfield was conscious of his navy-blue custom-fit suit. A matching felt hat, a cream with crimson print vest, and a peach ascot tie were touches Oldfield was convinced established him in society. The dockhands pointing at him probably thought he owned a shipping company.

Puffing on a snugly rolled Monte Cristo, Oldfield steered with his left knee when he needed to manage the cigar and his umbrella at the same time. The diamond-sapphire gold ring on his right pinky had turned inward to the palm of his damp hand. He rotated it around again with his thumb. John should see every detail of his success.

Stopping his Winton touring car near the old wooden lunch wagon, Oldfield stepped out and sauntered over to John. Bursting with the thrill of his position in the world, he anticipated the fat vendor's reaction to his conspicuous wealth and importance.

But John just wiped mucus from his nose on his sleeve. Residue from his cooking sausages coated his face, and Oldfield thought it gave his skin an unhealthy shine. John coughed and looked faint as he wobbled on his feet. The grill's smoke rose only a foot or so before it blended into the day's dullness and disappeared. Oldfield guessed John saw him but was ignoring him.

"Hey, Red Hot…you still selling this horsemeat?"

"Big shot."

"World champion big shot," Oldfield said with a smile.

"What the Hell are you doing on this side of town? Nobody down here gives a damn what kind of champeen you think you are."

"You aren't too good to sell me a red hot, are you?"

Big John wheezed and coughed.

"You okay, Red Hot?"

"Yeah, yeah. Sandwich, huh? You a big enough deal to pay for your own nowadays?"

"Plenty big enough. I'm just not sure those hot dogs will taste as good as when you gave 'em away, though."

Finally, "Red Hot" John smiled.

"I'll tell you what. I'll make you the last red hot of the day. I'm tired, I'm sick as Hell, and I want to go home to that dump apartment and get some sleep."

"You need some whiskey," Oldfield offered. "That'll cure what ails you."

Oldfield extracted a jeweled, pewter flask from his coat inside pocket, but the big man waved him off. Red Hot plucked a sausage off his grill and stuffed it into a sliced bun with a fork. He picked it up with a piece of newspaper and handed it to Oldfield. John asked the driver what he had been up to as he cleaned his grill.

Oldfield wallowed the meat and bread around in this mouth as he told John about Empire City, Indianapolis, Cleveland, and Alexander Winton. He liked the way John encouraged his reports as if the fat man took pride in the younger man's achievements.

"We're running out at Grosse Pointe tomorrow, Red Hot. You ought to come out and see us."

"Some of us have to work, Barney."

"Well, you know what you got to do," Oldfield said. "But John, this time, I am paying you for the food."

Red Hot continued cleaning his grill. Oldfield stuffed a bill into the older man's breast pocket. As John pulled at the cash, the driver backed away quickly.

"You keep it Red Hot. I owe you more than that. Come on out to the track tomorrow. Hell, you could set up your rat trap out at the track."

Red Hot's eyes bulged, and his jaw slackened, examining the money, he blinked to re-focus.

"A hundred dollars! Have you lost your mind, son?"

"I wouldn't yell that too loud around here, old man, you got all kinds of toughs on these docks. Take a few days off and get over that cold. You don't want to get the consumption!"

(Grosse Point Horse Track, Michigan, Tuesday, September 8, 1903)

Nothing was going right. The Bullet was still in the Winton shop, John Jack was an asshole, and Jules Sincholle had beaten Oldfield in his first race, a five-mile open event. Worse, when Oldfield won the next race, the third one of the day, he couldn't get a rise out of the crowd, even though the stands were pretty full. Close to five thousand people, the promoters said.

"It's because you took up with a damn Cleveland company, Oldfield," Tom Cooper explained. "Nobody from Detroit can stomach Clevelanders. You're a damn traitor."

Stuck listening to Jack's smart-ass comments and only winning because Sincholle's Darracq had motor trouble at the start, Oldfield was glum. At Cleveland, whenever Jack or Shanks pissed him off, he would just get the crowd riled up to drown out their bullshit. Michigan fans didn't care about them. But Detroit didn't seem happy with Oldfield either.

The rains of the previous day had turned the dirt into the muck, and the high humidity and clouds that still hung over Grosse Pointe, Michigan did little to dry the track. Mud clung to everything, and Oldfield, who had mastered the hard, dusty surfaces, couldn't feel the track anymore.

Damnation! This forty horsepower Pup doesn't have the grunt to plow mud.

Mud was everywhere, and he felt it matt down his hair. Grit crunched when he put his teeth together. He chewed off a wad of tobacco, which helped him spit. Using an old hunting knife, he kept in a toolbox, Oldfield squatted at the side of the Winton and scrapped at the thick mud coagulated around the spokes of the Pup's artillery wood wheels. Tom Cooper's voice came from over his shoulder.

"Mighty lucky, Barney, that's what you are, mighty lucky."

"What are you talking about, Cooper?"

"Well, I figured you knew, Barney. I figured you were awfully relieved to see Sincholle miss the race."

"I don't give a damn who's in the race or who isn't."

Cooper gave him that smile like he knew the truth about what Oldfield was thinking. He didn't like that about Cooper. He didn't like his friend to know what he was thinking.

"So, Barney, are you still glad you went to Winton?"

"I make ten times the money, and I get to drive five times as much, Tom."

Oldfield paused and looked at John Jack, who was twenty paces away.

"But some of these Winton guys sure are a pain in the ass."

Cooper smiled and then shrugged.

"They don't know how to have fun like you do, Cooper."

"You mean they don't like to get all corned up on whiskey and fuck low-down women?"

Oldfield laughed.

"Yeah. Those fellas don't know how to have fun."

Oldfield watched Tom smile and stroke his chin. He knew Cooper was hatching something.

"I was thinking, Barney, since you and I are running in this Diamond Rubber challenge cup in the last go of the day, why don't we make it more interesting? If you win, I'll not only get you drunk and laid for free, I'll pay for two women. But if I win, you do the same for me. Is it a deal?"

Oldfield smiled. Nobody was more fun than Cooper.

(Detroit, September 7, 1903)

A heavy-set woman opened the door to a tall, narrow Victorian house at the corner of a street of similar houses a few blocks south of Detroit. She wore a scarlet red gown with a neckline that prominently displayed her ample breasts, which Oldfield judged to require firm support. Surely, she was on the far side of forty years, the driver thought. Her hair was a surreal black color, like paint, piled high on her head and held in place with several combs.

Oldfield lifted a whiskey bottle and took a big drink, and immediately heard Tom Cooper's voice.

"Go easy, fella, save some for the rest of us."

"Are you boys drunk?" the woman asked in the flat, bored tone of someone who dealt with drunken men regularly.

"No, but by God, we're working on it, aren't we Spider?" Oldfield said, looking at Huff and offering him the bottle. Spider took a short drink, nowhere near the volume of the tongue swisher Oldfield had just consumed.

The woman's eyes searched the men like she could see their souls.

"Uh-huh. House rules. No fighting, no spitting, and no puking on the premises. Understand? My girls are clean and healthy, and so is my house. They both stay that way, or I make damn sure the person who crosses me is handed his head."

"Oooo...I love it when a woman talks mean," Oldfield said as he and Cooper laughed, but Spider's chuckle sounded nervous. Oldfield gave him a soft punch in the shoulder.

A giant black man emerged from behind the woman. Dwarfing her, he stood head and shoulders over the top of her piled hair. With arms folded across his chest, he pierced the men with unflinching eyes.

"Damned if that isn't the biggest nigger, I think I've ever seen," Oldfield said, thinking only seconds after he spoke that what he said might piss someone off. The man stared coldly at Oldfield.

"You don't waste words, madam, and I respect that," Cooper said. "All three of us do.

We're not crazy, and we do have money. We just want to be with some ladies this evening, and have a good time. Then we will be on our way. You can believe we will play by your rules."

Oldfield surveyed the giant behind the woman.

"Yes, Ma'am. I'd have to be a helluva lot drunker than I am now to bust up your house."

The woman offered a sardonic smile.

"Well, then, you will excuse my plain talk," she said. "But as I said, I run a clean business, and as long as everyone understands the rules, everyone leaves here real happy. You may call me Madam Winfield."

Stepping back from the doorway, she gestured for the three men to enter. Oldfield took in the grandeur of the house. Red dominated the décor. The wallpaper was blood-scarlet with an odd black insignia print spaced out to a four-point diamond design and repeated endlessly. Crimson draperies ran to the floor and more, piled like laundry. A wire drooped in gentle loops across the ceiling to a chandelier of cut glass that dominated the foyer.

Electrified and everything.

"Nice place," Oldfield said.

The black man's eyes trained on him.

"Ah…I am Mr. Cooper, and this here is Mr. Huff, and my more talkative friend here is Mr. Oldfield."

The woman smiled, nodded, and directed them into an adjoining parlor, where a half dozen girls sat on a love seat and three wingback chairs. Oldfield judged none was over twenty-five.

In the room were two large potted plants, one distinctively healthier than the other. A three-foot plaster statue of a nude woman rested on a table between the chairs. Two large paintings of naked women hung on the wall.

"When I buy me a house, I'm going to get me pictures like that to put on my wall," Oldfield said. Taking another swallow of whiskey, he then handed the bottle to Cooper, who took a swig and kept it.

The woman cleared her throat.

"As I said, my girls are clean. They are the prettiest in all Detroit. They are seven dollars by the half-hour, and ten for an hour. For twenty-five, she will keep you warm all night. Before anything happens, you need to drop your drawers, and I am going to give you a yank to make sure you aren't dripping. I run a clean house."

All three men obeyed the woman. As Madam Winfield performed her inspection, Cooper spoke.

"How much for two?"

"Two hours or two girls?" Winfield asked.

"I don't need two hours, that's for sure," Cooper said, "Remember, Barney, you're paying."

"With pleasure, Tommy boy, with pleasure."

Winfield smiled and turned to the girls, who Oldfield felt were very casual about all the interactions before them.

"You hear that, girls? It sounds like we got ourselves a real he-man come to a visit. And I am happy to say these boys are as clean as the driven snow. You've got nothing to worry about with these fellas."

Winfield turned to Cooper.

"Why mister Cooper, how far did you get in school?"

"What's that got to do with it, Ma'am?"

"Well, if you know how to multiply, all you have to do is double everything I told you."

"Sounds fair to me," Cooper said with a big smile directed at Oldfield. "Dig deep, buddy. Looks like me winning the old Diamond Rubber Cup is gonna be pretty expensive for you, huh? You pay for old Spider, too?"

"I don't give a shit, Tom. Sure, yeah, let's just get to it."

Cooper studied the girls carefully. Oldfield knew which one he'd take. One clearly stood out. She had smooth, creamy skin and wore a silk blouse with delicate frills that blended with the gentle, bouncing ringlets of hair that descended down her neck.

"I want that little Gibson Girl," Cooper said.

He surveyed the others. All were in various stages of undress, with garters and bustier on display. It seemed that Cooper somehow knew Oldfield's favorites before he said anything. One girl smiled, revealing a chipped tooth that curled over the one next to it.

"That one, too," he said, "She looks kinda mean, don't you think, Barney?"

"You're getting all the good ones."

"That's what winners do, Oldfield."

Madam Winfield motioned for the girls to come to Cooper. She extended her hand out to Oldfield, who filled it with greenbacks. Cooper tipped the whiskey bottle with a clumsy toast to Barney.

"Thanks for the whiskey, Barney," he said.

"Aw come on, Tom, that ain't fair."

"Sure, it is. That was the deal, besides you drank most of the other one."

Oldfield extracted his flask from his jacket pocket and tilted it back to take a long drink. He had learned to relax his throat and aim for the very back to keep most of it off his tongue. The liquid-fueled intense burn in the middle of his chest subsided quickly. Oldfield shook his shoulders vigorously and then his head, contorting his face into a grimace the entire time.

"Damn, that's nasty."

Cooper glanced back at his friends and smiled like he owned the world as he disappeared up the staircase with his girls. Oldfield shook his head and turned to Spider.

"Okay, Spider, now it's our turn. Looks to me, these ladies are getting lovelier by the minute."

Chapter 7 – A Cruel Sport

(Grosse Point Horse Track, Michigan, September 9, 1903)

The rear axle of the Winton wobbled so badly Barney Oldfield felt like he was driving on cobblestones. In the fourth mile of Wednesday's second event, his car slid in black mud that flipped off his front wheels and pelted his face. A faint scent of horseshit made him spit.

That damn Frenchman, Jules Sincholle, in his Darracq, skidded through the first corner way ahead of him in the distance. Directly in front of him was Henri Page, running second in the Decauville.

Another damn Frenchman, whooping my ass again.

Slowing, Oldfield pulled low on the course and headed toward the paddock, bouncing around on his seat like he was riding his bicycle over railroad ties. Stopping the Winton, he stormed off.

"Shit, goddamn it to hell, Shit!" the driver screamed, grabbing a rag and wiping the putrid mud off his face.

John Jack and George Hill, a Winton mechanic, ran to the spot where Oldfield stopped.

"What happened?" Jack shouted.

"Hell, I don't know," the driver fumed. "The damn thing is a piece of junk! It hasn't been running right since we got here! And now it's wobbling around like a goddamn duck!"

"Relax, Barney, yelling and cursing isn't going to help," Jack said.

Oldfield stopped and looked at his shoes and the dirt around them. His hands pressed on his hips as his face tightened, and he ground his teeth. An urge to hit Jack almost overwhelmed him. Head throbbing, he stared into the dirt and saw tiny grains of minerals that vibrated.

A mechanic's voice from under the car sounded miles away, "It's an axle bearing. It looks like it's melted."

"Barney. Barney."

Another voice filtered through his thoughts like someone stirring him from a dream.

Someone gripped Oldfield's arm and pulled him around. He was face-to-face with Tom Cooper.

"C'mon, Barney, let's fix the goddamned thing. You and me have a match race coming up. Don't you dare try to get out of me giving you an ass-whipping."

Oldfield sighed and ran his fingers through his hair and felt the dirt in his scalp.

"Bad day, Tom. Bad, goddamn day."

He followed Cooper to the car. Jack stepped in front of them.

"We won't require your assistance, Mr. Cooper," he said.

Oldfield hoped Cooper would hit Jack, but he just looked at him square in the eye, cocking his head sideways like he was studying him. While he continued to stare Jack down, he called to the mechanic, who was under the car trying to get at the bearing.

"Hey, buddy, under the car," Cooper shouted. "Could you use another set of hands?"

"You bet I could, Mr. Cooper, and the name is George. George Hill."

"Stand down, Jack," Oldfield said.

Jack shook his head and walked away. Cooper and Oldfield crawled under the car.

"George, do me a favor and go find some bearings in the tent," Oldfield said. Cooper touched a bearing and quickly pulled his fingers back, wincing in a hurt tone.

"You're a pussy, Cooper! You afraid of a little hot bearing? Did you burn your little fingers, you big sissy?"

"Shut-up, Oldfield, or I'll quit helping you. You're so goddamn dumb you could never figure this out without me. I'm going to fix this piece of shit, and then I'm going to get you out on that track and show everybody who the better man is."

"You go look at whose name is on all the tickets to this here race, Cooper. I'm Barney Oldfield. They got my picture on those tickets."

"Big deal. I'm Tom Cooper, and I'm going to kick mud in your face."

Oldfield grabbed a screwdriver lying on the ground and pried the bearing loose. It fell into the muddy grass, and smoky steam arose as the wetness cooled it. Now an oblong shape in its center, it was warped where the axle had eaten it. From under the Winton, Oldfield saw George's feet, and then his legs as he kneeled down to rest on his knees.

"Hey, fellas, I got a couple new bearings from our parts box. How does it look under there?"

"It's fixable," Oldfield said, extending his hand outward to grasp the bearings. Hill brought a ball-peen hammer, and Oldfield used it to tap the new bearings in place. The process went smoothly, and soon the wheels were back on the car, and it was ready for the next event, a match race against Cooper and the Nine-Ninety-Nine. Cooper frowned and started talking as they cleaned their hands with rags.

"Barney, I'm gonna lay it out straight for you. You ain't gonna beat me with the Nine-Ninety-Nine, and it ain't because I'm a better driver. I got twice the horsepower you do in that little Pup, and you don't have a prayer."

"You're probably right, Tom, but there are over two thousand people in the seats out here today, and we came to give 'em a show, and that's what we're gonna do."

"And we will, Barney. But I got one more thing to say to you. Them bearings ain't gonna last long. There's a lot of wear on those axles; they ain't right. I say they'll eat up those new bearings. And you're gonna get bounced around. And you better watch your tire wear, too, because when the wheels bounce, they get eaten up."

Hill stood beside them, listening.

"He's right, Barney, we should keep an eye on those tires."

Oldfield liked the Wednesday weather much more than Monday and Tuesday, the sun was finally shining again, and the temperature was over eighty degrees. The track dried considerably near the outer fence, but down near the poles, it was still soft and muddy. Chasing Cooper on the first lap of their match race, he skidded the Pup in a dusty, predictable slide up high near the fence and felt the track for the first time at the meet.

The Pup clung close to Nine-Ninety-Nine's rear through the first lap, and then Oldfield thrilled at the thought of passing Cooper. Suddenly, the impossible seemed possible. The Pup surged ahead in the first corner when Cooper hung lower on the track and furrowed his tires through the soft mud as he came down near the pole in the middle of the corner. Oldfield ran down the backstretch just in front of the Nine-Ninety-Nine.

Even with the throttle mashed, the little Winton could not shake Cooper in his big Ford. In the first corner of the fifth mile, his old friend pulled even.

"Goddamn it! Goddamn it to hell!" Oldfield moaned.

As they entered the backstretch, Cooper and the Nine-Ninety-Nine passed from the corner of Oldfield's eye to the center of his vision – directly in front of him.

"Fuck!" he shouted.

As they skidded through the second corner, a weak, empty spot grew in Oldfield's belly. Cooper had him beat. Oldfield backed off his accelerator and headed for the paddock gate, not bothering to cross the finish line. Cooper continued on, and Oldfield saw him take the flag in the distance, further down the straightaway.

Oldfield pulled the Pup to a stop near Hill's feet. Jumping from the car, he flipped the cowling open to remove the spark plugs and clean them. Time accelerated as he heard Detroit Automobile Club barkers shout into megaphones for him to return to the track. The final round of the best-of-three-match race event with Cooper was to start in minutes.

Oldfield thought about how he had only won the first race on Tuesday because the

Nine-Ninety-Nine fouled a plug. But he kept thinking about how he passed Cooper in the second race. As he scrambled back on top of his Winton, his mind conjured up images of making a pass on Cooper and then blocking him.

Oldfield watched Hill turn the crank as he flicked the spark lever, and the Pup's little engine gave a throaty yelp. The Winton Pup whipped out the paddock gate and with Cooper already on the track, waiting. Oldfield pulled alongside him, and the two began to slowly roll toward the starter.

From the corner of his left eye, Oldfield saw Cooper keep pace with him as he crept away from his starting spot at the head of the homestretch. Suddenly, Oldfield stomped on his accelerator and jumped ahead of his friend before he thought about what would happen next.

Of course, the Triple-A men would be pissed off but screw them. Oldfield leaned over his steering wheel and squinted at the road, surging toward him. Three car lengths ahead of the Nine-Ninety-Nine at the tape, Oldfield saw A. J. Picard, the starter, desperately flailing his arms in a signal for them to stop.

The sight of the frantic Picard gave Oldfield a sense of power for the first time that week. Laughing like a kid playing a prank, Oldfield imagined Cooper doing the same thing with the Nine-Ninety-Nine because he ignored Picard too. For three laps, Oldfield checked over his shoulder at Cooper on the straightaways and saw his friend continually chipping away at his lead.

Glancing back as he came out of the second corner, he groaned as Cooper was so close his front wheels almost touched Oldfield's rear tires. As they came back to the front stretch, Oldfield heard a mixture of cheers and boos. Picard waved his hands again as the cars passed nose-to-tail to complete the fourth mile. Oldfield laughed again as he saw Cooper ignore Picard and continue at full speed.

Tom and he could lick the world.

Cooper, down low on the track, once more appeared in the corner of Oldfield's eye, but halfway through the first turn, the rear of the Nine-Ninety-Nine slid around and skidded broadside. Oldfield pressed hard on his accelerator, feeling like he was escaping the grip of a wild animal. Cocking his steering wheel, Oldfield slid the Pup smoothly through the turn to pull nearly a hundred yards ahead. Stealing another glimpse over his shoulder, Oldfield spied his friend skid his wooden carriage. Cooper gathered up his car and got pointed in the right direction to pick up speed again.

As Oldfield crossed the finish line, he was surprised to see Picard waving the checkered flag like the officials agreed it was a real race. Quickly glancing back, there was Cooper, who had closed the gap, but was still more than thirty yards behind.

Oldfield coasted down into the still soft, muddy edge of the inside track where people extended their hands to touch him. Fans booed as the Pup came down the home stretch to stop in front of the judges' stand.

Oldfield squinted into the sun, his eyes tracing the grandstand steps up to the judges' box and gave the men sitting there a flippant salute. A big man with a Teddy Roosevelt mustache sat with his arms crossed, puffing on his cigar and staring at him. Another judge sat beside him and appeared half asleep with his right arm propping up his head.

Oldfield sat on his Winton at the starting line, waiting for the next event of the day – a ten-mile open handicap. Every time he saw those Frenchmen Sincholle and Gerard Papillion in their Darracqs, he wanted to yank the steering wheel off his car.

Damn it! What made them so much better here than at Cleveland? How could they improve so much in just a few days?

Frank Prong in the tiny, four horsepower Oldsmobile started down the track. Still, Oldfield's mind was on the Frenchmen. The promoter had him starting from scratch, giving Papillion a minute head start, and thirty seconds for Sincholle and Harry Cunningham. Oldfield sat silently in his car, watching the French mechanics starting the other machines. His teeth ground together, and his fingers tapped on his steering wheel.

"Bullshit!" he shouted and waved for starter A. J. Picard to come to him. Cooper, Hill, and Spider were in the corner of his eye, standing around the Winton with clueless facial expressions.

"What do you want, Oldfield? I've got a race to flag," Picard shouted over the revving engines.

"I'm going to go when Sincholle goes."

Picard waved for Harry Miller, clerk of the course, to come to him. Miller ran to where Picard stood, near the Winton.

"You deal with this son-of-a-bitch. The bastard says he won't start scratch behind Sincholle. I say he does, or he doesn't run at all," Picard shouted to Miller.

He turned to Oldfield, "You do as I say, Oldfield. So, help me God, I'll see that you never race at Grosse Point again."

Picard walked toward Dave Wurgis in the second Oldsmobile, checking his watch.

"You heard the man," Miller shouted to Oldfield.

The driver shut his motor off and stood up on his car.

"I guess I got some motor problems, because I'll be damned if I'm going to let that Frenchman whoop my ass again, and give him a head start when he's got the better car."

Oldfield jumped down from the Winton and marched away. Cooper's almost breathless voice followed him from behind.

"Barney, you're kidding, right? You can't just walk away like that, everyone's going to think you're yellow. It's your job, Barney."

Oldfield picked up the pace of his step. Jack stormed up to him in the opposite direction.

"What the hell are you doing, Oldfield? You can't just desert your post like that."

"Get away from me, John, or so help me, I'll knock your lights out."

Jack stopped in his tracks. From the grandstands, Oldfield heard a round of boos. Cooper pulled at his arm. He stopped walking but did not look at his friend.

The engines of the cars circling the track roared in the background as the two friends stood silent for several minutes. Oldfield's tense muscles relaxed, but he counted on Cooper to know he didn't want to talk just then. He just stared at the track.

Sincholle's Darracq crept by the finish line the first time, its engine misfiring. Oldfield realized that the cars that raced at Cleveland were showing the stress of all the miles.

Resting his arms on the rail fence, Oldfield leaned his forehead on them to feel the cushion of his skin and muscles. Cooper stood silently with him as they watched the other cars. Papillion led in the second Darracq until the ninth mile when his motor mysteriously fell silent. Cunnigham in the Packard Gray Wolf passed the little Oldsmobiles of Wurgis and Prong, and they finished one-two-three.

After everyone stopped, Oldfield focused on the judge's stand and noted that the big man with the Roosevelt mustache had descended down the steps to the paddock. The man appeared angry and very determined.

"Oldfield!"

Oldfield locked eyes with the advancing official.

"You know this fella?" he asked Cooper.

"He's Art Pardington, the referee. He's a big shot in the Triple-A, and he doesn't look happy."

"I ain't happy either. He better not cross me."

"Don't you get in a fight with this guy, Barney. I ain't your second if you do. This is way more trouble than it's worth. You just eat his shit and go on, you hear?"

Pardington was upon them before Oldfield could answer. He was about as tall as Oldfield and Cooper, but his limbs were like sticks, and he had a middle-age paunch. Weathered skin hung like drapes from his prominent cheekbones, and his eyes looked a size and a half bigger through his thick wire-frame spectacles. The Teddy Roosevelt mustache hid his lips but revealed big, long teeth just like the president. His voluminous voice boomed with authority.

"Who the hell do you think you are, Oldfield? You think you're above the rules of the Triple-A?"

"I'm Barney Oldfield, and I risk my neck so fat boys like you can sit up in the judges' box and be big shots."

Pardington's bony index finger poked at Oldfield's chest like a woodpecker.

"Listen up, farmhand. I don't take crap from people that don't show the Triple-A respect."

Pardington's arm reeled back like a piston on its downward stroke and then thrust toward Oldfield's chest for another stab. But Oldfield was faster. His hand clamped around the referee's wrist and stopped him short.

"Nobody lays a hand to Barney Oldfield."

Oldfield stared straight into Pardington's eyes, determined not to flinch. The referee appeared startled that anyone would challenge him. Hesitating, he then wrenched his arm free from the driver's grasp and raised his voice.

"Listen, you little weed bender. Do you understand why you have what you have? Do you know why Alex Winton hired you? It's because of all these people out here!"

Pardington gestured back over his shoulder to the grandstands.

"You hear them booing you today? Without them, you're nothing. Without them, you go back to plowing dirt or whatever you were doing before. You think about that. And then I want to see your ass in that car, where it belongs, for the next race. And you respect my starter and my clerks, and everyone else in the Triple-A, you got that?"

Pardington paused. Oldfield tilted his eyes away and downward. He shrank smaller before the man, thinking about his cars, his money, and if Pardington had the power to stop him from racing.

"I'm talking to you. Do you understand me? Because if you don't, I'll make trouble for you like you haven't seen before."

Oldfield took a deep breath and muttered, "Yes."

"Fine," Pardington barked and stomped away.

Cooper didn't say anything; he just walked beside his friend as they traced their steps back to the starting line. Of the ten cars entered, only Sincholle's Darracq and Cunningham's Gray Wolf were preparing for the next event, a ten-mile open run. Oldfield and Cooper walked to the Winton, where Hill and Jack were waiting.

"Nice of you to join us, Barney," Jack said.

Oldfield ignored the remark and asked Hill where the other cars were.

"I think everyone is wearing out. Page is done, and Papillion broke a piston. Too many miles on these cars. Too many miles on your car, Barney."

The Darracq mechanics began to push Sincholle's car toward the paddock gate. They, too, were withdrawing. As they rolled the car past the Winton team, Hill asked what the problem was.

"It is the tires," said one of the Frenchmen in a heavy accent, "They are too tired. It is too dangerous."

Oldfield turned back to Cooper and Hill.

"All right, fine, they want a race, I'll give 'em a race," Oldfield said, "I'll have a go with Cunningham. Let's fire this little buggy up."

Hill turned the crank with three big thrusts before the Pup fired, and he stepped back. The little Winton rolled slowly out on the track to join Cunningham's dull, dingy Packard Gray Wolf. The twenty-four horsepower Packard motor barked like one of those little dogs that try to assert his presence.

Oldfield studied Picard, who held a pistol in the air. The starter extended one finger, then two, and then popped the gun. A spark appeared at the tip of the barrel. Oldfield released the clutch, but the pedal slipped off his muddy leather sole. The Pup lurched forward before stopping and falling silent. While pounding his fists on the steering wheel, Oldfield watched Cunningham surge ahead.

In the distance, Cunningham skidded smoothly through the first corner as Hill once more cranked the Winton to life. Oldfield again released the clutch, pushing the car into first gear, and the Winton began to roll. It picked up speed toward the first corner, but Cunningham was so far ahead he was nowhere in sight. Worse, the Winton slowed and stalled as Oldfield neared the turn.

"Goddamn it! I'm sick of this shit!"

Oldfield reached behind his seat for a small box of tools. Jumping from the car, he unfastened the cowling and tossed it over the fence. The sound of heavy breathing came from behind him.

Hill, panting, with a handful of tools and spark plugs, appeared at Oldfield's side. They went to work replacing the plugs as the Gray Wolf circled the track.

The hopelessness of the situation made Oldfield more determined to fight. Tossing the old plugs over his shoulder, he screwed each new one in by hand and motioned for Hill to follow behind him and cinch them down with a wrench.

Oldfield heard the Gray Wolf coming down the homestretch toward him. Cunningham wrestled with the wheel, spewing dirt with his narrow wire-spoke wheels as he skidded through the corner.

Down by a fucking mile. I'm going to go pass that bastard!

Finished with the plugs, Hill ran to the front of the car to crank the engine but got no response. Another yank and the motor finally fired. Oldfield started to roll his Winton's wheels, but by that time, Cunningham was coming around again. Down another fucking mile, Oldfield mashed the throttle and fidgeted in his seat as the Winton struggled to come up to speed.

Two miles behind, Oldfield felt a sense of relief combined with an intense desire to attempt the impossible. There was nothing to lose. No one could expect him to overcome such a huge disadvantage, and if he did, he would redeem himself for everything that had happened at the meet.

The Winton hugged the inner fence as it slowly picked up speed around the first corner. Faster. By the time he got down the backstretch, he was going close to a mile a minute. He flung his car into the next turn, skidding out to the fence in a wild manner he knew the railbirds loved. Two men who sat on the outside track railing briefly zipped through the corner of his eye.

Dumbasses!

Oldfield cut a perfect arc around the outside of the corner and drew the Gray Wolf into view. Gaining on Cunningham, he hunched over his steering wheel, focused his eyes like hooks to draw Cunningham to him like a catfish.

I'll pass him if it's the last thing I do.

The ride grew more jarring as that confounded vibration started up again, violently pounding on his ass. Still, Cunningham grew larger and larger. Onto the home stretch to finish the Gray Wolf's sixth mile, the dueling cars were neck and neck, with the Winton car still two laps behind. Oldfield passed Cunningham in front of the stands, to ignite roars of approval.

Oldfield pulled three car lengths on Cunningham as he went into the first corner. Clearing the fence post and entering the backstretch, he stole a glance back at his rival, who grew smaller still. The biggest dust cloud of the week trailed him, and Oldfield pointed his head forward to see the drying brown road cascading under his wheels. Confident he was going faster than a mile a minute; Oldfield bore down on the second corner.

Throwing the Winton sideways, he powered his arc through the turn. Shockingly, the right front tire exploded. The Winton's steering wheel jerked out of his grasp.

The Pup shook violently and refused to yield to Oldfield's commands. He rushed to the fence like he was strapped to a cannonball. Nothing was in focus because his entire world shook harder than an earthquake.

The constant bouncing slammed his teeth together, and chips broke off in his mouth. Oldfield gripped the steering wheel as if its hard-oak wood could ooze between his fingers like clay. Forget control; now he just to struggled to hang on.

The Pup slammed into the fence, shattering boards into splinters and knocking down posts like matchsticks. With a soft thump, the Winton hit a dark object, but nothing made sense as Oldfield tried to sort out images that looked like a man flying in the air and toppling downward.

The absurd blob briefly rode atop the big, creamy-red Winton's nose, and then fell underneath. The racer thumped and hopped as pieces of the machine broke off around him, flying with the fence splinters in a tornado. Now his car was cascading downward, picking up speed like falling from the sky.

Oldfield froze, his hands locked on his wooden wheel as he took an interminable ride of launches into the air and slams back against the Earth. Surreal sounds of the car's wood frame snapping and crackling filled his ears.

Beyond the track, Oldfield couldn't believe where he was. Downward, he rode this bucking beast as another fence appeared, and he punched through it like it was Paper Mache.

Horrified, Oldfield saw a large rock flash into his path, and he braced himself. His eyes closed as a sudden, powerful jolt ripped the steering wheel away and launched him into feeling insignificant.

Sensations came and left quickly as something new and terrible was happening to him faster than he could think. He thumped to the Earth. Eyes closed; his body became a cocoon. From the darkness of his mind, he couldn't tell what was happening to him other than he was being scraped, poked, and stabbed.

Tumbling downhill, shrouded in darkness, Oldfield finally had a sensation that lasted long enough for his mind to process. Incessant, probing scrapes tore at his skin. Grasping at the straw he was mowing through, he felt it rip through his hands and slice his skin. Mercifully, at long last, everything stopped.

Breathless and swallowing back burning vomit at the back of his tongue, Oldfield moaned and grunted. He instinctively filled his hands full of weeds and yanked handfuls from the Earth as if that could give him a handle on the world. Wondering if this was what it felt like to die, he panicked and gasped for air. Cycling his legs like the futile flailing of a deer being devoured by a grizzly, he searched pointlessly for comfort. When he opened his eyes, he couldn't see anything but the brittle, yellowing weeds he floundered in.

A voice in the distance yelling at people to stay clear overcame the ringing in Oldfield's ears. As he lay in the grass, he felt the warmth of oozing blood pasting his shirt to a spot on his back.

Another blood leak emerged, then a third, expanding like ripples in a pond formed by a tossed stone. Oldfield's chest heaved as he fought to extend his short breaths to a controlled pace. Slowly, as he lay on his back, looking up at soft clouds, he realized that rocks and sticks had pierced his skin as he tumbled out of control.

Finally, Oldfield pushed up with his hands, feeling a sharp pain in his ribs and stinging in his palms, cut by grasping at the weeds. Dizzy and unsure, he stumbled to stand above the tall grass and spat out bloody chips of broken teeth. His inner cheek and tongue stung, feeling like pulp exposed after losing teeth as a kid. Stunned, Oldfield stood at the bottom of a ditch and wondered if he possibly could have rolled down such a hill. A mounted policeman pulled his horse near.

"You okay, Barney?"

Oldfield couldn't find the breath to speak, but nodded and waved to indicate that he was. At least he thought he was. Around him were red fragments of metal and wood that used to be part of his car. He scanned the immediate area, foolishly holding out hope that the Pup wouldn't be too beat up, but he couldn't find it.

A twisted, red lump rested against the boulder. The wreckage was like a memory from the previous night's drunk. All the wheels were knocked off the crushed hulk, and the shattered wooden spokes of one rim were about twelve feet from where he landed.

"Oh, shit," he murmured in resignation.

Stumbling up the hill, Oldfield emerged from the weeds to notice the astonished expressions of dozens of people who seemed stunned into silence that he was still alive. Not giving a damn to talk to anyone, he just wanted to sort out what all this meant for himself.

People shouted his name and asked if he was okay. Oldfield only nodded as his mind took an inventory of the pains that sprang up and became more acute as the minutes passed. The throbbing in his rib cage made him wince through every step, and the holes in his back stung relentlessly.

The new white shirt he had ruined the day before with mud splatters in the front, was now soaked with blood in the back. As he shuffled past people, he heard shouts for a doctor.

Oldfield pushed his way out onto the track and sensed the awe of everyone around him. Stumbling down the center of the homestretch, Oldfield came into view of the grandstands and heard the crowd begin to cheer. The blood-drenched white shirt was now matted to his back and felt heavy and sticky like it was soaked with glue.

The more time people had to absorb Oldfield's image, the cheers turned to gasps and screams. Scanning the stands, he saw a woman faint into the arms of her companion. Cooper, Spider, and Hill ran out onto the track to him.

"Jesus, Barney, are you okay?" Cooper shouted. "Goddamn, I never saw anything like it."

The cacophony from the grandstands and the people surrounding him suffocated Oldfield. He searched Cooper's eyes.

"I never had the crap kicked out of me like this."

John Jack drove a Winton Touring Car to where the three men stood. People swarmed around them, pointing to the bloody shirt and yelling.

"Barney, let's get you out of here," Jack said, for the first time not sounding like an asshole. "George, talk to the Triple-A guys and let them know we'll be at the hospital or the hotel. See what we need to do about the car. I'll come back and help you later."

Hill nodded, and Jack looked at Cooper.

"Do you want to come?"

Cooper and Oldfield stepped up into the tonneau, and the people who had poured out onto the track parted to make way for the Winton car.

In the Detroit Hotel, Oldfield lay in his bed, propped up with extra pillows, and facing Cooper, who sat in a chair beside him. Earlier, the doctor that had stitched the deep slices in his back told the driver that the pain in his ribs was understandable because they were cracked. Oldfield was supposed to lay still and not bust his stitches.

He struggled to eat the food Cooper had ordered to the room. Electricity surged through his skull intermittently when he chewed. His beat-up pulpy tongue was ineffective in maneuvering food away from his ripped inner cheek and chipped teeth. Oldfield never realized before how much his ribs moved when he swallowed. Cooper handed him a fifth of corn mash, and despite the fierce burning of his shredded inner mouth, he kept drinking it every time it was offered.

Oldfield thought about what John Jack said when he visited earlier. Jack said the name of the man he hit at Gross Pointe was Frank Shearer of Barberton, Ohio.

Never met the man before and I killed him.

Jack had also said that Shearer's brother was the man who sat next to Frank on the rail, but he only had a few scrapes. Oldfield couldn't get the sickening, soft thud of when the Pup hit Shearer out of his mind.

"They warned people not to sit on the rail, goddamn it. This almost happened at Cleveland when that little Baker Electric slipped under the fence."

Oldfield paused and studied the reflection of his face in the amber fluid-filled bottle he held in his hand. He tipped it to his lips again, using his tongue to try to shield the injured side of his mouth. The technique failed once more as the alcohol stung like battery acid.

Goddamn, that hurts. Just one more and I'll stop… Goddamn this Shearer fella anyway.

"You know, I don't think I ever realized how fast I was going until the tire blew out. When I couldn't control it anymore, I couldn't believe how fast things happened. Faster than I could think. Why didn't this Shearer fella listen to what they told him to do?"

"He sounds like you, Barney. Look, he wanted to be close to everything. A lot of them do. You can't hardly blame them."

"Well, I'm quitting. I've had enough of this game. I can do other things than risk my neck so other people can watch how men die."

"Funny, but I was thinking I might sell old Nine-Ninety-Nine," Cooper said. "I've been talking to Frank Day, and he's looking at buying it. He's going to take a run at your five-mile record at Milwaukee on Saturday. I think I've had enough, too. I might as well sell Nine-Ninety-Nine while I can still get something out of her."

(Zanesville, Ohio, September 9, 1903)

Carl Fisher hoped the blurry picture was another deception of his myopia. Mounted National Guardsmen waded into an angry, confused crowd at the county fairgrounds in Zanesville, Ohio. A dozen people or more lay scattered on the ground, several with strangely twisted arms and legs. One of Fisher's eleven hundred cubic inch Mohawk racers that he called "the most powerful car in the world" was now on its side, fuel and oil leaking out of the vents in its engine cowling.

Fisher squinted his feeble eyes in frustration as he searched for his friend, Earl Kiser. His weak eyes sorted through a pile of bodies amidst clucking chickens apparently liberated through some collision with a coop. Retracing the invisible pattern he had drawn with his eyes, Fisher passed over a limp figure in brown clothing obscured in the dirt of similar color. A nervous jolt automatically swung his head back again.

Kiser!

His friend lay beside the car, about fifteen feet from a pulverized wooden rail. The last Fisher saw Kiser he had pulled a good one hundred yards or more ahead of him going down the backstretch in their five-mile match race.

Damn! Everything had been so good.

Fisher had ordered the cars from Mohawk Cycle Company in Indianapolis, and they were fast as blazes at this little hippodrome. Now, his friend blasted through a fence and mowed down a pack of people. Everything happened so quickly his mind grappled with collecting it all. Out of nowhere, people screamed, "Murderer!" Some of them began breaking pieces off the stricken Mohawk.

Goddamn souvenir vultures!

Fisher clenched his fists and felt an explosion of blood and adrenaline rush to his head. Only briefly did he think that he might be taking on twenty or more men alone. His brother Earle pulled at his arm to restrain him.

"Goddamn bastards! I'll kill any man that touches that car."

A guardsman, perched high on his horse, shouted down to Fisher.

"Don't be a fool, fella. Move your partner, these folks are out of control."

Fisher studied Kiser, who grimaced in pain and lay helpless in the dirt. Knowing the nature of angry men, Fisher realized he needed to cut his losses and get Kiser and the surviving car out of the area.

"Earl! Jesus Christ on a bicycle! Let's get you up!"

A couple of drunken men with sticks moved toward Kiser, but the Guardsman came between them with his horse. Twisting his head over his shoulder, the horse-mounted man shouted to Fisher a second time.

"Goddamn, you idiots! I won't tell you again! Get the Hell out of here! I won't be responsible for what happens to you!"

Fisher took one of Kiser's arms and helped him to his feet. Motioning for his brother Earle to help, they drug Kiser to their Mohawk, which sat idling on the track.

In the background, Fisher heard a pistol shot. The Guardsman must be warning people to stay back. Almost immediately, though, a dozen men came running from behind the destroyed fence in their direction. Fisher gathered a handful of Kiser's collar into his fist, and with one mighty shove, he thrust his friend onto the front seat. Kiser screamed in agony as his injured leg bounced against the Mohawk's wood bench.

"Oh, God, Oh God, Carl, I think my leg's about broke off," Kiser screamed.

Fisher ran around the car to get to the controls ahead of the approaching men.

"All our legs are gonna be busted up if we don't get the Hell out of here."

Leaping to the steering wheel almost like he could fly, Fisher quickly slipped the machine into gear and started to roll. Earle ran alongside the car, just ahead of the mob. Fisher craned his neck to judge his distance from his pursuers while driving slow enough to let his brother jump aboard.

"Come on, goddamn it, Earle, hurry up, or I'll leave you behind!"

Like a hobo hitching a ride on a freight train Earle jumped aboard, and Fisher accelerated, his necktie slapping his face in the breeze like a flag in kite weather. Fisher saw Earle clinging to a trunk affixed to the back of the seat. The mob was within ten feet of them as Earle screamed for his brother to speed up and pull him away from grasping hands. Fisher cut down a service road that had a slight incline. He knew he could scale it much easier than men on foot. The pack of drunks and toughs fell back in the distance.

Fisher continued to drive over fifty miles per hour, almost as fast as he had raced. The stiff, wagon-like car bounced mercilessly, and he heard his brother screaming to slow down, that he couldn't hold on any longer.

The racetrack grandstands grew steadily smaller, and Fisher lightened his foot on the accelerator. Kiser writhed in pain beside him, and Earle screamed for joy – or just relief. Fisher peered out over the long, black, vented cowling and tried to focus on the rugged, winding country road.

Where is the goddamn road?

"I can't see a goddamn thing! How's a person supposed to know where the goddamn road is when it doesn't look any different than any other goddamn piece of Earth? How is this country ever going to have an automobile industry if there aren't any goddamn roads?"

Fisher wasn't talking to his brother or Kiser or anyone in particular. The brown edges of the dirt road blended into the brown, rugged terrain on either side. Earle shouted over the engine.

"Where are we going, Carl?"

Fisher raised his right arm and pointed straight ahead.

"Indianapolis."

"Have you lost your mind? That's a couple a hundred miles! I can't hang on to the back of this car that long."

A sudden jolt reverberated throughout the wagon frame, and both Earle and Kiser screamed. Kiser winced, and his face contorted in a grimace. Fisher, feeling pressured, explained what he meant.

"Alright, alright! I didn't mean we were just going to keep driving. I just want to get as much distance between Zanesville and us as I can. Hang on. We need to get Kiser to a doctor, and then we'll get him on a train. Then you and I will drive this wagon back to Indianapolis."

Fisher squinted at the road. Another monstrous jolt sent his heart racing, and he squeezed the wheel so tightly his knuckles turned white. The Mohawk bounded into the air and crashed back down as his brother and Kiser screamed in the background.

Fisher's heart continued to pound, and he held his breath like he was jumping in a lake. Glancing over his shoulder, he saw Kiser's face splattered with blood. He must have smashed his nose on the wood trunk when the Mohawk landed.

"Goddamn roads."

His breath returned as the Mohawk pointed straight again, and the exhilarating power of the engine momentarily distracted him. His mind drifted back to the track and the mess. The other car was destroyed. A picture of those people lying on the ground became more vivid as he reflected on it.

Real, living, breathing people, with jobs, farms, and kids.

"Jesus Christ. I wonder how many are dead?"

Chapter 8 – The Punished and the Adored

(Sunday, January 24, 1904)

Special Florida trains commissioned by railroads like the Seaboard Air Line absorbed an exodus of industrialists from the great Annual New York Automobile Show at Madison Square Garden on Sunday, January 24. Barney Oldfield and Tom Cooper joined most of the leaders of the industry, and many private automobilists on their way to the significant speed tournament on the sands of Daytona and Ormond Beach. Billed by promoter William J. Morgan as the "fastest racecourse in the world," there seemed little doubt to Oldfield that this was more substance than braggadocio.

He had stuffed his new leather briefcase full of motor journals and flipped through them as he sat on the train. Oldfield read about Packard's Charles Schmidt and his January 3rd speed trial. All the periodicals raved about how the little twenty-four horsepower Gray Wolf came within a fraction of the world's record for straightaway miles, at forty-six and three-fifths seconds, just a tick of the watch slower than Maurice Augieres' forty-six-second run on the Dourdan Road in France more than a year earlier.

The cacophony of voices hummed in the background and energized Oldfield. He loved the idea that so many people were coming to see him set records. Unlike any race meet crowd he had seen before, a palpable holiday mood infused the excited chatter as women and children traveled with husbands and fathers, asking questions like how far it was to Ormond Beach. A boy asked his father if it was true Barney Oldfield and William K. Vanderbilt, Junior was going to square off once and for all.

First-class accommodations were more crowded than usual, and when Oldfield rested his boot on the armrest of the bench directly in front of him, the middle-aged man in the seat turned around and scowled. Oldfield just shrugged his shoulders and said,

"Cramped, ain't it?"

A couple of rows forward, the little boy he heard earlier peered over his seat at the driver and pointed. Oldfield watched him for several minutes then decided to give the kid a thrill. Motioning for the youngster to approach him, the child drew near. The boy's eyes were like saucers, and his radiating, scarlet face flushed bright enough to warm the entire passenger car - he was breathless.

"Mr. Oldfield, my father and I were at Empire City last June when you set that world's record. You were going great guns! I read you busted that mile record again out in California. A track mile in fifty-five seconds flat! You must be the bravest man in the world! Bigger than anybody."

Oldfield talked to the boy for several minutes, savoring his admiration. Men stopped as they roamed the car, shaking his hand. The driver noted their suits, shirts, ties, and jewelry. Oldfield had large diamond rings on the pinky fingers on both his hands and sported a wide-brimmed gray felt hat because he thought the typical bowler was for ginks. A gold chain weaved through his vest buttonhole attached to a gold fob in one pocket, and a gold watch on the other end. One man, observing that Oldfield's cigar was short and unlit, offered him another.

"Monte Cristo, the finest in the world," the man said.

Since the accident at Grosse Point, Oldfield always had a lit or unlit cigar in his mouth, especially when driving. A fresh cigar clenched directly over his chipped molars cushioned the jarring to his sensitive, damaged teeth.

"I clamp it in the Southwest corner of my mouth," Oldfield explained.

An admiring man scraped a wooden match with his thumbnail and carefully lit a cedar stick he kept in his breast pocket. Fire kissed Oldfield's cigar, and the champion inhaled. People he didn't know knew him by reputation, but it was a different crowd than at his races. Their clothing was better and, for the most part, their language too. They pretended not to get excited about things, and throughout the trip, Oldfield noticed people pointing in his direction and whispering – but many turned their heads when they saw him look their way.

John Jack and Charlie Shanks sat together several rows ahead of Oldfield and Cooper. They had grown increasingly distant over the months, never attending the race meets, especially after Oldfield announced that Cooper was his manager. Oldfield yelled to Jack, "Finest cigar in the world, John."

Oldfield wanted the Winton executive to know who got free cigars and praise. Jack did not acknowledge him.

"Is Ford coming down here?" Oldfield asked Cooper.

"Nope. He's awful busy with his business. He set that record a couple of weeks ago, and I think he's going to wait and see what happens down here."

Cooper talked about how on January 12th, Henry Ford again emerged with the infamous Nine-Ninety-Nine. He skidded and slid over a measured mile of Michigan's frozen

Lake St. Claire at the astonishing time of thirty-nine and two-fifths seconds, for a new land speed straightaway record.

"Nine-Ninety-Nine," Oldfield said. "How many Nine-Ninety-Nine's are there now, Tom?"

"I don't know that there's even one now. There just seems to be one around when somebody needs one. After Frank Day killed himself up in Milwaukee when he was thinking about buying mine, old Spider and I spent better than a month patching it up. But you know that's just pieces. It isn't that same car. So then I sell it to that promoter, Will Pickens. Next thing I know, Spider's back working for Hank, and they say they have Nine-Ninety-Nine running a new world's record. It was really the Arrow. Don't that beat all?"

Cooper had a habit of talking differently depending on what mood he was in, or who he was with. He spoke smooth as silk around the Society Swells, but when he was with Oldfield and Spider or other racing friends, he was down on the farm.

"So, Barney, what's the betting line on busting Hank's record? Can you do it?"

"I still need to figure out how this beach racing works. I don't figure sand for anything but soft, but I hear this stuff is special. I hear it's hard as concrete when it's wet and baked in the sun. I'll tell you what, if that little Packard can run a mile in forty-six seconds, my Bullet is going to be awful strong."

"Word is, Willie K. Vanderbilt is gunning for the record. He's got that new ninety horsepower Mercedes. The thing is made of aluminum, they say."

"Is that supposed to scare me?"

"He's a Swell, to be sure, but he's not like the others. He knows how to drive. He runs over in those big European races. I hear the boy finished third in Belgium July before last."

"Third?"

"I'm telling you, Barney, those races are big derbies. It ain't these deals where we go five or ten miles at pumpkin fairs. Those fellas go for a couple hundred miles and more. And some of their races have fifty, sixty cars."

"I ain't afraid of him or any man alive."

"Good. Because if you whoop these fellas, we'll go on a big tour and let the weed benders get a load of you. That'll be good business."

(Ormond Beach, Florida, Wednesday, January 27, 1904)

The Winton Bullet II didn't arrive at Ormond until late Tuesday, and Oldfield, Cooper, and George Hill worked late into the night to prepare it. Just after dawn the next morning, Oldfield and Cooper took a walk on the beach to see a handful of racers practice. As they trudged through the powdery sand well apart from the shoreline, they saw a young man in an ankle-length duster and black leather cap pacing beside a table.

"Willie K," Cooper said.

"So that's what the richest man in the country looks like," Oldfield replied.

As they drew near, Oldfield shouted out, "William K. Vanderbilt, meet Barney Oldfield."

Vanderbilt did not seem to notice. At first, his eyes fixed on the men sitting at a table filled with electric timing equipment. In a delayed reaction, he cocked his head in Oldfield's direction and furrowed his brow as if contemplating profound literature. Then his eyes widened in recognition.

"Mr. Oldfield! Bully good! I heard you took the challenge to run the gauntlet, and I am pleased to see it is so. I shall be even more pleased to defeat you in combat."

"I'm just here to race, Mr. Vanderbilt," Oldfield said. "And if there is going to be any defeats going on around here, it's going to be me doing it. This is my manager, Tom Cooper."

Vanderbilt laughed a tempered but good-natured sportsman's laugh that revealed white teeth below a well-groomed thick, black mustache.

"And it would not be an American race without you, Mr. Oldfield. It shall be an honor to engage you. And welcome, Mr. Cooper."

Vanderbilt stared intently down Ormond Beach, toward Daytona Beach, seven miles away. Pointing to two tiny specs on the horizon, he identified them as his friend Gould Brokaw's Renault, driven by his chauffeur, Maurice Bernin, who was well ahead of a Bernard Shanley's Decauville, with his chauffer, Edward Fredericks at the wheel.

"They run down seven and one-half miles marked by a fifteen-foot ladder, and then they turn back. It's a private challenge. You know we amateurs, Mr. Oldfield, we're very sporting. A trophy and some wagers, a 'best of three heats' challenge."

Oldfield had read more about Vanderbilt than he admitted to anyone. The millionaire was twenty-five, a year younger than him, and was the scion of America's wealthiest family. His great-grandfather, Cornelius "Commodore" Vanderbilt, earned a fortune of over $100 million in steam shipping lines, and later, railroads. By the 1860s, he was the wealthiest man in America. Born into the fortune, this man, the newspapers sometimes called "Willie K," had gone to Harvard and married San Franciscan Virginia Fair, an heiress to a $200 million silver mining fortune. The story went that the people in Newport, Rhode Island, had practically run Willie K out of town for scorching their roads with the fastest cars he could buy. While Vanderbilt spent a lot of time in Europe, he had an estate in Long Island and a mansion on Fifth Avenue.

Vanderbilt abruptly turned his attention back to the timer's table, where there was a commotion between two men and officials from the Florida East Coast Automobile Association. The men argued, and it was apparent that they owned the cars in the match race. One of the men was upset that the officials had started the race without setting the Mors electric timer.

"How can you run a proper motorcar contest without recording a time?" he shouted.

The other man rolled his eyes.

"The tide is coming in, Bernard. Do we really want to delay this further? We have two cars. Don't you think it will be readily apparent who prevails in the end?"

Vanderbilt, appearing anxious, intervened.

"Mr. Shanely, won't we get enough of this nonsense when those professionals take to the course? Can't we have one day off from this sort of common behavior?"

Oldfield felt a jolt of anger. When it came to racing cars, nobody was more of a professional than he. This was a thoughtless insult – it was like he wasn't even present. Vanderbilt, who seemed welcoming and respectful at first, revealed himself as precisely what Oldfield expected: a snob who thought he was better than him.

Bernard Shanley stood tall, like a soldier coming to attention. He adjusted his tie and tilted his head toward Vanderbilt.

"Very well, then. And I shall expect the same consideration directed at me in the event of the next controversy."

Cooper looked at Oldfield and rolled his eyes, muttering, "Swells."

Soon, the roar of the Renault grew louder. Far and away in front, Brokaw's car had the better of Shanley's and decisively won the first heat.

As the second heat got underway, with the timing apparatus under the close scrutiny of Shanley, Vanderbilt pulled one of the Florida officials aside. Despite the seashore breeze, Oldfield could hear them talking.

"I should like to take a run at old Henry Ford's record, Sir. I should like to see the fastest mile not just possessed by the United States, but this great state of Florida."

Oldfield studied the official. A short, doughy man whose sport coat was a size too small, except the sleeves, which extended well beyond his wrists, grimaced as he listened to Vanderbilt.

"Can't do it. The tide's coming in, and it will take us too long to reposition the timers from the seven-mile stretch to your measured mile."

"Can't do it! Can't do it! Are you telling me that Florida's world record is in jeopardy because you can't plan? Because you are incompetent?"

The little man wiped his runny nose on his excessive sleeve and looked helplessly up at Vanderbilt.

"Mr. Vanderbilt," boomed a voice from several paces behind. Oldfield pivoted to see the source. The relentless sound of the surf and the silence of the sand had cloaked the approach of Art Pardington.

Oh God, it's Pardington, here to play God, Oldfield thought.

"Mr. Pardington! Bully good! You are always here when I need you," Vanderbilt's voice shifted from a tone of irritation to cheerful enthusiasm. "How are you, my good man? I hear you had a rough night of it. What's this about parking your car in the surf?"

The men talked as if Oldfield and Cooper weren't present. Pardington saw them – of this Oldfield was sure - but made no attempt to acknowledge their presence.

"This packed sand makes the best speedway in the world until the ocean covers it. Last evening, I showed that Motor Magazine newspaperman Al Reeves the course, but we got caught up in the rainstorm, and the wind blew out our headlamps. It was dreadfully pitch-black, and the next thing I knew, I was bailing her out like a leaky rowboat. We ended up walking four miles back to the hotel. I ruined a perfectly good suit and shoes and was quite miserable."

Vanderbilt poked Pardington's paunch belly and smiled.

"I don't suppose your newspaperman will write much of a story. But what of it? It sounds like a bully-good exercise, Pardington! If you want to exercise, I can soon have you out on the polo field with a fine steed."

"If you were anyone else, Mr. Vanderbilt, I would suggest the notion absurd. But your penchant for doing the impossible makes me question such a judgment. But I approached you to see if I could be of service. I could not help hearing your discussion with the gentleman from the Florida..."

"The buffoon!" Vanderbilt snapped. "Arthur, I need your help. The tide is narrowing the course as we speak. But the wind is calm and the visibility quite good. I feel the world's record is within my grasp. Won't you be a good man and accommodate my request?"

"Allow me to propose a solution," Pardington said. "When Ford made his run in that ridiculous contraption, there were no electric timers. He was on a frozen lake, for Christ's sake!"

This time, Oldfield reached out to Cooper and put his hand firmly on his shoulder. Calling Nine-Ninety-Nine ridiculous! The bastards! Cooper and Oldfield exchanged angry looks as Pardington continued his proposal.

"The officials there used eight skilled timers with split-second watches, which they all struck their timers simultaneously. There were three at the finish, and five at the start. It was perfectly official, all sanctioned by the Automobile Club of America. I have eight good men here for just such purpose. Since we can't re-assemble the electric timers, we can do it the old-fashioned way. Be assured it is all according to regulation."

"Good show! Good man! We must look sharp; the tide will not wait."

"I'm curious to see how this works," Oldfield said to his friend. "Let's stick around."

"Yeah, let's stick around and see this ridiculous contraption run," Cooper said.

Oldfield struck up a conversation with Al Reeves as they stood among a group of men at the starting tape. Reeves had participated in these timings before and knew Oldfield quite well from covering his races. The old newspaperman explained the timing procedure.

"Vanderbilt's up the beach about two miles. In a little bit, they'll give a signal, and he'll get a flying start by the time he gets here," Reeves said. "That Mercedes may be the most powerful car in the world. Four cylinders, two thousand pounds, and ninety horsepower, it's got an aluminum frame."

"Say, Al, I want to see the end of this. Can somebody drive Tom and me down to the finish?"

"Sure. I'm supposed to stay here, but I've got my Cadillac right over there. Drive it down to the end of the mile and just leave it there."

The day was bright but still chilly for Florida. All the men wore flannel overcoats, and many had gloves. The stiff breeze Oldfield felt to his back let him know it would push Vanderbilt along. An unpredictable wind could make for a harrowing experience, as the big cars jump enough on their own at top speed.

Oldfield imagined that to be caught broadside by a gust at precisely the worst time could brush a car off the road like crumpled paper. He knew, too, that a strong headwind could anchor the vehicle to the course, but the wind to Vanderbilt's back was worth as much as a second.

The beach offered miles of perfectly straight speedway, narrowing at the tide's tedious advance. At low tide, the width of the billiard-table smooth surface between the lapping waves on one side and the loose sand on the right was well beyond one hundred feet. Oldfield judged that little more than fifty feet were available at that moment.

A couple of loud blasts like gunshot drew Oldfield's head away from the shoreline view. It was Pardington, who arrived in a backfiring touring car. The chauffeur remained behind the wheel as Pardington bent his knees to extract himself from the machine. Clearing his throat, he prepared to address timers gathered there.

"Gentleman, Masseurs Thompson, Adams, Reeves McGuinness, and Leighton will time from the starting tape. After these instructions, I have directed Masseurs Batchelder, Smith, and Hall to depart to the finish line," Pardington said. "Before they do, however, each of you will start your watches simultaneously. Each man must strike his watch in absolute synchronicity with all the others, or this vital record will be rendered invalid. Is that clear?"

Oldfield stood among the huddled men, all dressed in overcoats nearly as long as their pant legs. They nodded and grunted in a way that affirmed their understanding of the instructions.

"Good," Pardington said as he began again. "Shortly after our timers are at their stations, the contestant will be instructed to start his motorcar and proceed. When he reaches the starting tape, the timers stationed at that point will stop their watches. At the instant, he completes his measured mile run, the timers stationed at the finish line will stop their watches. We will record the average time among the timers at each location, then subtract the time at the starting tape from the time at the finish line, and that calculation will produce a time that I will review for certification. Is that clear?"

Another chorus of affirmative grunts affirmed their understanding.

"Very well then, gather close to me and with absolute concentration, study your watches and listen carefully to my instruction," Pardington said. "At the count of three - at the instant, I say three - you are to start your watch. Is that clear?"

Oldfield watched Pardington as he counted off the numbers, and the men dutifully struck their timers. Pardington lumbered into a touring car. His chauffeur drove him in the direction of Vanderbilt and his Mercedes. Oldfield and Cooper took Reeves' Cadillac in the opposite direction to the finish line, where they climbed out and walked to the timers' station, consisting of a table and half a dozen wooden chairs.

From the finish line, Oldfield saw a dust cloud hugging the northern horizon and knew it was the big Mercedes kicking up sand. Pushing his way through a crowd of men, he asserted his right to a clear view.

Oldfield's eyes swept the beach behind him and guessed there was a crowd of nearly three thousand gathered with lunches on dunes safely distant from the course. Word must have spread fast that Willie K was on a record-breaking rampage.

The tiny sandstorm loomed more substantial on the horizon, and while it was difficult to tell from a mile away, Oldfield was sure Vanderbilt had passed the starter's tape. He stared at the tires of the German car, watching to see them bounce, and swore he saw daylight under them at least once. The dull roar of the enormous engine grew into an angry, ear-splitting cry as the white machine closed in on them.

When the Mercedes passed under the tape, no one could be sure that the record was busted. The timing committee was instructed to report to Referee Pardington at the Ormond Inn, so they could publicly record the individual watch times and make their calculations of averages and subtraction.

Willie K continued down the beach, his arm striking at the air above his head. As the car grew small again, Oldfield closed one eye and squinted the other, imagining that Vanderbilt was a tiny figure he could pinch between his thumb and index finger and flick into the ocean.

Several men ran alongside the Mercedes shouting congratulations and some yelling that Willie K had the new world's record, even though there had been no official announcement. Vanderbilt came to the finish line and pulled his car to a stop, shutting down the engine.

From behind, Oldfield heard a voice shout, "Bring on the professionals!" Then came another yell, "Gould Brokaw! Clear the way for Gould Brokaw!"

A man shouting, "Bring on the professionals," brushed past Oldfield as he pushed his way in front of others to hop into the mechanic's seat of the big Mercedes. Brokaw extended his right hand to shake Vanderbilt's and gripped the millionaire's elbow with his left, tugging at him to bring him closer so he could say something into his ear.

Several other men crowded around the Mercedes, shouting the same question about how it felt to go so fast. Vanderbilt shouted back, and Oldfield hated to admit to himself that he wanted to hear Willie K as he struggled to listen over the roar of the wind and surf.

"Whatever the time is, I feel that a faster time yet is possible," Vanderbilt shouted to the crowd.

Oldfield could tell Vanderbilt thought he was pretty important, as the millionaire continued to tell his story.

"I swerved once to avoid a wave, but struck it and got a shower. At times I bounced some, clearing the track, I should say, about two feet high. In traveling one hundred thirty-five feet a second, a man does not estimate at the time how far the car leaps."

Oldfield fidgeted and ground his chipped teeth watching Vanderbilt revel in the adoration. A photographer snapped several pictures at a distance and then approached Willie K about a posed shot. At first, Vanderbilt refused, but the photographer continued to press. Oldfield guessed the fella to be no more than eighteen; his cherubic-like cheeks gave him a babyface.

Brokaw whispered something in Vanderbilt's ear, and they laughed as they studied the boy. Vanderbilt sounded like he was on stage as he played to the crowd.

"Well, I really do not want to, but I will tell you what I am willing to do," said Willie K. "I will leave it to the toss of a coin. If the coin lands heads, I pose; but if it is tails, I don't."

The photographer agreed, and Brokaw flipped the coin, and everyone fell quiet. Oldfield glanced at Cooper and then rolled his eyes in disgust over the contrived theatrics.

"Say cheese, Mr. Vanderbilt," Brokaw said with a laugh.

Vanderbilt frowned and then said, "Go ahead, then, quickly."

Oldfield thought Vanderbilt looked surprised when the young man shouted for one of the women in the crowd to loan him the blanket she had used to sit on the beach. The young photographer folded it to an extra thickness and draped it over the cowling of the Mercedes, much in the fashion of saddling a horse. With great agility, the boy scrambled atop his car and straddled it. For an instant, Oldfield thought Vanderbilt stared at him as he directed his comments to his audience.

"Well, isn't he quite trusting, or perhaps foolish. Do you not know, young man, I could start this beast and shake you off like an insect?"

"I will have my picture and be gone from you before your chauffeur can turn the crank," the young photographer said, catching Vanderbilt in a candid smile. As he took the picture, Oldfield and Cooper stood silent as cheers erupted, and applause enveloped them.

As the minutes passed, Oldfield heard the chatter among the thousands of onlookers intensify. Clearly, some kind of news was spreading, he thought. Within minutes, Pardington's touring car appeared.

Carefully, the lanky official balanced on the running board until he planted one foot in the sand. Oldfield knew something was up.

Pardington sported a broad smile and the look of joy reserved for a reprieved man as he walked to Vanderbilt, who was now standing with Brokaw at the side of his car. Shaking the millionaire's hand, Pardington tilted a megaphone to his lips and faced the audience. When Pardington cleared his throat, Oldfield knew old shit-head thought he had something monumental to say.

"Mr. Vanderbilt, it gives me great pleasure to officially announce that on this date, on the sands of Ormond Beach, USA, you have earned the right to call yourself the speed champion of the world."

Pardington was interrupted by loud and spontaneous applause.

"With an official time of thirty-nine seconds on the measured mile, as recognized by the American Automobile Association, the Automobile Club of America, and the Florida East Coast Automobile Association. I crown you, William Kissam Vanderbilt Junior, the world mile speed champion and fastest man on mother Earth."

A sustained outburst of cheers drowned the relentless sounds of the surf. Pardington waited for another opening for one last megaphone proclamation, "Faster than any Frenchman, or any professional, and done in a proper motorcar, not some wagon monstrosity."

Oldfield looked around him to all the faces of people celebrating Vanderbilt. Nobody was paying him any attention. They didn't even know Barney Oldfield stood among them. The sight of Pardington and Brokaw laughing pissed him off, and he wanted to shut them up. Cooper looked madder than a wet hornet as he leaned toward Oldfield's ear.

"Wagon monstrosity. That fucking son-of-a-bitch. Let's get out of here, Barney, we need to get you ready to race these bastards."

Wednesday night, the National Good Roads Association staged a subscription ball in the casino of the Hotel Ormond. The casino was beautifully decorated in a tropical theme, with lush palm trees positioned carefully about the perimeter of the room. Bouquets of colorful flowers from the Floridian jungles provided stunning arrangements at each table. Wives of the millionaires and industrialists joked and commiserated about not having time with their husbands.

Like the other men in the room, Oldfield and Cooper wore black tuxedos, while the women donned elaborate gowns with sequins, ribbons, bustles and trails, many bare-shouldered and low cut for a display of flesh Oldfield delighted in.

Winton Motor Carriage Company had two tables, both near the center of the room. At their primary table, a round of eight, Alexander Winton sat with his stunningly beautiful nineteen-year-old daughter, Helen Fea. Joining them were Mr. and Mrs. Charles Shanks, Mr. and Mrs. John Jack, Barney Oldfield, and Tom Cooper. Shanks and Jack excused themselves from the table after taking a drink order from their wives.

Oldfield knew they were leaving to talk about him. George Hill told him earlier that he heard them talking about Oldfield and Cooper's plan to ask Alexander Winton to let them open a Winton Motor Carriage sales office in New York. Hill said Shanks had "put the fix in" on that. Oldfield watched Shanks stop to shake hands and chat with Howard Gould and Jay Santos-Dumont. Shanks beamed a great smile as he shook the hands of millionaires.

Back at the table, Abigail Jack moved to her husband's seat next to Cooper. Oldfield watched as she laughed and leaned her ear closer to his friend's mouth, apparently to hear him over the orchestra. While she was preoccupied with Cooper, Oldfield hungrily studied the cleavage of her breasts as they danced in step with her laughter. Then he ordered a bottle of Lucien Faucauld Petite Champagne, 1893, paying particular attention to fill Abigail's glass.

"Why, how thoughtful of you, Mr. Oldfield," Mrs. Jack said.

"I like to see people happy, Ma'am. Especially the ladies. Hey, Tom, why don't you tell that story about old Hank Ford setting the world's record again?"

"You shoulda seen ole Spider, Barney," Cooper said with a laugh. "Hank paid him fifty greenbacks to hang onto the side of the old Arrow, bent over the carburetor, holding down the throttle with his hand. The damn car was bouncing around so much, Hank couldn't keep his foot on the pedal."

"Spider?" Oldfield said. "Hell, you remember how scared he'd get riding with me? I'll bet his damn eyes were bigger than these dinner plates. Man, oh, man, I would have paid him another fifty bucks just to let me watch. Was he drunk?"

They laughed again, hard and loud. Oldfield noticed Abigail laughed at their story, made funnier by alcohol.

"Spider," said Abigail. "What a peculiar name. Surely his mother didn't name him Spider."

"What the Hell is Huff's name, Tom? I've known the man for nearly three years now, and I hate to admit I don't even know," Oldfield said.

"Edward," Tom answered.

Oldfield took a drink of bourbon, and nearly sprayed it out of his mouth when he heard the answer.

"Edward? Spider is Edward?" Oldfield was almost cackling. "Naw, he's Spider. Spider is a better name for him."

"Do you like your friends to have insect or animal names, Mr. Oldfield?" Abigail asked.

Oldfield felt a fresh trace of the bourbon glistening on his lips as he smiled.

"And you should have seen that track we made on the ice," Tom continued, re-starting the story of Ford's January 12 record.

"First, we scattered hot cinders, about fifteen feet wide, for pretty near five miles. They melted into the ice. Then, we laid down the sand. We swept all the loose stuff off."

"So, did that work pretty good?" Oldfield asked.

"Hell no! He was sliding all over the place. It's a good thing he had Spider on there, or Hank probably would have parked it. I think they both got so damned scared, they just kinda froze in position. Hank at the wheel and Spider perched on the frame. But I will tell you what, I am right proud of old Hank; he hung in there. We sunk the seat of the old Arrow and replaced the tiller with a wheel, and it's a whole new car."

"You don't care Ford called it the Nine-Ninety-Nine?" Oldfield asked.

"I don't give a good rat's ass," Cooper said, suddenly looking at Abigail.

"Pardon me, Ma'am. You're such pleasant company, I forget myself. I meant no disrespect with the language," Cooper said.

Oldfield was intrigued when Abigail reached out and squeezed Cooper's forearm. If she wasn't another man's wife, he knew his friend would take that as a signal. Maybe he would anyway.

"I'm a lady, but I'm an adult woman too. I enjoy your adventures," Abigail Jack said.

Cooper smiled and nodded.

"So, why should I care if he calls the Arrow the Nine-Ninety-Nine?" Cooper continued. "The real Nine-Ninety-Nine was a pile a junk after ole Frank Day smashed himself up last September. Hank wanted to hop up the Arrow, and that's what Spider and I did. That old wagon monstrosity got Ford a world record, for a couple of weeks, at least."

Cooper used a particular inflection on the word "monstrosity" that only Oldfield understood.

He slapped Cooper on the back.

"Yes, and let me see any of those big shots build a car that can set a world record, Tom. They can buy cars, but you can build 'em."

Oldfield looked across the table at Elizabeth Shanks. She was the dutiful company executive wife, listening to the brilliance of Alexander Winton.

"We are on the brink of huge technological advance," Winton said. "Our Winton products are increasingly accessible to more common citizens, and soon all cars will be cheaper than horses are today. But there are military applications as well. There will be huge forts on wheels that will dash across open spaces at the speed of trains. And soon you will see the demise of streetcars in our cities. There will be huge underground or overhead streets that will teem with capacious automobile passenger coaches and freight wagons. I am looking at automobile boats as well. I believe there will soon be fast ships crossing the Atlantic to Europe in less than two days."

"That's fascinating, Mr. Winton," Mrs. Shanks said. "And what do you make of this nonsense of flying machines? Surely this is a novelty!"

"Oh, I take those machines more seriously than that," Winton said. "The necessity of lightweight design prohibits their use in any meaningful way for transportation or freight delivery, but I believe the military will certainly be interested. But other fields will provide a startling change in our lives. For example, I believe there will be many wireless telephone and telegraph circuits that will span the world. Even people of common means will be able to talk to one another from across the ocean. More exciting than that, men will see around the world. Persons and things of all kinds will be brought within focus of cameras connected electrically with screens at opposite ends."

"You mean that new cameras could share pictures just as we can now hear voices over these telephone wires?" Elizbeth asked.

"Precisely. And what is more, the pictures will be in color and move!"

Helen Fea Winton appeared the bored daughter that had heard her father's prognostications many times at home. Oldfield studied her, and their eyes briefly met, but she quickly turned the other way.

"I want to tell you of changes that perhaps are more relevant to your fair gender," Winton said. "I see a time when hot or cold air will be turned on from spigots to regulate the temperature of a home, just as we now turn on hot or cold water to regulate our bath. And there will be liquid-air refrigerators to keep great quantities of food fresh for extended intervals..."

Helen looked back at Oldfield. He had never taken his eyes off her. The driver riveted his stare into her eyes and then winked. Helen instantly turned away, and her pale white skin began to flush a vibrant shade of red. This coloring did not decrease, but extended down the length of her long, supple neck to form blotches, some beneath her diamond clasped black velvet choker. The coloring complemented the ringlets of red hair that cascaded down from the sculpted pile she had pinned up in the style of a Gibson Girl.

At that moment, Oldfield saw Charles Shanks and John Jack return to the table. He almost chuckled when he saw Jack contort his face when he discovered his wife sitting close to Tom Cooper and whispering in his ear. Extending a glass of champagne between them, Jack gestured to his wife to take it.

"Oh, thank you, dear, but Mr. Oldfield already purchased a bottle of some exquisite champagne for the table," Abigail said. "It's really quite superior, won't you have some?"

"Uh-Oh. It looks like we drank it all, Abigail," Cooper said, examining the empty bottle.

Jack frowned and asked to see his wife in private. Oldfield smirked and then turned his attention back to Helen. He rose from his seat, his eyes fixed on his boss' daughter. She looked at him, then looked away, then looked back again. Oldfield nodded, reached out, and boldly squeezed her bare shoulder with his steady, rough hand. He said nothing and took a step beyond her seat to address her father. Winton was still prophesizing, this time about machines of invisible light, to enable physicians to study living human hearts inside a man's chest.

"Mr. Winton, sir. May I have the honor of a dance with your daughter?" Oldfield asked.

For the first time that evening, Winton was unprepared with a ready answer to a question. An awkward moment lingered as he and his driver locked eyes. Winton seemed to be calculating the odds of Oldfield absconding with his eldest daughter. Finally, the industrialist consented on the condition that his daughter agreed to the invitation. Oldfield turned and extended his hand.

Even Oldfield felt he looked deceptively proper, clean-shaven, well-groomed in his tuxedo with his hair neatly swept back and tamped down with just enough tonic. The girl probably lacked the imagination to conceive of the reality of Barney Oldfield. His vulgar, drunken, whoring ways had to be beyond her tender experience.

"Miss Winton, I would be honored," Oldfield said.

Helen was shy, but said, "Yes," and took the driver's hand. They interlocked arms and walked to the dance floor.

"I have to tell you something."

Helen studied at him, looking a little anxious. Again, she offered a faint, "Yes?"

"I don't know what I am doing."

"Why, what is it that you mean, Mr. Oldfield?" Helen said. "Are you not a professional?"

"I'm talking about dancing. I have never done this before."

Helen laughed. The comment changed everything. Suddenly, she seemed at ease or less intimidated. Her voice now had a lilt, and Oldfield felt a real grip in her hand as she clasped his. As they entered the dance floor, he glanced about and imitated the pose, if not the steps of a waltz. The famous driver grasped Helen's right hand with his left and gently encompassed her back with his right arm. Almost imperceptibly, he shifted his feet.

"We seem capable of perpetrating this fraud without detection, Mr. Oldfield. That is provided you don't draw attention to yourself," Helen said. "What on Earth possessed you to ask me to dance if you don't know how?"

"I don't know. I didn't think about it a whole lot. I guess I kept looking at you from across the table, and I wanted to talk to you alone and hold you in my arms," Oldfield said.

The red blotches resurged. Oldfield enjoyed the idea of stirring such a reaction in a woman. They talked more, and stayed close to the edge of the dance floor, moving cautiously and out of the path of those more skilled. A third, deeper voice brought Oldfield out of the trance he had melted into while searching Helen's eyes.

"Well, well, a professional race driver in a tuxedo, and dancing the waltz, no less. That is what you are doing, isn't it, Mr. Oldfield? Dancing the waltz?"

Oldfield looked at the man who was talking. His face was only vaguely familiar. He recognized Maurice Bernin, W. Gould Brokaw's chauffer, who stood behind the man.

"Who in the Hell are you?" Oldfield asked.

"W. Gould Brokaw."

Oldfield ignored Brokaw's extended hand. Brokaw seemed at a loss for words.

"I'm surprised you don't recall. It was my Renault that won the silver cup today."

"With your chauffeur driving," Oldfield said. "Congratulations, Bernin."

"Yes, proper sportsmen frequently employ chauffeurs. Excuse me, there is someone I want you to meet."

Vanderbilt was just leaving the dance floor. Seeing Brokaw gesture to him, he excused himself from a woman who continued back to her table. Vanderbilt approached Oldfield, Brokaw, and Miss Winton. Before greeting the men, he bowed and took Helen's hand to kiss it.

"William K. Vanderbilt the second, madam," he said, "If I may be so bold, I believe you are Miss Winton, the daughter of the exemplary captain of industry, Mr. Alexander Winton."

"You are quite correct, Mr. Vanderbilt," Helen answered. "May I congratulate you on your achievement this afternoon."

"Thank you, madam, an accomplishment born of much dedication and the support of many dear friends, I assure you," Vanderbilt said.

Oldfield studied Vanderbilt. Deep inside, he was intimidated. Vanderbilt had the grace and eloquence of an upbringing focused on etiquette and classical education, not slopping hogs on a farm or mopping vomit in an insane asylum.

The millionaire possessed a worldly awareness of customs and culture that could only be acquired through numerous trips to the Continent, escorted by family and associates that put an emphasis on the subtleties of social graces. To Oldfield, it was bullshit made all the more frustrating because he understood so little of it. He wanted to fit in, but every time he tried, there was somebody like Vanderbilt or Brokaw to make sure he didn't.

"I'm sorry our conversation was so brief this afternoon, Mr. Oldfield. What do you think of my record?" Vanderbilt locked eyes with Oldfield in an intimidating stare.

Oldfield hated feeling nervousness under Vanderbilt's gaze. He knew this was all part of a game in advance of their competition the following day. Vanderbilt wanted to make him feel uncomfortable, and Oldfield was frustrated that the millionaire was succeeding. His throat tightened, and he feared his voice would tremor when he spoke. A waiter with a glass of champagne walked near him, and he took a step, snatching it off the serving tray. Frowning, the waiter moved on.

By not answering Vanderbilt immediately, Oldfield realized that he came off as aloof and distant. While it wasn't intentional, he quickly surmised that it was a perfect impression. The drink helped relax the tightness in his throat.

"What do I think?" he said. "I think you could have done a thirty-eight if you hadn't let up when the car bounced."

Helen and Oldfield laughed, but the other men were silent.

"Of course, you were quite comfortable watching with the other spectators," Vanderbilt said.

"I'll be driving tomorrow, Junior."

An awkward pause settled over the conversation. Many people called William K. Vanderbilt, Junior 'Willie K,' but he had not granted anyone permission to refer to him as 'Junior.'

"It seems likely we three shall be locked in competition tomorrow," Brokaw said.

Oldfield gave Brokaw a puzzled look.

"We three?" he asked. "You mean, Vanderbilt here, me, and your chauffeur?"

Brokaw's countenance fell.

The waiter walked by again, having replaced the champagne Oldfield had snitched. This time, Vanderbilt snatched a glass of champagne from the waiter's serving tray. The waiter stopped, shook his head, and backtracked his paces to the bar to replace the drink a second time.

Raising the glass in toast, Vanderbilt said, "Que le meilleur gagner."

Oldfield felt the blood drain from his face, and his mouth drop.

Brokaw laughed. "It seems our professional track racer was never schooled in the Romantic languages."

"Pardon me, Mr. Oldfield, allow me to translate…" Vanderbilt said but stopped when he heard Helen Winton speak up.

"Are you trying to suggest that the best man win?" Helen asked without waiting for an answer. "Be careful what you wish for, Mr. Vanderbilt."

Oldfield looked at Helen and smiled until he heard Brokaw's voice.

"My chauffeur drives for me, but women speak for Mr. Oldfield."

With impressive speed and agility, Oldfield rocketed his arm to a spot just below Brokaw's bow tie. Gathering a handful of the millionaire's white silk shirt, his hand popped three silver buttons into the air. Bernin, the chauffeur, jumped forward, but Oldfield threw Brokaw into him with one mighty push.

Brokaw fell on his back, but not before he slammed into Bernin, who then stumbled into the waiter Vanderbilt and Oldfield had stolen drinks from. His tray bounced out of his hands, splashing champagne on a man and woman sitting at a nearby table. The woman screamed, as did Helen.

Within seconds, John Jack was at Helen's side, informing her that her father insisted that she return to their table immediately. Vanderbilt disappeared into the party, and Bernin helped his employer to his feet. Two wait staff dabbed champagne from the man and woman in the background. Cooper bounded from the table to his friend's side.

"You dolt! You uncouth idiot," Brokaw shouted as the room otherwise fell silent.

Even the orchestra stopped playing. Oldfield felt the weight of every eye in the room. A bald-headed man from the National Good Roads Association sprang up and gestured to the orchestra to resume. They did, and he walked through the casino, reassuring everyone that everything was under control and to relax and have a good time.

Moments later, Art Pardington stomped across the room to Oldfield. He leaned into his ear.

"Oldfield! You leave immediately, or I will suspend you from this meet. Go! Now!"

Oldfield nodded unenthusiastically and shrugged his shoulders at Cooper. As they walked to the door at the front lobby, John Jack stepped into pace with them. He spoke to the driver in the same demanding tones as Pardington.

"Because of your misbehavior, Mr. Winton has no alternative but to send Miss Winton home to Ohio on the morning train. You are not to speak to her ever again. Am I clear?"

Oldfield continued to walk without acknowledging the question.

John Jack stopped walking, but Oldfield heard him shouting at his backside.

"Am I clear?"

Chapter 9 – Broken but Unbeaten

(Ormond Beach, Florida, Thursday, January 28, 1904)

A yellow-orange streak extended across the surface of the Atlantic Ocean, narrowing to the hazy originating ball that had progressed only slightly upward from the horizon by 6:30 a.m. Barney Oldfield felt revitalized after a splash of cold water, a light scrubbing of his chipped teeth, and two cups of black coffee.

Dressed in a red leather suit that matched his Winton Bullet II, Oldfield walked with Tom Cooper down the beach access path from the Hotel Ormond, all the while trying not to let on that he was excited to see how people would react to his new outfit. The frigid wind – the locals said unusually cold for Florida even in January – failed to penetrate his leather suit, leaving only his now ruddy cheeks exposed.

Bonfires dotted the landscape and cast light against the purple sky of incomplete dawn. The morning was quiet, and as he walked, Oldfield noted how the glow of the fires on the dunes highlighted the people around them. How many times had he nurtured a campfire throughout the night, just like these folks? People lined the path leading to the beach, and the red outfit drew attention.

"Barney Oldfield! Barney!"

"Barney, let me shake your hand!"

Oldfield grabbed Cooper's arm, and they stopped to talk to a cluster of people at the picket fence that marked the access path. Two men and five young boys stretched their arms over the barrier to shake hands with the champion. One young boy poked his arm through the slats, and Oldfield laughed as he shook it. They told him they were from two families who owned an orange grove.

A short middle-aged man looked up to Oldfield and extended him a metal cup filled with black coffee. A weathered, portly woman with a headscarf shielding her ears from the wind told him she had some milk.

"No thanks, Ma'am, I'm allergic," Oldfield said.

A Cheshire-Cat grin expanded over the face of the man Oldfield took to be the woman's husband. A pewter flask appeared from the breast pocket of his dark blue felt navy jacket.

"I got something for the cold, Barney."

"Yessiree, a man's man!" the driver said, extending the dented tin cup for a shot. Oldfield liked it when people were honored to meet him and share their things with him. The man's face was frozen in a great smile.

The coffee was lukewarm with a taste reminiscent of aspirin. Oldfield drank most of it and handed the rest to Cooper, who pressed it to his lips before turning the cup upside down and giving it back through the fence. They thanked the people, who seemed to be trying to stretch out their time with the champion by asking him if he thought a man would ever go two miles in a minute, and if he felt he could beat Willie K.

"Mr. Vanderbilt shows a lot of speed, but my car wasn't named the Bullet for nothing."

Their smiling faces beamed like lighthouses as he spoke. Hopping awkwardly, the woman had one lame leg, but she clapped her gloved hands. The children giggled and chattered.

"You give 'em what for, you hear, Barney?" the man with the flask said as Oldfield nodded and turned back to the path with Cooper.

Oldfield walked about ten paces and turned back to face the group.

"Barney Oldfield can lick any man alive!"

Dutifully aroused, the huddle behaved as if they were of one mind, cheering and dancing simultaneously.

"Hey, big shot, don't you wish that crowd was at the party last night?" Cooper said.

The two racers nodded at each other and resumed their walk. Smoothed and tamped down, the widened access path accommodated cars. Oldfield had told George Hill to drive the Bullet II out to the beach a half-hour earlier and give the machine a once over with oil and wrenches. When the red Winton car came into his view, officials grouped the Bullet with five other teams. All of them gathered for the first scheduled event of the day, the American One Mile Championship.

"George! Are we ready to scorch some sand?" Oldfield asked.

"Yes, sir, Barney. She's battened down and lubed."

"Have you seen Mr. Winton?"

Oldfield tried to ask the question without giving away his regrets about Wednesday night. Feelings of anger resurfaced when he thought about Brokaw, but he wondered how angry Alexander Winton was and if Hill knew why he was asking or how important the question was to him. Studying his face, Oldfield guessed the young mechanic didn't have a clue.

"I haven't seen Winton, but you should have seen General Pardington! He was fit to be tied. He walked by here yelling about these Florida auto club boys. He says they don't know what they're doing. The word is, they haven't set up their timers, and the tide's coming in."

Beside the Winton was Frank La Roche's forty-horsepower Darracq, while Brokaw and Bernin parked the thirty-horsepower Renault an additional space over. Sammy Stevens and Harold Bowden came prepared with their identical sixty-horsepower Mercedes. Vanderbilt's more massive Mercedes sat unattended just above the tide line.

Oldfield saw Cooper looking at something over his shoulder and turned to see Brokaw and Bernin moving toward them. Oldfield playfully punched his shoulder and winked at him.

"C'mon, Barney. Let's you and me take a walk down the course. We need to see what kind of bumps this here speedway has this morning."

Cooper lowered his voice so Oldfield could barely hear him and moved a step closer to Hill. "George, you see these two sons-of-bitches coming this way? You don't trust them an inch further than you can throw them, you hear? You keep a watch on the old Bullet while Barney and I take a walk. We don't need their aggravation."

As they walked, Oldfield noticed an undulating pattern in the glistening sand that wasn't there when he drove the Bullet up and down the beach early on Wednesday, north of where Vanderbilt made his run. The rain that pelted his hotel windows early that morning had done its work. Cooper stopped at one particularly pronounced indentation and pointed toward his feet.

"What do you make of this?"

"It doesn't look like much walking, but it'll chip your teeth at ninety miles an hour," Oldfield said.

Pulling two fat Havana cigars out of his inner coat pocket, he handed one to Cooper. Oldfield licked his and stuffed it in his mouth without lighting it. Immediately, he felt the saliva build inside his cheeks, and the stream grew dark and potent by the second. The taste was never what he thought it should be, but for some reason, he couldn't explain, he expected it to somehow get better someday.

"The locals call these spots washboards," Cooper said. "You remember yesterday when you saw our buddy Willie K bounce? You said he backed off."

"Probably shit his pants. You know we're giving up ten horses to Junior. If I had him on a dirt track, I'd piss all over him. But this is just a straight line, for Christ's sake."

Cooper planted his boot in the puddle that had collected in the indentation, pointing at it with a big grin. Slowly, Oldfield began to smile.

"I get it, Tom. Damned if these bumps aren't my buddies. More than anything, this just might be a game of chicken."

Down the course, the men saw Vanderbilt and two other men coming toward them. The distance rapidly closed as they approached one another.

"Good morning, Mr. Oldfield!" Vanderbilt said. "I trust you had a restful night."

"I got a good sleep in if that's what you mean," Oldfield said. "Fighting don't bother me none."

"I would hardly call that a fight, Mr. Oldfield," Vanderbilt replied. "And just between you and me, such an incident can have wonderful health benefits. It makes the blood flow! It's certainly out of my mind now."

Vanderbilt's two companions stood several paces back, and Oldfield guessed they despised him and Cooper. Vanderbilt paused and appeared to study him.

"I must say, you have a very colorful…wardrobe," Vanderbilt said.

Damned if Vanderbilt didn't do it again. Oldfield walked onto the beach, thinking about how the people marveled at his boldness, and now Vanderbilt was saying he looked like a clown. Riveting his eyes into those of the millionaire's, he spat a brown stream downwind.

"Well, Junior, it keeps me plenty warm."

Vanderbilt blinked.

"I take exception to your reference to me as 'Junior,' Mr. Oldfield. I believe you are familiar with my name, and I suggest you use it. I expect that you will address me in a respectful fashion hereafter."

"Okay, Vanderbilt. I'll make you a deal. You show me respect, and I'll do the same for you. No more talking French at me and no more comments about my clothes or wagon monstrosities."

Oldfield grew tense as Vanderbilt fixed his eyes on him. After a pause, the millionaire broke his silence.

"Yes. Yes, I believe we can manage that, Mr. Oldfield. Well, if you excuse me, I will continue to catalog the speedway's imperfections," Vanderbilt said, looking over his shoulder at the other two men and nodding forward.

"Yeah, I'm cataloging, too, Vanderbilt."

The American Mile Championship was the feature event of the day. Oldfield knew why the officials had separated him and Vanderbilt into two preliminary heats. Everyone wanted to see them square off in the final.

Like a lot of men among the seven or eight thousand spectators, Oldfield placed a bet on himself to win the championship final. Hundreds like the family that had given him coffee over the fence had probably done the same. Within minutes, the first heat, featuring Vanderbilt, was organized.

Oldfield leaned on the right front wheel of his Winton and watched Vanderbilt accelerate down the beach at the wave of the starter's flag for the first heat. A cloud of dust and smoke obliterated the racers on the horizon, and the roar of engines faded with distance. Word quickly came back that the millionaire had won the first heat, his time fully nine seconds slower than the previous day, at more than forty-eight seconds. But Oldfield knew this mile was a rolling start, not the flying two miles Vanderbilt had the day before.

Oldfield finished watching the first heat from behind the wheel of his Bullet, about one hundred yards north of the starting line. Maurice Bernin, Sam Stevens, and Frank La Roche sat in their cars as well as their mechanics yanked mightily at the crank handles of their engines until cannon blasts and exhaust smoke polluted the air.

The beasts throbbed and edged forward, each seeking an advantage on the other for the start of the second heat. Bernin jumped ahead, clearly a car length in front of Oldfield when they reached the tape, and the starter waved off the run. Oldfield grew frustrated as a second attempt failed for the same reason.

Twice, Oldfield circled back the one hundred yards before the starting tape with the three other cars, each driver still revving his engine as they anticipated a signal to start again. As they prepared for the third attempt, an orange flare expanded in the corner of Oldfield's left eye, and he felt a flash of intense heat.

Flames suddenly erupted from under the cowling of the Darracq, and Frank La Roche leaped off his car and into the sand. Several men with blankets beat at the vehicle, and others doused the flames with buckets of water.

The engines were all shut down as a group of men pushed the Darracq some fifty feet up into the loose sand. The cacophony of explosions abruptly decreased, and Oldfield again noticed the muted sounds of the surf and people talking, as if he had just entered a new room.

As they waited the starter's signal a third time, Oldfield studied Bernin, who wore a strange mask with a leather flap that extended down from his goggles. Oldfield continued to focus on the hood. Bernin stared back.

He probably thinks I'm trying to stare him down, Oldfield thought.

What kind of man would work so hard for a prick like Brokaw? Bernin's focus broke when the starter walked between the Bullet and the Renault and yelled at the French driver, threatening to disqualify him if he jumped the start again. Oldfield shouted to the starter.

"I don't give a crap what he does! I'll give this little gink a goddamned head start. Let's roll!"

Bernin kept even on the third attempt, and his underpowered Renault quickly faded. The speedway was rough, and the Winton bounced violently, making Oldfield's vision flicker like a nickelodeon.

Clamping down on his unlit cigar, Oldfield leaned forward to put more of his weight on the accelerator so his foot wouldn't slip off. His stomach felt light at thrilling intervals, and the Winton glided over dips in the sand. Almost as fast as a rattlesnake, Oldfield's head darted over his right shoulder to glance back as Sammy Stevens fell in behind the Winton. As he turned forward, the finish line raced toward him and then vanished, and Oldfield heard cheers.

Coasting the Winton further down the beach to slow down, Oldfield then circled back. A mob of people pouring off the dunes and directly into his path obscured the empty, flat horizon he faced just minutes prior.

Oldfield slowed the car but did not stop it because he wasn't sure what the people hurrying toward him wanted. The crowd parted just enough for the Winton to continue, but many ran alongside the racer.

Some screamed that he was faster than Vanderbilt. Oldfield knew that with the Mors electric timing apparatus in place, news of the timed runs came with the speed of electricity. Driving slowly down the beach, he waved and nodded at the people. They shouted, "Forty-three seconds."

Could it be true? Could I have run six seconds faster than Vanderbilt?

The championship was down to three cars, which included Sammy Stevens' Mercedes, as he was the faster of the two second-place finishers in the heats. The crowd of people near the starting tape swelled steadily, and Oldfield tried to focus on his car as he worked with Cooper and Hill to check bolts, fuel, spark plugs, and tires. People crowded around and yelled words of encouragement or even stupid questions, and he just wanted them to go away for a little while.

A megaphone-wielding official shouted for teams to gather to review the procedures to start the race. A couple of hundred people crowded around them, with the race teams in the center. Oldfield impatiently listened as the official explained the same starting procedures, they used in the first two heats. When he finished, Vanderbilt spoke.

"If the contest is a close finish, we should be careful to know the position of everyone's car," Vanderbilt said. "I submit that our mechanics ride with us."

Oldfield agreed, and Vanderbilt extended his hand. The professional locked eyes with the millionaire and squeezed his hand firmly. Willie K squeezed hard as well.

"I will be riding with the World Speed Champion," Brokaw announced.

"Sorry, there's only room for one more in the Winton," Oldfield said. "And Cooper's got my shotgun."

"We'll see about that, Oldfield," Brokaw said.

Brokaw turned abruptly, and the gathering parted as he stormed back to the Mercedes, but Vanderbilt lingered.

"Mr. Oldfield," he said. "May I speak to you privately?"

Oldfield nodded, and they took a few steps as Vanderbilt continued.

"We have engaged in some verbal jousting over the past two days. I should like to put that aside for now. I would like to set an example for everyone here that while we come from different origins, we can be gentlemen to each other. You have my word of honor that I will hold even with you to the tape, race you clean down the beach, and leave the result to an honorable finish."

"An example for everyone?" Oldfield asked. "For your buddy Brokaw, there?"

The crowd obscured Brokaw.

"An enthusiastic chap, to be sure," said Vanderbilt. "Yes, for Mr. Brokaw most of all. Do we have a bargain?"

"I'll have a cheroot lit up and ready for you at the finish line, Willie," he said, winking and extending his hand for a shake.

Within minutes, the engines again fired, and Oldfield felt the world close off except for Cooper beside him and the haunting presence of Vanderbilt. Fixed on Vanderbilt, who stared back, Oldfield thought for a second of Stevens in the other Mercedes and then threw him away like a broken car part.

Oldfield wanted only to beat Vanderbilt with no question about a fair fight. As they edged forward to the tape, it seemed they were crawling, and Oldfield's heart raged in his chest. His hands shook so much he was grateful just to have the steering wheel to hold for security.

I have to beat this man!

The starter's flag waved, and as the line passed under their wheels, Oldfield mashed his throttle just as Vanderbilt must also have, as they held even for at least one hundred feet.

Stevens quickly fell behind as Vanderbilt and Oldfield bounced along the washboard surface. Steadily the Winton's wheels thumped, and the car lifted and dropped back down. Oldfield felt his butt bounce clear of his seat cushion, and in the corner of his eye, he saw Cooper use both hands to grip the car frame like he thought the bumps would toss him out.

A familiar surging of emptiness in his stomach reminded him of when he was a kid and jumped from a rope into the lake back in Wauseon, Ohio. All four wheels were off the ground in an instant, and Oldfield leaned forward to put all his weight on the throttle, so his foot never slipped off. The course dissolved into a giant gray vibration.

Gritting his teeth deep into his cigar, Oldfield felt a stream of brown saliva creep out the corner of his mouth and wrap itself around his cheek. His chest touched the steering wheel as he hunched over it like he was bear-hugging the big car. Oldfield leaned so far forward his butt was off the seat, and he pressed all his weight to mash the throttle. Another washboard and the Winton lifted off the ground. The car flew, and he knew all four wheels had cleared the sandy speedway.

Bam! They landed again, and for a brief, terrorizing instant, the car seemed to twist as it would go sideways and rollover. Oldfield kept his foot planted, never lifting, and with a twitch, the Winton found traction and continued its harrowing ride.

Halfway through the mile, Oldfield saw his gains of inches over the washboards added up to a car length lead. Suddenly Vanderbilt's Mercedes paused like it was out of gear, and the Winton surged one hundred feet ahead.

Again, the Winton bounced and glided over the hard sand. Oldfield felt his stomach's empty surge.

How much longer can a mile last?

A big cluster of people must surely mean the finish line. Beside Oldfield, Cooper lifted a fist in triumph as the Winton sped through the finishing tape. Oldfield lifted his foot and took a deep breath, and then released a torrent of screams and shouted, "Nobody's better than me! Goddamn bastards…"

"Barney!" Cooper screamed over the engine. "It's alright! You won! You showed them, Barney! It's okay now!"

As the car slowed, Oldfield arced a considerable U-turn, and a panoramic view of Floridian jungles on his right, and the endless ocean on his left unfolded like he owned the world. Steering back to the finish line, they passed Vanderbilt, and Brokaw still headed south. Cooper waved jubilantly, while Vanderbilt gave a quick salute, and Brokaw ignored them. Hundreds of people ran toward the Winton.

Oldfield pulled his racer to a stop, and fans and officials swamped him. A man with a green auto club brassard shouted into a megaphone, "Oldfield, Forty-six and three-fifths seconds, Vanderbilt, Forty-nine and three-fifths seconds." People began chanting, "Oldfield," and "Winton!"

The megaphone again pierced the pandemonium.

"Oldfield, new competition mile world's record!"

Like he was watching someone else, Oldfield was surprised when he erupted in another burst of screaming and jumped on his car with so much force Cooper briefly lost his footing and clutched the back of the driver's seat.

Oldfield's arms and legs began moving before he had a chance to tell them what to do. As if he heard about the most magnificent surprise he could imagine, Oldfield realized all over again that he had beaten the King of the Swells. His own screaming swept over him as he yelled and demanded that the crowd celebrate louder.

Cooper helped a boy of about twelve to the top of the car with Oldfield. The driver looked at the boy and tossed his hair. He ignited a match with his thumbnail and drew the fire into a fresh cigar as Stevens drove by and waved.

Cooper lit another new cigar as Oldfield bit off the end of a third one, stuffed it into his mouth beside the other, and lit it as well. A new wave of laughing and cheering erupted when he stuck one of the cigars in the boy's mouth. Then he screamed animal noises.

"You know me; I'm Barney Oldfield!"

(Ormond Beach, Florida, Friday, January 29, 1904)

William K. Vanderbilt, Junior wheeled his giant Mercedes to within Oldfield's sight near the starting tape. Gould Brokaw rode beside him, smiling as he instead of his friend

Willie K had just won the fifth event of the day, the Five-Mile Invitation for Gentlemen Operators. A full seven seconds faster than Sammy Stevens, Vanderbilt completed the five miles of the final heat in three minutes, thirty-four and three-fifths seconds.

Even though the big celebration was more than a mile south at the finish line, people still ran alongside Vanderbilt's car, cupping their hands around their mouths to shout congratulations. Professionals like Barney Oldfield were ineligible for competition.

"They got you pegged, Oldfield," Cooper said. "They know you ain't no gentleman operator. You're just an operator."

For Oldfield, it was one more brick in the invisible wall separating him from something he couldn't find the words to describe. Earlier, Vanderbilt had won a mile invitational for gentleman operators. No professionals were allowed to stink up their fun.

Vanderbilt and Brokaw laughed and joked with their smartly dressed friends, with Oldfield relegated to the sidelines. Dignified, they displayed an air of camaraderie they never showed him. When he won, people he didn't know ran off the dunes to meet him, but the automobile men and Society Swells shook Vanderbilt's hand.

Hell, Alexander Winton was the only big shot that congratulated him after he won, and that was just a handshake with "bully good" thrown in. Oldfield knew Winton was pissed off about Wednesday night.

And then there was Art Pardington. Word was he had a come-to-Jesus meeting with the promoter, "Senator" Morgan, about the race organization. By the end of the day Thursday, only the American Mile Championship had been completed. Pardington took over from the Florida East Coast Automobile Association on Friday. And much as Oldfield hated to admit it, Pardington had things ship-shape on Friday, and by 9:30 a.m., four one-mile events were complete as well as the five-mile invitational.

"General Pardington. He never misses a trick, huh, Barney?"

"I just can't sit for the way he has to control everything," Oldfield said.

Oldfield and Cooper turned away from Vanderbilt and his friends and returned to the Bullet II, just a few yards away. Hill polished her into a shine that bounced back the sun every time it burnt through a spot in the morning ocean clouds.

The sixth event of the day was the five-mile free-for-all, the next chance for Oldfield and Vanderbilt to compete head-to-head. The races came in three heats, and still, and again the two rivals were in separate heats with the hope of setting up a confrontation in the final.

Oldfield lined up with La Roche, Bernin, and Louis Ross in a Stanley steamer. The heat started with little trouble, and Oldfield surged quickly ahead. With his foot pressed down hard, he found the course far smoother than the day before. While leading, the Winton coughed and slowed at the three-mile mark of the run. Puffs of smoke appeared under the engine at the finish line, but the Bullet was still a reasonable distance in front of La Roche.

Circling back to the finish line to check his time, Oldfield continued toward Ormond to take a look at the engine and prepare for the final.

The time was three minutes and forty-eight seconds. Damn, that's slow. Something's wrong.

Suddenly, the engine rattled with a sound like his toolbox might make if somebody kept rolling it over and over. Oldfield stopped the car and threw open the engine cowling. Steam billowed from a cylinder like a piston rod had cracked through.

People ran near Oldfield, asking questions, but he just stared at the ground until they stopped. Oldfield remained beside his broken Winton as Vanderbilt roared by in his Mercedes to win the final, setting a new five-mile speed record in the process.

(Saturday, January 30, 1904)

Barney Oldfield sat at the window of the train headed to Atlanta. Cooper and Hill sat by the aisle, so it wasn't so easy for people roaming the car to stop and chat with him. Normally Oldfield craved attention, but today he wanted to think. Hill lazily strolled up to the front of the car and returned with some newspapers.

"So, Barney, did you see this?" he asked, tossing a January 28 copy of the New York Evening World into the driver's lap. It was an article praising William K. Vanderbilt, Junior's daring drive at the meet. Cooper snatched it.

"It says here that old Willie K won five events over two days, at one, five, ten and fifty miles, including two events reserved for Gentlemen Operators. Willie K and his Mercedes heralded as the stars of the meet."

"So let's talk about what we do next to make a lot of money," Oldfield said. "We all wish we could have stuck around to clean Vanderbilt's clock in the other races, but I showed them in the mile run. We showed who's the champion. Now, it's time to take our show out to the weed benders."

"I've been thinking about that," Cooper said. "A few months earlier, I sold the re-built Nine-Ninety-Nine to Will Pickens, one of the best barnstorming promoters in the business. Pickens hired a young driver by the name of Ed Hauseman. Hauseman's willing to do just about anything for money, and driving the big Nine-Ninety-Nine sounds like easy money to him."

"Sounds good for them," Oldfield said. "Tell me why I should care."

"Simple. I told Pickens we could do a Southern tour during the winter months to pick up some extra cash before the northern racing season starts. The idea is to partner with Pickens and stage match races out where some folks haven't laid eyes on an automobile before. Pickens knows how to drum up a crowd, and that means everyone gets a payday."

Oldfield smiled and winked at Cooper.

"It'll be great to cut deals with the track promoters and not have to put up with bullshit out of General Pardington and the Triple-A," he said. "Count me in."

Chapter 10 – Banished

(Savannah, Georgia, February 26, 1904)

"Death Defying Daredevils," Tom Cooper read aloud from the manila broadside pasted outside a saloon in Savannah, Georgia. Leaning with his hand pressed against the saloon's unpainted rough-hewn planks, Oldfield peered over his friend's shoulder to see the photo of himself at the wheel of the Winton Bullet.

The image of the Bullet flying just above the ground, running side-by-side with Ed Hausman in the Ford Nine-Ninety-Nine, made him feel like a big deal. Standing just behind Oldfield and Cooper was the master of the ballyhoo, impressively obese, double-chinned, and indomitable, William Hickman Pickens.

"I have these broadsides plastered all over town," said Pickens. "I got the kids of every stable hand, carpenter, and blacksmith into action. Just a few dollars can unleash the infinite energy of youth!"

Cooper continued reading.

"The World Champion Barney Oldfield versus Challenger Hausman on the Freak Nine-Ninety-Nine. World Speed Records Assured, Brave Young Men Cheat Death."

Cooper stopped and looked back at Pickens. "World Speed Records Assured?"

"Of course. I hold the stopwatch, don't I?" Pickens laughed. "Keep in mind we're pasting up twenty-four sheets, not affidavits."

Oldfield nodded. He liked the posters and the reception in town - kind of like royalty. People were always running up to him and shaking his hand, telling him they were honored him.

Honored to meet Barney Oldfield.

Gazing at Pickens, Oldfield thought about how he must have put on over a hundred pounds since they raced bicycles together just eight years before. Pickens' gelatinous belly dripped over the waistband of his pants, which surely would have tumbled to his ankles if not for the brilliant red suspenders pulling northward. Oldfield chuckled when he thought how Pickens told the story of the end of his bicycle racing days.

"My loss of athleticism did not immediately curtail my career," Pickens had said. "I had the advantage of serving as a reporter for my hometown newspaper back in Birmingham, Alabama. I continued to record an impressive string of victories until my editor double-checked my reports to uncover colorful embellishments. I was only thinking of the pride of my hometown citizenry."

Cooper motioned to Oldfield and Pickens to hop on the Winton touring car parked on the red clay road just outside the saloon. Oldfield was in a good mood after a couple of beers, and now it was time to put on a little racing exhibition. He yanked the crank, and then Cooper revved the engine.

Bouncing over the rough clay road in the rear seat of the Winton touring car, Oldfield watched Cooper's head as he steered into the paddock at the Savannah track. Pickens' fat ass was sprawled all over the other seat up front, one of his thick legs dangling out the side of the car. He shouted to the gate guards, but Oldfield didn't hear what he said, and he wasn't sure if Pickens even knew them. The fat man talked to everyone like he had known them all his life. If you listened to what he was saying, you realized it was mostly hogwash.

February 26 offered dark clouds and a muddy track, but the rain held off, and nearly three thousand people squeezed under the grandstand roof of Savannah's fairgrounds track. At least that's how many Pickens said was there.

Oldfield trusted Pickens for the most part. Track promoters had a habit of lying and screwing him out of his gate share on several occasions. There was that asshole in Denver that left with all the receipts before Oldfield even finished winning the feature. Someday he'd catch up with that bastard.

Pickens probably wasn't any more honest than the rest, just smarter. He knew that Oldfield could make him a lot of money if they worked together for a good long time. Still, it was insurance to have Cooper around to help keep an eye on the guy.

"I wandered town since a week before last; haunting saloons, barbershops, and the general store," Pickens said. "The legend of Barney Oldfield grew with each conversation. And I never set out to hoodwink anybody. But when the facts interfered with the truth, I discarded them both."

Oldfield wanted to make as much money as possible in 1904, and then partner with Cooper on an automobile sales business. Barnstorming sounded like a damn good idea. Everybody wanted to see the world's record holder. And with only one other car on the track, the show would be safer.

Oldfield even shook hands with Hausman with the understanding that nobody bangs wheels with anyone else. By promoting and organizing the races themselves, they did not have to pay the Triple-A sanction fee. More for the people risking their hides, Oldfield thought.

Everything felt different than at the other race meets. Some touring cars probably driven by doctors and lawyers or Swells were circling the track. They weren't as loud as race cars, and there were only two real race cars on the grounds, the Bullet, and the Nine-Ninety-Nine. George Hill was already there, and the Bullet was polished so hard it was as redder than it ever had been before.

By the amount of noise the crowd made, Oldfield guessed some had never seen a car before. Screams vibrated off the slate-gray ceiling of the sky when they finally pushed the Bullet onto the track.

Hill rotated the crank, and the deep throat of the big Bullet again barked as Oldfield rolled away. Nearly two minutes later, he was roaring down the front stretch, and his wave to the stands ignited another round of eardrum rattling noise. Pickens had paid some skinny little farmhand to wave a flag, and he ceremoniously unfurled it at Oldfield.

Oldfield charged into the first corner, deliberately skidding the car with dramatic flair. The mud made it easy and fun. When he flashed by the grandstand again, he decided not to wave, but to appear very serious and hard at work. Pickens was at the edge of the track with his megaphone to his mouth, probably blathering something about world records.

Oldfield slowed and pulled to a stop in front of the grandstand at the end of the next lap. Pickens waddled to the side of the Bullet, extending his hand to Oldfield as if to congratulate him.

The fat man mumbled something about weed benders, but Oldfield couldn't make it out. The whole time, though, Oldfield noticed that Pickens' eyes were wide and wandering like he was taking the entire picture in like it was a symphony, and he was the conductor. After a few minutes of cheering, Pickens waved his arms over his head in a signal to get people to quiet down. He motioned to Oldfield, still seated at the Winton.

"Barney, get off the car and follow me," he said, walking around the Winton and between it and the grandstand. Oldfield leaped down, feeling particularly athletic next to Pickens.

"I'd climb up on the goddamn car with you, but I'm too fucking fat," Pickens said with a laugh.

In the style of a boxing match, he grabbed Oldfield's right wrist and yanked it above his head. Screaming into his megaphone, Pickens announced, "Faster than a mile a minute, we have a new world's record right here in Savannah, Georgia!"

More thunder from the grandstand and Oldfield responded by waving with his free left hand.

"What was the time, Will?" he whispered.

"Hell, I don't know," Pickens replied. "I forgot to click on the damn watch! Too many things going on, I guess."

Within minutes, young Ed Hausman pulled the Nine-Ninety-Nine beside Oldfield's parked car. Hausman was a big brute with a face like a twelve-year-old who stood better than six feet five inches.

"He knows he's second place, right Will?" Oldfield asked. "If he doesn't know the script, I'll put him through the fence and give this crowd something to write to their friends about."

"The vagaries of chance are left to other games, Barney," Pickens replied. "We understand who this crowd came to see, and the customer must never be disappointed."

Pickens announced the main event, a ten-mile contest between the stars of the meet, the world champion Barney Oldfield and the challenger Ed Hausman in Henry Ford's world record-busting Nine-Ninety-Nine. Hill appeared at the front of the Winton and pumped its crank vigorously until the brilliant blasts of its engine again overwhelmed all other sounds in Oldfield's ears.

From that point on, the world took on a comical nature like a silent motion picture, only in color. Oldfield thought about how so much he understood about the world came through sound, and the views alone took on a ridiculous nature, like being the only sober man among a bunch of drunks.

Chuckling, he observed Will Pickens clumsily bending over to yank at the Nine-Ninety-Nine's crank. How amazing it was that this big ball of a man could even bend over enough to reach the crank, let alone ignite the engine with but one deft twist of his thick wrist.

Oldfield led Hausman away from the line and intended to keep it that way. Both cars slithered through the muddy turns. Oldfield saw Hausman in the corner of his eye and then pressed harder on the accelerator as the thick, sticky red clay flung back from his front tires and further behind him.

Hausman was a good boy, and although he stayed close, he only pulled even once on the backstretch, as they had all agreed would make a good show. Afterward, Pickens summarized the ten-mile demonstration.

"Fair women, gallant colonels, and dusky cotton pickers alike have cheered our boys today," he said. "I believe we can find similar enthusiasm in Macon. Perhaps we should consider establishing some new track records there. Maybe even another world's record!"

At the train depot, while Hill directed some hands Pickens paid to load the cars as freight, Oldfield, Cooper, and their fat ballyhoo man reviewed a map between Savannah and New Orleans.

"I'm your advance man, Barney," Pickens explained. "See these red circles? Some of these places aren't even on the map. These farmers and their people in those parts will pay good money to see you and these machines. We're performing a public service of education to these unfortunate souls as yet untouched by the newest marvels of the Twentieth Century!"

"You talking about me?" Oldfield asked and winked at Cooper. "A marvel?"

"You're damned right. I'm talking about you! You're the world champion! And it is our duty, indeed, our calling, to demonstrate your mastery of these magnificent innovations of locomotion! And our financial rewards for such an important service should be commensurate with its momentous significance."

(Cleveland, April 11, 1904)

Barney Oldfield paced the length of a long, narrow runner that covered the distance of the hardwood floor hallway leading to Alexander Winton's office. Stopping in front of the mahogany door, he stared into the wood grain, as if it was possible to peer through it and see what was keeping Winton.

Winton wired Oldfield in Detroit, telling him to report to his office on April 11. There was no further explanation, but since the Triple-A announced April 5 that Oldfield and Ed Hausman were banned from competition, he knew what had to be on Winton's mind.

"Barney!" came the authoritative voice of Alexander Winton, accompanied by his robust, determined footsteps marching up behind the champion driver. Surprised to discover Winton outside his office, Oldfield turned around. Eyes unflinching and fixed directly ahead, Winton did not pause to shake the driver's hand. Walking past, Winton turned the doorknob to the massive, substantial door of his office.

"Enter!" Winton wasted no words.

The masculine Victorian office exuded opulence with dark rich wood, lush maroon Persian rugs, and thick draperies, with extra length gathered on the floor. Behind the executive's neatly organized desk were bookshelves that reflected the habits of a well-read man. Winton looked down at a couple of piles of papers on his desk, plucking with precision a particular item from the stack. Clearly, he had more than one thing on his mind.

"Sit down, Barney," Winton said, his voice carrying the tone of command.

"I'll be brief, Barney, I won't have scandal connected with the Winton Motor Carriage Company. I spoke to you about your behavior at the Ormond Inn, and I know Mr. Shanks has tried to reach out to you."

"Shanks," Oldfield spat out the name like spoiled milk.

Winton's cold stare penetrated him.

"There is no man I respect more than Mr. Shanks," he said in deadpan. "As I said, you have put me in a most difficult situation. I cannot afford or tolerate difficult situations."

"What is this about, Mr. Winton, Pardington?"

"I have talked to Art, and I understand his position," Winton said. "He feels you compromise the Triple-A's ability to direct racing contests in a manner that is both safe and proper sport."

"He's just sore because people want to see me, and he doesn't control the show."

"I'm not going to engage you on the merits of Triple-A management, Barney. My concern is how your behavior reflects on the integrity of the Winton Motor Carriage Company."

"If you're going to fire me, be done with it," Oldfield said.

"I am afraid you're done driving the Bullet," Winton said flatly.

"Fine with me. I know damn well Lou Mooers wants me at Peerless," Oldfield said. "Nobody ever welcomed me here. Jack and Shanks had it in for me from the beginning. And I'm guessing me dancing with your daughter at Ormond didn't sit too well with you."

"I wish you well, Barney. I understand you better than you think. I, too, came from a humble background. Perhaps you will understand in a few years. But right now, you lack the necessities to work and live under the standards of the Winton Motor Carriage Company. I think you will be happier somewhere else."

Oldfield hung his head and looked at his left shoe, resting on his knee. His throat swelled. Silent, he thought about how it seemed like yesterday he happily signed to drive the Bullet, and he still felt it was something new in his life. Abruptly, it was all over. Oldfield respected Alexander Winton, and his mind played back everything that had happened in the seven months he had worked for him.

"I wanted to race the Bullet overseas in that big Gordon Bennett Cup coming up in June. I know I could give those Europeans what for…" Oldfield's voice trailed off.

In the next instant, he jumped up and smiled at Winton. The two men shook hands, and Winton's face softened like he was relieved the conversation was over. The industrialist told Barney he would honor their contract, which was good for five more months.

"You better get somebody good to drive that Bullet, Mr. Winton," Oldfield said. "I'm going to go talk to those clowns in New York, and then I'm going to get another car. I'll be back."

(New York, New York, April 15, 1904)

The thirteen-hour train ride to New York from Cleveland gave Oldfield and Cooper plenty of time to discuss their future. Both men interrupted each other in their enthusiasm for business ideas, especially an automobile sales business, and accumulating the money required to set up the store the way they wanted. They talked about where they wanted to live, and, of course, they discussed women. No matter what subject they explored, they eventually came back to Art Pardington and Triple-A.

"Like him or not, he holds a pretty strong hand," Cooper said. Oldfield closed his eyes and felt the rhythm of the iron wheels grinding over the rails. "I don't give a crap about the Triple-A," Cooper continued. "But he can put the screws to us if he stops tracks from letting us put on our races."

Cooper said he spent time talking to track promoters, among them Alfred Reeves of the

Empire City track. Reeves urged him to get Oldfield to "kiss Pardington's ass or anything else" to get back to the racing. Reeves said that he, like most promoters, felt squeezed because he knew what a draw Barney Oldfield was. But he also said he saw no percentage in making enemies with the Triple-A.

"The promoters know you could break your neck any day," Cooper said. "But the Triple-A will keep on organizing races. The thing we have to do is tell Pardington whatever he wants to hear, and get back to racing because that is the fastest way to make money. What else are we going to do?"

"That's what I keep thinking about," Oldfield said. "What else could I do?"

(New York, New York, April 15, 1904)

Oldfield and Cooper waited in Art Pardington's office after his secretary showed them in. Smaller, less comfortable, and more cluttered than Winton's office, Pardington stacked piles of papers on the floor beside his desk, on it, and across a credenza behind him.

Oldfield scanned some of the stuff while they waited. Technical documents ranged from reports on the use of aluminum in automobile design to the durability of new rubber compounds and mixed with trade publications. At the same time, other piles had reports on car sales, manufacturing techniques, and Standard Oil. A large stack contained proposals for funding quality roads and legislation for government assistance. In front of a wall, a projection lantern rested on a long, wooden table.

Like Winton, Pardington kept Oldfield waiting. Unlike Winton, Pardington insisted on Tom Cooper's attendance at the meeting. When Pardington finally entered his office, he found Oldfield and Cooper sitting at chairs around the table.

"Over here," Pardington said, dispensing with salutations. He gestured to two chairs parked in front of his big, mahogany desk. The racers moved from the table and settled into the chairs, noticeably lower to the floor than the big, high back, leather upholstered chair that loomed over Pardington's substantial desk.

"As you can see, I am a busy man. You requested this meeting, and I granted it," Pardington said. "Don't keep me guessing your purpose."

"I came to apologize for my actions," Oldfield said. "I know it was wrong to barnstorm those towns down South last month."

Pardington looked blankly at Oldfield. "Is that all?"

"Well, no, Mr. Pardington," Cooper said. "First, we should say that we appreciate you making time for us today. And we just want to promise that we will abide by the rules of the American Automobile Association if you would be so kind as to reinstate us in your competitions."

"I hear that you and Mr. Winton are no longer associated, Barney. How would you do any racing if I were to allow it?"

"Well, Mr. Pardington, we are taking one problem at a time," Oldfield said.

"The big thing for us now is to have your blessing," Cooper said.

"My blessing, huh? What do you think I am a fucking priest? I run the racing board of the American Automobile Association," Pardington said. "That means I enforce its rules and do everything in my power to upgrade the standards of this new sport. The best I can do for you is to take it under advisement and have someone from the board get back to you."

"Get back to us?" Oldfield said, irritated.

Pardington exploded.

"Do you understand who you are talking to? Do you understand that in the comprehensive view of this industry and this sport, what an insignificant speck you are? You are nothing. The automobile industry and motorsport have every opportunity to blossom into grand sectors of this nation's economy. This is a momentous occasion in history, and I will not allow some share-cropping hick to sabotage the hard work of visionaries like Mr. Vanderbilt and other members of our board."

Oldfield felt his face flush red like a thermometer. At the instant, his fists reflexively clenched into balls, he felt Cooper tear at his arm through his shirt to get his attention. It worked. Oldfield turned his head in the direction of his friend.

"It will help your cause, Oldfield, if you demonstrate a repentant attitude so I can report my observations to the board," Pardington said.

Cooper looked at his friend and nodded his head. Oldfield sighed and looked into his lap.

"I said I was sorry. I said I was wrong, and I won't do it again," Oldfield said.

Pardington's eyes fixed unflinchingly on the driver.

"I'm not sure you understand the gravity of this situation, Oldfield," he said. "This sport needs a guiding hand, a governing body. That is the only way to operate safely; that is the only way anyone can measure progress or trust outcomes. All of this is important to advancements and innovations that will improve the breed, and that means you have to follow all the rules, not just ask forgiveness for the latest ones you violate. I demand that you respect American Automobile Association officiating, and the necessity of our involvement in any American racing contest."

"You have my word," Oldfield said, his voice trembling but respectful.

Pardington's eyes landed on Cooper. "You as well?"

"Yes, sir, you're the boss."

"Good answer. As I said, I will take the matter under consideration with the board," Pardington said. "Now, I must move on to other business. If you gentlemen will excuse me..."

(Cleveland, April 24 - 25, 1904)

Barney Oldfield's mind churned on ways he could sail off to Germany and compete for America in the biggest race in the world, the James Gordon Bennett Cup. All the trade papers billed the big derby as an epic European road race that attracted the finest cars and drivers anywhere. Only three cars from each country could compete for the prize, and Oldfield wanted to be the hero that finally elevated America from laughing stock to champion.

He knew the pride of America hung in the balance, and wanted to put the recognized superiority of the French automobile to the test. He wanted to beat those Europeans to teach the French who Barney Oldfield was.

"The best in the world? I'll show them the best in the world," Oldfield thought.

Because of his desire, his skill, his confidence, and his April 20 reinstatement by the American Automobile Association, his availability, Oldfield knew he must be a topic of discussion at the Cleveland headquarters of the Winton Motor Carriage Company.

"Oldfield, what are you going to do about Old man Winton's telegram saying he wants you back - to go after that Bennett Cup," Cooper said as they ate a meal at Jack's Chophouse, their favorite restaurant.

"What do you think I'm going to do?" Oldfield said, tipping a mug of beer to his lips.

"I think you have the brains to know this is a big chance for you. I think you know that if you go over and whoop those European fellas, you can write your own ticket," Cooper replied.

The next day Oldfield agreed to meet with a Motor Age newspaperman at the Hotel Hollenden at Superior and East Sixth Street. Acting aloof, but bursting inside that the man would be writing about Barney Oldfield's big decision to fight for America's honor, he tried to think of something that would look good in the newspaper.

"This is the world's great automobile derby, and in this big international event, all the famous drivers get pitted against one another. I expect to make a great showing, not alone because I have confidence in my ability, but because I appreciate the Bullet is one of the fastest cars in the world," Oldfield told the writer.

Scribbling furiously, the Motor Age man hung on his words, but Oldfield didn't want to talk too long. He knew the longer he spoke, the more likely it was he would say something stupid. After ten minutes, the newspaperman thanked the driver and disappeared. Oldfield ordered a shot from the bar and waited for Cooper to come back from Western Union.

"Done," Cooper said when he arrived. "I wired Winton that you are back with him for the Cup. I also wired Will Pickens and told him to start talking to promoters again while we're in Europe."

"Good, Tom," Oldfield said. "Pardington can talk big, but even he knows I'm the biggest driver in America, and I draw the crowds. That's why Pardington reinstated me.

Besides, if I win the Bennett Cup, nobody, not even Pardington and every gink in the whole Triple-A can tell us what to do."

(Cleveland, May 07, 1904)

Oldfield, Alexander Winton, and Charles Shanks waited outside the main entrance to the Winton Motor Carriage Company in Cleveland, Ohio. Oldfield felt awkward with Shanks, but Winton seemed okay. He was a polite enough guy and never held any hard feelings.

As they sipped coffee from Winton's ceramic mugs, Shanks stood to the side, smoking a cigarette. Soon officials of the Automobile Club of America, recognized in Europe as the international automobile club of the United States, would arrive to inspect the Bullet.

"I don't know these ACA guys too well," Oldfield broke a silence that he felt contributed to the awkward feeling he had inside.

"There doesn't seem to be too much love lost between them and the Triple-A," Winton responded.

"Well, maybe I have something in common with them," Oldfield said with a wry grin.

Winton took another sip of his coffee. If it was anything like Oldfield's, it had cooled to an unappealing lukewarm temperature.

"Well, they call the shots on who represents America overseas, so let's keep that in mind," Winton answered. "The Secretary of the ACA, Sam Butler, has always presented himself to me as a fair but cautious man. He'll lead a team of three other officials for the trials. Dave Hennen Morris and William Gotshall will represent their racing committee, and William Kennedy, a mechanical engineer, is the technical supervisor.

"That Morris fella, he's in with the Vanderbilts, right?" Oldfield asked.

"I'd say so, he's married to Alice Vanderbilt," Winton answered. "That would be your friend, William's cousin."

Oldfield smiled to encourage any light-heartedness in Winton. He didn't like things being so serious for very long.

"Morris is a particularly bright man. He graduated from Harvard and is a lawyer. And most certainly, he is not to be taken lightly. While pleasant enough, I find him to be very political with a calculating mind. I will see if I can understand his motives because I believe that it will be important to achieving our objective."

On moments like this, Oldfield appreciated how intelligent Winton was. How great it would be to understand how the man's mind worked.

In the distance, the distinctive sound of an automobile engine disrupted the pleasant morning chirping of birds. Butler, Morris, and Kennedy rode in a Peerless with Lou

Mooers driving. Moores stopped the car in front of the Winton Motor Carriage building within a few feet of Oldfield. After a brief round of introductions, Kennedy began to inspect and weigh the cars.

George Hill stood near the Bullet, almost like a soldier on duty. Smiling when Oldfield and Kennedy approached, he said, "It's great to have you back, Barney."

"You ready to go to Europe and put a whooping on those Frenchies and Krauts, George?"

Hill smiled enthusiastically.

Oldfield hovered over Kennedy as he popped the Bullet's cowling.

"Bill, I want to make sure you take in the improvements since Ormond Beach," Oldfield said. "We have strengthened her a considerable bit. She now weighs fully one hundred pounds more. We built up the frame, and the crankshaft is a quarter of an inch thicker. We enlarged the drive shaft. The axles are stronger, and we put in new bearings. We also fitted it with a 1905 Winton carburetor and oiler, both great improvements."

Kennedy focused on his work, merely muttered, "Uh-huh."

Mooers joined the three Winton men as they watched the officials. Butler asked them if they knew a good place to run.

"You mean to tell me you have not selected the venue for this test?" Winton asked, his patience tested.

Shanks left, saying he would phone the Glenville track to inquire about its availability. Upon his return, the report was not good. Groundskeepers were working on the track, and it was plowed up and not available.

"Wherever we hold the trials, I want everyone to appreciate that the Bullet design is for track racing and fine European macadam. The Bullet design isn't for rough country roads; its muffler pipe only clears the ground by three inches," Winton said.

"Clifton Boulevard was one of the finest pieces of road in the country, and a good measure of it asphalt," Moores injected.

"That's a fine idea, Lou," Winton said.

He nodded at Shanks, who knew that Winton wanted him to speed ahead with one of the Automobile Club of America men to stake out the stretch.

"There's a stretch of several miles that has few houses or cross streets," Moores said.

They all agreed that Clifton Boulevard sounded like an excellent place to run the American trials for the most significant race in the world. As Oldfield observed, he silently wondered if when it came to any rivalry between the Automobile Club of America and the Triple-A if it wasn't a case of "Dumb versus Evil?"

Engines snarling, Sam Butler joined Oldfield in the Bullet to start his review of the trial. Oldfield sized up Butler through his goggles and then suddenly screamed like a bronco-busting cowboy. The Bullet roared as it leaped forward and jumped ahead of Mooers, who drove with Dave Morris in the Peerless. Oldfield mashed the throttle and cackled when Butler nervously gripped his seat as he bounced up and down.

Twisting his head backward like it was on a coiled spring, Oldfield again burst out in laughter when he realized that as he entered Clifton Boulevard, the Bullet was well ahead of the Peerless. Kicking up dust and stones, the Bullet unflinchingly put an end to the life of a scrawny chicken that chose the wrong time to cross the road.

An Automobile Club of America official had marked off three and a half miles of road, most of which was asphalt. Oldfield knew that only one home was adjacent to the course, at least an acre away.

Two side streets intersected the stretch, and two volunteers among some men and boys who gathered to watch were stationed there with flags. Butler had told Oldfield to drive at top speed down Clifton Boulevard until they saw a red flag inserted in a wooden platform, which marked the turning point. Each stretch up and down the boulevard was three and one-half miles.

Oldfield came to the first checkpoint, and the Automobile Club of America inspectors surrounded the car, making notes.

What bullshit, Oldfield thought.

As soon as they waved him away, Oldfield pounced on the throttle again. The asphalt was so smooth he wondered if this is what it would feel like to fly. The Bullet hardly bounced, even at more than eighty miles per hour. The surface at the turning point was macadam, and Oldfield liked that because it was easier to slide his tires when he cocked the wheel. In the corner of Oldfield's right eye, he saw Butler lose his notebook when he grabbed at his seat again on the turn.

Oldfield hollered and whooped as he slid the Bullet around the flag, noting that Butler's straw hat flew off, and his exposed brown hair danced crazily with the wind. His rear tires slid over the gravel, and Oldfield screamed like a cowpoke urging his horse and a herd of cattle along. Butler waved a hand in front of his face as dust boiled over the car.

The two cars sped up and down the makeshift course, the best roads in Ohio. Oldfield noticed a crowd was growing, as about twenty young men and boys climbed the trees that lined the wooden stretch to gain a better vantage point. Lifting his head to peer into the trees, Oldfield conjured up a cheer when he gave those hanging there a salute. Gradually extending his margin over Mooers, Oldfield's daring in the turns accounted for the big difference.

Lap after lap, Oldfield stormed around and saw Winton and Shanks as they stood at the start, talking and counting circuits. The Automobile Club of America men had told them the cars needed to complete one hundred miles at high speed to prove they were worthy of the international competition. Oldfield saw Winton busily scribbling in his lab book, probably recording the times Shanks captured with two stopwatches.

On the course, Oldfield picked up speed, and he guessed the big Winton was hitting over eighty-five miles per hour. Suddenly, a large black dog pranced on the course, less than a hundred feet from the speeding Bullet. The dog froze in its tracks, and Oldfield twisted the wheel violently.

For an instant, he lost control as the car's right side lifted off the ground. The big Winton felt terrifyingly light, and then the right wheels thudded back to Earth. Oldfield hit the accelerator with lightning speed, and after a lag, the motor carriage responded. Butler tucked his head between his legs and was clutching the underside of his bench.

"Goddamn mutt. Should have hit the Goddamn thing," Oldfield said.

After a while, Oldfield became bored with the road and tormenting Butler and decided not to push the car as he had at Ormond. Somewhere around fifty miles, he saw the Peerless had ground to a halt. When Oldfield stopped at a checkpoint, Hill told him that Mooers thought it was gravel in the chain drive – but later said it was an imperfection in one of the pistons. Mooers had argued with the Automobile Club of America men, who only credited him with fifty-one miles, and he insisted that he had done at least sixty.

Alone, Oldfield droned up and down the course, occasionally pressing harder in the corners just to keep sharp. Now, all four of the Automobile Club of America officials took turns with him, jumping in at the checkpoints. Without warning, an ominous hot mist began to escape from the engine cowling at eighty miles. Oldfield guessed a connecting pin in the water pump had broken, and cooling water stopped circulating.

Having experienced the problem before, he knew there was a chance to finish the one-hundred-mile goal before the car would stop and press on. Now the Bullet looked like a steam car, with a white vapor trailing it as they thundered down Clifton Boulevard.

Despite nursing the Bullet along, Oldfield, fearing engine damage, pulled to a stop when he felt the motor tighten. By Alexander Winton's count, his Bullet gave up the ghost seven miles short of the goal.

(Empire City, New York, May 19, 1904)

After much deliberation, the Automobile Club of America announced a second opportunity for American teams to live up to the rigors of their review for European competition. The venue was the Empire City track, which was heavy with mud on May 19 due to an unrelenting mist.

Oldfield guessed there were at least two hundred automobilists gathered to watch the three cars that invited to meet the challenge of a one-hundred-mile grind. Oldfield, Cooper, and Hill arrived early, and once again, Moores had the Peerless on hand. The third car, the Christie, was tested on a five-mile stretch of Merrick Road on Long Island May 10. The story Oldfield heard was that it had broken down as well.

The Christie was an intriguing car, and Oldfield looked forward to seeing and getting underneath it if the owner would allow it. Technical Supervisor Kennedy told Oldfield he admired the Christie, named after its creator J. Walter Christie.

"I think this car is a breakthrough in design. It has front-wheel drive, which just might be the best for traction," Kennedy explained. "The engine is mounted vertically to the frame and drives the wheels directly."

"That's a lot of weight on the front axle," Oldfield challenged.

"It is," Kennedy acknowledged. "But spiral springs are placed close to the front wheels, with one above and one below the spring block on each side, to cushion upward and downward motion. Frankly, I'd like to see you drive that Christie, so I know what it can do. Walter's a little eccentric. He's a perfectionist, always changing things. I'll bet that's why he's not here yet. He's probably still working on the car."

Kennedy explained that during Christie's Long Island trial, a defective oil feed forced it to stop for repairs. Until then, it ran impressively. The problem, combined with inefficient carburetion due to an equipment change from a European product to one of American design, convinced the Automobile Club of America committee to require the second trial of all three cars on the Empire City track.

As time crept closer to a scheduled one o'clock start, Oldfield and Cooper, combed over the Bullet, checking everything. Moores and some Peerless mechanics were doing the same thing. There was no sign of Christie. As they prepared to start the car, Oldfield motioned to his friend to come close.

"Guess what?" Oldfield asked without waiting for a response. "These ACA jackasses may have screwed everything up. I was over talking to Kennedy earlier, and he says Butler told him there is some kind of legal issue with the track."

"What?" Cooper asked, his face looking like a kid in school when asked an impossible question.

Behind them, Hill cranked the Bullet to life, and its engine began snorting.

"It's something about liability for today," Oldfield said. "I guess if I get killed or something, the track and the ACA are arguing over who should take the fall."

"Oh, Christ…" Cooper said. "Can't we just fucking race?"

"Well, it turns out they want Winton and Moores to take on this liability. Moores was grumpy about it, but he just signed this legal document the ACA put in front of him. I saw Winton's guy, Percy Owen, and asked him if it was true, and to just sign it."

Within minutes Oldfield was aboard the Bullet and entered the thick muddy track. A round of cheers acknowledged him as the Bullet toured the oval.

Because the Automobile Club of America trial moved to New York, Winton sent one his executives, Percy Owen, to represent him. Oldfield did but one slow lap around the gumbo-like track when he saw Owen on the outside of the fence and Hill and Cooper on the inside, signaling him to stop.

He knew this was not good news. Stopping the racer, Oldfield followed Owen into the track office. They entered the building, its wood plank floors occasionally squeaking under the weight of their feet. Owen took a seat at a desk. Bespectacled and looking more accountant than race driver, he had driven one of two Wintons in the 1903 James Gordon Bennett Cup.

Sitting on the desk was a legal document. Expressionless, Owen removed his glasses and locked eyes with Oldfield. Frowning, he said, "I can't sign this."

"Come on, Percy, sign the goddamned thing and let's be done with it."

Owen refused and asked that a telephone operator arrange a call to Alexander Winton at his office in Cleveland. When the track phone rang nearly forty-five minutes later, an operator patched the connection together. Oldfield anxiously followed Owen's end of the conversation.

"Good day Mr. Winton!" Owen said. "Yes, sir. Yes. Well, the track and the club want us to indemnify...yes. Well, allow me to read the portion of the contract, I believe, is a problem. Yes, it says...the parties of the second part – that's us, Mr. Winton – agree and covenant to indemnify and save harmless the parties of the first part – that's the track and the Automobile Club of America – of and from any and all claims for injuries, damages and all claims whatever to person or property, or otherwise, which may be made by corporations or other parties arising of, or in connection with, the holding of said speed trials, or any acts, negligence, mismanagement or omissions in connection therewith, or defects in the condition of the aforesaid grounds or structures thereon."

Owen paused, obviously listening to Winton. Oldfield impatiently leaned over the Winton executive, trying to interpret the exchange. Owen assured Winton he understood his directions and hung up the phone.

"He says to tell them to strike the clause. If they don't, he said to pack up and return to Cleveland."

"We can't do that. We've worked hard on the Bullet! She can win this derby!"

Owen shook his head and rubbed his right temple.

"Mr. Winton is the boss, Barney."

Oldfield stormed out of the office, slammed the door, and kicked a doorstop off the porch. The dull roar of Lou Mooers' Peerless moaned in the background as Oldfield mumbled curses to himself. He knew the situation was hopeless.

Oldfield watched Charles Wridgeway, hired to drive the Peerless for Lou Mooers, run the track alone. The Peerless slithered through the deep mud at a subdued speed, and the whole affair seemed ridiculous.

Oldfield wondered why Mooers would take on the risk when Winton would not. Maybe Mooers thought the same thing when, as Wridgeway came down the front stretch, he stepped out into the ankle-deep mud, his arms flailing. He called the trial off.

The Automobile Club of America ruled there would be no American representatives headed to Germany.

Chapter 11 – Prest-O-Lite

(Indianapolis, June 1904)

Carl Fisher strutted out of Fisher Automobile Company and headed next door for lunch at "Pop" Haynes' Restaurant at 114 North Pennsylvania Street in Indianapolis. His dim eyes spied the blurry image of an old man struggling to load his wagon with several bulky boxes, and he paused to study the geezer.

Within moments at least a half dozen people Fisher didn't know took advantage of his rare stationary pose and greeted him. Everybody knew Carl Fisher, and he was used to it. He was a success, at age thirty, a young business wizard – people said as much to his face.

Around the city, many called him "Crazy Carl," which Fisher took as a compliment – it didn't matter that not all of them meant it that way. Fisher performed attention-getting stunts, like riding a bicycle on a tightrope twelve stories up between State Life Insurance and Odd Fellow's on Washington Street. It had been all about publicity for his first business – a bicycle shop. People talking about him just confirmed the promotions were successful.

One young man no more than twenty charged toward Fisher.

"You're Carl Fisher!" he announced.

"And so I am," Fisher said, inhaling to fuel the fire at the end of his cigar and then releasing a cloud of smoke to billow forth almost immediately.

"I was maybe ten or twelve when I saw you ride that 'world's largest bicycle.' I saw you climb out of that second-story window, right over there, to get on it," the young man said as he pointed.

"Yep, yep. I sold a lot of bicycles with that trick. My brothers Rolla and Earl built that thing," Fisher said, all the time thinking about breaking the conversation off.

The young man cocked his head and squinted at Fisher like he had lobsters crawling out of his ears.

"You fellas used to throw bicycles off buildings. And I remember one time you let pretty near a thousand balloons loose in the air, all with coupons for free bicycles in them. My Daddy shot at a couple of them with his shotgun, but they was clean out of range," the nameless boy recalled.

Fisher briefly thought about how he had put his whole business in hock for five hundred dollars to pull off that stunt. Business deals were all a big bet to him, and one he relished because he believed Carl Fisher would always win.

Excusing himself, Fisher told the boy he had an appointment pending. A strange feeling about the old man with the boxes welled up inside him, and Fisher had learned to pay attention to his gut feelings.

"What do you have there, old-timer?" he asked the gentleman with the boxes.

"My name is Percy Avery, not old-timer," the sweating elderly man said, continuing his work and never making eye contact.

"I meant no offense. I beg your pardon. So, Mr. Avery, do you care to tell me what you have in those boxes?"

"You'd know what's in these boxes if you were smart enough to recognize opportunity when it bites you in the ass."

"You trying to sell me something, Percy? Because if you are, you got a damn sure funny way of going about it."

Fisher studied an open box lying on the dirt and macadam street. In it were two beautifully crafted brass cylinders, with fittings and connections of the same metal.

"Yeah, I know what this is. These are acetylene canisters for headlamps. So, you're the one who's been trying to sell us this stuff. My boys tell me these things are liable to blow up like a bomb and take somebody's head off. They don't want to monkey with them."

Fisher noticed how ashen and gray Avery appeared. Disheveled in wrinkled, loose-fitting clothes, the old man seemed tired. Startling Fisher, Avery suddenly reached into the box and threw a canister on the crushed stone street between their feet. The canister bounced once and landed.

"Blow up," Avery said, and then spat in the dirt. "Hogwash. This device is the latest thing from France. Your boys are dumbasses."

Any tension Fisher felt about being split up the middle by an explosion was gone in an instant. His imagination swirled around the image of the canister. Picking it up, he examined the dent in its formerly pristine structure.

"Come to my office tomorrow at eleven o'clock, and be prepared to put on your best show. I'll arrange a meeting with a partner of mine. Be sharp!"

The next morning, Fisher, who regularly arrived at his office by 5:30, had shut the door to place a couple of phone calls and read some material one of his men gathered for him on headlamps and acetylene gas. At about 10:30, he noticed the shadow of a man through the opaque glass window of his office. Excitedly opening the door, Fisher shouted at the sight of Avery.

"Avery! Jesus Christ on a bicycle, that's what I like, goddamn it! A man who is early to meetings!"

Fisher knew his voice filled the entire office area, but he didn't give a crap. His secretary, accustomed to his language and ways, did what he expected – continue to tap on her Remington typewriter, unfazed. Fisher welcomed Avery and liked that he was better dressed today with bow tie and jacket because it meant the old man was working harder to sell him.

Fisher was ready for a demonstration. Once his mind fixed on something, he saw no reason not to alter his day at a moment's notice. His partner could catch up at eleven o'clock.

"Mr. Fisher," Avery began, "I believe you'll agree that one of the principal drawbacks to motoring is the danger of driving at night by the poor light of carriage lamps."

"Yeah, I can't see shit," Fisher inserted.

Avery, who had no reason to be aware of his prospect's severe myopia, announced, "Well, you're going to see clear as day with this lamp! Watch this!"

Balancing with one hand on Fisher's desk, the old man struck a kitchen match off the bottom of his shoe. Applying the flame to a fork at the end of the brass tube, he smiled. With the sound of a child's popgun, a brilliant white light burst forth.

"I'll be damned!" exclaimed Fisher, shielding his eyes as soft purple shapes projected the bruises on his retinas.

Avery laughed and turned a knob to adjust the gas flow from the canister, and consequently changed the brightness of the flame. As he turned it off, he began to explain how the canister worked.

Minutes later, Fisher's business partner, Jim Allison, the president of Allison Perfection Fountain Pens, entered the office without knocking. Tonic, meticulously applied, tamped down Allison's hair, as always. Fisher liked that Allison always presented himself as the successful man he was.

Dispensing with introductions, Fisher struck a match on his dark wood desk and turned the canister knob. With another popping sound, light flooded the room. Allison, obviously startled, shielded his eyes and instinctively stepped backward.

"Look at this, Jim! You light a match, and presto, you can drive in the dark! Imagine this in a reflecting cone with a sheet of glass to block the wind. Hell, you can see for miles! And no more goddamn wind blowing out the goddamn lanterns!"

Allison waved his hand in front of his face with a downward motion.

"You're blinding me! Turn it off!" he said. "So, Carl, you want to sell headlamps now?"

"I feel a hen coming on, Jim! These will be the best in the world!" Fisher shouted.

Avery introduced himself to Allison, and the three men began to talk. Allison had read enough to know that compressed gas was dangerous and potentially explosive.

"Percy here threw this same can we used today in the street yesterday, and nothing happened!"

"Acetylene gas has been around for a long time, but it now has practical applications," Avery began. "It is composed of equal parts of carbon and hydrogen and has an illuminating power approximately twenty times greater than coal gas. It mixes water with calcium carbide, which is a combination of lime and coke. Acetylene generators do this very precisely, measuring the water down to the drop. There have been a lot of advances in these generators and problems with waste lime clogging up the works have been eliminated. No more excess heat and decomposition of the acetylene. But the big breakthrough came when some French scientists figured out how to store the gas in these pressurized containers."

"So, you're saying the canister can be fastened to a car to fuel the headlamps?" Allison asked.

"Precisely," Avery asserted. "What the French did is absorb the gas in acetone, which is four times more effective than any other solvent. One unit of acetone can absorb three hundred units of acetylene under one hundred seventy-six pounds of pressure at sixty degrees Fahrenheit. The stuff used to blow up at thirty pounds. That means you could leave one of these little twelve-inch cylinders on for over two weeks, and she still burns."

"But at that kind of pressure and temperature changes, aren't we strapping bombs onto carriages?" Allison said.

"That's the big difference in what the French have done, Mr. Allison," Avery said, picking up the cylinder to stress his point. "I purchased the patent rights to a great safety feature in this product. What you see here is filled with a porous material known as asbestos. It prevents excess gas from collecting in the cylinder, and still gives off just enough to produce the light you saw with your own eyes."

Fisher, Allison, and Avery discussed the business possibilities. Avery explained how financially strapped he was after purchasing the patent. Since he had failed to sell the product to car companies, he didn't have the five thousand dollars required to build the acetylene generator, hire an operator and a salesman. They talked again about the safety of the canisters. Still, Avery, who appeared to Fisher to be just short of losing patience with Allison, told them if they were worried about safety, they weren't thinking.

"The manufacturing process is the safety issue," Avery said. "This stuff is volatile, and I will have to personally train whoever we hire to charge these cylinders. That's what you need to worry about. After the stuff is in the canister, the asbestos makes it safe."

Fisher and Allison looked at each other, nodded, and told Avery they were interested and would get back to him soon. After Avery left, the two men talked about how they wanted to find new business, and this looked promising.

"He doesn't have the automobile connections I do, Jim. Hell, I can start offering his headlamps as an option in my shop today. It's a damn fine sales feature. Everybody is going to want this as soon as it is on the market. We need to be first. I know I can find a couple of thousand dollars. I feel a hen coming on!"

"I am well acquainted with your hens. The potential is obvious, Carl," Allison said. "But I'm still worried about the safety. If I can be comfortable, it is safe; then, I will find the money somehow because I believe this will be big. Let me take it with me tonight, and I will find out if it's safe."

The next morning, Allison was at Fisher's office shortly after six o'clock. Already there, Fisher read the Indianapolis Star and sipped his black coffee. Allison laid a severely dented canister on Fisher's desk.

"We're in business!"

Allison said he conducted a scientific test. He explained that he had taken the cylinder to the West Washington Street Bridge, where the White River trickled down to a creek, weaving its way between big boulders thirty feet below. Convinced no one was nearby Allison stood on the bridge and gave the canister a heave, bashing it against the rocks below. It collected dents as it bounced around, but landed out of the water, enabling him to retrieve it.

"Well, I'm glad you didn't blow up the goddamned bridge, Jim," Fisher bellowed.

In the coming weeks, Fisher, Allison, and Avery incorporated the new company and named it "Concentrated Acetylene Company," calling the first product, "Prest-O-Lite." Fisher ordered his men to begin fitting Prest-O-Lite headlamps to cars in his shop.

The bent and damaged canister was in a glass cabinet in Fisher's showroom and used as a sales demonstration for anyone inquiring about the product's safety. Fisher sold the headlamps to the manufacturers of the cars in his store, and soon the new company issued stock, attracting investors looking for an opportunity in a world that was rapidly leaving the faint of heart in the dust.

Chapter 12 – Death and Romance

(Cleveland, Peerless Motor Car Company, Monday, July 22, 1904)

In a garage at Cleveland's Peerless Motor Car Company, Barney Oldfield contemplated the face of Lou Mooers, the Peerless head engineer, as the designer puffed on his curved, twelve-inch churchwarden. The pipe's stem disappeared into Mooers' un-groomed and graying mustache. His bushy eyebrows touched the top of his cheeks as he studied the green racecar the driver sat in.

Oldfield returned his eyes to the prominent, spring leaf-colored torpedo cowling that extended before him. Tom Cooper traced the pointed bodywork with his fingertips. The perspective was strange to Oldfield after driving atop the Bullet.

As Oldfield sat at the wheel of the reconditioned Peerless racer that Mooers drove to an embarrassing defeat in Ireland, he glanced at his new, pipe-smoking boss and wondered how his engineering mind worked. Mooers had designed the car. For the first time, Oldfield felt more inside a racecar than sitting on top of it.

Next to the Peerless leader stood Ernie Moross - promoter extraordinaire - with his boyish, cleanly shaved face and slight stature. Moross named the car The Green Dragon. Mooers said Moross was the best publicity man in the business, and he wanted to make Peerless known for its engineering excellence.

"She's a whole new car from what I drove in Ireland Barney," Moores said, his voice bursting with an energy that belied his passion for machinery. "We replaced the steel armor and wood frame with pressed steel. The motor hangs considerably lower than before, and the flywheel clears the ground by only three inches. Now, the exhaust at the side flows through a single muffler parallel to the frame. She's stout."

Oldfield read about Peerless before he shook hands with Moores in the deal to drive the

Dragon. The company was founded in 1869 and produced bicycles until moving to the car business in 1900. An agreement to build cars under French De Dion patents yielded a machine on a De Dion frame, and it was not until October 1901 that the company released a car of its own design.

The racing Peerless history was a disappointment.

Mooers came to Peerless in 1902 to get them into racing. As well as driving himself, he hired others such as Charles Wridgeway. He told Oldfield he never thought the cars had the right driver. It was clear to the driver he was expected to be that man.

"We'll take her out to Glenville this week and put her through her paces," Moores said. "You'll see."

"You're going to make a lot of money, Barney," Moross said. "The Green Dragon is going to get a lot of attention, and by the end of the year, everybody will know her name."

"She had better be good, or we're going to look pretty damn silly with a name like that," Oldfield said.

"Word is, Earl Kiser's going to race the Bullet," Cooper said. "You know those guys are going to be gunning for you, Barney."

Oldfield shrugged his shoulders.

"Him and everybody else."

(Saturday, August 27, 1904)

The rhythm of the iron wheels of the St. Louis-bound train out of Detroit vibrated through Barney Oldfield's leather sole boots and into his feet. Two new diamond rings joined others on his fingers to complement the newness of his gray wool suit that became increasingly damp from his sweat. Soot sifted into the rail car, but the windows had to be open to relieve the stifling heat.

The wardrobe of his parents was markedly improved, his mother rustling in lavender satin while sporting a full bonnet and veil. His father, more understated in navy blue, retained the long, grey beard so typical of the Civil War veteran, but now presented it in the trim of a skilled barber.

Oldfield was solemn. His chance to show-off in front of his parents had disappointed him. Ma and Pa Oldfield had joined their son for an inconclusive confrontation with the new record-setting Bullet driver Earl Kiser the previous day at Grosse Pointe, Michigan. Regardless, their excitement stemmed from the St. Louis World's Fair visit. That would come after Oldfield's run in the Louisiana Purchase Trophy Race in St. Louis the following day.

Oldfield glanced at his parents from across the aisle as he talked shop with Moross and

Cooper. Despite the new clothes, his father still looked disheveled like an insane asylum janitor.

"I wish you'd knocked Kiser off in the fifteen-mile go yesterday, Barney," Moross said. "You had him two out of three, and that would have said something to beat him all three times."

Oldfield felt an irritating pang jolt from his gut, and he fired back at Moross.

"You trying to tell me I don't give you enough to work with, Moross? Hell, I won my fourth Diamond Cup Trophy Friday and busted the five-mile record doing it. In the Buffalo August 15 meeting, I won the five-mile free-for-all and the fifteen-mile free-for-all and then ran twenty-five miles in twenty-six minutes.

You told me yourself we drew around seven thousand Canucks up in Toronto for that exhibition a couple of weeks ago. It hasn't been a week since I set the mile record for half-mile tracks in Omaha, and they loved it. What the hell do you need, Moross?"

"Relax, Barney," Moross said. "Nobody's taking potshots at you. This is just business talk. Let me show you something."

The promoter reached under his seat and pulled out a leather briefcase, extracting a copy of the August 27 The Automobile trade journal. He began to read.

"Cleveland, August 22. Earl Kiser clipped two full seconds from the world's record of fifty four and four-fifths seconds. He established beyond question that it has been the car and not the driver that has been responsible for the long series of victories and records that have gone to the credit of the Bullet-Oldfield star combination."

Moross gave Oldfield a blank expression. The driver stared back.

"Earl Kiser was the star of the August 22 Cleveland meet when you were in Omaha. In the final event of the first day, Kiser set a new world's track mile record at fifty-two and four-fifths seconds. But it's better than that," Moross said.

"What he did was the stuff of legend. His car failed to start for the five-mile Diamond Cup run, and he didn't get underway until the others had a five-eighths mile head start. Kiser picked 'em off one-by-one, just missing the win by no more than a yard to Herb Lytle in the eight-cylinder Pope-Toledo."

"What a crock of shit," Oldfield said, feeling frustrated that Moross had a point. It gnawed at him that what Kiser did was so good Oldfield wished he had done it.

"It says here that Kiser has proven himself to be the peer of any driver on the American track. And I've got a copy of the August 25 Motor Age. In there, your old boss Winton is quoted saying, 'Kiser is King.' That's catchy. I wish I'd thought of that."

Oldfield didn't know why Moross thought it was catchy, but he didn't want to say so because he felt dumb. He quickly realized his facial expression gave him away.

"Kiser, Barney. You know, like the Kaiser of Germany, get it?" Cooper said.

"What a crock of shit," Oldfield said again.

"The point is, Barney, it doesn't matter what I think. You're still the best draw in the game. But if you think you have more pull with these rags then the Triple-A, then you're fooling yourself. You need to make sure they don't change people's minds about you. They do their talking here," Moross said, flicking the paper with his index finger, "you're going to have to do yours on the track."

"Are you saying Pardington can get them to put me down?" Oldfield asked.

"I'm saying Pardington and the whole damn Triple-A for that matter have little interest in you being bigger than the sport - bigger than them. They want to develop some other stars. And Kiser fits the bill right now. Winton will help them, too, because he doesn't want anyone thinking it was all on you that the Bullet was so fast."

"The new eight-cylinder Green Dragon is full of pep. Sometimes too much," Oldfield said. "She's a handful on the tracks. The car has better than eighty horses, but the brakes aren't any good. The truth is, I think the Bullet is the better car. But what really bothers me is that record. Something's fishy."

"Well, you may be right about that, Barney. I talked to Jay Collister, one of the timers in Cleveland, and he tells me that there were some discrepancies. It seems he clocked the fourth mile faster than the others, and the fifth mile slower. The times were weird, too, because the fourth mile was a minute three and change. And then the fifth mile is faster by eleven seconds and sets the record. But the point is there isn't much we can do about it unless you just go out and break the record."

The big race coming up the next day in St. Louis was just a few miles from the giant St. Louis World's Fair. Oldfield knew that a lot of people said the biggest track crowd ever would be there. Moross reminded him this was the best opportunity yet to show everyone that Barney Oldfield was the greatest driver in the country.

(St. Louis State Fairgrounds Track, Sunday, August 28, 1904)

Fresh from a three-mile exhibition run at the St. Louis State Fairgrounds track, Barney Oldfield skidded the Dragon to a stop on the home stretch in front of the grandstand to a cascade of cheers. When he got out of the car, he was surprised over the thick coat of dust on the Dragon's cowling. He blew on the hood and dirt scattered like powder.

Moross reported there were better than twenty thousand people filling every box in the place, and there must have been seventy-five automobiles loaded with people parked on the lawn near the clubhouse veranda. Oldfield raised his voice more than usual, so Lou Moores could hear him over the constant chatter.

"Dust," Oldfield said. "I've never seen anything like it. And she's a handful, Lou. She's got plenty of spunk, but she jumps around on the turns. I can't always be sure she'll go where I point her."

"I don't think any of the cars like this dusty surface. There's nothing to get a hold of, so they jump around. I'd hate to follow somebody out there," Moores said. "That cloud you kicked up must have been fifty feet in the air. If you get a jump at the start, nobody will be able to catch you in that dust."

Even the light machines boiled up clouds like a forest fire, and two races for smaller cars followed Oldfield's exhibition. Oldfield couldn't see any racer, but the leader, the others obscured in dust so thick it could choke a man. People around him talked of sprinkling the track with water to weigh the dust down, but Cooper and Moores were concerned the hard surface would just get slippery. Word was, the other drivers felt the same way.

As shadows of a sunny, warm day elongated into distorted shapes, officials called on four teams for the big event on the card, the ten-mile run for the Louisiana Purchase Trophy. Oldfield said all day long people had talked about the match-up between the Green Dragon and the massive sixty-horsepower Pope-Toledo driven by Missouri native Alonzo Webb. Most everybody agreed the other drivers, Webb Jay in a White steamer and G. P. Dorris, in the twenty-four horsepower St. Louis racer, were hopelessly outclassed.

All of the cars fired up and were quickly away. Oldfield could tell Webb was keeping an eye on him as carefully as he was studying the Pope-Toledo. Webb was a clean competitor, and they held their speed around the corners to hit the tape fifty yards ahead of the other two drivers.

The starter waved his hands furiously but disappeared from Oldfield's eyes into the billowing dust. The Pope-Toledo entered the first turn leading, grabbing the pole position and broad-sliding in front of Oldfield.

"Goddamn it!" Oldfield snarled to himself.

Now he would have to pass Webb in the thick dust cloud that overwhelmed the bright day to a frightful khaki gloom. The nose of the Green Dragon jumped to the right without warning as the driver cranked the wheel steadily to keep the car reasonably straight.

Webb came back into view on the backstretch as the cars kicked up less dust when pointed straight than when turning. Oldfield searched carefully to see how close to the fence Webb drove, hoping to find a spot to squeeze the Dragon by on the next corner.

Webb took the turn nearly flawlessly, cocking his wheel to the right as the rear of the car swung out into a controlled skid. The outside coming off a corner would be the only way around.

The two big machines charged down the front stretch, and Oldfield saw the crazy starter in the middle of the road, only to disappear in the Earthen fog as the big racers approached. Oldfield tensed as he dashed through the spot where the starter had been. Squeezing the steering wheel in anticipation of hitting the man, he felt nothing. Intense, his eyes riveted on Webb's tail. Oldfield swung wide, again trying to visualize how to pass on the outside.

Once more on the backstretch, he pulled his front wheels even with the Pope-Toledo's rear. Together they charged into the second corner, and Oldfield saw his world turn into a terrifying sandy-tan screen devoid of shape or structure.

Holding his foot down on the throttle, Oldfield wanted desperately to break through into the sunlight and put Webb and the cloaking powder behind him. In his blindness, Oldfield cocked the Dragon a little further to the right to be sure not to hit the Pope-Toledo.

Just as in the exhibition run, the Dragon stepped to the right, and Oldfield's heart raced. Still blinded like in a sandstorm, he tensed and then relaxed, relieved again not to have met with disaster.

Suddenly, he heard the terrifying sound of splintering timber, just as at Grosse Pointe a year before. The clouds parted, and the track's bucolic setting transformed into a bizarre obstacle course as Oldfield tried to comprehend the absurd sight of giant trees rushing toward him.

Instinctively covering his face with his arms, Oldfield doubled over as the Dragon absorbed an angry thud. Jerked like a puppet, he was lifted from his seat with the same terrifying sensation he had felt at Grosse Pointe.

Oldfield's sight was useless in the blur of colors and sensations of scrapes against his scalp and chest. The world champion thudded to the ground and tasted a warm, salty liquid on the back of his tongue. Rolling over and over and over, he melted into the darkness.

"Barney, Barney," the familiar voice of his old friend Tom Cooper called. Still dazed, Oldfield thought he and Cooper were out somewhere getting corned up on whiskey. Then he asked about Nine-Ninety-Nine.

"Nine-Ninety-Nine? Hell, you are loopy, boy. Last I heard old Will Pickens got thrown in jail back in Terre Haute for promising a Nine-Ninety-Nine exhibition and selling a thousand dollars' worth of tickets. But he couldn't get the car to run. He doesn't know how to work on those cars."

"Will Pickens?" Oldfield asked. "Who the hell is Will Pickens?"

Breathless, an elderly couple rushed into the room. Oldfield wondered who these fashionably dressed people were.

"My Baby! The newsboys are telling everyone you're dead! Praise the Lord!" the woman said.

Stupefied, the driver searched his mind for why his mother would be working on Nine-Ninety-Nine.

A doctor stepped between him and his mother and braced her, telling her something about a punctured lung. Oldfield started to talk but felt a searing pain in his ribs.

"The doctor thinks you busted a rib, Barney," said Moores. "That's why you were bleeding out of your mouth. He thinks you better lay still to heal up. We're going to get you over to Missouri Baptist Hospital."

Wait a minute. Ma and Pa came to St. Louis to see me race.

The pictures filling Oldfield's eyes possessed a disturbing stark quality that was so real they were hard to believe. Like a light coming on in a dark room, he became intensely aware of his mother, the doctor, and racing Webb in the dust. Oldfield whispered to Cooper, asking where he was and what happened.

"You're at the clubhouse at the St. Louis track, Barney," Cooper replied.

Sarah Oldfield sat beside her son's cot, clasping his hand as Cooper continued.

"We lost you in the dust, and you crashed through the fence. Webb came back around and picked you up and brought you here. You were talking crazy, and you just dozed off for a little bit here."

Oldfield felt bandages on his head. He touched their strangeness. "You nearly scalped yourself on a tree limb, Barney. And part of the fence scrapped your chest up. All in all, though, I'd say you were pretty damn lucky," Cooper said.

Oldfield glanced at Moores, painfully whispering a question.

"How's the Dragon?"

"She's done for, Barney. She nearly climbed an Oak. What that didn't take out of her, the souvenir hunters did."

A picture of dozens of people attacking the Dragon came back to the driver, people pulling parts off the car and running as he lay at their feet. Remembering an army of boots stepping around his face, he recalled struggling to shout as people ripped the Dragon apart.

Another cold memory came to the surface. One man bent a dented section of the Dragon's cowling back and forth until the crease broke a piece off. The man handed it to a boy who must have been his son and then resumed his work.

"Goddamn vultures," the words punched his lungs from inside.

"There's something else you better know, Barney," Moores said. "The Dragon took a man and a negro down. They're both dead. It was bad, awful. The fella's name was John Scott, and he worked here. The Negro worked in the stables. They were leaning on the fence when the Dragon went through. It took Scott's legs clean off. I saw them load him on the stretcher and then put his legs on his chest. You're better off not to remember, but I had to tell you. The Negro was mauled something awful."

"I'm quitting this game, I swear Ma. I had enough. Damn vultures just want to see people killed anyway. I ain't given them the satisfaction."

(St. Louis, Missouri Baptist Hospital, Monday, August 29, 1904)

A gray-haired nurse in a white uniform and cap that reminded Oldfield of something a nun would wear poked her head into his room at Missouri Baptist Hospital to announce the arrival of a guest, Mrs. Holland.

"I don't know any Mrs. Holland," Oldfield said, gritting his teeth from the pain that shot through his ribs. "What does she look like?"

The nurse frowned and disappeared. In a moment, a tall woman with a vaguely familiar face entered the room. Oldfield, as he did with every woman he met, evaluated her carefully.

A soft, voluptuous figure, the woman wore a navy-blue flannel skirt with a white linen blouse secured under her neck by a cameo broach. Her curly brown hair was pulled back and collected well above her collar, and as with the light top, was a choice, no doubt made in deference to the stifling heat of the late summer day.

Oldfield's eyes lingered on her full breasts before looking into her face, which was strangely round, much like his own. The woman asked Oldfield if he remembered her, and he had to admit he did not.

"We met at the reception Saturday night. I was introduced to you as Rebecca Gooby. But that's my maiden name. I am a widow."

The nurse's announcement of a married woman visitor had tempered Oldfield's enthusiasm even for female company, but the latest revelation cast the meeting in a new light. He smiled effortlessly and disregarded the inconvenience of pain when he spoke.

"Well, now, little honey, what can I do for you?"

"Mr. Oldfield, please call me Bess. And I came to see if I could be of service to you."

"What you're doing right now is a lot of help, Bess," Oldfield said. "If you keep doing it, I'll get better twice as fast. By the way, you call me Barney, won't you?"

"Well, Barney, you seem to have great confidence in the medicinal powers of my mere presence."

"Honey…excuse me…Bess, I have a feeling you could cure anything."

Oldfield delighted in the color that burst into Bess's face and neck, and he remembered how Helen Winton had blushed at Ormond. Bess was more composed, she did not giggle, and there was no awkward pause or change in the tone of her voice. But the blush meant everything to him.

Bess Holland returned every day for the week Oldfield was in the hospital. She eventually told him how she admired his confidence and how his inner strength was so evident in the courageous way he drove cars. Then she asked him how quickly he would drive again and if she could come to see him.

"Just as soon as you spring me out of here, you and I are going to the races. I don't know what they're holding me up for, anyhow. What do they know?"

Chapter 13 – The Vanderbilt Cup

(Long Island, New York, Friday, October 7, 1904)

Since spring, it seemed to Barney Oldfield that all he heard people talk about was the big international road race William K. Vanderbilt, Jr. and Art Pardington planned on Long Island, New York. Modeled after the James Gordon Bennett Cup races that ran in France, Ireland, and Germany, this was America's first international road race. Called the William K. Vanderbilt, Jr. Cup, the competition attracted entries from France, Germany, and Italy, as well as the United States.

Oldfield steered a twenty-four-horsepower Peerless touring car onto Creed Avenue in the village of Queens on Long Island, New York the day before the big race. The Peerless passed a large wooden barn-like structure that housed an old wagon-building company and towered over the church, train station, and general store next to it.

"Stop, Barney!" Lou Moores shouted from the tonneau.

Moores stood up in the car's backseat and waved his arms like a windmill in a thunderstorm at a fast-approaching Mercedes. The driver raised his hand, and the gravel road popped and scattered under his three-foot-tall artillery wood wheels as their tires gripped the Earth to stop.

The driver looked angry as his giant face had cheeks so red and pronounced, they were like apples. Brilliant blue eyes pierced the glare of his goggles.

"Wilhelm!" Moores shouted. "What do you think of the course?"

Moores paused and then said something in French.

The driver spat and wiped his gloved hand over his oily, thick blonde mustache.

"Mauvais!"

Moores and the driver exchanged a few more words in French before the Mercedes sped away, its wheels coated with oil and gravel. Oldfield, with Tom Cooper beside him in the front seats, asked Moores why a man so pissed would say the course was marvelous.

"Mauvais means rotten in French," Moores said. "That's Wilhelm Werner, the top driver of Germany. The fella that owns his car is Clarence Gray Dinsmore. It's the car Camille Jenatzy won the James Gordon Bennett Cup with last year and finished second this year. It's the biggest Mercedes in the race, with over ninety horsepower. He's got to be a favorite to win this derby."

Oldfield did not like hearing about another man being the favorite. Moores was barely seated again before the driver punched the throttle, and the Peerless picked up speed. Cooper pointed to signs on a tree in front of a church that shouted in bold block letters, "Warning! Stay off the road!" Oldfield thought of St. Louis and how this course seemed even more dangerous.

"It'll take more than a goddamn sign to keep people from coming out on the course," he said. "People are damn fools."

The turns in Queens were tight with loose, sharp stones on a downgrade that led to a railroad crossing. The Peerless picked up speed headed down the hill.

"Are the trains running during the race?" Oldfield asked.

"That's what they say," Moores said. "They have flagmen stationed all around it, so I guess they should be alright."

The Peerless exited Creed Avenue and entered Jericho Turnpike. Moores talked about how the course was just a little less than thirty and a half miles long and roughly triangular in shape. Sharp corners connected basically straight road.

"Keep going down Jericho Turnpike for a piece," Moores said. "It's a reasonable distance. About twelve-and-a-half miles, and it leads to the start-finish at a village called Westbury. It ends in a bigger village called Jericho. Then, turn right on Massapequa Road for six miles. That will take us to Bethpage Turnpike and Plank Road, which goes on for fourteen miles according to the map. That will give us a lap back at Queens."

Oldfield thought about how long the course was and how big a deal Vanderbilt was to stage this derby. By comparison, he felt small, and he didn't want anyone else to know.

As they approached a train viaduct, Oldfield had to zigzag abruptly to dodge holes as large as five-feet wide. Oil was everywhere and overdone in spots. It collected like rainwater in some of the holes, and a black mud mix splashed into the car.

The story traveling across Long Island was that Oldfield's St. Louis accident convinced the Triple-A to tamp down dust by oiling the entire course with ninety thousand gallons of raw petroleum.

I'm more famous than ever because I nearly killed myself, the driver thought.

Shortly after the viaduct, the surface was smoother, broader, and gently rolling. A roar grew louder from behind until a flash of white soared past the little Peerless.

Oldfield couldn't believe his eyes.

"Vanderbilt!"

Instinctively, Oldfield mashed his throttle, and his anemic machine offered pathetic acceleration. Helpless, he watched Willie K's white Mercedes disappear over the crest of the gentle hill in front of them.

"Goddamn it!"

Oldfield felt Moores reach over the backseat and firmly grip his shoulder.

"Come on, Barney, what are you thinking? That big Mercedes has better than ninety horsepower," Moores said.

At the Westbury start-finish, Oldfield brought the Peerless to a halt. Carpenters scurried about, putting the finishing touches on a grandstand on the right side of the road, and smaller stands for the press on the other side. Piles of scrap wood rested on either side, apparently awaiting final use as bonfire fuel.

Between two telegraph poles on either side of the road, a giant banner announcing the start-finish caught the brisk wind like a kite. There was Vanderbilt's name, the letters so big they shouted. A cluster of men stood in front of the press box, and Oldfield recognized Carl Fisher among them.

Another face from home! Fisher was someone who understood him.

Removing his wet, unlit cigar from his mouth, Oldfield stashed it in his shirt pocket, ashes smearing a gray smudge just above it. Inserting two fingers in his mouth and he emitted the high pitch whistle, he used to call his dog after blasting ducks out of the sky near the lake back home in Wauseon. Fisher's group turned their heads, and soon the Indianapolis businessman joined the Peerless men, greeting them as friends.

"New two-mile record for the lightweights out in Chicago last week, huh, Carl?" Oldfield said, offering a cigar that Fisher accepted.

"Two minutes and two seconds. I brought it in on the second mile at fifty-nine and four-fifths. That's all she had."

"That's all you can do is get all she can give you."

Oldfield knew the record was a big deal for blind Fisher, who he thought was as brave as any man, but never won much in racing cars. Oldfield chuckled and encouraged his friend, who talked about driving his Indianapolis-built Premier Comet to his biggest day a week earlier at Chicago's Harlem horse track. Fisher bragged about beating Henry Ford's new driver, Frank Kulick, two out of three five-mile heats in a match race.

Listening to Fisher helped drive out taunting thoughts from Oldfield's mind. Painful feelings that reminded him that Willie K owned everything – including the ground he stood on. He laughed again.

"You had a big day, didn't you, Carl?"

"Congratulations, Carl," Moores said. "Did you see Willie K scorch through here? Oldfield's still kicking about him dusting us before the train tracks at Mineola. He thinks he can run him down in this little touring car if we all pedal hard enough."

The men laughed until Oldfield finally joined them.

"Old Willie K's having a high time, isn't he? This is a damn big show," Fisher said.

"Nothing else like it in America. I've been here since Wednesday, just nosing around, talking to folks. I tell you, boys…and no offense, Moores, but America better get serious about its auto industry, and its roads or these European boys are going to walk all over us. They're going to get rich telling us what kinds of cars to buy."

Lou Moores did not argue. Even though Moores never said it, Oldfield knew the Peerless engineer understood the Green Dragon had little chance against the Europeans. Moores assured Fisher that he understood the situation.

Appearing unconvinced that Moores – or anyone – really grasped his point, Fisher pounded his right fist into his open left hand as if to emphasize the seriousness of the matter. Oldfield felt a surge of patriotism as he listened to the Indianapolis businessman talk about the possibilities if America would invest in public roads and understand that race competition was essential to improving the breed. Many in the industry believed racing had little to do with the development of cars needed to travel American roads.

"And I'm telling you," Fisher said, "These Eastern fellas just aren't cut of the same cloth you and I are."

Intrigued, Oldfield asked what he meant.

"Well, look at this grandstand. It's the only paid seating. Four-hundred-eighty individual seats, and eighty-three boxes seating six each. The seats sold for five dollars, and the boxes went for fifty bucks. That's going to barely cover expenses. Hell, the goddamn Tiffany's trophy cost twenty-five hundred dollars. Most everyone is going to watch for free. There's going to be twenty or thirty thousand people here."

Fisher lowered his voice and looked both ways like somebody was spying on him. Oldfield leaned forward with the other men. There was something about Fisher that made you think everything he said was vitally important.

"They take a lot of pride in being amateurs and gentlemen sportsmen. I'm here to tell you, there isn't a damn thing wrong with making a buck. It's American, for Christ's sake! Jesus Christ on a bicycle, how the Hell does old Willie K think he got his money? His great-granddaddy hustled for it. That's how! Got his hands dirty!"

Fisher always made Oldfield laugh. He told Fisher he had room for one more in the Peerless, but he declined. Fisher wanted to stay in Mineola and Westbury, where most of the automobile men were. He said he had to figure out how to keep America in the auto game.

When Oldfield pushed the Peerless in gear, the wheel spun on the shiny oil for a second before catching traction – but there was no dust. Driving on, Long Island unfolded before them, the road slicing through vast, open spaces save for the rare roadhouse or village.

Jericho was little more than a few houses and a post office. Bored, Oldfield picked up speed as they traveled south on Massapequa Road, past cabbage and cornfields, and open grazing land. Pushing the little Peerless to the limit, he tried to get a feel for the road at speed. Smooth traveling at twenty miles per hour, but as he topped forty, the tiny car bounced sideways and briefly got off the ground.

Cooper and Moores gripped the sides of the carriage tightly and continued to talk about cars and racing with no apparent concern for safety. Oldfield was comfortable around men like that.

At the rough Bethpage turn, Oldfield slid the Peerless on large, sharp stones that proved far more treacherous than any of the men had assumed. Finally, Moores spoke up.

"Take it easy, Barney! Goddamn, this stuff will blow the tires."

On the right side of the road, a team of horses pulled a massive metal cylinder. Apparently, they were attempting to crush new stones that had been laid to fill holes and even the surface. Cooper sat up in his seat, surveying the turn and the roller team.

"They're going to race on this shit?" he asked.

Oldfield pressed on to the town of Hempstead, where Moores told him he would find one of two control points on the course. This is where he wanted to watch, to see the competitors in the heat of battle, and observe how officials managed them. Word was they would stop the cars here because they were population centers in the towns of Hicksville and Hempstead.

Filled to capacity for days, the hotel in Hempstead and the roadhouses along the path had "no vacancy" signs posted. Oldfield and his friends didn't care. They had everything they needed: blankets, jerky, beans, coffee, and whiskey.

They parked the Peerless and walked among the teams from the car and tire companies who had supply stations crewed by mechanics to fuel cars, replace tires, and make repairs. The stations were positioned at the entrances or exits of controls where the racers were most likely to slow or need service.

Later that night, Oldfield and his friends stopped at the Continental Tire depot, just outside of the Hempstead control. They knew the five Mercedes entries used Continental tires.

Without the sun, a chill settled onto cloudless empty fields, now dotted with campfires. The Peerless men approached the Continental tent, handled by eight mechanics, four German, four American. Moores introduced himself, and then Cooper and Oldfield. When Moores mentioned Oldfield, the Americans looked at each other in apparent surprise, smiling.

"Barney Oldfield? You're kidding, right? This here is Barney Oldfield?"

Crowding around the driver, the mechanics turned away from Moores and fired questions.

"How come you ain't racing, Barney? Hell, I'm working for the Kaiser, but I can see America needs you."

Oldfield poked at Cooper.

"Kiser is king, huh, Tom?"

Oldfield turned back to the tire men. He enjoyed the way they looked at him, sensing admiration and awe. They smiled and shook his hand and asked how he was feeling after the spill at St. Louis. Judging them to be regular fellas, Oldfield opened the trunk on the back his car and removed a quart of corn whiskey.

"Would the Kaiser mind if you fellas had nightcap? I'm buying it."

Everyone crowded around the fire to pass the bottle. The German team leader, a Mr. Bäcker, spoke English and had heard of Barney Oldfield.

Everyone, especially the Americans, was eager to share with the driver. Some drank from his bottle; others poured his corn liquor in hot coffee as the dark cold intensified.

Oldfield talked about whipping Alexander Winton and Vanderbilt and hitting the mile-a-minute record in old Nine-Ninety-Nine. He told everyone Tom Cooper built Nine-Ninety-Nine with Henry Ford, and then he and Cooper argued about who was the better driver.

Moores lay on the ground, wrapped in a blanket with another one rolled up under his head. He was soon quiet and unresponsive even though Oldfield occasionally poked him. Oldfield, Cooper, and two of the tire men talked into the early morning.

Finally, only Oldfield and Cooper remained awake. As Oldfield lay on his back near the fire, his eyes fixed on the sky, and the harder he stared, more tiny dots of starlight revealed themselves to his eyes. And then, he focused on the vastness of the space between the small dots.

"Tom, coming here makes me think."

"I could say something, Barney, but I won't."

"I'm serious. Driving around this big old course and seeing all these people lined up to run this giant race is something else. I was thinking about what Fisher said. I mean, think about how much money Vanderbilt has. He doesn't even have to worry about making money. He buys a fancy trophy from Tiffany's, and people come from around the world to run this race with his name on it. And did you see the way he shot past us down Jericho Turnpike?"

"And you whipped his ass in Ormond. Did you see these guys here, the way they looked at you? The way they talked to you? They think you're a big deal, Barney."

Oldfield's eyes began to close. He didn't want to say to Cooper that he was afraid and felt small, although he thought his friend could tell. No one should know of his thoughts of St. Louis and how he missed Bess - or that deep in his heart, fear he could never measure up weighted his spirit.

(Long Island, New York, Saturday, October 8, 1904)

A thin line of pink softness marked the eastern horizon as Carl Fisher, and Art Newby warmed their gloved hands in front of a bonfire next to the Westbury press and officials stand. The flame cast an uneven orange glow over the faces of other men standing there, as it altered the shadows of their noses and hat brims continuously.

Fisher watched Triple-A Secretary and Starter Charles Gillette sort brassards of green, blue, and red as he talked with Art Pardington, Chair of the Triple-A Racing Board. Pardington, as head of the race commission, already had affixed his blue brassard to his coat sleeve.

By Fisher's count of the pile of remaining brassards, several officials had not yet arrived with little more than an hour before the start of the race. All around him was a commotion as pedestrians roamed the area, and a curved stream of lights from automobiles and horse-drawn runabouts flowed toward them from the direction of Queens.

His fingers wrapped around a steaming ceramic-coated metal coffee cup; Fisher glanced at Pardington. The condensation of his breath dissipated in the crisp air.

"So, Art, tell me about this telephone system you have to keep you in touch with what's going on around the entire course."

Fisher was curious about how electricity could make voices travel across wires, and he knew Pardington was a former manager of the Long Island Bell Telephone Company. Pardington explained the system was a state-of-the-art telecommunications network designed by New York and New Jersey Telephone Company.

"Over five hundred miles of wire connects timers and judges around the course to the officials' stand," he said. "This is the latest in advanced technology. I have four telephone company men stationed on motor bicycles ready to rush to any point of malfunction."

Fisher was about to ask Pardington how quickly every home would have a phone, but he noticed the referee was distracted by a commotion behind them. Something had his attention.

Fisher pivoted to see a massive, gleaming-white Mercedes weaving between surreys and horse-drawn buses as pedestrians scattered to the shrill sound of the car's horn. Beside the driver was a large man with a Red Cross brassard. The ninety-horsepower Mercedes was William K. Vanderbilt Junior's calling card, and it was apparent Pardington lost all interest in the bonfire discussion as he tossed what was left of his coffee in the dirt and walked toward his boss.

Pardington's abrupt departure didn't faze Fisher. His active mind shifted as he surveyed the setting. The sense of spectacle made him envious that it was not his creation.

Oil street lamps still shone brightly in the dim pre-dawn light, as did dozens of campfires dotting the big fields behind the stands. The substantial river of tiny lights on Jericho Turnpike continued to inch closer from the north as pedestrians, wagons, and automobiles loaded with people ostensibly bent on finding choice vantage points arrived. Automobilists clustered around the reserved stands, where Society distinguished themselves from common folk that rested on blankets or in wagons.

An ominous rumble filled Fisher's ears as bright orange bursts of flame from an exhaust pipe shone brilliantly in the pre-dawn gray. He squinted to bring the number five Mercedes into focus. Young millionaire amateur George Arents was the first competitor to arrive. Fisher walked to the side of the press stand, where his friend Art Newby stood.

The structure broke a persistent and chilling wind.

"I can't say I've seen anything like this, Carl," Newby said. "And all those people sleeping in the lobby and lawn at the Garden City Hotel this morning. I don't believe even Willie K himself thought he'd draw this kind of crowd."

"I'm not sure he gave it much thought, Art. You and I put on a show, and our big concern is counting the gate receipts and making sure everybody gets their money's worth. But these guys don't have any gate receipts. And what they are doing is entertaining themselves. It's kind of like looking at the world in reverse."

As the minutes passed, the grandstands across the road filled. John Gerrie of *The New York Herald* approached Fisher and congratulated him on his wins in Chicago. But Gerrie quickly turned the subject to the members of Society gathering in the stands.

"Actually, I am amused at the idea of cute little Mrs. Willie K over there with her dainty ass on those dewy rough planks," the newspaperman said.

Gerrie nodded his head in the direction of a woman in a black and white shepherd plaid tailor suit, with a box coat and short skirt, a red velvet toque, and a long black veil.

"That's little Mrs. Willie K. And sitting beside her is Elsie French Vanderbilt, the wife of her husband's cousin, Alfred Vanderbilt. Alfred owns the ninety horsepower Fiat Paul Sartori is driving. She's the one in a pale blue cloth tailor gown and pale blue toque."

Fisher squinted at Gerrie, wondering why someone could give a shit what kind of clothes these people wore. He turned back to study the women, but they were too blurry to tell if they were good looking.

What Fisher could see was that the women were both animated, even giddy, and shouting and waving at friends. Gerrie waved at a man in a black suit and tie who tipped his bowler in an almost imperceptible way that made it unclear whether it was a response or an oblivious adjustment performed in boredom.

"That's John Jacob Astor. What a rogue's gallery, huh?" Gerrie said as he laughed. "It's all worthy of opening night at the Metropolitan Opera, don't you think? See the couple there just off to the left?"

Fisher, never envious of Society, but always bored with their frivolous ways, barely nodded. Newby, more interested, encouraged the reporter.

"That's Mr. and Mrs. Oliver Belmont," Gerrie said. "She's Willie K's mother. Her name is Alva, and she married Ollie back in ninety-six after she caught Willie Senior, giving away her jewelry to some showgirl he took a fancy to."

"Talk about ambition. In ninety-five, Alva forced her daughter Consuelo into a marriage with the Duke of Marlborough so she could be the mother of a Duchess. Apparently, she spent two and a half million dollars to renovate his castle and still pays him a one-hundred-thousand-dollars-a-year annual lifetime salary. Now she gives speeches talking about how women should be allowed to vote. They're silly people, really."

Fisher barely heard the man as he focused on the cars gathering at the starting tape. While he didn't know all the men personally, he knew who owned the racecars, and who drove them.

Feathering the throttle of Sam Stevens' red Mercedes, driver Al Campbell appeared impatient to get underway. Starter Gillette and another official began counting down the seconds to the start with their fingers. Their bodies were like shadows in the gathering exhaust smoke as Gillette waved the flag to send Campbell on his way.

Fisher was almost startled by a roar that suddenly erupted from the grandstand. Next up was crowd favorite Fernand Gabriel, his reputation enhanced by his victory in the tragic 1903 Paris-Madrid fiasco that cost eight people their lives and inflicted a dozen more injuries.

People at the Garden City Hotel had talked about how Gabriel had beaten a train across the tracks by mere inches during practice earlier in the week. Just as Gabriel came to the tape, a maroon-colored White steam touring car rolled onto the course alongside the grandstand.

"Jesus Christ on a Bicycle! Who in the Hell does that idiot think he is?" Fisher yelled.

"Augustus! No, no, no!" Gerrie screamed.

The bizarre sight was even more surreal as it first appeared in Fisher's feeble eyes that a bear was driving the car. People in the grandstands began to throw paper and fruit at the steamer and scream for the man in the bearskin coat to be arrested.

Only the starter, Gillette, remained in place as the other officials descended on the car. Still, the driver surged forward, pinning a man against the wooden barricade in front of the grandstand. Willie K, wearing a fur coat, turned cloth side out, ran to the driver, and leaned into his face. The man backed down.

"Do you know that man?" Newby asked.

"Augustus Post. He's the chair of the Triple-A Touring Committee. He doesn't get along with Pardington, so he wasn't appointed to the Race Commission, and he's been pissed off about it for months. He's been drinking. He thinks he ought to be allowed to come and go as he pleases," Gerrie said.

More thunder emanated from the seats as Gabriel accelerated away. The cars continued to start in two-minute intervals until there were no more. Then there was silence. A slender man with a huge megaphone was apparently shouting updates relayed to him through the phones, but he was too far away to hear. Eventually, all the drivers that could start were on their way.

"This is going to get tiresome when some of these cars drop out. All people will see is a car shoot by and then wait in silence for another one in ten minutes or so. There's nothing to see, so how the Hell are you supposed to know what's going on?" Fisher asked.

People walked onto the track and leaned forward in the direction of Queens, straining to look around the other people making up a long tunnel doing the same. All the talk around Fisher and Newby was that Campbell would come back around first.

Three minutes after William Wallace, the last driver to start, left the line a car approached to complete the first lap. The two or three thousand people in the area screamed when they realized it was Gabriel. In Fisher's weak eyes, the crowd on the road blurred into two dark, shadowy accordion-like walls of flesh, expanding to barely accommodate the speeding racer, and then closing again the instant he passed. Fisher looked at Newby.

"Jesus Christ on a bicycle! Somebody's going to get killed! They think they should stand on the course to watch the race!"

"Car Coming!"

A tall, thin yachtsman with a long marine glass shouted from within the branches of a large tree near the two telegraph poles marking the entrance to the Hempstead Control. Barney Oldfield tilted his head up toward the man, and then his eyes darted back to the road as a red Mercedes flashed around the bend, swerving as it neared the entrance. The driver braked, and the car careened to the left, then to the right, skidding past a tape marking the twenty-five yards required braking distance.

Oldfield cringed as the car skidded backward and bounded up onto a sidewalk, some fifty feet beyond the tape. The riding mechanic flew from the machine as it bounced over a gutter, but he quickly sprung up and shouted to the driver to take it out of gear. Several bystanders eagerly joined in as he pushed it back to within the tape so the timers would shut the clocks off.

"George Arents," Oldfield said to Tom Cooper, who stood with him on the opposite side of the road.

"I saw in the *Brooklyn Eagle* he's another Swell, a millionaire who thinks because he can buy a car, he can race it. This is his first race."

Once within the tapes, an official recorded the arrival time of the car and handed the driver a yellow card. The mechanic restarted the engine, and they headed toward the control area's exit more than a mile down the road.

Within minutes, the yachtsman, who Oldfield realized had no official capacity at the race, was shouting that another car was coming. Apparently, the official checkers, posted in a small wooden stand near the control entrance, realized he was useful, nicknamed him "Bill," and encouraged additional reports.

Alonzo Webb, in the sixty-horsepower Pope-Toledo, skidded to a stop well within the tapes. Oldfield nodded at his friend and ran over to Webb as the timer handed him his card.

"Barney! You're looking fit! How are you feeling?"

"Better than you, Al. I don't have to worry about these idiots – watch out for that fool just ahead of you."

Webb asked his friend if he wanted to hitch a ride through town, and Oldfield waved to Cooper to let him know he was going. When Oldfield started to climb up on the fuel tank behind the seats, Andy Anderson, the mechanic, objected.

Anderson explained that a week earlier, while riding in the same position with the other Pope-Toledo driver, Herb Lytle, he was thrown on top of Harold Rigby, Lytle's riding mechanic, when a steering knuckle broke and they slammed into a ditch. Rigby's chest was crushed, and he bled to death. Oldfield thought of St. Louis, nodded, and stepped onto the running board.

Clinging to one side of the car while balancing his right foot on the mechanic's running board, Oldfield felt the car jerk as gears engaged. Webb took a leisurely pace down the main residential road, bordered by charming homes set back on well-kept lawns lined by large shade trees.

This went on for nearly a mile and a half until two looming telegraph poles with a white canvas banner marking the control's exit came into view. Oldfield shook hands with Webb and Anderson and then hopped off. Coming around the car to Webb's side, he asked about the European racecars.

"I hate to say it, Barney, but everything I've seen all week long says we don't have a prayer. Our cars are underpowered, and we're not used to these long races like in Europe. Hell, maybe Lytle in our touring car will be the only American around at the end, and they don't have the horses to keep up. The Europeans have us covered."

"I'd like to see them try to take on Alonzo Webb on a mile track," Oldfield said, giving Webb a wink. "Good luck, my friend."

The timing official deposited Webb's freshly marked yellow card into a copper box on the side of the car. Webb started again, shifted through his gears, and the big Pope-Toledo gradually grew smaller into silence.

As the race progressed, Oldfield noticed the control became more crowded. The officials looked like weak bunglers as they struggled to keep fools from running into the road to touch the cars or push them without being asked. Screams filled the air regularly as drivers, barely in control, skidded into the area, scattering clusters of idiots that filled the roads the cars were supposed to travel on. Oldfield again thought of the two men he struck in St. Louis.

He marched through the town to return to the other end of the control where Cooper and Moores were. He found them near the entrance to the Pope-Toledo depot just outside of town. The Pope-Toledo mechanics prepared for Alonzo Webb's return.

When the Pope-Toledo appeared, Oldfield studied the mechanics as Webb rolled in for service. Half a dozen of them jumped for the car as if to storm it. One had the wrench to remove the tank cap, the other a funnel to direct the fuel, and a third had a fuel hose connected to a tank on a stand eight feet high. Three other men squirted lubricating oil at a dozen points on the car. Oldfield thought about everything it would take to win a race this long. All the equipment, the people, and the money seemed overwhelming.

As Webb prepared to leave, the man with the hose shouted as a steady stream of gas poured from a hole in the tank. Someone yelled for chewing gum, and another pulled the sagging tank level and lashed it with ropes. The excitement and energy in Webb's face on his first Hempstead stop was gone, and he stared forward grimly, shaking his head.

Within minutes, George Heath, the American-born French Panhard driver living in Paris, masterfully slid his car to a stop within the tapes. With the most powerful car in the race, Heath, lapped everyone by his fifth tour of the course. Oldfield noted how he subtly turned his wheel as his tires briefly slipped in oily mud. Self-doubt crowded its way into his thoughts – could Barney Oldfield drive like that? The cars were huge, and the race, at three-hundred miles, was almost incomprehensible when he thought of his five or ten-mile runs.

As Heath slowly proceeded to the other side of town, Oldfield studied Moores's face and wondered if his private doubts were obvious. His boss had entered him and the old Green Dragon in a race at Pittsburgh the week before against weak competition. None of his miles were under a minute. He didn't want to say to Moores or Cooper that he dreaded the idea of racing wheel-to-wheel again, but he wondered if they already knew.

Was the Pittsburgh meet an attempt by Lou to build back his confidence?

Oldfield was startled back from his thoughts as Albert Clement, at twenty-one, the youngest driver in the race, screeched his Clement-Bayard to a halt in front of him. Animated, Clement was obviously not pleased with the officials about something. His face as black with oil as a minstrel, he cursed in French. Oldfield imagined Clement was wholly involved in what he was doing, and the thought of wrecking, of getting hurt or even death, was the furthest thing from his mind.

In the end, it was Heath who won the race, barely a minute faster than Clement. Riding mechanic Carl Mensel, a husband and the father of three children, the youngest two months old, had been killed. He died when his head was crushed after his driver, millionaire George Arents lost control and flipped his Mercedes between Hempstead and Queens. Arents was in the hospital, and some said he would not survive.

Seeing Oldfield, newspapermen wanted to know if he would run the race the next year. "I can lick any man alive," he said to *The Automobile* newspaperman stationed in Hempstead.

Did he sound convincing?

Chapter 14 – America's Pride

(Brighton Beach, Saturday, October 22, 1904)

Almost in a daydream, Barney Oldfield fixed his eyes on Bess Holland, who sat on the front row of the grandstand at New York's Brighton Beach horse track. From his vantage point at the starting line more than a hundred yards away, he felt safer with his questions than if he was sitting beside her.

A peculiar vague sensation nagged him about why she was there, and his mind tried to categorize this woman but found no ready labels. She satisfied his urges, and while he wanted to run away, he did not want her to leave. She was not the beautiful woman he wished for and yet confiding in her made him feel that someone understood.

A wicked, cold west wind swept over the track and reminded Oldfield of where he was. Despite the blustery blasts, the ground was still mud from rainstorms on Thursday, and he said to himself that he thanked God there was no dust. Glancing back at Bess, Oldfield wondered how comfortable she was in the biting cold as he saw her reach up to secure her big bonnet from flying away like a kite.

People milled around the track, and the paddock, some associated with teams, some officials, and others just wanted to be near the cars. Ernie Moross strolled by with a guest, Frank Maney, of the Energine Company. Maney had started providing his company's product, gasoline, to Peerless without charge so he could use Oldfield and the team in his promotions.

Maney waddled over to Oldfield and shook his hand. Fat as a pig for market, he was one of those guys that were always moping little dots of sweat off his forehead and flushed face with a handkerchief, even in the cold wind.

"Congratulations on whipping Kiser and the Bullet last week at Cleveland, Barney,"

Maney said. "How do you like the new Dragon?"

"I like her fine, Mr. Maney. She's light and strong, barely seventeen-hundred pounds. From the success of the Pope-Toledo and the Packard Gray Wolf finishing third and fourth in the Vanderbilt, the light cars look to be the way of the future. And with rounded sidebars, V-shaped radiator coils for a torpedo nose, and canvas wheel covers, she just glides through the air. She sits low, too, barely four inches off the ground."

"She powerful?" Maney asked.

Oldfield thought it was a stupid question, but he played along with the man.

"She's got sixty horses and pulls three-hundred pounds less weight than the old one. We put both the intake and exhaust valves up top on the head, and we think we get better carburetion."

"Hellfire, boy, you get better carburetion because you use Energine gasoline," Maney said, turning to Moross. "Isn't that right, Ernie?"

Moross laughed and slapped Maney on the back. He positioned himself behind Maney, but in Oldfield's line of sight. Moross could read the driver's face, so he knew when he had enough conversation. Moross would wink or nod and always come up with a creative way to segue and move a guy away. Since St. Louis, Oldfield felt anxious and skeptical of anyone pushing him. People didn't care if he got hurt. He liked Moross for helping to move everyone along.

"What we need is that mile record, Barney," Maney said. "Let's take that one away from Kiser once and for all."

The mile record chewed at Oldfield. At Cleveland, he ran his fastest mile ever against Kiser at fifty-three and four-fifths seconds and still didn't believe Kiser had really run a full second faster in August. None of that mattered, though. Kiser had the record, and the pressure was on Oldfield to break it.

Running against Kiser at Cleveland wasn't difficult because the Bullet misfired with a faulty magneto. Oldfield was comfortable when he ran by himself, but the vision of breaking through the fence with the trees rushing at him at St. Louis came back to him when he ran side-by-side with someone. Moross pulled Maney away to see the Peerless stock car that Charles Wridgeway drove at the meet.

The red Renault of Maurice Bernin and Alfred Vanderbilt's black Italian Fiat, driven by Paul Sartori, was positioned beside the Dragon. Both drivers and cars had competed in the Vanderbilt Cup, and the New York area was still buzzing about the great race. Lou Mooers, who had disappeared to find a wrench for the spark plugs, returned to loosen the leather belt straps and peel back the Dragon's cowling.

"How does she like this mud, Barney?"

"I haven't let her all the way out yet, Lou. She seems a little nervous."

Moores, with his churchwarden clenched between brown teeth, had been in a good mood since the previous Saturday at Cleveland when Oldfield met Earl Kiser and the Bullet head-to-head and won two straight five-mile match races. Peerless' new success and the palpable excitement of the patriotic crowd were most likely the inspiration for the smile that overwhelmed Moores's unmanaged whiskers and his crude whistling of an unrecognizable tune.

Much anticipated was the featured International Cup between the heat winners for America, France, and Italy. Sartori's Fiat was the only Italian car. Still, Oldfield had won the American qualifying heat against Wridgeway in the little Peerless, and Bernin had prevailed against Guy Vaughn's forty-horsepower Decauville in the French heat.

Oldfield glanced at the opposing teams lined up beside him. Bernin was on the inside, with Sartori in the middle. W. Gould Brokaw stood with Bernin, and pointed at Oldfield, then said something into his driver's ear and they both laughed.

"They're just a pair of jackasses, Barney," Tom Cooper said. "Come on, get in the car, and I'll crank it."

Oldfield got a great start in the five-mile International Cup and stormed into the first corner leading. Dust and dirt flipped off the Dragon's tires as he rounded the corner. The track had dried some since morning. From over his shoulder, he saw Bernin about one-hundred-fifty feet further back, and Sartori trailing him. Wanting to build his lead to avoid running wheel-to-wheel, Oldfield pushed hard into the second corner. To his disappointment, Bernin clung tenaciously to the Green Dragon's tail.

Oldfield held the lead until the third mile, but when he swung wide again in the second corner, Bernin dashed the Renault to the pole and pulled even. The red car and the cloud of dust and dirt that traveled with it surged like Oldfield's personal sandstorm back toward him, and an electric jolt shot through his arms, and they froze, his fingers gripping the steering wheel tight enough to squeeze off pieces.

Corners at Brighton were only eighty feet wide, more than twenty feet narrower than Empire City or some of the other tracks. When Bernin swung the ass of his car to slide through the corner, he rocketed into the Dragon's path. Instinctively, Barney pulled his brake lever, and the Dragon slipped on the damp earth up near the ominous fence.

The fierce pounding in Oldfield's chest choked at his lungs, and his rapid breathing yielded little air. He hacked at his steering wheel like a novice, making a jagged path through the turn. Sartori shot by on the front stretch.

"Goddamn it!" Oldfield screamed. "Fucking bastards!"

Bernin won easily, with Sartori second, well ahead of the Green Dragon. Oldfield imagined Bernin and Brokaw laughing at the start-finish line with the crowd cheering their names. He couldn't stand the thought of watching them and quickly drove by into the paddock.

(Sunday, October 23, 1904)

Lou Moores sat in a different passenger car than the one Oldfield was in on the train ride back to Cleveland. A chill had fallen over the Peerless team after losing the International Cup and gone were the bush-faced Peerless engineer's whistling tunes.

Oldfield hardly spoke a word to Bess. He got on the train with her but moved to a different seat with Moross and Cooper after they traveled just a few miles. Bess seemed disappointed in him, and her eyes were red. Oldfield figured she'd move on anyway, probably because she thought he was yellow. Women don't want anything to do with cowards.

"So, Barney, what do you want to do next?" Cooper asked.

"What, you think I'm washed up, Tom? I told you, I'm not risking my neck for vultures. Those other fellas haven't been through a fence, they don't know."

"You're right, Barney, they don't know. But that doesn't change what happened," Moross said. "Do you want to keep driving, or do you want to do something else? There's no in-between in this game."

"Sure, there is. I'll just do exhibitions and put up some records."

"That's not going to work, Barney," Moross said. "People want to see the champion. Champions race. Every once in a while, you're going to have to lay it on the line."

"Why don't you put it on the line, Ernie? Why don't you go out there and crash through fences and kill people and get yelled at and called yellow? Did you hear those people booing me yesterday? I'm not killing myself, so those vultures can pick my bones."

"Oh, quit your bellyaching about vultures, Barney," Cooper said. "That's not what's bothering you, and you know it."

Oldfield furrowed his brow and raised his voice.

"Oh, okay, Mr. Fortune Teller. You know what I'm thinking now, huh? Why don't you drive the Dragon and see if you could do better? You bust through a fence or two."

"Barney, you're scared," Cooper said. "You lost your nerve. Just admit it. Now you have to decide if you want to race cars. And if you do, you're going to have to face it."

"We can make hay with this Barney if you feel up to it," Moross said. "I'll talk to Al Reeves at Empire City. Get this; Leon Thery is visiting New York. The Gordon Bennett Cup winner, for God's sakes! We get Bernin and Sartori to go along with this, we can bill it as the greatest match-up in the annals of international motorcar matchmaking. There's lots of money to be had making book on this."

"Barney," Cooper said. "Empire City is a good track for you. It's a full twenty feet wider than Brighton, and the corners sweep around and don't cut off tight like Brighton. There's plenty of room to race side-by-side."

Oldfield felt cornered. If he said no, he was yellow. But if he said yes and got spooked again, he would be washed up.

"What do you say, Barney? I'll ballyhoo this to China if you just say go," Moross said.

Silently, the driver nodded his head.

"That's great, Barney. I'll call Reeves tomorrow and take the train out to Yonkers. Tom, you should get Barney out to Glenville and work up to some speed. I'm going to find Lou."

Oldfield felt Cooper staring at him, but he sat silent, looking into his lap.

(Cleveland, Monday, October 24, 1904)

Oldfield sat at the bar of the Hotel Hollenden, better than halfway through a bottle of corn mash. He had already burned through one Havana special and was puffing furiously on a second. His cigars contributed to the thick haze that hung over the bar.

Tom Cooper told him he was lousy company and left him to drink alone. Oldfield didn't want to talk to Bess; besides, it was apparent she thought he was yellow. She didn't try to put her head on his shoulder, and her voice didn't carry that lilt it used to.

She was more interested in that stupid book she was reading than him. Now, she saw right through him. She understood what she was getting herself into. Cringing when he walked into the room, she must be figuring when and how to leave and head back to St. Louis.

A couple of men in the bar wanted to talk about cars, but Oldfield told them he was busy. He listened and laughed at a drunk and his companion who sat at the bar beside him as they railed on about what a sissy Alton Parker was - the Democratic candidate for President against Teddy Roosevelt in the upcoming election November 8.

"He ain't no man! Now TR, that's a man. He don't take shit off of nobody, you just ask those Spaniards!"

Oldfield laughed the big kind of laugh that bounced off the walls so he could hear himself above the other noise. It felt good to laugh, and not to have to think about racing or talk to anyone involved with it.

"If Alton Parker was a Rough Rider, we'd all be speaking Spanish, for Christ's sake," the drunk continued.

"Yeah," his companion said with a slur. "He's a Soft Rider…"

As they cackled, Oldfield felt a poke in his left kidney. The bartender, a large Italian man with black hair and a red striped shirt, wiped the bar with a towel as he walked toward him.

"Excuse me, Ma'am, but this bar is for men only."

Oldfield looked over his shoulder and saw Bess, her eyes red and glistening.

"We need to talk," she said.

Oldfield looked at her, trying to think of a way to avoid conversation. He wasn't sure whether she would leave him, or talk about how a man who loves her should behave.

Maybe she would ask him a bunch of questions about how he felt, and he didn't want to tell her. He didn't even want to think about it long enough to figure out what he was thinking. Worse, suddenly, he didn't feel like he could laugh again if he tried.

The bartender interrupted them again, asking Bess to leave. There were women Oldfield would have ignored, and there were bartenders he would have hit in the face. He did neither. He left with Bess.

When Oldfield was in Cleveland, he always had a suite at the Hotel Hollenden. The staff knew to keep the liquor cabinet stocked with whiskey, and a few bottles of stout ale. An ice bucket sat on top, with several glasses. Without hesitation, he walked directly to the glasses upon entering their room, grabbed one, turned it over, and dropped chips of ice in it.

"Barney, please, no more drinks, at least until we're finished talking," Bess said.

Oldfield wasn't used to complying with a woman's wishes, but he stopped what he was doing and turned to face Bess.

"I felt like we had grown pretty close in a short time, Barney," she said. "But these last few days, you don't seem like the same person."

"Didn't know I'm yellow, huh? Is that what you're thinking? You thought I was courageous, but now you're finding me out, is that it?"

Oldfield anticipated that Bess now saw through him, she could see he was afraid, and he wasn't who she thought he was.

"What are you talking about? Do you think I think you're a coward because you got scared at Brighton Beach? Is that what this is all about? Tom said…"

"Tom. He thinks he can read my mind. So, you're talking to him about me behind my back now, huh?"

"He's a good friend to you, Barney. Let me ask you a question. Do you want to race on Saturday?"

Oldfield turned his back on Bess and instinctively reached for the whiskey, pouring it over the ice.

"Let me tell you something, and you better believe me or I am going back to St. Louis tomorrow morning," she said.

Oldfield kept his back to Bess, half-heartedly sipping at the whiskey, not gulping shots as was his style.

"If you want to quit racing, that's fine with me," Bess continued. "I never said I wanted to watch you do something you didn't like. If you're too nervous about doing it again after everything you've been through, it doesn't change a thing about my opinion of you. I still think you're courageous. You're the only man in the world brave enough to have gotten back into that car after what happened in St. Louis. And that's the part of you I love. It's the part of you that would be the same if you were a farmer or a shopkeeper.

That's who you are. Driving race cars is just something you do. Do you understand me, Barney Oldfield?"

Oldfield turned and faced Bess. The sensation of his eyes filling to the brim like a shot glass was strange and awkward. He swallowed hard and looked at his feet for nearly a minute to relax his tight throat so his voice would not crack. A drop descended from his head to splash on the top of his leather boot.

"I never told a woman I needed her to back me up before."

Bess walked to him, hugged him, and said, "Is that what you are doing now?"

He didn't respond, except with a weak smile, and he didn't want to say anything. Bess seemed to understand, and he liked the motherly tone she took with him.

"Barney Oldfield, you listen to me. If you don't want to race, then don't. We'll think of something else to do. But if you want to race, then you go into it knowing nobody in the world can drive a car as fast as Barney Oldfield. I know some of those people like to put on that they're high and mighty, but you know what I think?"

Oldfield wrapped his arms around her and squeezed her softness against his chest. He wanted to hear what she thought. Everything she said made him feel the things he did were entirely justified. Not just justified, but righteous and great.

"I think they're afraid of you. Those drivers know you're special, and they know when you're at your best, they don't stand a chance. Barney, you are a bona fide, twentieth century man. You were born to race these machines."

His mood changed without him making any effort for it to happen. Bess could flip a light switch on the back of his collar. Within minutes, he went from not wanting to talk about cars to wanting to jump in one and charge into the first corner at Empire City.

"Tom and I will go out to Glenville tomorrow. Then we'll load her up and head for New York on the evening train. Pack your bags, little honey, because you're going to watch old Barney take those foreigners down a notch or two. I can lick any man alive."

(Empire City, Saturday, October 29, 1904)

Despite the eagerly anticipated Yale-Columbia football game scheduled for the same day as the big international motor racing match-up, every seat at the Empire City track was filled. Moross told Oldfield that the Astors and the Vanderbilts, including Willie K, were among those in the judge's stand.

"I don't know if they want your blood or your patriotism, but the highest ranks of Swelldom want to see you drive Barney," Moross said.

Moross had that edgy, jittery look of a man with too many cups of black coffee in his belly. He was always that way when he thought he was onto something huge. The paddock was packed more than any place Oldfield had seen other than the Vanderbilt

Cup. He wanted to get back to join Moores and Cooper at the Dragon, but Moross had brought Bess to his side at the clubhouse veranda and told him to wait. She had no idea of what Moross was up to either.

All about them were people, talking, pointing, and generally milling about. Clearly, someone or something not too far away was carving a path through the crowd. Like a field of corn lying down before a giant combine, the crowd parted for someone. People shouted and pointed, moving quickly and respectfully to make a path for two large young men in uniform who instructed the group to "gangway" and "look sharp."

Just behind them was Moross. Dwarfed by the bigger men, he beamed a big smile like he was about to announce the biggest promotion of his life.

Just behind and towering over Moross was a stately man, in the full-dress uniform of a high-ranking officer, looking distinguished with snow-white hair and immaculate mustache.

"Admiral Dewey, sir, I give you the track racing champion of the world, Mr. Barney Oldfield," Moross said.

Oldfield was prepared for many things from Ernie Moross, but not the hero of Manila Bay, the great Admiral credited with single-handedly destroying the Spanish Asiatic fleet in May 1898. Admiral Dewey, a favorite of President Roosevelt, and a hero to Americans throughout the land, now extended his hand to Barney Oldfield.

Oldfield looked at Bess like she should confirm what he couldn't believe, but she just smiled and gazed at him with soft, warm eyes. The two men stood eye-to-eye, and Barney noticed the confidence of a substantial handgrip.

"Beautiful Indian Summer day, isn't it, Mr. Oldfield? Perfect for a victory celebration. Tell me, Mr. Oldfield, is America going to prevail today?"

"I have five thousand dollars riding on Barney Oldfield, Admiral. I appreciate the sportsmanship of these gents, letting me back in the game, but I will show them no mercy."

"That's what I like to hear! A man with confidence in his abilities and the courage to show it! I have placed a wager on you myself, Barney. I'll bet on an American in an American machine every time."

Only then did Oldfield notice Brokaw and William K. Vanderbilt, Jr. trailing Admiral Dewey. They looked uncomfortable and surprised to hear the Admiral had bet against them. Still, the crowd was louder than any he had heard before and mixed in all the noise he distinctly heard different voices anonymously shout his name.

"I'll be up in the judge's balcony with these European car owners. I expect you to drive by and park that American car in front of me after winning this contest. Is that understood?"

Dewey reminded Oldfield of Alex Winton. When he winked at him, he felt like the Admiral knew with uncompromising certainty who would win, and anything less was not just unacceptable, but incomprehensible. The men saluted each other, and Dewey moved on, cutting through the crowd, waving and nodding his head to acknowledge shouts and cheers.

Oldfield, Cooper, and Moores joined Bernin, Brokaw, Leon Thery, Sartori, and Alfred Vanderbilt in front of the grandstands to draw for starting positions in one of two preliminary heats. Old Art Pardington was referee; Oldfield was sure he just wanted some of the spotlight so he could feel like a big man in front of all the Society that had turned out.

Pardington decided to divide the international match-up into two preliminary heats. The men reached into a hat full of little folded papers with numbers as the wind swept back their hair and kicked up dust at the edge of the track.

"And we want a standing start," Brokaw said.

"Let them have whatever they want," said Oldfield. "I'll race them any old way for any old thing to prove that they haven't got me down and out by any means."

Lou Moores frowned. The Green Dragon had but two gears, and the European racers had four. A standing start was a decided advantage for foreign cars.

"We only have two gears, Mr. Brokaw, but I am sure you know that. Nonetheless, I shall grant your request, provided teams are allowed to push their cars to get underway," Moores said.

The usual grumbles and grunts followed, but the ever-impatient Art Pardington interceded. He pronounced that to refuse the push was pointless because the Dragon would incur an excessive handicap.

The first heat matched Thery in his Gordon Bennett Cup-winning Richard-Brasier, and Sartori in Alfred Vanderbilt's Fiat. Other than a brief skirmish on the backstretch, Sartori steadily pulled away from Thery. Oldfield studied the Frenchman, who sawed at his steering wheel in the corners and skidded badly, costing him time.

"He doesn't have much experience at track racing. Give him a week, and he'd be a terror."

Moores added that Thery's car wasn't geared right, and a delay in customs didn't allow him to drive on the track until Thursday. Sartori continued to extend his lead, but his time for the ten-mile run was an unimpressive nine minutes, forty-five and four-fifths seconds.

When the drivers came to a stop on the front stretch, newspapermen swarmed them. Despite his loss, Gordon Bennett Cup winner Thery attracted the biggest crowd. Oldfield elbowed his way through the group to compliment the Frenchman on his grit. Thery dragged the back of his gloved hand across his oily, dusty face and then spoke.

"I have no excuse to make," said Thery. "I did the best I knew how, but I had not had a chance to learn much and no opportunity to rig my car for track speeding. I am glad if the Americans got any pleasure from seeing me. I certainly enjoyed my try at track racing and hope for a chance at more of it someday."

Just a few yards away, Moores and Cooper quickly prepared the Dragon for its big opportunity. Oldfield jogged to the car and jumped in. The Peerless engine fired, and all eyes were on starter Fred Wagner. A spindly man who liked to be called "Wag," Barney thought he reminded him of an old schoolmaster from his youth.

When Wag fired his pistol for the second heat, between Bernin and Oldfield, four husky lads rounded up by Tom Cooper pushed the Green Dragon for nearly twenty yards. Bernin refused such assistance, and Oldfield gained an advantage, rushing to the pole of the first turn a full car length ahead.

Oldfield flew down the backstretch, the vast, sweeping corner rushing at him as he steered the Dragon into a gentle slide. He powered a reasonable distance from the outside fence smoothly. Wagner stepped back from the track as Oldfield approached the end of the first mile.

Mile-by-mile, he extended his lead, his eyes fixed relentlessly on his line around the track, focusing so hard he drove thoughts of accidents from his mind. The dirt was smooth and moist, not muddy, just enough to keep the dust down. Oldfield peered over his shoulder as he exited the corner to enter the home stretch of his fifth mile and couldn't see the red Renault.

Screams intensified as he approached the grandstand and then dissipated as he dove into the first turn. Brimming with confidence, he felt so powerful the next time around he raised his left hand off the steering wheel as he headed down the front stretch and commanded thousands of voices to shout louder.

Cooper held a chalkboard out at near the start-finish. At fifty-three and one-fifth seconds, the lap was the fastest mile Oldfield had ever run. By the end of the ten miles, Barney Oldfield and the Green Dragon owned the world's track record for one to five miles from a standing start. Pandemonium welcomed him, and as he slowed the Dragon, people overwhelmed soldiers trying to enforce order and poured onto the track.

A thick crowd smothered the green car, with the driver still sitting in it. Hands thrust at him, clutching, clawing, and reaching over each other. Too many voices made it impossible to hear any one of them.

Oldfield stood on his seat, his eyes searched the stands for Bess, and finding her, he waved. She was smiling and jumping in place, one hand on her hat, and the other arm across her chest, attempting to control her full, undulating bosoms.

In the distance, Oldfield spied Moores and Cooper with Sartori and his people in a cluster around Art Pardington.

That can't be good.

Ernie Moross squeezed and ducked his way through the people around Oldfield. He was small enough to worm and jostle through holes with little notice.

"What the Hell is going on?" Oldfield asked.

"They're protesting your pushed start. These guys want you to come up through the gears."

Over the next fifteen minutes, the Fiat and the Green Dragon lined up, and Pardington issued his decision. The Peerless could be pushed until its rear wheels hit the starting tape, anything further would be a false start. Three false starts by one competitor would be a forfeit.

Cooper's pick-up crew of four again pushed the Dragon, but this time for just a few short feet instead of the several yards as before. The Dragon whined, its engine straining to overcome its tiny first gear, and then, when Oldfield shifted, his car stumbled and stuttered as it tediously labored to produce the revolutions to drive the taller gear.

Advantaged, Sartori jumped into the lead by three lengths in the first corner. He hugged low on the track while Oldfield accelerated in his old style out to the outside fence. The Green Dragon entered the backstretch at full tilt, and Oldfield laughed as he realized he was traveling much faster than the Fiat.

Bastards. Try to mess with my start.

Inching closer and closer to the big, black Italian machine, Oldfield could almost touch it. His heart pounded like a racehorse when the wheels of the two cars nearly interlocked. Jittery, the Fiat, looked nervous as its wheels cleared the ground on bumps, and it jarred back down on the track a foot or two sideways from where it started. Oldfield knew it could hit him.

Steadily, the nose of the pea-green Peerless pushed ahead and came into the second corner, clearly leading. A thrilling surge shot up his spine as Oldfield claimed the inside line. Exploding in a cackle, he then shouted, "Fucking bastards!"

Down the front stretch, he heard the grandstands thunder, and he delighted in the noise. Indomitable, mile-by-mile, he raised his hand to command the crowd and hear the reaction.

Admiral Dewey was in the stands, for Christ's sake! Bess too! Relentless, Oldfield refused to let up on Sartori. He mashed his throttle, and steered his light, bouncing machine out to the edge of the track in the corners so he could enter the stretches at full speed. Running at a track record pace, he ticked off the final laps just above fifty-three seconds.

After Wag waved the flag, Oldfield coasted the Dragon around the track and back to the judge's stand as Dewey had commanded. People again flooded toward him, but his eyes fixed on Admiral Dewey, who was beside Vanderbilt and Brokaw. Oldfield stood on the Dragon's seat and saluted the great Naval hero and screamed, "You know me, I'm Barney Oldfield!"

Dewey made a show of a vigorous salute in return, and another wave of noise erupted from the people around him because they noticed too. Oldfield's keen eyes detected Dewey's smile as he laughed and applauded. Searching for Bess, her face was lost in the boiling turmoil of people jumping and stepping over each other in the grandstands.

Peter Prunty, the famous Vanderbilt Cup announcer, scampered onto the track with a giant megaphone half as tall as his six-foot frame. A round of gunshots rang in Oldfield's ears as two soldiers on either side of him fired rifles into the air to quiet the crowd. Prunty shouted into his megaphone, and in a few minutes, pandemonium subsided.

"Ladies and gentlemen," Prunty shouted. "Allow me to introduce the new world's track record holder for ten miles, at nine minutes, twelve and three-fifths seconds, America's Monarch of Motoring, Barney Oldfield."

As if all the sound in seven thousand voices could be pent up for one, giant explosion of screams and cheers, a roar erupted at the proclamation. Moross wiggled his way to Oldfield's side, and the driver sat back in his seat to shout instructions in the diminutive publicity man's ear.

Agile Moross quickly relayed the message to Prunty, who waved for the crowd's attention and then announced, "Mr. Oldfield informs us that he is ready to meet any man in the world on any track at any time."

(Denver, Sunday, November 6, 1904)

The booming howls coming from the packed Overland Park grandstand in Denver, Colorado, eclipsed the thunder of the Green Dragon's engine every time it tore down the front stretch. After Barney Oldfield set several records on Saturday, even the Sabbath couldn't prevent an overflow of people from squeezing into the boxes to see the world champion run.

He ran over ten miles before megaphone barkers in the stands shouted the news that somewhere along the way, Barney Oldfield became the new track mile world's record holder at fifty-one and one-fifth seconds.

Oldfield saw everyone in the grandstand standing and Tom Cooper at the inside edge of the track giving him signals with five fingers in one hand, and one in the other. The next time around, Cooper held up a chalkboard with "11-15," on it, the signal they had agreed to tell him what mile records Oldfield had broken. The driver decided to press on for twenty miles.

Oldfield trained his eyes on his tires on the stretches to see if there was any sign of wear. Still, he could not view the rears. He had worked them hard to set the mile record and wondered how much longer they could last. At that point, he was lowering his own records set the previous day.

By the end of the twentieth mile, Cooper waved at him to slow down, but suddenly the right rear tire exploded. Like rolling downhill in a wooden cart, the Dragon bounced violently. Oldfield kept both hands on the wheel, aiming as straight as a tightrope.

Gradually pulling the brake lever to scrub off speed, Oldfield, at last, slowed the car to a point where it was easy to control. Shredded to rags, what was left of the tire slapped the ground as the wheel rotated. The Dragon limped around the track to where Cooper stood.

The tire failure thrilled the crowd, amplifying their plaudits and chatter. Cooper scurried around to the right rear to see if there was damage.

"It looks okay. It looks good. Great job, Barney! It's too bad Lou is off with those Detroit investors and isn't here to see these records."

"It's too bad Bess is off apartment hunting," Oldfield said, "I've got some ideas for how we could celebrate."

"I'll wager we can find some female companionship appropriate for the occasion unless you feel like you're married or something," Cooper said. "I'm feeling kind of restless and ornery, myself."

His cigar still clenched between his teeth; Oldfield felt the grimy dust coating on his face when he smiled at Cooper.

"Just like old times, huh, Tom?"

Moross scurried over to the two men, breathless.

"Now, that's the ticket, Barney! That's what we've been talking about! It looks like we got another reason to raise the price on having Barney Oldfield on the next promoter's card."

"Damn right!" Oldfield shouted. "Seeing as how I spend just a little bit more than I make, whatever that is! And, you take a note, Moross, I don't have to race nobody. Running out there by my lonesome is the way I like it."

Oldfield returned to the track later in the day to run another ten miles, refusing to participate in a ten-mile handicap because he only had one remaining set of fresh tires. By the end of the day, he had broken over a dozen records and unseated Earl Kiser as the world's track mile record holder.

"Kiser ain't no king," Oldfield told a cluster of newspapermen Moross gathered.

Joyously Toying With Death

Chapter 15 – The National Championship

(New York, the Bronx, Morris Park Track, Saturday, May 20, 1905)

Shaped like the blade of an ax, the nose of the Green Dragon split the yellow dust of the Morris Park track as the brown dirt path flowed past Barney Oldfield. Down the back-stretch, the sixty-horsepower car twitched as it confronted a stout headwind. In the face of the current, combined with an incline entering the track's sweeping second corner, Oldfield felt like he could get out and push to go faster.

Without lifting off the accelerator, he cranked his steering wheel and slid through the vast, sweeping bend. The wind now to his back, the front stretch was more comfortable but not enough to make up for the time lost. After coasting to a stop near start-finish, Tom Cooper and Lou Moores eagerly scurried to Oldfield's side.

"I hate to tell you this, Oldfield," Cooper said in his typical candor. "You're barely under a minute."

Moores puffed on his churchwarden, expressionless, and awaiting feedback.

"I don't like it, I don't like it at all," Oldfield grumbled. "This place is too big. What is this, a mile and a half?"

"A mile and five-sixteenths," Cooper responded, even though Oldfield wasn't looking for an answer.

"The Dragon is all wound up before she gets to the end of the stretches. Hell, with that hill on the backstretch, I could run ahead and get a red-hot and then catch-up later. And then there's this damn wind..."

"Okay, I get the picture," Moores finally interrupted. "I don't have any answers for you, Barney. We can try another gear, but we sure as hell can't build another engine today.

We're stuck."

Oldfield felt stuck. Surrounded by new cars, he sensed more was at stake than in his previous three years of racing. Foreign cars and drivers like that Chevrolet-fella and his ninety-horsepower Fiat had come out of nowhere. Then there was his match race against Charlie Basle in the ninety horse power Mercedes.

Basle will whoop my ass down that backstretch.

(New York, the Bronx, Morris Park Track
Saturday, May 20, 1905)

Louis Chevrolet's big Fiat sounded faster than the Dragon. The brutish twenty-six-year-old's arms wrestled the Fiat's steering wheel as Oldfield and Cooper observed him from the side of the track on his record trial run.

"Another damn Frenchman," Oldfield grumbled.

"Actually, I understand he was born in Switzerland," Cooper corrected.

Oldfield frowned. "Another damn foreigner with a big engine is what I see. He wants what's mine."

From in front of the judges' stand near where the two men stood, a big, rotund figure filled Oldfield's ears with a megaphone blast.

Shouting to an estimated crowd of some seven thousand spectators, the fat announcer screamed, "Ladies and gentlemen, we have a new world mile track record of fifty-two and four-fifths seconds. This bests Barney Oldfield's record for the same distance by a full one-fifth of a second!"

"The events of this day aren't making me happy, Cooper."

"You're still the star of this meet, Barney. Everybody came to see you in your match race against Charlie Basle, so let's get you ready."

(Peerless Motor Company, Cleveland Ohio,
Thursday, June 1, 1905)

"Lou, I agree with Barney. Look, going back to Morris Park on the tenth…," Moross paused, eyeing Oldfield cautiously. "What I mean is…he's just going to get his head handed to him again. Basle beat him in that match race, but he's not half the driver Barney is. Our sixty can't handle those ninety horsepower cars on that long track. We need to stick to the short tracks."

Oldfield was glad Moross threw in that line about Basle not being half the driver he was. Now he wouldn't have to yell at the little guy for saying Chevrolet would whip him again.

Puffing on his weathered churchwarden, Lou Moores avoided eye contact and presented only a blank expression. All of that told Oldfield the old engineer wasn't happy. That didn't mean the driver was ready to jump into the conversation just yet. He just sat quietly and diverted his attention by scanning the room.

Moores' office was a mess of drawings, some tacked to the walls. Diagrams of frames, suspensions, and engines seemed the perfect motif for such a mechanical mind.

Finally, Moores broke the silence, summarizing what he had heard. Recounting how Oldfield thought he could make more money by putting Moross to work with track promoters around the country, Moores made it clear that his primary objective was not to make his drivers a fortune. He said he liked Oldfield's argument better, that it was no good for business for Peerless to go to places where they stood to get beat.

Oldfield knew that Moores was mostly interested in the national track championship the Triple-A had announced in May. Robert Lee Morrell, the new chairman of the Triple-A racing board, shared a schedule of five to ten-mile races to be conducted through September.

Moores explained that the owner of the winning car would be crowned champion along with his driver, all based on points. At each national championship race, the winner would be awarded four points for first, two for second and one point for third. In the end, a special trophy would be presented to the champions. Although he didn't say it, Oldfield was far less concerned about winning the championship for Peerless than going to the tracks that would give him the most significant percentage of the gate receipts.

"We'll win the championship, Lou. But let's pick up on it after Morris Park."

Moores did not respond, and there was an awkward silence. Oldfield knew that wasn't what the man wanted to hear. Much as he didn't wish for his boss to be disappointed, he wanted much more not to lose again at Morris Park.

(St. Louis, Missouri State Fairgrounds Horse Track, Saturday, June 10, 1905)

The business district of St. Louis was a human tunnel of contiguous bodies, all clamoring for a glimpse of Barney Oldfield, and he loved it. Riding at the end of a towrope pulled by a bus-wagon Ernie Moross had rented to parade up and down the street for three solid days prior, Oldfield knew he was what the people were waiting for.

His eyes penetrated the surging walls of bodies to sort out the women he found appealing. Oldfield removed the stub of his unlit cheroot to spit the brown mixture of saliva and dissolved tobacco to one side. Simultaneously, he lustfully locked his eyes on one young woman he judged to be his age or younger and smiled at her.

A mental image of his expectations for time with Bess in the hotel room that night overwhelmed his eyesight for several seconds and then was gone. The sound of people screaming his name, calling for his attention, brought him back to the moment.

Moross's plan was working. Like the story of the Pied Piper, people followed the Green Dragon to the track. Once inside, the stands grew fuller as Oldfield inspected his racer. Moross estimated there were upwards of seven-thousand people at the race.

"And I get a twenty-five percent guarantee on the gate, right Moross?"

"We get the thirty percent and thirty-five percent if you win," Moross responded, "And you and Tom get eighty percent of that. You guys decide how to divvy that up."

Oldfield feigned disgust with the deal but kept it to himself that he was pretty happy. Cooper could have fifty percent of their split since they were going to invest in a business together the following year.

"We could probably do better if you would go wheel-to-wheel with these guys instead of just doing handicap races," Moross said.

"I told you, Moross, I don't race side-by-side with anybody if I don't have to. I have to look out for myself because nobody else does."

Moross could be a greedy little bastard, but he usually caved-in when Oldfield raised his voice at him. He did what Oldfield wanted, and it was a good crowd. The little man recruited Alonzo Webb and Earl Kiser to agree to race Oldfield, both for a fifteen percent share. Oldfield was okay with all that. They were both damn fine drivers, and he knew people would pay to see them. Most of all, Oldfield liked knowing he got the lion's share.

He liked that the other two drivers were running stripped-down stock cars. That way, when he caught up to them, it should be easy to pass and not one of those deals where they run neck-and-neck for most of the track.

As the start of the race drew near, all the cars were pushed in front of the grandstands. From behind the other two cars, Oldfield saw Moross explaining to Kiser his starting procedure, and then he walked to Webb to repeat the instructions. Following that, he approached Oldfield.

"Look, Moross, you don't need to tell me nothing. I'm counting to ten when you let Webb go, and then you wave the flag because that's when I'm going. I want to try the new gearing since Empire City," Oldfield said, amused by his game of worrying Moross.

"Don't be an asshole, Barney," Moross snapped, obviously irritated. "I'm serious, don't pull that shit because other people can count too, and we could end up in a big argument over the gate receipts. We agreed that Kiser gets thirty seconds head start, and Webb gets fifteen. Okay?"

The driver smiled and winked at Moross.

"You just wave that flag when I start moving, and everything will be okay."

"Barney, I'm telling you, don't do it. You can catch these guys fair and square."

Enjoying the exchange, Oldfield told Moross to "go wave your little flag."

The promoter shook his head as he stomped back to the starting line to wave off Kiser.

The Packard kicked up dust and grew smaller as Moross studied his watch. After dutifully waiting fifteen seconds, the active little man twirled his stick with red cloth, and Webb was underway.

Oldfield eased the Green Dragon to the starting line. Moross was obviously nervous. Counting to thirteen, Oldfield started to roll his car. Moross panicked and abruptly swung the flag back and forth in a hurried manner, absent of any hint of style.

Oldfield chuckled and stomped on his throttle. Directing the Green Dragon down a narrow lane of packed dirt, he shifted his weight in his seat, bent his left arm, and stiffened his right as he set up to enter the first corner. The Green Dragon had three miles to catch the others.

Webb disappeared behind the first turn railing just as Oldfield entered the homestretch. Oldfield sensed that people were cheering from the stands as he shot by them, but his eyes locked on the driest lane of the track.

On the backstretch, Webb was closer still, but also Oldfield could see Kiser. Webb's Pope-Toledo was all over the back of the Packard. By the time Oldfield reached the home stretch again, Webb was in front of Kiser and obviously pulling away.

At the rate the Green Dragon closed on the Packard, Oldfield knew Kiser should have gotten a more significant head start. Kiser's Packard grew steadily larger, and Oldfield knew he could overtake him in the first corner. Instead, he waited until they were on the backstretch. Gunning his Peerless, Oldfield was forced into the soft, moist dirt out of the main lane. The Green Dragon labored but overcame the Packard before the next corner.

As he entered the homestretch, Oldfield saw Webb starting his third and final lap, about an eighth of a mile ahead. The Green Dragon's engine barked like a bitch but had nothing more to give. Oldfield's teeth ground at his cigar butt as he urged his machine forward.

Down the backstretch, both cars soared, the Green Dragon steadily closing. Entering the final corner, Oldfield surged up on Webb's Pope-Toledo. Feeling like he could choke up his heart for fear of ramming Webb from behind, Oldfield lifted his foot. Webb inched further ahead as they entered the homestretch.

Swinging the Green Dragon wide off the final corner, Oldfield felt his car's wheels plod through the moist dirt beyond the dry lane they had been using. His more powerful engine's advantage dulled, Oldfield was reduced to closing on his rival by inches.

"Shit!" he screamed as Webb ducked under Moross' flag first. Moross seemed to shrug his shoulders at Oldfield when he stormed by.

Still screaming "shit" as he wheeled his green and yellow-brass racer into the paddock, Oldfield ignored Cooper as he parked the car. Tearing off his goggles, he threw them into the car seat. Still, Cooper said nothing and kept a distance.

Oldfield stormed around the car for no particular reason. He kicked at the ground and then crossed his arms as he leaned his butt back against the left rear wheel. Cooper stood at the front of the car, his arms on his hips.

"Well, aren't you going to say anything?" Oldfield demanded.

"What for? You're too pissed to talk to right now, and besides, you know what you did."

Before Oldfield could respond to Cooper, Moross jogged up and interrupted.

"What did you do that for, Barney? You could have had him. Why did you back off in the last corner?"

Oldfield spat his wet cigar at the promoter's feet.

"Where do you get off telling me how to drive a race car? What the hell do you know?"

"Ease off, Barney," Cooper interrupted. "We know you don't want to go into the corners side-by-side. The fact of the matter is, though, there are going to be times when you have to. And don't you go spit at me, or I'll knock your lights out."

Moross, his mind always angling, offered up their story.

"Look, you were the fastest car out there. You only had three miles to catch up, and you did, really. Another inch or another second, and you would have won. You're still the champ."

Even Oldfield couldn't say why he would never admit he found Moross useful, but he did.

(Empire City Race Track, Yonkers, New York City, June 26, 1905)

"C'mon Tom, I'm kicking in six hundred bucks," Barney Oldfield urged.

"Yeah, but you're stupid. Why do I want to throw money away to watch Chevrolet whoop your ass? Makes no sense," Tom Cooper replied.

Oldfield didn't want to think Cooper was right. Ever since Major Miller, who owned Louis Chevrolet's Fiat, had goaded him into a bet the night before, Oldfield's mind had been machinating over how to shut him up. He finally concluded that if he could get a jump on Chevrolet, he could kick up enough dust to blind the foreigner.

"Look, Barney, you put a thousand dollars at risk just because you had too much to drink, and you let that goofball Miller get to you. You haven't been close to Chevrolet yet this season."

Lou Moores, sitting on a bright red wooden folding chair and smoking his pipe, had apparently heard enough.

"Barney, I want you focused on that championship as we agreed."

His boss only momentarily distracted Oldfield. Chevrolet had won the first national championship race at Morris Park, but Oldfield had equaled the score by winning the second race at Hartford – mostly helped by Chevrolet breaking a gear.

"I told you I'd take care of that, Lou," Oldfield snapped. "We can shut these guys up by taking a thousand greenbacks out of their wallets."

"Will you shut up if I give you the four hundred?" Cooper asked, extracting a roll of twenties and fifties bound by a string.

Oldfield knew Cooper would eventually chip in. His friend knew money was for having fun, not for saving. Cooper just wanted to hear him beg.

Oldfield shrugged at Moores and noted that they were at his lucky track, Empire City, where he had won the international track race the year before. Eager to find Major Miller and Chevrolet, Oldfield took Cooper's money and promised to be right back as he began a determined walk across the paddock.

Miller, a "sport," was dressed in a navy-blue suit and tie with a startling-white silk shirt and navy bowler hat. The hat had a diamond pin in it. As Oldfield approached, Miller's back was to him, his hands on his hips, creating a kind of winged-look as the sides of his jacket rested on his wrists. Miller was peering over a mechanic who had the hood of his Fiat open, exposing the big ninety horsepower engine.

"Ok, Miller, let's see your money!"

The major turned with a quizzical look on his clean-shaven face, which was quickly overwhelmed by a sinister smile that Oldfield thought made him look too eager. Miller extended his right hand for a vigorous shake.

"Oldfield! I'm pleasantly surprised. And here I thought your enthusiasm for wagering last night was exclusively fueled by alcohol! You are in earnest!"

Oldfield knew a lot of slimy characters, but somehow Miller made him want to take a bath after talking to him. Word had it the guy was only a major in the army reserves because his daddy – who had actually worked to make millions and earn a place in society – was a general. Oldfield didn't like calling him, "major" even though most others did. 'Miller' was good enough.

"Show me your money," Oldfield did his best to sound demanding, but he knew damn well Miller could light cigars with thousand-dollar bills. Miller extracted a thick leather pocketbook from his coat and fanned ten one-hundred-dollar bills like a deck of cards. Oldfield displayed his money, a mixture of tens, twenties, and fifties in a similar, but more jumbled fashion.

From the other side of a truck painted the same pearl-white as Miller's Fiat walked a burly young man with an absolutely out-of-control thick black mustache – Louis Chevrolet. Although he wasn't much taller than Oldfield, he just seemed bigger, especially with arms that looked like thighs.

"Burr-nay!" Chevrolet shouted in a thick French accent. The tone of his voice seemed pleasant enough, but he was incomprehensible – at least to Oldfield. Chevrolet continued to talk in a stream of words spewed so quickly Oldfield gave up trying to interpret them. Amazed that Chevrolet thought anyone in America could follow him, he decided to turn back to Miller for translation.

"Do you understand him?"

Miller and Chevrolet looked at each other and laughed heartily. Oldfield had the feeling of being left out of a joke.

"We have an understanding, Oldfield. An excellent understanding. I especially like the way Louis speaks to me on the track. I trust you understand that language?"

(Empire City Race Track, Yonkers, New York City, June 26, 1905)

Coughing on dust, Barney Oldfield couldn't see much of the track, but his eyes locked on the white Fiat's swaying rear end. He spat a viscous mix of saliva, dirt, and tobacco onto his steering wheel – there was no time to turn his head. The grime dripped down his chin past the front of his neck and under his shirt.

Fuck that.

Oldfield felt he could reach out and grab at the Fiat. He wasn't going to back down this time. This time he would pass him anyway, anywhere he could.

Clearly faster in the turns, Oldfield was gaining on this big foreign brute in his big foreign car. Damn, he would do anything to get by that Fiat. The Green Dragon's rear wobbled and sunk without warning.

Flat tire. Goddamn flat tire!

Instinctively Oldfield lifted his foot. The car slowed, and his mind struggled to accept that he would not pass Chevrolet. Alert, keenly alert, Oldfield felt a mixture of anger and exhilaration. He knew he was faster than Chevrolet in the corners. He knew he could beat him.

In the paddock, Moores and Cooper stood on either side of a space wide enough for Oldfield to park. Both were shouting, but the driver couldn't hear before he turned the engine off.

"Okay, Barney," Cooper shouted. "We've got two more heats to get these guys. You were looking good out there."

Cooper handed the driver a cup of water, and he swished it around in his mouth and spewed out a muddy stream. Moores studied the tires in his stoic way. Waving at a Peerless mechanic, he pointed to the wheels.

"You're driving the Hell out of the car Barney. That's what you're supposed to do," Moores said. "But you're tearing up the tires. We're going to put on a fresh set – but we need something for the national championship race, and we don't have any extra ones."

Oldfield nodded his head all the time, thinking he didn't give a damn. The next heat was ten miles, and he wanted Miller's thousand dollars. Even more than that, he was determined to whip Chevrolet's ass.

As the Fiat and the Green Dragon rolled toward the starting line, Oldfield yelled from his cockpit, "Come on, come on!" with no expectation of anyone hearing him let alone responding. Chevrolet was vulnerable, and Oldfield ached to attack.

Plunging into the first turn, Chevrolet had the inside, forcing Oldfield to the high lane if he wanted to avoid the haze of dust trailing the Fiat. Ahead by fifty feet on the backstretch, the white car was faintly visible just beyond its dusty wake.

Oldfield hung low in the corners as the Fiat slid sideways in the turns, kicking up earth toward the top of the track. The Fiat pulled away from the Peerless' sixty horses on the stretches, with Oldfield closing the gap on the corners setting a frustrating rhythm for each lap.

Almost imperceptibly, it seemed the Dragon was gaining, and the sixth mile convinced Oldfield it was. Inching closer, he caught sight of the big Swiss driver's shoulders shifting like he was swinging an ax. With each turn, the Fiat drifted higher up the track. Sensing that Chevrolet was struggling, Oldfield realized something was amiss.

Tires! His tires!

Oldfield assaulted the corners, seizing the inside, braking late, and maintaining the Dragon's revolutions by keeping his foot on the throttle. The green racer responded, pulling even with the Fiat in the corners but slipping back on the stretches.

Sweeping off the final corner of the ninth lap, the stubborn Fiat was a nose behind but steadfastly clung in the corner of Oldfield's eye. At last, the big car no longer flung dust back at Oldfield, but irresistibly crept ahead as they passed the grandstand.

Oldfield clung to the inside pole of the track as they hurtled into the first corner, slicing his wheel into a precise drift. Abruptly, the Fiat disappeared from Oldfield's peripheral view as it wobbled and ascended toward the outer fence. Without flinching, Oldfield continued to apply pressure to the accelerator until he was flat just before entering the backstretch. Staring straight ahead, he did not take the time for even the briefest glance behind.

The Green Dragon smoothly traced its arc through the final corner and soared toward the finish line. A glimpse to the left revealed Cooper and Moores jumping with their fists in the air as he swept by.

Back in the paddock, Cooper excitedly shook his driver's hand, but Moores silently studied the tires. He didn't have to say anything, his face made it clear any satisfaction he got from watching his car overcome the Fiat was overwhelmed by his worrying about not having enough tires for the national championship race.

"Barney, you're beating him in the corners, but you're wearing out the tires in the process," Moores said, his voice ranging to that higher octave that told Oldfield his boss was getting upset.

"I got him, Lou! I got him!" Oldfield tried to sound more excited than irritated. "Peerless beat, Fiat!"

The Peerless engineer paused and then posed his big question.

"If you run this final heat, I don't think you're going to have enough tires to run the national championship race as well."

"I'll win that championship for you and Peerless, Lou. I will. Let me stick it in these guys and turn it a few times."

"Uh-huh. What will it be next time, Barney? Another bet? Will another promoter offer you more money to run somewhere other than the Triple-A championship? I told you what I wanted weeks ago."

Moores didn't wait for a response. He turned his back and walked toward the track gate. Oldfield did not see him as he lined up for the ten-lap third heat but decided not to think about it.

Oldfield figured Chevrolet changed tires because he was back to the inside of the track on the corners and holding the Fiat down to the pole. As the laps unfolded, the Green Dragon squealed through the turns, barely gaining inches on the Fiat while down the stretches Chevrolet leaped ahead by yards.

Given the option to choose a distance of five or ten miles, Oldfield selected ten. Chevrolet seemed to lose his edge after five miles. Despite the Fiat's fresh tires, the pattern of the Green Dragon closing on the corners and Chevrolet creeping ahead on the stretches developed again.

Oldfield tried to evade the encroaching dust clouds cast off by the Fiat by holding low in the corners and pointing the Dragon's nose to whatever lane Chevrolet was not in on the stretches. Grit coating his teeth and his dry mouth proved his strategy was not entirely effective. Still, the Fiat was coming back to him, like he was reeling in a big fish.

Oldfield pulled within inches of the Fiat's tail as both cars thundered down the home stretch to begin the final lap. The two drivers went to the pole entering the first corner, and again the Fiat had the edge on the backstretch. Determining his only chance was to skirt the edge of the track and come off the final turn without lifting his foot, Oldfield swung his racer directly into the billowing dust cloud following Chevrolet.

Blind, Oldfield cut his wheel at the angle he believed would form the arc at the perimeter of the track – and not into the fence. Refusing to think of the possibilities, he called on his sense of timing to decide when to straighten the wheel. Emerging from the cloud and pointed toward the finish line, his eyes frantically searched for the Fiat.

Chevrolet was still more than a car length ahead and slipping further from Oldfield's grasp. Relentless, his mind searched for another way – another lap, another heat.

"Goddamn it to Hell!" he shouted as Chevrolet took the flag a split second ahead. Fuming and damning his fate over and over, Oldfield coasted around the track to return to the paddock gate.

(Fisher Automobile Company, Indianapolis, Indiana June 28, 1905)

A shadow through the opaque glass of Carl Fisher's office door gave evidence of his secretary on the other side. Sauntering from his desk, he turned his doorknob counterclockwise and peered around the oak door. Fisher paused – only briefly – to soak in her image, features softened by his dim eyes. She was not only quite lovely but also an excellent typist, and she ran a tidy office.

"Margaret, honey, can you get Jim Allison on the phone? Is there any more of that coffee left?"

"Yes, Mr. Fisher," Margaret Collier responded, dutifully picking up her phone to call the operator.

Fisher turned, the door abruptly shutting behind him. Returning to his expansive mahogany desk, he sat in his leather chair and flicked at his June 27 copy of The Automobile trade paper he had been reading when he decided to call Jim Allison. The peal of his black candlestick phone's bell disrupted the silence of his office.

Picking up the receiver, he heard a young operator say, "I have Mister Allison on the phone for you, Mister Fisher."

Fisher leaned closer to the mouthpiece. "Thanks, Doll," he responded, quickly shifting to the more masculine tone of business in greeting his Prest-O-Lite partner. Collier was back with coffee, but Fisher hardly noticed.

"Jim! How are you today? Good, good. Say, I need to tell you I am going to Europe for about a month. I've been on the phone with Colonel Pope."

Fisher didn't expect any complaints from Allison. Avery was doing a good job setting up shop for charging the compressed gas canisters, and they had added an extra salesman because the uptake was healthy on their headlight product. Still, Fisher wouldn't make a big move without alerting Allison, a man he revered more than any other.

Deadpan Allison responded without voice inflection.

"So, Carl, are you going off to play with race cars while I'm left working?"

Feeling not the least challenged, Fisher continued the conversation much as he would if Allison had said nothing.

"I'm going to help the Pope-Toledo boys in their shot at the Gordon Bennett Cup. The Colonel likes our headlights, and I want to get a look at those European teams up close. I'd like to expand into Europe someday and certainly supply their imports over here. It'll be a good idea to have relationships with their home base. Besides, I might lend a hand driving."

A long pause from Allison made Fisher think they lost their connection. Finally, his business partner broke the silence.

"Developing business certainly has merit, Carl. I would only suggest that you leave the driving duties to their chauffeurs. Herb Lytle and Bert Dingley, I believe?"

Feeling annoyed, Fisher challenged Allison.

"What are you talking about? I set a world record last year at Harlem. Goddamn mile-a-minute! How many men do you know can say that?"

"Do not take offense, Carl. Since you first started contemplating this idea, I have done a little reading. This Auvergne circuit certainly is not a nice, smooth horse track. They're going to be climbing a mountain for Christ's sake."

"If I wanted this advice, I'd call my mother," Fisher replied.

"Just use your head, Carl. At points, the altitude is over fifteen hundred feet with just a precipice to your side."

Fisher didn't want to admit it, but Allison had a point, still he wasn't going to let him know he thought so. He changed the subject.

"Well, I've booked passage with the White Star Line. We embark on Tuesday. I'm traveling with Cliff Myers at Diamond Tires as well as the Locomobile boys. I guarantee you we'll see business from this."

"Knowing you, Carl, I have complete confidence we will. You're a good man, and you are important to our success."

Fisher hung up the phone.

Allison's a good man. He's a little stiff, but a good man.

Glancing back at The Automobile, he noted Leon Thery had won the French elimination trial to select that country's representation in the Bennett Cup. Wondering if the Americans could even stage a respectable performance, he folded the paper and placed it at the corner of his desk.

(Brunot Island Race Track, Pittsburgh, June 28, 1905)

Lou Moores stopped attending his driver's races after Empire City. Barney Oldfield had not heard from Moores since that race meet. The question of what that meant crept into his thinking – and then he thought of something else. Two Peerless mechanics joined Oldfield, Cooper, and Moross on their train rides to places with horse tracks, like Brunots Island across the Ohio River from Pittsburgh.

The mechanics could whip the Green Dragon into racing trim, and then there was, of course, Ernie Moross, who could fool people who did not know anything about cars into believing he did. Moross incessantly connected people, always looking to add two and two and come up with sixteen.

Cooper once said to Oldfield that half of what Moross said was bullshit, but he wasn't always sure which half. When Moross walked into the Peerless compound at the Brunot Island paddock, Oldfield knew by the look on the little man's face he was angling.

"Barney…do you have a few minutes?"

Oldfield nodded, yelling to Cooper that he was taking a walk. As they strolled together, Oldfield focused on a circle of the scalp at the top of Moross's head that was becoming increasingly visible through thirty-one-year-old thinning hair. Oldfield thought it would look pretty damn near like a bald spot when wet.

"I've been talking to Earl Kiser, Barney. You know there's another national championship race at Morris Park next week."

"Morris Park..." Oldfield's voice trailed off. He knew he need not say anything more for Moross to understand his lack of enthusiasm for the place and its confounded, interminable stretches and narrow turns – it was the perfect place for the Green Dragon to look like a pig.

"Yeah, I know, Barney," Moross frowned. "Well, it seems Alex Winton is more interested in running at the meet in Columbus on that July fourth weekend than going to the Bronx. He's partial to Ohio. Kiser too."

"Well, if you've worked something out with Winton and the Columbus folks, I'm not losing any sleep over being a no-show in New York – I'd rather jab a stick in my eye than go back to Morris Park. All that is providing you can make it worth my while. I go where the money is."

Moross assured Oldfield the 'Columbus Motor Derby' would be very lucrative and more rewarding than anything he could find at Morris Park. It would benefit Moross as well, of course.

"Remember how we split up the receipts, Barney? I'm sure Lou would not be happy knowing I am pulling you away from the national championship. I just figure Morris Park is not the best place to run the Green Dragon, and the Columbus Motor Derby people are more flexible. They like their odds of drawing a big crowd if you and Earl Kiser run a match race."

As they talked, they approached the Winton Motor Carriage Compound, and Oldfield recognized Earl Kiser moving toward them. A compact, stocky man, Oldfield never told Kiser that his abnormally long arms made him think of an ape. Kiser, he judged, was about the same age and was one of the drivers he truly feared in a match race. Oldfield never wanted to admit that Kiser was getting just about as much or more out of the Bullet as he ever did.

"Barney! It's been a while," Kiser said, extending his hand.

The two racers pressed palms and clasped. Oldfield always made it a point to lock eyes with another driver. He didn't want anyone to get the impression that he wasn't confident, or worse, would back down in a tight spot at speed.

"Ernie tells me he's worked out a deal with you, Winton boys for Columbus on the fourth of July," Oldfield said.

"So, you understand you, and I split half the gate?" Kiser asked.

"Well, we didn't get a chance to discuss the details..." Moross's voice trailed off.

Oldfield stroked his chin, conscious of the three diamond rings on fingers of his right hand.

"Like I just told Ernie; Earl, I go where the money is," Oldfield said, electing not to share his distaste for Morris Park. He didn't want that issue to become a negotiating point.

"Well, you guys take a look at it," Kiser said. "I'm sure we can both do a lot better together than apart. Let us know by tomorrow before noon. If not, we'll talk to Major

Miller. Or we might reach out to the White steamer people. There's a lot of interest in that Whistling Billy steamer job Webb Jay's been driving."

Oldfield winked at Kiser, putting his arm around his shoulder.

"Let's talk about something else," he said. "Let's talk about Miller and Chevrolet. I'm getting awful tired of eating dust off that Fiat."

"Well, I don't plan on being behind that Frenchman," Kiser replied.

"I hear he's Swiss," Oldfield corrected.

"Switzerland?" Kiser appeared surprised. "Now, I wonder why he speaks French?"

Oldfield shrugged his shoulders. Moross started to interject, but Oldfield put a firm grip on his arm.

"Never mind, they are all foreigners to me. What I want to talk about is dust and how we stay out of it, you and me."

Kiser encouraged Oldfield to continue.

"We kicked up a mountain of dust at Empire City. It took me a week to get that dirt out of my ears. The way I figure it, we might as well be in a cloud of locust with three cars running together. Miller likes flying starts because he thinks Chevrolet with those ninety horses can get the jump in the first corner, and then we have to ride in his dust. What I want is a standing start or race in heats two at a time."

(Brunot Island Race Track, Pittsburgh, June 28, 1905)

"Boys, it's high time we resolve this. This start was scheduled for a half-hour ago, and the folks in the stands are getting restless," Event Starter Charles Gillette inserted himself into the protracted exchange between Oldfield, Kiser, Major Miller, and Chevrolet.

"The plan always was for a flying start," Miller asserted. "No rule changes now. Let's race!"

Miller's voice projected a loss of patience and the build-up to a shouting match.

"Rules? Who in the hell said there were any rules?" Oldfield replied.

Something about what he said, amused Kiser and he laughed. Oldfield briefly wondered what he said that was funny, but returned his focus to the debate.

"Charlie, I crashed through enough goddamn fences. People tend to get killed when you do that. You don't want that here," Oldfield said.

Gillette grimaced, but Oldfield didn't think he was concerned about people dying. He was just getting annoyed.

"Here's what we're going to do," the starter announced. "You three line up at the half-mile post, and then we start at the judges' stand. That way, they'll be less dust than if you do a full warm-up lap."

"Who are you bullshitting, Charlie?" Oldfield shouted. "I'll tell you what; you guys just have a two-car race if you're going to do it that way. Three cars in the kind of dust that's going to get kicked up is suicide, and I don't want any part of it."

Oldfield turned, with Moross running alongside.

"Okay, Barney, I'll talk to them. We'll work something out."

Behind them, Oldfield heard Miller call him "yellow," and he pivoted abruptly, staring at the Major. Eyeing the massive Louis Chevrolet standing with his car owner, Oldfield shouted from fifteen paces, "Okay, Miller, you come right here and say that. You come right here, and we'll see who's yellow."

Miller, appearing surprised Oldfield heard him, fanned at the air, saying, "Oh, forget it."

Judging that was enough to save face, Oldfield continued his walk, ignoring Moross. Returning to the Peerless camp, he shared the exchange with Cooper, and the more he talked about it, the madder and louder he got. Somewhere along the way, Moross disappeared, and Oldfield figured he was back with the Winton group - maybe with that asshole John Jack.

Cooper suggested they walk to the fence trackside and watch Kiser and Chevrolet race. As Gillette had ruled, the two men started on the backstretch and came roaring around the last corner to bear down on the starter. Entering the first turn, Kiser got the jump and pulled ahead, hugging the track at the pole.

"The Bullet III has at least eighty-horsepower," Oldfield said, leaning into Cooper's ear.

Kiser continued to pull away from Chevrolet, leaving a rooster tail of dust to rain down on the Fiat driver. Down the home stretch, Oldfield saw Chevrolet wipe his sleeve across his goggles.

"I'm enjoying this," Oldfield shouted and then laughed.

Oldfield felt a tap on his shoulder. Moross had returned.

"Here's the deal, Barney. You race the winner of this heat. Looks like that will be Kiser," Moross said.

"I've got two eyes, Moross," Oldfield growled and then paused. "Okay, tell them we're ready to race."

On the track, Kiser pulled far enough ahead his dust thinned before Chevrolet passed through. He finished a quarter mile ahead of Chevrolet by the end of five miles.

Within forty minutes, Oldfield lined the Green Dragon up against Kiser, this time in a standing start. With Kiser on the inside, the racers charged into the first corner neck and neck. With dust so thick he could see little more than the Bullet hugging the rail, Oldfield edged in front and came out of the first turn with more momentum.

Breaking free of the dust, Oldfield was soon out of the second corner and onto the home stretch. Pulling further ahead through the first turn and backstretch, he sensed something was wrong with the Bullet. His suspicion was confirmed when he glanced over his shoulder. Kiser was coasting to a stop at the three-eighths-mile pole.

After pulling up near the judges' stand, Oldfield saw Major Miller flailing his arms with two officials. Cooper trotted over to Oldfield as he climbed off the Dragon.

"That pain-in-the-ass Miller is protesting," Cooper said.

Oldfield scrunched up his face, pondering Miller's scheme.

"He claims there's a Triple-A rule against not carrying a reverse gear. Since we don't have one, he wants you disqualified."

Oldfield spat out his cigar stub and stormed toward Miller. He felt Cooper at his side.

"Miller! What is your problem?"

"Mr. Oldfield," came the deep baritone voice of a judge with bushy sideburns and tiny wire spectacles and oval lenses. "Is it true your Peerless entry has no reverse gear?"

"How the Hell do I know?" Oldfield feigned. "I'm not in the habit of driving backward."

"You know damn well what gears you have in that car!" shouted Miller. "I demand that all entries comply with the rules of the Triple-A."

"Oh, for Christ's sake, Miller, were you dropped on your head as a child? Why don't you go fly a balloon or something and bother somebody else?"

The bespectacled judge waved his hand with authoritative flair.

"We shall have no more of this discussion," he said. "Because the regulation in question here was only recently enacted, I am inclined to suspend any penalty with the understanding that the Peerless entry is brought into compliance by the date of its next appearance in a Triple-A event. Can you live with that, Mister Oldfield?"

Oldfield smiled at Miller and nodded his head at the judge. Un-tucking his shirt, he released dust that collected inside it. Oldfield then brushed the dirt off his sleeves in Miller's direction.

"See you tomorrow in the ten-miler, Miller."

(Brunot Island Race Track, Pittsburgh, Pennsylvania, June 29, 1905)

Barney Oldfield braced his left foot on the Dragon's floorboard. He pushed his accelerator flat with his right boot as he straightened his racer coming out of the corner and onto the backstretch in the final heat of the national championship race. Surging ahead of Chevrolet, he thrilled at the notion of dumping dust on his competitor. With the Bullet III still out of commission with a broken driveshaft, the race was left to Oldfield and Chevrolet.

Relieved to be clear of dust, Oldfield continued to pull away from the Fiat. Refusing to ponder what might be wrong with Chevrolet's car, he focused on the track and watched for Cooper's chalkboard each time around to count the first six laps.

Bam! An explosion erupted from behind, and the Green Dragon whipped violently around at the head of the home stretch. Oldfield felt his ass lift from his seat, but he clung tenaciously to the steering wheel. Briefly tilted on two wheels and at the brink of overturning, the Dragon bashed down again and broke the right rear wheel.

Just as abruptly as the car had twisted, it ground to a halt. Oldfield was sideways on the track, parked at the end of a sizable rut in the dirt leading up to his right rear wheel. The tire with the most weight pressed against it in the corners had proven not up to the task. Turning his head, the other way, he saw Chevrolet disappearing into the first turn. Oldfield had not noticed the Fiat passing him.

Hopping out of his car, Oldfield paced around it, his eyes assessing the damage.

Not too bad. Have to get it back to the shop and tear it down and see what's bent.

The pop and rumble of the Fiat in low gear approached Oldfield. Chevrolet brought his racer to a stop, the engine idling.

"Are you well?" the big man asked through a cumbersome French accent.

Strange. I hadn't really talked to Chevrolet before – just that shit Miller.

"Thanks for asking, Louis. Yes, I'm fine. I'm doing better than my car, but we will race again."

"Good. I like to race you," Chevrolet said. "Can I drive you somewhere?"

"No," Oldfield said, considering his options. "No, I'll stay here with the car. I expect somebody will come by to fetch the Dragon and me. Thanks."

From the other direction, a Winton touring car came to a stop. Turning, Oldfield saw Earl Kiser and Bess. Bess was obviously distraught. Chevrolet gave something of a salute, and Oldfield nodded his head as the big Fiat went on its way.

"People in the grandstands were saying the Dragon turned turtle and crushed you," Kiser reported. She's pretty upset. I told her it was likely nothing. Damn, people are always talking, making the worst of things."

Oldfield walked to the passenger seat of Kiser's Winton. Squeezing Bess' hand, he detected redness about her eyes, which glistened with moisture. In her other hand, she held a handkerchief.

"Somebody's awful sweet on you, Oldfield," Kiser said, smiling. "You sure as hell don't deserve it."

Oldfield knew Kiser was joking, but he believed it was true, too. He stood in front of her, hesitating.

What in the hell do I do now?

"Barney!" Bess blurted, her voice trembling.

Everything he did felt false and strange – like he was watching someone else. Opening his arms, he wrapped them around Bess's broad shoulders, drawing them together and pressing her round face to his.

"Ah, now, honey. You know me. I'm Barney Oldfield. I'm doing fine."

(Hotel Hollenden, Cleveland, Ohio, July 19, 1905)

From behind Bess, Barney Oldfield reached around and above her bosom and drew a brilliant, sparkling diamond necklace to her neck. Fastening it, he gently pivoted her to face him.

"Beautiful," he said, melting into her eyes.

"Oh Barney, it most certainly is, but should you? I mean, this is something for a queen or a Broadway actress," Bess said.

"And it is for Bess Holland, soon to be Mrs. Barney Oldfield. Now how would it look if the woman of the world champion race driver wore anything but the best? Besides, we got plenty left over after that deal we made with Kiser in Columbus."

"And this dress..." Bess said, obviously self-conscious.

"What? It's beautiful. You deserve it! That black velvet looks like the black velvet in the display case at the jeweler. It really makes those sparklers dazzle."

"Well, it is stunning. But it is so tight and low cut. I'm afraid it is too much," Bess said.

Oldfield smiled and stroked his chin, his fingers now sporting another set of ostentatious rings. Reaching behind Bess, he gave a sharp slap on her ass.

"Look, honey, I'm with you, and you look beautiful, and I am keeping you all to myself. I want everyone to see how lucky I am."

Oldfield was sincere at the moment as he examined the brave display of flesh, the form-fitting black dress provided. Few women could compete with Bess's cleavage, especially when her breasts were propped up in such a tight gown. Somehow, she looked thinner, more shapely than usual.

"C'mon, we have dinner reservations downstairs with Tom in fifteen minutes. He tells me he has some cute young filly he's seeing."

"I wish you wouldn't call women fillies, Barney. I've told you that before. No woman wants to be compared to a horse," Bess admonished.

She asked him to be "nice" as she adjusted his navy silk jacket by tugging the lapels. She told him he looked like a gentleman and that all he had to do was act the part.

Oldfield opened the door of their room at Cleveland's Hotel Hollenden and gestured for Bess to go first. As she passed him, he again slapped her bottom.

"Yes, dear. Let's go meet Tom's girlfriend for this evening."

Entering the dining room, Oldfield spotted Cooper waving from a table. Next to his friend sat a delightfully youthful woman, looking very Irish with red hair done-up Gibson Girl style, with gentle ringlets cast against cream-colored skin. She was beautiful – and familiar.

Holy shit! Helen Winton!

Cooper stood up, and Helen remained seated.

"Miss Bess Holland, may I introduce you to Miss Helen Fea Winton," Cooper said.

"Helen is a member of a very famous family in this neck of the woods. She is the daughter of Alexander Winton. Oldfield, Helen, I believe you two have met."

The unsuspecting Bess graciously greeted Helen as Oldfield watched, feeling stunned. Oldfield said he was going to the bar for a particular drink order and asked Cooper to join him.

"What the hell are you doing, Tom? Why didn't you tell me you were with Helen?"

"She asked me not to tell you. I think she wants to see you, Barney."

"Yeah?" Oldfield said, intrigued, and feeling guilty about it. "And what about old man Winton? You think he is going to take kindly to his sweet young daughter in the company of thugs like us?"

"She says she's twenty-one and free to make her own choices. She likes racing men, Oldfield. If you're not interested, I am."

"Of course, I'm interested, but this is not the situation."

Oldfield felt angrier with Cooper than he had in a long time, maybe ever. Stopping at the bar, the two men ordered shots and tossed them back as quickly as they arrived.

"This is really stupid, Tom. I'll bet everybody in this room knows who she is."

"And everyone knows who you are, too. So just be a gentleman and let's talk racing. She likes that. I'll escort her home and find out what she thinks after dinner. You may thank me for this someday."

Recognizing that he might well thank his friend down the road, Oldfield gulped a second shot. The two men then returned to the table.

Gazing at Helen, Oldfield worried if Bess would notice his eyes lingering. Occasionally, Helen's eyes would pierce Oldfield's, seeming to set a hook for an instant, and then in the next moment, she would appear no more interested in him than Bess. She occasionally reached over to squeeze Cooper's forearm and laugh with a guttural tone that slowly kindled a warm glow in Oldfield's body, like the soft light of a gas lamp turned down low.

"So, Mr. Oldfield, Thomas has told me of this amazing steam car," Helen said. "I believe the papers refer to it as 'Whistling Billy.' I should like to hear your opinion."

"Thomas?" Oldfield asked.

"Me, Barney, me," Cooper responded as if he anticipated the question. "Miss Winton is being formal."

"Oh, yeah," Barney said, glancing at Bess. "Can we drop the formalities? Please call me, Barney."

Bess appeared comfortable, but apparently less interested in Whistling Billy than Helen.

"Well, that steamer has some real get-up and go. White claims they set a new track mile record at Morris Park on July third. Forty-eight and three-fifths seconds. Now, people talk about freak machines, that there is one for sure."

Oldfield explained that Whistling Billy had a large boiler and no transmission because the power was delivered directly to the wheels.

"They say it is twenty horsepower, but that's ridiculous. You can't get a real horsepower reading off that thing because it all depends on the amount of boiler pressure the engine's carrying at any moment."

Cooper added that while the steamer shot off like a rocket, the dissipation of pressure after a few miles made it difficult for such engines to be competitive in long-distance races.

"But as long as they're running these short races and hill climbs or speed trials like down at Ormond, they are damn hard to beat," Oldfield said, glancing again at Bess, who appeared ready to yawn.

"Now for some gossip," Oldfield announced. "First, I hear that our old friend Major Miller absconded with Bob Fitzsimmons' wife."

Helen looked askance, and Oldfield guessed she was unfamiliar with Fitzsimmons. Eyeing Bess, he winked, knowing full well she had heard plenty from her boxing aficionado boyfriend about Fitzsimmons.

"They call him the Freckled Wonder," Oldfield explained. "He's a New Zealander who won the middleweight, heavyweight and light-heavyweight world boxing championships. Can you imagine that little dandy Miller if Fitzsimmons catches up to him?"

The more important story, Oldfield and Cooper, explained, was that with Miller on the run, nobody knew what was happening with his Fiat, or with Louis Chevrolet.

"Morris Park was pretty rough on the Fiats. Paul Sartori in Alfred Vanderbilt's Fiat hit a sixteen-year-old kid." Cooper added. "Broke both his legs, I hear. And then Jay in the steamer put a whipping on Chevrolet in the same race. The Fiats didn't have a good day."

"Do you know this boxer, Fitzsimmons? Is he likely to go after the Major?" Helen asked.

Before anyone could answer, Oldfield felt the grip of two strong hands firmly squeezing his shoulders. He turned his head to look to his left, but the man behind him dodged his peripheral vision like he was ducking behind the corner of a building. Examining Cooper's face from across the table, Oldfield saw a smile, and then came familiar laughter from behind.

Kiser!

Bess stood up and offered a hug, obviously still grateful for the kindness Earl Kiser showed her by driving her to Barney's side after the wreck at Brunot Island.

"Earl, you old dog! What do you mean showing your ugly face around here, scaring our women-folk?" Oldfield said, standing to shake his hand.

"Why I just thought I'd come by and thank you for being so slow at the Columbus Motor Derby. You know the one I'm talking about, the two-thousand-dollar Columbus Motor Derby, right?" Kiser jabbed.

Oldfield felt his countenance fall. He had a tough time joking about getting beat. There just wasn't much funny about it to him but knew to let his frustration show would only yield more ribbing. He promised to whip Kiser the next time they raced, but the exchange was chilled by the abrupt arrival of John Jack.

At Bess's request, Barney introduced Jack to her, but the interaction was as lifeless as a dead possum at the side of the road. Jack requested to see Helen.

"Mr. Jack, it is no business of yours with whom I consort," Helen asserted. "And given that I regard this as a social occasion of no business importance to the Winton Motor Carriage Company, I shall ask you to excuse yourself from our conversation and allow me to enjoy the company of my friends."

Jack's face flushed red, and his eyes darted back and forth like he was looking for a fire escape in a burning building. Stammering something about Mr. Winton's disappointment, he retreated to another table, mumbling like a playground bully who finally had someone stand up to him.

"He does have a habit of spoiling the most enjoyable of evenings, doesn't he Barney?" Helen asked in a manner that suggested the comment was a private joke.

Feeling her eyes on him, Oldfield glimpsed at Bess. From the expression on her face, he knew Helen's remark would trigger a question he would have to deal with back in their room. Oldfield quickly turned back to Kiser.

"How do you put up with that toad?"

"I just ignore him, Barney. He's just a runt who hides behind a big company and a great man like Mr. Winton because he can't really be his own man. Nothing he says has anything to do with me – it's all about how he feels about himself."

"You're quite the philosopher, Mr. Kiser. Well put," Helen said, briefly clapping her hands.

Kiser's cheeks flushed as bright as two red apples, and he smiled to reveal yellow and brown teeth. He bid everyone a good evening and warned Cooper and Oldfield to have the Green Dragon in tip-top shape for their return to Cleveland the following month.

"I don't know about you, Oldfield, but I am not letting some car that whistles like a tea kettle lay claim to the world mile track record for long. You watch me at Glenville in August."

(Grosse Pointe, Michigan, August 7, 1905)

Webb Jay's cream-colored steamer shrunk to a dot in the distance up ahead as Barney Oldfield slid high coming out of the last corner and onto the home stretch on the final lap of the open class ten-mile race at Grosse Pointe. The steamer was a rocket, its dust dissipating before the Green Dragon could pass through it. The starter had already flagged Jay the winner before Oldfield was close enough to see it.

Stunned, Oldfield lifted his foot and reflected on his frustration with Chevrolet. At least in those races, he felt he had a chance if he could drive harder in the turns. This freak steam car was impossibly fast. Getting whipped so convincingly didn't anger Oldfield as much as it drained him. It would have been more frustrating to come close and lose, but against the steamer, he wasn't even in the game.

After parking the Dragon, Oldfield pulled his goggles off and somberly slogged his way to the judges' stand where officials presented Jay, who donned an ankle-length khaki linen duster, with a silver cup. Cooper met Oldfield halfway, his demeanor reflecting his friend's disposition.

Ambling over to Jay, Oldfield extended his hand. Jay was a tall, slender man with coal-black hair and the grip of a bear but a quiet, modest nature. He even told Oldfield he was glad he had the steamer and not the other way around.

Once beyond earshot, Oldfield broke his silence with Cooper.

"Fucking prick. At least he could be asshole enough to get me mad at him."

Cooper laughed like he needed to laugh.

"Tomorrow is another day," he said.

(Grosse Pointe, Michigan, August 8, 1905)

Waiting for the starter's flag for one of the top attractions of the day's card, the five-mile open race, Tom Cooper leaned his head close to Oldfield, who sat in the Green Dragon.

"Four cars. Are you going to be okay with all the dust these boys are going to kick up?"

To the inside was the White misting steamer of Webb Jay, and to the right of Oldfield was Dan Wurgis in the REO Bird and Charlie Burnham in a stripped-down stock Peerless. Oldfield grimaced and nodding his head; he admitted he didn't like it but figured Wurgis and Burnham in cars of about thirty-horsepower would be left behind, and he wouldn't have to race near them.

With the starter's flag Oldfield pushed the Dragon in the first corner in a desperate move to seize the lead from Jay. The powerful steamer's boiler must have been at full pressure. The low-slung white car easily out-pulled the Dragon and hugged the inside lane at the first pole. Onto the backstretch with his right foot flat, Oldfield followed the ever-shrinking tail of the puffing Whistling Billy.

Oldfield adjusted his ass in his seat and leaned into the second corner. Suddenly, the Dragon slowed as if a cylinder died. In an instant, Wurgis and Burnham were upon him. Oldfield saw Burnhman's Peerless enter the periphery of his vision just as he felt a brutal slam lunge his head forward. The screech of metal crumpling from behind pierced his eardrums and tingled down his spine.

The Dragon's tires howled in high-pitch protest, and Oldfield gripped his steering wheel as his racer whirled like a pinwheel. The abrupt motion blurred the track and stirred a sensation of free-fall in his stomach. The too-familiar sound of cracking timber followed as the Dragon burst through the infield fence and began to tumble in a tall stand of weeds.

Had it been hours?

A man with a long nose pointing into Oldfield's face appeared just as a burning sensation shot through his sinuses and into his eyes. He smacked at the man's hand, who withdrew a small amber bottle, inserting it into his coat pocket.

"Lay still Barney," the man said, his nose not nearly as long and pointy as a minute before. "You have a nasty scalp wound, lay still and let me have a look at you."

"Burt! Is that you?"

"Well now, that's a good sign," the man replied. "You remember our bicycle racing days. It sounds like you'll be all right. I'm a doctor now, Barney, Dr. Burton Parker, at your service."

Oldfield started to sit up, but Dr. Parker pinned his shoulders down. A sizzling hot pain raced through his left shoulder. In the meantime, at least two dozen bystanders had crowded around the drier and the Dragon.

"Goddamn it! I think my arm's broken! Burt, don't let any vultures strip my car!"

"It will be okay, I promise Barney. Let's get you over to Harper Hospital and bandage you up."

As the pain in his shoulder and arm grew more intense, Oldfield moaned. Lying back, he felt the blades of grass brushing his scalp and ears.

(St. John's Hospital, Cleveland, Ohio, August 12, 1905)

The blanket over Earl Kiser's right leg poked up at his foot like a tent on a campground, but gone was the symmetry on his left side. Cascading down from just above where his knee should be, the cover over his left leg gave the impression that there was a hole in the mattress, and surely his shin and foot dangled below. Oldfield studied the disparity, fighting off thoughts of the possibility of permanent disfigurement to his own body.

Bess shooed a fly away from the open cuts and swelling that closed Kiser's left eye. Vibrant blue and purple tones extended into bright redness and a puffy cheek that could have been struck by a hammer. Kiser's right eye peered out from his beaten face.

Winking at his former competitor, Oldfield gingerly fished inside his suit pocket, trying not to disturb his sore left arm still in a sling from his wrenched shoulder. Clumsily, he extracted a cigar and extended it to the wounded man. Bess smacked the hand of his good right arm like a schoolmarm.

"Barney! For Heaven's sake, don't you have any sense?"

Oldfield shrugged his shoulders, feeling a shot of pain from his left side. Jokingly he sought Kiser's support by insisting the disabled racer would have taken the smoke. The faintest smile traced across Kiser's lips and gave Oldfield the sense of doing a good deed. The expression immediately dissolved as Kiser winced. Oldfield could only guess the injuries to his face were so sore it was painful just to move his lips.

Kiser was so pitiful Oldfield wondered if he was doing more harm than good by hanging around. Bess leaned over the stricken driver and kissed him on the forehead while Oldfield squeezed his right hand. He promised to be back before he left Cleveland. Kiser thanked them. He weakly waved as they passed through his hospital room door. Strolling with Bess down the wood floor hallway, they encountered Cooper and Moross approaching Kiser's room.

"How's he doing?" Cooper asked.

"Okay, all things considered. The man is awful beat up. The leg's gone, of course, and he has a dislocated shoulder. His face looks like somebody took a mallet to him," Oldfield replied.

"It's funny, he loved that Glenville track. So does Winton, it's their home track really. Nobody knows what happened. One second he was warming up; the next, he crashed through the fence. Maybe a steering linkage broke. It's just too bad all the way around," Cooper said.

Moross tentatively cleared his throat.

"Barney, I have to ask you something. This may not be the best time, but it's the only time to bring this up. I was talking to the promoter out at Glenville. With Earl gone and you out of commission, they think they have a big hole in the program. They're wondering if you would just do a five-mile exhibition. That will help the gate."

Oldfield fixed on Moross's face and then surrendered to the inexorable magnetic draw of an emerging idea. Moross continued to talk, but Oldfield calculated rough numbers to determine how much he could demand from the Glenville promoters.

As Moross continued his spiel, Oldfield blurted, "Fifteen percent."

Moross shut-up and with a blank stare gawked at the driver, as did Bess and Cooper. From the expressions on their faces, Oldfield thought his nose and ears might as well be green with pink polka dots.

Moross broke the silence, "You want fifteen percent of the entire gate for five exhibition laps?"

"No, I want fifteen percent for Earl. What if you were in that hospital bed a cripple for life? What if you were lying there, not knowing what you were going to do next and thinking nobody gives a damn?"

Her eyes glistening, Bess shuffled to Oldfield's side, intertwining her right arm with his left. Kissing his cheek, she whispered, "I love you," into his ear.

"Well, I'll be damned, Barney. That's a damn fine idea," Cooper said as Moross nodded. "Either that or that slam to your noggin was even harder than we thought."

Grinning, Oldfield knew his expression gave away how proud he was of himself. Disengaging his arm from Bess, he motioned for Cooper to walk a few feet further down the hall.

A quick glance over his shoulder revealed that Bess was discussing the possibilities of the decision with Moross.

"Tom, we haven't had a chance to talk, and we can't right now, but you need to tell me what Helen said the other night," Oldfield asked.

"Thank God. I was afraid you were turning into a saint on me," Cooper said, obviously keeping an eye on Bess. "Let's see if we can talk tomorrow. I think you'll like what I have to say."

Aroused, Oldfield briefly mulled over the notion of stealing more time to hear about Helen. Cooper smirked, patting Oldfield on his good shoulder, telling him they would talk soon.

(Glenville Horse Track, Cleveland, Ohio, August 14, 1905)

Barney Oldfield, his head swathed in bandages with just a hint of maroon dye to accentuate the seriousness of his condition marched out to the Green Dragon, where it was parked squarely in front of the grandstand at Cleveland's Glenville horse track. Like a round of Midwestern rolling thunder preceding a late spring storm, the people packed in the stands made clear their admiration for the wounded hero.

"I give you credit, Moross, you got the word out about me running here," Oldfield said as they stood next to the Dragon. A large man with a yard-long megaphone bellowed out ballyhoo about Barney Oldfield's brave deeds and warm-hearted generosity for his stricken comrade.

"Well, we had Sunday to work with the newspapers since nobody wants us racing on the Sabbath," Moross said. "You give me enough time; I can work wonders."

A Peerless mechanic folded the cowling of the Dragon shut, tightening the leather straps. Nodding at Oldfield, he pronounced all plugs clean and gapped; tire pressure perfect and just enough gas to do five miles.

Giving Oldfield the once over with his eyes, Cooper shook his head.

"Looks like you're already too, Barney," Oldfield said. "That bloodstain is a nice touch – but how's the arm? Now, how's that going to work steering with your arm in a sling?"

"The same way it always does," Oldfield replied while flexing his fingers. "It feels better today. But imagine what they're seeing now. Their bloodied, battered hero is risking his life to benefit his fallen rival."

While Oldfield's head only hurt when he touched the scalp wound, the shoulder raged like fire as he began to circle the track. His left shoulder, with his arm now unfettered from the sling, protested with pain in each corner. Still, the clear track beckoned Oldfield, and the discomfort gave way to his urge to slide through turns.

Clear of dust and unhampered by other cars, the pain passed from his mind, and Oldfield began to enjoy the feeling of a figure skater as his wheels danced on the dirt. He went high on entry, close to the pole at the apex, and high on exit. He avoided his brakes and feathered his throttle keeping all sixty of his horses at the ready.

Without the interruption of a slower car or guessing where the rail was amid dust, Oldfield felt a musical rhythm and deliberately slid the Dragon sideways on the final turn of the five-mile run. As he approached the judge's stand, Oldfield saw Cooper and Moross running out on the track and the megaphone-equipped barker to the other side.

Rushing to his side, his friends appeared giddy enough to be at a party. Cooper grabbed the driver's sore shoulder, and he let out a yelp.

"Oh…sorry, Barney, I forgot," Cooper said, still grinning like the Cheshire cat. "You really had 'em going, buddy! That was the fastest five miles of the day!"

Cooper's comment sounded strange to Oldfield as he had never considered going fast.

Why did I forget it's fun to drive this thing?

A swarm of people swelled around the Green Dragon as if they sprouted up from the ground. An official had a medal with a red, white, and blue ribbon, and there were newspapermen and photographers and hangers-on. Oldfield slipped his arm back into the sling and stood up on his seat.

"You know me, I'm Barney Oldfield," he howled.

A newspaperman yelled out, asking Oldfield if he knew he had set fast time for the day. Oldfield feigned ignorance, explaining that he and the Dragon were just having a dance out there. He liked the excitement, but also knew that other than Webb Jay's steamer, all the other cars were just stripped-down stock machines and that Jay had broken down before finishing the five-mile national championship race.

The promoters milked the moment, the megaphone announcer stoking the crowded grandstand with embellishments on Barney Oldfield's death-defying drive. "One-handed and with worn tires," were among the colorful exaggerations.

On the path back to the paddock, Oldfield and his friends passed a man wailing and chanting while twirling a black umbrella. Dressed like a state fair midway barker in a checkered sports coat with a handkerchief in his breast pocket and a straw hat, he looked exceedingly grumpy with a scowl on his double-chinned face.

Pausing, Oldfield contemplated the man. Figuring Moross most likely to know about such matters, he sought the promoter's opinion.

"Him? His name's Ned Broadwell. Kind of a kook if you ask me. Claims he can make rain. One of the churches hired him and sent him over. After Earl's accident, they think they're doing the work of Jesus to stop the races."

"Well, I've heard about such people," Oldfield said. "I'm surprised management hasn't thrown him out on his ass."

"They think he's harmless, and they know the church would probably get even more riled up if they give him the hook," Moross explained.

Oldfield inspected the sky, noting a gathering thick cloud cover so dense it was black in spots, like cotton balls soaked with dirty motor oil. Eyeballing Moross, he inquired if his promoter had taken a gander skyward.

Moross shrugged his shoulders. In the background, a car's engine growled as it circulated the track. Oldfield peered between the stables in the paddock and saw the cream-colored White Sewing Machine Company steamer of Webb Jay toying with Charles Burman in a stripped Peerless stock car. Oldfield knew what Jay was doing, slowing on the stretches just to make the race look more interesting for the spectators. He had done the same thing a hundred times.

By the time they had returned to the Peerless compound in the Paddock word was that Jay had won handily. Tiny droplets began to dot Oldfield's face with pinprick coolness. Grinning, he winked at Moross, who shrugged his shoulders as if he questioned his earlier assessment of Ned Broadwell.

As the two Peerless mechanics pushed the Dragon and Burman's stripped stock car into the stables for shelter from the weather, Oldfield tugged at Cooper's arm. His friend appeared to know what he wanted. Reaching inside his jacket, he extracted an envelope and handed it to Oldfield.

"Helen told me to give this to you," Cooper said. "She wants to see you. I'd love to treat her like a lady, but she's got some cockamamie idea that you're the one she wants. Bess is a fine woman, but this here is one sweet young thing. Either way, I am out of it from now on. The next move you do is entirely on your own."

Oldfield said that was fair enough. He tucked the envelope in his pocket.

Chapter 16 – Around-the-Clock

(Indiana State Fairgrounds Track, Thursday, November 16, 1905)

An indigo National touring car emerged out of the pitch of night and came into the range of Carl Fisher's weak eyes. Fisher recognized the vehicle and who was in it less because of what he could see, but what he knew. He was expecting Art Newby. A pop and a flash distracted him momentarily as Frank Wheeler, sitting across from him, tossed another piece of a dead tree branch on the bonfire that warmed them. The light it cast bounced back at Fisher from the brass fixtures of the National car. Embers wafted into the crisp November air.

Newby pulled his car to a halt and then turned down the acetylene gas-fueled flame of his headlamps. Two figures approached Fisher and Wheeler, and as they drew close, the faces of Newby, as well as Jim Allison, became recognizable. In the background, one of Newby's Nationals, a four-cylinder Model C, droned along at nearly fifty miles-an-hour on the Indiana State Fairgrounds dirt oval. The track was dotted with dozens more Prest-O-Lite headlamps mounted every twenty-five feet on the inside and outside railings.

Fisher and Newby arranged for two Nationals to begin a twenty-four-hour drive cutting laps around the one-mile circuit in a quest for a new record for mileage covered in a day. One of the cars, driven by "Jap" Clemens, broke a steering knuckle at dusk and ended up crashing through the fence to destroy Newby's machine.

"Jap okay?" Fisher asked.

"Yes, thank God," Newby said. "He came onto the front stretch, and the darn steering knuckle snapped."

Newby screwed his face up, furrowing his brow and chewing at the inside of his cheeks. The expression was exaggerated into thorough strangeness by the dancing flames that incessantly altered the shadows of the men's noses, ears, and hat brims. Fisher knew his colleague was thinking about how bad this would make his car look to customers.

"We're going to get that record, Art," said Fisher. "You can count on it. And when we do, we'll run some ads and put the car on display in my showroom. You still have that Merz kid driving? How old is he, sixteen?"

"Charlie's seventeen, and one hell of a mechanic," Newby replied. "He can drive, too, but Jap's an old hand. He climbed out of his car and immediately asked about getting a crack at the other National. I told my boys to call Charlie in. It's brutally cold though, we'll probably end up having them spot one another."

The men huddled by the flames, more a raging bonfire than a simple camping arrangement. The night was unseasonably cold, sinking toward freezing, but the flames were vibrant, and it did not take long for a thin coating of sweat to bead-up on Fisher's forehead. He asked Newby, Allison, and Wheeler to huddle with him just outside the track after the drivers settled into their challenge. The accident delayed the meeting, pushing it back into the concluding hours of that Thursday evening.

"Gentlemen, I feel a hen coming on," Fisher began.

Allison interrupted.

"Oh, Christ, Carl, what now? Aren't you busy enough with Prest-O-Lite and the sales garage?"

"Now, hear me out, Jim," Fisher said. "I've been thinking a lot about the state of the racing game. It has some serious problems, and we might be able to take advantage of the situation. Look at what the press is saying about track racing. They are comparing it to the Roman gladiators, Christ's sake."

"All that boiled over after those accidents in August," Wheeler said. "Kiser, Oldfield, and Webb Jay. It was one after another. How is Earl doing? Have you talked to him?"

"He's in good spirits for a peg leg," Fisher said. "Earl's a good man, good head on his shoulders. He knows cars inside-out and already has a job. Did you fellas see Jay got sprung out of the hospital after a couple of months? They say he was out cold for weeks."

"I think where you're headed with this is that track racing is dead," Allison inserted.

"Well, it is," Fisher replied. "Dead except for record runs like what we're doing here. There have just been too many accidents. Jesus, I still have visions of those dead people at Zanesville a couple of years ago."

Allison presented his usually stoic face, but Fisher knew when he had listened enough, he would bring things to a point.

"What do you want to do, Carl, build a track just to race cars on?"

"Not just a track. I want to build a big speedway, now that's the ticket! These mile tracks aren't big enough to really unwind an engine. Racing on these horse tracks is going away. The press says so. Hell, Barney Oldfield is even talking them down. He says he's quitting and going out to Broadway to take up acting."

Allison shook his head and looked between his legs at the ground he was sitting on.

Fisher chuckled a bit, knowing his partner was reacting to the thought of Oldfield acting. Yeah, that is funny.

The National's engine continued to emit its dull roar in the background. Fisher looked at the other men, but all of them were silent. Finally, Newby spoke up and confirmed what Fisher suspected.

"I'm tapped out, Carl," Newby said. "The car business is okay, but there's a lot of competition out there. Where would we get the kind of capital we need to build this speedway you're talking about?"

"Jesus Christ on a bicycle, Art," Fisher raised his voice again. "Let's just talk about it. People still like to watch the races. The car companies need a speedway to really test their engines. The horse tracks are for horses, for Christ's sake. They aren't safe, and neither are those road races like that crazy Vanderbilt Cup. This is a business opportunity!"

"Well, Carl, as usual, you bring up some good points," Wheeler offered. "I'm open to talking about it. What do you have in mind?"

Fisher sparked at Wheeler's encouragement to keep the conversation going. While he had no business plan, he had given considerable thought to the idea of a speedway.

"It needs to be big and smooth as a billiard table. Bigger than anything going. Three miles around in oval style, with a road course connecting in the middle. It needs mile-long straightaways to let the factories bring their cars out and push the engines to the limit. Also, we can set up a giant grandstand behind fences and gates, so people have to pay to get in – not like Vanderbilt, where they watch for free. I know people would pay good money to see the top cars and drivers going like Hell at such a place. Between the car companies and spectators, it will more than pay for itself."

"So, do you expect the manufacturers to invest in this big speedway you're talking about?" Newby asked.

"I don't want to carry any debt if that's what you mean," Fisher asserted. "I'm prepared to invest. Art, you should be first in line to pony up. Car factories don't have a good place to test their cars. America's public roads are a mess, that's another reason the road races here don't measure up. There are only a couple hundred miles of paved roads in the whole damn country. All the others are dirt or Macadam. Hell, they're mud gumbo half the time. The Europeans are going to run National and everyone else out of business, Art. You know if you think about it."

Newby cast the blank stare that Fisher recognized that his friend thinking. He just wasn't ready to sign onto the idea just yet, but he was thinking.

"Look, you fellas all know I went with the Pope-Toledo folks to France for the Gordon Bennett Cup race last July," Fisher continued. "I wish you had been there; you'd know for yourselves. The Americans were outclassed. All the Europeans have had good public roads for years; they are even and not all rutted up. Not only do we need a big speedway with long stretches, but also it has to be smooth and water-resistant. I want a speedway that lets our boys go great guns."

"Is this just an interesting conversation, or do you want to do something about this scheme you are trying to hatch, Carl?" Allison asked.

"Goddamn it, Jim! How long have you known me? Do you take me for a man that likes to talk people to death?"

"Okay," Allison returned, obviously pausing momentarily to form his next thought. "Let me and Art sit down with this thing and put some numbers on paper. We can't make any decisions until we understand all the costs involved and how to raise capital. There's the cost of land acquisition and then developing the terrain. There will be buildings, garages, and grandstands. I am sure there will be a lot more as we think about it."

Wheeler appeared agitated. Fisher guessed he was feeling insulted that Allison had not suggested he work with Art and him on putting a plan together. On the other hand, Fisher had no such hurt feelings. He counted on Jim and Art to sort out the details. He couldn't sit still long enough for that.

"What about me?" Wheeler said with a tone that sounded simultaneously angry and hurt.

Allison and Newby looked at one another. Newby shrugged his shoulders.

"Sure, Frank, if you want to help on this, that's fine," Allison said. "We sure as Hell need Wheeler-Schebler Company on board with us. I'll ring you up next week. We'll get a handle on this crazy Carl Fisher idea."

The next day, at 2:45 in the afternoon, Jap Clemens and Charlie Merz completed their twenty-four-hour drive to earn a new record of 1,094.56 miles covered for an around-the-clock endurance drive.

Chapter 17 – Broadway Barney

(New York, Wednesday, January 10, 1906)

The rotting carcass of a horse, its body, twisted into contortions, and its flesh pecked at by birds, lay sprawled at the curb of Astor Plaza. Barney Oldfield stopped, and looking down on the beast, the dim glow of the streetlights revealed swarming maggots feasting on the putrid flesh. He stretched to step over it, but momentarily struggling with his balance, he planted the heel of his right boot firmly into the animal's bloated abdomen, forcing an explosion of flatulence out of the deceased creature's anus. A dead horse fart. Tom Cooper covered his nose and scurried around the lifeless form to the crowded sidewalk full of people busily heading home or out to some nightspot.

For Oldfield and Cooper, their destination was the swanky Astor Hotel – a recommendation of Will Pickens, who was managing their stage production. After breaking off rehearsal of their proposed Vaudeville act at a playhouse a few blocks from Broadway, they decided to take in the after-hours revelry their rehearsal schedule typically denied them. A steady drizzle, the din of city sounds, and the general gloom of an overcast night was an appropriate setting for the unpleasant obstacle of a large, dead animal.

As Oldfield and Cooper entered the main entrance to the Astor Hotel off-Broadway, the towering colonnade of marble and gold shouted a grand statement. Both men paused, tilted their heads upward to absorb the massive, thick structures that loomed above them. Four expansive wall panels of art depicting both modern and historic New York cast an undeniable air of grandeur.

This sure as Hell wasn't the Hollenden Hotel, Oldfield thought.

All along the lobby perimeter were entrances to rooms of different themes, some designed for women, others for men. There was a Louis XIV-inspired ladies' lobby, along with a restaurant and a reading room exclusively for women. Men could choose from a German Renaissance hunting room, an Elizabethan Men's lounge, a Flemish barroom, and a Pompeian billiard room. To get to the thematic rooms for gentlemen, they had to pass through the banquet hall, the first of several in the multi-story building.

The two men wandered into the banquet hall, their eyes wide and absorbing Gotham ambiance. Within a few seconds, a portly man, exquisitely dressed and ostentatious with sparkling jewelry, stood up from his seat at a table to wave, and shouted, "Oldfield!"

"Diamond" Jim Brady. Oldfield had gone out of his way to introduce himself during his trips to New York and had struck up a friendship. Brady was a very successful industrialist and a patron of the arts – Broadway was his stomping ground. He was well worth knowing. As Oldfield approached, he heard Brady excuse himself from a table of other well-dressed men, all smoking large cigars.

Charging up to the drivers, he extended his meaty hand, several fingers adorned with diamond rings. One ring's band was so thick, and full Oldfield wondered if Brady could bend that finger as it covered a joint. Brady also sported a diamond pin on his tie and several gold shirt studs with sets of diamonds and rubies. His cuff links glittered with precious stones.

Faster than a rattlesnake, Brady plucked the cigar Oldfield had in his mouth and shoved a replacement at him. Dashing Oldfield's cigar in a coffee cup on the table behind, Brady turned back to Oldfield, who was surprised, but jovial.

"Get rid of that turd!" Brady shouted. "Lillian Russell cigars, that's what you need!"

"But that was a La Intimidad," Oldfield responded. "That's a damn fine Cuban smoke."

Brady waved him off and handed Cooper another cigar.

"Lillian Russell, Barney," Brady said. "Be honest, would you turn away Lillian Russell?"

"Well, you do have a point, Jim," Oldfield said as he studied the flamboyant millionaire's double chin and fleshy frame. His rotund middle rivaled that of Will Pickens.

Brady led them to the billiard room, more upscale than Oldfield's usual haunts, but he also felt very much at home. The three men approached the dark mahogany bar to a spot with two open stools. Brady stopped, looked at a man sitting on a stool just adjacent to one of the unoccupied seats, and waved his hand, saying, "shoo." Dutifully, the servile man tipped his hat and walked away.

Oldfield sat down, scanning a ceiling adorned with crystal chandeliers and potted ferns hanging well above his head. He glanced at Cooper and then turned his attention to Brady. A burly bartender with the typical handlebar mustache of the trade swaggered over to where the men rested, asking what they wanted to drink. Brady said, "the usual," while Cooper and Oldfield requested bourbon.

"It's on me," Brady announced. "They just run a tab and send the bill to my office at the first of the month."

The bartender returned with a pint mug full of a stout-looking beverage for Brady and shot glasses of bourbon for the drivers. He also shoved at them a massive platter of oysters on half shells with a bowl of lemon butter. Brady took a big gulp of his drink and applied a long, rectangular white linen napkin to a spot under his second, flabby chin. The cloth cascaded down his ample belly that tumbled over his waist to shield a perfectly laundered shirt and suit. Oldfield and Cooper tossed back their drinks. Brady then motioned to the bartender for another round as he began voraciously sucking down oysters after pouring the melted butter over the lot of them.

"Well, thanks, Jim, you're very generous," Oldfield said. "The cigars, the booze."

Brady put his diamond ring adorned right hand on Oldfield's shoulder and winked. He took another swig from his mug and then gestured for them to sample the oysters as he would sure as sunrise eat the whole damn platter if they didn't. Cooper and Oldfield complied, tipping their heads back and taking the shells to their mouths, to allow the buttery, wet mollusks to slide down their throats.

"You bet," Brady said without a pause. "So, you boys are doing Vaudeville, now, huh? I hear you have a provocative act."

"Not much around here gets by you, does it, Jim?" Oldfield replied. "Yeah, Tom and I shipped a pair of cars out here and have set a great stage effect. I drive my old Green Dragon, and Tom here is in the Peerless Blue Streak. We got them on treadmills, so they run in place, but a carousel of scenery circles around in the background, and it looks like they are really going. We even rigged a couple of bags of dirt to spill out behind the wheels and kick up a bunch of dust. People are hacking up a storm, but they want to see it."

Brady stroked his chin, and the wideband diamond ring glistened. Smiling, he asked Oldfield and Cooper if they wanted any advice. They eagerly nodded their heads.

"I know you know Jim Jefferies. Look at old Jeff; he's playing Davy Crockett on stage. Right on Broadway! Jim Corbett has been doing a fine job as well; that man was a smart boxer, and it turns out he's a fine actor. Bob Fitzsimmons is at it too. Fellas like you two are big-time too, right? You auto racing boys shouldn't be selling out to Vaudeville. You should do what these boxers are doing. You could be big-time; you could be part of a Broadway production. You two ever hear of the Vanderbilt Cup?"

Both men said they had been to the race. Cooper added that he had even tried to qualify with the Matheson team in the American Elimination Trial a couple of months prior, but the car broke.

"No, I'm not talking about the race," Brady returned, an oyster tucked into his bulging cheek. "I'm talking about the stage play that just started. It's a George Dillingham production called the Vanderbilt Cup. What you have would be a perfect addition, he'll grab your act for the show, and you'll make more money than you ever could playing Vaudeville. Tell him I sent you."

Cooper and Oldfield looked at each other and nodded their heads as Brady downed his third mug of black fluid. He had finished the oysters as well. They thanked Brady, and Oldfield told him he had one question before he left.

"What is it that you're drinking here?" he asked. "Is that Guinness or some kind of black ale?"

Brady, his upper lip glistening with butter, asked Oldfield if he could keep a secret and then moved closer to whisper.

"Root beer," he said, withdrawing his face from Oldfield's ear. "I've never touched a drop of alcohol in my whole damned life."

(New York, Astor Hotel, January 20, 1906)

"The big effect comes in the second act," Oldfield read out loud from the New York American Newspaper. "Barney Oldfield, the famous driver and his Green Dragon racer that holds every record in auto circles from one mile to fifty, is introduced in a contest with another machine driven by his longtime sidekick, Tom Cooper. The giants are seen together on the stage traveling at a lively clip, spitting flame and sparks while the roar of exhausts fairly shakes the building."

Oldfield peered over the top of his newspaper at Bess. She sat across from him on her wingback chair in the parlor of their apartment at the Astor Hotel. Like Diamond Jim, more sparkling diamond rings had found their way onto Oldfield's fingers, and he felt comfortable in his throne, a custom brown leather recliner. Bess, too, looked striking in her red satin dress clasped at the neck with a large diamond and ruby broach.

"Did you hear what I read, here, little honey?" Oldfield said. "I'm a big effect!"

"Yes, and you are a giant, too," Bess said.

"Don't be so smart," Oldfield replied. "I don't hear you complaining about me pulling a thousand greenbacks a week."

"Oh, Barney, of course, I am glad you are doing something you enjoy, and they pay you well," Bess replied. "I do wish you would stop spending as fast as you make it, though. I like the gifts, but I never wore this much jewelry before. It just doesn't feel right. And look at you with those thousand-dollar suits and that floor-length sealskin coat. Then you come home with that scraggly little red-haired Irish terrier. Whatever possessed you?"

"Hypo? Everybody loves Hypo!" Oldfield said in a jovial tone. "Look, I'm a Broadway star, my love. A man's got to look the part, doesn't he?"

Bess frowned and shook her head. She focused her eyes back into the book she had in her lap but then shot her head up again.

"I just want us to set something aside for a rainy day."

"Rainy days? Barney Oldfield doesn't have rainy days! Hey, hear what the New York World said about our show."

Seizing a second newspaper, Oldfield began reading as if to make his case.

"These racing machines rock and roar and spit blue fire, enough to shake the gold fillings out of one's teeth, while the scenery whizzes by at a mile a minute. As a sporting thriller, this Cup contest has the chariot race of Ben-Hur beaten to a frazzle."

Oldfield felt like Bess was studying him. He paused and then asked her what she was thinking.

"Are you sure you're happy, Barney? Is this an adventure or a new career?"

"I'm happy enough for now, but I want some lines in the play. Jeff has lines in the Davy Crockett play. I'm glad they got my name on the marquee, and I'm not kicking about what they're paying Tom and me. I just don't feel like I'm really in the play until I have a speaking part."

Hypo announced his entrance to the room with a high-pitched yap. He trotted to Oldfield's feet, his tail wagging and tongue out.

"What's the matter, boy? Do you want to go for a walk?"

Oldfield stepped over to a corner hat stand and grabbed a leash. There he found his sealskin coat from one of a row of hooks on the wall. Within minutes Oldfield and Hypo descended down the elevator of his apartment building and were out in the street.

Oldfield was amused by the cadence of Hypo's strut and his short stride. The dog tugged at the leash as if to pull his master along. After about a city block, Hypo paused, circled around, and sniffed at the corner of a brick building. He hiked his leg and began to pass a remarkable stream of urine for a tiny dog.

A tall man in a trench coat approached Oldfield and his pet from the opposite direction. Looking down at Hypo's display, the man began shouting.

"What in the Hell are you doing stinking up the neighborhood with that goddamn mutt?"

Indignant, Oldfield shouted back to assert that he lived on that block, and he had the right to do what he pleased. Besides, a little dog piss isn't going to hurt anyone.

The man growled something unintelligible. He then kicked Hypo in the rump, causing the little dog to yelp and scurry behind Oldfield. Without hesitation, Oldfield cocked his arm and delivered a blow to the man's jaw hard enough to knock him down. Stunned, the man sat up, and realizing his pants leg had brushed into Hypo's puddle, he withdrew a pistol from a holster inside his coat.

Oldfield abruptly yanked at Hypo's leash and began running.

"Damn, it's dangerous business walking a dog in New York City!"

(New York, Murray's Restaurant, 34th & Broadway, February 1, 1906)

Tom Cooper traced the lip of his beer mug as he listened to his friend, Barney Oldfield. The tip of his finger collected the residue of Pabst Blue Ribbon and transferred a thin film around the edge of the glass.

"I'm getting bored," Oldfield announced. "I hope going on the road brings back some of the enthusiasm I had for this acting job in the first place."

George Dillingham had informed the Vanderbilt Cup cast that after a few weeks on Broadway, they were going to take the show on the road, the first stop being Parsons Theater in Hartford, Connecticut. From there, they would make stops across the continent until they ran out of the country in San Francisco.

"San Francisco," Oldfield said. "Bess told me she's really looking forward to that."

Cooper smiled in a way Oldfield didn't like. He interpreted it to mean that Cooper thought he was dumb. What the Hell smart-ass comment would he make next?

"So, Barney. We've only been doing this stage stuff for a couple of months, and you say you're bored? Do you really think traveling around is going to make that much of a difference?"

Oldfield wasn't comfortable with his friend confronting him with his feelings. He felt cornered like he needed to convince himself, not Cooper, that his new career could prove to be what he had hoped. It was just that he simply couldn't come up with the words to convince himself. The driver was just hoping that changing the play or where they performed would somehow make things better.

"I'm bored," he said again. "They won't give me any lines, for Christ's sakes. Jim Jefferies has lines in his play! Corbett too. That fucking stage manager Hugh Ford called me a ham."

Cooper studied the Murray's Restaurant menu like he had heard everything his partner had to say before – so there was no need to give him attention.

"I see they have live lobster for a buck," Cooper said. "But the Lobster Newburg is only twenty-five cents more, and I'm kind of hankering something spicy."

Oldfield didn't like Cooper responding to him like he didn't hear him, because he knew he did. Clearly, his friend wasn't interested in what was pissing him off.

"Let me tell you a little story. The other day, Hypo and I were taking a walk, and some guy pulled a revolver on us. Shit, it isn't any safer to walk around New York than it is to race the Dragon."

Cooper showed a blank face like nothing Oldfield could tell him – not even that someone had pulled a gun on him – was a surprise. Sarcastically, he said that he was sure Oldfield had done absolutely nothing to stir up such a response from this anonymous man.

"Well, I did hit him in the face. But that was because he kicked Hypo!"

Cooper shook his head and asked his friend what he was going to eat. Hungry, Oldfield turned his attention to the menu.

"Those fried scallops with bacon sound good," he said. "And I think I'll have me some of those frog legs too. Now, aren't you bored with this stage stuff too? I mean, it was kind of fun at first with all those theater ginks acting all amazed about how loud and smoky our cars are, but that's nothing like hearing them cheer when I set records and whatnot."

Cooper confessed he was bored as well. He had been in touch with the Matheson Company managers and planned to help them with the cars during the year. He was especially interested in bringing them to the Vanderbilt Cup. The race, not the stage play.

"That doesn't mean you're quitting the show, does it Tom?"

Cooper paused, and Oldfield riveted his eyes on his friend's face. The idea of not having him around when he was stuck with theater types like Dillingham and Ford was not appealing.

"I'm not saying that, Barney. I just don't get to work on engines as much as I want. Tuning those old Peerless cars for the stage is a far cry from racing. I'm willing to stay with the stage for a while, anyway. I'll go on the road with you and Bess, and let's just see what happens. I'm still going to tinker with the Matheson fellas, though."

Oldfield was somewhat relieved, but he could tell his partner wasn't going to last in the stage play game more than the rest of the year. He would worry about that later, maybe November.

"Let's change the subject," Cooper said. "Whatever happened between you and Helen Winton? Did you two get together?"

Oldfield frowned at the thought of talking about his former boss' daughter. He and Helen had been together before he left Cleveland for New York, but anticipating the encounter proved more satisfying than living through it.

"Well, there's not much to say, just that she's not as playful as I thought she'd be. I think we both decided there wasn't much of a point. No hard feelings, either side."

Oldfield felt Cooper studying him. It must have been because he was disappointed at not hearing more details.

"No hard feelings, huh? And what about Bess?"

The mention of Bess's name brought a smile to Oldfield's face. He was a little amused that a skirt chaser like Cooper would even think about the wife's feelings in such a situation, but he was seeing something he hadn't noticed before in his old friend.

"Bess said she never thought I was the kind of man she could expect to come home every night, put his house slippers on, and relax in a chair."

Cooper rarely appeared surprised by much of anything, but the look on his face indicated he was.

"You know Barney, I have to admit I am jealous. I hope you realize what a great lady you have there with Bess."

(San Francisco, Palace Hotel, April 18, 1906)

Barney Oldfield thumped and hopped as pieces of his car broke off around him, flying with the fence splinters in a tornado. Now his racer was cascading downward, picking up speed like falling from the sky.

Oldfield froze, his hands locked on his wooden wheel as he took an interminable ride of launches into the air and slams back against the earth. Surreal sounds of the car's wood frame snapping and crackling filled his ears.

Beyond the track, Oldfield couldn't believe where he was. Downward, he rode this bucking beast as another fence appeared, and he punched through it like it was Paper Mache.

Suddenly, Bess clutched him, her shrill screams an alarm of terror.

What the Hell?

Oldfield opened his eyes with Bess wrapped around him like an anaconda as a thick cloud of plaster dust scattered down from the ceiling. Still dulled from several glasses of champagne to celebrate their latest San Francisco performance of the Vanderbilt Cup the previous evening, he struggled to gather his senses as his room quivered like gelatin. Mother Earth was a rumbling freight train, but shaking more violently than the relatively puny locomotives that passed his parents' house. Paintings danced on the wall before tumbling to the floor with the disturbing sound of shattering glass. The crackling sound from the splintering walls around him was too familiar from the accidents that had destroyed his cars.

The Palace Hotel! San Francisco!

Oldfield, at last, turned his attention to Bess and began squeezing her as hard as she had coiled around him as the dull rumbling and shaking intensified. He wanted to say something to reassure her, but talking now made no sense. Like his disintegrating Winton at Gross Point, they could only hang on.

The canopy above their king-size bed was an umbrella to the plaster dust. Mercifully, the hand of God jostling the world subsided.

Bess still clung tightly to her husband as he began to blurt out a torrent of "goddamns" and "Jesus Christ!"

"I think we just had a goddamn earthquake."

"My Lord," Bess shouted. "I never in all my life..."

Gradually, Bess relaxed her squeeze, and Oldfield sat up, sweeping the room with his eyes. Books and paintings were on the floor, as well as one of the gas lamps. The large rug under and around their bed had a coating of plaster dust that reminded him of the snows back in Ohio. He reached for his pocket watch that had bounced but remained on his nightstand. 5:26 am.

Sirens were already alert to devastation. Oldfield, with Bess shadowing him, even tugging on his nightshirt, nervously shuffled over to the window that faced the street. Pulling aside the drapes, the emerging light of dawn revealed a battlefield-like scene of destruction. Bess peered over his shoulder. Gone were the hundreds of cars, trolleys, horse-drawn wagons, buggies, and countless pedestrians of the day before. The buildings of April 17 had been replaced broken boards, rubble, and dismembered blocks.

A fire wagon whirled by, its bell peeling out its approach. Within a minute, another followed. There were fires blocks around as wood structures gave way and fueled the conflagration's relentless advance.

"Good Lord, how could this happen? There are more buildings down than standing," Bess said.

"Yeah, little honey, which tells me we need to get our asses out of here because I don't know what's going to happen next. We don't want to be inside this place if it suddenly decides to let go."

Tom Cooper rapped on their door to the hallway and simultaneously tried the doorknob. Oldfield scurried across the room and let his friend in.

"Jesus Christ, Barney, did you look outside?"

"You bet, Tom. Bess and I are grabbing a few things and our suitcases. You better do the same, and we'll meet you in the hallway in two minutes."

Soon the three friends were bounding down the stairs, bags in hand, to find their way to the street. Doors flung open, and others, many from the Dillingham stage production, did the same. Some women were crying, and men tried to compose themselves to not belie that they were pissing their pants as well.

There were no lights, and the stairwells became clogged and dark. The process slowed down, but people were generally respectful and ignored jostling and even toes that were inadvertently stepped on.

After more than a half-hour, Bess, Oldfield, and Cooper emerged from their stricken hotel and into the dusty morning air. The wind whipped up clouds of dust from the rubble and fires to dim the sun. At least the temperature was comfortable.

A roar alarmed the people in the street, but it was not another shaker. A severely damaged building, with one of its sides standing alone as if deserted by it three companions, buckled to punctuate the brief calm.

Hundreds of people continued to pour forth onto the street, where the trolley car's tracks had in one spot been bent into a backward letter, "Z." People were bloodied and sat on the ground or large piles of blocks. In general, people were slack-jawed and stunned.

Oldfield raised his voice above the din as he put his hands on both Bess and Cooper's shoulders.

"Well, okay. Our first job is to figure out how to get out of here and head home," Oldfield announced. "This isn't our home, and it never will be. We can just leave; a lot of these poor bastards are stuck. And as far as this stage business is concerned, I am through with it. To Hell with it. Racing is a Hell of a lot safer."

Chapter 18 – In the End, Death Always Wins

(Hawthorne Horse Track, Illinois, Tuesday, July 3, 1906)

The Green Dragon's hood vibrated, and its tires kicked up clouds of dust and quivered like a gob of gelatin as they strained to grip at the Hawthorne Horse Track, especially when Barney Oldfield stood on its throttle. He wrestled the wheel, correcting first one way and then, with quick hands, to the other. He wanted that one thousand dollars track owner, old Ed Corrigan, had promised if he could run faster than the record for his rival Chicago track, Harlem.

Accelerating toward the finish line, Oldfield saw "fat boy" Will Pickens standing at track's edge. It was easier to spot Pickens' mass than the relatively slight Tom Cooper who stood beside him. He even saw Pickens pumping his fist in the air. He did not find a pit board, but that fist had to mean good news.

Oldfield's run for the record was the highlight of the track's July 3 card, and he could hear the railbirds shouting. Slowing on the backstretch, he coasted the Dragon to a stop near where Pickens and Cooper stood.

"What do you think of that, ladies?" Oldfield said. "Me and the old Dragon haven't lost a step after all that acting."

Cooper did not say anything but stroked his chin as he circled around the green and brass car. Oldfield knew he was checking out the tires.

"You would have been even faster if I had been holding the stopwatch," Pickens said. "You clocked in at three-ought-six for the three miles, and all three laps were faster than anything at Harlem. Old man Corrigan owes us. We're a thousand dollars richer."

Cooper paced to the other side of Oldfield's seat.

"Tires are shot. I'm glad you shut it off when you did. We might be off in the field somewhere untangling you from a tree or something."

Oldfield frowned. He was disappointed Cooper was so quiet. No handshake. No nothing.

"Tom, we had a good day. I just busted that Harlem record and Corrigan will make good on his promise. I also won those two heat races. We had a good day, right, Tom?"

Cooper frowned. Oldfield sensed his partner had not been the same since the San Francisco quake, even before. He looked a little lost. Pickens picked up on Cooper's attitude as well, and although he did not say anything, Oldfield could tell he was listening.

"Barney, I've been thinking," Cooper said. "Getting back to where we were with racing isn't enough. I need to carve out my own way for a while."

Oldfield felt a jolt like he had been punched from inside his chest. There was a minute of excruciating silence.

"What the Hell does that mean, Tom? I thought we were partners. You said you wanted to get back to racing. Well, look around. That's where we are."

Cooper bowed his head, averting Oldfield's stern stare. Nobody said anything. Sounds of people talking, engines rumbling from various distances away, even the laughter of people filled Oldfield's ears and angered him.

"Well, to Hell with you, Tom," Oldfield erupted. "I guess I was pretty goddamn stupid to think we were friends!"

Cooper remained silent and turned to walk away. Pickens' eyes widened, and he shook his head at Oldfield. He followed Cooper, walking faster than Oldfield ever imagined the fat man could muster.

Pickens caught up with Cooper, pulled at his elbow, and the two, just out of earshot for Oldfield, began to talk. The driver kicked at the dirt, scattering up a little dust. Cooper turned toward his friend, and the two met in the middle of the distance between them.

"Listen, Barney," Cooper started. "I'll always think of you as my best friend. We've been through a lot together. We've raced bikes and cars, whored around, acted on Broadway, and even worked a gold mine, for Christ's sake."

He stopped, staring into Oldfield's eyes, who extended his hand. They shook and then leaned forward to slap each other on the back.

"The Matheson brothers are offering me a pretty good deal. I worked with them some before, and I know they are good fellas. It's not like we will never see each other again. Unless you go off and do something stupid like get yourself killed."

(Detroit, Woodmere Cemetery, November 20, 1906)

Oldfield's raging headache was a painful alternative for the aching hole in his spirit since November 17. It was as if he was outside his body and observing as he and five other men let the black webbing that cradled the casket gradually settle down the full six feet into the Earth. Ever since Will Pickens placed a phone call to him at the Hotel Hollenden on November 17, he had been knocking down bottles of corn mash.

"Dead soldiers," he called them looking at the empty bottles.

Pickens always seemed first to learn news and never struggled to put words together – but November 17 was different. It was different because Tom Cooper was dead, killed in New York City.

Oldfield looked across to the other side of the grave at Pickens. Beside him were Spider Huff and Frank Matheson. At Oldfield's right was Ernie Moross, and also nearby was bicycle champion, Eddie Bald. For an instant, Oldfield thought Cooper should be there beside him or across from him, helping.

The casket disappeared below the edge of the grave to a dark spot at the bottom. A minister said a few words, but Oldfield was not listening. He watched the first few shovels of dirt scattered over the side and then abruptly walked away.

Since they received the news, Bess was leaving Oldfield be. Now, though, she approached him, her eyes red and moist.

"Barney, dear, I met someone you may wish to speak with."

Oldfield gave her the cold stare he knew Bess would recognize. They had been together long enough that sometimes they didn't need words. He was in no mood for conversation.

"You should know there is a woman here that was with Tom when it happened. If you don't want to talk, I will tell her. I know that it won't bring Tom back. It's just that listening to her may help you come to terms with what happened. It may make you feel like you had a chance to say goodbye."

Silent still, Oldfield did not move. Again, that was enough to let Bess know he would listen if just for a while.

"Her name is Virginia Vernon. She was sitting next to Tom and was hurt in the accident, too," Bess said. "Come, walk with me. She's in a wheelchair with a leg fracture, and we should walk to her."

A group of people parted way and Virginia Vernon, a young woman of about twenty in a wheelchair, came into view. What looked like a forced smile spread her lips briefly, and she extended her hand to Oldfield. He gently squeezed it.

"Mr. Oldfield, I am honored to meet you," Virginia said. "Bess told me you might want to hear my account of what happened, and I said that I would, of course, be of service to you, if you would like. Before I start, though, I want you to know I don't blame Tom for anything that happened. I really thought he was a gentleman, and, honestly, I was excited to be around him. He was funny and smart."

Oldfield soaked up her words like a tonic. He knew she had seen something he hadn't, and really, was glad to be spared that. He had learned from the funeral home director that Cooper's neck was broken. A portion of his skull had been crushed when he was tossed from the car. Oldfield had seen men die brutal deaths, but never a friend. He felt he shared empathy for Cooper with the woman, and a sensation of being closer to his friend came over him. He kneeled to her side, resting his weight on one knee like he was proposing marriage.

"I don't quite know where to begin, except that there were four of us. Tom, myself, my friend Helen Lovett and Mr. Barlow, who was very well-to-do. Mr. Barlow passed away too, I am afraid. We had just left the Hotel Wroxeter, and, to be honest, we had been drinking. We were in one of Mr. Matheson's cars, and suddenly there was another car with people in it. Tom and the driver were yelling at each other."

Oldfield leaned forward. He wondered if Cooper was arguing with the other driver and if they were fighting mad.

"Nobody was mad, Mr. Oldfield. Everyone was laughing. It's just that the people in the car – I don't think Tom knew them – were egging him on. They were daring him to race with them, and both started picking up speed. We were all laughing and thought it was fun."

Oldfield smiled before he realized it. Cooper could never resist a good race.

"Our car and the other one was racing down Eighth Avenue toward the intersection with the exit road from Central Park. Suddenly, the other car shot ahead. Then Tom tried to get up alongside them again, and that's when the rest started yelling for him to stop. Both cars were going pretty fast, and we were so close. I thought I could reach out and touch a woman riding in the other car. As we neared Seventy-Seventh Street, our car gained on the other car, and as we came close to a curve, our front wheels ran up on the rear wheel of the other car. After that, I just remember waking up in grass beside the road. Mr. Barlow and Helen both had head injuries, and I just knew Tom was gone. It was horrible."

There was really nothing more to say. Oldfield knew Virginia was the only one of the four lucky enough to survive. He wasn't interested in more details of hospitals and doctors. His friend was dead, but Virginia's story made him feel he knew his friend's final chapter. Oldfield stood up and then leaned forward to kiss the woman on her left cheek.

"Thank you, Virginia. Thank you very much. God Bless you."

(Detroit, Cadillac Hotel, November 20, 1906)

Darkness and silence were friends to Barney Oldfield. Another dead soldier sat on the secretary desk nestled into the far corner of his room at Detroit's Cadillac Hotel. A fresh bottle, open and only barely sampled, stood ready for duty.

Rapping at the door from the hallway punctuated the silence, Oldfield was only aware that his ears had a faint ringing when the space around him was void of sound. Bess's dress rustled as she appeared from the adjoining room to answer the knock her husband was prepared to ignore.

Hinges protested only faintly as Bess at first cracked the door and then opened it broadly. Will Pickens. Oldfield heard their whispers, but only picked up fragments of the exchange.

"I've let him alone…but glad you are here."

"I hate this, Bess…I just wanted to check on him."

Oldfield poured his shot glass full of Green Brier Tennessee Sour Mash. He felt the considerable presence of Pickens beside him. Oldfield glanced to his side where Pickens was planted and then tilted his head upward in the direction of the secretary desk's cabinet. The desk cabinet had glass windows, and visible were two shelves of books, but the bottom one was stocked with two more bottles of Green Brier and an assortment of shot glasses as well as a beer mug.

Oldfield muttered, "Pour one if you like."

Pickens didn't have to be asked twice. He awkwardly swayed forward, his gelatinous belly briefly leaning on the extended desktop. Oldfield watched as the amber liquid flowed into the ounce container.

"Barney, I just wanted to come to see you," Pickens said. "I know we're all toughs, but this hurts like Hell, and I know you feel it worst. Tom was the last man the game could afford to lose."

Oldfield swallowed hard. He wasn't silent just because of his dark mood. His throat tightened as if something was choking him from inside his neck.

"I can't help but think of things we did," Pickens continued. "Remember a couple of years ago when we did that southern barnstorm that got you in hot water with Winton? Oh, and remember that time we were in Reno for a race meet, and those cowboys wanted to know where the notches were on the Dragon because you killed so many people?"

Pickens chuckled, and Oldfield thought the big fella was trying to fight off a cackle.

"Tom and I went over to livery stable where we had it stored and brought a file. Yeah, we put some notches in the tail. It was a convincer and brought people around."

Oldfield did like remembering the story. Pickens was doing the right thing – somehow.

"I remember Tom and I paying the bond to get your fat ass out of jail," Oldfield tossed into the exchange.

"That was unfortunate," Pickens said. "Such a misunderstanding."

"Yeah. Everyone misunderstood that after giving you a one-thousand-dollar advance to put on an auto racing exhibition that you weren't going to do it."

Pickens poured himself another shot.

"My mechanical abilities proved inadequate to the challenge; I do confess. However, I never intended to cheat anyone."

Oldfield mustered a smile. He filled both shot glasses with more whiskey. As he raised his glass, Pickens met him with his.

"To Tom Cooper, one Hell of a man and a damn fine friend," Oldfield announced.

Pickens nodded, winked, and tossed back his drink.

(Horace "Pop" Haynes' Restaurant, Indianapolis, November 23, 1906)

Carl Fisher stormed through the door of "Pop" Haynes's restaurant. He was hungry and late – something he detested in others. Peeling off his overcoat, Fisher marched to the table Haynes and his crew always reserved for him. Keeping pace behind him was William Galloway, Fisher's favorite waiter. He let his coat slide down from his arms, and without saying a word, Galloway caught it and draped the collar over a peg in the wall designed for precisely that purpose.

Already seated were Art Newby and Jim Allison.

"About time, Carl," Allison deadpanned. "Our time is valuable too."

"Okay, Okay, Jesus, Jim, don't get your bowels in an uproar. Where's Wheeler?"

Allison rolled his eyes, and Fisher knew it was a dumb question. Wheeler always held things up.

"Did you fellas order yet?" Fisher asked as Galloway again approached from behind. This time he balanced a copious plate loaded with a large baked potato with a sixteen-ounce steak partially extending over the edge. Fisher turned his attention to the waiter before waiting for his partners to answer.

"Galloway! Good man! Always on-the-spot with what I like!"

Fisher jumped into his chair and, without hesitating, started to devour his blood-rare meat. His table, his personal waiter Galloway, and his favorite meal of steak and potato were always ready for him at Hayne's place. Galloway took Newby and Allison's order.

As Fisher chewed, Allison confirmed they were there to talk about his speedway idea again.

"You bet," Fisher pronounced with a mouthful of chewy beef. "Look at what's happening, you fellas know. Somebody finally got killed at the Vanderbilt Cup. Big surprise, people walking out onto the road and they couldn't figure out that was going to happen? So now they are talking about building a concrete speedway?"

"It's hard to say what they are planning," Newby replied. "I hear a lot of different stories. Vanderbilt has Pardington managing the project, and Art is a good man. The big problem is they are trying to get right of way from a bunch of Long Island farmers. Some are easy to work with; others are bull-headed and trying to hold out for big money."

Galloway returned with two more steaming plates of hot food. He quietly put them in front of Allison and Newby.

"I want to watch what's happening out there. If those fellas want to take on the cost of building the speedway this country needs, then let 'em do it. I'm just not sure they really know what they're doing. Most of those fellas are Swells who never really worked to make a buck."

"True," said Newby. "And I can tell you as a man who runs a motor vehicle manufacturing company, it would be nice to have something proper in our backyard."

All three of the men fell silent. Fisher thought about the expense of building the three-mile track the men had discussed months prior.

"So, you fellas are thinking three-quarters of a million dollars?"

Newby shrugged as Allison began to speak.

"That's just a rough estimate, Carl," Allison said. "We can't kid ourselves. Something like what you described could easily top a million. A good thing to keep tabs on is what we are hearing is going on over in England. I see they want to build something with big banking and paved with concrete."

"Honestly, Carl, if we did that, I could see it double the price, maybe it would cost us two million," Newby inserted.

Fisher frowned. If the men weren't his friends, he might have started yelling. He set his teeth together like a clamp and held his breath. It was so damned frustrating to talk. There were a thousand things to do, and he just wanted to hear how to get things done. That's all, nothing else.

"I want to keep an eye on what they're doing in England. When they get that thing close to finished, I am going over there. That Locke King fella that's putting up all the money is likely to do everything first class."

"Well, I've been thinking of heading east and visiting Pardington," said Newby. "I want to hear what he has to say about getting that speedway built. I've also been thinking about sending a couple of my boys to run Nationals out there. This will give me a chance to take a look at the situation for both reasons."

Galloway checked on the men, inquiring if they needed anything else. Fisher ordered a round of bourbon shots, but Newby protested. Just then, Frank Wheeler arrived.

"I'm sorry, gentlemen," Wheeler apologized. "It's the pressures of business, you know."

"No, we don't have any idea, Frank," Fisher said. "We just fuck ourselves all day waiting on you. Here, sit down, I have something to say. And Art, I'm putting a drink in front of you whether you join us or not. This is important."

Galloway returned promptly and placed the shots in front of the men, including Newby. Fisher reached out to take Galloway's arm.

"William, would you like to join us as I propose a toast?" Fisher asked.

"Thank you, Mister Fisher," Galloway said. "But please understand it just wouldn't be proper or respectful to Mr. Haynes. I'm one of his wait staff."

Fisher took a moment to study Galloway's black countenance, one he judged to be about fifty years old. It had a great character with deep lines that gave him an attractive and wise look. He respected the man. Fisher nodded but asked Galloway to remain. He then turned his attention to his three colleagues. Wheeler had taken his seat in the dark-grain wooden chair at the table.

"Gentlemen, this is the first occasion we have had to be together since we lost a good man, both professionally and to me personally. I know all of you heard about Tom Cooper's passing last week."

Everyone became solemn, and even Newby joined the men in raising his glass.

"To Tom Cooper, a great champion, a good friend, and a master of the internal combustion engine."

With a round of affirming, "hear, hear, cheers," Newby, Allison, Wheeler, and Fisher clinked their glasses and then drank. All but Newby tossed their bourbon back in a full-throated gulp. Newby took a sip and then covered his mouth as he coughed.

"That was a fine thing you did, Mr. Fisher," Galloway added. "Will that be all, sir?"

Fisher again pivoted his head to the older servant.

"Galloway, how much money does old man Haynes pay you?"

"It would be six dollars a week, Mr. Fisher."

"What would you say if I asked you to come run the Fisher household for twice that? I live with my mother, and she's getting along in years and could use the help."

Open-mouthed, the servant looked genuinely stunned.

"Well, Mr. Fisher, are you sure?" he asked. "That sure is generous, and I would enjoy working for you."

Fisher and Galloway shook hands. He left it to Galloway to speak with Haynes and then let him know when he could resign from the restaurant and start working for him.

His colleagues were quiet, and Fisher knew he was almost surely shocking them with the idea of letting a Negro in his home to run and organize it. Their facial expressions were emblems of surprise. Newby broke the silence.

"He's a good man, Carl, and I am certain he will serve you well."

"He will. He shows up on time, and he'll help me to do the same, right, Frank? The man isn't perfect, but I never hear excuses. He just works harder, and I like that."

Chapter 19 – Life Goes On

(Cleveland, Ohio, January 1907)

Bright white, scripted letters shouting "Blue Streak," and "Green Dragon" jumped off the dull, barn-red painted boards of Barney Oldfield's railroad boxcar. A plume of smoke emerged from Oldfield's lips, where his teeth clinched an ash-tipped La Reina. The two race cars were now his since his contract with Peerless expired. Now he was in business for Barney Oldfield only. The sight of "Oldfield Amusement Company" on the side of the big car made it feel real as if he needed to prove it to himself. He savored a long look.

Ernie Moross, also puffing a cigar, but somehow more tentatively than Oldfield, looked up at the driver and winked.

"We're in business now, Barney. We're going to tackle every pumpkin fair in the south this winter and then just stay on those railroad tracks north and west in the spring. Pickens will be running just ahead of us to do the advance work, and we'll pack 'em in, guaranteed. We're going to make a lot of money."

Oldfield returned a glance at the promoter and nodded. He felt like Moross expected him to laugh and slap him on the back, but he did not. Oldfield was glad to have the little man at his side. Moross knew the business and had big ideas. It was just that Oldfield expected Cooper to emerge from around the far side of the boxcar and offer his opinion. It probably would have been to tell him some word was misspelled or something, but he'd smile while doing it.

Moross must have sensed Oldfield's melancholy, or maybe he just felt he had to fill up the silence at the moment.

"Say, Barney, how's married life? That was a swell wedding you and Bess had. The folks at the Hollenden really lit up the room and put on a nice spread. She's a great lady, that

Bess. You're a lucky man."

"Thanks, Ernie. Bess keeps me grounded, and I need that."

Oldfield thought briefly about saying he didn't feel lucky after Tom Cooper died – but he held back. Something made him feel guilty about that emotion because he was, in his heart, grateful that Bess wanted to share her life with him. Bess did not bitch, she let him do what he wanted, and that was the kind of woman he needed.

Still, Oldfield could not shake the image of Cooper at the funeral home, looking pale and with that big gash across his cheek. Sometimes he even had dreadful dreams of when he, Moross, and the other pallbearers lowered the casket into the Earth. Cooper was gone, and now his old friend had a yearning to drive his cars faster than ever. On the track, there was nothing, except speed.

The Dragon and the Blue Streak peeked seductively out of the boxcar's open, tall sliding doors. They were familiar to him – they were like old friends.

(Hotel Portland, Portland, Oregon, July 6, 1907)

Oldfield fumbled with the hefty skeleton key to his room at the Hotel Portland. His hand involuntarily waved it like an impotent magic wand incapable of finding the keyhole.

With his left hand, he attempted to steady his right arm as he stabbed at the lock, finally dragging it like a piece of chalk until it found its mark. With a twist of his wrist, the lock clicked, the hinges whispered a squeak, and the door swung open into his Hotel Portland room. Bess stirred, pressed the electric light button, and the light at her nightstand illuminated the room. Oldfield cringed as she fixed her eyes on the clock on the dresser.

"My Lord, Barney! It's two o'clock in the morning!"

"I can read the goddamn clock woman. Don't be a nag."

Oldfield turned his back to Bess. He did not understand why he was speaking harshly to his wife, but mostly he did not care. Or maybe he just wanted to dump some of his pain on someone else.

Instead of sitting down on the bed, Oldfield shuffled his feet to where he was confident of his position and then collapsed his weight onto the side of the mattress like an old man with atrophied legs. He half-expected to land ass-first on the floor and was briefly pleased with himself that he had successfully sat down on the mattress. Bess was quiet, but he could feel her riveting stare shooting through him from behind.

"Goddamn Evening Telegram…accusing me of being a thief," Oldfield muttered. "Accusing me of lying."

"That's no excuse for giving in to your weakness. And don't you dare raise your voice to me again, Berna Eli!"

Oldfield scooted along the edge of the mattress, leaned over, steadied himself with a hand on the footboard bedpost, and shakily rose to his feet.

"I'll show you how weak I am," he snarled.

Abruptly, Oldfield launched across the room and put both fists through the terrace glass windows. Scarlet blood emerged from slashes on his hands from shards, but he continued unabated like he was watching someone else take control of his body. Somehow it made sense to follow through on his destruction, beating through the remaining jagged glass with his forearms and leaning out the third-story window.

Bess screamed from behind him, but he did not want to figure out what she was saying. He jutted his head out of the window into the darkness, pierced only by a sliver of the moon and two gas lamps at the hotel's gated entrance below. Wind tussled his hair. Two feet down from the window was a narrow ledge, and while he had not considered it before, the idea of stepping out to balance on the precipice made him feel less foolish than retreating to his wife's pleas.

As he lifted one leg up and out the window to find his footing, he felt Bess frantically pulling at his coat and screaming for help. She continued to scream and tug at his back, and Oldfield knew he did not want to dive, but somehow succumbing to her strength made him feel weak. Suddenly, two big, irresistible arms emerged from behind and locked around his chest. Oldfield fell backward into the room and realized that a man had rushed into the situation.

Bess was blubbering. The large man in their room reached out to her as he leaned the weight of his body on her husband's chest through his knee. Even in his madness, Oldfield's mind tried to determine who this stranger was and how he got into the room. The light was dim, and his features unfamiliar. Bess began thanking him between sobs.

The man told her to get some towels to try to cover Oldfield's hands. The driver's energy was gone, and a sense of embarrassment came over him. He surrendered any resistance, rolling his head back and forth, muttering curses.

"Goddamn. Shit. Jesus Christ."

Bess rushed back with the bathroom towels and began to wrap Oldfield's hands. With each passing second, the sting of his lacerations expanded its intensity.

"Are you okay, ma'am, was he attacking you?"

"No, no," Bess replied. "He's been drinking. He's distraught, but the drinking isn't making anything better. This is Barney Oldfield, my husband, the racing driver. He was unfairly arrested today after the newspaper said he cheated everyone at Irvington Park. He's not normally this way, he lost a dear friend a few months back, and now he has people accusing him of being a swindler. He's not, he's a good man."

The man kept Oldfield pinned to the floor as he looked into his face.

"Mr. Oldfield, if I let you up, can you promise to compose yourself?"

The driver nodded, yes.

The man stood up and turned back to Bess.

"I'm the hotel detective, Mrs. Oldfield. I'm glad I was roaming this hall when you screamed. With all seven floors here, I could have been anywhere."

"We're both grateful for your help and your understanding, sir," Bess said.

"It's part of the job," the detective returned. "I won't lie and say it's the fun part, but you take the good with the bad. We have a nurse here. She won't be happy with him either, but I'm going to wake her and have her come to tend to those cuts. He's going to need some stitches."

Bess thanked the detective and then directed her stare to her husband, who closed his eyes.

Chapter 20 – Conflagration and Challenge

(Indianapolis, Pearl & East Streets, August 17, 1907)

The fire was dead, but the lingering scent of smoke, ash, and chemicals invaded Carl Fisher's nostrils. Several feet away, Frank Sweet, his vice president of Prest-O-Lite, was poking through debris and some charred wood with a stick.

"It was a hell of a blast, boss," said Sweet. "Little bits of metal and all kinds of pieces were flying everywhere."

Looking over his shoulder to the opposite side of East Street, Sweet raised the stick and pointed to the dented and beat up twenty-five-pound brass tank that gleamed in the sun despite the dulling black smoke residue that covered at least half of it. A gaping hole better than a foot wide had been punched into a railroad boxcar about one hundred fifty feet away.

"I was trying to call you, Mr. Fisher, and Mr. Allison, too, just as soon as it happened," Sweet added. "I left that tank right where it landed, just to give you an idea what a big powerful mess this was. It was just about the damnedest thing I have ever seen. Praise the Lord nobody was seriously hurt."

Fisher yawned. He did not get much rest on the overnight train ride from New York, where he had been visiting another Prest-O-Lite factory. He rubbed his eyes and shook his head. Another goddamn problem that just wasn't necessary.

"How is everybody?" Fisher asked. "I hear Emma sprained her ankle."

"Yeah, she had to jump off that fire escape ladder. The end of that thing is a good eight feet off the ground," Sweet said. "And Kate jumped too. She scratched up her arm pretty good, but no stitches, the Doc just wrapped it up."

Fisher scanned the area. Charred boards were lying about, and metal fragments embedded in the ground sparkled in the sunlight. Pools of water from the firemen's hoses dotted the yard in front of the building. Several of the windows in the old converted veterinary college Fisher had gotten for cheap were blown out. There was that goddamn fire escape ladder. Jesus Christ, that's a leap of faith. Why the hell didn't somebody think of fixing that goddamn thing? Jesus Christ, do I have to think of everything?

"Goddamn it, Frank! What the Hell is this mess," Fisher shouted. "I put you in charge of this plant, aren't I paying you enough to look after things?"

Sweet tilted his head to the ground. Fisher continued venting.

"I'll get the ladder fixed, Mr. Fisher," Sweet said. "We'll fix it all, and I promise to go over it with a fine-tooth comb."

Fisher frowned, shaking his head.

"How the Hell did this happen, or have you bothered to figure that out yet?"

"Claude Hess, the new hire, thinks we had a leaky tube from the compressor feeding the tanks," Sweet reported. "John Lucky was training Claude and was able to get to the electric cord and pull it from the wall, but not soon enough to stop some of the explosions."

Hearing that a trainee was involved in the mess set off an explosion in Fisher's brain.

"You mean you turned a trainee loose on the riskiest part of the process? Use your head, man!"

Sweet's jaw dropped as his eyes opened wide. Fisher could see the man was astounded.

"Mr. Fisher, a man's got to learn by doing. John was watching closely, but it just happened so damn fast, there wasn't much anyone could do."

"You're on thin ice, Sweet," Fisher said. "What's your estimate on what this is going to cost? How long until we can get back to production? We couldn't get any insurance. This is coming out of my pocket for Christ's sake! Speak up, man!"

Sweet appeared genuinely afraid of his boss's next reaction.

"It's just my first estimate, Mr. Fisher. I'm putting the loss of equipment at about fifteen thousand dollars. I also believe – and this is rough until I get a contractor out here – that the damage to the building will set us back another ten thousand. It's going to be close to a week before we can get any production going."

The numbers did not infuriate Fisher as much as Sweet appeared to think they would – but he was careful not to let the man know he was actually relieved. Turning his back and heading toward East Street and his parked Stoddard-Dayton, Fisher told Sweet to get busy and provide him a report by the next day. His mind began churning about calling New York and a couple of other charging centers to tell other vice presidents to pick up the slack. He heard Sweet begin to speak again from where he left him.

"There's one more thing, Mr. Fisher," Sweet said. "That Fire Chief Charlie Coots says we're going to have to move outside of town."

Fisher didn't look back at his employee.

"You let me worry about Coots."

(Indianapolis, Pearl & East Streets, December 20, 1907)

The tires of Carl Fisher's Stoddard-Dayton screeched in protest as he skidded to a stop in front of his Pearl and East Street Prest-O-Lite facility.

"Not again! Goddamn it! Jesus Christ on a bicycle, not again."

Immediately, a massive explosion erupted with a flash of flame. Fisher slogged toward the conflagration and gradually felt the chilly December air warm. Fire Chief Coots stood facing the building with his hands on his hips, his eyes fixed on the flames. His men scattered about with hoses, showering the walls. Occasionally, Coots waved his hands or pointed and barked orders to firemen. Beside him were Mayor Bookwalter and Police Chief Robert Metzger. Again, there was another blast with subsequent flame like the building was under bombardment.

As if he could sense Fisher's approach, Coots turned abruptly and locked eyes on the businessman.

"Goddamn you, Fisher, you greedy son-of-a-bitch! I warned you about this operation."

Fisher felt an electric surge of anger emanate in his stomach and shoot through his spine to his limbs. His heart raced with fury and frustration.

"Fuck you, Coots. We did everything to fix this since August. We cleared the upper floors and limited the canisters we stored here. You don't know your ass from a hole in the ground, and I'm not taking any guff off the likes of you."

"You don't give a shit about anybody but yourself, Fisher," Coots screamed. "Now you got a man dead. You feel good about that?"

Metzger and Bookwalter stepped between the two men. Fisher noticed Metzger was wheezing as he breathed. Bookwalter spoke before Fisher could ask about Coots' claim a man had died.

"One of your men, a fella named Elmer Jessup, got burned really bad, Carl," Bookwalter explained. "He was literally a human torch running down towards Washington Street."

"Is he going to be okay?" Fisher asked. "Where is he?"

Metzger shook his head as Bookwalter pointed to the drug store across Pearl Street.

"A transfer man leaped off one of those boxcars over there and tackled Jessup with a blanket and smothered the flames," Bookwalter said. "He was on fire for quite a while before that. Doc Ketterhenry took him over to Mueller's drugstore with another one your men who got burned."

Fisher pivoted abruptly and began to sprint back toward Pearl Street and the drugstore across from it. Bursting through the door, he immediately halted his momentum upon seeing Jessup, who was moaning and calling out for someone.

Ketterhenry was intent on his work, cutting and wrapping gauze around blistered, bursting, scarlet flesh that covered Jessup from his feet up to the top of his head. Fred

Mueller peered at the morbid spectacle from the opposite side of his counter. Sitting quietly nearby was another man with red blisters erupting from his face. The man looked familiar to Fisher. He seemed stunned.

"How bad is he?" was all Fisher could think to say.

Ketterhenry dismissed the Indianapolis businessman with a sweeping wave.

"Doc has both your boys on morphine," Mueller inserted. "I think that's why Van Garder, there, is so quiet. Drugs and shock. He tried to tackle Elmer there, but didn't have a blanket like the other fella who got to him."

"John Van Garder!" Fisher announced when Mueller's mention of the man's name triggered his memory. Craning his neck as he surveyed the room, not so much with purpose but just fidgeting as he searched his mind, he scanned the array of pill bottles, supplies, and instruments. Kneeling by Van Garder, Fisher carefully placed his hand on the man's shoulder for fear of inadvertently touching an injury.

"You're going to be alright, man. You hear me? I'll pay your doctor bills, and you're going to heal up just fine."

Van Garder stared straight ahead, not making eye contact.

"I did everything I could, Mr. Fisher. I heard an explosion, and then we were all waist-deep in flames. Elmer was at the back of the room, the furthest from the door. He got out, but not fast enough. I tried to stop him, but the fire…he's going die, isn't he Mr. Fisher?"

Fisher frowned. Conscious of discouraging a man fighting for his life, he squeezed Van Garder's hand but remained silent. In the background, he heard Jessup moan again and call out a woman's name. Fisher realized the stricken man was probably asking for his wife. Standing up, he walked to the store's front door and then out to the sidewalk, stuffing his hands in his pockets because he felt like he should do something with them but couldn't think of what it could be.

Across the street, the firemen were still dousing the blaze but making progress. The blasts stopped, and Fisher surmised that there were no more canisters to explode. The bell on the storefront door chimed behind him. He glanced over his shoulder to see Doc Ketterhenry.

"His feet are the only spots where he isn't seriously burned," Ketterhenry reported. "Most of the burns are second and third degree. There isn't the slightest hope for him."

Fisher tilted his head down, his brown leather boots coated with dust and soot, came into view.

"I'm sorry, Carl," Ketterhenry said. "He was a good and honest man, a father. I just wanted you to know so you can begin thinking about anything you can do for his family."

Fisher thanked the doctor and dragged his feet back to his burning building. There was not a sense of urgency as when he raced to the drug store just minutes earlier. Dreading another encounter with Coots, he waved at Bookwalter and motioned to him to meet in the middle.

Bookwalter approached, with Metzger shuffling behind. The police chief hacked gurgling phlegm from the back of his throat and bent over with hands on his thighs to spit the mucous on the brown, muddy ground.

Fisher frowned.

"Jesus, Bob, you need to go to bed, you're going to die of pneumonia."

Turning to the Mayor, Fisher looked for support from a friend.

"Damn, Charlie, I thought we had all the bases covered. We limited the number of canisters from three thousand to three hundred and blocked everyone from using the top two floors so it would be easy to get out. I only had maybe a dozen men here, no women. Everyone else is over at our fireproof concrete building on South Street."

Bookwalter's face was blank, expressionless.

"What do you want me to tell you, Carl? Do you want to hear that you and Jim did everything perfectly? That it is just bum luck?" Bookwalter asked. "The outcome speaks for itself. What you did wasn't good enough."

Metzger, hoarse, and wheezing appeared agitated.

"I think you owe old Charlie an apology, Carl, this is the second big mess you have created for this city in four months. And you talk about your South Street plant all you want, but just because concrete doesn't burn, that doesn't mean we won't have more big explosions. That building is right across the street from St. Vincent's Hospital for Christ's sake."

"We'll be fine. I'll have a crew over here tomorrow to clean this mess up, and we won't ever be back."

(Hamline, Minnesota, April 7, 1908)

"I couldn't be happier at this moment," Barney Oldfield announced as he leaped from the running board of his new, one hundred horsepower Stearns stock car. "These cars can take a beating and not give me a lick of trouble. That's what I need for my plans."

He shoved his leather-gloved and dirty hand toward Charlie Soules, who had exited Oldfield's other Stearns, a smaller sixty-horsepower machine. Both hefty drivers gripped hard and cranked their arms like they were working the water pump at a farm.

Soules' goggles were pushed to his forehead to reveal the only portion of his face that wasn't coated with oil and dust. Oldfield felt the film over his own face and knew he looked the same.

Simultaneously, both men swatted at their linen dusters, ushering forth clouds of Earth. Bess Oldfield, sitting in the passenger seat of the big Stearns, waved her hand in front of her veiled face.

"I'm delighted you're in such a good mood, Barney," she said, beaming. "I suppose many women wouldn't be so thrilled to drive from Cleveland to Minnesota on these dusty roads, but I guess loving a race driver makes me silly."

Oldfield cocked his head toward his wife and cracked a smile with his unlit and dirty cigar stub clenched in the corner of his mouth. Ernie Moross, who rode with Soules, stepped from behind his driver, also smacking at the sleeves of his duster to shake off the coating.

"Roads, huh?" Moross said with a smile. "Is that what you call what we've been driving on?"

Oldfield surveyed his two new cars, both coated with layers of splattered mud and dust. His first order of business would be to wash and polish them. They had to be presentable for the weekend's races at the Minnesota State Fairgrounds.

Scanning St. Paul, Minnesota's Selby Street, where his cars were parked, Oldfield traced his glance across the buildings of sandstone, brick, and wood. He hoped his eyes would land on a garage, but nothing jumped out. Above him loomed the red brick Blair Flats residential hotel, where Moross had arranged rooms. Someone inside would know where he could take his cars for a good cleaning, fuel, and space to tune the engines.

"Walt Christie is supposed to be staying here, too," Ernie announced. "Do you want to go into the lobby and look for him while I register our rooms?"

"I need a beer," Oldfield replied. "That was a long trip, and that's what the doctor ordered. You go ahead and register, and I am going to stop at the lounge to quench my thirst."

Oldfield raised his voice, so Soules, who was rummaging through the toolbox on the other side of the smaller Stearns, could hear him.

"Hey, Soules, you want to get a beer with me before we get all cleaned up?"

The other driver waved with a smile, indicating that he thought it was a good idea.

Oldfield strolled to the other side of the car he had driven to extend his hand to Bess and help her step from the passenger seat running board.

"Now, Barney, only one, please," Bess said with a worried look. "Promise."

The driver frowned and nodded affirmatively.

"And at least take that duster off and wipe your face. Please...throw away that filthy cigar; it's disgusting. I'm going to get our room and take a bath. That's what you need to be doing," Bess said.

"Kiss me, my love," Oldfield said with a cackle.

Bess playfully pushed her husband away.

Oldfield spat his cigar stub onto the street. Tossing his leather cap into his car, he pulled the duster up and over his head. Bess stepped away as Oldfield unfurled his duster and immediately produced a cloud of grit. He removed a towel from behind his car seat and wiped his face and hair.

Moross and Bess disappeared into the hotel entrance as Oldfield and Soules followed from several feet behind. Oldfield's eyes instantly widened upon seeing the trademark unruly graying hair between the nose and chin of John Walter Christie, the man joining him to thrill railbirds with their wheel-to-wheel dueling. At times it appeared Christie had no mouth at all. It was obfuscated from view by the thick and unattended patch of hair.

Christie was an elder among the drivers. At nearly forty-three, he was thirteen years Barney's senior. He had a reputation for being both brilliant and crazy, always experimenting with his car designs. Christie was famous for his behemoth front-wheel drive creations with the differential contained in a big, bulky casing at the front of the car that was about the circumference of a small drainage pipe.

Christie had raced in the French Grand Prix a few months earlier, and also the Vanderbilt Cup in '05 and '06. His car was powerful, fast, and never reliable. The critical thing to Oldfield was that it was such an odd-looking contraption, and so loud, it always attracted attention. Its speed, too, proved it was a man-eating monster.

"It's good to see you, Walt. Are you ready to give these Minnesotans some thrills?"

"Oh, I am sure that we can provide some drama for the masses," Christie replied. "I am glad to see you with the Stearns, it seemed to me the Peerless was getting long in the tooth."

"I had a lot of good outings with those Dragons," Oldfield affirmed. "Of course, there were others I'd rather forget. But yes, time marches on, so I sold them. I was thinking about quitting the game until Harlan Whipple called and pointed me to the folks at Stearns. The trip from Cleveland was a good test, and I want to take them up to that big derby at Briarcliff at the end of the month. I can prove to those bastard Swells up east that I can drive with the best of them."

"And well you can, Barney," Christie replied. "But this weekend is about theatrics, and you are a showman, to be sure. Our ventures have been lucrative and my business needs that for funding. Maybe someday you will be at the wheel of a Christie automobile."

"Maybe, but until then, I'm happy to drive in front of yours."

Christie shook his head to dismiss the idea.

"We take turns, Barney, we take turns," he replied.

Barney winked at Christie, revealing a big smile. Both men laughed.

(Briarcliff, New York, April 24, 1908)

"Go ahead and hit 'em, Charlie," Oldfield shouted. "They're goddamn vultures."

Charlie Soules marched around the one-hundred-horsepower Stearns racer swinging a small sledgehammer to put space between the machine and a hoard of clutching souvenir seekers. Oldfield stepped on the running board of his car, using it as his pulpit to shout at hundreds of people surrounding him.

Between warnings of, "Don't touch my fucking car," Oldfield looked at the column of twenty-two racers in front and behind him. All along the line, there was pushing and shoving as people closed in around the cars. Some sought to tear parts from the racers, while others intervened to stop them. The drivers and mechanics struggled, turning tedium into madness as they waited to be signaled into their single-file start for a two hundred-sixty-mile battle over a craggy, treacherous thirty-two and four-tenths-mile course through the hills surrounding Briarcliff, New York.

A man lost in the crowd shouted, "Don't worry, Barney, we'll stop these bastards!"

A Triple-A official wielding a megaphone scurried past the Stearns and the other cars shouting at the crowds to "gangway." Suddenly, a tall man swatted at Oldfield's face with an open hand. It barely touched his mouth, but broke his cigar. Oldfield kicked at the man, who was grabbed from behind by others.

In the chilly pre-dawn darkness, lantern-wielding officials weaved through the crowd. The fighters and general commotion jostled the illuminators and produced constantly changing shadows of bizarre contortions that made the moment surreal. Nearby, Oldfield saw the short, stout, and barrel-chested driver Herb Lytle scuffling with a spectator. Another onlooker grabbed the intruder from behind, and Lytle remained on guard.

Suddenly and above the din, Oldfield heard the familiar voice of Triple-A Starter, Fred Wagner. He, too, held a megaphone to his lips and shouted for people to stand aside from the racers. Behind him marched two columns of boisterous militia-marshals, pushing their way through the crowd and yelling, seemingly with delight, over their authority.

Wagner's army-style march, along with the hammer-wielding drivers and mechanics, proved useful as the crowd pushed back enough to clear the way for the cars. Just past five o'clock a.m., engines started to roar at the front of the field. In one-minute intervals, Wagner released the drivers into the competition.

Ernie Moross emerged from the crowd and the darkness to step up on the Stearns running board. Oldfield seated himself behind the wheel.

"General Pardington told the press there will be a control in a stretch of about two and three quarter-miles through Mount Kisco. I asked Pickens to camp out there. There are some tire and fuel depots on either end of the control. You have to stay there for ten minutes and can't work on the car, and they stop the clock on your race time for that stop. Everything else is set. You should be in good shape."

"We'll be in good shape when they get this derby underway," Oldfield said. "Thanks for the tips, I have to think right now, so leave me alone."

Moross patted his driver's shoulder and hopped down and melted into the crowd. With the guards still lining the starting area in front of the grandstand, Wagner walked from car-to-car, shouting instructions to each driver and his riding mechanic. Finally, he approached Oldfield, with Soules beside him.

"You got this derby under control, Wag?" Barney asked.

"Always," replied Wagner. "The Triple-A runs a tight ship, you know that."

"Is that what you call it," Barney replied with only the hint of a smile.

"Listen up, Oldfield," Wagner was quickly down to business. "Mr. Pardington just announced the race has been shortened to eight laps, not ten. You've seen the course, but

I am obliged to remind you it is treacherous and raw. You'll find narrow bridges, stone walls, and a generally rough surface with tree roots, crevices, and loose gravel. There is an active train track, and you need to pay attention especially hard until the sun comes up because there are boulders at the side of the road that can put your car out of commission. Art also decided to make about three miles at Mount Kisco village a ten-minute control, so the course is thirty-two and a half miles in total. You know what a control is, right, no work allowed on the cars, right?"

Oldfield showed Wag a deadpan stare and then acknowledged that he understood the control points were for safety and timing and that he would be stopped until ten minutes after his entry.

"Okay then," Wagner finished. "Fire this beast up, and I wish you the best of luck. This is your first big road race, but I know you're ready."

Wagner extended his hand to Oldfield, who had located a new cigar and clamped it between his teeth. He nodded and shook Wagner's glove. Soules was stroking furiously on the oil and fuel pumps as Oldfield flicked the spark lever, and the engine erupted with the robust sound of cannon blasts.

Despite his loud engine, Oldfield heard people cheering near him and wondered how many of them had earlier tried to dismantle pieces of his Stearns. Wagner stood at the tape, officiously waving a red flag to alert Oldfield the timing watches were on for him. He released his clutch and, skidding his rear tires, the Stearns fishtailed briefly before shooting forward. He jerked at his shifter and quickly rifled through gears to soon top fifty miles per hour.

With the sun peeking over the horizon, gentle orange light rays illuminated the undulating, winding road. Oldfield saw Montague Roberts, who started a Thomas a minute ahead of him, sliding through twisty curves. The Stearns bounced over a shallow crevice, and he felt the wheels lift and then crunch gravel as his racer closed on the car in front.

Soon, the railroad crossing loomed, and Roberts slowed. Oldfield gave his wheel a slight turn to the right and bounded over the tracks, again hopping off the ground. Soules's hand slipped off the fuel pump nob for an instant. The mechanic immediately recovered and resumed pushing and pulling on it.

The jarring ride continued through countless curves and only short stretches of straight road. Thousands of people lined the running surface wherever the terrain made it feasible to stand or sit. In several areas, tree limbs hung overhead, looking like skeletal hands in the distance as Oldfield focused on the road. Soon, the narrow wood-plank bridge over Murray's Creek appeared, and the driver tensed as he threaded a needle without reducing his pace. The boards protested ominously, several of them flapping and popping nails.

"Jesus!"

He continued to gun his big Stearns, sliding through the dirt and loose stones on curves until the control at Mount Kisco, where he saw men waving their arms and flags to alert him to slow. A giant banner with "Control" spelled out in huge, bold, black letters stretched across the road, suspended by two tall telegraph poles on either side. A throng of people, many shouting Oldfield's name, parted like the Red Sea and then closed in on the Stearns again. The unmistakably rotund and substantial form of Will Pickens waddled out from the horde. Oldfield considered steering directly at him to see him jump and run but thought better of it.

Pickens shuffled up to Soules' side of the car and yelled into the cockpit.

"How do you feel? I see you got around a couple of cars."

"She's really stout and fleet and hugs the curves. Who's leading?"

"That kid, Lewis Strang," Pickens responded. "He's leading, and by a bunch – probably a minute ahead of everybody already."

Oldfield digested the information. He didn't want to make excuses but also wondered about the speed of Strang's Isotta. *Was the kid that good?*

"Pardington dispatched some carpenters to repair that old bridge over Murray's Creek," Pickens added. "I hear tell it's falling apart."

Oldfield nodded and was more delighted to hear about the repair work than he let on. Flicking a wave to Pickens, he depressed his clutch and slipped back into gear. People waved and cheered as Oldfield crept through the village. Boys ran alongside and behind his car. Along the dirt road were clusters of wooden homes, a livery stable, a general store, and a small bank constructed of Portland cement.

At the Control exit, an official handed Soules a card that was a record of the time he came in the control area to indicate when the watches were stopped but would continue ten minutes later. A man with a Triple-A brassard on his arm stood to the side of the Stearns. He signaled with his fingers the minutes and then seconds until his release. With another wave of a red flag, Oldfield rolled forward and worked his way through his gears.

On the second lap, he rocketed up a small incline to the railroad tracks where he saw a man frantically waving a pair of yellow flags. The man jumped in a frenzy as if he was dancing to the whistle blasts of the approaching locomotive.

Knowing there was no way to stop his car from its full-pace without crashing, Oldfield jammed his throttle to the firewall. Soules showed no signs of flinching as he focused on pumping fuel and oil. The train's big engine ground to a halt, but its prodigious cow cutter protruded, blocking half the intersection.

Oldfield gripped his steering wheel and aimed at the narrow opening between the boulders at the edge of the road and the stationary behemoth. Suddenly the right rear of his car violently bounced as he clipped the cow cutter.

With a jolting thump, the left rear of the Stearns lunged off the ground. Within seconds the tire forcefully crashed back to the road. A vision of spokes cracking into splinters flashed through Oldfield's mind. He let up on his throttle and kept the machine pointed straight. His heart rate surged, but it was thrilling to feel the rear wheels finally grip the road, and he rapidly returned to speed.

His pace quickening, Oldfield melded into the Stearns and the road. Nuances of the running surface, with its ruts, varying mix of dirt and gravel, gnarly tree roots, and constant abrupt turns, were a part of him. He slithered through bends, driving with his throttle as much as the wheel.

Oldfield's heart surged to see the Italian Isotta of Hugh Harding as he steadily chipped away at the distance between them. Weaving at Harding's rear on a short stretch, Oldfield pulled around and was quickly half a car length ahead as they approached a sweeping bend at the intersection of Mount Kisco Road and Old Street. The spot could have been designed as a passing lane, and with his well-honed dirt track flair, he slid around the Italian car. Eagerly, the driver peered ahead to a subsequent set of curves. Like a rapid current of water charging through the meandering river, he overwhelmed the path before him.

Oldfield's charge continued on unabated until lap four when the Stearns began to chug and hesitate. With only that few seconds of warning, the engine fell silent as snow, and suddenly its driver was aware of the sounds of people along the course yelling.

"Shit!"

Soules glanced at Oldfield, and without speaking, he jumped on his seat and crawled on the back of the car to remove the gas cap. Reaching for the tool trunk at the rear of the vehicle, Soules cursed.

"You're not going to like this, Barney, but the goddamn toolbox is missing. I'm guessing the leather straps loosened when we hit that stupid train."

Stunned, Oldfield charged to the back of his racer. There he saw the leather straps dangling like a ribbon removed from a gift box.

"We've got gas," Soules proclaimed. "I can't measure it, but there have to be several gallons in the tank. I see it swishing around in there."

Both men dove at the engine cowling. With those leather straps removed, Oldfield's eyes feasted on the engine, scanning each familiar component in detail. Soules jostled spark wires, the battery, and the magneto.

Oldfield leaped into his driving seat, and, taking the car out of gear, he flicked the spark lever off and on, while Soules yanked at the crankshaft handle. The engine faltered and died.

"Well, we got spark," Soules said. "There must be something clogging the gas line."

Oldfield pounded his steer wheel. Reeling, he could not let go of how good it felt to command the twists and turns – and how fast he knew he was going.

Behind them, the explosions of a healthy engine grew louder. Harding's Isotta soared past. Oldfield jumped to Soules's seat and furiously pumped fuel. Soules stomped around to his side.

"I'm not sure that's going to help, Barney. Oh, Hell, without our tools, I don't have any other suggestions."

Painfully, nearly twenty minutes elapsed as the two men punctuated work at the fuel pump with attempts to start the silent engine. Finally, a promising chug, a sign of life, struggled into their ears. The engine erupted with a sudden, vibrant sound, and the two men cheered. Still, Oldfield couldn't muster his previous exhilaration after losing an unrecoverable amount of time.

He resumed his chase with vigor, taking solace in the idea that he had nothing to lose. Clearing everything from his mind, Oldfield locked his eyes forward to weave his racing line with impeccable precision.

Skidding to a stop at Mount Kisco, he saw the corpulent Pickens shove his way through the mass of humanity milling about.

"What the hell happened?" Pickens shouted.

"Gas line clogged, I think. We're guessing the goddamned toolbox fell off after we hit that goddamn train."

"Okay," Pickens responded. "I'll rustle up another trunk and some tools, so when you come around again, we can strap them on."

Nodding, Oldfield asked, "What's my position in the race?"

"Most embarrassing!" Pickens announced with a smartass cackle.

"Not funny, fat boy."

Oldfield shifted back into gear and rolled to the other side of the village. As the race progressed, he found his earlier speed, but the quest was hopeless. On the sixth lap, he felt a tire let go, and he skidded to a stop just off the road. Soules pulled a pre-mounted spare from the back, and the two men bolted the tire with its rim to the wooden wheel. Again, about eighteen minutes were lost.

When Oldfield charged onto the final stretch to the finish, he was greeted by hordes of people who had swarmed the course. Triple-A officials frantically waved yellow flags. Exhausted and feeling defeated, he did not care. It had been nearly six hours since his start, and his delays put him a lap behind the leaders.

Slowing, but determined not to stop, Oldfield kept the Stearns rolling at nearly twenty miles per hour to give people the choice of getting out of the way or being trampled by his wheels. People shouted his name, and he responded with half-hearted waves. Many also yelled, "Lewis Strang," for the man who won the contest.

Soules leaned up in his seat and then pointed with jabs into the air to the sign marking the Stearns camp. Creeping closer, they saw Ernie Moross waiting. Oldfield shut off his engine and rolled to stop in front of a white cloth Stearns tent.

"How are you feeling, Barney?"

"Okay," was all Oldfield gave him, not wanting to invest in a conversation.

Moross seemed to understand, but offered, "You had some hard luck out there, Barney, but people could see your speed. I was talking to John Wetmore. He's doing a great article for The Automobile newspaper. He said you really showed them today. Everybody wants to see you do more of these big road race derbies."

Moross's words made the driver smile if only faintly. He wiped his gloved hand across his grimy, oily, and dust-covered face. Moross extended his hand and said, "Good job, champ."

For the first time, Oldfield treasured a handshake with the little promoter, part of him wanted to make it last. He could make something of this day.

(Indianapolis, Fisher Automobile Company, June 7, 1908)

Heads buried in the Indianapolis Star, Carl Fisher, and Jim Allison sat across from one another at the table at the Fisher Automobile Company. The phone on Fisher's desk rang more times than he could count, but he had no interest in answering. The last thing he needed was more shit from Coots, Bookwalter, and anyone else.

"Prest-O-Lite is done in this city, Carl," Allison announced. "Are you reading that article about that fella Neukom calling a city council meeting tomorrow night? They want to run us out of town."

"If we fight it, we lose," Fisher said. "Blasting out the windows of the St. Vincent's Hospital Chapel was strike three. It doesn't matter; nobody got killed or even injured really bad."

Fisher paused, shaking his head. He hated being wrong, but he knew he was.

"I honestly believed that concrete and steel could contain any blasts. Hell, we damn near knocked down Coots' fire station next door. Chunks were shooting like missiles through the walls of that hospital, the goddamn fire station, and buildings all around."

Allison dipped his newspaper down to allow his stony face to peer over the top of pages.

"You got to know when to fold 'em, I always say. Besides, let's get this operation out of town. That location off Kentucky Avenue out near White River is pretty promising. That's far enough away we could detonate the building ourselves and not bother anyone in the city. I'm tired of people saying we don't care about human life, even our own employees. That's bullshit. We're making the charging process safer every day."

"Are we?" Fisher asked, not really expecting an answer. He thought about a fix on how to stop the constant criticism.

(Indianapolis, Fisher Automobile Company, October 7, 1908)

Inserting her head around Carl Fisher's office door, his secretary Margaret Collier announced that Mr. Trotter had arrived for their meeting. Lemon Trotter, no stranger at Fisher's office, hovered over the woman from behind, and immediately followed her inside. She retreated back to her desk in the open office area.

Fisher cast aside a paper map, nearly as large as the surface of his desk, of the west side of Indianapolis. He sprang from his polished wooden chair and swaggered to his portly friend for the manly greeting of a firm handshake.

Trotter was a welcome guest. He knew every acre of central Indiana, and that also meant he was well acquainted with extraordinary people. Real estate expert extraordinaire, Trotter knew their opinions, their proclivities, and much of the stuff no one would talk about in the company of anyone but the closest of allies. He was a big man, physically and financially substantial. His paunch both underscored his success and his age, as, at thirty-eight, he was four-years Fisher's senior and creeping up on forty.

"Lem!" Fisher announced with a full-throated volume totally unnecessary to be heard in his private office. Still, his booming voice served notice of his enthusiasm, his affection for a friend, for a man he respected.

"You ready to go look at some land?" Trotter inquired, knowing the answer. "I got about three-hundred and forty acres of nice, flat farmland you can build a circular parkway on."

Just days earlier, the two men had taken a business trip across the state line and into Ohio. The roads were typical Midwestern cow paths of dust, ditches, and rocks, with streams to ford. With his Stoddard-Dayton chugging up hills and boiling its water, Fisher cursed at each delay to replenish the radiator. One of his tires proved unworthy to the task as the rubber burst, and Fisher blasted a rapid-fire round of hearty expletives. Trotter helped his friend apply the spare wheel, and Fisher noticed he had let the barrage of cursing run on without interruption. That did not stop him from continuing.

Outside Fisher Automobile Company, its owner scurried ahead to his Stoddard-Dayton parked at the curb. He noticed that Trotter was several feet behind, sauntering along with no effort to match Fisher's frenzy. He was one of a handful of men Fisher let get away without showing some pep. Fisher scrambled into the driver's seat and shouted at one of the mechanics from his garage to turn the crank. The Stoddard-Dayton shifted its balance only just perceptively as the substantial form of Trotter settled into the passenger seat. The engine roared to life. On the road again, Trotter provided direction.

"Take Michigan Street out to Indiana Avenue and then turn left on Crawfordsville Pike. It's the old Pressley Farm, you know, right? It's about five miles northwest."

Fisher knew, but he didn't mind Trotter's instructions. He didn't want to admit he couldn't see the road markers and was happy to have Trotter warn him about an upcoming turn.

Autumnal leaves, mostly dead brown, on the road and at its side scattered and mounted to the sky as the Stoddard-Dayton stormed by. They moved further west, and trees grew scarcer and the road rougher as the men entered farmland that had been clear-cut long ago.

"Up here, Carl, this is the first vantage point I want to show you," Trotter said as he gestured.

They came to a halt near the railroad tracks. Trotter lumbered from the vehicle as Fisher bounded to Earth. With his back to the rails, Trotter pointed at the horizon across the expanse of a big farm field.

"This whole area is three hundred and twenty acres, divided into eighty-acre tracks," Trotter said, pointing to a structure in the distance. See that big old farmhouse over yonder? That's the only structure out here. It's a poor farm now. You got the Ben Hur streetcar line over there, and the Big Four rails could practically come to your doorstep."

Fisher extracted two cigars from his breast pocket and extended one to Trotter. He pivoted back to the car as he mulled over how to pitch the idea of investing to his favorite business partners. Stoughton Fletcher from the bank would be right. Allison, of course, and Newby. He already talked to those fellas.

Plucking a wood match from his pocket, Fisher placed his thumbnail on the sulfur tip and deftly flicked it to a flame. He sucked smoke into his mouth, and an orange glow brightened on the opposite end of the cigar. He motioned for Trotter to approach and use Fisher's cigar to light his.

"What do you think, Carl?" Trotter asked. "You're always bitching about the public roads, and you seemed downright depressed when you came back from that big concrete Booklands track over in England last year. You can swing it, what are you waiting for?"

Fisher slowly nodded his head and peered through Trotter like he was transparent window glass to soak in the expanse of the setting. He visualized gates, ticket booths, and a big grandstand out there in the field. He thought about a banner saying, "Speedway," not far from where he was standing.

"You're damn right, I can swing it," he shouted, not so much to Trotter but to the ground from which he would raise America's first superspeedway.

Chapter 21 – Balloons and a Speedway

(Indianapolis Gas Company, Northwest Avenue Near Fall Creek, October 30, 1908)

A large vermilion mushroom cap sprouted up from the ground near the massive fueling tank at the Indianapolis Gas Company. Carl Fisher studied the swelling bag, anticipating its one-hundred-ten-thousand cubic foot capacity. He glanced at George Bumbaugh, the man who, with his family, had stitched it together in his home that was primarily converted into a gas balloon workshop. They named it, "The Chicago," at the request of millionaire Charles Coey, part-time race driver, part-time aviator, and full-time sportsman.

Bumbaugh was frequently referred to as the Captain, although he admitted he had no military service record. Fisher gathered his friend liked the moniker and had shortened it to, "Cap," when he addressed him, more out of efficiency than a term of endearment.

Bumbaugh was burly and stout, taller and rounder than Fisher. He always wore a military-style cap, with a brim to shade his eyes, but not running the full circumference of his head in the manner of Fisher's floppy felt hat.

Fisher reveled as much in the horde of people that gathered to witness the inflating of his air vessel as he did in the grandeur of the immense red ball. His lips spread into a beaming smile and revealed teeth that clinched a cigar.

"There might be five thousand people here," Fisher said, nodding at Bumbaugh as ash tumbled from the tip of his smoke. "We should have sold tickets."

"I think you're going to sell a lot of cars once we pull this off. And Carl, you might want to put that fire-turd out before we blow everybody here to kingdom come."

Fisher dreamed up another spectacular, attention-getting stunt. This time he was attaching one of his Stoddard-Dayton cars to the balloon in place of the conventional wicker basket. Within minutes Fisher and Bumbaugh planned to take seats in the vehicle and attempt a flight over Indianapolis. He discarded his cigar and obliterated it with his boot.

When the vast bag of gas fully inflated, the two men swaggered to the Stoddard-Dayton. Both sank into the front seats of the vehicle, the balloon's rope controls dangling in front of them. Fisher was still working on his pilot's license, so every regulation of law and policies of the Aero Club of America required him to ride with an experienced pilot. Bumbaugh was nothing if not an experienced balloon pilot. His reputation for building and flying the old gasbags was known throughout America.

Glancing upward at the giant gas tank that loomed in their path, Bumbaugh shook his head. Fisher always listened to Bumbaugh's ballooning opinions. That was gospel.

"Even with no engine in the car, she's a real boat anchor. We could clobber that big old gas tank, and then God help us."

Fisher nodded, knowing that neither of them wanted the word to get out about the Stoddard-Dayton's missing engine. They had even pumped its tires full of the same gas that was in the balloon for more lift. He motioned to his assistant, Galloway, who rushed to his side.

"Galloway, rustle up some good men to give us a hand. We need some hefty manpower to take hold of some of these tow ropes and guide us clear of that gas tank tower."

Galloway nodded dutifully and was off in a flash. Within minutes the familiar faces of six men surrounded the vehicle. Bumbaugh instructed them to grasp several ropes scattered around the perimeter of the car and attached to the balloon above them. He told the men to slowly walk in unison, all the while pointing to Fall Creek.

"Prepare to get a little damp, boys. But we need to be on the north bank to be sure we don't slam into that gas tank."

The husky team performed remarkably well for having been assembled impromptu, especially as they waded through the stream with its abundant slippery flat rocks. Within fifteen minutes, they were across the water and in a launch position. Several hundred people also crossed Fall Creek just to stay close. Soon, the balloon and the attached car were released to the sky.

Fisher surveyed the area, taking in a panoramic view as best he could with his infernal vision. Thousands of people shrank progressively smaller, along with their cars, buggies, and bicycles. There was a mild breeze at about one hundred feet above the ground. Bumbaugh, studying his gauges, estimated that they were traveling six miles per hour. In the distance, even Fisher's dim eyes spotted the Soldiers and Sailors monument, the tallest structure in downtown Indianapolis.

Ascending still higher and drifting south, people and objects on the ground became almost indistinguishable from the general terrain. Fisher knew, though, the brilliant red enormous orb with a car dangling from it was still prominent to people below. They did not need to see him, but their ability to read the gigantic bright white letters that spelled, "Stoddard-Dayton," was paramount.

Eventually, Bumbaugh estimated that they had climbed to twenty-eight-hundred feet. The air at that altitude was surprisingly still. Fisher noticed the brim of his felt hat tapping at his forehead but never suspected it might blow away. Bumbaugh did what he could to find a meaningful current, but the atmosphere offered unrelentingly calm. After traveling about seven miles in roughly ninety minutes, the balloon captain suggested they descend. Soon, teams of people in all manners of conveyance entered the realm of Fisher's squinting eyes as they chased down his balloon.

The Chicago's dissension was painstakingly slow and to Fisher's liking. Within twenty-five minutes, they gradually sank to the ground. During that time, the Indianapolis businessman knew he was giving the hundreds of people and a handful of photographers who had followed him a memorable eyeful of his car and its mentally indelible brand name on the side of the balloon.

The wheels touched Earth with a pleasingly gentle bounce. People rushed the landing spot, and Frank Moore, who managed Fisher's automobile business, slowly parted them at the wheel of a second Stoddard-Dayton. He gave his boss a knowing nod. The men planned to swap the balloon with the car for an identical one Moore would arrive in.

Fisher jumped on his leather seat to punch at the air with his clenched fist.

"I'm here to tell you boys, this car is the first in all of history to fly over our grand Hoosier capital! We were in the air so high that the sun shone upon us much longer than it did on the ground beneath us."

The owners of astonished faces in the horde clearly hung on every word. The air travelers jumped out of the machine, and Fisher stomped off paces with authority. He continued his barrage of increasingly more enormous exaggerations intending to create distractions while his brothers Rolla and Earl joined one of Bumbaugh's assistants in unhooking car and balloon. Moore then backed his car away in reverse for several feet as the Fisher brothers pushed the other Stoddard-Dayton away from the landing spot. Moore then inched his car into generally the same place where the other had landed.

Some people were still entranced by Fisher's double talk, and others were distracted by efforts to anchor and deflate the Chicago. No one seemed to show interest in what Moore was doing with his car. A quarter of an hour passed, and Fisher wound down his colorful spiel. It was six p.m., dusk had given way to darkness, and it was time to drive back to the Fisher garage. Moore cranked at the front of his car until its engine came to life. Fisher ignited the Prest-O-Lite headlamps, as Moore joined him and Bumbaugh, taking his spot in the tonneau. The hundreds of enthusiasts who had scurried along to track the balloon jumped and cleared the way for the magnificent flying automobile.

(Horace "Pop" Haynes' Restaurant, Indianapolis, December 4, 1908)

Carl Fisher clutched his wool overcoat about his neck in a futile attempt to stave off the frigid December wind as he pounded his boots on the sidewalk as much to circulate blood into his ever-numbing toes as to pace off the steps to Pop Haynes' Restaurant. He burst through the double doors several minutes early for a lunch meeting with the men who agreed to partner with him in the Pressley Farmland purchase and race track construction. He liked to arrive early; he loved being first.

To his surprise, he saw Stoughton "Stoat" Fletcher, scion of the Fletcher National Bank family, clutching his bowler and appearing sheepish next to Fisher's usual table. Fletcher's face remained cherubic despite his twenty-nine years, but his thinning hair belied the passage of time. Fletcher nodded at Fisher and extended his hand for a grip. Fisher instinctively anticipated news he did not want to hear but held his silence to put the onus on Fletcher to speak first.

"I knew you'd be early, Carl, you almost always are. Honestly, I am a bit embarrassed, but I have some bad news. I can't make good on the real estate investment I promised. My family is against it."

"So, they are in the snob club of Indianapolis' high and mighty that think Carl Fisher and his friends are just poor boys with big ideas, eh?"

"Oh, Carl, it isn't that," Fletcher snapped, apparently relieved to have broken his news. "Dad told me to tell you that we will still make good on the construction loans you want if you still want to do business with us. It's just that they think having me involved isn't in keeping with the bank's image."

Fisher nodded and deliberately stared into Fletcher, who appeared to shrink.

"All right, Stoat. I guess there is no need for you to stick around. We will find what we need to purchase the land, and I will be back in touch with you about the loans."

The truth of the matter was that Fisher did not want to discard Fletcher. The bank loans he could arrange could come in handy.

Only a trifling of minutes passed before Allison and Newby arrived. Wheeler was last, but not particularly late. Fisher was already seated, cradling a shot of whiskey in his right hand. Wheeler pivoted his head as he dragged a chair across the wood slat floor and away from the table so he could sit down.

"Where's Fletcher?" he asked. "I thought Fletcher was coming."

"Come and gone," Fisher replied.

His colleagues studied him, apparently awaiting an explanation.

"There's not a lot to say. It seems his daddy spanked him and told him he couldn't play with us."

"Oh, well, that's just dandy," Wheeler pronounced. "And I suppose we're supposed to make up the difference? What is that, another twelve-thousand dollars on top of the fifty-thousand share we already discussed?"

"More like twelve-thousand-five-hundred each," Newby injected. "That's sixty-two-thousand-five-hundred dollars each unless we find another investor."

Wheeler furrowed his brow.

"Gentlemen, with the seventy-two thousand dollars required to secure the deed on the land, Jim and I talked to some friends in construction and came around to a conservative estimate of an additional one-hundred and seventy-thousand dollars to build the place," Newby continued. "That's if we agree to Carl's suggestion that we surface the track with crushed stone. Concrete, like they used out in Long Island, would be considerably more."

Fisher brushed his hand across the table, scooting plates, saltshakers, and cutlery away. He extracted an Allison Perfection fountain pen from the breast pocket of his jacket and began sketching on the tablecloth. With flair, he directed the implement across the white cloth. Soon, a rectangle with rounded corners took shape. Then he squiggled a line within the interior of the boxy-circular shape.

"The track should be five miles long, counting the curves going right and left in the middle. The circular course should be three miles around. I have already spoken to the world's top civil engineer, P.T. Andrews, in New York, through the long-distance telephone lines. I told him I would mail him our rough depictions of our vision of the racing facility. We will have him visit us in a few weeks, and he will survey the tracts of land we have and prepare his proposal."

"What, you're going to send him this tablecloth you're ruining?" Wheeler cracked.

Fisher frowned at his partner, rolled his eyes, and went on with his work. After illustrating the course, he began to fill in details. A smaller rectangle was, Fisher explained, a grandstand. Across from that on the other side of the front stretch was a square, he called a judges' stand. That facility would have the latest in telephones and telegraph equipment. There would be garages, bridges, and maybe an aerodrome. The corners, he added, "will be banked like Brooklands."

"Carl, you said you saw for yourself the Brooklands track was concrete with banking so high you couldn't walk up the incline," Allison challenged. "How will this track compare to that? Banking like that requires steep grades, which are a lot of work and materials. I don't see how what you are proposing will mount a challenge for world records."

Fisher shook his head, all the while frowning. He knew Allison could read him. His silence wasn't hiding anything from his partner.

"Our track is going to be the greatest in the world!" he asserted. "The fastest! It's going to be the first speedway."

The word, "speedway," hung in the air in front of him. He could swear the other three men saw it there too. Almost like they were of one mind, they nodded their heads affirmatively.

"Look, I may be the only man in America that has even seen Brooklands," Fisher announced. "We already have the greatest speedway in the world, we just have to build it!"

Fisher rolled the fingers of his right hand into a fist and brought it down on the oak wood table like a judge's gavel. The gesture surely proved the truth of everything.

(Fisher Automobile Company, February 8, 1909)

Park Taliaferro "P.T." Andrews stood like he was posing for a photographer on the Persian rug in the middle of Carl Fisher's office. He puffed on his pipe and hugged the gleaming brass spittoon, usually stationed beside Fisher's desk. Andrews paced off the half dozen or so steps to the meeting table and chairs occupied by the Speedway Company's partners – Carl Fisher, James Allison, Art Newby, and Frank Wheeler. Plunking the spittoon down, he sat in the chair provided to him, unclenched his yellow teeth, and removed the pipe. Lifting his left leg, he planted it on his right knee and began tapping his pipe on the heel of his boot. Spent ash cascaded from the bowl and into the spittoon.

Fisher studied the man rearranging his office. Carrying his spittoon around was a little odd, but odd never bothered Fisher. Despite several weeks of long-distance communication through every modern means, including at the speed of electricity with telephone and telegraph, he had only met Andrews the night before over dinner at the Claypool Hotel.

Fisher always looked for an honest man, a straight shooter with confidence. Too many times, men he met were boastful like they were trying to cover up for something they knew in their hearts they lacked. That's phony. Fisher saw some of that in Wheeler, but the man was a risk-taker, had money, and was therefore useful.

Andrews was another thing altogether. He was a contractor, and if their new company committed to him, they had to be sure there would be no surprises halfway through the project. What's more, Fisher wanted the best. He tried to not just listen to Andrews, but also assess his mannerisms, how he carried himself.

"P.T. and I had a nice long talk over dinner last night. It was casual, just to get to know each other. But now that we are down to business, I did not want to speak further without you gentleman involved in the conversation."

His pipe emptied, Andrews leaned forward and shook each man's hand. His grip was firm, and his eyes never blinked as he looked them squarely in the face. There were the perfunctory expressions of pleasure over making one another's acquaintance, and a brief exchange about the train ride in from New York. Andrews complimented Indianapolis on having a beautiful Union Station.

"Crossroads of America," Fisher remarked. "That's why it makes sense to have the greatest speedway in the world right here where the corn grows so tall."

Andrews nodded and then began.

"Gentleman, I have taken your conceptual drawings into consideration and surveyed the grounds where the track will stand. You have some fine, flat real estate, which is an asset. But I see you have announced intentions to have your maiden auto race around the fourth of July. I want you to reconsider that date and delay your debut."

"What?" Fisher exclaimed, his mind suddenly recalibrating his impressions of Andrews. "We can't do that. We need this place up and running. We need to see a return on our investment!"

"I understand, but the problem is you don't have enough time," Andrews returned. "You don't have a snowball's chance in Hell of getting done by July fourth, even if you work twenty-four hours a day."

"We can do anything, goddamn it!" Fisher insisted. "We'll get more men, more mules, and machines. It's essential to our business we get the track in operation."

Allison spoke up, pushing back on Fisher.

"Carl, listen to the man. He knows a lot more about the problems involved with this kind of project than all of us put together."

Apparently unfazed, Andrews started up again in a business-like tone. There was no hint of emotion over being challenged.

"Your biggest single problem is the creek at the south end of the property. That's no simple job a typical culvert will resolve. You're going to need to build a bridge over it. That takes time, especially since it is a confined space. It doesn't matter how many men, mules, or steam shovels you have, there's only a small number of them that will fit there before they start getting in one another's way."

He would never admit it, but Fisher felt the weight of Allison's stare. His throat tightened, and his temples pounded to the point of explosion. Fisher swallowed and tensed his grip on his chair's armrests. There was something about clenching the chair that helped him contain his frustration. Out of the corner of his eye, he saw Art Newby nod in agreement with Andrews.

"Move your first automobile races to August, at least, right after those motorcycle races you've been discussing," Andrews offered. "We will move Heaven and Earth to provide you with a useable track by then."

Allison, Newby, and Wheeler almost simultaneously nodded their heads and muttered approvals. Fisher scanned their faces, recalculating his timeline and finances.

"We don't need the track finished to conduct the balloon races, just enough grandstands to sell tickets," Allison inserted. "That puts us open for business in June."

Fisher had already figured the balloon contest into his hurried-up, silent calculations. He didn't bother to say anything other than to agree with Allison. Thinking he had enough of the meeting and that there was nothing left to discuss, he began to stand up from his chair.

"There's something else that's fundamental to this project we need to discuss," Andrews added. "It's about the circular track's length. I think we should scale back from the three miles to two and a half."

Fisher dropped back into his chair, shaking his head. *What now?* He hated sitting still and talking. Busy men get things done, talking men just talk. Andrews plunged one hand into his jacket pocket, his fingers busily squirming around under the wool weave. A second later, he extracted two pieces of carefully trimmed cardboard that reminded Fisher of horseshoes. Andrews then removed a folded piece of paper from his breast pocket and placed it on the table. As he positioned the cardboard U-shapes on top of the drawing, Fisher realized it was a scale model of the track that had been in his head for years.

"We could squeeze a three-mile track onto the real estate we have to work with," Andrews said. "But the shape of the grounds will force the track out to the edge of your property."

The two pieces of cardboard touched in the middle from opposite sides of the paper. The cardboard pieces extended out to almost either end of the model. Andrews then placed the edge of one of the shapes on top of the other and began pushing until it reached a straight pencil mark on the lower piece.

"If you want to give yourself room for growth, you better leave space to build more grandstands."

Andrews plucked a charcoal pencil from his breast pocket and quickly sketched rectangles in the space created by sliding the cardboard templates together.

"See those?" he announced. "Those are your future grandstands. Those are the seats people will someday pay money for."

Fisher's eyes absorbed the model, and his speedway became clearer like it was completed, and he walked the grounds. The word "growth" appealed to him. That was one of his favorite words. P.T. Andrews persuaded him that his track should be two and a half miles long.

(Fisher Automobile Company, Indianapolis, March 18, 1909)

Carl Fisher thought Ernie Moross, who scooted up to the edge of one of the chairs in his office, reminded him of a child trying to sit at the dinner table and reach his cutlery. It was his first formal meeting with the company partners, and Fisher was literally sizing him up. Along with Margaret Collier, his secretary, they squeezed around a meeting table with Jim Allison, Art Newby, and Frank Wheeler.

"Gentlemen, it is done," Fisher began. "We have filed our papers with the state, and this is the first official shareholder meeting of the newly formed Indianapolis Motor Speedway Company. I have asked Mr. Moross to join us because, as we all have agreed, we need a professional manager dedicated to overseeing the operation and promotion of the great speed plant we have envisioned. Margaret is capturing the minutes to meet our legal obligation in the event of an audit. She will keep us all pointed in the right direction."

Moross was no stranger to anyone in the room. His reputation as a ballyhoo genius for Barney Oldfield lodged his name in the minds of racing people across America. He cleared his throat.

"Gentlemen, I want to first say how honored I am that you have placed your trust in me to take on such an important role in this inspiring enterprise. We will waste no time in creating the facility and winning the hearts and minds of everyone in Indianapolis and throughout the automotive world. I have already commissioned a scale model of the rectangular, oval speedway on the grounds, just off Crawfordsville Pike."

Moross further shared that after the meeting, he would head downtown to Union Station to pick up America's top racing driver, Lewis Strang. Strang was to pose with the track model for photographers and newspapermen the next day.

Fisher nodded his approval.

"Ernie is a fine asset to our enterprise. He also has shared that his parting with Barney was most amicable. Mr. Oldfield is now the grandmaster of racing drivers and is a promoter's dream."

"He is at that, Carl," Moross replied. "And Barney is eager to help our efforts any way he can. As for Mr. Strang, he and George Robertson are widely viewed to be the top American race scorchers of the day. Between the two of them last year, they accounted for victories at most of the top auto races of the season – Savannah, Briarcliff, the Vanderbilt Cup, and the Fairmont Cup. I intend to have all these brave men and many others active at our Indianapolis Motor Speedway."

Heads nodded around the table with acknowledgments of "bully good."

Within a second, Wheeler waved an index finger.

"Please tell me there are no surprises after starting construction that the level of financing we have agreed to will change."

This time it was Fisher who scooted up to the edge of his seat to emphasize his prowess.

"You have no need for concern, Frank. As agreed, Jim and I are the senior partners with an investment of fifty-seven thousand dollars each. Your share, Frank, is the previously agreed-upon forty-six thousand, and Mr. Newby has agreed to invest twenty-five thousand. We have obtained thirty-six thousand in bank loans secured against the land from Fletcher National Bank for a total of seven hundred and seventy-two thousand dollars in capitalization."

Wheeler frowned at Newby.

"No confidence, Newby? Too rich for your blood?"

Observant that Wheeler had a habit of picking on Newby, Fisher reasserted his leadership in the room.

"Margaret, please note that our investment group appreciates the financial, time, and skillful contributions of Mr. Newby."

The secretary dutifully nodded her head, continuing to scribe. Fisher also asked her to record that the founding officers of the company included himself as president, Newby as first vice president, Wheeler as second vice president, and Allison as secretary-treasurer.

"We are setting a goal to have our speedway operational by August," Fisher asserted. "I am requesting an approved date with the Federation of American Motorcyclists for a motorbike race in August. Given our cash outlay, I have no intention of allowing the land to lay fallow until then. As discussed, we can commence generating revenue with a national championship balloon race by early June. Let the record show that I intend to take part in that competition with the assistance of Captain George Bumbaugh. Furthermore, my affiliations with Indiana Aero Club and the Aero Club of America, I am confident we will enjoy an exciting and profitable event."

(Indianapolis Motor Speedway, March 19, 1909)

Blustery kite-flying weather made ruddy the faces of Carl Fisher, Ernie Moross, and a cluster of newspapermen who huddled close to hear the impressions of Lewis Strang, the scorcher who had won so many races the year before. Strang gestured at Moross's model of the proposed speedway created on the length of ten square feet of ground directly behind him.

"This scale model clearly shows the intended length of the two stretches to be better than a half-mile," Strang explained. "The corners will be steeply banked so drivers can continue at speed with minimum braking."

George Bretzman, a well-established Indianapolis photographer, shouted to Strang to assume a studious posture near the model. Two other photographers, Ed Spooner, and George Grantham Bain scurried around Strang to put their backs to the sun. Patiently, Strang mustered up a thoughtful expression as he riveted his eyes on the model, bending over toward it to appear to be in thoughtful examination. He relaxed that stance and returned to a typical posture. The photographers busied themselves, capturing a variety of angles.

Fisher strode to Peter Paul "P.P." Willis of the Indianapolis Star to make a point. No newspaperman in Indiana had a better grasp of the automobile industry and motor racing than Willis. His ability to turn a phrase was almost poetic and always packed with insight.

"I have to hand it to you, Carl, you always think big," Willis said, shaking his head.

"Hi, P.P., I trust you are well. What are your thoughts about our big project?

"That's what I'm here to determine. I have no doubts that the speedway will be the world's greatest when you're done, but that August date seems ambitious. Do you really think she'll be in a suitable condition to conduct breakneck speed races by August? That's only about five months."

"We've commissioned with King Brothers Construction for over one hundred laborers, seventy-two mules, and three steam engine shovels to be on the job within days. I'll bring in more if need be."

Even while conversing with Willis, Fisher overheard Ed Spooner as he directed a question to Strang.

"Ernie tells me that you are the only American pilot to have driven the high banking of that Brooklands concrete track over in England. How do you think this project compares?"

Strang glanced at Fisher and Moross, who joined him, with Willis, in drawing closer.

"I think it compares very favorably," Strang began. "Standing here today, I am confident saying that all the Brooklands speed records will be crushed before this year is out. I also want to recognize Mr. R.H. Losey of the Losey-Buick garage right here in Indianapolis. A lot of my confidence comes from joining the Buick racing team for 1909."

Losey nodded and waved his hand as Strang continued.

"Mr. Losey can confirm that Mr. Durant at Buick headquarters in Detroit sends his greetings to Mr. Fisher and everyone at the speedway," Strang added. "He has instructed me to share with all of you that the Buick Motor Company is entering its full team in all events to which its stock and special racing cars are eligible. As I am sure you know, I have some very daring and skillful teammates with Bob Burman and Louis Chevrolet joining me."

Willis turned to Fisher, squinting his eyes. Fisher, preferring to talk than field a question, preempted the newspaperman.

"P.P., here's the deal. I expect this track to be two and one-half miles around on the circle with a road course connecting it so we can do road racing as well. This track will have the length and smooth surface to allow the factories to stretch their engines to the breaking point."

"Breaking point?"

"Sure. That's how you find a weakness in the construction. I intend to leave the gates wide open every day so the factories can bring cars here to test to their heart's content. This track is essential to the American automobile industry!"

(Indianapolis Motor Speedway, May 21, 1909)

Carl Fisher shouted so the other men in his Model K Stoddard-Dayton could hear him over the firing pistons in the car's engine. He couldn't stop talking about his new Speedway as he drove the rough surface of the track. At the end of the straightaway, Fisher slowed to a near stop. Peter Paul "P.P." Willis sat beside him, and behind them in the backbench were photographers Ed Spooner and George Bretzman. Trailing the Stoddard-Dayton were two Overland Model 30s, one with Ernie Moross driving and the other with Overland Vice President Will Brown at the wheel. All three vehicles carried a collection of reporters and photographers.

"Look at these beautiful, green grounds," Fisher exclaimed. "Isn't that inner area of clover fields brilliant? Churchill Downs has nothing on us."

The clover showed a vibrant, verdant hue under a cloudless sky. The field was radiant in contrast with the tall white fences around much of the perimeter of the property. White-with-green trim buildings had sprouted up like the cornstalks that had erupted from the very same soil in decades past. Fisher thrust his index finger at the structures on his facility, raving about restaurants, observation posts, billboards, garages, and the grandstands. His weak eyes could not bring the aerodrome near the north end of the course into focus, but he pointed in the general direction believing his passengers could see it. Fisher shouted about it as if it was as evident in his eyes as in his mind. There, he assured his guests, were several of the great gasbag vessels that would burst forth to the skies in June to compete for the national championship of ballooning.

Fisher settled back into his driver's seat and inched forward to the end of the straightaway to the point of the most significant construction commotion. He coasted to a stop to where the elevation increased for the entrance to the sweeping but incomplete turn. Gesturing out to the men, mules, and machines between turns one and two, Fisher assured everyone that the bridge under construction was nearing completion. It was necessary, he explained.

"This is our biggest challenge," he announced, pointing to a steam shovel surrounded by several mule teams and thirty laboring men. "We have a creek running nearly the full distance of the grounds. It crosses the track here, between the first and second turns to the circular track. We would have this whole speedway done if not for this."

The ponderous, mechanized shovel scooped up another hefty load of earth and pivoted to deposit it in one of several sturdy Oakwood carts. His passengers gaped in awe. It was evident that while all had seen projects like the downtown limestone Soldiers and Sailors Monument arise from piles of stone, this emerging cathedral of speed was another matter entirely.

After giving the men several moments to fill their eyes and pose questions, Fisher again returned to his seat and steering wheel. He shepherded his car to the bottom edge of the track, where it was most comfortable to navigate past the King Brothers crew. Charging down the backstretch, the white and green wooden aerodrome, looking much like a giant horse track stable, came into view on the left. Fisher assured the men that they would do another lap to stop for Spooner and Bretzman to take photos.

"Gentleman, we are approaching the third turn, and for today, this is our first high-banked turn," Fisher hollered. "Hold on, because I need to pick up speed, so we don't go sliding down the bank."

Fisher noticed Willis immediately clutched his leather armrests.

"Carl, are you sure this is safe?" the newspaperman challenged, his voice shaky.

The businessman smiled, taking some satisfaction over poking at the Indianapolis Star reporter.

"No faith, P.P.? I've been driving cars for a long time. Everything will be fine."

The Stoddard-Dayton accelerated to some forty miles per hour, and Willis clasped harder at his seat as he leaned to the left and into the turn. Fisher felt the tires trying to skid on the dirt and loose gravel surface. His passengers said nothing – as if they were holding their breath.

The running surface declined slightly at the exit of the turn as the Stoddard-Dayton bounded across an eighth-mile short stretch to the fourth turn. Fisher smiled as he peered over his shoulder to see that he had distanced himself from Moross and Brown. They entered the long front stretch, and he glanced at Willis, who had relaxed his grip on the sides of his seat.

"What do you think, gentlemen? Can you imagine this track once it's finished?"

Fisher answered his own question before Willis, and the others could speak.

"It'll be the greatest speedway in the world! We'll have all the world records!"

Fisher relaxed his foot on the throttle, and the Stoddard-Dayton began to wind down. The car crawled to a stop in front of the judges' stand. Green and white like all the other structures, it stood three stories.

"Right there, in that magnificent judges' stand, we will have telephone and telegraph lines to communicate to all corners of the Speedway and tell the world about all our races as they are happening. Set up your cameras, gentleman, this is our first stop on your picture-taking tour."

Spooner and Bretzman hopped out of the back seat, tripods in hand. Soon, the others from the Overland cars joined them, and all the photographers went to work, documenting what they knew would sell newspapers.

(Indianapolis Motor Speedway, June 5, 1909)

Barney and Bess Oldfield craned their necks to take in the gargantuan gas-filled passenger balloon that towered over them in the infield of the Indianapolis Motor Speedway. Its owner, Charles Coey, one of Oldfield's old racing buddies, claimed it was the biggest in the world. "Chicago" was emblazoned across the massive bronze-colored orb.

"Barney, this is as big as they come," Coey pronounced. "What you see here is one hundred ten thousand cubic feet of capacity. This is the mighty Chicago, and she stands as tall as an eight-story building."

Oldfield had no doubt that Coey's claim was fact, no brag. Everyone said this man was a millionaire. He owned the big Thomas Motor Company dealership and garage in Chicago.

"Damned if that don't beat all," he said. "Eight stories, you say!"

Coey nodded and started up again.

"She's so big the Aero Club of America boys won't allow her in their national championship main event. They say she doesn't fit regulations. They got her in a handicap trophy with two of the other balloons. I don't give a crap, I just want to get in the air and go sailing."

Bess tugged at her husband's coat sleeve, and he turned to see her pointing at nothing in particular, but the spectacle in general. The scene was like nothing he could recall. Nine huge gasbags tugged at their tethers as though they were alive, thriving, and eager for their leap heavenward. Thousands of people looking awed meandered through the zig-zag, random lanes between giant balls of yellow, sparkling white, brown, cream, and red. In the darkness of the previous night, the flaccid silk and rubber-coated cotton containers arose to glory as hydrogen gas from a network of pipes engorged them. They stood tall and proud, decorated with strings of pennants around their circumference. Flags hung from the wicker baskets soon to be occupied by daring pilots and their assistants.

"Thanks for bringing me, Barney," Bess said. "This is amazing. Why I think you should have to go to a World's Fair to witness this. It's another world, this whole place. It's so big, so modern."

Oldfield nodded his head in concurrence. When he arrived the previous day, Ernie Moross took him on a tour of the grounds. This Speedway, with its fifty-foot wide track, the steeply banked corners, and the dozens of buildings, garages, oiling stations, and grandstands, was clearly a twentieth-century complex. The champion dirt track barnstormer felt he was seeing the future. It was the ultimate shrine to track racing.

Carrie, Coey's young, beautiful wife, eagerly ran to Bess to embrace her bear hug style. She was a small woman compared to Bess, and full of energy with a beaming smile.

"It's wonderful to see you again," she said breathlessly. "Both of you. Isn't this exciting."

"Well now, little lady, I hear tale you had more excitement than this just a few days ago," Oldfield said with the smile of a teasing older brother. "Charlie tells me he took you for a trip through the clouds right here the other day."

Mrs. Coey blushed, but the smile never relaxed.

"It was so exciting. Why I never could think of how to pilot these big balloons like Charles does so masterfully! And to see this amazing new speedway from the sky! It's so big, so modern. The aerodrome. The grandstands. All these other beautiful buildings. It really is a new day!"

Oldfield smiled and nodded at the woman. Carl Fisher was good on his word. He could be full of ballyhoo, but here it was, the great track, the first true Speedway of America. Thoughts of going to the Vanderbilt Cup years earlier entered his mind. Yes, Fisher really had outdone old Willie K.

(Indianapolis Motor Speedway, June 5, 1909)

"Carl, your Speedway is a new wonder of the world," said Charles Glidden, the founder of the famous Glidden Tour reliability run. "What you've done here exceeds all the press agent reports."

Fisher inhaled a significant volume of air like he could snuff up Glidden's praise. For him, any compliment aimed at the Speedway was a personal plaudit, especially from an Eastern automobile man so favored by the Triple-A. He pumped Glidden's hand and told him he'd be honored to launch the next Glidden Tour from the new Speedway.

Glidden, at fifty-one, was sixteen years Fisher's senior, but both men shared a sense of mission to re-shape the world using the latest advancements in a new age of invention. With Alexander Graham Bell as his mentor, Glidden became a millionaire by building telephone companies and launching electrified communication across great distances.

Eight years earlier, in 1901, Glidden sold his interests in the telephone industry. He traveled to Europe as a motorcar pathfinder carving through the continent in a horseless carriage. Returning to America, Glidden was bursting to show everyone the power of the new transportation vehicles. Soon car companies throughout the nation poured their entries into the Glidden Tour reliability run.

Now Glidden filled his eyes with a new colossal Speedway not for the sake of automobiles, but for ushering mankind into the skies. He was an aviation enthusiast and an experienced balloon pilot. Fisher was sure the massive gasbags, having expanded like giant peacocks into a glorious mix of colors, fueled Glidden's imagination and sharpened his vision of a new world for a young century. It was essential for Fisher to recruit the enthusiasm of men like Glidden.

The blue-sky day with its pleasant jacket-weather temperatures made everything brighter in color and possibility. Giant balloons strained at their moorings and swayed with a soothing breeze that seemed to Fisher like a mother's gentle kiss. The only thing missing was for Ed Spooner to show up with his camera to take Glidden's picture to record the splendor. He snorted in another deep breath of perfect air through his nostrils. Glidden's voice brought Fisher back from a rare peaceful moment for his kinetic brain.

"So, Carl, I hear you just earned your pilot's license," Glidden said. "And today is your first race? Are you excited?"

Actually, Fisher had only completed his tenth and final ascent required for his international license just four days prior. He assured Glidden of his excitement, but also his confidence in his assistant. George Bumbaugh was a match for any pilot in a balloon, and he had flown with him more times than he could remember.

"I suspected we would find you two conspiring together," the booming voice of Alan Hawley turned the attention of the conversing men. Hawley was an expert balloonist and one of the founders of the American Automobile Association.

"Freeloading again, huh, Hawley...you old son of a so-and-so," Glidden said with a chuckle.

"You can go back to sleep now, Glidden," Hawley playfully returned.

Both men were lending a hand to organize proceedings, and when anyone asked Carl Fisher, he vehemently pronounced them and all the officials as the best in the business. Hawley played the role of an official judge, laying down the rules for pilots and assistants alike. Glidden was the event's official timer.

As the men clustered together, Fisher felt someone gently wrap herself around his right arm and then burrow her head into his shoulder. It was Jane Watts, a young woman eleven years his junior who seemed to have a habit of appearing at his side out of nowhere. Fisher was expressionless over the attention, but the truth of his heart was that he liked it. He did not want her to stop, but he was careful not to show enthusiasm. Glidden raised his eyebrows and then smiled upon Jane.

Clusters of onlookers – a mix of farmers, businessmen, their wives, and children – continued to swell around each of the nine balloons. All the while, everyone was wide-eyed as if they were walking through the wonder of a child's fairy tale. Growing with the horde was the din of human voices occasionally punctuated by a horn blast or whistle. Suddenly he heard someone close by shouting his name.

Photographer George Bretzman's goatee was the first thing Fisher's eyes recognized. The bearded snapper motioned for the men to move a little closer. Spying fellow aviator Charles Edwards just within arm's length, Fisher reached out and tugged his elbow.

"Come on, Charlie, let's get our photograph taken," Fisher said. "Us birdmen need to flock together!"

As Edwards greeted Glidden and Hawley, Fisher remembered Jane was standing quietly at his side. He turned and looked down into her smooth, innocent face.

"This is business, little honey. How about if you stand just to the side while we get this picture taken for the newspapers?"

(Indianapolis Motor Speedway, June 5, 1909)

The stark alabaster whiteness of A. Holland Forbes' big balloon New York was camouflage to Carl Fisher's straining eyes as he searched to distinguish it from the cotton ball clouds well over one thousand feet above. Fisher wanted to keep an eye on Forbes because everyone who knew anything about balloons was going around saying he was the favorite. It was paramount to get the best of the favorite.

Fisher scrambled into the big, substantial rattan basket he would share with George Bumbaugh for more than two days if everything went to plan. The light breeze wafted fine dust back at Bumbaugh's face as he poured sand out of bags to lighten their balloon,

Indiana, for their precisely timed 5:05 p.m. ascension. Snatching a bag from the side of the basket, Fisher emptied its contents. With each release, the Indiana tugged more determinedly to be set free. Nearby, a military band played the Star-Spangled Banner.

Beside them and just outside their basket Alan Hawley held a starter's pistol above his head, and Charles Glidden studied his stopwatch to ensure the accuracy of the interval between the New York and the Indiana. Rules of the event assessed performance for both duration of flight and distance covered. Given the puffed-up personalities of the men involved, accuracy was essential, or there would be Hell to pay.

Around the scene, soldiers gripped thick, rough ropes to mark off a distance to the balloons and restrain the crush of onlookers. Many shouted at Fisher, and he saluted and waved. Without warning, a bosomy, curvaceous woman in the bluest of satin dresses, too formal for the occasion, burst forward carrying a dozen long-stemmed vividly red roses. The blaze of color was undeniable, even to Fisher. Distracted with his launch tasks, he at first did not recognize her. Then it came to him.

Gertrude Hassler, the opera singer he had grown tired of as a paramour, was making her dramatic, stupefying entrance. Fisher had not set aside the time to inform her to his changed heart, but he sensed that she was worried over his coolness in recent weeks and was clinging to a role in his life that he had never fully granted her. He leaned forward and down as she heaved the roses upward to him in the basket. Hassler awkwardly clutched at his neck to kiss him, but only managed a tangential smear of red lipstick to Fisher's right cheek. A soldier approached from behind to politely but firmly escort her beyond the restricting ropes.

"Well, Carl, are there any other women in your life that we need to wait for?" Hawley chortled. "I will fire this pistol in less than a minute, so the next lady is going to have to be quick."

Fisher disposed of one more bag of sand. He glanced at Bumbaugh, who said nothing, but smiled and pointed upward to the sky with his right index finger.

Hawley's blank exploded, and the Indiana's two pilots released the ropes to the basket that tethered them. The balloon swiftly mounted to the sky as if it had been eagerly anticipating its emancipation from Earth.

The unanticipated roses suddenly fit into Fisher's ascension plan. He began casting them one by one into the gathered spectators below. People scrambled like refugees fighting over morsels of food spilled out into a street. While the roses cascaded downward, Fisher scanned the grand vista of the giant track he had willed into existence. Laborers swung picks and shovels alongside mules, two-ton rollers, and steam shovels, and it all moved with synchronicity worthy of stage play choreography. The laborers remained clustered at the south end as they had for weeks, busily assembling the bridge that spanned the wide culvert they had dug to channel the relentless creek.

Now five-hundred feet above, the new vantage point revealed that the entire grounds contained a small assemblage of humanity that felt deceptively suffocating at ground level just minutes before. The grandstand held a scattering of spectators.

The shingled rooftops of bright white wood plank garages, oiling stations, the restaurant, were all in place on the forty-one finished structures. In the distance, the judges' stand to the west and the magnificent aerodrome near the backstretch facing east were substantial and faultless in the full-dress of snowy white with green trim. The stand of trees at the north end exulted in the soft greenness of their young spring leaves. The clover shared that fresh color and texture, as the ravages of the coming summer sun had not yet baked them into maturity. Instead, the Hoosier rays of early June soaked everything Fisher could see in resplendent vivid illumination. For a moment, his frustration over the lack of spectators fell away as the view demonstrated his great Speedway was more complete than not.

Rapidly the Indiana floated directly over the grandstand and roses streamed from its basket. People scurried through the bleachers like they were chasing a foul ball at an Indianapolis Indians baseball game. Surmounting the stands, Fisher widened his eyes as Crawfordsville Pike and the tributaries feeding it came into view. The hordes of people he had expected to purchase tickets and enter the gates of his new palace were now clearly visible outside the confines with staked-out vantage points and improvised seating.

Automobiles, cabriolets, ordinary buggies, and farmers' wagons lined the road. Spectators stood on them, and several wagons had kitchen table chairs in their beds where people were comfortably taking in the spectacle of the balloons. Fisher flashed a glance to Bumbaugh, who simply shrugged.

"Jesus Christ on a bicycle! You put on a show for people, and they take advantage of you."

Several farmers constructed makeshift refreshment stands where they sold God-knows-what, food Fisher couldn't make out. Whatever it was, the whole situation exasperated him.

"Jesus Christ on a bicycle! They're a bunch of poachers down there."

Bumbaugh leaned toward his partner and tugged at his coat sleeve. Fisher turned and followed his co-pilot's pointing gesture to a higher altitude spot where the New York's name, blazoned in black on the shimmering white balloon, was barely visible against the fluffy, obfuscating clouds. Fisher spun around to scatter a stream of sand into the current.

"Easy on the sandbags, Carl," Bumbaugh shouted. "That stuff can be like gold later. If we shoot our load now, we won't be able to make her lighter when we need to."

Fisher closed the bag but continued to look upward at Forbes. He knew height was not the metric of success, just speed, and duration. The job was to find the best air current at whatever altitude. Old Cap was right again.

The barometric gauge steadily ticked down, and at thirty inches, Fisher knew they were at roughly one thousand feet. The Indiana continued its climb to three-thousand feet, and from that height, the comprehensive panorama of the Speedway's glory grew smaller in the distance. The sight heightened Fisher's queer sensation that always overcame him when ascending in a balloon. The Earth and everything he knew seemed to slip away from him. The sky was a new world without limitations or grounding. A man could do little to control his destiny because, in the clouds, he was subject to the currents, the weather, to nature's insensate whim.

For miles around the Speedway in every direction, crowds on foot and in automobiles tried to follow the Indiana. Many of those in cars gave chase apparently to see how long they could keep the lofty globe in view. They were confined to the necessities of the terrain, roads forcing them to slow, to turn, and to take a more meandering course than a crow could fly. Fisher suddenly became aware that Bumbaugh was studying him.

"The roads of the sky are not beset with turns and curves, bridges and hills," Bumbaugh announced. "You don't meet passersby and have to slow to let them pass. Here we have wind and limitless space, both beautiful and sometimes terrifying."

The Speedway passed from view in the Indiana's basket, but all eight of the other balloons, each released at five-minute intervals, were well into the sky and visible. Fisher and Bumbaugh rose to three thousand feet, where they found a wind current that ushered their vessel along. Gradually, all the competitors dispersed in various directions depending on the vagaries of the wind at their respective altitudes. By 6:30 Fisher and his partner were alone in the sky, rising to eight thousand feet where it seemed even birds dared not to venture. The sensations were not entirely unlike the embrace of the wind from a sailboat skimming over calm lake water.

Fisher was calm now as the annoyance of the poachers at his Speedway diminished in his mind. The distraction of the sensuality of his ballooning experience relaxed him. He fell into one of his rare trances, where he felt a kind of infinity to a moment and oneness with everything.

"*Man has never really lived until he has floated high over the terrestrial ball*," he thought.

A crescent moon in the clear sky proved insufficient illumination to see the ground, but only occasional clouds and the confines of the Indiana's basket. The brush of the wind overcame the silence so appropriate as the darkness lured the Earth to sleep. Far enough from Indianapolis now, there were no city or town lights to provide evidence the planet had not disappeared into a mysterious abyss.

Bumbaugh jarred Fisher back to reality with a nudge on his shoulder. He thrust forward a sandwich layered with steak and lettuce and partially wrapped in wax paper. Fisher grasped the food and deftly directed it to his open mouth. The steak was a little chewy, but rare, which was his taste. The sliver of the moon and a sky dotted with stars were like diamonds on black velvet.

"This is why I do it, Carl," Bumbaugh mused. "The skies are kind tonight. This is as peaceful as a sailboat on a smooth lake. There are times when mounting the wind keeps you so busy you don't have a moment to think about anything but escaping its peril."

The carrier pigeons in the basket at their feet fluttered their wings and caught Fisher's attention. Their job was to communicate with a world now so remote. Among Hawley's admonitions was for pilots to use the feathered creatures to carry messages about the time and location of specific vessels.

Indiana. 8:15 pm. Entering Brown County air space.

Extracting the birds from their cages of sticks and twine revealed their distinct lack of enthusiasm – more like terror – about taking to the air in the dark from eight-thousand feet. Released, they ventured no further than the edges of the wicker basket. Fisher went to one of the birds and, grasping the ball of gray and white feathers, perched it on his left index finger. Little feet clasped so tightly to his skin, he thought it could draw blood. Warm piss trickled from the terrified diminutive creature and ran over Fisher's hand.

"Shit! This thing's pissing on my hand! Okay, it's back in the cage with you!"

Without saying a word, Bumbaugh reached into a box and extracted a small loaf of bread and a paper bag. He deposited another message of location and time. In one deft motion, he tossed the wireless signal over the basket.

Hawley had prevailed upon the newspapers from Indiana to Florida to alert their readers that carrier pigeons and paper bags with bread loaves would sail from the skies .with valuable information about the whereabouts of the brave pilots. Prizes were promised for those retrieving the messages and ushering them to the nearest newspaper office. The papers trumpeted the excitement and drama of the race in the clouds. Readers were eager to savor every detail.

"We should balance up for the night, Carl," Bumbaugh announced.

Sunset had brought on the inevitable cooling of the air, and this congealed the buoyant gas in the balloon to bring on a sharp descent if no ballast was dispensed. The pilots settled on the release of forty-five pounds of sand. Shedding too much weight might send the big bag shooting in a terrifying, uncontrollable rush to the upper regions of the atmosphere.

"I'd be pissing like that damn pigeon," Fisher said.

Their work complete; the men began considering shifts for slumber and vigilance. Despite the dim light of the moon, Forbes came into view again at about 1 o'clock. He had apparently abandoned the southwest current. They had last seen him riding to drift back to the southeast flow. Bumbaugh estimated the balloons were traveling at about ten miles per hour.

At dawn, the Hoosier came into view, but Forbes' New York had disappeared. Fisher leaned on his basket's edge, watching the sunrise from an advantaged height. Small streaks of light began to steal over the horizon. Relaxing his weight on the rattan, Fisher was enchanted by the glory that was unfolding below him. The entire world had awakened. The grand expanse of the Ohio River came into view. The pigeon, so nervous before, was delighted to be released into daylight.

Without warning, the distinctive pop of long rifle reports originated from somewhere below. Hunters and farmers embedded in the rolling foothills of the Southern Indiana woods most likely believed the ball in the sky was an errant circus balloon now only worthy of target practice.

The volleys continued for hours. After passing the sight of one shooter, another commenced as if on a relay team. While the gunfire was unnerving, the Indiana was most likely out of each shooter's range.

The pilots began to toss confetti into the air to find a swifter current. The Indiana settled at ten-thousand feet; the men pleased with newfound speed. This continued for two hours until, without warning, the current dissipated, deserting them some forty miles from the point where they had been over the Ohio River. The air was still. Bumbaugh had worked through the night to ready their balloon. He now drifted to sleep while standing up, leaning on the edge of the basket with his arm hugging a stay rope.

With Fisher pouring more sand, the Indiana was able to ascend two-thousand additional feet. At twelve-thousand, five-hundred feet, they found a current blowing eighteen miles per hour. By Sunday noon, the pilots drifted back above the spot they had abandoned the previous day. The price was hours and wasted ballast. Fisher silently studied his partner and fought back his anxious emotion to blame him. Cap was a good man, though, and a friend. He resolved to swallow his frustration and keep his mouth shut.

The Indiana sailed on, but its lofty altitude created new challenges. Above a full cover of fleecy white clouds, the sun bounced its thermal energy back to the pilots after already baking them on the way down. Fisher's tongue was dry and felt thick. He kneeled to twist the cap of one of their metal cans of water. He tipped a sample into a cup, but when he pressed it to his lips, he immediately spat.

"Oil! Goddamn motor oil is in our water. We can't drink this shit!"

Bumbaugh ambled over to the other two cans, opening them and repeating Fisher's tasting process. He shook his head and offered the speculation that the person providing the cans didn't realize they had been used to store mechanic's oil.

The Indiana continued to drift southeast, and its occupants saw the Village of Shackle Island, Tennessee come into view. Fisher began to release gas from the balloon to allow it to descend to about two hundred feet. Curious onlookers emerged from their homes and shops to soak in the strange sight. Bumbaugh lashed a wooden bucket to a rope and slid the hemp twine through his hands and slowly downward.

"Water! Water, please," both men shouted.

They were now close enough to the ground that they could shout to the people there – and be heard. They quickly learned from the people that they were over Northern Tennessee. Two men dutifully untied the rope and ran to a nearby well. As Bumbaugh pulled the line that had been re-attached to the bucket upward, he glanced at Fisher.

"You're not worried about being disqualified?"

"We didn't touch the ground, did we? Besides, I'm more worried about dying of thirst. We need this damn water."

Expending more valuable sand, they rose to six-hundred feet, hoping for a southeasterly current. Fisher had a vision of traveling some five-hundred-fifty miles south to the Gulf

Coast. Without warning, the Indiana commenced spinning around. It shot straight upward. Fisher, his heart pounding like it wanted to crash through his breast bone and ribs, fell to the basket floor, all the while searching Bumbaugh's face for an answer. His mentor grabbed at stay ropes to balance himself long enough to read the barometer.

"Eddies," Bumbaugh announced. "Eddies like I have never seen before!"

Fisher stumbled to his feet as the air current shot them straight upward. It was blowing so hard he surmised from the barometer that they might be ascending at a rate of eight-hundred feet per second.

Bumbaugh, panting, shouted that he had never seen anything like the vortex they were trapped in. As they climbed steadily through the atmosphere, the air became frigid. Fisher could not control his teeth from chattering as he stared at the barometer with a sense of panic.

Twelve-thousand feet!

The unrelenting surge compelled both men to grab coats Bumbaugh had packed, just in case. Their advance had continued with no release of ballast, and as they climbed, the gas congealed, producing a vapor that looked like campfire smoke. Nothing in Bumbaugh's cumulative experience of three-hundred ascensions had prepared him for this situation.

The balloonist's eyes shot upward to fix on the balloon. Terror swept over his grimacing expression. Like a bubble ready to burst, the sphere's diameter swelled at an alarming rate.

"This damn thing is going to explode," Bumbaugh cried out. "We have to release some of the gas!"

He seized the valve rope to ease the accelerating pressure. Knowing that they could be dashed to their deaths if too much gas was discharged, Fisher locked in on his mentor's hand. He swung around the center of the basket to inspect the barometer. The reading indicated they were at fourteen-thousand feet, but within minutes it was clear they were in descent. An involuntary sigh emerged from his lungs that surprised him.

"If I was a praying man, I'd thank God."

Both began dispersing six bags of sand to the winds. Like casting gold dust into an ocean, they had to lighten their vessel to check the drop-off from releasing gas. Far from a plummet, though, their downward pace was so slow Fisher could barely see their instrument's needle moving.

Houses in Cumberland Valley finally came into view, and for Fisher, the sense of being near the Earth again was a comfort. Leaning his elbows on the side of the basket, he let go of another sigh. The thumping in his chest had subsided.

With no warning, the Indiana began to spin violently once more. The air rushed past them, casting Fisher's hat backward.

"We must get out of this," Bumbaugh shouted. "We can't afford more gas and ballast!"

Zeroed-in on the barometer needle, Fisher marked with relief that when they arrived at nine-thousand feet above the world, they leveled off. Within minutes measured dissension commenced, and at eight-hundred feet, the balloonists worked to level off their vessel.

"I'm not ashamed to admit I am an exhausted nervous wreck," Fisher shared. "I don't have any stomach for more shooting the chutes of the clouds. Let's drop a rope and try to anchor to the trees."

The men slid their four-hundred-foot rope over the side of the basket, and it tumbled down into the tops of a large clump of hardwood trees. In tangling with the branches, it slowed their progress. The Indiana drifted southwest, and by morning they had covered thirty-five miles to arrive over Island City.

"I want to land this rig," Fisher said.

"Ready to throw in the towel, Carl?" Bumbaugh asked as if he was skeptical of Carl Fisher quitting on anything.

Fisher felt like he had survived a deathtrap. Below they spotted a cluster of colored plantation workers and began to hail them. The laborers appeared reluctant, apparently disbelieving their eyes. Finally, three of them latched onto the rope, pulling the balloonists closer to the point of nearly kissing Mother Earth. Bumbaugh tapped Fisher's shoulder and pointed to what appeared to be a tall pile of railroad ties.

"Ask them if they can pull us over there," he directed. "I feel better about that pile as a landing platform than this terrain. Let's try to avoid damaging the basket."

The Indiana, at last, landed on the ties. Fisher leaped over the basket and crawled down to the ground. He had a cigar in his inside coat pocket and was aching to smoke it. His legs felt unsteady as he negotiated the plowed dirt in the direction of an appealing shade tree. There Fisher collapsed to extract his cheroot. A flame sparked as he flicked his wrist to scrape a wooden match on the sole of his oxblood boot.

Bumbaugh shrugged and also climbed down to the workers. Bringing two buckets, he asked if they had a brush to scrub them. Fisher puffed and smoke ascended over and past his eyes. Bumbaugh appeared as if in a fog as he meandered to a well to replenish their water. Extracting his cigar from his mouth, Fisher called out to his friend.

"I want to go back up."

Apparently incredulous, Bumbaugh pivoted beside the cobblestone well, directing his eyes to their balloon.

"You're joking, right? We landed, Carl, our race is over."

Fisher shook his head and began rambling about extenuating circumstances that might enable them to argue that they should be given an exception. He knew he was talking faster than he could think. Fisher had not sorted out his thoughts. Rooted in emotion, the foundation of his argument vaguely rotated around the outrageous atmospheric vortex he would insist had nearly taken their lives.

"It's not going to work, Carl," Bumbaugh said. "But if that's what you want, okay. I will always look for any excuse to fly."

The pilots returned to their basket, and one of the farmhands released the rope that moored the Indiana to the massive, creosote-soaked lumber blocks. All the black workers halted their labors to gawk at the strange, giant ball. They remained in place, gaping upward as the two men again ascended.

"Carl, we don't have enough ballast to ride through the night. I think it best if we continue on to sometime around dusk if we can."

"That's okay, Cap. The way I figure it is that if we deduct thirty minutes from the time we landed in Island City, we'll be about forty-nine hours in the air. That should put us well ahead of Forbes or anyone else for the duration award. I'm sure we won't win on distance because of the time we spent backtracking in Southern Indiana."

Bumbaugh rolled his eyes and shook his head. Fisher guessed he was privately debating on whether he should say anything.

"C'mon, Cap! Out with it."

"It just doesn't work that way, Carl. The first time we paused to get drinkable water was the end of our race. And then when we landed on those railroad ties, well, there's no talking your way around that, I don't care if you are the president of the Indiana Aero Club."

The Indiana drifted into the mountainous terrain around Tennessee City, gradually descending as the buoyant hydrogen seeped from its giant container. The pilots traced the ground with their eyes and finally found the clear-cut acreage of a family farm. Bumbaugh timed the approach and pulled the valve rope to release more gas. Two girls rushed from the farmhouse, and, after looking upward at the ominous orb, screamed and ran back in.

The girls again ran outside, gesturing and looking all about on the porch. One of them grabbed the rope of the dinner bell, clanging with high energy apparently to attract men working in the fields.

Fisher cast their mooring ropes over the side of the basket, and, pressing his megaphone to his mouth, shouted to the teenagers to run to the nearest tree and wrap the end portions of the rope around the trunk several times. By this time, the girls seemed calmer, and the Indianapolis businessman guessed that they recognized he and Bumbaugh as too harmless white men and their fears had abated.

A sturdy-looking man with a thick beard appeared with two younger men. Fisher's guess was that the man was the girls' father, and the two companions were probably his sons. Four other men charged forward to the scene. Soon the Indiana's basket lay among some shrubs on the ground. The balloon deflated, and all the strangers seemed delighted at the opportunity to assist in folding the silk bag to a size that would fit a wagon bed.

"Damnation," exclaimed the farmer who shared that his name was Burgess. "I never saw such a balloon that people could climb into. Hell, we thought it was just a stray circus balloon. We had our long rifles cocked and ready to have at it."

With the Indiana packed in the family wagon, Burgess was agreeable and happy to take everyone and everything into Tennessee City, some ten miles away. They rambled and bounded along rocky paths and descended into a valley where they found a place to camp at half-past ten o'clock. The following morning it was a tramp across seven hilly miles to the town. There, Fisher found a telegraph office and discovered the race results had already been posted. Somehow the officials had learned of the Indiana's mid-race descents to the ground and issued a disqualification. Pilot John Berry and his assistant Paul McCullough had been declared the big winners with their St. Louis balloon, dubbed University City. They landed on Lookout Mountain near Fort Payne, Alabama.

Chapter 22 – Motorcycles

(Indianapolis Motor Speedway, July 29, 1909)

A solitary indigo dot emerged from turn four of the Indianapolis Motor Speedway to storm down the homestretch. Carl Fisher squinted to see its swelling color and shape, but the increasing decibel level of blasting pistons was all the evidence necessary to foretell of its approach. Fisher turned his head slightly askew to steal a furtive glimpse of the man at his side, Peter Paul "P.P." Willis' face, all the while searching for clues about the newspaperman's impressions. The Indianapolis Star reporter's eyes fixed on the approaching midnight-blue National Motor Vehicle Company car driven by the company's star driver, "Happy" Johnny Aitken.

The lusty engine sound grew ever louder and then dampened as it again shrank in the distance during the quarter-mile charge into turn one. A cloud of engine smoke and track dust hung in the air before them, but none of the men were fazed by the haze. Art Newby, vice president of National, examined his stopwatch.

"Two and a half minutes," Newby announced.

Willis furrowed his brow and turned back to Fisher.

"Well, a mile-a-minute is still some get up and go, but this is supposed to be the greatest track in the world. Aren't you expecting speeds up to around one hundred miles per hour?" Willis challenged.

Fisher acted nonchalantly but privately was disappointed. He did not want Willis walking away to write any crap about the track not being up to snuff.

"This is all just a test, P.P." Art, here, wants his cars shook down for the races next month, and we all want to see how the track holds up under the scorching of powerful racers. We just invited you out here to be a part of the first laps of the track at speed."

About three minutes later, Aitken again appeared, this time slowing down to join his boss and the other men in the pit area in front of the judge's stand. Newby and two of his younger drivers, Tom Kincaid and Howdy Wilcox, dashed to the side of the parked car.

Willis scanned the immense Speedway and then locked eyes with Fisher. Bending toward the ground, he filled his hand with a large rock and stood up to display it on his palm.

"I've told you before, Carl, you and your boys have done a yeoman's job pulling this speed shrine together just since April. But let's be honest, this track looks like it needs more work. Do you really think it will be ready for scorching speeds in just a couple of weeks?"

Fisher paused to contain his frustration. Still, he saw in Willis' expression that his own tone of voice belied his real feeling. Nonetheless, look 'em in the eye and show only confidence.

"Of course, it will be ready. We will spare no expense to get it right. This is the greatest Speedway in the world. You have to know that, Willis."

Willis smiled and raised his eyebrows, nodding in a slight, almost undetectable manner.

"Relax, Carl. I'm not going to write anything bad about your Speedway. All of Indianapolis wants this place to be successful. I've seen a lot of racing, I've seen a lot of cars. I hope what I say is useful, that's all. I look around, there are a lot of rocks like this one that needs to be crushed and smoothed out. The surface is lumpy. Heavy cars might be able to handle this, but I don't know about those motorcycles."

Fisher gently patted Willis' shoulder. He knew the best way to get good press was to show men like this newspaperman respect and be thoughtful about what they say. Together they stepped to the side of the big National. Aitken with his lanky, lean form climbed out of the car, and after conferring with Newby, Kincaid, and Wilcox appeared to understand that Willis needed a quote.

"The Speedway looks pretty bumpy out there, Johnny. Did it give you any trouble?"

Aitken's ever-present smile stretched the thin, dust-coated grime that had started to build on his face.

"Nah, Pete. This is all just standard procedure testing. Yeah, the track can use some smoothing, but I know Mr. Newby and Mr. Fisher will take care of those details. Before they're finished, Indianapolis will have the fastest Speedway in the world. I hit it up today, but nowhere near what this National will admit. Besides, what you have here is a true stock car, not some freak machine. It's our new sixty horsepower touring car, and anyone with enough greenbacks can buy it."

Willis scribbled on his notepad.

"What about the motorcycle boys, Johnny? Don't you think the big cars will do better on this track than those little light bikes?"

Aitken again flashed his toothy grin.

"That's something you're gonna have to ask those fellas, I don't know much about those motorbikes. But I will tell you this, those boys know what they're doing. They're the best there is. I'm sure they will do just fine."

(Indianapolis Motor Speedway, August 2, 1909)

Carl Fisher slammed the door of his Stoddard Dayton Model K roadster and scurried down the pit road of the Indianapolis Motor Speedway in the direction of two men standing with Ernie Moross. Fisher was not in a hurry because of any concern that he was late to a meeting. It was just another goddamn thing he had to squeeze into an overstuffed day. Charles Wyatt, president of the Indiana Motorcycle Club, and the group's vice-president, Harry Dipple, had their heads down with hands in their pockets, studying the ground.

Wyatt and Dipple craned their necks upward as Fisher approached. Hands extended, and the perfunctory grips, shakes, and greetings of, "good to see you," were exchanged. Fisher gave Ernie a nod just to let him know he was acknowledged. The men all wore white linen suits in deference to penetrating rays of the sun and the eighty-eight-degree temperature. Fisher removed his wide-brim felt hat and mopped his forehead to sop up streams of sweat.

"What do you think, gentlemen?"

Wyatt and Dipple, seemingly uncomfortable, glanced at each other. It was as if they were hoping the other one would speak first.

"Come on, gentleman. Out with it."

Wyatt cleared his throat and took a step, so the bright sun was not directly in his eyes.

"Well, Mister Fisher, we have some concerns."

Fisher studied Wyatt's face. The man may have been the far side of twenty-five, but he looked to be about seventeen.

"You do, huh? So, are you going to tell me? I don't like to guess what people mean."

"Well, Mister Fisher, it's like this. Harry and I – and it's not just us, a lot of the local riders, too – are concerned. We're a little worried about the track conditions."

"Look here, what you are standing on right here and now is the finest Speedway in the whole goddamn country. You can take that to the bank."

Fisher glanced at Moross, who stood dutifully to his side.

"It's just all these loose stones, Mr. Fisher," Dipple inserted. "A lot of them are rocks, really. The fellas are liable to fall because we expect the stones will shift around quite a bit. We figured all this would be crushed into a limestone screen."

Fisher rolled his eyes. He knew he looked impatient because he was. After a moment's pause to consider the best answer that would avoid a dispute, he spoke.

"Now, Charles, Harry. First, you fellas call me Carl, okay? Now, let me ask you when are our motorcycle races supposed to start?"

Without waiting for a reaction, Fisher answered his own question.

"They start August 13, with our tune-up day on August 12. I'm an expert at construction, and I have hired Mr. P.T. Andrews, the best engineer in the world. We have about two weeks, and that's plenty of time to put on the finishing touches."

The two motorcycle officials looked at each other but held their tongues.

"Now let's talk about something important," Fisher inserted. "How do you see all the other motorcycle events going on in the city? We have a lot of out-of-towners coming into Indianapolis. We need everything about their visit to be top-notch."

"Honestly, Carl, all of that is the least of our worries," Wyatt started. "Ernie, here, he's been a great help, and we thank you gentleman for that. Red, white, and blue streamers and bunting are already up on the business buildings around Monument Circle. More will be going up in the coming days, all along the motorcycle parade route through the city on August 12. We expect upwards of a thousand bikes in that. Every newspaper and professional photographer for miles around is coming out. We're setting up one of those panoramic photos to squeeze everyone in. That's important."

Fisher nodded. He had not heard the latest tally of riders for the parade, and he liked the number.

"How's that endurance run coming in from Cleveland taking shape?"

"That's coming along nicely, too," Wyatt asserted. "We could have one hundred motorcycles in that thing. Overland has loaned us a pathfinder car. We're going to finish up at the downtown Denison Hotel on Wednesday at about 5:30. The route is three hundred and ninety miles, so it'll be a real test."

Fisher continued to ask questions he mostly knew the answers to.

"Your convention is all planned, I am sure. You'll be electing a new slate of officers on the national level of F.A.M. I even hear the F.A.M. headquarters could move to Indianapolis."

"That's an open question, but we are certainly under consideration. We're doing it up big to prove to everyone Indianapolis is the right home for motorcycle leadership. The night of the finish of the endurance run, we're hosting the riders and convention delegates at the German House for a vaudeville act. If that's not enough, we're doing a smoker and another vaudeville show Thursday night after tune-up day out here. We would really like you, Ernie, and your partners to join us for any of the convention or entertainment."

Fisher peeked at Moross and winked.

"Well, now, Charles, Harry. Sounds like this here Speedway is mighty important to you, boys."

"Of course, it is, Carl," Wyatt replied. "We just want this race meet to come off without a hitch, and everyone leaves happy. With so many of our members expressing doubts, we felt obligated to let you know what folks are saying."

Fisher pointed down the straightaway and motioned for the men to follow him. The gravel crunched and shifted under their boots. In the background, carpenters hammered down the last of the roof shingles on garages and other buildings. Fisher loved the constant clamor of pounding. It was progress music.

"Look down there at the south end. We had a railroad siding set up, and that's where those fifteen boxcars are sitting. We laid forty carloads of pitch down first. Then we started applying ninety thousand cubic yards of stone. We cover that with more pitch taroid at the rate of two gallons to the square yard. We have three sizes of stone covering the track, but our forty-ton steamrollers are pulverizing it all into a limestone and granite screen."

Wyatt and Dipple looked at each other, apparently reassured. At least it was clear they wanted to believe.

"Carl, everyone at the Indiana Motorcycle Club and F.A.M. wants you to succeed. We're all in this together, we want to put Indianapolis on the map. We will tell everyone we are reassured by our conversation and what we see here today. Still, surely you know some of the F.A.M. men will be visiting you soon, just to check on things."

(Indianapolis Motor Speedway, August 11, 1909)

The light emanating from a series of Prest-O-Lite burners cast elongated shadows of an army of laborers wielding sledgehammers. The men heaved them over their heads and behind their backs and then swung them violently forward, delivering crushing blows to pulverize piles of rocks in tight spots the forty-ton steamrollers could not reach. Some of the shadows stretched to maybe eight feet tall, with long, skinny hammer handles at times stretching another five feet and pointing well above them.

The sky was clear, and with no blanket, the heat of the day dissipated to a more comfortable sixty-five degrees. Carl Fisher paced along his Indianapolis Motor Speedway, shouting encouragement, but mostly he wanted to let workers know he was with them even deep into the night. Occasionally, he called on a man to come to a spot he felt presented a treacherous pile.

Fisher was interested in the conversation Ernie Moross was having with P.P. Willis some twenty feet away, nearer to the outer edge of the track. Moross was gesturing in some exaggerated manner he must have thought served a point as Fisher strode toward them.

Willis' back was to one of the lights, making his body a black silhouette with radiance outlining his form. The glare played havoc with Fisher's astigmatic eyes, and he motioned to Willis to reposition himself more to the side of brilliant illumination. Now, he could make out the man's face. It's always essential to see a man's face, especially the eyes. Willis pivoted his head as if he was panning the entire Speedway all at once.

"How's it going, Carl? You're cutting it a little close, aren't you? I mean, the races are in two days. You have tuning day for the bikes tomorrow, right? Those boys are supposed to be going some."

"C'mon, Pete, we give you a lot of insider dope. What's with the constant needling?"

"I'm a newspaperman, Carl. Did you forget? Just because I ask questions doesn't mean I'm going to run back to my desk and start flailing away on my Remington. I just want to understand the deal."

Fisher scrunched up his face. He glared at Moross.

"Ernie, what were you talking about with Pete? What you had for lunch?"

"Carl, of course, I told him we are on schedule, and everything is going to plan. Pete just wants to hear it from you."

Fisher shook his head for effect, looking down at his shoes. He deliberately remained silent for what he thought was the better part of a minute. It was all so bothersome.

"Well, here's the deal," Fisher began. "We are on schedule. These are finishing touches. For Christ's sake, it isn't easy building the greatest Speedway in the world in just a few short months. And then you get stupid things popping up, like today we had five cars of taroid held up in shipment. I had to commission a special train to haul in five more, but they're here now. We'll apply all of it after sunup, while you're still asleep. But we expect those kinds of snags. It's just part of the job."

Willis appeared incredulous.

"So, tomorrow is tune-up day," Willis persisted. "Will all that tar and stone be cured?"

Fisher paused. His impulse was to lash out at the man, but he knew that would lead nowhere. Or worse.

"P.P., it's like I said. We know what we're doing. All of this is more like an extra precaution."

Willis continued to scribble in his notebook.

"Okay, Carl, final question. And I ask this out of humanitarian concern, I won't even take notes. What happened with that Negro that fell in the big vat of boiling tar? I understand he didn't make it. It just sounds horrible."

Fisher's body acted on its own with a rush of the fury he felt that night a few weeks earlier. Again, he was silent, but not for some kind of effect. Was this worth explaining again? Feeling Willis' presence, he broke his sullenness, but with none of his characteristic verve.

"He was on a ladder leaning up against one the big dispensing vats and just lost his balance. I was here but didn't see it. I sure as Hell heard the screams."

Moross stepped away to begin what looked to be a spiritless tramp down toward turn one. Willis hung his head, but once Fisher started, he had to finish. He had a message he wanted the journalist to hear.

"I had some of the boys help me load him in the car and took the man over to the nearest hospital. You know the one. Pete, some of the flesh on his arms fell off down to his bones. The man was screaming something terrible. More terrible than I have heard from anyone or any animal."

Fisher paused. He had to; his voice was quivering. After a moment, he gathered himself and calmed the choking in his throat.

"I raced him over to the hospital, and a couple interns come running out with a stretcher. Then, when they get a close look at him, they tell me to take him over to City Hospital because they don't treat niggers at their place. I screamed and cursed like you never heard me. I didn't want to waste more time, so I just took off like a rocket. He was dead before we got there. I swear to God, I'll shut that place down if it's the last thing I do."

Fisher averted his glistening eyes from Willis. He felt a firm hand grip his shoulder.

"God bless you, Carl," Willis said. "I'll pray for you and for the very best possible races this weekend."

(Indianapolis Motor Speedway, August 12, 1909)

Popping reports like a cadre of musket-firing soldiers announced the approach of what the press had already nicknamed "monster two-wheelers" as they bounded over the undulating gravel surface of the Indianapolis Motor Speedway. Carl Fisher, his arms crossed over his chest, puffed mightily on his La Corona, and squinted with his dim eyes trying to determine just how much bouncing was going on.

Several men had joined him on the platform of the second floor of the white and green-trim open-air judges' stand. Among those crowding onto the wood plank floor were Fisher's partners, Art Newby and Frank Wheeler, along with Ernie Moross. Newby had two of his executives at National in the mix, Guy Wall and George Dickson. Other auto men in Fisher's circle, such as Howard Marmon, and George Weidley, the Premier engineer who designed his disqualified Vanderbilt Cup racer four years earlier, had volunteered for race management duties. All had accepted roles as judges, timers, and scorers. Ernie Moross was the starter, and Federation of American Motorcyclists National Chairman Earle Ovington was the event referee.

Fisher occasionally glanced at Ovington, not so much to smile or welcome him, but to read his demeanor. Ovington reminded him of Wheeler in appearance - a stout, barrel-chested man with a robust and carefully groomed mustache. Charles Wyatt and his men at the Indiana Motorcycle Club shared the scuttlebutt among the bikers that Ovington was not impressed with the Speedway, at least not when it came to their bikes.

Fisher's mind churned as he studied the riders and their bikes zip past. There was that seventeen-year-old kid, Ray Seymour, and the amateur champion Stanley Kellogg on his Merkel. Fred Huyck on the Indian was impressive. But that California champion Ed Lingenfelder was going some. He looked strong.

"I feel a hen coming on," Fisher muttered to Moross.

The rat-a-tat-tat of engine pops reverberated on Fisher's eardrums as he sauntered to Art Newby's side. A nod at Moross was his signal for him to join them. Newby, who agreed to serve as a timer, saw his partner approaching and looked up from his stopwatches.

"How are those boys doing, Art?"

"You mean, how fast?" Newby asked. "They're going a good clip, Lingenfelder ran about two minutes and twenty-five seconds a couple of laps ago. Not quite a record for two and a half miles, but close. He's the fastest boy out there."

"I think we need to prove a point, Art. What do you think about a record for say, twenty-five miles? Ten laps."

Newby's eyes traced Fisher from head to toe. Fisher knew he was reading him.

"A record would be fine, but there are no guarantees."

Wheeler approached from behind Fisher, who looked over his shoulder to see who was listening. He told Newby a "guarantee" was essential to their business. Ovington needed to understand the track was ready, and the papers needed a good story for their readers. Newby shook his head in the negative.

"I can't abide by it, Carl. I'm an honest man, and we need to get what get on the up and up."

Before he could respond, Wheeler intervened.

"Oh, quit being so holier-than-thou, Art," he said. "We all have a little of the cutthroat in us. It's business, all's fair."

"No, Frank. Go away," Newby said, turning his attention to Fisher. "I can't do that, Carl. I know other people do, but nothing-doing for me. Respect that I am a man of principle."

"Art, I truly admire you," Fisher resumed. "You're a better man than me, I told you that before. How about if I ask Ernie here to do the timing?"

Newby turned his face back to the track. His chief engineer at National, Guy Wall, appeared at his side, clearing his throat.

"Excuse me, gentlemen," Wall inserted. "Art, I just want you to know I'm going to drive down to the first turn and watch the bikes there. Riders throw their weight into those turns, you can't believe they don't just fall over. It's a hell of a thing to watch."

Wall gave his boss a wink, and Newby apparently took it as his cue.

"Good idea, Guy," Newby replied. "I'll go along with you."

Turning back to Fisher, Newby spoke softly but firmly.

"I don't have anything to do with whatever timing scheme you are hatching. I don't want to know about it; I don't want to hear about it."

"Ed's as good and as brave as there is on these bikes," Fisher replied. "He's liable to set a new record or two today. We won't do anything we don't have to."

Newby said not a word but paced off the steps in as close to a stomp as Fisher could imagine Art Newby ever doing. He felt a pang as Newby and Wall disappeared down the stairs. Carl Fisher never gave a shit what any man thought, except for Art Newby. He was a man of high ideals Fisher could not bring himself to fully emulate.

His moment of self-reflection was fleeting. Fisher pivoted to Moross and Wheeler.

"You two head downstairs and flag down Lingenfelder. Frank, tell him we'll make it worth his while if he's willing to gun for a record. A couple of hundred bucks should do it. Ernie, you flag and time. Make sure we get what we want, we're just going to have to hope he stays on the bike."

Within minutes, Moross and Wheeler dashed down the stairs and were trackside flagging Lingenfelder to a stop. Fisher scrutinized from his perch in the judge's stand. He was conscious of Earle Ovington, the F.A.M. chairman, advancing to his side.

"Carl, a word with you, please."

Fisher turned to meet Ovington's eyes.

"What are your men down there, huddling with Lingenfelder?"

Fisher bristled. It was his track, and he did not answer to anyone. After offering Ovington only a blank stare, the F.A.M. officer rephrased his question.

"Carl, I've got no issue with you working directly with our riders. It's just an honest question because I'd like to know."

Fisher, comfortable he was back in control of the conversation, smiled.

"It's simple, Earle. We thought we'd offer your Western champion a little incentive to post a new record. The press will pick it up, and it should be good for business. You like what's good for business, don't you?"

"Of course, Carl. None of that presents any problems. The problem is that some of those boys are getting real hesitant. They're not used to such a big track and racing on gravel."

"Crushed stone."

Fisher's abrupt and curt insertion seemed to throw Ovington off balance.

"Excuse me?"

"Crushed stone, Earle. The track is smooth crushed stone."

"As I was saying, these boys run on big plank saucers, on beaches, and sometimes dirt tracks. This is new, and it is speedy."

"What are they yellow?"

Ovington came back, this time sounding irritated.

"You and I aren't the ones risking our hides."

"I thought your boys were brave. I've seen them leaning sideways running full tilt on those board circles. I used to race at places like that with the bicycles back in the nineties. It's not like it's a picnic if you fall down on one of those tracks. Those planks have splinters so big they're like daggers."

"Carl, there's talk of moving the race out to the dirt track at the Fairgrounds. We're having a meeting at the Denison tonight with our officers and some of the racers. You should be there. Bring anyone from your company that you like."

"Earle, that is about the goddamned stupidest thing I ever heard. Tomorrow is the first day of the race meet. Do you know how long we've been ballyhooing this show? Do you think it's a good idea to move the whole thing to another track the night before the races? We'll have people coming to our gate and getting really pissed off."

"You, know, Carl, all your promises about being better than that big track over in England made the riders expect everything to be perfect. What you have may be fine for the big, heavy cars you're used to, but not these bikes. They're disappointed, Carl."

Adrenaline surged through Fisher's veins. Fighting back an urge to choke Ovington, he instead stepped close to his face.

"The Speedway will positively be in finished condition and ready for the record-breaking time. The track is better now than Brooklands ever was. I know, I've been there and you haven't. We have double the force of men working day and night smoothing out the few remaining defects. There is no goddamn reason real men can't break records. The races on the track tomorrow will prove it."

Ovington, apparently startled by Fisher's aggressiveness, stepped back.

"You need to come to the meeting tonight and tell the boys that. You're the one that needs to say it."

The sound of a substantial man stomping up the stairway behind them distracted them from their exchange. Frank Wheeler was back, reporting that Lingenfelder was well on his way to a twenty-five-mile record run. Moross was still trackside with his watch. Fisher returned his attention back to Ovington.

"You're damn right, I'm going to that meeting. I'll set those fellas straight."

"I'll join you at whatever meeting Carl," Wheeler said. "I promise to let you do the talking. Lingenfelder should finish his run soon. He looks strong."

The rapid-fire popping and cracking of motorcycle engines continued unabated. Fisher had nearly exhausted his cigar and fished around in his inside coat pocket for another. Gesturing to Ovington, he extended one to him, almost a peace gesture.

"I don't mind if I do, Carl. Although I probably should slow down on these things. My chest is still rattling and wheezing from that smoker the other night."

Fisher fixated on Lingenfelder but said nothing. Soon, the star rider coasted to a stop in front of Moross. The men appeared jovial, shaking hands, and Moross even slapped the rider's back. They both trotted over to the judges' stand and were soon up the stairs to join the officials.

Moross's face was stretched out of shape by a huge, toothy smile. Putting his arm around Lingenfelder, it was apparent he had something important to announce.

"Gentlemen, you are now looking at the new American speedway record holder for motorcycles over twenty-five miles."

Fisher almost pounced on the bike jockey, shaking his hand like it was the lever on a water well pump.

"Twenty-five miles in twenty-five minutes," Moross yelped.

"How was the track, Ed? It's obviously plenty fast."

Lingenfelder peered at Moross like he wanted some kind of support or permission.

"It's plenty fast," Lingenfelder started. "My Lord, Mr. Fisher, you built those straightaways over a half-mile. I had my engine all stretched out about halfway down them. I felt like a jackrabbit, hunched over my bars bounding around those turns."

"Did you feel safe?" Fisher asked.

"I never feel safe, Mr. Fisher. There's no safety in motorcycle racing. I know some of the boys are getting cold feet, but I don't have any time for that. If you're going to be a scaredy-cat, you need another line of work."

Fisher beamed. He wanted to hug Lingenfelder. Both his hands gripped each of the small but sturdy man's shoulders.

"I want you to come to the Denison Hotel tonight and help me calm everyone down. We are going to have a Hell of a show this weekend."

(Indianapolis Motor Speedway, August 13, 1909)

Carl Fisher turned to Fred Huyck, the jockey-sized Indian Motorcycle rider out of Chicago, seated beside him, hoping he would tell him what he wanted to hear. Together with Indianapolis Police Department motorcycle patrol officer Albert Gibney, their eyes swept the third-turn banking of the Indianapolis Motor Speedway. A light mist born of the slate-gray skies darkened the crushed limestone and gravel chunks making up the track's surface. It also appeared like tiny water blisters on the black leather upholstery of Fisher's pearl-white Model K Stoddard-Dayton. None of them complained about that small nuisance, all three were accustomed to any manner of weather. Besides, it kind of felt good with the eighty-degree air temperature.

"What do you boys think?" boomed Fisher. "You see any problems? Do you think you can race on this deal?"

Huyck's face beamed a pleasant, even amused expression like he was about to laugh over a joke.

"Mr. Fisher, it wasn't that long ago my job was setting up pins in a bowling alley for three bucks a week. I've had to work hard to get a chance on these bikes, and I'm never looking back. You need to know I can race my bike on anything. I'm ready to go if you say the word."

"I agree," the policeman offered. "I'm new to this racing game, but I have seen all kinds of roads. Hell, I came in on that four hundred mile endurance ride from Cleveland Wednesday evening. Some of those roads were wicked. Riders gave up and pushed or carried their bikes for a spell."

This was what Fisher wanted to hear. Before he could move on, though, Huyck spoke up.

"Now, Mr. Fisher, I ain't gonna sit here blowing smoke and tell you that you got it all perfect. I can see room for improvement right here."

Fisher paused to encourage the rider to elaborate.

"Well, a lot of this gravel isn't broken up nearly enough. See that pile over yonder?"

Huyck was pointing, but the truth of the matter was that Fisher, despite some determined squinting, could not see. He asked Huyck to walk to the spot and show him. Their boots crunched over the loose, wet stone until Huyck stopped and pointed down. Most certainly, there was a mound of rubble.

"Okay. I see what you mean, Freddie. I'll dispatch some men with hammers to break it up when we get back to the stands."

"Understand, Mr. Fisher, that there are a lot of these spots. This is just an example. It's also that even the truly crushed stone is too loose. This tar you put down isn't strong enough to hold it in place. The fellas hit the same spots lap after lap, and it breaks free."

Huyck's comments seemed like doublespeak to Fisher, and he felt like someone had cranked up the temperature.

"Damn it, Freddie, which is it? Is the track in good shape or not?"

Huyck frowned at Fisher and quickly shifted a glance at Gibney.

"I meant what I said earlier, the track is good enough. I'll race on it, and I'll win on it. Hell, I'll set records if I can."

Huyck thrust his right arm forward, pivoting on his feet and sweeping the air with his hand as if he was surveying the entire Speedway.

"I see all these men out here still working. I see that big steam roller over there. You don't have them out here because you think things are perfect. I won't speak for Gibney, here, but I got to expect you wanted me to help you figure out what to work on."

Gibney nodded.

"Mr. Fisher, I'm with Huyck here. I just want to help. But I'll also say I think we can use the track as is. I'm prepared to take a tour of this speed plant with your engineer or a foreman and try to catalog the rough spots."

Fisher was encouraged by the exchange. In fact, it was almost exactly what he wanted to here. He had been telling people the track was in good shape and would get better in the coming months with some seasoning.

"How about if your boys do a little work, and then we go out and test it?" Huyck asked. "You know, since the races are postponed today, we can still give your Indianapolis newspapers something to write about."

Once back at the judges' stand, Fisher tramped up the plank steps to the hum of familiar voices upstairs. P.P. Willis and Ernie Moross spoke in low tones, but he could hear them, if not distinguish their words. Fisher paused halfway up the flight to consider what to say to Willis. Once he appeared on the platform, Willis abruptly broke with Moross and rushed to his side.

"Carl! Where have you been this morning, I've been looking for you."

"I've been working, Willis. Some of us actually do things. Others just have opinions."

Fisher had the kind of relationship with Willis that allowed him to needle him. Although he was never plain-spoken with him on the point, it seemed to Fisher that he and

Willis had an understanding. They weren't always jovial about it, but never afraid to be direct.

A handful of men were on the platform. Wyatt and Dipple were among them, but nowhere near the crowd that was straining the boards a day earlier. Fisher's voice carried, and the others fell silent and examined the situation as if they expected fisticuffs. If the remark annoyed Willis in any way, he didn't seem to want to waste an instant thinking about it.

"So, Carl, the scuttlebutt is that you postponed the event card today because your track isn't ready. You told everyone that one of the features of your paving is that it can dry fifteen minutes after a rain shower. What say you?"

Fisher frowned, deliberately exaggerating an expression of annoyance. He wanted to intimidate Willis from pressing such questions.

"What's your point, Willis? You just want to put me on the spot? It can't be that you're so fencepost dumb that you can't figure out that the track is fine, but we wanted dry weather for the spectators."

"So, Carl, you're saying that the bikes could be out there running, but you just don't want to let your ticket buyers get wet?"

"You need to understand, Willis, I have a business to run. I have to consider ticket sales because that's important to this outfit's operation. But you don't have to worry about that, do you? Understand that this is a testing facility as much as a stage for speed contests. Our doors are wide open every day. Factories that want to test a car or a bike can come out and run around. It's good for them to know they can get right back to testing promptly after a shower. Hell, Gibney and Huyck are getting ready to go out and do some testing right now."

Fisher paused, but he wasn't finished. There was more he wanted Willis to hear.

"Look, P.P., I'm okay with critics. But be reasonable. Look around. The buildings and fences are all completed. The main grandstands can accommodate thousands, and all under an awning. Surely you see the other stands at other points around the course. Look at the clubhouses, garages, office buildings, and this judges' stand. Everything is spick and span."

"Carl, I have congratulated you many times on the great work you and your boys have done. You've raised this place up from a fallow cornfield to a speed plant in a matter of weeks. I want you to succeed, but I wouldn't be doing my job if I didn't look into concerns when I hear them."

Their conversation was interrupted by the popping and cracking of motorcycle engines below. Moross nodded at Fisher and took a beat down the stairs.

"See, Willis? The track is ready, and two of the boys are going to give it a go. That cop Gibney and Freddie Huyck. Stick around, you're going to see some speed."

The two bikes came storming out of the garages nearly at full speed even before getting on the track. Huyck was some fifteen yards ahead of Gibney, who exaggeratedly crouched over his handlebars and looked determined to close the gap. Two minutes passed, and two dark dots swooped out of turn four and onto the main straightaway. As they approached, Gibney, who wore a white shirt, black trousers, and eye goggles, flicked his handlebars and, charging up from the outside, caught even with Huyck, who briefly turned his head to steal a glimpse of his opponent.

The competitors continued on, their little motors growing louder as they approached the start-finish line, and then faded as they headed south to turn one. Lap after lap, they diced, but Gibney began to get the upper hand, and stretching out a distance from Huyck. Fisher turned to Willis to needle him about being a pessimist.

Abruptly, the peal one of the track's farm bells announced its alarm. The alert was faint because it was in turn one, but ominous because Fisher knew it was a declaration of emergency. Moross yanked the bell at the judges' stand, and those standing with him clamped their hands over their ears. Still, no one complained because they knew the purpose of alerting the track ambulance and rescue cars. One of the phones on the stand rang its bell, too. Fisher quickly picked up the receiver to the wall-mounted, walnut wood encased device. A voice on the other end shouted, "It's Gibney. He's down hard."

Willis tore out for the stairs as Huyck brought his Indian to a halt below. The man hardly had a chance to dismount his bike before Willis was on him. Fisher wasted no time watching but bounded down the stairs two steps at a time. He ran to the rider to hear what happened.

"It's like I said to Pete here, Mr. Fisher, Gibney fell down hard. I pulled up and was going to stop, but your rescue boys were on him in a second. I decided to just stay out of their way and let them do their jobs. I did get a look, though. He's alive and moving, but he was cut up bad, especially his left arm. He was bleeding something awful, and it looked like one of the doctors was fixing to put a tourniquet on him."

"Jesus Christ on a bicycle!" Fisher shouted.

"He was pushing it like he wanted to prove something, Mr. Fisher," Huyck offered. "And he kept futzing with his oil pump in the corners, which is just flat stupid when you've got these long stretches. They give you plenty of time to get all situated for the turns."

Fisher said nothing and instead immediately beat a path to his car behind the judges' stand. He could hear someone else running behind him. Willis, of course.

"How about a ride, Carl?"

Fisher said not a word, figuring that not objecting was as good an invitation as he cared to give. He spun his machine around with flare that bounced Willis on the passenger side of the bench and a rooster tail of loose stones launched into the air in their wake. Out onto the Speedway, Fisher was unrelenting with his throttle, racing through the Stoddard-Dayton's gears and accelerating until there was no reason to go further. Track workers loaded a stretcher with Gibney on it in the horse-drawn ambulance. The rider pumped his legs, sliding the bottoms of his feet on the stretcher. From that Fisher surmised, he was in tremendous pain. Instinctively, he started to dart to the vehicle but heard

Earl Ovington's voice from behind.

"Leave them be, Carl. He needs to get over to the hospital so the doc can stitch that arm."

Fisher skidded his shoes to a stop. His own breathing resonated in his ears like he was listening to someone else's body from the inside. Everything had caved in on him with such relentless suddenness. He just wanted to gaze into the stones beneath his feet. Ovington approached; Fisher did not need to see to feel he was there.

"This is what you get, Fisher."

Before he could say another word, Fisher stepped into his face and shouted.

"Goddamn you, Earl, you speak to me with respect, you got that? I'm holding everything together here, and the least you could do is not be a pain in the ass. If you got something to offer that helps us, show me. Otherwise, shut the Hell up and get out of my way."

Turning to Willis, Fisher maintained the volume and strain in his voice.

"You didn't hear a goddamned word of this, you hear me? I don't want to read a goddamned word of this in the Star tomorrow."

Willis appeared stunned and was silent. Fisher stomped back in the direction of his car. Coming around to the driver's side, he glared at Willis and Ovington.

"I'm going to the hospital to look in on Gibney. Are you two going to stand there with your goddamned mouths gaping, or do you want to get the Hell in the car and join me?"

(Indianapolis Motor Speedway, August 14, 1909)

"Billy!" Carl Fisher bellowed as he approached the Knox garage behind the judges' stand at the Indianapolis Motor Speedway.

"Moross talked to you about doing a couple of exhibition laps, right?"

William "Billy" Bourque, a handsome driver of nearly thirty, had a strong reputation as a scorcher who could wheel a race car anytime, anywhere. Behind him, a Knox mechanic had peeled back the cowling of the big car and was bending over headfirst, his elbows cycling a wrench like he was swimming into the engine. Bourque dabbed a handkerchief at the streams of sweat stemming from his hairline and descending down his forehead. Unlike the previous day, Saturday brought on the glaring, unrelenting sun, baking the Speedway and everyone in it with ninety-degree heat. The sleeves of the driver's white linen shirt were rolled up, putting the cords of his lean, powerful arms on display as he rested his fists on his hips.

Bourque nodded, indicating that he not only knew what to do but when to do it. Fisher wanted some excitement to fill the void of a dull day. Only nine riders of the original thirteen entries lined up for the first race of the day, a five-miler for private owners. Worse, the second contest, the one-mile F.A.M. national championship, saw only ten of an expected twenty-nine bikes in front of the starter.

"You're a good man, Billy. Give 'em Hell and show these railbirds what race drivers can do. Too many of these two-wheeler boys are showing their yellow streaks."

"I don't know what the problem is, Mr. Fisher. I'm not partial to these little two-wheel jobs. I like four wheels under me. Anyway, I'm happy to help, and every lap I take around this place teaches me something. I want an advantage when you have the car races next week."

Fisher nodded, feeling satisfied. He needed to hear a helpful voice because he was tired of Ovington's bullshit and stupid questions from newspapermen, like Willis. Fisher roamed the garages for a short walk, collecting his thoughts, before returning to the repair pits near the starting line. Inserting his finger between his collar and neck, he felt the dampness of his skin and the cloth as he surveyed the twelve-thousand-seat grandstand, little more than a third full.

"Jesus Christ on a bicycle," Fisher muttered to himself.

Moross was at the line, firing off his starter's pistol to send nine Indianapolis Motorcycle Club riders into their five-mile, high-speed clash. He launched the bikes one or two at a time because it was a handicap race. Again, six riders from a list of fifteen chose not to show up.

Fisher strode to Moross's side as the little motorcycle engines whirred at speed in front of them and then disappeared into the first turn a quarter-mile away. Silent, he stared at the bikes, spaced well apart, as they zipped past.

"Jesus Christ on a bicycle."

Moross turned his head toward Fisher, who was once again puffing on a La Corona. He shrugged his shoulders and raised his eyebrows.

"This is fucking boring," Fisher issued from the left corner of his mouth.

"I have to agree, Carl. It doesn't help that these boys keep backing out. Hell, we had three hundred bikes here yesterday, but most of them have loaded up and left."

Fisher searched the vast expanse of his mind as Paul Koutowski on a Minneapolis bounced by to win the two-lap go. The white stone surface looked deceptively smooth – even like concrete – as it glistened in the glare of the sun. Watching the bouncing bikes, Fisher could barely admit to himself that treacherous bumps belied the danger of the apparently smooth running surface.

"Okay, Ernie, here's what we do – we do something spectacular with what we have. There are two boys here that aren't afraid of anything. Jake DeRosier and Eddie Lingenfelder, and they're the biggest names we got. Lingenfelder's from California and DeRosier is on the other side of the country in Massachusetts, at the Indian factory."

"A battle of champions?" Moross was clearly enthused.

"Go to work, Ernie. Do it up in style. Make it spectacular. I'm going to tell Ovington what we're up to."

Fisher mounted the steps up to the second floor of the judges' stand. No sooner had he entered the room, a cluster of men fell silent, and Ovington stormed forward so quickly Fisher felt like he was going to pounce.

"Carl, we need to talk. I'm calling this disaster off. The track is just too damn dangerous."

"What?" Fisher deliberately raised his voice to strengthen his argument.

"I won't have it, Carl. It's not worth it. All the riders are upset, and most of them are leaving anyway. Nobody wants to break their neck for this insanity."

"You can't do that! People paid good money for tickets to come to see your show. Look, we have an idea. DeRosier and Lingenfelder aren't afraid of anything. We will announce them in a match race between the champion of the East and the champion of the West. I'll post whatever bonus I need to for the winner, and we'll call him F.A.M.'s national professional champion."

Ovington, although he was shaking his head, backed down. He seemed resigned and shuffled back to the group of men he had been conversing with.

"Earle, this will work," Fisher announced. "This will be a big deal, and nobody out there in those seats is going to walk away feeling cheated."

Ovington kept his back to Fisher. Apparently, he had heard enough.

Out on the track, Moross had sent away a small field of riders on fifty-five cubic inch bikes for a five-mile contest. The dwindling crowd revived as Fred Huyck, and A.G. Chapple ran inches apart on a pair of Indians. Hyuck came to the line almost side-by-side with Chapple but crossed clearly a wheel ahead. The eruption from the grandstands was an elixir to Fisher, administered through his ears. He thrust his fist in the air and screamed. Turning to Ovington, he winked. The motorcycle man did not appear enthused.

Within moments, Moross pressed a megaphone to his mouth and began shouting in the direction of the grandstands. A runner darted across the track to relay the message to several barkers, also with megaphones, who enthusiastically repeated the call to arms. Moross loved theater at moments such as these, and Fisher nodded approvingly with the announcement.

"Ladies and gentlemen," Moross bellowed. "By special decree of Indianapolis Motor Speedway management in company with the Federation of American Motorcyclists, there will be, at last, and finally, the much demanded once-and-for-all titanic ten-mile showdown by motordom's two greatest professional riders for the right to claim the title of world's champion!"

Runners scattered to the barkers roaming the grandstand, but most were already repeating the message and doing their best Ernie Moross impersonation. Simultaneously, the band the track had hired struck up "The Star-Spangled Banner," as first Lingenfelder stormed out on the track, his engine responding to his twist of the handlebar throttle of his German-made N.S.U. Bike. Lingenfelder, dressed in a stark white uniform, almost blended into the track surface of the same color. The N.S.U. acronym shouted its blackness in contrast to the rest of his outfit. He fashioned a circular path around the starting line and stopped.

Fisher observed as Lingenfelder's assistants strapped his feet to the bike pedals. He must be damn sure that bike won't come out from under him.

Suddenly, DeRosier, a Canadian, burst forth more dramatically, highlighted by his red tights and the American silk flag stitched to the back of his navy-blue jacket. A wave of delight swept through the grandstand as onlookers erupted in cheers and chants. Along with the steady musket-fire of the two engines, DeRosier's patriotic apparel and American-made bike garnered the favor of the spectators.

With another pop of his starter's pistol, Moross unleashed the two bike racing heroes. At no surprise to anyone observing, the two stayed close together as they stormed about the track. Fisher pivoted and marched over to the open window on the backside of the judges' stand, squinting to see what he could of the two riders. Art Newby was there as well, donning his trademark straw hat and manning a stopwatch while supervising three other men doing the same. Noticing Fisher, he turned his head to the two tiny dots on the back straightaway. The small lenses of his thin wire-rim glasses reflected the sun's glare, and it was hard for Fisher to see the eyes behind them.

"Lingenfelder by a nose," Newby said in a low, business-like tone that Fisher interpreted as his friend's private helpfulness in consideration of his poor eyesight. Fisher nodded and returned to his vantage point at the other side of the stand.

Fisher heard the bikes before he saw them. They grew steadily closer, passing under the pedestrian bridge just north of the starting line. The riders completed their first lap with Lingenfelder clinging stubbornly to his slim lead. Fisher was back at the other side of the stand to gather what he could from that spot. Soon the little dots appeared on the backstretch.

Newby grabbed Fisher's right bicep, apparently out of excitement. Pointing, he declared, "DeRosier's in the lead! He passed Eddie!"

Fisher did not care who would prevail, but he wanted a close, exciting contest. He also wanted it over without an accident. The day could be saved.

Again, engine sounds preceded the two dots emerging from the fourth turn at the head of the front stretch. Both tore forward, but before they were under the pedestrian bridge, it was apparent something was horribly wrong. In the distance, one of the riders flew over his handlebars as both bike and man slammed to the sharp stone surface and slid separately forward for what seemed forever.

One of the bikes blew past the judges' stand. Lingenfelder. Newby darted to Fisher's side.

"Oh my God, oh my God."

Ovington, also in the stand, shot by Fisher, shouting.

"Never again, Fisher. Goddamn it, never again. You shut this down. Now!"

Fisher nodded at Frank Wheeler, who stood nearby. Wheeler took it as a cue to escort the angry motorcycle man. Fisher heard Wheeler tell Ovington he would ride along with him and make sure there were no delays in arriving at the track hospital promptly.

Newby continued with his observations. In the distance, he described DeRosier slowly standing up, but apparently quite wobbly as he stumbled toward the ditch at the side of the track. Abruptly, DeRosier lurched and then tumbled into the ditch.

Within minutes the track's emergency car was at the stricken man's side, its attendants armed with a stretcher. Newby shared with Fisher that the men had descended into the ditch and extracted DeRosier. Soon, an ambulance arrived, and the rider was carried to it on the stretcher.

Fisher had heard enough. Before Newby could continue his narration of the grim scene, he interrupted.

"It's not going to end this way, Art. We cannot let it end this way, I don't give a rat's ass what Ovington has to say. This is our Speedway, goddamn it!"

Convinced that Ovington, who had hopped in a car with Charles Wyatt, was on his way to the track hospital, Fisher sped over to Moross.

"You keep this show running, Ernie. You hear me? Get that five-mile open handicap started, and let Bourque out on the track directly afterward. We need people to start imagining the great auto race meet we'll have next week for them."

Moross did not appear fazed. He had seen everything at race tracks and gave orders to the clerk of the course and his runners to notify the riders and Bourque to get to the starting line. By the time Ovington and Wheeler returned, Moross and Fisher had staged the five-mile handicap, a ten-mile amateur championship, and Bourque's exhibition laps. Privately, Fisher clung to a modicum of satisfaction that Bourque cut his lap at a pace well above a mile-a-minute.

Ovington skidded to a stop and immediately launched out of his car with Wheeler trying to keep up. He was livid, and his arms flailed. Fisher guessed that the F.A.M. official had heard that there had been another accident when J.F. Torney fell from his Peugeot motorbike at the north end of the Speedway. The good news was that he was not seriously injured.

"Goddamn you, Carl! We're done, do you hear me? Done! Forget about the second day on Monday, we are moving our show out of here."

Ovington stomped off, and that was fine with Fisher. Moross cocked his head at the Speedway president and then shrugged his shoulders.

"It's academic, Carl," Moross said. "Only four of the forty-six bikes entered showed up for that ten-miler. Nobody was willing to do the twenty-five-mile race. It doesn't matter what Ovington says, we just don't have any bikes."

Wheeler, panting, jogged to Fisher's side. Before Fisher had a chance to ask, he volunteered a report on DeRosier's condition.

"The front tire blew and got stuck in the fork. The bike went from sixty miles an hour to almost stopped. He's beaten up bad, Carl. Those stones sliced him up something awful, from head to toe. It doesn't look like he broke any limbs, but he did crack a rib or two. The big worry is internal injuries. He coughed up a little blood, so the doctors just want to wait and see. He's over at Methodist."

Fisher felt a wave of pressure emanating from his gut. He clenched his fists and wanted to stamp his feet or hop in his car and drive it off a bridge. He retreated to the only thing he knew how to do – busy his mind with his next project.

"Okay, we need to visit Jake at Methodist and do the right thing by him. We also need to turn to the auto race meet. It's only five days from now. The cars are heavier, and they have four wheels. They'll be fine. Let's do everything in our power to give everyone the best damn racing show anyone has ever seen."

Chapter 23 – Gladiators and Adoring Boys

(National Motor Vehicle Company, 22nd Street, Indianapolis, August 16, 1909)

"Old Glory" was a streak of color without even moving, Barney Oldfield thought as he examined his new National "Six" race car in the National Motor Vehicle Company factory on 22nd Street in Indianapolis. A smile stretched his lips and exposed his yellowed teeth as he clenched his unlit cigar stub at the southwest corner of his mouth. Thinking of the crowd's reaction at the Indianapolis Motor Speedway later in the week was nearly as satisfying as the idea of unwinding his new acquisition's engine on the track's long straightaways.

Beside him stood the company's vice president, Art Newby, whose dour appearance belied his kind heart. The factory floor was spotless, and all around them were laborers, hands busy with tasks associated with cars at various stages of assembly. The faint smell of machine oil made him feel at home. Weeks earlier, Oldfield had purchased from Newby his dark blue machine with its distinctive red, white, and blue star-spangled banners painted onto each side of the engine cowling.

"So, are you anxious to show off Old Glory out on our new, big, Speedway Barney?"

"I think the railbirds will love it, Art. It will call a lot of attention to National, too, so that shouldn't hurt your feelings any."

Newby nodded in the affirmative, and then mopped his forehead with a handkerchief. The big electric fans in the windows of the brick building could only do so much to combat the day's ninety-degree heat. He motioned for two of his men to pull open the big door leading to the loading dock.

"I know you fellas had a rough time with those bikes this weekend, Art. How is everyone holding up?"

"It's a hard game; I don't need to tell you, Barney. Those bikes just weren't up to tackling a big track like ours. And then, like the Indianapolis Star said in one of their articles, there's a nigger in the woodpile somewhere among those F.A.M. men."

"There's always somebody aiming to knock a fella down when he's trying to build something up. That's especially true when nobody else has done it before. I've been out to your Speedway, and I know it's the finest there is."

"Thank you, Barney. Sincerely. We know the track is a little rough. It still needs some seasoning, but we believe the big cars will do alright on it. We appreciate you being here. As far as I'm concerned, you are part of the National team. All you have to do is ask, and we'll do everything we can to help. You have a lot of fans in the city, no more than if you were a native son."

Oldfield winked at Newby. Those last few words were good as gold, and that made him feel at home among the Hoosiers.

Sunlight flooded a corner of the factory as the men threw open the massive garage door. Oldfield instinctively squinted to give his eyes time to adjust. He and Newby paced off steps alongside Old Glory as four National men pushed the big machine into the summertime blaze. The area was industrial, and dominated by the National factory. So it seemed strange to Oldfield to see a boy of about twelve running toward him and away from the bordering Monon Rail Line. Newby must have noticed the quizzical expression on Oldfield's face.

"The boy's name is Toby. His father works for me. I hope he can come work for National someday. He's not short on enthusiasm. He's one of your biggest fans, Barney."

Oldfield glanced at Newby, who smiled, his eyes fixed on the kid. He thought about his upbringing in Wauseon and how ideas in young minds can swell up into some pretty big things. Regardless, he got a kick out of sharing his interest in cars and racing.

The boy ran so fast he crashed into Oldfield's side.

"Mister Oldfield, Mister Oldfield," he blurted out, panting. "Are you really Barney Oldfield?"

"Why, I believe I am, son. Thanks for reminding me. Mr. Newby tells me your name is Toby."

"That's right. And you're Barney Oldfield! I mean, you're the world racing champion Barney Oldfield!"

Oldfield smiled and removed his soggy cigar stub from his mouth to give it a toss on the street. The National men cranked Old Glory, and the six-cylinder engine exploded in the throaty roar that resonated in his chest.

Newby shouted above the engine's clamor to ask Oldfield if he was taking the car out to the Speedway.

"We'll get there eventually. Today, I mean," the driver yelled back. "I'm going to tour the city first. Hey, do you think the boy's father would mind if I took him along?"

Newby was amused.

"A ride with Barney Oldfield? The world champion, Barney Oldfield? I'll let him know. You can drop the boy off at his house on Illinois Street. He knows where it is."

Toby was off and running to the car. He hit the running board like it was a spring and landed in the passenger seat. Oldfield was nearly as spry and inspired by the youthful eagerness, slammed into his seat as well. Double-clutching, he found first gear, and Old Glory rumbled off.

Making his way to East 12th Street, Oldfield then cornered onto Delaware Street. The foot traffic was thicker there, and soon heads were turning. People waved, some shouted his name, or, "Give 'em Hell on that Speedway, Barney."

There were few things Oldfield enjoyed more. He glanced at the boy beside him, whose eyes were so bright they could light up a night sky. Oldfield tipped his driving cap to the people and shouted his trademark phrase, "You know me, I'm Barney Oldfield!"

The sidewalks thickened with bodies as everyone came rushing out of shops and restaurants, pointing and waving. Cars and carriages on the road slowed or paused so the occupants could gawk. Soon, a cluster of boys, many Toby's age, began chasing the car, their little legs pounding on the macadam street. The boy twisted backward; his knees buried in its leather upholstery. He, too, waved, all the while grinning like he just escaped with a million dollars.

Oldfield guided Old Glory onto Sanders Street to wheel up before the Wheeler-Schebler Carburetor Company. He had earlier confirmed with Frank Wheeler they could meet at 10 o'clock before both headed out to the track. Oldfield wanted a gander at the much-talked-about silver trophy Wheeler had commissioned. Toby appeared in a whirlwind, his head spinning with mouth fixed in a bright smile.

Good on his word, Wheeler emerged from the giant building's lobby door, with no jacket, but sporting a vest with the gold chain connecting pocket watch and fob exposed. His sleeves were rolled well above his elbows. The two men firmly gripped hands. Oldfield extracted two Lillian Russells from his jacket pocket and extended one to Wheeler, who was happy to accept. Oldfield struck a match on the building wall, cupping his hand around it to keep the flame alive long enough to do its work. He puffed slowly two or three times to build a good ember and then handed it to Wheeler to begin the burn on his.

As Wheeler puffed his cheroot to life, he asked Oldfield who his little friend was.

"Why, this is Toby, Frank. Toby, this is Frank Wheeler, a very important Indiana businessman. Ever hear of him?"

"Heck yeah, Mr. Oldfield, everybody in this city knows who Mr. Wheeler is."

Oldfield and Wheeler nodded at each other, chuckling, their heads now cloaked with a cloud of tobacco smoke. Oldfield could tell Wheeler was amused, and he was as well.

"He's a National man – or at least his Daddy is," Barney shared. "He's embarking on a career of working on cars and driving them, right, Toby?"

The child nodded and said he wanted to be like Barney Oldfield someday.

"Be careful what you wish for," Wheeler said with a smile and a wink at Barney. "It's good to know the whole story before you dive into something. So, do you work on cars with your father?"

"No, sir, not yet. Father says he can't afford one just yet, but he's saving up for one. Mr. Newby says he'll give him a good deal on one of them."

"A good deal, huh? Why I'm going to talk to Art and tell him he ought to be giving his men Nationals," Wheeler replied. "As long as they come equipped with Wheeler-Schebler carburetors."

Toby beamed as Frank put his arm around Oldfield's shoulder and welcomed them into his building. With the boy trailing, they swaggered into the Wheeler-Schebler Company lobby. There stood the most magnificent example of silversmithing Oldfield had ever seen. It gleamed in the electric lightning Wheeler had strategically placed all about it, showing off its ornate design. The trophy included a scantily clad woman that looked to be a Greek Goddess perched at the structure's pinnacle, with two other figures, one of them a Native American Indian with headdress, resting on the loving cup-style handles just below her. It towered over their heads, an imposing structure, with the Wheeler- Schebler Company name boldly inscribed at its midsection.

"You're looking at one thousand pounds troy silver in seven foot of artistically sculp-tured statuary, Barney. I commissioned Tiffany to design and build her. She's worth ten thousand dollars."

"Well, goddamn, Frank. You just plain outdid yourself. You have the best darn trophy I have ever seen. You've put the plain-Jane Vanderbilt Cup to shame. But I got one ques-tion."

Wheeler briefly interrupted from his proud-as-a-poppa grin, inquired as to what was on the driver's mind.

"What's that Injun on the left there all about?"

Wheeler appeared amused.

"Well, those snobs out east call us, 'Westerners,' you know. And we know they don't mean that as a compliment. We figured we'd show 'em we're proud of who we are, and we don't give a lick what they think of us."

"That's the way to be, Frank. I say, full speed ahead and let 'em eat dust. You need to know I intend to win this trophy. It would look nice back in Cleveland."

"Well, if you or your team win it three times in a row, she's yours. That's the deed I signed. Until then, the trophy travels under bond with the last winner who holds onto it until the next run for it."

Their conversation shifted to matters at the track, Oldfield asking for the straight dope on what the deal was with its condition. Wheeler repeated what Newby had shared, and Oldfield knew things were not perfect. He heard about the dust. He hated dust. You could not see, and the shit got into your eyes despite goggles.

"Okay, then. It sounds like I need to get Toby home and go on out to the track. Thank you for your time, Frank, and keep this masterpiece polished up for me, okay?"

"It'll be glowing so fierce it will bruise your eyeballs. And Barney, take care of yourself out there. Our race is three hundred miles, no need to rush until near the finish."

Oldfield paused and locked eyes with Wheeler. The businessman wouldn't have said that if he didn't mean it. Oldfield nodded. He had a good idea of what he was getting himself into at the new track.

(Indianapolis Motor Speedway, August 17, 1909)

Carl Fisher studied Bob Burman's Buick as he skidded the car to a halt near the starting line in the repair pits at the Indianapolis Motor Speedway. He was most interested in the newspaperwoman sitting at the driver's side. The whole idea was to stir reporters into a frenzy.

Ernie Moross hurried to the car ahead of Fisher, because he had arranged for the petite woman in the riding mechanic's seat to experience a few laps with one of the bravest scorchers in one of the fastest race cars in the world. She was Marie Chomel but insisted on being addressed by her pen name, Betty Blythe. She reported for the ladies' section of the Indianapolis Star. Fisher liked the idea because a lot of women swooned over the mysterious speed devils at the wheels of fast cars. He was delighted to see the brightly colored Japanese parasols twirling as mothers and daughters went on their promenades in front of the grandstand. He knew all along the fairer sex were drawn to the men and their fast cars.

A shower of oil droplets pasted dirt to Blythe's khaki linen duster. She used a small handkerchief to wipe her face. All that did was stain the cloth and smear her cheeks. Moross handed her a towel, but the newspaperwoman again spread the oil.

"My Lord, this oil is nasty. It reeks!" Blythe said. "It was like rain, the way it sprayed back at us. It wrapped me in a cloud!"

Fisher extended his hand to the reporter to help her out of the Buick. He felt the slimy lubricant on her fingers. She turned to wave to Burman, who had kept his engine running. He flashed a broad smile that appeared bright as his teeth contrasted with the dark grime on his face. Burman was soon back in gear, motoring in the direction of the infield garages.

Blythe looked to be about thirty, but the gossip was she was thirty-eight. The duster, along with the oil and grime, obfuscated her pretty face and slight build. Still, she brimmed with an afterglow of energy and enthusiasm from her ride.

"Well, young lady, I hope 'Wild' Bob warned you that riding in race cars is a messy business," Fisher said.

"Oh yes, he did, but my lands, there is just no way to understand until you do it for yourself. Riding in a racecar with a crack driver has been quite an experience, Mister Fisher. There's just no other such sensation in the world. Riding in a touring car hardly compares. Talk about going like the wind. Talk about thunder!"

"What did you think of 'Wild' Bob?" Moross asked.

"I don't know that he said two words the whole time. He's very focused on his driving, and for that, I am thankful. I don't know that I can say much about what he even looks like - I couldn't do an accurate description of him. His face was filthy, and honestly, I could only catch an occasional glimpse of him, and a blurred one at that. I do know he has great muscles in his arms. The cords stand out from his iron grip on the wheel. He just stared straight ahead, seeing only the track."

"Are you ready to go again?" Moross quipped.

"Well, I should say I would, but not today. I need to catch my breath. I'm tired of holding onto my seat to stay in the car. You're never in the car, you're on it, and I feel like you are more likely to fall off than stay on. I confess pictures flashed in my mind's eye of my body lying out there on the road, squashed flatter than any pancake."

Chuckling, Carl said, "Well, we certainly would not want that happening, especially to such a fair young lady."

"It's the road that I don't understand. It looks so smooth until you are in a car going a mile-a-minute. It does not go any definite way. Sometimes it goes up; sometimes it goes down. You can never tell which way until you hit it. Then you learn its direction through painful jolts. I wrenched a few muscles in my back, for certain. I was holding on hard and still was afraid I'd be tossed off and land on the largest pile of rocks. I moved my foot, too, because the heat of the engine radiated through the floorboard."

"Well, Miss Blythe, I was worried you would change your mind and not get on the car," Moross said. "But I suppose you did not know what you were getting yourself into, did you?"

Fisher was surprised to see that, for the first time, Blythe appeared peeved. Her radiant expression melted like a candle as she apparently felt Moross' comment was condescending.

"Did I not know? You can always trust cheerful idiots to make things look as black as possible. They try to frighten you to death like they think it is fun. Well, I'd rather be a coward than to have some people's idea of humor. Do you think me some kind of a dunce, Mr. Moross?"

Usually, never at a loss for words, Moross appeared flabbergasted. He clumsily asked Blythe's forgiveness and all the while apologized for, "planting his foot in his mouth."

Blythe paused, her arms crossed, locking her azure eyes on Moross's bowed head and then shaking hers in the negative. Fisher mulled what she had said about cheerful idiots. He had met many of those in his life, especially when he announced, "I feel a hen coming on!"

"Ernie, I know you know better, so let's forget it," Blythe said. "Remember, though; I require your respect."

Fisher caught Blythe's eye and simply nodded. Silently, he felt a twinge of anger at his contest director. He should know better. Pissing off the press was not in his plan.

"I take a lot of heart that you would be willing to go back out on the track another time. You felt good about your ride?" Fisher asked.

"Oh, very much so, Mister Fisher. I knew this to be a risky business when I agreed to it. But I believed and still do that Mr. Burman has tremendous skills, and besides, he doesn't want to harm himself, I am sure. I'm also sure he doesn't want to damage that Buick race car. If I do go again, though, I might request Mr. Oldfield. A woman at a party last night asked me about my chances this morning. She said she would prefer to be steered into eternity by a handsome man. She said Mr. Oldfield is the best-looking of any of the drivers."

"For God's sake, don't tell him that," Fisher laughed. "Besides, she may have old moon-face confused for someone else. His head is swelled-up enough."

As Moross spoke to Blythe, Fisher saw another Buick parking nearby. The driver was Louis Chevrolet, and beside him was Roland Mellett of the Indianapolis News. Fisher trotted to the car, eager to hear what Mellett had to say. Fisher first arrived at the driver's side to greet the brawny Swiss driver now firmly American. Chevrolet always showed enthusiasm when meeting Fisher, and his stretched lips revealed his giant teeth that rarely appeared from behind his bushy mustache. He rubbed at his oily facial hair with his brown leather-gloved hand as if those strokes were part of his grooming process.

"Bonjour, Monsieur Fish-air!" boomed Chevrolet's resounding baritone.

His was one of the few voices Fisher had encountered that could overcome the cannon blasts of an engine like the Buick. Fisher liked Chevrolet and knew the French talk was an act, something he did if he liked you. If not, the Swiss driver might go thoroughly French, to talk past a person he despised just to piss them off. His English had improved mightily in the five years he had been in America.

"How do you find the track, Louis?"

Chevrolet shut down his barking engine. He shook his head and leaned down closer to Fisher's left ear. Other cars continued to roar around the track, and, along with sounds of other crews and railbirds, he still had to shout.

"Have your men continue to work on it. There are piles of rocks out there, so crush them, please. Some rocks and stones were shooting off the other cars at me like bullets. I am concerned that this will be worse as the races go on. Your track is not as fierce as Crown Point, but it bumps me around so much it reminds me."

Chevrolet had won Indiana's first major road race at Crown Point, Indiana, just outside Chicago two months earlier in June. It was a public road course through the city and out into the surrounding countryside. The craggy terrain was utterly unsuitable for racing, and Fisher had heard all about it. The constant jarring had nearly destroyed the Buick - it finished with only three of its four cylinders still running.

Fisher didn't want to ask any more questions. He shook the driver's hand, thanking him and wishing him well. By that time, Mellett had climbed off the car and was standing on the other side. The Buick crew swarmed Chevrolet's car and began pushing it back to the garage. The obstacle cleared, Fisher strode to Mellett and, shaking his hand, asked what he thought of his Speedway. The newspaperman rubbed at his face with a handful of his duster while shaking his head.

"You fellas have done tons of work in a short time. It's amazing, Carl, but I'm no expert. I've never been on a race car or a race track before. It sure seems dangerous to me, but those boys are the experts. That Chevrolet fella doesn't seem to be afraid of anything or anybody."

"He isn't. He's ornery as Hell, but he's also as good as there is."

"Well, he spooked me. I've been wondering about riding with a famous driver at full speed, but he cured me of that. I have no further wish for that kind of joyriding. I never before experienced a sensation like circling this two-and-a-half-mile course in little more than two minutes."

Fisher searched his mind to phrase his next question in a manner that would elicit the answer he desired. He sure as Hell did not want another newspaperman telling him how dangerous the track was – how alarmed he was about being thrown off the car.

"Going a mile-a-minute unnerved you, huh?"

"It's not as much the speed as to how rough the track is. I suppose maybe the faster you go, the more you notice undulations in the surface. It looks pretty smooth until you get up to speed, but molehills are converted to mountains when you hit that mile-a-minute pace. I held on with grim determination, all I could muster. Still, I felt like I could lose my seat at any time. Several times my foot was jolted free of the foot brace outside the car, and a couple of times, my hands slipped off the side of the seat. And the dust, my Lord, when we came upon that other car, it was just an impenetrable white screen. I don't know how those boys can see to drive at all, let alone at breakneck speed."

Fisher's impatience sprouted up like tall rows of Indiana corn in June. Mellett's description slashed at his pride - it was not what he wanted to hear. The newspaperman must have picked up on Fisher's anxiety.

"Carl, I don't want to be one of those killjoys. I'm just a cowardly writer. These boys are heroes and daredevils. Hell, the extent of my experience with this line of work is the three laps you just arranged for me with maybe the bravest man alive. I predict a grand spectacle for the lookers-on."

Mellet finally said what Fisher wanted to hear. He wanted to astonish people, and the good thing was that Blythe and Mellett were stunned by speed, by danger. Tell the world, he thought.

(Indianapolis Motor Speedway, August 17, 1909)

Stripped racing cars in brilliant shades of red, yellow, blue, white, gold, and green, thundered past Carl Fisher and Park Taliaferro Andrews as they supervised the work of dozens of laborers, most bare to the waist with the sun glistening their sweaty backs. Like in a prison yard, they vigorously swung massive hammers on the stubborn stone track. Spurred on by Fisher, they desperately endeavored to pulverize the treacherous surface. Men were all about the track, some three hundred of them, but Fisher privately confessed to himself that those where he was, at the entrance to turn one, were at most considerable risk.

J. Walter Christie, in his brilliant red Christie IV racer, stormed into the corner just a few yards from Fisher and Andrews. His front wheel drive "freak" racer slid almost sideways, and Fisher heard him ease off and then start accelerating as his tires kicked off stones in his wake. Just seconds later, the lusty, raucous engine of Barney Oldfield's "Old Glory" National was upon them as well. Oldfield nearly traced Christie's path, both taking a lane down near the infield to steer clear of the toiling hands. Fisher judged that both drivers had slackened their pace a smidge as a precaution, but he also knew they still carried high speed.

For days, drivers were unrelenting as they expressed their disappointment in the new track's craggy, treacherous condition. In the face of the obvious, Fisher remained insistent all was well. The running surface was fast and safe for racing. Goddamn drivers had stirred up those infuriating newspapermen.

"I don't mind admitting, Carl, this entire situation makes me nervous," Andrews said. "Look at those men. If one of these cars blows a tire, we could be standing here watching people cut down like a field of hay."

That was what Fisher could not stand to hear. Certainly not from a man he hired. He had listened to enough of it not just from Andrews but of all the do-nothing naysayers telling him he was impatient, that he was wrong, that he was reckless.

"Goddamn, it, Park, just get this shit smoothed out. We're running races tomorrow come Hell or high water. Understand?"

Fisher paused, watching Andrews shake his head. Abruptly, and not to Andrews or anyone, he shouted, "Goddamn it!"

Fisher felt bound in chains. The rage of the volcano in his gut rose, his mouth spun out of control like he was watching someone else speak. Suddenly, he stormed away, stomping his feet on the infield grass to grow his distance from Andrews and the situation.

Eventually, Fisher reached the repair pits, his spirit buoyed by the activity he found there. Finally, his imaginings came to life. Cars thundered down the grand front stretch, and as they came to a stop in the pits, mechanics pounced upon them with monkey wrenches and other tools. They clamored around open engine cowlings and wheels.

To Fisher's eyes, the gleaming white, lengthy straightaway was solid concrete, and he wished it was. Len Zengel on the big red Chadwick roared out of turn four and devoured the straight road ahead of him. Swooping past Fisher, the engine's gun blasts diminished in the distance.

Barney Oldfield, now in his pit, stood on the opposite side of Old Glory, apparently surveying the car's condition. A National mechanic was prostrate under the machine; his head obscured as only his legs and feet protruded into view.

"You got time for a walk, Barney?" Fisher said.

Oldfield shrugged his shoulders and then nodded as if he was dubious that their exchange would lead to any conclusions, but he always had time for Fisher. The two men strolled to the garage area, which was teaming with men at work and too busy to pay much attention to them.

"What's your verdict on the track condition?"

"Carl, do you want some bootlicks or just some plain, old, unvarnished straight talk?"

Fisher cast a glare at his old friend.

"The goddamned truth, Oldfield. Why the Hell did you think I asked?"

Oldfield stopped near the Buick garages to lock eyes with the Speedway president.

"Carl, I like these long stretches. I can open her up. The problem is, it's still rough. I don't worry about beating up my ass. At least not as much as what that jarring is doing to the car. We bounce like balls out there, sometimes my tires leave the ground like I'm going to end up saying hello to one of the Wright Brothers. I think we're beating these machines to death. I'm not saying we don't race. I am here to race. I've seen my share of rough tracks, but you need to tell everybody to use their heads."

Fisher paused. Oldfield's expression was deadpan, and his face soiled with oil, tar, and dust. He mopped it with a towel. There wasn't another driver in the paddock he believed would tell him the straight dope better than Oldfield. Some would kiss his ass; others would play games like they thought they could gain a leg up, and others were just too damn stupid to be of any use.

"We got a lot of people coming to Indianapolis from out of town. The Chicago club has a caravan of a hundred cars or more coming down. Newby is hosting them. Stoddard-Dayton says they're coming in from Ohio with all their employees on a train. Other groups are coming in smaller bunches. The hotels have booked up all their rooms, and some people are opening their homes for rent. The trains are making special runs every fifteen minutes tomorrow. Hell, some people are sleeping in passenger cars on the rail siding just outside the south end we set for materials shipments. Now they use it as a hotel. The show must go on."

"Well, I see old "Wag" is here," Oldfield said. "He takes that starter job pretty damn seriously. He takes himself pretty seriously. And General Pardington is here too. The Triple-A stuck you with him for a judge, I understand."

Fisher nodded in the affirmative. "Don't you worry about them. I'll handle them."

Oldfield chuckled, which gnawed at Fisher. He couldn't read minds, but he perceived that the driver doubted him. Never mind that.

"They're going to be a pain in the keister, Carl. They always are. That's their hoity-toity specialty."

Rotund and massive, William Hickman Pickens emerged from the white-and-green trim wooden Buick garage and marched toward Fisher and Oldfield. Pickens had signed on to manage the Buick team, perhaps the most formidable on the grounds. Or anywhere. They had three young but seasoned scorchers everyone respected. Bob Burman, Louis Chevrolet, and Lewis Strang – all were coming with high expectations.

Pickens' soggy cigar was little more than a stub, and spots of tobacco juice stains marked the corners of his mouth. Two fresh cheroots protruded from the outside pocket of his white linen jacket, soiled with smudges of nondescript grime in various places, most notably at his elbows. Oldfield deftly plucked the two cigars from Pickens' pocket and extended one to Fisher, who mustered a smile as he accepted it.

"Well, now, you old son-of-a-bitch, help yourself," Pickens said with a hint of a yellow-tooth grin.

"Don't give me any crap, Pickens, you still owe me for bailing you out of jail out in Wyoming," Oldfield snapped back.

"Good to see you, too, you old moon face. You are sure as Hell are not any better looking since I saw your mug last. You too, Carl. Good to see you, I mean. I can insult you some other time."

"I don't think Carl's in any mood to be amused, Will. He's got a lot on his mind."

Pickens squinted at Fisher like he was looking for some kind of clue. He followed that up with a statement, not a question.

"The track."

"Don't speak too loud. You got something to say, keep it between us. Both of you need to put the best face on things if any of these nosy newspapermen come stalking us. What are you hearing?"

"Present company excluded, I have the three best drivers you can find anywhere," Pickens began. "I'm sure you've heard it from Barney. This place has their attention. It's rough, but all of them are telling me the tough part is all the shit that comes flying at them. We got dust, but we got dust everywhere we go. Here, though, they're constantly getting pelted with pieces of stone like buckshot. Sometimes a big chunk of rock comes flying back at them. My boys aren't backing down like those yellow-belly two-wheel little jockeys you had out here a week ago, but I'm here to tell you, Carl, they are going to want to see big improvements before they come back."

"We're working on it; goddamn it. I've got three hundred men out here working like dogs and dodging your cars to make the track safe."

Before Oldfield or Pickens could respond, a breathless Peter Paul Willis rushed up to Fisher.

"Carl, I've been looking all over for you!"

"I know, that's why you haven't found me until these lunkheads distracted me. What do you want now?"

The newspaperman went straight to work.

"Word's getting around you have your first casualty of these races. Did you hear?"

"What in the Hell are you talking about, Willis? I've been out here all day trying to get work done. Everyone's fine. Hell, Zengel ripped off a lap at seventy-five miles an hour. This track is fast, Willis, or do you care?"

"Carl, the man who got hurt, and he got hurt real bad, is a Stoddard-Dayton mechanic by the name of Cliff Litterall."

"I'm telling you that's impossible. Nobody's hurt out here today. You got it all wrong."

"The accident happened in front of your dealership near the corner of Capitol and Vermont. Some of the Stoddard-Dayton boys were driving cars out to the track. I'm hearing Litterall was riding on the fuel reservoir of one of the cars and slipped off. The car just behind ran over him and crushed his chest. He's out at Methodist."

The explanation rang true. Fisher had thrown the doors of the Fisher Automobile Company open to the Stoddard-Dayton crew when they arrived the previous evening. He sold their models, and their success was also his. He retreated from banter with Willis, who continued to speak, explaining that Litterall probably wasn't going to make it, that he was twenty-seven years old with a wife and kids.

Fisher announced he was headed to Methodist before Willis finished speaking. He abruptly pivoted to sprint back to a garage where he kept his touring car, a Model K Stoddard-Dayton. He shouted instructions as he paced off his backward steps.

"I hate this. But goddamn it, Willis don't you dare pin this on the Speedway. This is a street accident, and I am going to the hospital to try to help. I don't want to see the paper tomorrow and read that this is somehow the track's fault. Don't you do that to us, Willis."

(Indianapolis Motor Speedway, August 19, 1909)

Carl Fisher imagined this day for months, and now his satisfaction in seeing it unfold was blunted by dread. Consciously considering his facial expressions, and his words, he projected calculated confidence in his voice. A yawn, though, escaped as he hurried about his giant Speedway in his Stoddard-Dayton with Park Taliaferro Andrews at his side. Both men had been up all night, but now in the gleaming morning sun of ten o'clock, the condition of the track was easily discernable. Irrefutably, the late summer rays revealed a stark contrast to the artificial illumination with its dancing shadows projected by Prest-O-Lite lamps just hours prior. Shifts of workers toiled around the clock in the Speedway owner's desperate attempt to will the latest, most fabulous American racing plant into existence.

Some one hundred men, stripped to the waist, their increasingly scarlet backs bathed in sweat, labored with rakes and sledgehammers on the backstretch and front. Steam rollers lumbered behind them, tracing their work to pulverize stone further and mash it into a layer of sticky tar. Thousands had already arrived with their automobiles, their horse rigs, and the regular stops of the Big Four rail lines and interurban passenger cars. Fisher found some comfort in the ignorance he ascribed to most ticket customers and wanted to believe that they would see his brinksmanship preparation as merely a matter-of-fact procedure.

"Carl, I still think we should have oiled the entire track, not just in front of the grandstands," Andrews said. "We're going to have a dust storm on our hands in that three-hundred-mile race."

"That's just fine, Park, but I own this track, and I have to make decisions. You can just have personal opinions. I wanted oil on the front stretch to keep it clean and clear for the fans. We got a lot of women out here."

"I take my profession very seriously, Carl. I don't appreciate any insinuation that I speak carelessly. You paid for my advice, and I expect you to respect that."

"Park, I understand English. You need to understand that I listen to your advice but make my own decisions. I'm spending a fortune out here that wasn't in the budget. Hell, I thought we would have that inner track constructed by now, but we barely started because of the gravel you recommended."

"Bullshit, Fisher. In April, I told you we should use concrete as they did at Brooklands. I gave you a macadam alternative because you wanted something less expensive and quickly up-and-running so that you could see a return on your investment."

The conversation drained Fisher. He had made his decision and did not care to indulge anyone in debating it two hours before the first race. Even though Andrews' recollection was accurate, Fisher's emotions propelled him well past facts. Getting through a safe weekend was all that mattered. The track just needed seasoning, and that takes time. He coasted his car to a stop in the repair pit and turned to Andrews.

"Look, Park, I'm not in a good mood, but I will put my best face on. I need you to take this car and get out to the crews and start moving them off the track. Park it over there, near the judges' stand when you come back. You're a good man. I just have a lot on my mind."

Fisher bolted out of the car without the lightest step on the running board. All the crap stewing inside him fueled him forward, despite a sleepless night observing the exertions of his hired hands.

Andrews darted the vehicle away as Fisher turned his back to the engineer, absorbed in assessing the scene. A large number of women occupied the grandstand - as many as men. They filled the giant wood plank structure in their gala attire and multi-colored millinery. Most shielded their faces from dust with automobile veils, and some with Japanese parasols of vivid red, yellow, white, green. Speedway pennants atop the track's forty-one buildings accented the white and green trim of the structures.

Dozens of flags of many nations, each fluttering in a gentle summer breeze and added to the color palette of the scene. The race cars, such as the indigo National, mustard Marmon, white Buicks, and variants of crimson for Fiat and Marion, moved through the paddock and garages to stir a dynamic sensory mix.

Fisher toured the pits and then the garages to witness mechanics at work grooming the big racers. They tightened hubs, pumped tires, and poured gasoline through enormous metal funnels to fill the hefty barrel gas tanks. The clamor of twisting, pounding tools, and shouts across cowlings or from under machines stepped up as the noon hour neared.

His tour provided a spiritual tonic from the taxing track scenes that tortured him from dusk-until-dawn. The laborers struggling to repair ruts in the track or smooth its gravel surface – and what that might mean for his races – preyed upon his emotions. Fisher's eyes recognized the ever-officious Triple-A starter, Fred "Pop" Wagner, along the path between the garages and the repair pits.

Wagner, a man Fisher found pompous more-often-than-not, flailed his arms, each holding a red flag tied in a neat roll around wooden sticks. He directed the five cars of the first race out to the track with the help of a horde of scurrying, panting course clerks. Abruptly, he swiveled his head in Fisher's direction, his recognition of the track president punctuating his work. Wagner purposefully trotted toward Fisher. Without a formal greeting, he plunged into his message.

"My boys are upset, Carl."

"Well, Pop, maybe you ought to brush your teeth and take a bath."

Wagner squinted at Fisher from under the brim of his flat wool hat as if what he said was a ridiculous non-sequitur. Beads of sweat on his forehead and temples formed rivulets down his cheeks to his collar. His curious expression transformed into a scowl.

"You damn well know what I mean, Fisher. My boys are saying the track isn't safe. They know about that motorcycle fiasco you palmed off on everybody last week, and none of them want to end up sharing a room with DeRosier in the hospital."

"First, none of these brave men are anymore your boys than mine, so knock off the fatherly crap. Second, you have a job, and I suggest you do it. I have mine, and I've been up-all-night supervising track conditioning work to make this place safe for everyone."

"I love these young men, and many of them call me "Pop" for a reason. I look out for them. You mark my words, Fisher; I don't want you playing roulette with their lives."

From the corner of his eye, Fisher noted a third man's approach. William Kissam Vanderbilt, Jr. extended his hand. His greeting came in a dignified, even tone.

"Carl, I wanted to seek you out and congratulate you on such a large endeavor. You've literally grown this fine facility out of the fertile soils of the West. My hat is off to you."

"Willie K, it is always a pleasure. Have you visited your box seat accommodations yet? I trust they are to your liking."

"I did so yesterday, and yes, I am quite pleased. I noted your structures and personnel for crowd control. The blue coats and brass buttons of your city's policemen seem to be everywhere, along with the olive uniforms of your state militia. Their rifles and bayonets speak volumes without so much as firing a single shot. The fences and signs telling people to stay back would seem to provide ample warning. I am painfully aware of the challenges of controlling unruly crowds."

Fisher did not know what to make of Vanderbilt's intentions. Wagner would tell you what he thought, voicing his opinions most vehemently on matters he of which he knew little. Vanderbilt's poker face could be disarming if you did not realize his stories varied depending on who he addressed. Still, there was no reason to offend the man.

"I shall be watching everything with keen interest, Carl," Vanderbilt said. "I plan to observe your shorter contests from the repair pits and may join you in the judge's stand if you will have me. However, I fully intend to be in the fine private box seats at the banking of turn one for the arduous two hundred fifty-mile Prest-O-Lite Trophy competition. I see the trophy is one hundred fifty pounds troy silver and valued at ten thousand dollars. Most impressive!"

Fisher mustered a smile. He had not fully forgiven Vanderbilt and Art Pardington for denying his Premier racer for the 1905 Vanderbilt Cup for excessive weight. Having Vanderbilt around was not his first choice for companionship, but he remained a man of tremendous influence.

"You are more than welcome to join me in our judges' stand. I can introduce you to some of our Indianapolis officials you may not have met before. The platform will be a bit crowded today, but there is always room for my friend, William K. Vanderbilt, Junior."

"I am relieved you gentlemen will be comfortable," Wagner interrupted. "You'll forgive me; I have a race to conduct. Don't you forget what I said, Fisher. I don't want any of my boys injured. There will be Hell to pay."

Fisher again shook hands with Vanderbilt, and without a word to Wagner – who had already turned to stomp away – he paced off steps to the judge's stand. Once there, he waded through a crowd of officials and hangers-on, some he did not recognize. His eyes landed on Jim Allison, who leaned on the bottom panel that framed one of the open-air windows that faced the repair pits. Allison, donned in a light gray summer suit with a white straw hat, motioned for his partner to join him.

On the track, Wagner struggled to get the first race, a five-mile go for one-hundred-sixty-one to two-hundred-thirty cubic inch displacement engines, underway. He wanted a flying start with the cars neatly aligned, but after two attempts, he asserted his authority and organized a standing start. Two Stoddard-Daytons, one in the hands of Louis Schwitzer, the other driven by Carl Wright, accelerated away from the other starters.

"Granted, I sell Stoddard-Dayton, Jim, but I have to tell you I want to see these boys prosper after what happened to that Litterall fella."

Stoic Allison nodded in his usual stony, expressionless manner.

"That mechanic that fell off a car in front of your automobile business. I heard he died. Sad story."

"It makes me sick. The man was gone by the time I got to the hospital. He had a wife and kids. I want to do something for her with funeral expenses or whatever. I can't bring him back, but I feel like I have to help."

"If that's what you think is appropriate, Carl, I approve."

"Thanks, Jim. And that's why I want these fellas to win something. A lot of them are friends of mine. All good people. The company shut down their factory out in Dayton and shipped just about every employee to Indianapolis by train. Hell, they had a caravan of maybe one hundred cars come in too, with the company executives riding along. I know it won't fix anything, but all those people need something to cheer about."

The two Stoddard-Daytons streaked past the judges' stand nose-to-tail. George DeWitt in a Buick was some distance back in third. Velie driver John Stickney trailed, and John Ryall's Buick had pulled off the course. Allison had seen him drop off the banking and coast into the infield adjacent to the southwest turn and nudged Fisher.

Vanderbilt was good on his word, finding a place on the judges' stand and in the company of Art Pardington. The two New York men shuffled to a spot behind Fisher and Allison, excusing any interruption they might have created.

"Any word on the condition of your course?" Pardington asked.

"It's in better shape than your annual romp through the Long Island villages and cabbage fields," Fisher shot back.

Allison, his right arm still leaning on the window frame, squeezed Fisher's forearm. Not many men could put their hands-on Carl Fisher, but coming from Allison, he knew it was a signal to back off. No need to pick a fight.

If two jaws could drop simultaneously, Vanderbilt and Pardington had accomplished the choreography. Pardington glanced at Vanderbilt for a signal, and the millionaire gave him one. He smiled.

"Now, Carl, Art was maybe a little indelicate, but not contentious. We're just making conversation. You are quite correct that we have both shared some of the same challenges in racecourse preparation. We make such inquiries with empathy, not contempt."

Fisher deliberately fixed on Vanderbilt's eyes. No man would intimidate him. Still, he checked his words and voice inflection as deference to Allison. Jim had good judgment, of this Fisher was sold.

"That's fine, then. So, you already know the answer to your question, Art. We are moving heaven and earth to make this right for our drivers, our teams, and our spectators."

"To safe, fair sport," Vanderbilt said. "Art and I would expect nothing less from our Western brothers in speed."

The howl of the Stoddard-Daytons grew loud as they stormed by the judges' stand for the final time. Wagner hopped and danced on the track, making a show of his checkered flag for Louis Schwitzer's victory, and the conclusion to the first automobile race at the Indianapolis Motor Speedway.

Fisher excused himself, saying he had business to attend. Spotting Ernie Moross, he wanted to collar his contest director about gate receipts. Beside him was the thin, graying, and effeminate Ad Miller, manager of the downtown English Opera House. Moross had recruited Miller and his staff to manage the gates and to sell and take ticket stubs. Moross spied Fisher's approach and preempted any greeting when he drew near.

"I know what you're looking for, Boss. You want to know about the gate. Ad and I were just chatting on that. It's too early for a final count, but I estimate we will see at least fifteen thousand people here."

"Not bad for a Thursday," Fisher acknowledged.

"I think we're going to hit over one thousand automobiles in the infield before we end the day," Miller said. "I'm figuring the average is three people per car, but we'll know when we count the receipts tonight. I walked the road through the infield just to get a gander at our customers. Walked past those three thousand hitching posts, and rigs took most every spot. The horses were busy swatting flies with their tails."

"We know we have ninety-five hundred grandstand seats, and another four thousand in the balloon race bleachers," Moross added. "The trains are still bringing loads of people. I'm confident we finally have a good crowd. The refreshment stands are doing brisk business." Fisher thanked the men and returned to the open-air window facing the track. Louis Chevrolet's Buick emitted a throaty growl as the Swiss blasted past Wagner's checkerboard flag. Art Newby, sitting with the timers, yelped out, "It's a new record for ten miles."

Fisher savored the instant. The struggle with the track shrunk in the context of the event. Beautiful day, profitable crowd, and now records he could shout about to claim he had the fastest track in the world. Would this get everyone off his back?

(Indianapolis Motor Speedway, August 19, 1909)

The air streaming off Louis Chevrolet's gleaming red Buick added fury to the unfurling of Fred Wagner's checkered flag, and the starter leaped into the air for dramatic showmanship. It was Barney Oldfield's queue to button up his one-hundred-twenty horsepower Benz. Oldfield polished the glass lenses of his goggles as his mechanics, the Hill brothers – George and Jimmy – finished fueling the spotless, stark white racer. Dust was everywhere, but the Hills gave the shimmering car a once over with rags. The sparkling machine, parked in its trackside repair pit, reflected the sun like a mirror, and Oldfield squinted when he looked up from his work with the goggles.

George Hill, wiping his hands with a rag, strode to his driver's side.

"She's tuned up, Barney, ready and waiting. If she could talk, she'd be yelling at you to hop in and turn her loose."

"I never had a car wait on me my whole damn life, George. If you got her all timed and she doesn't miss a beat, I am going to blast that mile record to kingdom-come. That gold-plated prize car is going to be mine. I'll give it to Bess for all the shit she puts up out of me."

"It's a beauty. I walked through the Overland display tent and saw it there in among their other stuff. That gold plating is on all the fixtures, the headlamps, the horn, the radiator cap, and the trim around it. The body is as white as the Benz here. That sets off the gold."

The Overland car, with the very idea it boasted gold, was generally regarded as the best trophy to be found anywhere. All a driver had to do was set the fastest mile time during 1909 at the Speedway. The track previously announced there would be two more big race meets in September and October.

Wagner marched with an exaggerated appearance of importance to Oldfield's side. Here come the official driver instructions.

"Everything ready, Barney? It looks like you might be the only driver to attempt a run. DePalma's Fiat crapped out, a broken cylinder or something. Maybe Christie will roll up here, but I never know about him. Aitken and Strang got a look at that Benz and figured you had too much for them to handle."

"They're smart fellows, Wag. They know they can't catch me."

Wagner seemed to ignore the response and displayed a serious face.

"Your job is to beat Webb Jay's old 1905 record of forty-five and a fifth second. Your competition is a performance from four years ago."

"Thanks for the tip, Wag. I was there."

Wagner continued his instructions without pause.

"Okay. Just fire this beast up and get her up to speed. I will give you a running start. We have an electric time wire up there on the north end and another at the south end. We have one at the kilometer mark too. You'll be doing some wheel work, but for the most part, it's a straight line."

Oldfield thought about yawning but decided to give the starter a break.

"Barney. I got something else to say. Be careful out there."

"Careful? Wag, I'm going out there to set the mile track record."

"You know what I'm saying. Don't take any unnecessary risks. Be aware of the track. I'm hearing from some of the drivers that it's rough and getting rougher with ruts and whatnot."

"Don't worry about me, Wag. I'm not ready for the dirt nap just yet."

Wagner abruptly turned, and Oldfield imagined the guy had put up with a good deal of guff all day. His arm shot out from his side before the starter got away to clasp his big hand around Wagner's elbow. Wagner twisted his head in Barney's direction.

"Wag," Oldfield said, and then paused. "You're doing a good job."

The starter nodded, darting off to a waiting car. The timers had to be in place and ready, and Oldfield knew Wag wanted to scrutinize their work. Jimmy Hill watched Wagner's car grow smaller in the distance and then bent down to the crank at the front of the Benz.

He yanked it once, twice, and then again before the German engine responded with piston blasts. Oldfield fed the four in-line cylinders just enough gas to idle until he pulled his gloves over his fingers, scanned the oil pressure gauge, and performed his little rituals like turning the wheel – slightly – back and forth.

Motioning to his mechanics, the Hills and a third man put their shoulders to the big machine to push it as Oldfield eased it into gear. A tide of dust engulfed the men as Oldfield stole his last backward glance. A few small stones kicked up off the front tires, and he imagined following cars in traffic would produce a storm of grit. At this moment, with no one in front of him, the big track stretched out to the horizon, clear as crystal.

Down the front stretch, into the first turn, and through the short chute, the south end time trap loomed. Triple-A officials stood to the side in the grass, waving and applauding. The Benz' tires skidded only a bit as Oldfield rounded turn two and began to put on speed. He knew he had to be at racing speed to hit the starting timer at a record pace. The rear wheels skidded exiting turn three, but with no more violence than Oldfield had felt hundreds of times before on dirt tracks.

Oldfield approached turn four a shade high, pinching down to the apex and then out again toward a ditch at the outside of the corner. The Benz thundered onward as it devoured the distance unfolding before him. Under the pedestrian bridge for an instant of shade, and then back out to the glaring sun, Oldfield clamped down on an unlit cigar as he peered unwaveringly over the cowling of the Benz. Recalling the washboards of Daytona Beach when he saw an uneven pile of stones, he pushed more firmly on his throttle and ground his teeth into a dissolving cheroot. Jostled about, but relentlessly soaring forward, the Benz doggedly advanced and surpassed the kilometer time trap.

As turn one approached, Oldfield again entered the corner high and swooped down the banking toward the spot of the last electric timer. Immediately past the timer, Oldfield eased the throttle as his momentum spoke to him about the perils of turn two.

Brimming with confidence that the record was his, Oldfield raised both hands into the air down the backstretch. Returning one hand to the wheel for turns three and four, he waved to a smattering of people there. Entering the pit area, Oldfield heard cheers and commotion from the crowded grandstand as he shut down his engine. The reaction convinced him of his success and was eager to learn by what margin.

Wag was there, clapping, as well as the Hills, Carl Fisher, Art Newby, and a horde of others. Oldfield coasted to a stop as the officials swarmed his car. Hands thrust at him, and Fisher clasped his left shoulder to give him a good shake. Just outside the men that encircled him, Oldfield spied Indianapolis Star reporter P.P. Willis and, along with him, was a cluster of scribes and photographers, including George Bretzman and Ed Spooner.

"Forty-three and a fifth," Wag bellowed. "Three seconds faster than the record. You're the fastest mile-man in America!"

There were handshakes all around until Oldfield broke free by standing up in the car to tower over the others. He bounded down, and the newspapermen's questions ensued.

Aside from inquiries about the sensation of speed, they all wanted to know about the condition of the track. Oldfield paused, locking eyes with Fisher.

"The Speedway men have done magnificent work. The track is already the fastest one going in America, and with more seasoning, I guarantee I'll be back out here with faster times."

Carl Fisher sprinted down pit lane, all the while focused on the chocolate-brown Knox of Billy Bourque as the driver brought his big machine to a halt. Art Newby scurried along, too, following the Speedway president.

Fisher was delighted with Bourque's win in the just-completed five-mile race for more than one reason. First, it was quickly the best show of the day as Bourque and "Wild" Bob Burman had jockeyed like a pair of racehorses the entire distance. The Knox driver nipped Burman's Buick by a fraction of second at Wagner's checkered flag. Fisher broke through a cluster of Knox people to collar the winner.

"Billy! Bully good race, my friend. I just want you to know I was pulling for you the whole way. I remember men that do me a good turn like you did for me at motorcycle races. You showing off your Knox helped us bring in all these people in the stands."

Fisher was conscious of Newby behind him. Swinging like a door, he opened Newby to Bourque's view. Newby thrust his hand forward for a shake.

"I guess I'm allowed to congratulate you because none of my Nationals were in the race," Newby inserted with a smile. "Seriously, Billy, you are a friend to our Speedway, so let us know anytime we can be of assistance. Watch out, though, I have a pair of my boys lining up for the Prest-O-Lite go in an hour or so. They'll be ready."

Newby turned his head to keep an eye on Wagner, who was organizing the next race. National driver Charlie Merz was in the line-up.

"I have to go keep an eye on Merz," Newby added. "Congratulations again."

Fisher slapped Bourque on the back.

"Hey, Billy, I got another favor to ask. How about coming up into the judges' stand. I got Willis up there, and we could use some good press. I know Allison would like to shake your hand as well."

Bourque wiped his face and hands with a rag, affirming the request with a nod. Together they began their walk toward the stand as engines started roaring on the track. Wagner had sixteen cars lined up for the start of a ten-mile contest. He dropped his red starting flag before Fisher and Bourque were up the steps of the wood-plank judges' stand.

Fisher made a show of draping his arm around his latest "scorcher" hero as they entered the second-floor platform with officials and newspapermen. Willis rushed forward, pencil and notepad in hand.

"Give us a minute, P.P.," Fisher said. "First things first. Jim! Come say hello to the most exciting speed demon of the day!"

Allison strode the distance of his spot at the open-air window to the center of the floor.

"Good show, Billy," Allison said. "Everyone at our Speedway couldn't be happier than to see you dash to the front of one of our races. I hear you have wedding plans."

"I sure do, Mr. Allison. We're getting hitched next month. She's a wonderful girl."

Allison put his hand on the driver's shoulder and gave him a jostle. Allison winked and turned him over to Willis.

"Great job, Billy," Willis started. "Everyone wants to know – how is the track?"

"It's fine, P.P.," Bourque asserted. "Regardless, though, don't you want to know about how Burman and I was dicing it up the whole time."

"Sure, I do, Billy. I'm doing my job. I have to ask about things that are on everyone's mind. So, tell me, how did you get the edge on Burman there at the end? He's one tough customer."

"You newspapermen don't call him 'Wild' Bob for nothing. He's as good as they come. I think I just came out of that northwest turn with a little more momentum. I went high there, up near that ditch at the side of the track. I think by doing that, I didn't have to back off as much and got the engine running harder when we came out on the straight. It was just enough. Boy, that was close."

Their exchange was punctuated by the growling engines of the ten-mile handicap race out on the track. Fisher turned his attention from the interview to the vista from his window. Ray Harroun, who started with a fifteen-second head start, maintained the lead as the fourth and final lap began. This result was more good news for Fisher because Harroun was at the wheel of a locally-built yellow and black "Yellow Jacket." As much as he wanted the Speedway to save the American automobile industry, the success of Indianapolis car companies was foremost.

"Hey, P.P.," Fisher shouted. "You need to pay attention to this race. One of our Indianapolis race teams is going to win it. That'll make good copy for your readers!"

Willis nodded and shook Bourque's hand another time. As he headed for the stairs to return to the track, two more scribes approached Borque, but after a few minutes, the driver extended his hands to signal to excuse himself.

"Gentlemen, I have to go get everything in order for the big race of the day," he announced. "The next time you see me, I hope to be with that beautiful silver Prest-O-Lite Trophy.

"You're only three hundred miles away, Billy!" Fisher shouted.

(Indianapolis Motor Speedway, August 19, 1909)

Carl Fisher anticipated this moment since breaking ground to build his Speedway in March. The feature event of the first day of auto racing at the new track was minutes from launching. Newspapermen, poised to telegraph their stories across America, buzzed their chatter while outside the din of thousands of race fans filled the air. The featured prize at stake was the One hundred fifty-pound troy silver Prest-O-Lite Trophy from the company Fisher founded with Jim Allison. The one-thousand-dollar trophy gleamed like a star, reflecting brilliant Indiana summer sun. Allison paced off the steps alongside his partner as they approached "Pop" Wagner's lineup of the nine starters in front of the main grandstand.

Fisher and Allison mingled with the cars, drivers, riding mechanics, and team members. First, there was Fred Willis in the Jackson, and then a special stop in front one of the hometown favorites, Fred "Jap" Clemens, the old man of the bunch at forty-five. Clemens was born during the Civil War and was well into his twenties by the time the first car traversed the streets of the Hoosier capital city. He was a mechanic working with a variety of machinery before taking up driving. Fisher had a soft spot for him since his twenty-four-hour drive with Charlie Merz back in ought-five when they set a world record in one of Newby's Nationals.

"Hi, Jap," Fisher announced, propelling his hand for a greeting. "My condolences for the loss of Cliff Literall. I didn't know him, but his family is very nice, and everyone at Stoddard-Dayton says he was a good man."

Clemens scrunched up his leathery face. Allison bowed his head in a silent, supportive gesture.

"I didn't know him well, Carl, but everyone in Dayton respected him as one hell of a mechanic. I've seen a lot of men die in my time; it don't get any easier."

Carl nodded and tipped his felt hat. He didn't want to send a man off into a big race with death on his mind, but he did want the Stoddard-Dayton people to know of his sympathy. Shifting to small talk about the hopped-up Stoddard-Dayton's engine, he wished Clemens well and reminded him that a win would help him sell a half-dozen cars at Fisher Automobile Company. The two track founders then proceeded on to the Buick drivers, Bob Burman, Lewis Strang, and Louis Chevrolet, whose three big machines lined up side-by-side.

"Monsieur's Fisher and Allison," Chevrolet bellowed in his rugged baritone. "This so-called wild man Burman and I thank you so much for building this magnificent track."

"This magnificent, gritty track," Burman added.

"And what does that crack mean?" Fisher asked.

"Relax, Carl," Burman returned. "I'm not poking you; I'm just saying it could do with some water or oil to tamp down all this dust and the stones. We're getting pelted out there."

"Yes," injected Chevrolet. "But I have seen worse. Crown Point just about beat my kidneys to mush. And the Vanderbilt is always rugged. I ask of you please, for all of us, find a way to repair ruts that will form. The wheels grind for so many miles, and this track is high-speed. Three-hundred miles is a great distance."

Beside them was the third Buick driver, Lewis Strang, who was listening and nodding. Fisher admired him for his flair in adorning his linen skullcap with a long red streamer of cloth. He liked anyone with the pizzazz to stand out in a crowd. More substantively, Fisher commended any man such as Strang, who lost his parents as a teenager and went to work to scratch out a living, never leaving his siblings behind. He was an American success story, which is how Carl Fisher saw himself.

"We want to give you boys the best track you've ever raced on. We'll do everything possible to make things safe. You have Carl Fisher's word on that."

Allison had already moved on to the spot where Art Newby stood – between his two National entries. The drivers, Charlie Merz, and Tom Kincaid were both young enough to be Jap's sons, but they were among the bravest and fastest scorchers in the sport. Fisher wrapped up his exchange with the Buick men and then strode to his partners, slapping Newby on the back.

"Everything in order, Art?"

Newby mustered a smile, but his expression quickly turned to a grimace. Fisher noticed his friend's apparent pain.

"You okay, Art? Sun getting to you?"

"It's my stomach again. It feels like it's on fire, and I keep having to go to the sheds."

"I wish I could help. Once you see your men off, I hope you join us in the judges' stand. The shade and breeze might do you some good."

Again, Newby forced a smile and nodded in affirmation. Fisher turned his attention to Merz and Kincaid.

"You boys chomping at the bit?"

He followed his question with a statement that sounded like an order – even though he was smiling and chuckling.

"Now, you men have an assignment. One of you needs to win one for your boss here; he's a good man."

Almost simultaneously, the young pilots cried out, "Yes, sir, Mr. Fisher!"

Loyalty is laudable, Fisher thought. The three founders commenced to walking to the judges' stand at a pace to suit Newby. Once to the second story platform, Fisher saw Frank Wheeler and waved him over.

"Listen, Frank, I want you to lay off Art today," Fisher whispered.

Wheeler, visibly affronted, asked, "what the hell" Fisher was trying to say.

"His stomach is acting up again, and I don't want you needling him. He may be a church-goer, but he's never been a nut about it to me. He's a good man."

"Fine. I won't talk to Art then. I got other people up here I can spend time with."

Fisher shook his head as Wheeler turned his back to storm off to a cluster of Triple-A officials and George Schebler, his partner in his carburetor business. Newby was leaning against the column of the window overlooking the pit area. A pair of binoculars rested on his chest; a leather strap affixed to them draped around his neck. Allison approached, a box in hand. Extending it forward, he told Fisher to open it. He did, revealing a new set of binoculars.

"I brought you a present to mark the occasion. These boys are going to put over a hundred laps in, and I want you to have a clear view of who gets our trophy. These binoculars are a gift I am giving most of the men up here. See the Prest-O-Lite name etched on it? There isn't anyone up here that can see the fourth turn clearly without some kind of telescope. These binoculars are the best around. Now you can see who is doing what before most the people here today."

That was a damn good point. Fisher was going to be able to see as well as anybody.

"Thanks, Jim. You know, I guess I ought to break down and get me a pair of spectacles to wear all the time."

Allison smiled and excused himself to personally hand a box to Wheeler, who was at the far side of the plank floor. Simultaneously, an eruption of blasting engines filled the air with delightful cacophony. The racers were gunning for another of Wagner's standing starts.

Within minutes, the horde of mechanical beasts charged toward the first turn, Chevrolet's white Buick clearly in front. Even with his binoculars, Fisher could barely see only one other car, as all of them continued into the south end short chute – Burman was second. Visibility was not about Fisher's eyesight, but instead, the billowing dust clouds kicked up by rapidly rotating wheels. The phenomenon had been a factor all day and was suddenly made more startling through the clarity of binoculars. As all the cars rounded the turn, the deafening clamor dissipated to a decibel level that allowed the men to speak to one another.

"Jesus Christ on a bicycle!"

Like a general lowering his field glasses, Allison pointed to turn two, where the diminishing racers disappeared behind a stand of maples and sweet gums.

"Those cylinders are hammering cranks!"

Flashes of indigo, white, red, and copper peeked out of the raging dust storm for partial seconds at a time. The men aimed their lenses at the fourth turn, where Burman was in hot pursuit of Chevrolet. Their teammate Strang was within range as well. Their trip down the front stretch was markedly visible. Fisher cringed as he thought about his conversation with Park Andrews earlier, who challenged his decision to only sprinkle petroleum on the straightaway in front of the grandstands.

For an hour and a half, all nine machines thundered on, the dust dwindling as the racers spread out along the track. Still, it appeared ominous, and Newby wrapped his arm around Fisher's shoulder to say, "I'll be darned glad to see this marathon behind us."

Fisher was not challenging, just silent. Only sequestered in his private thoughts did he allow himself to agree. Just get it over with, and we'll oil all two and a half miles for tomorrow. Pointing his binoculars to the north end of the track, Chevrolet again surged into sight, and then, quickly, Burman was in pursuit. Where was Strang? He had been running closer to his teammates the whole time.

Strang emerged into view at a markedly slower pace, his car in flames. His riding mechanic removed his jacket and beat back the fire that emanated from the engine. Strang shot into the pit area, slowing to the spot where the Buick crew stood ready. One man dashed forward, spraying a fire extinguisher into the blaze, abating the devouring inferno, but not squelching it. Other drivers not entered in the race and their crews swarmed in with more fire extinguishers and blankets until they extinguished the conflagration.

Strang and his mechanic grabbed blankets to fling the smoldering metal cowling open. These fires were frequent when an errant spark or intense heat triggered a flame nourished by copious coatings of oil and grease. After strapping the engine cover back into place, Strang jumped behind the wheel as his mechanic began to circulate the crank handle. Immediately Triple-A men bolted to the front of the car to form a blockade. Allison lowered his lenses and turned to Fisher and Newby.

"What do you make of that?"

"I can only assume those Triple-A officials believe Strang broke their rules by letting other men work on their car during the competition," Newby replied.

"Jesus Christ on a bicycle," Fisher uttered. "What are they supposed to do, let the car burn to the ground?"

"I'm speculating, Carl, just trying to answer Jim's question. I'm not agreeing with what they're doing. Maybe not disagreeing either. If you don't like it, take it up with Frank Trego over there, or one of the other Triple-A men."

Fisher was not in the mood for another argument. Instead, he simply shouted out to Trego and told him he ought to get on the track phone system and call the post near Buick and ask them to give Strang a break. A goddamned break, for Christ's sake! Trego remained focused on the Warner electric timing apparatus, oblivious or just ignoring the track president.

Lap after lap for another hour, Chevrolet and Burman stormed by, filling Fisher's binoculars with images of their darkening white cars as they twisted their steering wheels. Shrieks erupted, and the track farm bells pealed out their alarm. Fisher was stunned by what he saw through his Prest-O-Lite glasses. Bourque's copper-brown Knox skidded off the track and then barrel-rolled into the fence at the outside of the course. Fisher's mind struggled to comprehend what he saw, what looked to be two giant rag dolls thrown from the car as it flopped over them. The phone in the judges' stand vibrated its chime, another sensory embellishment of the surreal cruelty of the moment. After fifty-eight laps, the monotonous pattern of the race had brutally changed.

"Did you see Chevrolet go by?" Newby shouted.

"That wasn't Chevrolet, that was Bourque."

"It was, yes. But did anyone see Chevrolet?"

"I only saw Burman," said Allison. "But I'm like everybody else. That mess down there coming out of turn four distracted me."

"That's about the spot where DeRosier nearly killed himself last week," Newby added.

Fisher couldn't stand not knowing, not being able to control the situation.

"Goddamn it! I'm going to the infield hospital," he announced. "I want to head the ambulance off and find out about Billy and Harry first hand. Jim, you need to stay here so you can present our Prest-O-Lite Trophy to the winner."

Leaping down the stand's steps two at a time, Fisher yelled, "Moross," and then heard the little man scurrying behind him as their feet pounded the planks. Both scrambled to his Stoddard-Dayton, Fisher to the steering wheel, Moross at the crank handle. The engine rumbled to life, and Fisher had the car in gear and rolling before Moross hopped onto the running board and bounced into the passenger seat.

Within minutes the two men crossed the track's inner field and skidded to a halt on a grassy spot near the hospital tent at the south end. It was set up like a battlefield hospital, white with a bold red cross on the roof. Fisher sprinted through the canvas door flap to chilling screams of pain. Struggling to sort out the sight before him, he realized that the ambulance had not yet arrived. The man sitting on an examination table with his eyes bleeding was Louis Chevrolet, not Billy Bourque. His riding mechanic, George DeWitt, stationed himself like a soldier at his driver's side. Fisher glanced at Moross.

"What the hell happened?"

"There's a lot of dust and stones flying around out there, Mr. Fisher," DeWitt began. "We were coming up to put a lap on one of the Stoddard-Daytons when the left rear tire on that car flung off a good-sized rock smack into Louis' goggles. Shattered the lens real good, and some glass slivers got into his eyes, as well as dirt and oil. We coasted to a stop after turning off the course on the backstretch. I helped him find his way over here."

Ola Slaughter, a nurse, refilled a large glass syringe for another go at flushing out Chevrolet's eyes. It was relatively quick work to wash away the grit, but a couple of glass slivers pierced the skin just beneath both his eyeballs and required her to wield a pair tweezers for the delicate task of extracting them.

Chevrolet, a big burly man, was in tears. Not from wailing, but his body's natural reaction to foreign material.

"Okay, Mr. Chevrolet, I think I got it all," said the nurse. "Whatever you do, don't rub your eyes. I know they are plenty irritated, but you'll make it worse, especially if I left something behind. I recommend we wrap gauze over your eyes for at least a few hours."

Chevrolet did not respond. Instead, he vaulted off the table, all the time squinting like he was in bright sunlight. DeWitt offered his hand, but Chevrolet waved him off. He muttered a thank you to Slaughter and started to the tent flap when the commotion of an ambulance seized everyone's attention. Doctors Maxwell, Weyerbacher, and Fred Meyer heard through the phone line of what was coming their way and prepared for the arrival.

Everyone stepped back as the first man to push his head through the opening was police patrol officer John Weaver, who had witnessed the entire incident. Weaver gripped the handles of the stretcher, his back to Bourque, who was unconscious and lying down. A Ragsdale ambulance attendant supported the other end. Two of the doctors rushed to guide Bourque onto an examination table. Bourque's mechanic, his head disfigured, and face covered with blood was on a second stretcher. The attendants placed him on a cot. Dr. Weyerbacher shot to his side, kneeling beside the stricken man to put a stethoscope on his chest. As if to confirm the obvious, he simply shook his head.

All their attention turned to Bourque, who was still breathing. One doctor examined a pair of head wounds; the other two tore away at his pants to reveal compound fractures to both legs—the shin bones of both legs pierced through his flesh for an alarming display of white and scarlet.

Bourque's breathing became imperceptible as awful gurgling bubbled from his throat. Streams of scarlet traced down his cheeks from the corners of his overflowing mouth. They ripped open his shirt, and Chevrolet, Moross, and DeWitt stepped outside the tent.

"He's drowning in his own blood," said Dr. Meyer.

"Well, do something!" Fisher shouted.

Dr. Weyerbacher put his hand on Fisher's shoulder and asked him to leave.

"There's nothing we can do," said Meyer. "He has crushed ribs, and at least two of them have punctured his lungs."

Fisher pivoted toward the exit, muttering "Jesus Christ on a bicycle," to no one in particular. Outside, the roar of the engines was less muffled, more distinct. Moross looked ashen, and Fisher began to imagine a confrontation with officials and press back at the judges' stand. Chevrolet and DeWitt had disappeared after one of the Buick managers arrived in a car. Fisher was silent, his mind ruminating on how to handle all the critics and their accusations. Patrolman Weaver followed them outside.

"Mr. Fisher," he said haltingly. "I was standing at post twelve and witnessed the whole thing. The driver looked back. It seemed that his car was unsteady. When he twisted his head backward, he turned his wheel, and the car shot into the ditch, turning turtle and landing against the fence. The two men flew out of their seats. I did not know which was which, but one of the men struck a fence post with his head, and the other landed under the car. The car broke her axles, one wheel flew onto the track. The axles landed in the ditch."

Fisher thanked Weaver, told the shaken man to go home, have a drink, and get some rest. Moross said nothing, dragging his feet to the Stoddard-Dayton crank handle. A twist got the engine barking, but this time there was no urgency to scurry away. Fisher dreaded dealing with Wagner, Willis, and other Triple-A men or press reporters, and a little more time to sort his thoughts was welcome.

Back on the platform, Fisher found himself at the center of a cluster of reporters, all clutching their little notebooks. Moross intervened, motioning them to another corner with the promise "to share what we know."

Wheeler, Newby, and Allison drew to Fisher's side.

"Tell us what you need, Carl," Wheeler offered.

"We need a safe race track," Fisher muttered. "I need some back-up when this thing is over because you can be damn sure those Triple-A men are coming after us."

Wheeler extracted a pewter flask from his breast pocket and extended the vessel to Fisher. Simultaneously, he surveyed the room and discreetly expanded his gullet to pour half of the contents down his throat.

"I called over to the hospital and spoke with one of the doctors," Newby said. "Everyone up here knows Billy and Holcomb are goners. They said Chevrolet had cuts on his eyeballs?"

Fisher grimaced. "It's a madhouse over there. A rock busted Louis' goggles, and glass slivers got into his eyes. The glass scraped his eyeballs so much there was a little bleeding. A nurse tweezered the shit out. I think he's going to be okay."

Cars continued their clamor as they whirled by outside the judges' stand. Burman had been untouchable since Chevrolet pulled aside. Behind him, Jackson driver Fred Ellis was second and relentless in his pursuit. With but six of the nine starters still running, long gaps formed between their appearances on the front stretch.

Fisher traced Burman through his binoculars until unexpectedly, the driver darted into his repair pit. His mechanic scrambled to the right rear of the car to jack the wheel off the ground. Burman slid a funnel into his fuel tank and immediately hoisted a gas can above it, emptying the contents into the car. Ellis circulated the track from nearly a lap down and took the lead on the eighty-third lap.

Burman charged out of his pit, and Fisher imagined the driver's determination. With fifteen laps remaining, "Wild" Bob was closing, but the task before him seemed more than immense – most undoubtedly impossible. The desperate pace went on until the ninetieth lap when the Jackson, its engine silent, coasted listlessly to its repair pit.

Fisher scrutinized the situation through his binoculars. Ellis stumbled from his seat, looking shaky. His mechanic poured fuel through their funnel and into the car's tank. Ellis grasped the crank handle and then collapsed.

Alarmed, Fisher shouted and pointed as did everyone on the platform that wasn't studying the electric timer. A collective gasp emanated from the grandstand as Ellis was helped to his feet and into the Ragsdale ambulance. Everyone on the grounds was riveted on the fourth turn, anticipating, until Burman surged past and into the lead. Steadily, he ticked off the final tours of the circuit nearly a lap ahead of Jap Clemens.

Fisher and Allison descended the steps until they were trackside, flanking their sparkling silver Prest-O-Lite Trophy. Burman was prompt to arrive like he had scouted the location of the trophy before the race.

Fisher couldn't shake the image of Bourque and Holcomb's broken bodies. He consciously let Allison praise and congratulate. Privately, his mind spun up a course of action to condition his track for racing by the following morning. On the other side of the car and to Burman's back, a man waved at Fisher.

Wagner.

The starter pointed at Fisher in a jabbing gesture and then shifted his hand upward at the judges' stand. Fisher, with an exaggerated gesticulation and in an almost violent manner, waved the man off. Nobody pokes at Carl Fisher, even from a distance. To hell with that jackass.

Wagner swaggered over behind Burman, slapped him on the back, interrupting the Speedway founders' conversation. Burman swiveled around, and upon recognizing the flagman, he speedily extended his hand for an aggressive shake. There was an exchange of words Fisher could not make out. Wagner lingered, and Fisher knew he was asserting his position in the pecking order above Fisher. Not a chance.

At last, Wagner disappeared, headed to the judges' stand. Newby arrived at Fisher's side after completing a conversation with his drivers, Merz and Kincaid, who finished third and fourth.

"Wagner has made it damn clear that he wants to meet with us up in the judges' stand," Fisher said. "I'm in control here. We're in control here; this is our track. He's just a pencil-neck New Yorker."

"We have to be respectful, here, Carl," Newby said.

"I respect Billy Bourque and his mechanic. I hate what happened to them. But by damn, I am not going to let him use this tragedy to bludgeon what we have built here."

"Carl, I believe you care. I am just sickened by these deaths. Did you know both of these boys had wedding plans next month? They were just getting started in life. We can protect our business, but we need to demonstrate compassion for this terrible loss. Praise the Lord for sparing me from what you saw in the hospital tent."

Fisher studied Newby's face and then glanced at Allison. Inhaling mightily, his enthusiasm for the confrontation welled up. His chest puffed, and power swelled in his limbs. Newby was right, as usual. He would contain his contempt, and his most potent stance would emerge with measured force. He wanted to do the talking, but he knew that the ultimate demonstration of authority came with a united front of intelligent, dynamic men.

When the three founders reached the second floor of the judges' stand Frank Wheeler was already there. With cheeks flushed and rosy, he scurried to his partners.

"Wagner wants to shut us down," Wheeler shared in a guarded tone.

Fisher smiled and winked.

"We'll see about that."

In the far corner, a gaggle of Triple-A men was buzzing. Wagner flailed his arms, but the others were less animated. Among them were men more local than the others. Dave Beecroft, Frank Trego, and Charles Root were out of Chicago, along with George Cox of Terre Haute – all men he knew well. Still, the Triple-A chair, Lewis Speare, and Frank Hower, head of the contest board, were the officers he needed to convince.

Without hesitation, Wagner raised his voice in a scolding tone, "I told you, Fisher, not to kill my boys. Now there's hell to pay."

Looking past Wagner, Fisher directed his attention to Chairman Speare.

"Lewis," he began. "I think we should all pause a moment out of respect for the loss of two of our sport's bravest men."

Wagner was slack-jawed, appearing stupid, which satisfied Fisher. No one seemed comfortable with the requested pause, but there was no way to object. Fisher knew it asserted his command of the room, and his respect for the seriousness of the situation.

After a minute, Wagner blurted out, "This moment of respect is appropriate, but we need to ensure that this doesn't happen again this weekend. I move that we shut the entire race meet down. Call it off."

Again, Fisher deliberately did not acknowledge Wagner. He retained eye contact with Speare and sensed the other Triple-A men were taking cues from the big boss. Flamboyant Wagner was the exception.

"Lewis," Fisher began. "I assure you and all the executives in this room that I understand the seriousness of this situation. I witnessed the injuries at the hospital firsthand. It swirled my guts like a butter churn, and I never want to see such a scene again."

Wagner shook his head, rolled his eyes, sighing. Fisher continued stating his position without allowing the distraction of Wagner to disrupt the cadence of his delivery. He maintained eye contact with Speare.

"Gentlemen, I have developed a list of precautions for conditioning and staffing the Speedway I will share with you. We are seasoning our track every day, and I can assure you that by tomorrow morning, it will be in tip-top condition. We have lighting that enables us to work through the night. We have done it before, and we will do it again. Our commitment is to a fast, safe facility."

Wagner appeared ready to speak, but at last, Speare raised his voice.

"We understand your dedication, Carl, and want to help this Speedway live up to its potential. What's this I hear about a two-foot ditch at the west side of turn four?"

"Two foot is an exaggeration. Some of the laborers may have dug up and transferred earth to the heart of the turn to fill in ruts. We'll fix it, pronto, and you can be damn sure it won't happen again. I will personally inspect every inch of this track."

"Art, Jim, we heard from Frank before you gentlemen joined us, and he has been clear the Speedway officers will make good on your promises for a great race track. You've been quiet here," Speare said. "What do you think? Can this track be brought up to snuff by tomorrow?"

"I wouldn't put my National boys in the middle of all this without believing we are doing everything we can to give them a safe track to race on," Newby said.

"Our engineer Park Andrews has already assembled a team of good men filling in rough spots, and doing whatever is necessary," Allison said. "They're out there now. We'll patch everything and have the course oiled before the races tomorrow."

Wagner found an opportunity to inject himself into the conversation.

"We should hear from Mr. Vanderbilt. And Mr. Pardington."

Speare cast a stony gaze on Wagner, and the starter seemed to understand that he had overstepped. The chairman transferred his eyes to the Speedway founders.

"Gentlemen, the American Automobile Association is invested in the success of the Speedway. We want this grand experiment in race track design to be successful. America and its automobile factories need it. However, we cannot sit by and tolerate the kind of carnage we have seen today. Let's continue with our races, but we need a safe day tomorrow."

Fisher knew he could only promise precautions, not provide life and death guarantees. He saw no reason to say anything else except, "Good evening, gentlemen."

(Indianapolis Motor Speedway, August 20, 1909)

Carl Fisher, his mind foggy after his around-the-clock vigilance to will his Speedway into racing condition, glanced at his fellow founders as all four of them sipped coffee out of tin cups and rested their arms on the window sill of the second-floor judges' stand. Fisher had the morning Star newspaper, its pages fluttering in the wind as he tried to focus on a particular article. The men never made a habit of huddling together unless over lunch or in an office to talk business. Today, all of them knew what was at stake, perhaps even the future of their enterprise.

"I spoke with George Crane at Knox," Allison remarked. "He says they're through."

"Packing up and heading home?" Wheeler asked.

"Nope. It looks like they are quitting the game entirely," Allison continued. "Crane telegraphed the Knox vice president right after the accident, and that's the reaction he got."

Fisher did not look up from his newspaper but was listening.

"That's my understanding as well," Newby inserted. "I saw Al Dennison in front of their garage this morning. He took it hard; he and Billy were teammates for years but also friends like brothers. They shared an apartment back in Massachusetts."

"W.E. Wright," said Fisher. "If that's the Knox man you're talking about, I'm not surprised. He doesn't have much stomach for this kind of thing."

"Carl, if something like that happened to one of my men, I don't know but that I would do the very same thing," Newby said.

The voices of three men grew louder as they ascended the steps behind the Speedway owners. Rounding a left turn from the stairs and onto the second floor, Fisher recognized two of them immediately. The first was Harry Stutz, the Marion Motor Car Company executive engineer, and Howard Marmon, also an engineer. Still, more than that, he was part of the ownership family of Nordyke and Marmon, which produced Marmon automobiles. Both were prominent men, well-known in the Hoosier capital city and beyond. Each had wire spectacles hooked over their ears, evidence of their many years sitting at drafting tables for the tedious, close-up work of creating detailed blueprints, studying them, and revising. The third man Fisher recognized as Charles Jeffery, second only to his father Thomas at the Gormully and Jeffery tire company.

"We're just showing Charles around this incredible Speedway you men have so impressively brought into the world," Marmon announced. "We picked him up at the train station last night and whisked him out here this morning in one of my cars."

Stutz, his eyes noticeably widening, said, "And I will take him back to the Claypool in my Marion Flyer this evening."

The remark brought chuckles from all around.

"Charles, before we say anything else, I think I can speak for my partners and everyone at the Indianapolis Motor Speedway Company. We are mighty pleased that G and J commissioned a beautiful trophy for our feature race today," Carl said.

Jeffery said it was his honor. He congratulated the owners with an enthusiastic handshake – like he was closing the deal all over again.

Stomping feet on the wood plank stairs behind them grew louder with each step. The heads of Lewis Speare and Frank Trego appeared above the wall lining the stairwell.

"Good morning, gentlemen!" Speare announced. "I am delighted with how the track looks this morning. We took the liberty of a lap tour. It looks like you laid down the oil as we asked, I didn't catch much dust. Some of your men and mule carts are still out there with the finishing touches, I presume."

"Good morning to you both as well," Fisher returned. "Yes. Last-minute details. We still have a couple of hours before the first race at noon. I don't see any reason to waste any time bringing this track to perfection."

"Carl, there is something we need to discuss," said Speare, with a solemn expression. "We need to shorten the G and J Trophy to fifty miles."

Fisher blurted impulsively, "What the Hell are you talking about, Speare!"

Behind Speare, Trego nodded his head. The image of what Fisher deemed ass-kissing behavior incensed him to his bowels. Speare replied in a measured tone.

"Carl, it's the responsible thing to do after yesterday," Speare continued, apparently unmoved by Fisher's visceral reaction. "Especially with the Wheeler-Schebler Trophy tomorrow. We don't want to overstress the cars or the drivers before that three-hundred-mile race tomorrow."

"Have you spoken with the teams involved," asked Marmon. "We'll have Ray Harroun in both those races, and we are ready for a hundred miles today."

Stutz thrust his right hand upward, his index finger extended forward as if to put an exclamation point on his words, "Marion will be represented in both contests. We thrive on competition."

Fisher was grateful for the support of his colleagues. Glancing at them, he said, "Ask any of my partners if they like the idea of promising everyone that bought a ticket a one-hundred-mile feature race and then pulling a bait-and-switch."

Allison, Wheeler, and Newby uttered disgruntled tones denouncing Speare's proposition. Finally, Charles Jeffery spoke up.

"Gentleman, I want to be clear that this is a matter of honor and integrity. We agreed to commission the G and J Trophy on the premise that the Speedway and the Triple-A would conduct a hundred-mile feature race and nothing less. What you are proposing is unacceptable."

Speare appeared flummoxed. Swinging his head behind him and in the direction of Trego, he found only a blank face.

"Fine. You are all united in your position. I want you to understand we made our request with the sincerest best intentions for the safety of everyone concerned. I will pray for the best possible result from your decision. Now, I have work to do, and I am sure each of you has responsibilities to address. Excuse us."

Speare nodded, and he and Trego went about their work, testing the electric timer, and organizing scoring sheets. Fisher started talking about an article in his newspaper, raising his voice vigorously.

"Fellas, did you see this article? The headline is, 'Speedway Adds to Indianapolis.' All the hotels downtown are full-up to overflowing. People have spare rooms in their homes to let. Stoddard-Dayton had a big banquet last night with a couple of hundred people at the Denison for Jap Clemens finishing second in the Prest-O-Lite Trophy."

Allison cocked his head toward his partner, his face wrenched into a quizzical expression. Only Newby seemed to understand his friend's lusty proclamation was for Speare, and not him.

"I'm well aware of the enthusiasm for the Speedway, Carl," Speare said without looking up from documents scattered before on the Hickory table where he had grabbed a chair.

Fisher rolled his eyes but also recognized his foolishness and tucked the paper under his arm. Marmon, Stutz, and Jeffery pardoned themselves from the moment; their satisfaction with the conversation was palpable.

With his partners, Fisher returned his gaze outward to the track. The sixteen-thousand-seat grandstand across from them on the other side of the front stretch was filling up as the trains out of Union Station delivered their passengers every twenty minutes or so. Barely ten o'clock and the races were scheduled to commence at noon. Fisher found what he saw was gratifying; it was a good crowd for a Friday.

"Each of us takes a car and ventures out to the track for a final inspection?" Fisher said, lowering his voice. "If you see any Triple-A men out there, stop and have a chat. We need to make sure nobody stirs up trouble."

(Indianapolis Motor Speedway, August 20, 1909)

Barney Oldfield squeezed the tan-taped steering wheel of "Old Glory" as George and

Jimmy Hill ran a final check on wheels, tires, fuel, oil, and water. They cinched the leather straps holding the car's star-spangled banner cowling in place. Fred Wagner, his arms stretched around his back and his hands clasping his red starter's flag, paced in front of a row of eight cars. The other two indigo Nationals with Johnny Aitken and Tom Kincaid in their seats as well, with Art Newby's men tending to the machines just as Oldfield's mechanics were doing. Newby ambled between the three cars, treating Oldfield not as an independent, but one of the team drivers he wanted to prosper. National's top executive locked his right hand into vigorous handshakes, each followed by a slap on the racers' backs.

In the line were competitors and cars familiar to Oldfield, who had been at the sport longer than any of them, aside from Herb Lytle, who caught eyes with his rival and gave him a nod from his crimson Apperson. Ralph Mulford pointed at the front of his pearl Lozier to provide instructions to team mechanics. There was Eddie Hearne down from Chicago with his brick-red Fiat, and teenager Tobin DeHymel, up from San Antonio. The nineteen-year-old sat in one of two bleach-white with scarlet trim Stoddard-Daytons. The other identical racer was in the hands of Fred "Jap" Clemens, senior enough to be his teammate's father. Together they were ready to charge into the third race of the day, a ten-miler for stock chassis cars with engines smaller than six-hundred cubic inches.

Wagner curtailed his back-and-forth gait, and a clerk-of-course extended a megaphone to him. Shouting out instructions every driver had heard before, the starter asserted another standing start and uttered admonitions of disqualification for any driver daring to jump the gun. He then told the teams to crank their engines and prepare for battle. A series of exhaust explosions ensued as every cylinder blasted the smoky residue of gasoline, spark, and air.

The mechanics scurried back to vantage points behind their cars, poised for any engine malfunction or hesitation. Wagner extracted a six-shooter from his holster and pointed it above his head. In his other hand was his red flag as the combination gave drivers no excuse for missing the signal. His gun burst permeated the din of engine thunder, and simultaneously, Wagner sliced his red flag through the air.

Hearne bolted his Fiat into the lead in a clean start. The other cars stormed down the front stretch in pursuit, and Oldfield judged the distance between his wheels and Lytle's Apperson and those of Clemens on the other side. Hearne was safely in the lead heading into the first turn while the other seven cars converged for the three available lines through the curve.

Oldfield felt like he was in a game of chicken with the other cars as their wheels crept ever closer to his. He asserted his position on the inside as he was half a car length over Lytle. All the drivers around "Old Glory" masterfully steered their racers side-by-side without contact or turmoil.

Through the short stretch and into turn two Oldfield saw Hearne's red car grow perceptively smaller as the mining company millionaire extended his lead. Because of the short race distance, nobody had a riding mechanic, and Oldfield glanced backward to see the Stoddard-Daytons of DeHymel and Clemens closing in. Both drivers surged with strong momentum off turn two and then soared out onto the backstretch. Swiftly they were upon him, one on each side. They surged ahead as Hearne relentlessly lengthened his advantage.

Oldfield's pulse soared on his approach to turn three, as the star-spangled cowling lifted from the air that got underneath. Startled, he spied orange flames lapping at the underside of the hood. He abruptly lifted his foot and pulled low on the entrance to turn three as Aitken blasted by with Kincaid in pursuit. Suddenly, the cowling took flight, hurtling back at Oldfield's face. Instinctively, his right arm shot upward to deflect the makeshift guillotine. His quick thinking redirected the errant metal above to fly behind him.

Stinging, throbbing pain shot like a lightning bolt down his arm as Oldfield lowered it to grasp the wheel and steer off course at the north end of the oval. His forward motion halted, and the flames abated. Oldfield clutched the erupting gash in his right forearm as crimson rivulets flowed between his gloved fingers.

A mounted police officer galloped to his side on a gray stallion.

"Sergeant Metcalf at your service, Mr. Oldfield."

Oldfield removed his leather pants belt and tightened it on his arm above the wound. He circulated the now hoodless National racer looking for any severe damage. There wasn't any to his best assessment.

"Sergeant, I could use a hand here. Do you mind cranking my engine? I'm going to drive it back to my pit and then find a doctor to fix me up."

Roaring engines grew increasingly loud as the racers thundered toward them on their second lap. Oldfield paused to study the situation and found Hearne was missing and De-Hymel in the lead. Clemens, Aitken, Kincaid, and Lytle followed in an orderly succession.

The Sergeant dismounted and scurried to the front of the car. He appeared unsure. Oldfield climbed into his racer and shouted instructions.

"It's easy, just grip the handle and turn it like an ice cream maker. Just be sure to pull your arm back quickly. There's a lot of compression in these engines, and I've seen fellas break their arms if the crank kicks back."

Dutifully, the policeman labored at the unfamiliar task. He was a large man and up to the required exertion despite a distinct lack of confidence. Finally, and on the fourth turn, snarling growls burst throughout the air to announce the engine was alive. Oldfield saluted Metcalf and eased his car into gear. He glanced over his shoulder and saw the racecars approaching rapidly. Clemens had snatched the lead from DeHymel as Aitken crept up from behind.

The limb pulsated, and upon returning to his pit, Oldfield was in a hurry to have one of the Hill brothers drive him to the infield hospital tent. By the time they arrived, his arm was numb, but his tourniquet had sharply mitigated the flow of scarlet fluid from the wound. Pulling back the flap of the tent, he saw the doctors and nurses conversing among themselves and two patients, apparently spectators, with minor injuries.

"Hey, can someone patch me up?"

Everyone turned their heads toward Oldfield and appeared to recognize him immediately. Nurse Slaughter and Dr. Meyer advanced toward him.

"This belt needs to come off," Meyer said. "But before that, let's stitch the wound."

Taking her cue, Slaughter pivoted to a supply cabinet to extract a needle and thread. Meyer motioned Oldfield to a chair.

Oldfield winced as he watched the nurse weave the needle through his torn flesh. Piercing skin on one side, then appearing through scarlet crevice only to disappear into the other side. The meanest moments came as she pushed the needle up to puncture its way through and out of the previously unmolested tissue. Watching intently, he chewed on a fresh, unlit cigar.

Her work complete, Slaughter released the tourniquet and began to bandage and wrap the wound. The heavy flow of blood had abated, scarlet spots from both the injury and damaged skin from the stitches appeared from under the dressing.

"Rest your arm for a week or two," Dr. Meyer said. "You'll heal up nicely and be just as good as new."

Oldfield planned to drive his Grand Prix Benz in a ten-miler later in the afternoon. He saw no purpose in saying anything to the doctor because sure as Hell, a stupid cut on his arm wasn't going to change his plans. He nodded and then turned to George Hill, who had waited at his side.

"Let's head back to the garages, George," Oldfield said, glancing at Nurse Slaughter. "Thanks for your handiwork, Ma'am. You're so darn pretty I'd let you sew me up for fun."

Slaughter blushed. Smiling at the doctor, Oldfield thanked him as well. As he stepped out of the tent, he heard the doctor behind him ask if he planned to take their advice. Oldfield did not respond and kept walking to the National touring car Newby had provided him.

Back trackside, Oldfield ambled by the judge's stand. Hearing someone shouting his name, he tilted his head upward to see Carl Fisher leaning out of the second-story window.

"Barney! You got a minute for me? Come on up here."

Oldfield gestured affirmatively and told Hill to go to the garage and have the boys get the Benz ready. A fifty-mile contest for five cars was just beginning to start, and next on the schedule was the one Oldfield had entered the Benz. Oldfield scaled the judge's stand steps until he stood in front of Fisher and Allison.

"Who won the race?" he asked.

"Aitken ended up winning after Hearne, de Hymel, and Clemens all dropped out. Art's happy. Bully good for them, but I hated to see both the Stoddard-Daytons crap out on the last lap."

"Well, I'll have to congratulate Newby and Aitken when I see them next."

No one had time for more conversation, and Oldfield appreciated Fisher coming directly to the point.

"How are you, Barney? Meyer over at the hospital tent called and said you had to get a nasty gash stitched up. You feeling okay?"

"Do you mean, am I going to keep driving in your races?"

"You know me too well, Oldfield. Look, you're my friend, and I hated to hear what happened. I understand if you're not feeling up to it, but I won't deny you're one of the favorites with the railbirds."

"I'm going to give it a shot, Carl. I've been itching to bring the Benz out for a go," Barney said. "But, you have to let me get back with my fellas and get organized."

Fisher delighted to hear one of his star drivers would return to the track, laughed, and provided a vigorous handshake. Stoic Allison also shook the driver's hand, but with far more measured enthusiasm.

The Hill brothers had the one hundred twenty horsepower Benz gassed and ready to go by the time Oldfield traipsed into his garage stall. The men pushed the big machine along the path leading to the track as a pair of Stoddard-Daytons stormed to the finish line and Wagner's checkered flag to conclude the forty-lap race for small cars. They were the only two to finish out of five racers.

Again, Oldfield waited impatiently as Wagner tediously aligned the six cars in the race, a ten-mile free-for-all for all racing cars. That spaghetti-eater Ralph DePalma in his sparkling white jumpsuit sat high in his Fiat. There was something that pissed Oldfield off about that guy ever since he beat him in a match race at a dirt track the previous year. If there was one guy in that line Oldfield was determined to put down, it was DePalma.

Wagner droned on with his warnings about false starts and the procedure in general. Finally, his little blank gun emitted its snap and spark as he waved the red flag. Oldfield's big Benz had the horses to get a jump on the others as he stormed away toward the southwest turn at the end of the straightaway.

Oldfield's arm throbbed like a drum beat, but he felt he could hold on. Glancing over his shoulder, he saw Len Zengel following closely. Dust obscured the other cars as Oldfield pulled steadily away, the pain in his arm ever escalating. Still, he pushed on, despite the constant jolts and jostling from the rough track. Each bump was another stab.

Oldfield and his Benz ticked off the first lap in front, with Zengel, like a ghost lurking in the dust cloud, as the only challenger visible through the smoky veil from behind. He cranked his wheel and slid through turn one, with crushed stone flying all around the Benz, and especially in its wake. Hurtling through the south-end short chute, Oldfield again twisted his wheel for the second corner. Despite the growing protests in his right arm, his exit onto the backstretch was flawless. Only Zengel, undoubtedly being pelted with stone chips, hung on grimly.

DePalma's Fiat was parked on the grass a couple of dozen feet to the left. That was fine with Oldfield, let that son-of-a-bitch finish last. His momentum only increased at his approach to turn three, and again the oval presented a short straight and then turn four. Like an electric shock, searing pain flashed through his arm. Unconsciously, his right arm flited off the wheel as if on its own, but instinctively he raised his foot from the throttle and reaffirmed the grip of his left hand. The big car coasted toward the pits, as Oldfield now drove with his right hand, his left squeezing his wound as it wept more blood.

Zengel's Chadwick rumbled by, well in command. Aitken entered the home stretch at least fifteen seconds behind. Oldfield continued to creep along, not toward his pit, but his garage. George and Jimmy Hill scrambled up from behind as he stopped.

"What happened, Barney?" George asked. "Something break?"

"Yeah. My goddamn arm. I must have busted a stitch or two. It nearly launched me out of my goddamn seat. Fuck, it hurts."

Almost simultaneously, both the brothers asked their driver if he wanted to keep racing.

"That's what the Hell we came here for, isn't it? Jimmy, see that the car gets into the garage and start giving it the once-over for tomorrow. George, let's get in your car and drive me over the hospital tent to see that pretty little nurse."

(Indianapolis Motor Speedway, August 20, 1909)

Carl Fisher dialed in his binoculars to focus on Lewis Strang as he swept by the judges' stand with his red streaming ribbon affixed to his linen skull cap fluttering back over his red Buick's fuel barrel. Strang led an hour into the race, with his teammate George DeWitt and Marmon's Ray Harroun down by more than two laps.

"This should be over in about a half-hour by my calculation," said Jim Allison.

Hearing the comment, Frank Trego, who manned the official AAA electric timer, announced that Strang had broken every American track record after twenty miles. Nobody appeared to threaten his dominant grip on the contest.

"Well, it isn't close, but we can make hay with all these records," Fisher said, directing his comment to his partner. "The Indianapolis Motor Speedway is the fastest track in the country. The greatest race track in the world!"

Allison, who rarely appeared amused, allowed Fisher a glimpse of a subtle smile.

"Who are you talking to, Carl?"

"Anyone who will listen, Jim. Anyone who will listen."

Strang maintained his record pace despite being laps in front of his pursuers. His teammate, Louis Chevrolet, retired with a misfiring engine after only ten laps. Adolph Monson, in one of Harry Stutz's Marion entries, was gone after only four laps. Only four cars remained, making for tedious, extended gaps of relatively muted racket as the drivers droned past.

"Records, yes," Allison inserted. "And no accidents. The track is in good condition."

Leaning near Carl's right ear, he lowered his voice.

"And the Triple-A can stick that up their ass."

Fisher chuckled.

Strang ticked off the miles as they piled up to the point when Wagner, a tiny figure in gravel from Fisher's vantage point in the judges' stand, unfurled his green flag to signal the ultimate lap. The crimson Buick launched into its final round roaring with a delightful anger Fisher felt in his chest. Blasting pistons were at work, propelling the beastly machine precisely as intended. Strang refused to slacken his pace as he circulated the course's stretches and four turns with flawless flair accentuated by the red ribbon on his head.

Fisher nudged Allison, and the two men began their footslog downstairs to the platform and table where the G and J Trophy stood. Passing Lewis Speare, he said, "Great long, safe race, huh Lewis?"

Speare nodded affirmatively.

"Let's keep it that way, Carl. We have a race that's three times longer tomorrow."

Fisher said nothing as he and Allison continued their descent downstairs. Strang was just wheeling up to a halt in front of the trophy. Dust, dirt, and tire rubber coated the car, dulling what had been a lustrous shine under the Indiana sun. Strang wiped his face with a towel a crew member tossed him as he turned his attention to a beautiful young woman who simultaneously held her wide hat in place and jumped up and down.

"Mrs. Strang," Frank Wheeler announced after stepping to his partners' side. "Or Jeanne Spaulding. Or her stage name, Louise Alexander, if you prefer."

Strang embraced his wife, who still steadied her hat with one hand. The driver crushed her fluffy silk blouse, undoubtedly staining its gossamer whiteness with track grime. At the moment, she did not appear to mind. Three photographers huddled around the couple as the eager wife unabashedly planted a lingering, full-lipped kiss on her heroic husband.

Fisher raised an eyebrow as he cocked his head toward Wheeler.

"That'll make the papers. Mrs. Strang is quite lovely, an actress I hear."

"Yes. I saw her perform in New York last year before they were married," Wheeler added. "I believe he told her to give up the acting for the marriage. Too many romantic leading men in the plays."

"Well, all that matters right now is that it is a great story and a bully-good image for the papers. Let's find Newby and hustle another night of track repair. We need a great day of racing tomorrow. And records."

(Indianapolis Motor Speedway, August 21, 1909)

"It's a new speed record," Carl Fisher shouted.

James Allison peered over his partner's shoulder to see the time on the stopwatch. Eight minutes, twenty-three, and a fifth seconds for ten miles. Fisher and Allison caught Frank Trego's eyes. Nodding his head, Trego confirmed the electric timing device corroborated the pronouncement.

"Old Barney is scorching the track, sliced-up arm or no," Fisher said. "You got to hand it to the man; he's tough as nails. He's smashing every speed mark to smithereens!"

Both partners raised their binoculars to their eyes as Oldfield, and his pearl Benz emerged from the northwest, rounding turn four. The thundering machine grew more substantial in their vision and then passed the finish line with billowing dust and stones chips in his wake. Oldfield had led from the start over his two opponents, Len Zengel in the big Chadwick, and Ralph DePalma, back with the Fiat. He relentlessly extended his lead, amassing an advantage of at least a mile by the contest's halfway marker.

Trego got with the spirit of the moment, announcing the continuous stream of record-shattering progress. By fifteen miles, he declared another record of twelve minutes, thirty-two and two fifth seconds.

"If his arm or his car doesn't give out, he's got that Remy Brassard in the bag," Fisher said. "Say, I see the Remy brothers down there behind the trophy platform. Let's go have a chat."

Upon greeting Frank and Perry Remy, Fisher noticed they, too, had stopwatches.

"We've been up with the Triple-A timer in the judges' stand. Barney has smashed every speed record from one to fifteen miles," Fisher offered.

"Well, he just added one for twenty-miles, according to my watch," Frank Remy replied. "Sixteen minutes, and just a tad shy of fifty-four seconds."

Fisher nodded, his eyes scanning the gleaming, silver Remy Brassard, and Trophy perched on the table before them.

"Hey, fellas, do you mind if Jim here has a look at that brassard? He was too busy tending to our Prest-O-Lite business to see it in our meeting a few weeks back."

"Of course," said Perry. "Let me show you how carefully we handle the silver. No smudges."

Next to the awards, there were three or four jeweler's cloths. He unfolded one and wrapped it around the back of the brassard. Allison managed the careful handoff, only placing his fingers on the fabric.

"We thank you tremendously for your participation in our races," Allison said as he tilted the prize at different angles. "That and the seventy-five dollar-a-week salary for the winner until the next race is most generous."

"We have a great deal of respect for the men who pilot these mechanical wonders," Perry said. "Most of the attention goes to the cars and the factories who construct them, and that's fine. That's what our trophy is for. But my brother and I want to call attention to the brave drivers. Our brassard is a unique prize, and with the salary, we believe the winning driver will recognize our sincerity."

With that, Ernie Moross inserted himself amongst the men. He wielded a megaphone in apparent preparation for the awarding of the brassard and trophy. The rolling cacophony of the Benz approached the checkered flag. Fred Wagner waved it with spectacular flair. DePalma, a half-lap behind, finally crossed the finish line as well. Zengel followed him.

Oldfield coasted toward the sponsors and officials with his mechanics, the Hill brothers, trotting along as if in tow. The grime-coated car rolled to a stop in front of the trophy platform, its brilliant whiteness obscured by a veil of dust so thick Fisher thought he could scribble his name in it with his index finger. A clerk of the course scurried to Moross's side to extend a small note card. Moross scanned it quickly and then tilted his megaphone to his mouth.

"Ladies and gentlemen, may I have your attention, please," Moross bellowed out and then paused.

Across the track and among the grandstand-capacity crowd of spectators, young men also with megaphones barked the contest director's words. The din of the gathering diminished.

"It is my pleasure to announce that everyone's champion driver, Barney Oldfield, has not only become the first Remy Brassard winner but also has annihilated every speed record from one to twenty-five miles. We have a new American record for twenty-five miles of twenty-one minutes and twenty-one seconds!"

Delayed in relay for a matter of seconds, the approving cheers and applause from the grandstand made it clear people were getting their money's worth. Moross continued with his pronouncements, narrating the ceremony of awards presentation by the Remy brothers. Ignoring the jeweler's cloth, Oldfield clutched the brassard to slide it up the sleeve of his left arm, obviously sparing his injured right limb pain and discomfort. He pushed his award up his left arm and lines formed on his shirt, where the edges scraped away the dust, grime, and tire specks that had accumulated there.

Fisher nudged his way to the side of the Benz, extending his hand to the driver. He thought about Oldfield's injury as they clasped hands and gave a gingerly shake.

"How's the arm, Barney?"

"Better than yesterday. That little nurse gave me a few extra stitches and then wrapped me with this thicker cloth bandage. It still smarts some, but I've been through worse."

"Well, it's not affecting your driving, that's for sure. You set that new kilometer record in our time trial event this morning, and now you showed 'em what for in the Remy deal. The crowd loves it, Barney. They love you."

Oldfield scanned the stands across the way.

"You got them packed in here for this day of the meet, Carl. You and your boys are onto something here."

He then motioned for Fisher to lean close so he could speak in a subdued tone.

"Carl, I don't know what you can do about it, but that track is breaking up in spots. There are more dust and rocks and shit flying at us out there than any dirt track I've seen. That Wheeler-Schebler race is going to be a mess before we drive three hundred miles."

(Indianapolis Motor Speedway, August 21, 1909)

"Well, Frank, it's finally your turn," Carl Fisher said. "You too, George. Both you fellas outdid yourselves with this trophy."

The gleaming, ten-thousand-dollar Tiffany silver Wheeler-Schebler Carburetor Company Trophy towered over Fisher and its namesakes.

The Wheeler-Schebler prize was displayed on a roughhewn wooden platform at the base of the judges' stand. Unlike the rest, its sheer size accentuated its magnificence. Seven feet tall and boosted to the sky by the platform, Fisher positioned himself in the shade where it eclipsed the sun. He judged the award the pinnacle of silversmithing. A Greek Goddess stood triumphantly atop, casting her shadow several feet behind Fisher. Two other figures rested on loving cup handles just below the deity's feet. On the left was an American Indian in native dress and clutching a tomahawk. On the other side, another woman, again in a flowing robe, clasped the handle of a large sword.

Fisher squinted as he traced his eyes over each detail. Despite having examined it at least a hundred times, it irresistibly drew him back. His heart swelled, and he wanted to point to its ornate wonder as the crowning emblem of his achievement. The Wheeler-Schebler Trophy, provided by Frank Wheeler and his partner George Schebler, was worthy of his wonder-of-the-world Speedway.

"I want you gentlemen to celebrate today," Fisher said. "Come and walk with me through the cars Wagner has lined up. "We'll have just enough time to chat with a few of the drivers before I have to get up to the judges' stand for the start of the race. Today is truly your moment."

Wheeler took a step forward toward Fisher. It was apparent he did not want to be overheard. Coming close, he uttered, "I can't do it, Carl. You know how I've been scraping my skin and can't stop the bleeding? It happened this morning to my big toe, and my right sock is pretty soaked. I just can't put up with walking. You and George go. I'll stay here with the trophy."

"Jesus, Frank. The doc can't do anything?"

"Not really. He wants to put me on a diet. He thinks I've got diabetes."

"Yeah," Fisher whispered. "Doctors can be a pain in the ass. Half the time they don't know what they're talking about."

Fisher took a gander at Schebler, who seemed to know the essence of his exchange with Wheeler. Schebler, appearing older than his forty-four years, was a short man, and a genius. Their carburetor was the product of his inventiveness – Wheeler was the loquacious salesman.

Together Fisher and Schebler strolled the aisles between rows of four cars each until they had counted off nineteen. Their positions were by order of entry, and one of Art Newby's Nationals, driven by Johnny Aitken, was on the pole.

"Art!" Fisher yelled to get his partner's attention. Newby turned from his chat with Aitken.

"How are things shaping up for the team? Johnny, Charlie? Barney's got a National, too. Tell me you're confident."

Newby grimaced, and Fisher read into the expression. He didn't want any pessimism on the precipice of his track's biggest event. In one year, it had become one of America's biggest races with something like forty-thousand paying customers. The Vanderbilt Cup never did that; they let almost everyone in for free.

"Tell me you're optimistic, Art," Fisher repeated as if by doing so, he could will success into the moment.

"I am optimistic about my cars. It's this track I'm worried about."

"Oh, come on, Art. You know as well as I do, we had boys out there working all night again. We had some more oil laid down after the Remy race."

"Carl, this thing is three hundred miles. These boys will run hard; they'll go like bats straight out of the bowels of Hell. We keep patching ruts, and that's after just the sprint races."

"I'll be damned if we're going to shorten this race. We went through that yesterday with the G and J. We're going to do what we said we'd do."

Newby nodded, turned away from the conversation, and moved on to his next pilot, Charlie Merz. Disappointment, even hurt, welled up in Fisher. Newby's approval buoyed his enthusiasm, and his disapproval was even more powerful. He paused to collect himself, never to show how another man's opinion could make him doubt a damn thing.

"Carl?" Schebler said. "Are you okay? Do you want to keep walking?"

Fisher returned from his introspection. He studied the kindly, weathered face of George Schebler. Like everyone else, Schebler and all the people on the grounds were living in Fisher's vision. Everything had to work.

"Let's go chat with Oldfield," Fisher finally said. "He's always good for a boost."

Oldfield and Jimmy Hill sat side-by-side in "Old Glory." George Hill was checking the cowling back in form with the Star-Spangled Banner paint job refreshed.

"Tell me good news, Barney," Fisher said as he approached.

"George, have you got that big trophy all polished up for me? I plan to swing by in about four and a half hours and take it off your hands."

Schebler assured the Remy Brassard champion the Wheeler-Schleber was sparkling.

"You think you're going to get to take that one home too, Barney?"

"Well, I plan to turn left and go like Hell."

Oldfield seemed like he did not want to answer Fisher's first question. The Speedway president did not want to probe further. Oldfield had already told him about his concerns over track conditions earlier.

"Barney, I heard what you said after the Remy. We laid some oil and filled the ruts. We tamped it down, really hard."

"Carl, I've been around now longer than most of these boys. I can handle whatever comes at me. As I told Wheeler when I came into town, I'm not ready for the dirt nap, and I know how hard to push. I appreciate what you and your boys are doing. Listen, I need to collect my thoughts."

Fisher had heard enough. Everyone was too honest, and he had enough of that. Schebler strode at his side until they returned to the big trophy. From there, he went alone to his spot in the judges' stand.

Engines commenced their angry howls below, spewing exhaust smoke and obscuring the men surrounding them. Within seconds, mechanics came scurrying out of the haze like they were escaping some deadly fog.

Within minutes Wagner again shot his pistol and flapped the red flag to ignite the tinderbox explosion of the largest starting field of the entire three days. Aitken bolted from the pole position to a shocking jump on the others, and Fisher studied Wagner to see if he would try to call a false start. Nineteen unbridled machines defied official but feeble attempts to recall or dissuade them. The jockeys were hard characters hurtling their rides in relentless pursuit of the next car until nobody was in their way.

Aitken appeared through Fisher's binoculars at the end of the first lap from the distance of turn four. He panned his spectacles as the National grew ever-larger, drew nearer, and then diminished on its path to turn one. Perhaps twenty seconds elapsed before second-place Herb Lytle's Apperson crept into view, with Bob Burman in his Buick no more than a car length further back.

As the race carried on, the order of the first three did not change except that Aitken extended his advantage. Abruptly, at fifty miles, Lytle's car swerved unevenly, not far from the judges' stand. At first, the machine lunged ominously toward the packed balloon stands outside turn one, and then, as if in ricochet, it shot to the infield and stopped short of the creek there. Fisher focused his binoculars on watching Lytle jump out of the car and rush to the side of his riding mechanic, Joe Betts. The force of the accident had launched the mechanic from his seat. Betts stumbled to his feet, and both men returned to their errant racer, ostensibly examining for damage. The race fell into a rhythm of Aitken motoring away, with Burman holding the rest of the field at bay.

"Aitken just broke Strang's one-hundred-mile record from yesterday!" shouted Jim Allison, who had been looking over Frank Trego's shoulder at the electric timer.

Fisher involuntarily busted off a loud clap of his hands, thrilled with more evidence he had constructed the greatest track in the world. Like a sudden drenching of ice water to his spirit, he could see Aitken creeping around turn four and coasting to his pit. Burman devoured Aitken's advantage and surged into the lead within forty-five seconds.

After several minutes, the judges' stand phone rang. Ernie Moross answered. He said very little, and Fisher surmised that whoever was on the line was doing all the talking.

"That was Mr. Newby," Moross shared. "Aitken is saying he can't see a thing out there. He goes through dust clouds not being able to tell if there is an accident in front of him. He says if the race continues, someone is going to get killed."

(Indianapolis Motor Speedway, August 21, 1909)

Barney Oldfield squinted to peer through the glare of the sun on his goggles and the dense powder that enveloped "Old Glory" as he thundered down the backstretch to approach turn three. Jimmy Hill sat beside him, thrusting the rod in his brass cylinder oil pump while on the stretch, but letting go of its nob as the turn came upon them. Hill abruptly but routinely pivoted backward, clutching his seat to stay in the car while he tried to discern what might be approaching from behind.

Bam!

Old Glory bounded over a pothole at the point the turn straightened for the short stretch between them and turn four. Oldfield felt his ass lift off his seat but held tightly to the wheel.

"This is bullshit," Oldfield screamed to himself with no expectation of Hill hearing him.

As they rounded turn four, Oldfield felt a squeeze from Hill on his right bicep, a signal of another racer approaching. The yellow Marmon of Ray Harroun emerged from billowing dust to pull up to Oldfield's side and then slither ahead. Harroun cleared Oldfield's National and then steered back down in front of him. Dust and stone chips sprayed rearward to Oldfield and Hill, pelting their car as well as their faces. Oldfield cringed as the rock fragments chipped at his goggles, threatening to shatter glass into his eyes.

As Harroun disappeared into the debris cloud, Oldfield made the decision he had weighed for about sixty miles. Pointing his racer down the track to where he could see the inside edge of the running surface, he relaxed his throttle – but only slightly. Damn if he would get hurt for no good reason. He felt as though he was driving blind. Driving low on the track reduced the likelihood he would be surprised by a wreck blocking his way.

From his new vantage point, Oldfield had a better sense of where he was but had to let off the gas sooner going into turns because he was hugging the inside of the track. Just inside turn one, Herb Lytle and Joe Betts labored furiously with shovels to dig out their red Apperson, half-buried in a mound of dirt. The next time around, Oldfield saw them attaching a steering linkage.

As Old Glory's pilots forged on for another two hours, they endured a relentless pounding from the deteriorating running surface. Ruts that had battered them grew deeper while still more took shape to take their toll of bruises on the backsides of the men. Lytle was again on the track but barely visible in the distance. Oldfield took consolation that all the cars had scattered to positions on the track and away from one another.

Entering the front stretch, Oldfield screwed up his eyes not so much to see more clearly, but reflexively attempting to make sense of what was unfolding before him. Jimmy Hill waved frantically, an action punctuated by emphatic pointing. Oldfield lifted his foot as he could see flashes of midnight blue amidst the foggy veil that obfuscated what had become obvious was a car. A car was tumbling like a barrel on a loading dock, crashing to Earth only to bounce several feet into the air and continue.

The color was distinctive, the same as his car. Oldfield had seen Aitken's National parked in the pits when he had reported for tires several laps earlier. He knew the errant racer had to be Charlie Merz's machine. It continued its vicious path, crashing through a trackside fence in front of the grandstand – and into a massive cluster of spectators.

The carnage had ceased by the time Oldfield came upon the spot, and he surveyed the area to see how dangerous it might be when he came around again. People were lying all about the scene. Hill turned and leaned into Oldfield's ear. It was the first time since the race started that Oldfield could make out his mechanic's voice.

"Jesus Christ, Barney! Did you see that? That's Merz' car. My God, how could anyone survive? All those people…"

His voice trailed off. Oldfield said nothing and tried to blot his mind of the images. Images too familiar, too similar to some of his accidents.

(Indianapolis Motor Speedway, August 21, 1909)

"Jesus Christ on a bicycle!" shouted Carl Fisher. "Goddamn! No, no, no!

His burning La Corona dropped out of his mouth. The scything carnage came into focus through his binoculars. A two thousand-pound National rolled, bounced, and pirouetted in the air in a relentless pursuit of destruction.

A detached voice Fisher did not immediately recognize screamed, "It's number ten. It's Charlie Merz!"

Jim Allison darted to Fisher's side at the very edge of the judges' stand closest to the debacle. His steady, unemotional voice confirmed it was Merz. It had to be Merz. Aitken had dropped out, and Oldfield, in the third National, had just passed the scene at a measured pace. Fisher could hear wailing screams from people on the other side of his track, just north of the entrance to turn one.

Focusing again with his binoculars, he observed soldiers and police scurrying about, with no sense of organized movement. People, maybe now just bodies, were scattered along the path the indigo hulk had churned. Farm bells at the top of the buildings were urgently clanging their panicked peels for aid. Allison's binoculars had seemingly become affixed to his face as he searched for hope.

"Jesus Christ, Carl. I can't count all the people on the ground. The car is nothing but wadded up junk. Three of the wheels ripped off. Wait! I think I see Merz! By God, he just climbed out from under the car. That kid is the luckiest son-of-bitch in the world."

Fisher noted that one of the National's wheels bounced onto the track. The remaining racers picked up speed despite Ragsdale ambulance attendants scrambling across the track with their stretchers. Dust of the smash-up dissipated, and Fisher saw many of the people struggling to their feet. The phone reverberated with unprecedented alarm as if it, too, was pleading for help. Moross answered and immediately shouted expletives and dropped the earpiece to pivot toward his boss.

"Carl! It's the officer at the station near the pedestrian bridge. People are crowding onto it, and he thinks it's going to drop onto the track."

Fisher yelled for Allison to direct soldiers to the spot as he dashed to the stairs. Calling for Moross to follow, he bounded down the planks and then to the ground. In a full sprint, Fisher rounded the judges' stand to the spot where to his parked Stoddard-Dayton. Simultaneously he ordered the guard at the base of the stand to rush to his car and crank the engine. In it were Jane Watts and one of her girlfriends in the tonneau where they had been observing the races. Moross knew the drill and leaped into the front passenger seat as Fisher planted his foot on the running board and clambered to the steering wheel. The sturdy soldier fired the engine in one deft stroke.

"Hang on, ladies; you're in for a ride."

Jane and her friend seemed to understand anything was possible in the wake of the devastation they had just witnessed. Fisher stormed away on a service road to the south end of the track where the sagging suspension bridge was undoubtedly groaning under the excessive weight. Fisher swung his car off the service road to the undeveloped terrain that was the most direct path to where he needed to be.

"Hold tight to the car! Forget your damn hats!"

The Stoddard-Dayton violently bounded over its rocky path. For an instant, Fisher questioned his judgment in taking the crow's course. Undoubtedly, the terrain would destroy the bouncing car, along with its occupants. Nonetheless, he kept his foot planted on the gas pedal, ever-correcting at the wheel as the machine bucked like a bull. As they approached the bridge, the immediate danger was apparent. Indeed, the suspension bridge, packed with fools, creaked its cries for relief. Fisher skidded to a stop and sprinted to the back trunk behind the women. Unbuckling its leather straps, he flicked open the lid to extract his ivory-handled Smith and Wesson thirty-eight special, a box of shells, and a megaphone. Deftly, he commenced sliding blank rounds into the six chambers. Fisher grabbed a handful of real bullets and thrust them into his coat pocket – just in case.

"Carl, promise me you won't shoot anyone," Jane shrieked.

"Not unless I have to, little honey."

Furiously puffing his cheroot, reduced to a stub more by Fisher's intensity than elapsed time, he thrust the box of remaining shells and the megaphone to Moross and told him to hold onto them. Moross abruptly ran ahead, clutching the megaphone, as Fisher continued to load his weapon during his steady march. Moross' high-pitched voice emanating from the amplifier, pierced the din. He commenced to hollering out that the president of the Speedway had a goddamned gun and was mad as Hell.

Fisher nodded his head. Moross knew how to get people's attention. At the foot of the bridge, where the steps reached the ground, Fisher eyed a cluster of soldiers, young men looking bewildered.

"What are you men doing down here? These people need to get the Hell off the bridge."

Several of the men replied that the bridge was about to collapse. Pointing his revolver to the sky, Fisher fired off a round and shouted to Moross to follow him up the stairs. Moross grimaced but didn't argue. At the top of the stairs, Fisher rapidly blasted two more blanks toward the heavens. Shocked, the people quieted and fixed their eyes on an apparent maniac. Fisher spat his cigar out over the side of the bridge and took to bellowing expletives into the megaphone.

"Listen up; goddamn it! You're all going to die if you don't get off this damn bridge! Do it now...or so help me, God, the next shots are not going into the air!"

With his pronunciation of the word "now," his gun erupted again. Barking like a battlefield sergeant, Fisher demanded people move to the stairs closest to them. He tucked his Smith and Wesson into the waist of his trousers and grabbed Moross' right arm to pull him forward into the crowd as they advanced onto the structure. Fisher neared the middle and pulled the trigger another time, this one aimed above everyone's heads and toward the empty turn four infield. He extended the gun to Moross to reload.

Fisher's theatrics worked. The sagging bridge conspicuously snapped back as people rushed to descend the stairs. At last, the bridge's ominous protest of creaks subsided. The final person climbed off the bridge, and Moross, looking frazzled, studied the Speedway founder.

"Jesus, Carl, you scared the shit out of me. Were those real bullets?"

"Grow some balls, Ernie. This kind of crap is part of the goddamned job."

Fisher stormed to the far side of the bridge nearest the grandstands to fiercely jab his arms ominously toward the guards at the base of the stairs.

"Close this bridge for business for the rest of today, you hear me? Get your bayonets mounted to your rifles, goddamn it! Get tough. Nobody, not even your goddamned mother, gets through here, or you'll see me come looking for you."

Moross had disappeared down the infield side stairs, apparently headed back to the car. Fisher stomped down the stairs, shouting the same instructions to the men there. Jane had left the car and anxiously grasped at her man.

"Oh, Carl, oh, Carl! I was so afraid for you. You're so brave."

"Yeah. Don't you worry your pretty head, little honey. I have everything under control."

Scanning the area, Fisher spied Moross walking well ahead, in the direction of the judges' stand. Staying on the service road during the way back, Fisher rumbled along to Moross and shouted to him.

"Ernie, get in the car, for Christ's sake. What are you doing?"

"Go on, Carl. I need some time to walk this off."

Fisher punched his throttle and stormed off to the judges' stand. Leaving Jane and her friend in the car, he briskly paced off his steps to the judges' stand. The remaining racers droned on, with Leigh Lynch in a Jackson well ahead of Ralph DePalma's Fiat, and Bruce Keen's Marmon.

When Fisher reached the second floor, he felt everyone's eyes on him. Without asking, he surmised they all knew that he had successfully cleared the suspension bridge. Spying Allison, Fisher strode to his partner's side. Allison, usually as emotional as a stone, appeared ashen.

"Carl, we're getting calls from the doctors. More fools are storming the medical tent. Goddamn ghouls are wanting a glimpse of blood."

Enraged, Fisher slammed his fist down on the timer's wooden table. His instinct was to tear off to his car for another round of pistol blasts and shouting. Allison clutched his arm.

"Don't go over there, Carl. The doctors called to say they think the soldiers and police have things under control. We need you here. Speare and the other Triple-A men are talking about stopping the race early."

Within minutes the farm bells clanged their terrifying alarm again. Before they finished their peels, the phone rang with a report that Keen had slammed into the buttress supporting the pedestrian bridge Fisher had just visited. Keen was unhurt, but attendants scooped his riding mechanic into the Ragsdale ambulance for a trip to the hospital. The man had walked but did not seem to know where he was.

Lewis Speare approached Allison and Fisher with the look of a relentless man with a made-up mind. He shook his head as he began talking.

"Gentleman, this is it. We can't in good conscience allow this travesty to continue. The race is a no-contest. I am walking down to Wagner to flag this off."

Fisher could not muster any indignation. He scooted the chair Speare had sat in toward him and collapsed into it. Meeting eyes with Allison, they simultaneously shook their heads.

(Indianapolis Motor Speedway, August 21, 1909)

Fred Wagner's checkered and yellow flags slashed at the smoky veil confronting Barney Oldfield as he stomped his accelerator and hurtled to the finish line. The flags were visible well before the shadowy figure of Wagner emerged. Relief swept through Oldfield's constitution with the realization that at last, he would escape the dark, blinding curtain produced by the crumbling track and engine exhaust.

Beyond the line, Oldfield let up on his accelerator, and "Old Glory" relaxed its momentum to the point that the driver had to downshift. He glanced at Jimmy Hill, with his face concealed with a sticky muck held in place by the engine oil. Hill's eyes welled with tears, and Oldfield surmised that his mechanic was, like him, struggling with crud scratching at the whites of his peepers.

The car crawled as the airborne powder dissipated markedly. No other race cars were in view. A commotion surrounding the infield hospital tent was apparent as perhaps a thousand people clamored around the medical station.

"What the hell do you think is going on over there?" Hill asked.

"Five will get you ten that's a cluster of vultures wanting to see what dead bodies look like," Oldfield said, turning his head away.

No longer concentrated on racing, Oldfield's anxious feeling to get back to his pit for water to salve his eyes heightened. Up ahead, he spied Ralph DePalma's red Fiat entering turn three. Oldfield paced "Old Glory" to hasten his arrival at the pit while staying some distance from DePalma and the inevitable helping of debris his wake would churn back at him. Exiting turn four, Bruce Keene's trashed yellow Marmon appeared as its crumpled form lie motionless and silent at the base of the pedestrian bridge. The entire scene was a battlefield.

At last, Oldfield entered the pit area, and there he spied not just George Hill, but also Art Newby, Charlie Merz, and a police officer. Merz stood between the two older men, both with an arm around him. Oldfield halted his big National with both he and Jimmy Hill demanding water even before the car was parked. The National men had anticipated such an order and had two oaken buckets at the ready.

Oldfield bounced out of his driver's seat and, with a hand from George Hill, hoisted the three-gallon wood container above his head. Opening his eyes wide, he tilted the bucket into his face and immediately blurred his vision. The warm liquid, baked in sunlight, splashed through his thick brown hair over his face and soaked his shirt. Hill had a towel ready, and Oldfield commenced to scrubbing his face and dabbing his eyes. Newby approached with Merz and the officer.

"Is there anything I can do for you, Barney? Are you okay?"

Still comforting his eyes with the towel, Oldfield said, "Oh, Art, I imagine I'll be fine once this sting lets up. Nothing a hot tub of water, some soap, and a fifth of corn mash won't fix."

Newby, a decided teetotaler, assembled a patient but awkward facial expression.

"I praise the Lord; you have escaped worse. Today is a terrible day for the National Motor Vehicle Company. I regret to tell you, but I am suspending our race team. We are out of the racing game."

Oldfield scrunched his face but refrained from his temptation to challenge Newby's apparent decision. Thinking it might be a case of emotions getting the better of him at the moment, he did not pursue the topic. He was, though, eager to know of injuries in the big accident.

"I saw that huge wreck down near the first turn. Was that you, Charlie? Say, there's no problem with the police, here, is there?"

The three men looked briefly dumbfounded until Newby explained the portly man in the blue coat was John Merz, the driver's father. Visibly relieved, the elder Merz slapped his son on the back.

"It was me, Barney," Charlie confirmed. "My right front tire let go when I was at full tilt. It veered me directly at the fence in front of the grandstand. The wheel shattered, and that barrel-rolled me to where the car was chopping off fence posts like matchsticks. I can't even recall what happened; everything was a blur. I just clutched the steering wheel, but I can't tell you how I stayed in my seat. I can't even recall when Kellum went overboard. When everything was over, I was upside down in the mud near that little creek down there."

"Kellum? I thought Herb Lyne was riding in your car," Oldfield said, glancing at Newby.

"Lyne collapsed from exhaustion, and since Aitken's car quit, Claude just hopped in to fill the mechanic's seat," Newby said.

"I honestly thought I was dead when the car stopped," Merz continued. "I was sure, at the very least, my legs would be all busted up, but no. I just turned the engine off and crawled out from under the car. I saw Claude lying some fifty feet away and ran over to him, but he was gone. A bunch of people was down, some moaning and others silent. I do remember the car hitting one man, fierce. I hate to say it, but I have to guess two or three in that crowd are no longer with us."

"We have two fatalities from the crowd. Another man hurt badly. They're all at the medical tent," Moross confirmed.

Oldfield swung around to find Ernie Moross had crept up from behind.

"Ernie, where did you come from?"

"I don't want to talk about it—more of Carl's shenanigans at the suspension bridge down yonder. I'll fill you in later. I stopped at one of the guard stations and called the judges' stand to find out what was going on."

"Jesus," Oldfield said. "Well then, what the Hell is going on over at the medical tent? A bunch of vultures wanting to see blood?"

"I'm afraid that's the case, Barney," said the police officer. "When that fence got mowed down, people started following the ambulance to the tent. Hell, they were running across the track during the race when there was a gap between passing cars. I'd be over there now, but I had to come to see my boy."

The elder Merz's voice trailed off as he choked back tears. Without warning, Oldfield had to shuffle his feet from the force of a boy not quite five feet tall who tackled him at the waist and burrowed his face into the driver's stomach.

"Whoa up, little man," Oldfield said. "Do you have me confused with someone else?"

The child cocked his head upward to see Oldfield.

"It's Toby, Barney; you remember Toby?" Newby asked.

Looking downward, Oldfield recognized the boy he had taken for a ride to see the big Wheeler-Schebler Trophy just days before. It seemed like weeks had passed.

"Mr. Oldfield, are you okay? Are you hurt anywhere?"

"Son, don't worry about old Barney. I've been through much worse."

Oldfield glanced at the other men, aware that the deadly accidents of his career were well known. He embraced the boy with a reassuring hug.

Riveting his eyes into those of Charlie Merz, he said, "It may not seem like it now, but we'll see better days."

Making Mile Record at Speedway and Bundled-Up Driver

STRANG IN FIAT.

Chapter 24 – The Brickyard

(Claypool Hotel, Indianapolis, August 25, 1909)

"There's no end to what politicians will do to make hay out of a situation they think can advantage them," Carl Fisher asserted.

Jim Allison, Frank Wheeler, and Ernie Moross, showing grim faces, gathered around an oak table in the boardroom at the Claypool Hotel in downtown Indianapolis. Also present was the hotel manager, Henry Lawrence, who responded to Fisher's urgent call for private accommodations after hearing that Lieutenant Governor Frank J. Hall had called on the Indiana state legislature to ban auto racing.

Noticeably absent was Art Newby, who had shut down his factory to allow time for his employees to mourn the loss of Claude Kellum. Fisher telephoned Newby the previous evening, but his first vice president did not want to discuss his racing plans. He told Fisher he had just returned that day from Kokomo for Kellum's funeral.

"Before we get to what to do about Hall, I want to share the good news. First, despite our shoving matches with the Triple-A fellas the last few days, Speare told me before he left that he wants the Speedway to thrive."

"Okay, exactly what does that mean?" Allison inquired.

"Well, let's just say he's giving us all the opening we need to move full speed ahead."

"What does that mean, Carl? That we're just going to move forward with that twenty-four-hour race in a couple of weeks?"

"Since Speare says his Contest Board won't meet for a couple of weeks, I suggest we postpone the twenty-four-hour go until mid-October. We can finally run the Wheeler-Schebler race then as well."

"I'm not comfortable with doing it at all, Carl," Allison said. "All of us need to discuss this and weigh our options. We got ourselves in this fix by rushing things. Tell us, what did Speare say?"

Fisher explained that Speare had shared several conditions the Speedway had to meet for the American Automobile Association sanction of races longer than a hundred miles. Speare's view was that track racing was particularly dangerous because of the constant speed stressing both driver and car. The only sanction for races of long distances would come if the Speedway and the race teams agreed that at least two drivers share every car, changing after every hundred miles. At that time, expert judges would assess the condition of the cars for five to ten minutes. The fresh driver could then continue with the competition. Following the stop, physicians examine the first driver.

Fisher had grown weary of his contests of wills with Speare and a whole lot of American Automobile Association officials. Men like that ever-annoying Fred Wagner.

"I just agreed with everything Speare said, especially since it gives us the clearance to run the twenty-four-hour race and the three hundred mile Wheeler-Schebler Trophy September 24 and 25," Fisher said.

"Carl, I don't want to whitewash over what happened," Allison returned. "Five men are dead. Five men are no longer with us, no longer with their families. We need to take every precaution possible to ensure safety. For Christ's sake, Hall isn't the only person out to get us. Look at how that coroner John Blackwell released the testimony you gave him. He made it sound like we don't give a damn about who gets hurt or killed, and we're just making money over here. We have to think this through."

"Blackwell is full of shit; everybody knows that," Fisher replied. "Hell, he performs unnecessary autopsies so he can bill the State one hundred dollars each. Look at his report. He twists things around like saying that because we had a hospital tent and ambulances on the grounds, it proves that we knew people would get hurt and die. It's plain stupid."

"It may be stupid, but there's a lot of stupid people out there that believe whatever stories they hear. I'm with Jim, Carl. We can't afford any more bad publicity," Wheeler said. "The Jackson people are up in arms because we didn't award the trophy to them. They don't buy into the view that the race was null and void. They'll probably sue the Triple-A and us."

"I know all that. That's why I have Henry here with us. He's a good man, and I wanted to hear what he has to say about a campaign plan I have."

"Campaign?" Moross asked, apparently sensing that the word suggested assignments for him.

"Yes. A campaign. We need to reach out to the leaders of Indianapolis and get them on our side. We know everyone from Mayor Bookwalter to all the car companies, and other businesses like what Henry has here at the Claypool. Ernie, we need to get the newspapers on our side. Henry, you see how much commercial benefit the Speedway brings to Indianapolis, right?"

"Of course, I do, Carl," Lawrence said. "Your Speedway is the biggest advertisement for this city. It brings people from outside here, and they spend money. Everyone needs to understand that we all benefit. The business boon allows us to hire people. We need people to understand that."

"Yes, and gentlemen, we will do the right thing even if it means paving the track so it can withstand the cars digging ruts. That surface was rough. That was our problem. Now what we need is to divvy up a list of the movers and shakers in Hoosier land. Henry has agreed to rally the hoteliers."

"Carl, I just want to say I like this idea," Moross said. "I will get to Willis and the other newspapermen. What would be convincing is to show him and the others our list of power boosters vouching for us."

The door at the back of the room creaked. Art Newby snuck his head around the edge of the entryway. Everyone paused, and for an instant, there was a quiet stillness.

"I just heard what that idiot Hall had to say. I don't want to go to any more funerals, but by God, I can't abide by some politicians running us out of business. I'll decide when and where National races, not some pencil neck. We're in this game, don't doubt it. What's our rebuttal plan, fellas?"

(Indianapolis Motor Speedway, September 11, 1909)

Johnny Aitken's big National swayed as it labored like a howling leviathan demanding its freedom from chains. The restraints locked to its front and rear axles and then affixed to two thick iron posts sunk in several feet of concrete in front of and behind the racer. The rear wheels, unable to overcome the restraint, swung back and forth from side-to-side as the tires steadily churned out the smoke of burning rubber. The engine's relentless wailing continued unabated, and Carl Fisher tugged on the arm of Peter Paul Willis of the Indianapolis Star. He nodded his head toward the track infield, and the two men paced off steps until it was possible to hear a conversation.

"This is what I told you about yesterday," Fisher started. "Our three paving choices are creosote block, concrete, or brick. We may even invest in this bitu-mineral company in Paris, Kentucky, and move it here to make sure we have all the concrete we need. What you see here are three test slabs of each paving option with the same post and chain configuration. The Nationals are record-breaking cars, so when they grind a track, they will break it up if there is any possible way."

"Impressive, Carl," Willis replied. "I commend you for taking action to make this place as safe as possible."

"And fast!" Fisher stressed, pointing out that the hard surface should enable drivers to attain ever more speed.

"Yes. Tell me, how long will this paving project take?"

"About a month if we work around the clock."

Willis frowned with evident skepticism.

"Look, we have to give the boys something to shoot for, Willis. Don't publish this, but I'll cancel the twenty-four-hour race and the Wheeler-Schebler Trophy if we have to. That's why I have Ernie out in New York meeting with Glenn Curtis. Curtiss has airplanes. We can put on an air show if we have to. The Speedway is a business, P.P.; we have to keep it afloat."

Behind them, Aitken had mercifully shut down the National's engine. Art Newby leaned into the cockpit as a group of some twenty men scrutinized the brick test slab and the worn tires.

"Who are all those men, Carl?"

"They are experts from the American Paving and Manufacturing Company. You've met the engineer, P.T. Andrews. He's among them. They all have a keen interest in paving options for the track to learn and apply it to paving roadways. This track is a proving ground for all aspects of driving—engines, tires, metal parts, and even street paving. What's more, these hard surfaces are absolutely dustless. That will help the drivers tremendously."

"Let me think about this a bit. Let's take a walk, Carl. Suppose you tell me what other improvements you're planning."

As they strode the front stretch, Fisher pointed to the fences in front of the grandstands that now set back forty feet to keep the crowds further away. He described a sand cushion to be laid just off the running surface that would slow errant cars before reaching the fencing. Fisher and his partners had decided to expand the grandstands, adding boxes to the one-dollar section and erecting a steel scoreboard. A new aerodrome was under construction on the far side of the infield as well as additional restaurants and expanded garages.

"If you walk down to any of the turns, you'll see buttresses going up. They will support concrete walls to keep cars from going down the embankment. That's a Hell of a lot safer than flying off the edge at the top of the banking."

"You're expecting a lot of business, aren't you, Carl?"

Fisher felt a bit annoyed by the question as if Willis doubted him. He paused to shed that sensation and answered the question directly.

"You're damn right, I am. We have the greatest race track in the world, and that's what you need to be telling everyone. Our Speedway Company has the best interests in mind for Indianapolis, car companies, and fans. My partners and I are investing another seven hundred thousand dollars in making everything right. Everything the best, anywhere."

"That's a lot of money, Carl. That takes you up to a million and a half. I have to respect men who believe in themselves and what they are doing to put serious money behind it."

"I appreciate your help, P.P.," Fisher said. "The article reporting on how all the big businessmen, the Mayor, and other important people see the Speedway's great benefits to Indianapolis was personally important to me."

"Carl, I quoted those men because they wield a great deal of influence here, and also well beyond this city. Our readers know how big those men are, and I need to help them understand developments affecting this community. That's my job. I double-check my facts; I strive for balance. All I can ever promise you is a fair shake."

"That's all I ask, P.P. You tell it straight, and it will always be good news, I assure you."

(Atlanta, October 22, 1909)

Squinting did nothing to erase the opacity. Like sheer gauze wrapped around his face, Barney Oldfield blinked to wash away the film coating his corneas. Three shadowy figures leaned over him as he lifted his head from the uneven, splintery pine table. A stream of drool escaped from the left corner of his lips.

"Barney! Barney!"

The voice was strangely familiar and too loud for the furious thumping deep within his head. Someone or something annoyingly jostled him at his shoulders.

"We may have to carry him out of here. I don't think he knows where he's at."

Hands grasped Oldfield's arms and lifted him from under his armpits. Why are they doing this? Wobbly, there was no way to stand. The roughhewn, wood plank floor, coated in the grime of years of stale spilled beer and spat tobacco juice, tempted him. If only he could lie down.

The sickness that befell him earlier remerged with the change of his position. He gagged dry heaves and vaguely sensed that whoever was supporting him had shuffled their feet to spare their boots of any mess.

The dingy room was a modicum of comfort for eyes unprepared for sunlight. Gradually, Bess Oldfield's face emerged into focus. Her eyes were red, and she pressed a handkerchief to her nose in an apparent attempt to ameliorate odors. The voices of Will Pickens and George Hill were like pieces to a puzzle Oldfield assembled in his mind.

Tilting his head at Pickens, he angrily shouted, "What the hell did you bring her here for?"

"Jesus, we didn't know where you were. Do you know you've been missing for three days?"

"Missing! You dumbass, I haven't been missing. I've been right here."

"Barney!" Bess shouted. "I have had enough. Nobody knew where you were. Will and George called me because they hoped you had come home to see me. Fat chance of that. This drinking has to stop."

Bess rarely growled in authoritarian tones, and Oldfield opted to tread lightly. He did not have the energy for an argument, especially one he could not win. She continued to assert herself, telling the men to help her husband to a taxi waiting outside. As the two men wrapped his arms around their shoulders to assist his stumbling progress, they complained of the foul smell of vomit on Oldfield's jacket.

"Oh, my Lord," Bess reacted. "Have you lost all dignity? I am going to burn your clothes."

For Oldfield, it was more like he was eavesdropping than hearing his wife's criticism. Each step was a teetering trial aggravated by nausea and the relentless drumbeat in his head. The saloon doors flew open, and cruel, brilliant rays attacked his pupils, literally blinding him. Uneasy and helpless, his steps were now entirely trusted to his colleagues. The driver of a black Christie taxi hopped down from his seat at the steering wheel to open the coach door wide enough to stuff the drunken champion inside.

"Position him to the window, if you will. If he gets sick, I want him throwing up over the side, not in my cab."

Pickens and Hill complied, loading Oldfield in like freight. Bess made it clear she wanted no part of his filth and wished to ride furthest away from her husband's stench. Pickens, with his enormous girth, plopped down beside his old racing partner, and the cab springs noticeably compressed. Hill climbed into the bench seat beside Bess.

By the time they reached the Hotel Aragon, where Bess had taken lodging, Oldfield was more mobile but still leaned on Pickens at times. Bess stormed into the lobby, apparently on a mission.

As Oldfield shuffled along, Pickens and Hill kept pace in the event of a tumble. He knew he was a spectacle; the glares and stares from hotel staff and guests in the lobby were evidence of that.

"Where's Bess?"

"She ran ahead, Barney," Hill replied. "I have a room key. I think she's drawing you a bath. I'm sure that it's more for her than you. You smell something fierce."

Oldfield told Hill to shut up as they rode the elevator to the sixth floor. The bathwater proved chilly, but Bess gave no evidence of sympathy. As he slid into the porcelain tub, she threw a bar of soap, a scrub brush, and washcloth in after him. Her facial expressions were clear evidence of her disgust as she used a towel to pick up her husband's putrid clothing and deposit them in a sack. After tossing it in the hallway, she returned with a kettle of water she had steamed at the fireplace. Oldfield scrambled his legs back to his chest as his wife appeared to have little care as to where on his body, the boiling water might land.

"Damnation, woman! Are you trying to scald me?"

"Shut the fuck up!"

Bess stomped out of the room. Hill and Pickens pulled up chairs as if watching their friend bathe was as familiar to them as observing him eating lunch.

"Are you going to be up to racing tomorrow?" Pickens asked.

"I know you're worried about the gate receipts," Hill said. "But remember what happened in Buffalo when you went out on the track hungover? We don't need you mowing down any more fences."

Oldfield scowled at his mechanic as Bess returned with a cup of coffee devoid of color like the pitch of an abyss to Hell. She towered over him, silent, with menacingly crossed arms. Pickens punctuated the awkward moment.

"Now, Bess, you got every reason to be angry," Pickens offered. "We looked for him for two days before we called you. I just have to tell you it can be a rough life out here on the racing circuits. Heck, some clown threw a hammer at Barney up in Buffalo. While they were racing, Bess. While they were racing!"

She placed the coffee cup on a vanity next to the tub and then inquired if Barney was hurt.

"No, it just bounced off the radiator. It did give me a scare. I fixed the situation," Oldfield's voice trailed off.

The look on Bess's face made it apparent she was waiting for an explanation. Hill spoke up before Oldfield could gather words.

"Old Barney pulled up beside that jerk and put a wheel into the side of his car. He put him right through the fence."

Oldfield chuckled at the memory, despite the constant throbbing at his temples. That show of mirth ignited cackles from his racing partners.

"My lands! You didn't kill that fool, did you?"

"Nah, he's okay. His car got tore up, but he deserved that. You can't put up with that crap. Word gets around that you do, and more assholes will come out of the woodwork."

Bess sighed and paused. Pickens, in a rare somber moment, offered that Oldfield had reached a crucial point in his career.

"Listen, Barney; you need to clean up. I'm telling you that if you keep this crap up, nobody's going to want to have anything to do with you. I don't think what I have to say here is any shock to Bess. You need to get serious about things."

Oldfield sat up in the tub, the water now opaque with dissolving soap, and splashed his face. Sliding backward, he descended the curvature of the bath to submerge his head. He burst back above and simultaneously announced, "I'm bored!"

"You're bored, huh?" Bess said. "So, you get liquored up like a smelly pig?"

"I guess. I don't know. I just feel like I need something big to go after."

As Oldfield completed his sentence, his eyes landed on Pickens, who nodded his head.

"I want to be the fastest man alive. I want to go down to Daytona and set the world speed record."

"Isn't that about one hundred and twenty-seven miles an hour? You don't have a car that can go that fast," Bess said.

"I know where to get one. Will has been talking to Jesse Froelich at the Benz importer in New York. We think we can trade my Prince Henry Benz for that one. Plus, some cash, of course. Victor Hemery ran that car at Brooklands at nearly one-twenty-seven. I figure I could easily bust through that going straight down the beach. I may hit one-thirty-five."

"And what is the name of this world-beater car?" Bess asked.

"The Lightning Benz. The two hundred horsepower Lightning Benz."

(Indianapolis Motor Speedway, November 27, 1909)

Carl Fisher's Stoddard-Dayton, Ernie Moross at the wheel, kicked up cement dust as it chugged and belched its way closer to the judges' stand at the Indianapolis Motor Speedway. Fisher anticipated the arrival of former world boxing champion Jim Jeffries for well over a month. Finally, along with his sparring partner, Sam Berger, he was at last standing on the vitrified surface of the great, massive Indianapolis speedway.

Carl bounded down the steps of the judges' stand and skipped toward the man they called, "Jeff." Jeffries was distracted, his head pivoting like a weather vane in a strong wind as he took in the red brick Speedway vista. A yellow-stained toothy grin stretched Berger's face as well. Moross lurked in the background.

"Well, I'll be damned!" Jeffries exclaimed. "If this don't beat all!"

"I take it you're impressed, Jeff."

"You bet, Carl. This track is the damnedest thing I ever saw. Hell, it makes me want to give my gloves a toss and hop in one of your race vehicles."

Moross stepped forward to share the agenda of the day. The boxers were in town for a three-round sparring exhibition downtown at Tomlinson Hall. Fisher and Moross invited a few newspapermen to come to the track within the hour to witness Fisher taking the big men on a few exhibition laps. There was no doubt in Fisher's mind the program would beat the drum for both the boxing show and an upcoming Time Trial meet at the Speedway in December. He pointed to an elongated stable-like structure across the way to the backstretch.

"See that? That's our aerodrome where we house airplanes and balloons. After we do a few laps and talk to newspapermen, we'll take you over there, and one of our aviators has set it up so you can sit at the controls of a real aeroplane."

Squinting his eyes in the face of the sun, Berger asked about the balloons.

"You talking passenger balloons?" he asked without pausing for an answer. "Now how in tarnation do you squeeze those big balloons into that barn."

Moross appeared ready to provide a respectful, patient explanation. It was too late as Fisher and Jeffries erupted with laughter. The boxing champion planted a punch to his partner's shoulder.

"Jesus, Berger, have you been hit upside the head once too often? Hellfire, man, they deflate those orbs and fold them up like blankets. You need to get out more. Don't you know anything?"

Fisher figured it was a good time to intervene.

"Well, now that we have that mystery solved, can I escort you gentlemen to my chariot?"

Jeffries, all of three-hundred pounds by Fisher's silent estimation, had the Stoddard-Dayton frame and springs creaking in protest as he first stepped up on the sideboard and then collapsed into the front seat. He sure as Hell wasn't going to say anything, but Fisher privately mused over the notion of Jeffries being in fighting shape for his announced title challenge with the current world heavyweight champion, Jack Johnson. Berger apparently thought the car's tonneau was too tight a fit for his frame, nearly as robust as his partner. He motioned with his fleshy hand that they should proceed without him.

With Moross's assistance at the crank, the Stoddard-Dayton engine blasted to life. Fisher sped away, his tires chirping on the bricks, wanting Jeffries to experience acceleration followed by sustained speed. He noticed Jeffries clutching his seat with one hand and the car's side panel with the other. Swiveling his head in Fisher's direction, the champ beamed a great smile.

"I hear-tell that the locals nicknamed this place The Brickyard," Jefferies shouted. "I'm sure the newspapermen picked up on that right away."

"They did. I like it; it's clever. I wish I had thought of it myself. Repeat it every chance you get."

As the tires rotated over the bricks, a monotonous but rhythmic clipping sensation rumbled up the seat to Fisher's pants. He wasn't just proud; he was damn proud his Speedway allowed for the smoothest ride in all of automobiling.

Fisher now had his throttle to the floorboard as he exited turn two to storm down the backstretch faster than a mile-a-minute. Both men grew silent as the track founder concentrated on taking the long, sweeping corners with as much speed as he could conger up. Repeating the process for five laps, Fisher noticed a cluster of newspapermen with Moross and Berger in front of the judges' stand. The next time around, he made a point of skidding to a stop at their shoes. Some scattered as Fisher and Jefferies locked eyes and cackled. The engine now silent, the newspaper men clustered around the hot, smoking car.

The reporters began firing off questions at random.

"Hey champ, when did you get into town?"

"I just came over from Union Station."

"What do you think of Indianapolis?"

"Hell, I love you, Hoosiers, you know that. I will also say, Carl and his men have outdone themselves with this Brickyard Speedway. That was the fastest car ride I have ever had. Smooth as all get out. This track has to be the finest Speedway in America and the whole damn world."

"How fast did you gun it, Carl?"

"The champ deserves a real demonstration, nothing less. We were clipping along at better than a mile-a-minute down this straightaway, right here."

"It's the truth," inserted Moross. "I got a stopwatch right here that proves it. Fifty-three and three-fifths seconds. For those of you without a slide rule, that's about sixty-eight miles an hour!"

Fisher figured Moross was full of crap, but that's why he paid him.

"That's fast, champ, were you scared?"

Everyone laughed as Jeffries feigned an angry frown.

"Seriously, Jeff, let's talk boxing. When are you going to knock that nigger's golden smile down his ugly throat?"

"Mr. Johnson and I shall tangle in due time, that I assure you."

Fisher felt the gaze of Peter Paul Willis, who, through a sideways nod of his head, made it clear he wanted an aside with the Speedway founder. Fisher pulled at Berger's arm and asked him and Jeffries to talk about the sparring plans. He then strode over to his car as if he needed to retrieve something. Instead, he discreetly continued his walk around the car and toward the judges' stand. Willis followed.

"Clever ruse, Carl. Getting the champ out here to cast a little extra light on your Brickyard."

"Thanks. So, did you want me alone just to compliment me?"

"You don't take kindly to that kind of talk, do you?"

"Do you? I hate that word."

"Yeah, really, I just didn't want to stand around and listen to that bullshit. I don't have colored friends, but they're people too, like that Galloway man you have for a butler."

"Yes, William Galloway, and he's not my butler. He's my assistant. He looks after my property and checks in on my mother when I can't."

"You walk to your own drumbeat, don't you? Nothing wrong with that, I respect you for it. How's married life?"

Fisher studied Willis' face. He never trusted reporters. Never let your guard down.

"Married life is pretty much like my life was before. I had to make an honest woman of her, and there never seemed to be enough time to fit a wedding in."

"When was that, anyway? It happened so fast, and then I hear you took the little girl off for California for better than a week. You had the whole damn city shocked and talking. Is it true that you went to California because of your San Francisco Prest-O-Lite factory blew up?"

"It's been about a month. Is this some kind of story you're writing, Willis? Keep my personal life with my wife out of it, you hear me? You don't need to be talking about Prest-O-Lite way out in California. Nobody got hurt."

"Okay. On my honor, I won't write a word about your wife or that little Prest-O-Lite issue. Let's talk about this Brickyard."

"It's about time. Nobody in the world has a facility like the one you are standing on right now. We have the fastest, safest track in the world. We have that big aerodrome over there, so this is the biggest airfield in the country, too."

"It's impressive, Carl, I give you that. But what's your plan for racing? That's what everyone wants to know about after that sad affair in August. I hear you've got a notion to put on some kind of race meet stunt next month. December? Are you daft? Everyone will freeze their keister off."

"Maybe, but the last time I checked, we're all big boys here. What's important to this

Speedway and to the city you live in is that we firmly establish that the Brickyard is the fastest track in the world going into 1910. We're going to re-write the record books. I want to hold all the major track speed records for 1909—every damn one of them. Asa Candler's men down at their Atlanta speedway have had bragging rights long enough. The Indianapolis Motor Speedway is the world's greatest racecourse, and you need to tell everybody about it."

"I'll be here whenever you organize that ice cycle festival. It's up to you fellas to give me what I need to write the kind of story you're talking about. If not, I'm not making things up."

(Indianapolis Motor Speedway, December 17, 1909)

Condensation from the mouths of Indiana Governor Thomas Marshall and Carl Fisher briefly obscured the Speedway president's view of the gold brick, the final block of three million, two-hundred-thousand bricks as it sunk into place at the finish line. Marshall eased the block into place by gripping a handle on the end of a chain screwed into its side. He leaned forward, and Fisher instinctively crouched too, only recognizing that he had done so when he realized their foggy exhales mingled together before dissipating into the unseasonably frigid Hoosier air.

With the brick nestled in its space, muffled applause ensued from wool mitten and glove sheathed hands in the small gathering of people standing around them. Both men resumed their normal posture and firmly clasped hands. A vigorous shake by each was the exclamation point on the massive project finally brought to fruition. George Bretzman and three other photographers clicked the shutters of their tripod-mounted box cameras to record the moment for posterity. With Fisher to his right, the Governor cleared his throat and projected his voice.

"I am proud to mark the occasion of the completion of this grand facility. I have had the opportunity to inspect the rejuvenation of this phenomenal complex. It is a rebirth that distinguishes Indiana as the epicenter of the automobile industry. From what was until recently farmland, we will see a more promising, richer fruit sprouting forward to define the twentieth century. It is here Mr. Fisher and his associates have gifted our Hoosier capital with a massive laboratory to be used to great advantage for the betterment of our state's automobile companies, but also all of America. It is here that our finest engineers and mechanics will expand their body of knowledge to levels beyond our humble imaginations as they exist at this moment. Wonderful, profitable developments will be born on these grounds and bring America to the forefront of the greatest technology reshaping society in a new age of human history. What's more, every Hoosier here should applaud this valiant, noble, and altruistic turning point for mankind. Here we witness

Indiana greatness!"

When it was apparent that the Governor had said his piece, Peter Paul Willis burst forward to insert himself in the exchange between the two executives. Fisher intended to brush him aside, but Marshall spoke first.

"Give us a minute, P.P. I want an aside with the hero of the day."

Marshall nodded in the direction of turn one, some distance down the brick straightaway. Fisher noticed that two burly men who had accompanied the Governor had crossed their arms and cast menacing eyes at anyone who attempted to follow.

"So, Carl, play it straight with me. Are we to have any repeats of the bloodbath you staged last summer?"

"No, sir, your honor. We have spared no expense to make the Speedway both fast and safe. Our big problem in August was the running surface crumbling apart and the cars digging ruts. Well, no car in the world can dig a rut in these bricks."

"That's fine, but I'll be honest. If these damn fool drivers want to kill themselves, well, that's their business. I don't like it, but that's their trade. What I want to know is that the good people of this city and all other visitors expecting to enjoy their picnics and spectate these speed contests can do so with the peace of mind that you – you, Carl – have provided them with the protection to keep them out of harm's way. To keep them from being mowed down like tall grass by these behemoth machines."

"Yes, your honor. You have my word."

Fisher pointed toward the area between the edge of the track and the large grandstand.

"See there; we moved the stands back some forty feet to keep everyone at a safe distance. Just as important, as you can see, we have prepared sand pits on the ground leading up to our reinforced fencing. No car, no matter how fast, is going to plow through all of that."

From Marshall's furrowed brow Fisher surmised skepticism. Never one to talk too much, he paused, waiting for the Governor to reply. Finally, he looked into Fisher's eyes.

"I see the potential here. I value your efforts. What you built is an asset and distinguishes Indianapolis from the rest of the country. From the world, for that matter. If you and your boys can get this right, this whole operation can boost our automobile industry. That means jobs and a better economy for all Hoosiers. In the end, that's what is important to me. I have supported you. I told Hall to shut his trap about legislation to outlaw racing."

Marshall paused, sinking his eyes deeply into Fisher's.

"Don't make a fool out of me, Fisher."

"You have my word, sir."

"I have one more question. I saw you were claiming that brick is gold. I'm not stupid. So, what is it?

"Wheeler has the technical explanation, but the short story is that that brick is of the same bronze alloy as his Wheeler-Schebler Carburetors. That seems to be gold to him. His business is brisk. So, it is gold to me and all your constituents."

Marshall appeared pleased with the answer, and the two men paced off the distance back to the gathering. Before they reached the others, Marshall muttered.

"I need to get out of this infernal cold."

People stormed toward them, but Marshall's men intervened. Indiana's top executive veered off in the direction of the judges' stand, where a driver stood ready with a car with an engine that had been purring the entire time.

Willis returned to Fisher's side, casting a scowl that divulged his disappointment over the Governor's abrupt departure.

"So, that's it, eh?"

"I think he told you what he thinks. He's a smart man. He sees the value and the potential of what we have built here."

Fisher turned to stroll toward the judges' stand.

"It was cold, bleak, biting weather: foggy withal: and he could see the people in the court outside, wheezing up and down, beating their hands upon their breasts, and stamping their feet upon the pavement stones to warm them."

"You think I don't know Dickens, Willis? I've read more books than you have. Are you comparing me to Ebenezer Scrooge?"

"If the shoe fits. But let's just say it is the Christmas Season, and you go dragging us all out here in this inclement weather. It's barely twelve degrees! I feel like my face is going to freeze and fall off.

"Might be an improvement. Sorry, your delicate constitution is so gravely affected by a little cold and a breeze."

"Look around. Everyone that came to hear Marshall is leaving."

"That's what you newspapermen do. Whether you admit it or not, I know you know this is important to our city. You need to toughen up and tell this groundbreaking story."

The two men mounted the steps leading up to the second floor of the judges' stand. There Fred Wagner, Frank Wheeler, and Charles Warner, inventor of the electric timing device named after him, huddled around a coal-burning stove. The open-air windows of the structure mitigated the stove's warmth. Warner's arms noticeably tremored as he and the others out-stretched their fingers to the comfort of the flame-containing cast iron heater. Willis eagerly bounded forward, extending his gloved hands in with the others.

"Gentlemen," Fisher announced. "It seems this newspaper reporter doesn't understand how important these time trials are."

Willis rocked his head and rolled his eyes.

"He doesn't understand how important these time trials are to the automobile industry, to this city, and our sport of racing."

Wheeler nodded his head, uttering, "hear ye, hear ye!" The others studied Fisher as if they were intrigued to hear whatever yarn was as yet between his ears and not quite rolling off his tongue.

"I'm here, aren't I?" Willis retorted. "How about backing off on the sarcasm?"

"What we are about to witness is the clear evidence that these very grounds have spawned forth the world's greatest Speedway," Fisher continued. "The Indianapolis Motor Speedway will close 1909 and head into a new, bustling decade as America's first super-speedway – the fastest track in the world. After today, no one will be able to refute that there is no other such palace of speed and safety anywhere. I say that without equivocation as an irrefutable fact. You can bank on it."

"Let the races begin!" Wheeler pronounced.

(Indianapolis Motor Speedway, December 17, 1909)

Jane Fisher lay her head on her husband's shoulder, clutching a bear fur blanket and yanking it to her neck to shutter out the frosty air. She wore a thick mink coat, and her husband donned one of buffalo fur where she burrowed her head into his shoulder in a child-like embrace. The prodigious velvet ribbon affixed to her sable Vasselin Villetard brushed Carl's face, and feeling inconvenienced, he plucked it from her hat. It was an abrupt action that inadvertently jerked her headpiece downward and over her eyes.

"Carl! That's my favorite winter hat! Why would you do such a thing?"

"Relax, I'll buy you a new one. It was just in my way, and I want to settle in here and be comfortable with my wife."

He was pleased that her exasperation dissolved in an instant as a smile stretched her lovely lips. She was a good woman.

They cuddled in her Baker Electric car, with its tall, booth-like cab and completely enclosed coachwork. He had purchased the car just weeks before they married in October, thinking it inconceivable that his girl could manage a loud, smokey, oil-spewing beast like one of his gas automobiles. On the morning of the time trials, it occurred to him the vehicle would provide ideal shelter from a windy day when the atmosphere could freeze your lungs. It was suitable for a huddle with his girl to watch the spectacle.

Pulling Jane close to his side and with their coats, a blanket, and caps, they were undoubtedly more comfortable than anyone else on the grounds. Windows of the rectangular box-like automobile enclosed them from every angle, ideal for both shutting out the miserable wind and delivering ample transparency for a comprehensive view. The container muffled the thundering race cars shooting past them from their spot on the pit road. Fisher was pleased that his wife peppered him with questions because he wanted her to be interested, not nagging about nonsense.

"Carl, what is the difference between these cars? You talk about classes, what are classes?"

"It's simple, little honey. It's mostly about engine sizes. The first car out was my little Empire with Newell Motsinger. The engine in that car is only one-hundred-sixty cubic inches of displacement. It's the smallest car out here today."

"But what does that mean? Displacement of what?"

Fisher squinted and studied her sweet face. Should he even try?

"Look, every car has pistons that go up and down in cylinders, like tin cans. The size of all the cylinders adds up to a certain amount of displacement. The bigger the displacement, the more horsepower, and the faster the car can go. Make sense?"

Jane nodded her head in a manner that gave Fisher hopes that his teaching was getting through. After all, she was not a stupid girl, but a girl nonetheless. These mechanical contraptions weren't exactly women's work.

"There are different classes of cars sorted by engine size, by displacement. You already saw the Empire, and then we had the Class Four cars with engines up to two-hundred-thirty cubic inches. Then Newby's drivers Johnny Aitken and Tom Kincaid ran their Class Two cars. Those are four-hundred-forty-seven cubic inches."

"I saw Johnny earlier. I hardly recognized him. He grew a beard."

Carl sighed and frowned at his wife's non-sequitur. Had she followed anything he was saying about the car classes?

"Johnny started that earlier in the week. He thinks it protects his face from the cold. Look, do you want to know about what we're doing here or not?"

Fisher paused and studied his bride. She was so appealing; he wondered why he cared if she couldn't follow him – or in her heart did not want to. With their fur garments and her softness pressed against his side, he enjoyed a glowing coziness within the protection of the enclosed car—thick railroad passenger car glass used in the construction of the vehicle muffled the engine noises outside.

"I'm sorry, Carl. Forgive me. Johnny's beard just came to mind. Please do tell me about the cars."

"Okay, I'll begin again. The car circling the track is a Class One Packard. The engine has four-hundred-thirty-two cubic inches. It was the last entry, so it's just running by itself. After it's done, we will roll out the biggest cars, and they will get after the records I want. Those records will prove our Speedway is the fastest in the land. That will be Lewis Strang in the big two-hundred horsepower Fiat Giant and his uncle, Walter Christie, in a car of his design."

"Really? What does he call it?"

Fisher pivoted his head to look into his wife's sweet face.

"Why, dear, he gave it his name. He named it a Christie. A lot of people call it a freak, though."

"That's mean."

"They call it that because it can only be a race car. It is not a touring car. Christie designed it with one thing in mind - to go fast."

Out the right-side window of the Baker Electric Fisher spied Ernie Moross trotting toward their car, his breath puffing in the cold like a locomotive steam engine. He clutched a paper in his hand. Rapping on the door, he immediately opened it and inadvertently flooded the cabin with frigid air and into the faces of the Fishers.

"Carl, you wanted updates. Aitken just set a new stock chassis record."

Observing that Moross appeared ready to read details on his paper, Fisher shouted, "Jesus Christ, Ernie! Get your ass into this car! You're going to give Jane her death of cold."

Moross shrugged and planted his right foot onto the running board, then hopped into the bench seat across from Fisher and his wife. His ruddy cheeks evidenced the raw elements. He flexed his black wool-gloved fingers and clapped his hands.

"What do you have for me, Moross?"

Moross thrust the paper forward as he launched into his report.

"You wanted records. Well, Aitken is delivering them. His mile run cleaved ten seconds off the American Class Two record. It's now forty-nine seconds. That's going some for a stock chassis."

"I can read, Moross."

"I meant no offense, Boss," Moross replied. "I hope you understand I am enthusiastic about my job. I firmly believe we are writing history here. Forgive me if I can't shut up about it."

Fisher looked up from the paper and sunk a stare into his publicist. Recognizing that he was speaking without thought for how the other man might feel, he paused.

"Ernie. You're a good man, and I appreciate the enthusiasm you bring to your work and my company. It's why you are great at what you do. The best, I should add."

Moross nodded his appreciation. Glancing out the window, Fisher spied Christie rolling to a stop in front of his crew. Moross recognized where his boss was pointed and fired off another report.

"Yeah, Christie. That's why I ran over here. He just broke the American record for the quarter-mile. Eight and seventy-eight hundredths seconds. Can you believe he's up over one hundred and two miles an hour on our track!"

Fisher beamed.

"Now that's showing what a freak machine can do! He's going some! Tell Aitken I want him back out there. There's more in that car, I know it. Let's pile on those records so low it will take Atlanta or any other place years to challenge us."

"What about Art? Shouldn't we ask him?"

"He's not feeling well and is parked in front of his fireplace at home. Just talk to Aitken, he's the team captain. Tell him I asked as a personal favor. He can make his run after Strang goes out."

Moross nodded, opened the car door, and leaped to the ground in a sprint. Fisher turned to Jane.

"You're going to have to excuse me, Dear. I want to see Lewis in his Fiat Giant. The Fiat is the car I'm banking on giving us the national mile record."

Fisher plunged his right hand into his Buffalo coat and searched for an inner pocket to extract a cigar. Lighting it would be easier inside than out in the swirling gale. He did not wait for a response from his wife, who passively observed him. Swinging open the door wide, he bounced from the car to plant his soles on the brick surface. The smoke of his cigar melded with the condensation of his breath to produce a cloud. His pince-nez spectacles immediately fogged, and Fisher plucked them from his nose and withdrew a handkerchief from his coat pocket to polish the lenses. He saw so much better since purchasing them a few weeks earlier, it was hard to fathom why he waited so long.

Strang's Fiat engine fired, also generating smoke and flames out the exhaust pipe. Within seconds, the driver was away and soaring toward the first turn. The electric timer's tripwire was set up at the exit to the fourth turn to start the timed runs, with another at the entrance to the backstretch for a full measured mile.

The car's boisterous engine never entirely faded from Fisher's ears, but the angry roaring became decidedly less intrusive at the far end of the track. Strang appeared as a little red dot in turn four and steadily grew as he stormed toward Fisher, who studied it through the smoke of his cigar. The guttural growl rapidly and inexorably advanced, and then shot by him. Fisher sauntered to the judges' stand where he knew he could receive a timer's report and a warm from the cast iron stove.

Officials recorded the time before he arrived on the structure's second floor. Charles Root, the Triple-A officer out of Chicago was tilted forward and peering over Warner's shoulder.

"The boy covered the mile in forty and six-tenths seconds," Warner reported with Root nodding at his back. "That's better than Oldfield ran here back in August."

"But he didn't break his record from Atlanta last month," Fisher uttered in lifeless monotone.

Strang coasted his stout red and now silent car to a stop directly beneath the judges' stand. Several yards behind him, Johnny Aitken prepared his National for a second record run. A National mechanic yanked the crank handle, and after just two spins, the engine caught fire, belched smoke, and emitted thunder. Someone handed Aitken a chamois hood with holes for his eyes cut into the cloth.

After a while, Strang vaulted up the stairs to join Fisher and the officials near the stove.

"Gangway, gentleman, he playfully ordered. He marched to the stove and squeezed between Wheeler and Moross, who stood nearby. Fisher examined the young man's face and was astonished at the scarlet tone of his cheeks.

"Good God, man, what happened to your face?"

Strang responded with a tortured and weak smile.

"Oh, some of the boys are going down to the creek and splashing their faces with the icy water. They think it numbs them to the cold, but I'm here to tell you it just hurts like Hell."

Wheeler grimaced as if he could feel the intense sting the redness affirmed.

"Son, have you ever heard of frostbite? That's not something you want to fool around with. Now you stay near that stove and get good and warm, you hear me?"

Out on the track, Aitken had the National soaring. According to Warner's report, the driver peeled off a mile at forty-five seconds – a full four seconds faster than his record from earlier in the day.

Fisher ambled to Strang's side. Curious to hear first-hand from the man with the most potent and fastest machine of the day, he wondered aloud how it was the young driver had been three seconds faster for the mile on the Atlanta two-mile circle.

"I never raced on bricks before, Mr. Fisher. A mile is tough because we have to slow it up a bit to make two turns. I'm getting the hang of it, but I'm just more used to sliding my ass end out a bit in the corners. It was easy on that red clay last month, but these bricks are a different deal. I think I can do it, but I need a little more practice. Let me tune up the engine a bit and have another go tomorrow."

Moross descended the steps and out to trackside. Hollering into his megaphone, he joked with the few dozen onlookers that it was time to pass out the ice cream cones. Seven barking engines quickly rendered his projection device useless.

Aitken and Kincaid were back with their Nationals, as was Walter Donnelly in the Packard and Newell Motsinger in Fisher's Empire. In all, cars represented five classes. Wagner waved them off in staggered fashion. Fisher did not want a race; he preferred simultaneous time trials. The idea was to run the racers for twenty miles each, and see how many records fell. Onlookers appeared more animated than they had been all day. The sheer number of cars circling the course fed their eyes with speed and color, and Fisher knew it.

Fisher clutched the open-air window frame with his gloved hands. Warner studied his timer's reports as they printed. He plucked out the fastest times and yelped proclamations to the other men.

Fisher listened until the end and then announced to the other men he was headed home with his wife – and that he would see them early the next morning. The draining wind and bitter bleakness made him weary. He trudged to the black Baker Electric, where he found Jane's head framed in the window nearest him. Once in the car, he shared the good news with her and simultaneously wondered how much she understood.

"Well, our Speedway owns records up to twenty miles for two classes. Aitken just ran twenty miles in sixteen minutes and eighteen seconds. That's a new American Class two record. Also, Motsinger finally came through for my Empire. We now have the Class Five record at twenty-three minutes and fifty seconds."

Turning to Jane, her countenance was inscrutable. He wondered what she was thinking.

"I'm happy for you, Carl. But I'm also ravenous. Can we go home?"

(Indianapolis Motor Speedway, December 18, 1909)

Flames lapped at the top of the oil drum filled with wood scraps and trash directly behind the parked racers of Lewis Strang and his uncle Walter Christie. The two men and their mechanics busily swarmed the cars, perhaps more animated than usual, in an attempt to stay warm in the nine-degree deep freeze. Carl Fisher, his hands thrust into the copious pockets of his buffalo fur coat, warmed in front of the big container and peered at the scene through the black smoke emitted by the fire.

"Lewis! Walt! You boys have a minute for me?"

The two rugged drivers marched toward the Speedway president.

"Carl, I see your face, but did you get swallowed up by a buffalo or something? That's plenty of coat you got there," Strang said.

Christie extended a leather-gloved hand to grasp a handful of Fisher's buffalo fur. Chuckling, he confirmed that it was a beast's hide and that some animal did not consume Fisher.

"My mother didn't raise any fools," Fisher said. "Warmth is a comfort to my soul, and my soul can use all the comfort it can get. At least it's not blowing up a gale like yesterday."

"Where is everybody else, Carl? Are we the only ones to come back for more punishment?" Christie inquired.

"Motsinger will have my Empire out in a bit. Newby told his boys they accomplished all he could ask of them yesterday and that he'd rather see the cars parked than to stress them out on the frozen bricks anymore. Farmer Bill parked his Cole and drained all the fluids. He put it on blocks, and it's in one of our garages. Five will get you ten he's reclining in a comfortable chair right now in front of his fireplace. But listen, I don't want to take up too much of your time. But I am glad to have you both here; this is important to our business. Can either of you boys get me that American mile track record today?"

"Hughie Hughes is giving me a hand, and he's a hell of a mechanic. We found a couple of loose engine valves and tightened them up," Christie offered. "We plugged up some ventilation holes to keep us warmer. I'm willing to put up the cash that says we can top one hundred and twenty miles an hour today."

Strang studied his uncle and then rolled his eyes at Fisher.

"That would be quite a leap up from yesterday. About seventeen miles per hour," Fisher said. "It looked like you scared yourself skidding, in the first turn after coming through the time traps yesterday. You think you can maintain that kind of speed?"

"I found a broken spring, so I figure that might have been the culprit. Art may be right that the cold is affecting these cars. The metal in springs and axles may be getting brittle."

"What about you, Lewis? You told me yesterday evening that you might have some cards up your sleeve. I understand your mechanic that Scudellari fella is sharp as a tack. Did you boys come up with anything?"

"Tony and I fashioned a thick leather hood to insulate the carburetor. We also fabricated a pipe off the exhaust and pointed it at the carburetor to blast it with hot air. I just don't think the engine has as much pep as it did in Atlanta when the temperatures were a lot warmer. Heating the carburetor should make all the difference in the world."

Strang's words encouraged Fisher more than those of Christie. He always thought Christie had a screw loose – and not one holding his car together. Nodding at the men, he wished them luck and departed for the judges' stand. There he found his old friend James Allison huddled with Frank Wheeler, Charles Root, Fred Wagner, and Charles Warner around the big belly coal stove that cast out a thawing glow into the room. Fisher joined them briefly and then motioned for Allison to step aside to another corner of the room with him.

"What's the latest with Motsinger and our car?" Fisher asked.

"I did a quick once-thru. We adjusted springs, valves, spark plugs, and increased the tire pressure just a tad. We did everything we can."

"I know you did. It would serve us well if Motsinger can post a class speed record or two. It'll only matter if Strang brings home the big markers. If he does, Motsinger's work will pad our bragging rights."

"It's just so damn cold," Allison continued. "I can't help but believe this frigid weather does nothing to help carburation. And look at this place, it's deserted, there can't be more than a hundred people on the grounds."

"Can't blame them. The thermometer over there on the column reads nine degrees. I told the newspapers we were offering free admission. I don't know that we would have gotten any more if we paid them to come in."

Strang's engine boomed to life and then maintained a lusty rumble. Yards beyond the red Fiat, Christie's steel-grey, long-nosed machine blasted flame out its exhaust only to abruptly fall silent. Hughes threw open the bonnet, and Christie leaped out from behind the wheel and removed the chamois hood he wore to shield his face from the bitter cold. Fisher's attention turned to Strang as he rolled away. The plan was to do a warm-up lap and then start timed runs. Strang had agreed to two laps at full speed to have a shot at the five-mile record along with the others.

While Christie and Hughes flailed their arms, as they leaned into the freak racer's engine compartment, their elbows thrashed up and down like they were demonstrating to the pistons how they wanted them to behave. On the track, the Fiat engine grew louder, and then the sound dissipated after Strang soared by. The next time around, the timer was counting.

Fisher removed his pince-nez and inserted them in his breast pocket. Pressing his binoculars to his eyes, he trained his vision on the storming red car zipping down the backstretch. The red dot appeared at the north end of the track to hit the timing traps for a quarter-mile, a half-mile, kilometer and, deep into the south end, the mile.

"We have a quarter-mile American track record of eight and five-hundredths seconds," Root shouted as Warner nodded his head in affirmation.

"What about the mile?" Fisher exclaimed.

"No. Not this time. Let's see what Lewis does on this second lap," Warner announced.

Soon, Strang blasted by the judges' stand for the final time. He stormed into turn one and then through the last timing trap.

"Carl, Jim, you fellas are going to have to be happy with a new American record for five miles," Root reported. "He blew that one out of the water. Oldfield had it at four minutes and eleven seconds. Lewis just posted – get this – three minutes, seventeen and seven-tenths seconds."

Fisher turned to the judges' stand window facing pit lane. Waving his arms frantically, he caught Moross' attention, and the diminutive publicity man sprinted toward the steps outside. Within seconds he was on the second floor among the other officials, panting like a racehorse.

"Carl, before you get started," Root said, "Do you realize Strang's speed at the quarter-mile mark was one hundred twelve miles an hour?"

Fisher glanced over his shoulder at Allison, who brazenly clapped his hands. Moross, as well as Wheeler behind him, was beaming.

"Moross, I feel a hen coming on!"

"Carl, you don't have to say a word. I'll chase down Willis and the others," Moross said. "Charles, I need to scribble down those records. Willis and the other newspapermen need to get accurate, convincing numbers."

Wagner had already flagged Christie out onto the brick track. The Christie engine was firing with tuned precision. Regardless of its rhythmic sound, Christie could not match his nephew's speed. He improved his quarter-mile time by fractions of a second, still at one hundred and three miles per hour.

Fisher's mind played out his story. Strang's five-mile record was a big deal. If that were the first fact, he pushed on the newspapers, and it would imply Strang also bettered the American track mile record. Besides, he did beat Oldfield's mile record for the Indianapolis Speedway. The one hundred twelve miles per hour speed would get everyone to take notice.

The Speedway president hopped down the stairs to trackside. Hands in his coat pockets and puffing a La Reclama Cuban he saved for a celebration, a feeling of relief mixed with exuberance swept over him. Two days of practice, two days of time trials, and no accidents. Just one hundred and twelve miles an hour and new world records. His eyes did not have to search very long before he spotted P.P. Willis, who had been out and about sticking his nose into everything.

"Carl! Just the man I want to see," Willis hollered with open arms. "I just spoke with Wagner. You gotta be one happy buffalo!"

"Really, what did that old coot have to say?"

"Well, this may surprise you, Carl, but he was quite complimentary of your Speedway. He said you would attract many European entries because it is such a fast track. He called

Indianapolis a wonderful automobile center and better represented in racing than Detroit. Something else he said was even more important to me."

"Oh yeah? What's that?"

"He corroborated the time for Strang's five-mile record that Moross just shared with me before you walked up. He said he timed Lewis' run on his stopwatch, and it was nearly identical to the electric timer's report. Not that I don't trust you Speedway promoters, but it was important to have a second opinion. If nothing else, Wag is as honest as the day is long."

Fisher put on a poker face. He did not want his countenance to belie his joy to hear Wagner's compliment and the conviction Willis had that his Speedway was the fastest track in the country. Considering for a minute what he should say next, he conjured up a short speech he wanted Willis to scribble down.

"While I am exceedingly proud of our great records made in this season, yet I am more than ever delighted that this midwinter meet is over. It was my ambition to have the new season open with Indianapolis holding all the laurels. We now have a high prize that will make other tracks struggle to equal. Not only that, but I am sure we have a track now that will permit a much faster time under better weather conditions. I predict marvelous records on this track for next summer."

Willis dutifully scrawled each syllable until it was all recorded on the notepad, he kept in his breast pocket.

"Got it, Willis?"

The newspaperman nodded in the affirmative.

"Good. Now I'm headed back in town. It's colder than a witch's tit out here."

Chapter 25 – Speed King

(Daytona Beach, March 16, 1910)

The gusts of the gentle, lapping Atlantic tide were pleasant and insufficient to kick up gritty sand from Daytona Beach. Still, there was a frosty cheek-kiss from the forty-degree atmosphere. Barney Oldfield tugged at his stocking cap to shield his ears. Aligned beside him in a row were fellow drivers John Walter Christie, George Robertson, and twenty-three-year-old David Bruce-Brown, the most heralded young amateur in America. A dozen feet away, with his back to the glowing orb that grew ever more luminous as it rose from the ocean, Richard LeSesne fiddled with his big camera, all but his feet obscured by black drapery that concealed him. His hands emerged from under the cape to deftly adjust the oak legs of his tripod.

Well acquainted with the photographic process, the drivers held resolutely stationary through not just one, but three tedious snaps of the shutter. LeSesne flipped the curtain aside, and it momentarily gathered up the anemic breeze before relaxing to a flaccid state.

The photographer approached the four men to announce that his next subject would be Oldfield's pearl-white "Lightning" Benz. The brutish machine rested in the background as it was groomed by Oldfield's mechanics, Bill Healy and the Hill brothers, George and Jimmy.

"She won't bite you, buddy. But she might devour me," Oldfield said. "We'll have to see."

With a tip of his black bowler, LeSesne hoisted the tripod and its attached camera and swung it over his shoulder before marching off. Robertson, the 1908 Vanderbilt Cup winner, squinted in the face of intensifying sunlight, obviously studying the Lightning Benz.

"I should be in that car," he asserted. "Ernie Moross said he had ten thousand dollars of Carl Fisher's money to buy it. He had Jesse Froelich of the Benz Import Company ready to sell it and put me in it."

"Well, George, I hate to tell you, but you're not in it because I am," Oldfield said with a sense of fulfilling, deep satisfaction. "Besides, Froelich said he wanted me in it. He knows I'll whip that steed to tremendous pace and then do a better job than anyone telling the world about it. Look closely. The name on the side of the car is, 'Barney Oldfield."

Walt Christie inserted himself before Robertson could respond. The twenty-six-year-old was to drive Christie's front-wheel-drive creation, and Oldfield judged that he didn't much like his driver coveting the Benz.

"I see in the newspapers you bought the thing for six thousand dollars."

"Not quite. I also traded my Prince Henry Benz I drove last year."

The two veterans of the game paced off the steps toward the pearl racer gleaming in the morning daylight. Oldfield thought about telling him he was too busy for company at the moment but did not for reasons even he did not understand. Studying the German product just feet from the car, Christie fell mute. Oldfield knew the engineer was dismantling it with his eyes, and there was something uncomfortable about that like the man was seeing Bess naked. No matter. Christie was a mad genius, always dreaming up new marvels, none of which endured real tests.

"Big chain drive," he offered, breaking his silence. "I imagine the torque in this thing would twist a drive shaft like a pretzel."

Oldfield nodded but did not care to encourage more conversation. He told the older driver that he was about to get busy. His goal was to establish new land speed records. His goal was to rise to the summit of his profession as the fastest man in the world. After an awkward silence, Christie headed in the direction of Robertson and their mechanic, Hughie Hughes.

Will Pickens, the rotund wonder of the ballyhoo, accompanied the Lightning Benz on its transport from New York. He tended to details of the acquisition and prepared press announcements to deliver on Oldfield's – and Froelich's – expectations for promotion. The publicity push was aimed at heralding Benz cars and reinvigorating Oldfield's career, which had been tarnished by his alcohol binges, and their fixed barnstorming shows the previous autumn. A consensus had developed in the trade press that Oldfield, who had turned thirty-two six weeks earlier, was getting too old to keep up with the likes of Robertson and Bruce-Brown.

Oldfield toured the perimeter of the rectangle of sand now defined by his Benz. He shouted questions to pierce the general din of the ocean – wind gusts that always muffled words, the lapping waves, and the occasional squawks of seagulls. His inquiries met with affirmations from Jimmy at the front, George at the back, and Healy from underneath. Wheel mounts were torqued, oil fittings secured, tire pressure set to the driver's prescription. The timing of the enormous twenty-one-and-a-half-liter engine delivered a rhythmic growl that had Oldfield applauding impulsively. There it was. The modern-day chariot he would use to reclaim his reputation.

Nearby, Christie's car coughed and stuttered. He and his men furiously flogged the machine-gray behemoth with its body shaped like an upside-down canoe pointed at each end. One, two, three repeated attempts to sustain explosions in the cylinders failed. Robertson threw a tin coffee cup at the car's rear tire and stormed off. Within minutes Christie and Hughes hitched a jackass to the front of the vehicle and mushed through loose sand beyond the water's edge.

Behind them, several men pushed Hugh Donald "Huge Deal" McIntosh's one hundred twenty horsepower Benz for Bruce Brown. McIntosh, a ponderous man, cut an imposing figure as he strode beside his rolling machine with crossed arms. The Australian show-business promoter had provided the same car to Bruce-Brown the previous year with the outstanding result of a new amateur speed record at one hundred and nine miles per hour or thirty-three seconds.

McIntosh, the scope of his dimension undeniable, silently loomed over his employees' labors. He motioned at Bruce-Brown, who dutifully came to his side. They obviously had an exchange as the car owner puffed on a prodigious cheroot simultaneously. Free smoke quickly dissipated in the ocean breeze. Oldfield glanced at Pickens and then at the Triple-A timer's table where Charles Warner sat. The two men cleared the hard-packed shoreline and then trudged through white powder toward Warner. The Warner electric timer inventor looked up from his station and acknowledged the two men.

"Hey, Barney, Will. What can I do for you, gentlemen?"

"Just stay sharp when I tear down that beach," Oldfield said, winking. "Don't blink because you'll miss me."

"This isn't a stopwatch, Barney. I have traps set up for the measured mile and spots between. Unless you can exceed the speed of electricity, you can't escape our notice."

"Hey, Charles. Do you mind if we watch this kid Bruce-Brown with you? He's quite the wheelman. I just would like a peek at your report when he's done."

"I don't see a problem with that. I need to telephone the report down to the other end, so Hugh and David hear it first. Just stand over there, I want to get a good gander at how the boy does."

Bruce-Brown had circled his car back to a marked spot so he could get a flying start on his run. Soon, a brown dot sped toward them, growing larger in every fraction of a second, its engine ever more raucous. The Benz crossed the first timing wire and began to shrink and grow muted as it progressed south.

Oldfield observed Warner on his phone and could not resist advancing toward him. Before he was within ten feet, Warner craned his neck toward the driver and shouted, "He beat his own amateur speed record for the mile. Thirty-two and eighteen-hundredths of a second. That's eight tenths faster than last year and about one hundred and twelve miles per hour!"

Oldfield arrived at the table and peered over Warner's shoulder at the ticker tape. Bruce-Brown was a year younger than Oldfield was when he started racing. The kid probably couldn't remember a time before cars. Damn fast. Hell, a mile-a-minute used to be a big deal.

"You're up next, Barney."

"Thanks. I just want to walk the course a bit."

"We can give you some time," Warner said. "But don't take too long, or we will lose the speedway to the tide."

Pickens and Oldfield again marched through the loose sand; the gritty white powder clung to their dampened boots.

"You walking the course, Barney?" Pickens inquired. "You want some company?"

"No offense, Will, but I want to do this alone. Tell the boys to give me twenty minutes and meet me with the car running at the opposite end."

Pickens shrugged and then pivoted toward the Lightning Benz.

Maybe it was Bruce-Brown's run and thinking about himself coming to Daytona as a young man for the first time. Strolling the hard-packed, damp shoreline, he recollected how back in 1904 Tom Cooper pointed out washboards left the previous night by the retreating tide. A curious feeling swept over him as if he could feel Tom, not by his side, but within him. There had always been an aching void Oldfield had been unable to fill since lowering Tom in the ground. He searched for his Henry Clay Secretary of the Navy and stashed it in the corner of his mouth, not bothering to strike a flame in the face of the Atlantic breeze. Smoking was not necessary; the cigar made him feel all of Barney Oldfield was in place for his task.

The calm ocean had given little rise to washboard the shore with infernal ripples that became jarring hurdles that set cars to fly at high speed. Reassured that the course was in his favor, Oldfield privately resolved to focus on what was in front of him, hold his breath, and urge his new race car to its limit. As he finished the mile walk, Pickens had the car running and ready. Oldfield hoisted himself into the seat by gripping the steering wheel and planting his foot on the shoe-sized platform just for that purpose.

"Healy and the Hills are at the far end, where you make your standing start, so you're going full tilt by the time you get to the starting wire. Wagner is down there with his flag, and he's going to want to talk to you."

Oldfield nodded his understanding and commenced to put the engine in gear. Pickens, still fixed next to the driver's side, gently clasped his friend's left forearm.

"You feeling fit, Barney?"

"I haven't had a drop for three weeks if that's what you mean."

"Good. You are the man for this job. Go show them you're the fastest man on Earth."

Oldfield nodded and pinching the sides of his goggles, lifted them past his chin and over his eyes. Several hundred people had assembled on the dunes near the course, many with picnic baskets and blankets. Cheers and shouts blended into engine sounds, and the ocean as he made his way to the point of departure.

Fred Wagner and his mechanics hailed him. Swinging around them and circling back,

Oldfield came to where they stood. Healy and the Hills paced around the mighty Benz performing their visual inspection. Wagner leaned into the car, and Oldfield bent downward to hear the official over the engine.

"Okay, Barney, the car looks perfect. Hats off to you and your boys prepping it. You've been here before; you know what to do. I saw you walking the shore. I did that early this morning, and I don't think I have seen a better stretch of sand speedway anywhere. You have the right car, the right course, and you're the right man. Now go give the world a new land speed record!"

Oldfield cast his mind beyond distraction. Wagner's words had melted into the rest of the irrelevant background noise. Limitless packed sand, as hard as granite, extended before him. Full throttle, his Benz hurtled toward the starting wire. Oldfield's competition was the beach, demanding him to maintain his resolve or be jerked like a yoyo along random paths. The vibrating wheel wanted to whirl out of his fingers and required constant finesse with subtle input corrections – left, right, left, right.

Bam! The front wheels lifted off the ground, and for a fleeting fraction of a second, Oldfield lost sight of the beach to see only blue sky and cumulus clouds. There was another thud as the tires landed, and instinctively, the driver gripped harder on the wheel and mashed his accelerator to assert control. He braced for his tires to fly off the rims. They remained intact, and five eternal seconds later, he hurtled over the final timing wire to continue down the beach toward acres of undeveloped verdant jungle.

Oldfield figured he covered another mile just to decelerate to a moderate pace before he swung his big racer around to progress back toward the cluster of people at the finish. With the engine quieted from its anger, his senses were flooded with sounds, ocean waves, the fluttering wind, sea hawk squawks, and the raucous glee of spectators at his back in the distance. In his hellbent flight, he had forgotten the cigar clenched between his teeth. The fingers of his left hand traced the contours of his face to find a mix of saliva, melted tobacco, and sand. Tobacco juice was splattered on his shirt with grit adhered. With the crunch of sand in his teeth, he flicked the unsmoked stogie toward the advancing tide.

Pickens jogged in his direction and observing him, Oldfield concluded that but for his leather suspenders, his trousers would likely slide about his knees, and his overabundant form would plunge him face-first into the grit. Others Oldfield did not know engulfed and surpassed Pickens, shouting, "world record" in unison. Soon his Lightning Benz was surrounded by screaming and careless people, and he winced as one man placed his hands on two of the hot exhaust pipes. His face contorted, and he pivoted to dive through the crowd and race to the water to soak his burns. Oldfield stood up in his seat and shouted down to those all about his car.

"You know me, I'm Barney Oldfield!"

Panting, the giant Pickens literally tossed several men aside and elbowed his way to his driver. Oldfield studied his enthusiastic promoter.

"Jesus, Will, I don't know what's more amazing, me setting a world speed record or you running!"

Still breathless, Pickens mustered, "Twenty-seven seconds! One hundred thirty-two miles an hour!"

Oldfield pumped a fist at the sky, shouting about buying the house a round of drinks. He imagined all the celebrations, all the newspaper stories, the congratulations from people who mattered.

Three newspaper scribes shouted questions to Oldfield, eagerly scribbling down his dramatic description of his ride. Pickens again brushed people away so LeSesne could set up his camera. Oldfield continued his sensational tale of his drive.

"I let the great old car have its head. Down went the throttle, and I advanced the spark well along. We were shooting through space. I began to choke, everything before me enshrouded in a haze, and I suddenly felt as though I was in the middle of a nightmare about to jump off some mountainous precipice."

Oldfield's mind raced to stay just ahead of his hair-raising narrative as he embellished onward for several minutes. Somewhere, Pickens had glommed onto a megaphone, and reading from a notecard, he began to shout over his driver.

"Excuse me, Barney, but I have some official Triple-A news we should share with everyone gathered here. Ladies and gentlemen, you are looking at the newly crowned Speed King of the World! With an official time of twenty-seven and thirty-three one-hundredth seconds, Barney Oldfield is the new Speed King of the world at one hundred thirty-two and seventy-one hundredths miles an hour!"

(Ormond Hotel Casino, March 16, 1910)

"To the Speed King of the World," William Hickman Pickens shouted as he raised a glass of Champagne Delbeck. The dining room of the Ormond Hotel Casino was packed with automotive and racing people sitting at round tables throughout the banquet hall. Many heard Pickens' pronouncement. Some applauded, and almost everyone joined the toast with a chorus of, "For he's a jolly good fellow."

The men around their table, Bill Healy, George and Jimmy Hill, and John Walter Christie, along with Bess Oldfield, stood up and raised their flutes to a delicate clink with shouts of, "hear, hear." Oldfield felt the weight of Bess' consuming stare monitoring his behavior. He knew she was drink counting.

"Bess! It's a celebration! You are dining with the fastest man alive. Faster than anyone and anything!"

It was true. No other automobile, locomotive, motorcycle, or aeroplane had achieved such speed. Bess had said she was so fearful of her husband pressing beyond the known limits of man and machine that she had remained in her room, distracting herself with Henry James' "*Washington Square.*"

"Look around!" Oldfield shouted. "The last time I was here, I was with the Winton crew, and I was thrown out on my keister."

A thought of Helen Fea Winton crept into Oldfield's alcohol-fogged consciousness. He stole a fervent glance of Bess, who set at the other side of the table, glaring at him. Was he drinking too much? Did Bess know about his dalliances with Helen? They had never discussed the subject, and he sure as hell was not going to broach it. The best tactic was to carry on with his proclamations.

"Alexander Winton. Willy K. General Pardington. Where are they now? I know for sure; I am the Speed King of the World, and I plan to close this place down tonight!"

Christie and the other men applauded, but Bess sat silent.

"And I want to say one more thing. Someone who was with me today at one hundred thirty-three miles per hour, and is with me here right now – I feel his presence, I really do – is Tom Cooper. I want everyone to raise a glass with me to a great champion on both two wheels and four. A great man and a damn good friend to boot. Tom, I know you can see us, and we raise our glasses heavenward to you!"

At this, Bess finally joined in with a full heart. She and the others stood tall and toasted Tom Cooper. Appearing behind Oldfield came Fred Wagner, who joined the salute a trifling late. He then clamped his left hand on one of the new Speed King's shoulders and shook him.

"Barney, I am proud of you. You did it, son! You still have what it takes. Enjoy your Speed King title."

After a brief exchange, Wagner departed for his table while along came Charles Warner to repeat the congratulatory process. Several other men streamed toward Oldfield like he was standing in a reception line. One was a hotel bellboy with an envelope containing a telegram.

"From Germany, Mr. Oldfield."

The driver searched his coat pocket and planted a glittering silver dollar on the young man's extended palm. Tearing open the envelope, Oldfield read it aloud.

"Congratulations to a daring Yankee driving the German Blitzen Benz. Speed Kings of the world."

"Blitzen Benz?" Pickens inquired. "Now who in the devil sent you that."

"None other than Kaiser Wilhelm from across the ocean in Germany. What is this 'Blitzen' business? Is that a cuss word?"

Wagner returned to Oldfield's side and asked to see the message. Studying it, he expressed his doubt that the word could be construed as offensive.

"Hold on a minute," the Triple-A starter said. "I have been keeping a German cobbler who runs a nearby shop pretty busy with my men's shoes. I invited him to join us this evening, so let me go see what he thinks."

Wagner returned promptly and explained that "Blitzen" was German for "Lightning." Oldfield winked at Bess, who now looked to be casting admiration from her eyes and smile. He creased his telegram and slid it into his coat breast pocket. Still standing, the newly-crowned Speed King pondered the German word and stroked his chin. Looking at Pickens, he smiled and nodded.

"I like it. Bill, let's find a man who is good with a brush and change the name on the side of the car. From now on, I am driving the Blitzen Benz."

Chapter 26 – First Super-Speedway

(Chicago Blackstone Hotel, April 16, 1910)

"This place is impressive, Barney," said Ernie Moross from his stool at the mahogany bar of the tavern inside Chicago's new high-rise Blackstone Hotel. "How long have they been open?"

"About a week," Oldfield said before emitting a cloud from sucking on his Henry Clay Secretary of the Navy. "This is a big deal. Caruso performed at the opening. The tallest building in the world."

Window shades diffused the ten o'clock morning daylight emanating from the world outside, permitting only subdued illumination into a chamber that Oldfield deemed comfortable. The dim light from electrified sconces encircling the perimeter of the room cast a relaxing glow that soothed him. As he quaffed a hearty gulp of Old Style lager, he offered to procure one for Moross.

"It's a little early for me," Moross replied.

"Don't be a stick in the mud," Oldfield said while motioning for the barkeep to draw a pint from his cask. Soon the man produced a substantial glass stein filled with golden fluid and a frothy top that only just barely dripped over the brim. Moross rolled his eyes but seemed resigned to a drink.

"What have you been up to Ernie? I imagine that giant Speedway is keeping you busy."

"As a matter of fact, it is. We just wrapped a big Indianapolis auto show with all the car companies and sales agents two weeks ago."

"Auto show, huh? At the Speedway?"

"We had some events at the track. We ran obstacle courses, egg balancing, and I even got on a big teeter-totter with my Marmon."

Oldfield put on a skeptical face, complete with squinting eyes. Stunts Moross and Fisher hatched could never shock him. Still, he was in a mood to be amused.

"Egg balancing?"

"You know Barney. One fella drives, and another one rides shotgun balancing an egg on a tablespoon. If you don't break the egg, it shows your car delivers a smooth ride. The winner is the driver that gets through an obstacle course the fastest."

A huge smoke cloud billowed from the driver's lips and wafted in the direction of Moross's face. This was followed by a condescending smile that stretched his countenance.

"Eggs and teeter-totters. So that's what's keeping you busy?"

"Stop with the needling, Barney. That show did a lot to help the auto business in Indianapolis. It isn't New York, there's no Madison Avenue Garden, so we had to improvise. All the dealers dressed up their showroom floors and offered prizes and refreshments. We had a floral parade that ended at the Speedway. It was successful enough I can see us doing it again next year."

Oldfield thought the whole affair sounded dreadfully dull, but he decided it wasn't worth taking another jab. Instead, he inquired about a rumor he heard that the Speedway bricks were cutting and blowing out tires.

"Oh, that. We're fixing it. We're shaving the bricks."

"Shaving? What are you doing, crawling around on your hands and knees, soaping the bricks and scraping at them with your straight edge?"

"Very funny. Barney, this Speedway has the latest and best in paving technology. This isn't one of your dirt hippodromes or a wood plank track."

"Well, aren't you a genius with your highfalutin words - technology, huh?"

"Okay, fair enough. Here's the scoop. Some of the Marmon and National fellas were doing test runs when the weather got better last month. When they stopped at the pits, the mechanics gave their cars a once-over and found cuts in the tires and lots of abrasions. The engineers figured out that the winter cold and spring thaw crumbled the thin coating of concrete that was smoothed over the edges of the bricks. That left sharp edges exposed, and they were cutting into the rubber after just a few laps."

Oldfield shook his head and stared into his lap.

"Ernie, I'll be straight with you. Your bosses sunk a lot of money into that Speedway, but they better get it right for next month, or it's going to be curtains for the whole show. That fella Jack Prince put up his Playa Del Ray board track near Los Angeles in no time. Smooth as all get out, and it only takes a few weeks to build them. A million feet of lumber and a hundred tons of spikes and nails. Tell me, how do you shave a brick track?"

Moross explained that it was a process devised by track engineers. It entailed pulling pallets of bricks, scrap iron, and rocks at the back of a team of Overland motor vehicles. The heavy pallets bounced over the track, chipping at the edges of the bricks. Not every block had to be treated, just the ones in the lanes the cars drove over.

"It's going to be alright, Barney, trust me. That's not the reason I took the train up here to meet you. Our national championship races are coming up next month, and we haven't received your entries."

"Triple-A national championship races. What a crock of shit. Those clowns are just doing that to make me look bad. It's stupid. There's not even a points championship like they had in ought-five. That one didn't work out so well for them because I won the goddamn thing."

"I'm sure some it is directed at you, and any other outlaws who put on races outside their purview. You're cutting into their action, and they're trying to make your hippodroming out to be phony."

Oldfield hoisted his warming beer to his lips. Every time he thought about just up and quitting, his mind came up blank as to what he could do next. Besides, no matter how much money Oldfield made from driving, he never could put anything away. There were too many things to own, too many people he needed to make sure they knew he was a famous champion.

"Ernie, if you and Carl and the boys want me in Indianapolis next month, you're going to have to pay up. I spent ten thousand greenbacks to get that big Benz, and I have put money into it since. Probably a total of fourteen thousand dollars. I need to make some of that back, so tell Fisher he needs to make it worth my while."

"Barney, you didn't do yourself any favors letting that amateur kid Caleb Bragg hand your head to you last month in those match races at that Playa Del Rey board track you love so much. What is he? Twenty-three? He's already filed an entry for our races. People are going to think you're yellow if you're not there."

Oldfield riveted his eyes into Moross. He knew he could make the little promoter blink.

"Barney, come on. We can't give people appearance fees, no matter how big a name they are. We've got some nice purses for our races; you can make a lot of money. Besides, I need your help. I'm not getting along with Carl that well. I haven't been able to deliver the European drivers he wants. He shouts at me, and it's humiliating. Sometimes he apologizes later, but I'm really tired of it. If I can't convince you after all our time together, he'll sack me, I know it."

"Ernie, this isn't an easy life. You have to stand up for yourself and let the cards fall as they will. I can't help you with that. Just know I'm not asking for any damn appearance fee. What I want is a five-thousand-dollar prize for setting the track mile speed record. You do that and leave the rest to me."

"That's the best you can do for me? I'm not sure that's going to work."

"That's my offer, and, yes, I think it should be a lot of help to you with Carl and the other fellas. I'm the Speed King of the World. Everybody knows me. You just hang that big bag of cash at the mile marker, and I'll grab it as I go by."

(Indianapolis Motor Speedway, May 26, 1910)

A six-o'clock shadow cast by the bright sun now obscured by the half-filled grandstands across the front stretch was, like the Daytona tide, edging inexorably to the feet of the men surrounding a big yellow machine. Barney Oldfield traced his fingertips over the cone-like tail of the mustard Marmon race car at its Indianapolis Motor Speedway pit. At the same time, Starter Fred Wagner flagged the final practice day for the upcoming weekend's national championship race meet to a close.

Engines fell silent as drivers returned their machines to the pits. Just behind Oldfield, the nearby Buicks of Louis Chevrolet and Bob Burman were met by a swarm of mechanics. The crimson American of Herb Lytle coasted to his pit in silence at the other side of Marmon car, the engine switched off. Still chattering, thousands of spectators who had created the wall of color that washed across the corner of Oldfield's right eye when he was on track, now began to file out of their seats and set off to their touring cars, buggies, or the nearby rail station.

Little Ernie Moross and the rotund one himself, Will Pickens, strolled around the Marmon as Oldfield continued to examine the car with his hands as much as his eyes. Just weeks prior, Moross wrote an article about the new Marmon racer for the Indianapolis Star. In it, he called the car a "modern invention of restless humanity…designed to travel at record speed and still more speed in this desperate and dangerous sport…new lines to extract speed, speed, and still more speed from that invisible nowhere."

Oldfield was careful to show respect to the two Marmon men observing him, Howard Marmon and his driver, Ray Harroun. Several times he glanced to their eyes as if asking for permission. Gentle hands as if he were caressing a woman.

"I've never seen craftsmanship like this in an American race car," Oldfield said in earnest with no a hint of flattery. "Now, my Blitzen Benz is one hell of an example of the work of artisans, but that's the Germans for you. I just wonder, you only have one seat here. How do you fellas plan to race like that for two hundred miles?"

The bespectacled Marmon, with his cleft chin and brown hair tonic-slicked to one side, appeared older than his thirty-four years. He was the picture of an engineer, and Oldfield imagined him growing nearsighted from hours poring over a drafting table. His left cheek pulled a smile to one side of his face, and he nodded at Harroun.

"I should let Ray speak to that, but, yes, we fully intend to show well in the Wheeler-Schebler Trophy. He's the brave soul who will figure a way."

Oldfield saw Harroun as a stoic sort, rarely speaking other than to answer only the questions he found worthy. Harroun cleared his throat for the deadpan delivery of his brief response.

"I know where my car is in relation to others, and a quick glance is all I need to evade trouble."

"As usual, Ray is far too modest," Marmon inserted. "I'd say winning our first outing at

Atlanta a couple of weeks ago is a good start. We conducted some extended runs in heavy traffic today with fast laps of a minute-forty-five."

Oldfield unconsciously shook his head. Damn, that *is* fast. He studied Harroun, nicknamed the "Bedouin" by the press because of his rugged face, jet-black hair, and deep-brown eyes. His body had the sinewy look of an active man.

"Ray was the lead engineer on this masterpiece," Marmon continued. "We agreed the lean, cigar-shaped profile would give us an edge on getting through wind resistance. By eliminating the riding mechanic, we have the profile of an arrow. The pointed tail is part of the aerodynamic design. That shape rolls the air off the car to help us find speed. Looks like an insect stinger, don't you think? It's why we call it the Marmon Wasp."

Oldfield felt Harroun had grown weary of his inquiries. He glanced at Moross and Pickens and, after meeting their gaze, nodded. Apparently, Marmon took it as a signal he was about to depart.

"Now hold on, Barney," Marmon said. "We've peeled back the kimono on our latest speed machine and given you a good look to boot. It seems only fair that you tell us something about what you will be wheeling this weekend. Your Daytona speed record in the German car certainly has everyone talking. Can we see it?"

"It's in the showroom at the Conduitt Automobile Company downtown. I'll have it hauled to the garage here tomorrow. I'd be happy to give you the grand tour. The thing puts out two hundred horsepower. It's so much power it uses an old-fashioned beefed-up chain drive to the rear wheels. The torque is overwhelming and would twist any driveshaft into a pretzel."

"Barney's also racing a Knox Raceabout that Conduitt is providing," Moross inserted.

Marmon's eyes widened, and he nodded knowingly while saying he had come across the news in the newspapers. Oldfield wondered if Moross would offer too much information about his negotiations over compensation for showing up.

"Come on, Ernie, Will, let's hoof it back to the garage. These gentlemen have work to do, I am sure."

Barney felt the crunch of cement particles shaken off the bricks and now under his leather soles. The track was brick, and so was the pit lane they traversed.

"I don't want to talk to people about my business arrangements, Moross. You too, Will," Oldfield asserted. "Talk about the cars all you want, I don't care. But don't share anything about my deals."

Moross, visibly annoyed, snapped at his former driver.

"Oh, for Christ's sake, Barney, are you daft? There's no percentage in it for the Speedway or me to talk about any deals we strike. If you don't know me better than that by now, I've been overestimating your intelligence for years."

"To overestimate would be easier than underestimate in this case," said Pickens, smiling and appearing impressed with himself.

Oldfield halted and pivoted toward the hefty promoter. Feigning a glare at Pickens, he was not angry but wanted to see if the man would be intimidated. He wasn't.

"Listen, fat ass, you like your job as my manager? Keep your fucking opinions to yourself."

Oldfield only just got the words out before a laugh burst through his clenched teeth. Pickens cackled and shot a look at Moross, who shook his head.

"Nobody talked about the engine," Pickens said, obviously looking for a change of subject. "Why did you cut off the conversation?"

"Harroun was shooting daggers out of his eyes. I don't need to stick around with unfriendly people who don't want me," Oldfield replied. "What do you know about that engine, Moross? How much horsepower?"

"About fifty from four hundred seventy-seven cubic inches. It's six cylinders and is in a T-Head configuration. You know what I see, though? I see the future. I see a car this track was built to test and prove-in."

"Hey Ernie, snap out of it. Knock off the ballyhoo. I'm not one of your newspapermen you try to sell ideas and quotes to. Remember me?"

"I know all too well who you are. I'm trying to have an honest conversation."

"For shame!" interrupted Pickens. "There are no honest conversations in the racing game."

"I'm telling you boys, this here Speedway is going to make everything different. This brick surface is smooth and tough. Straightaways five-eighths of a mile – plenty long enough to let an engine stretch its legs to the breaking point. This track will change everything. And look at that crowd that came out here just to watch test laps on a Thursday, for Christ's sake!"

"It is one hell of a speed palace," Oldfield mused. "Right now, I don't have time for philosophical discussions. I'm thinking of Saturday. That Knox Raceabout you set up for me has some grunt, but I don't see it as a match for that Wasp car. My best chance is that they haven't had enough time to work out the bugs, and the damn thing breaks down. It's obvious they built it with this track in mind. It may be the first true Speedway car."

(Indianapolis Motor Speedway, May 27, 1910)

Newspapermen Peter Paul Willis, Harry Deupree, and C. E. "Heinie" Schuart, clustered together in the judges' stand, gesturing, whispering, and apparently forming opinions destined for a typesetter. Carl Fisher strode across the wood plank floor and, barely having gotten out of his mouth a perfunctory request to be allowed into their conversation, he inserted his voice with all the confidence of a man who owned the place.

"What are you ladies complaining about now?"

A hint of a smile graced Fisher's face, but the three reporters paid little notice.

"We're glad you stopped by, Carl," Willis said. "Perhaps you can tell us why there were only six cars in this race? Your one-hundred-mile Prest-O-Lite Trophy feature race? Is anybody going to make it that far? Fox in that Pope Toledo lost a wheel on lap seven. He's not coming back. You're down to five."

Nodding at American Automobile Association Event Referee Art Pardington, who stood with his back to them in the far corner of the room, Fisher insisted the decision was out of his hands. Pardington and technical inspector David Beecroft announced the previous day that entries by the Buick and American companies would be disallowed from stock car events. Regulations required manufacturers to produce at least twenty-five cars for consumer sales before the model could be considered stock. Factories were not allowed to claim their entries were stock unless they met the criteria. The three scribes were skeptical that the decision was out of Fisher's hands, but he held firm.

As if on cue, the electric warning horns stationed about the facility assailed everyone's ears and blasted a warning alarm to rescue crews around the brick oval. Men scurried to one side of the stand, all craning their necks to witness whatever their worst fears had conjured up on the projection screen in their heads.

Fisher clumsily pushed his binoculars to his spectacles and pointed them at the north end of the track. The image was spectacular as the shredded carcass of the right rear tire slapped violently at Tom Kincaid's indigo National. Kincaid veered into the infield grass but kept rolling, apparently headed to his pits. As they drew closer, Carl could make out that while Kincaid remained in the driver's seat and his riding mechanic, Don Herr was leaning to his right to steer the stricken car. Kincaid appeared to be holding his arm.

"So there, Carl," Willis continued, "another car bites the dust. I'm telling you; they are all going to be parked before a hundred miles."

With Kincaid stopped at his pit and the National team busily replacing the defective tire, Fisher turned back to the journalists.

"Two things, boys. One, we will have cars battling at the finish, be assured of that. Two, the Triple-A is the governing body of our sport. I choose to accept that. Of course, I like big fields, but this is a great race. Look at all the speed records we are setting today. The Speedway is the fastest race track in the country. That's what you should be writing about."

The short field meant conversations were more natural to conduct. The clamor of rumbling engines outside was punctuated by the relative silence of nearly a minute on some laps. Ray Harroun had things well in hand in one of the stock Marmon "Yellow Jackets."

"Ray just set a new twenty-mile American record that's under sixteen minutes," Fisher enthused. "We've already set five other American class track records in the earlier races today. This buffed brick track is smooth, fast, durable, and safe. No matter who wins our Prest-O-Lite Trophy, our Speedway will hold records for every mile up to the full one hundred."

"Stop selling us, Carl," Deupree said. "We understand and appreciate that you have built an awesome track..."

Deupree's voice was overwhelmed in mid-sentence by the barks and blasts of Kincaid's engine as he picked up speed along the pits and headed back to the running surface. He paused, shook his head, and continued.

"Nobody I am aware of has had anything nasty or unfair to say about your operation, Carl, but we have to report the facts. If we don't, nobody will believe anything we have to say – even when it's good news for you. Today is going tremendously well, as you say. But the fact of the matter is everyone wishes there were more cars in this race."

"And what's Oldfield's status?" Schuart asked. "He didn't even start the third race. I hear the Knox has a broken steering knuckle. Is that true? Is that car out for the weekend?"

"You so-called journalists always see things in the darkest light, don't you?" Fisher said. "I haven't had a chance to talk to anyone about the Oldfield situation. I'll predict he will be back out here tomorrow, mixing it up with the best of them. As for Buick and the others, you can see every one of them duke it out in the Wheeler-Schebler Trophy tomorrow because that's a free-for-all. You don't have to have a stock car."

The men chattered all at once and denied being pessimistic, just insistent on the facts. Fisher pointed at Pardington, advising them to go ask him. Abruptly, he turned his back on them and swaggered to a spot beside Jim Allison at the window overlooking the front stretch. Fisher removed his pince-nez, the lens smudged in his haste to focus on Kincaid through his binoculars. He polished them with a handkerchief and deposited them in his jacket's breast pocket. Grasping his binoculars, he pulled them up from their resting spot on his chest and returned them to his eyes.

"How's Harroun doing? Still on record pace?"

In a cruel coincidence, before Allison could respond and the moment Fisher trained his binoculars-assisted eyes on Harroun, the Yellow Jacket slowed exiting the northwest turn. Clearly, the engine was no longer firing. Although Harroun's pit was some distance away, he could make out the Marmon mechanics pouncing on the stricken machine and throwing open the bonnet.

Fisher scurried to the timer's table to reassure himself that Dawson could maintain record pace. The second Yellow Jacket stormed by the start-finish and continued to tick off laps at speeds not much less than Harroun's pace. Dawson surged onward unimpeded while the heavier Nationals of Tom Kincaid and Charlie Merz lost ground, hampered by retreats to their pit stalls for new tires. Relentless, Dawson continued his onslaught until just after setting the American track record for eighty miles when his Marmon faltered. Harroun had returned to the race, but hopelessly behind.

Fisher ground his teeth, thinking of the predictions by the newspapermen that no one would finish. Frank Fox in the Pope-Toledo was waylaid, Harroun and Dawson were struggling, and the other three cars of Kincaid, Merz, and Leigh Lynch in the Jackson had trailed most of the way.

Kincaid dashed by the judge's stand, and Merz followed within a minute. The National teammates appeared strong, provided there would be no more tire issues. Kincaid tripped the ninety-mile mark at a record pace, and Fisher was conscious of an involuntary sigh released from deep within his lungs. All the work, all the expenses - he simply could not tolerate anything less than all the American records for the distance. Not Atlanta, not Playa Del Rey, only Indianapolis. Dawson returned to the fray but was well over a lap in arrears.

Lynch in the Jackson trailed hopelessly behind in third with Dawson soaring, but with only nine miles remaining, the task of recovery was beyond reach. Fisher stomped over to the timer's table to peer over the Triple-A official's shoulder. Yes, Kincaid was under the record Louis Chevrolet set at Atlanta the previous autumn, but just barely - only twenty-seven seconds. The Speedway president paced the floor as the remaining three laps ticked off.

Returning to Allison's side overlooking the track, Fisher joined him when everyone burst into applause as Kincaid's dark blue machine passed under Wagner's unfurled checkered flag. The Speedway founders simultaneously bolted for the stand's steps and bounded down to the pit lane brickwork and sprinted to a platform reserved for trophies. The magnificent sterling silver Prest-O-Lite prize was perched there. Affixed to an oversized brick were bas-relief silver emblems of a car, wings, and "Prest-O-Lite" in bold letters shouting out at any eyes that landed there.

Fisher and Allison each gripped the hand of Prest-O-Lite executive Frank Sweet, who had transported and safeguarded the trophy. Both greetings were perfunctory and brief as Fisher, along with Allison, turned his attention to the indigo National coasting toward them. Kincaid had shut down the big engine and, with his mechanic Don Herr beside him, stepped up on his seat, leaning over with his left hand still in touch with the steering wheel and waving to applauding fans with his right arm. Herr stood too, his fists clenched and his arms extended into the air.

Fisher turned a sideways glance at Allison, who offered a rare smile and shrugged his shoulders. Applauding with more vigor, Fisher said, "Young men celebrating, bully good show. Good for them!"

Kincaid slid back in his seat to apply his brakes. He freewheeled to a halt in front of the trophy. The winning driver stood again, grasping his soiled skull cap with his left hand and yanking off his goggles with his right. Rivulets of sweat meandered over his cheeks and neck, mingling with the thin coating of oil and rubber bits that had collected there. Both daredevils again acknowledged the uproar from the grandstands.

Ernie Moross, armed with a megaphone, launched into his embellishments of the race excitement and the heroism of the drivers involved. He shouted about records and how the Indianapolis Motor Speedway was the fastest of all tracks. A cluster of photographers led by George Bretzman, Ed Spooner, and George Grantham Bain surrounded the car, and steady fire of shutter clicks ensued.

Fisher and Allison delayed their approach until satisfied the photographers had captured the moment that would play out in newspapers around America. Kincaid bounced from his car and accepted a towel tossed to him by one of the National men. Company vice president Art Newby stepped forward to clasp Kincaid's shoulders with both hands as his driver mopped at the grime coating his face. A gaggle of newspapermen, National crew-man, and those of social standing with dubious claims to credentials squeezed in tighter. Fisher grasped Kincaid's right hand and launched into his energetic pumping of arms.

"Easy on the arm, Mr. Fisher," Kincaid said, obviously wincing. "When one of my tires blew, the carcass slapped my arm and stunned it useless. Don, here, had to grab the wheel, or we would have been done for."

"You're all better now, right?"

"Yeah. It was just a bad deal. My arm got smacked, and then a second later, it felt like it fell asleep."

"Well, winning this trophy has to make you forget all that! How does it feel to be the fastest man in the country for one hundred miles? Boy, you're famous now! Your mug is landing on the front pages across America."

All Kincaid could do was laugh and try to shout a thank you over the celebratory din. Fisher studied the twenty-three-year-old driver's tousled brown hair and young, cherubic face, flushed with rose born of exertion, heat, and joy.

Turning to Allison, he gave Kincaid a playful jab and said, "This boy has one hell of a career ahead of him. He's the perfect picture of our sport. Daring young men are pushing American cars into a better future."

He felt the grip of Art Newby tugging at his arm and motioning to join him a few yards to the side. Art, with his manila straw hat casting shade across his bespectacled eyes, looked to be feeling more fit than usual. Winning is a tonic, Fisher thought.

"Carl, I found out what happened with Oldfield's car," he shared. "Broken steering knuckle. Ernie told me."

"Okay. What's his plan to fix it?"

"I'm helping him. I have his mechanics – the Hill brothers – over at my shop down-town. I have my best parts fabricator fashioning a sturdy replacement. He'll be back out tomorrow morning."

"Good. Tomorrow is Saturday, our big day, and expect State Fair-sized crowds. We need Oldfield on the track. We need as many cars running strong as we can muster. And we need Barney Oldfield because, as he'll tell you, everybody knows him."

(Indianapolis Motor Speedway, May 28, 1910)

Fifteen Overland touring cars with what company Vice President Will Brown dubbed "Rough Riders" at the wheel ran rapidly in choreographed form. The shot toward ten-foot-high wood-plank ramps stationed in front of the grandstands of the Indianapolis Motor Speedway. Carl Fisher continuously pivoted his head toward the board "mountains" and the cars scaling them, and then back to the nearly packed grandstands. Ernie Moross, stationed beside him, had done something right, Fisher thought. Not as good as attracting European teams, but it made the folks at Overland, the largest automobile factory in Indianapolis happy. That counted for something that could be measured in dollars.

Fisher and Moross positioned themselves at the top of the track, just before the sand traps leading to the fencing behind them for the best view of Rough Riders at work – and, simultaneously, the ticket-purchasing customers. Besides, Fisher found it satisfying to feel the bricks of the running surface just beneath the leather soles of his Italian-import shoes.

Up and down, the Overlands first surmounted the incline and then shot to the bottom of the leeward side. From there, they rushed to a second board mountain to repeat the process and land on the bricks just north of the first turn. A stanchion bedecked with red flags and a large sign boasting an arrow directed them toward the grassy infield.

The cars had been released with thirty-second intervals between them to avoid entanglement. The Overlands clipped through the grass, the makeshift course led the machines to the ditch that directed the creek out and beyond the facility. Each driver then dove down the trench, splashed through the creek, and temporarily disrupted its gentle, babbling sound that could be heard on any other day.

After plowing through the sludge and water for more than ten yards, another sign urged them to mount the far side of the creek trench and upward to the level ground of the infield. Tires churned up mud, the powertrains grunted, but the engine and gears proved more than up to the task, which, as Brown would say, "The whole point of owning an Overland vehicle."

The Overlands raced across the infield to the far side of the track. They returned to the bricks at the exit of turn two. Fisher grasped the binoculars he had grown to depend on in such situations to monitor their progress. Barely visible were two more ramps stationed near a cluster of bleachers on the far end of the track.

The now insect-sized dots again mounted the slope side and then plummeted almost uncontrollably on the descent. At that point, the drivers really cut loose and charged full tilt to the finish line in front of the judges' stand where Fred Wagner's checkered flag awaited them. In the meantime, Fisher and Moross marched briskly toward the spot where the starter stood. They arrived just as the final car got the flag.

Fisher saw that almost immediately, Wagner noticed them and jogged in their direction. He was not at all convinced he wanted to hear what Wagner had to say because he never seemed able to read the man's temperament in the moment.

"Carl! Bully good show!"

"Thanks, Fred, but Ernie here deserves the lion's share of any praise. This was his brainstorm."

Wagner waved him off with a hand gesture.

"I don't care who thought of it, I just want to say that in all my experience around races from coast to coast I never witnessed such a perfect exhibition of a car's possibilities. I think it marvelous that the winner was able to take the time required to climb those inclines and then make two and a half miles in a few seconds over three minutes."

"I'm glad to hear a Triple-A man say that, Fred. I know how much you appreciate automotive demonstrations that make a relevant point to the public. These Overlands can climb steep hills and manage the sharp declines. They can charge through tough terrain as well. Our creek down at the south end isn't much different than the goddamn roads in this country."

Wagner nodded, shook both men's hands, and excused himself. Fisher then turned his attention to his contest director.

"Okay, Ernie. It was a good show. Now you really have to go to work. We're on a tight schedule. I need you to break this setup down post-haste."

"As I said before, the ramps are on big castors. We just need to remove the wedges and blocks, and they will be out of the way."

"Fine, but I don't want to talk about it, Moross. I want it done. Now, chop-chop."

(Indianapolis Motor Speedway, May 28, 1910)

Only three engines fired, but together they generated a haze of billowing clouds of exhaust smoke that obscured all but the closest people and objects. Barney Oldfield remained fixed on Fred Wagner, and especially his scarlet flag. Paying little notice to his competitors – the two Nationals of Johnny Aitken and Don Herr – Oldfield knew that this five-mile, two-lap sprint race meant the first turn was for all the marbles. It was the fourth event of the day, but most importantly to Oldfield and his numerous fans, it was his first contest of the three-day race meet.

Sitting at the inside of the track, Oldfield visualized a path into and through the first turn. If he could remain even with his rivals, they would inevitably give way, and the corner would be his.

Wagner was in his classic theatrical form, pacing back and forth in front of the raging machines as if he could punch one into submission with his fist. He tucked his rolled-up flag under his left armpit with his hand plunged into his tweed suit coat pocket. Wagner jabbed at each of the drivers with his right index finger, and Oldfield tried not to think about the silly display. He studied Wagner's feet because he knew nothing was going to happen until he moved a safe distance to the side.

Seconds later, Wagner did just that. Abruptly and with an exaggerated flourish, he unfurled his flaming starter's implement, and Oldfield released the Knox's clutch with precision. Both he and Aitken were gone in a second with Herr not far behind. The race was for cars with engines of three-hundred-one to four-hundred-fifty cubic inch displacement. Oldfield was pleased to feel the pulling power of his six-cylinder Knox Raceabout, and he stole a swift glance at Aitken, who was at his rear wheels.

One thing was sure, Oldfield had no plans of backing off on the approach to the first turn. Aitken fell back only slightly, to a point directly at the rear of the Knox. At the front, Oldfield found little dust or debris. More than likely, if there was any cement dust or the like, it was flying back at his adversaries.

Through turn one and then the short chute at the southernmost point of the track, Oldfield led the way as the three cars plunged into the second turn. Once on the backstretch, he craned his neck backward to assess his lead. It wasn't much, but it did not have to be. Incrementally, the brown Knox piled up yards on the midnight-blue Nationals. Aitken had the edge on his teammate, but all three were so close that a mistake or misfire would cost them positions.

At the north end of the track, the Knox felt strong after building momentum headed into turn three. Soon, Oldfield swooped past the front stretch grandstands where the screams of an appreciative cluster of some twenty thousand spectators overcame the howling engines. Another glance at Aitken revealed that his rival had not grown closer but also had not lost ground.

The final lap was, to Oldfield's delight, a duplicate of the first. Again, he stormed down the front stretch, but this time Wagner's checkered flag awaited. One thing with Wag, he was never afraid to step on the track and drape his cloth over the nose of a car. Oldfield had told him he was one burst tire away from becoming splattered pulp, but the Triple-A official insisted it was the kind of dazzle lookers-on expected.

Oldfield eased his throttle and commenced to waving at folks. Some were at the end of the grandstand and others in the bleachers at the inside. He picked up the pace down the backstretch as there were no seats there, and virtually no one to see his gestures. He coasted into the pits toward his pit stall. George and Jimmy Hill scurried northward to greet him, their fists punching at the air. He slowed to their pace, and they ran alongside the Knox and down to their pit where the ponderously obese Will Pickens had decided jogging with the Hills might prove to be a humiliating experience. Art Newby wandered over from his National pit station. Oldfield's crew were appropriately deferential to the Speedway founder and executive, allowing him the first handshake.

"Congratulations, Barney. All of us at the Speedway wanted to see you make a splash. I have to say that while I never like second best, I take no small satisfaction, it was my boys back at the factory that fashioned you the new steering knuckle that made your success possible."

"The guys did a great job, Art. I'd like to stop by after this meet and personally thank them if you introduce me."

"That would be swell, Barney. I'll let you go for now. I think with all the noise from your fans, they want some of your attention."

As Newby turned to walk away, Oldfield removed the cigar he had clenched between his teeth throughout the five miles and thrust it up in the air like he was carrying a torch. His brilliant smile was genuine, but he stretched it even further than what came naturally.

"You know me; I'm Barney Oldfield," he bellowed as an elated Pickens slapped him on the back.

Impulsively, he bolted forward and over the pit wall, his cheroot having returned to his mouth and both arms in the air. He grasped the white wood railing that demarcated the pits from the spectator side and, with an athletic jump, swung his legs and hips over the barrier. From there, he darted into the bleachers and undertook to shake as many hands as he found feasible.

(Indianapolis Motor Speedway, May 28, 1910)

"I had a premonition that something would happen to me today," said driver Herb Lytle from his cot in the Indianapolis Motor Speedway's medical tent. "I was restless last night and couldn't sleep. I knew that something was wrong. I told my mechanic before the race that I thought I would get in trouble before the end of the day."

Carl Fisher emitted a sigh born of calm in his breast upon realizing that Lytle's injuries were far less severe than he had feared when nurse Ola Slaughter called the judges' stand to say that the doctors were treating the driver's broken bones. Like in August, the track president had gunned his Stoddard-Dayton and bounded through the infield straight as the crow fly. Doctor Weyerbacher made eye contact with Fisher, and with a hand on his shoulder, he made a reassuring embrace.

"He's going to be fine. It's a broken shin bone. Nothing pierced the skin, and I had an easy time setting it. In a couple of months, he'll be good as new. I gave him a little codeine for his pain."

Fisher returned his eyes to Lytle, who appeared to be fretting like there was a story he had bottled up in his soul.

"It was crazy out there, Mr. Fisher. The handicap race had my car at the back. I was flying by and dodging all kinds of cars. What were there, twenty? I don't know how those of us in the bigger cars, like Aitken and Oldfield, didn't hit anybody. We were coming upon them so fast that our brakes were useless."

Fisher squinted as he listened and tried to understand what happened. Did he hit another car and become tangled up?

"Honestly, I was coming up on Gelnaw in that little Hupmobile and tried to pinch the corner at turn one to get around him. The ground was soft down there, and it grabbed my left front tire and turned me over. It threw me and my mechanic clean out of our seats.

He just sprung his shoulder."

"Jesus, Herb. Thank Providence, it wasn't more serious. It was good to hear the doctor say you will be back in action soon."

"No, I should have learned my lesson last year at Riverhead when I hit my head and had that concussion. Hell, I nearly died," Lytle lamented. "It's all over. I am through with the motor racing game. Never again will I take a seat behind the wheel of a racing car in a contest. The game is alright for those who are lucky, but I seem to be out of luck every season."

Fisher shook Lytle's hand with a robust grip as if to reassure his unmitigated respect. Lytle had been through Hell. Doctors gave up on him in the big Riverhead wreck. None of them had seen a man recover from such a concussion. They said he had a crushed skull. His riding mechanic, James Bates, was crushed when their heavy Apperson racer turned over on him. Lytle had been thrown clear, but the landing fractured his skull.

Flipping the door flap of the medical tent, Fisher ducked his head and shuffled out into the sunlight. The track was quiet, at least of engine noise, because they were between races. Standing on just his right foot, he lifted his left boot and struck a match to its sole. Extracting a La Corona and a stick of cedar from his breast pocket Fisher set it aflame. He kissed it to his cigar and puffed like a fireplace bellows. Perhaps it was best. Men of so many accidents should no longer be in the game.

(Indianapolis Motor Speedway, May 28, 1910)

Up and down the front stretch of the Indianapolis Motor Speedway, the chock-full grandstands were bursting with color, especially with the Japanese parasols many women held to shield against a sun that only intermittently rested behind the occasional cotton-ball puffy clouds. Barney Oldfield soaked it in with his eyes and ears. The moment had vibrance and emitted constant, stimulating, beautiful images along with a jumble of the indiscernible racket. All of it rolled up into a ball of energy and enthusiasm ebbing within him. It was an energy he didn't understand – it just was.

Oldfield also knew he could ratchet up the din and the motion as if he was tuning an engine. The people's champion occasionally stopped to raise his arms as if to orchestrate a symphony to the crescendo of a performance. The clamor peaked and then modulated to the ubiquitous commotion each time he stopped and gestured.

"You know me; I'm Barney Oldfield!"

Oldfield was very much conscious of his trademark unlit cigar – or more how it distinguished him from his competitors. He understood mystique and played it to the hilt. He continued his confident march from his garage down to where Starter Wagner had aligned the nineteen cars for the Wheeler-Schebler Trophy from the outer edge of the track and into pit lane up to the wall crews stood behind.

Oldfield's chocolate-brown Knox was one of the machines resting in the pit lane with but one car closer to the wall. Will Pickens, and the Hill brothers, George and Jimmy, were stationed nearby. George, who would ride as a mechanic with Oldfield, appeared ready to pounce on the engine crank upon command.

"Well, Barney, you made a damn fine entrance. You get them all riled up. People at Monument Circle downtown could probably hear that commotion," Pickens said. "Damned if this crowd doesn't beat all. Eyeballing it, I'd wager there's at least sixty thousand people here today. It's more than I have seen anywhere this side of the Vanderbilt."

"Yeah, but those Long Island folks watch free. Fisher knows how to make us all some money," Oldfield replied.

His gaze landed on the Marmon Wasp. Envy swelled inside him as he could not deny his disadvantage. Harroun is going to take the trophy unless the new car breaks down. Oldfield knew he had to keep the yellow car in sight if he had a prayer.

Fred Wagner raised his huge megaphone to his lips to shout out warnings to the mechanics to fire up their steeds in anticipation of the start. It was all George Hill needed to hear as he leaped forward and grasped the engine crank to give it a mighty yank. Oldfield had taken his perch at the wheel and adjusted the spark lever as he gave the hefty Knox its gas. The six-cylinders exploded to join the angry cacophony of eighteen other howling power plants. Exhaust pipes belched forward a thick haze of smoke that engulfed everyone, making it difficult to see.

Oldfield fixed on Wagner, awaiting the dramatic unfurling of his red flag. Now that is all he would see, all he had room for in his eyes. Just as with the earlier sprint race he won against Johnny Aitken and Don Herr, Oldfield wanted to claim that first turn. It was his.

The bright red flag swirled like a Fourth-of-July sparkler in Wagner's hand. Oldfield jammed his throttle, eager to get clear of the other cars that had been lined up with wheel hubs just inches apart. Several racers darted in a cluster at the front, Oldfield among them. He could see the white Buick of Arthur Chevrolet heading the pack – he had managed a terrific start.

The hurtling cars swarmed together, uncomfortably close, as a couple to the right of Oldfield banged off each other in turn one. Instinctively, he eased his throttle, and immediately two racers shot past him. Ending up in a pile on the first turn was not a good plan. George Hill sat beside him, silent and unmoved. He'd ridden shotgun countless times before.

Upfront, Oldfield spied Harroun's stinger tail in pursuit of Chevrolet. He did not want to lose contact with the leaders, but their pace and the dense traffic was undoing him. By the third lap, they were barely in sight. Still, Oldfield found his attention yanked to another direction when he came upon Aitken, whose indigo National was stricken with a shredded tire that slapped at the air like a Barnum and Bailey ringmaster's whip. Oldfield closed on him instantly as Aitken decelerated near the start-finish line.

Incrementally, Oldfield picked off positions over the next several laps, and gradually Chevrolet came into view, but just barely. Harroun and the Wasp were out-of-sight. Storming into turn one on his sixteenth lap, Oldfield felt his axle collapse at the right rear. The big Knox waddled like it wanted to squirm away from his grasp. Bill Endicott in the Westcott and George Clark in his Cutting split the difference to soar past him on either side.

Oldfield let up on his throttle, staring intensely and managed to keep his racer pointed straight even though the corner necessitated a turn of the wheel. Hugging the inside at the short chute, the gritty, grinding sound of the metal rim at the edge of his wooden wheel became audible. Glancing over his shoulder, he spied sparks as the brick surface wore the rim into useless trash.

Cars continued to shoot past as he kept an excruciatingly moderate pace on his crippled machine. Jimmy Hill and Pickens must have seen them coming as Oldfield plodded along beside the pit wall because they already had a jack and tire irons on hand. Halting the car, both driver and mechanic leaped from their seats.

"As long as we stopped, let's change all the tires," Oldfield shouted as a pack of cars led by William Tousey in a National rushed by. Harroun coasted to his pit station nearby, and two Marmon mechanics pounced on the right rear tire, demounting it from the rim. Another poured a can of gas into the Wasp's tank.

Oldfield went straight to work on his damaged right rear. George Hill attacked the front two tires, demounting them from the wheel rims. Jimmy Hill sprang up to sprint around the back of the Knox and helped Pickens pull a new, heavy artillery-wood wheel with tire pre-mounted over the pit wall. By the time they had replaced the entire wheel-tire assembly, George Hill was cinching down the bolts that fastened the new left rear tire. Jimmy took the time to pour a five-gallon can of gas in the fuel reservoir. Well before they had completed their work, Harroun was back on track and up to speed.

Oldfield and George scrambled back to their seats. He studied the monster scoreboard to his left as Jimmy twisted the crank. Number thirty-two – Harroun – was leading. Behind him was Leigh Lynch in the Jackson and Arthur Chevrolet. The Knox engine howled, and soon Oldfield pulled the machine onto the track with purpose. Just as he did, Harroun in the yellow Wasp blasted past him before he was up to speed. Oldfield wondered how many laps he was down. Goddamn it!

"One goddamn tire!" Oldfield shouted. "Harroun only changed one goddamned tire!"

Beside him, Hill either thought the conversation was pointless over the loud engine noises, or he could not hear. Leigh Lynch, in his Jackson soon came by as well, with Aitken, recovered from his blown tire, keeping pace. Over the next several laps, Oldfield circled the big brick track, steadily passing one car after another, but never knowing his position because of the time lost. All he knew is that he was nowhere close to the leaders.

Rounding turn two, a crumpled midnight blue car came into view. The wood spokes were all snapped like matchsticks from each of the four wheels, the metal body was bashed in something fierce. Driver Joe Dawson was apparently assessing the damage, but he looked fit and able. Oldfield instinctively assumed the mess was the result of a blown tire.

As more laps passed, Oldfield finally hit his stride with his steed. Throughout the remaining miles, no one got by him – he did all the passing, and he derived some satisfaction over his recovery. Still, it was not enough, and Oldfield never saw the leaders again. Returning to his pit after Wagner's checkered flag, he examined the mammoth scoreboard. Tugging down his goggles below his chin, Oldfield squinted. There he saw the car numbers for Harroun, Lynch, Aitken, Chevrolet, Frank Fox, and Bill Tousey, all ahead of him. Seventh. He was seventh.

Pickens waddled up beside of him. Oldfield spat out his cigar alongside the Knox, and the fat promoter handed him a fresh one along with a towel.

"Light?"

Oldfield waved him off. Most times, he just liked to have one in his mouth. He did not bite off the tip, but clamped it between his teeth to let the saliva dissolve the brown leaf into juice he let collect in one cheek or the other until he had enough and spat it out.

"Barney, I know you're disappointed, but I have to tell you the last half of the race you were going great guns. Really, you were showing them."

Oldfield mopped the beads of sweat from his forehead and then examined the oily grime on the towel that came off with it. Sometimes he would tell someone to can their words of consolation, but at this moment, he was okay with it. Setting aside who was ahead of him, Oldfield had enjoyed the last several miles. It felt good, and he knew he was fast.

George Hill approached him, and instead of the handshake Oldfield expected, his mechanic hugged him.

"It was an honor to ride with you, Barney. You are a hell of a race driver."

"All right, fellas, thanks, but let's not get sappy. We've got a couple of those national championship races tomorrow, and more than that, I want to bust that mile track record."

(Indianapolis Motor Speedway, May 28, 1910)

Carl Fisher made a point of stepping back from the center of a cluster of racing and automobile men surrounding Ray Harroun under the shadow of the humongous and gleaming Wheeler-Schebler Trophy. It was a calculated move, but it brought about an odd sensation for a man who routinely surrendered to his nature of flooding all open ears with ideas and opinions.

He left it to Frank Wheeler and George Schebler to shake the hands of every Marmon executive while informing Harroun he had just set new American records for every mile between one hundred and two hundred. The result was a new standard in speed for the distance at an average of seventy-three and sixty-two-hundredths miles per hour in two hours, two minutes, and sixteen seconds of racing.

The race had been over for several minutes. Still, Fisher listened carefully to pick up the gist of what the group was saying over the top-of-the-lungs screaming going on in the grandstands across the track. Among the Marmon men were the Marmon brothers themselves, Howard and Walter, along with two executives that by all accounts they relied on most – Herbert Rice and Clarence Stanley. Newspapermen Peter Paul Willis, Harry Deupree, and C. E. "Heinie" Schuart fired questions and jotted down their records of what the champion and the makers of his mechanical marvel had to say. A cluster of photographers led by George Bretzman, Ed Spooner, and George Grantham Bain was busy with their shutter clicks, only occasionally shouting out a request like, "Ray, look over here."

Harroun's lips were noticeably chapped with one fissure deep enough to reveal a scarlet line. Willis was the first to call it out.

"So, Ray, how do you feel? It looks like the wind dried out your lips. Was it pretty rugged out there?"

Harroun instinctively ran his tongue around the perimeter of his mouth. It was as if he had not noticed until someone pointed it out to him. Still, his natural wax statue-like expression melted to release a wide smile.

"Oh, I feel fitt'n," Harroun said. "But this game is not for fools. It requires your respect and constant attention, or it'll bite you like a rabid dog."

"How was the track compared to last August?" fired Schuart.

Before Fisher could intercept that line of questioning, Wheeler spoke up.

"The track is the finest, fastest, and safest in the world," Wheeler asserted. "Ray and the boys proved that today. Can we talk about the titanic struggle we witnessed today and not rehash the unfortunate instances from last year?"

Before anyone could respond, Harroun continued.

"This is the finest speedway, the finest racecourse, I have ever driven," Harroun stated in his trademark deadpan tone.

Howard Marmon also chimed in, pronouncing the Speedway an invaluable asset to the Hoosier capital. The entire American automobile industry as well.

"How about your Wasp?" Willis inquired. "It looked to be running like a Swiss watch."

"It's a mechanical wonder," Harroun said. "Perfectly constructed and engineered. Our success was all about the car. The best in America."

"I only saw you at your pit once," Willis noted. "And you only changed one tire. Do you think the design of your car made that possible?"

"Damn right, it did," said Howard Marmon. "But you boys write this down. Ray Harroun is too damn modest. Ray Harroun is one fine driver and engineer, and he made this whole thing possible."

"We only had to change the right rear tire," Harroun added. "That's where the weight leans most heavily in these banked left turns, so it's hardest on that one. The others show little wear, you can look for yourself."

Marmon again added a point, saying that the Michelin tires were a high-quality product – but he wanted to find a reliable American brand.

"I've spent a lot of time speaking with Mr. Fisher and Mr. Wheeler here. This track was built for America. For American car companies to develop their products. That's why we want those fellas in Europe to bring their cars over here. You saw what happened today. We're ready for them."

(Indianapolis Motor Speedway, May 28, 1910)

Ernie Moross and Barney Oldfield scrutinized the gold-plated automobile before them. It was the central display in the colossal Overland Automobile Company tent near the garage area. Electric light bulbs overhead were obviously positioned to bring out the sparkle of the car. It was evident that all the fixtures of the vehicle were truly coated in gold. The headlamps, horn, acetylene tank, handbrake, the trim around the edge of the radiator, and even the radiator cap boasted genuine gold plating. Yes, with brass underneath, but undoubtedly a coating of gold.

Two other Overland vehicles, one of them the car that won the obstacle course trial – still showing the splatters of mud as evidence of the ordeal it had overcome – were at opposite sides of the canvas and wood pole structure. A banner hung above, spanning the distance from one side of the tent to the opposite. It read, in the company's cursive script, "Overland, the most popular car in America, one thousand to fifteen hundred dollars." Topiary and potted palms in wicker baskets dressed up the perimeter.

"Thanks for coming, Barney. I know Carl will appreciate you taking the time. He's anxious to speak with you."

Oldfield had never gotten over his amusement of toying with Moross. His tongue deftly shifted his cheroot from the south corner of his mouth to the north. He squinted at the short, thin contest director.

"Oh, he is, is he? Well, that warms my heart. But between you and me, I wanted to stop by here anyway to see this here automobile that Overland says will be an award to the man who sets an American mile track record. That's me. You know that, right, Moross?"

"That's what we're counting on Barney. If you set that record, what are you going to do with it?"

"I'm going to give it to Bess for putting up with a lot of shit from me."

"Where is Bess?"

Oldfield glared at Moross.

"That is none of your damn business."

As if that was his cue, Fisher emerged from the flap opening of the khaki canvas pavilion with wife Jane on his arm – dutifully quiet, even invisible. He, too, puffed a cigar – this one a deep chocolate Corona.

Fisher approached Oldfield with a well-considered pitch. He knew the man; he knew the words to incite and to motivate.

"Isn't she beautiful, Barney?"

Fisher amused Oldfield. The driver wasn't a weed bender stumbling into his car dealership in awe of all the sophisticated twentieth-century mechanical wonders surrounding him.

"It's alright, Carl. I have a lot of cars. How long do you think that gold plating stays on that brass before it wears off?"

Fisher made a point of casting a lingering smile within a deliberately quiet moment as he fixed his eyes into Oldfield's. Oldfield stared back.

"I see you're not easily impressed. Still, it's an outstanding prize. You've had a good race meet so far, Barney, by beating our National men to win a race. And you drove like the dickens in our Wheeler-Schebler Trophy race. I think you would have given Harroun a run if you hadn't had tire trouble."

Oldfield knew Fisher was flattering him but did not want there to be any signal that he liked it.

"You know, Barney, after the bloodbath last year, running that two-hundred-mile race today was a great statement to the world," Fisher continued. "It just goes to show everyone that we not only have the safest race track in God's creation, it's also the fastest too. We have every record, but one now."

"The mile. I feel like we've been here before, Carl. Well, I like to make records, and you like to have records set at your Speedway. You sell a lot of tickets here, don't you?"

"Barney, do you realize there's a big showdown going on among the speedways right now? Everyone wants to say they have the fastest track in the country. We've built the best damn Speedway in the world. We've proved a lot here so far in these first two days, but we need that mile record. If we can't claim the fastest mile, it gives a big opening to that damn Los Angeles board track and the dirt circle down in Atlanta."

"You mean Playa Del Rey? The track where I set the American mile record in March?"

"So, what are you saying? You brought your Blitzen Benz here just to sit in the garage?"

"Back in ought-three, when I set the mile-a-minute record on the fairgrounds track, it was important to your business. You made it worth my while. That was seven years ago! Things have changed. I need ten times that now."

Fisher paused. He paused to think, and he paused to get Oldfield to wonder.

"Barney, you got the appearance fee you wanted. We found you that Knox. I'm already paying you more than any other driver just to show up. Hell, tomorrow we're even giving the whole two and a half miles a gasoline bath and a good broom scrub to get all the oil and grease off. You racing men may take the Sabbath off, but not Speedway men. You will have a clean vitrified surface to speed over when you come back on Monday."

"I'll take you at your word. Look, Carl, I know that mile record is important to you. You know me, I make a little less than I spend. I'm in a little difficulty. I got some debts I need to pay off. Me setting that mile record would be good for both of us."

Fisher listened. He then glanced at Jane, who had an almost disinterested expression. The fact of the matter was, he had come to the tent prepared for an Oldfield shakedown – and was expecting it would cost him more. Thrusting his hand forward, the two men shook on the deal.

(Indianapolis Motor Speedway, May 30, 1910)

Horns all about the Indianapolis Motor Speedway blared their alarm, and the core of Carl Fisher's gut leaped into his throat like it could come out from between his teeth. The startling reverberation was jarringly chased by the ominous, annoying bleats of the telephone in the judge's stand. Fisher brushed aside Ernie Moross in his haste to grab the device's receiver. The voice on the other end came from one of the National Guard officers he had hired, uniformed, and stationed at the north end of the track.

"Mr. Fisher! Harroun just knocked down the concrete wall in turn three," the man shrieked, his voice quivering. "That Wasp car of his jumped into the air and almost sailed right of the Speedway."

"Jesus Christ on a bicycle! Is he hurt?"

"I don't think so, sir. He's out of the car and walking around it. The car looks pretty beat up, though, but I don't have a good line of sight from my station."

Fisher abruptly hung up on the man and announced to no one in particular that he was headed down to the north end. He elbowed his way through a cluster of Triple-A men and newspaper reporters. Bounding down the wood plank steps, he sprinted to his Stoddard-Dayton parked at the side of the structure. Another National Guardsman saw him coming and darted to the starter's crank. The engine responded with a growl.

Out on the brick surface, Fisher spied Fred Wagner waving cars off the track. The starter handed his flag to an assistant and signaled to Fisher with his two arms flapping above his head like some kind of giant bird. The Stoddard-Dayton halted its counterclockwise scramble, and Wagner hustled aboard without a word.

As they continued, Fisher sensed the steady rumble of his tires over the brick surface. So smooth compared to his excursions in the previous year around the original crushed stone track or his frenetic, bouncing rushes to the infield hospital. Speeding backward down the front stretch and through turn four, the devastated yellow Marmon Wasp came into sight. Harroun, hands on his hips and head pointed down at the spot of a missing wheel at the right rear, he was apparently assessing the damage.

Within seconds Fisher and Wagner were at his side, both asking for assurance that the driver was uninjured. Harroun craned his neck and expressionless countenance toward the men as if his deep concentration had been disturbed.

"I'm fine. I wish I could say the same for my car."

Fisher sprung out of his automobile to initiate his own assessment. The three wheels still attached were catawampus, tilting at odd and impossible angles. The chassis appeared intact, but Fisher knew that trained eyes in a severe appraisal could identify subtle twists devastating to the metal structure. The body displayed little evidence of damage, aside from a few scrapes.

"What happened, Ray?" Fisher asked.

"I made a stupid decision," Harroun said, expressionless. "I should have changed the tires before making this practice run. I thought after working perfectly for two hundred miles, they would be fine for just a few more this morning. We planned to swap them out for fresh ones in time for the national championship free-for-all race this afternoon. Well, she won't be available for that contest."

"Where's the fourth wheel?"

"It's in splinters, but parts of it flew over the wall there," Harroun said, pointing back at turn three.

"Can she be repaired?" Wagner inquired.

An Overland truck and the Marmon brothers, in one of their touring car roadsters, roared up to the scene with a photographer. Harroun acknowledged them with something akin to a salute.

"Wag, we're just going to have to get her back to the shop and take a good look. I want to lift her up and get a good gander at the underbelly. If I can work my will, the Marmon Wasp will win again. Excuse me, gentlemen, but I need to speak to my bosses."

(Indianapolis Motor Speedway, May 30, 1910)

Fred Wagner officiously flapped, fluttered, and swung his arms about in his exaggerated fashion of directing drivers and cars into alignment for the first competition of the day – the ten-mile free-for-all. Observing from the second floor of the judges' stand alongside his partner Jim Allison, Carl Fisher peered at the Triple-A starter through his Pince-Nez spectacles and shook his head.

Wagner must have thought he was impressing onlookers, and maybe he was, but they didn't know he was a pompous ass. An involuntary chuckle burst forward from Fisher's throat, which Allison witnessed and responded with a nod and a smile. Fisher knew Allison understood what he was thinking. Changing the subject without either man speaking a word about it, Allison inquired about John Newby, their partner Art's father.

"Do you have any updates on Art's father?"

"Not really. I stopped by the hospital yesterday to check in on the old man. Art was there and said that the doctors are calling it a cerebral hemorrhage. I guess that's a doctor name for what I call a stroke. Anyway, nobody there knows what's next. All anyone can do is wait."

"I suppose his age doesn't help any," Allison said. "What is he, seventy?"

Fisher nodded affirmatively. He pointed across the track to the big grandstand, which was already packed with spectators and remarked on how the elder Newby suffered his seizure right there on Saturday during the Wheeler-Schebler Trophy feature.

"Yeah, he's an old man. Maybe his constitution couldn't take the excitement. More than likely, though, it would have happened if he was just sitting on his parlor sofa. I don't expect to see Art here today; he's pretty distressed. That man is an empathetic soul. He's got more compassion than you and me put together."

Below them, on the bricks, Wagner had apparently completed his task of making the race cars just so-so in a line. There were five competitors – the Chicago millionaire Caleb Bragg in his blood-red Fiat, Ben Kerscher in Barney Oldfield's green 1905 Vanderbilt Cup-winning Darracq, and the three ink-blot blue Nationals of Tom Kincaid, Johnny Aitken, and Art Greiner, all aligned to Wagner's satisfaction.

The sight of gorgeous sunshine and the colorful, packed-to-capacity grandstand delighted Fisher. Even Allison relaxed his stoic countenance to muster a smile. A stir among the men behind them on the creaking wood flooring compelled the two Speedway founders to pivot. Will Brown, Overland's top executive at the Indianapolis factory, had escorted Blanche Scott, who had garnered the interest of newspaper readers across the country as she traversed the rough roads across America.

The Overland folks were making their presence known at the Speedway throughout the week with their service vehicles and the Rough Riders' obstacle course. The plan was for Scott to take a pass by the grandstands in her snow-white Overland Model 42.

Scott was a deceptively petite woman, barely five-feet tall and one hundred pounds. She was pretty, too, with dimples in her ample cheeks and hazel ringlets sprouting forth from the sides of a bonnet. Fisher had seen photos in newspapers, but to examine her stature in the flesh made him skeptical about her goal of driving from New York to San Francisco without the assistance of a mechanic.

Still, a cluster of men gathered around her as if to gawk at some kind of freak. In addition to Fisher and Allison, Frank Wheeler towered over her, and the new Triple-A Contest Board Chairman Sam Butler moved in as well. Peter Paul Willis of the Indianapolis Star crowded in amongst the circle, with an eager face, always looking for a story. His colleague Heinie Schuart squeezed in as well. Photographers George Bretzman and Ed Spooner were just behind the others as loose concentric circles began to form. Within a minute, all the men on the second-floor platform realized who she was.

"Gentlemen, please welcome Miss Blanche Scott, the most daring woman automobile driver in America," announced Brown.

"And just how many daring women drivers are there in our great nation," Butler scoffed.

Brown continued his introduction as if Butler had said nothing. Fisher bit the Corona in his mouth so that it pointed upward at a forty-five-degree angle. He had not considered the potential for confrontation. Still, it dawned on him that the only woman in judges' stand was unlikely to receive a warm welcome, especially since she was attempting a feat that few of the hard cases present would dare to try.

"Miss Scott is boldly spanning our continent's great distance from shore to shore. New York to San Francisco."

"Blanche, have you had any setbacks thus far?" Willis leaped into the conversation.

"Only what's expected. Tires are the most common affliction. I'm sure you gentlemen will agree there is an easy remedy for that. It's called a tire iron and a sturdy jack. The only attention it needs more frequently is gas and oil. I did have to stop in Ohio to cool…"

Butler, his face boasting a condescending smirk, turned to another Triple-A official just behind him and muttered something inaudible. Scott took a step forward to clasp his forearm and yank the man around. She pierced her eyes into his.

"Excuse me, but I was speaking. If you can't be courteous enough to give me your attention, then get your ass to the far end of the floor."

Slack-jawed, Butler said, "Now listen little honey...".

Scott interrupted her voice in a calm but stern tone. She pointed her finger upward in the direction of Butler's bushy waxed mustache.

"Don't you ever call me that. You address me as Miss Scott. Got it?"

"I meant no offense…"

"No. Hell, no! What you meant was to put me in my place, and I'll have none of it. I have a hundred dollars that say I can change a tire faster than you can. By damn, I'll do it right now."

Fisher, astonished by brashness in a female, involuntarily applauded. Except for the speechless Butler, the men laughed, but in a good-natured manner that the Speedway founder saw as supportive of the no-nonsense woman. He liked moxie in anyone and got a kick seeing it in a determined lady. To relieve the awkward moment, he steered the exchange back to inquiries concerning her journey.

"Miss Scott, why don't you tell my newspaper friends here about your preparations headed West. It's only going to get more rugged in that direction. There must be some spots out there with no roads, for Christ's sake. Hell, there are still some wild Indians out there."

Scott shrugged her shoulders. Fisher surmised that everyone there was convinced that she and the Overland people knew what they were doing. Most importantly, Scott had the confidence that propelled her to surmount any challenge.

"I don't imagine those poor Indians will be much bothered. Not any more than you fellas."

The men grew increasingly free with their laughter. Clearly, they were warming up to the anomaly standing before them.

"Let me say that the Overland Automobile Company believes in Miss Scott, and we are all proud she selected one of our new Model forty-two vehicles," said Brown. We also believe in our machines. They are robust and can tackle any terrain. I can't imagine this is a surprise to you, gentlemen if you witnessed our obstacle course on Saturday."

Willis and Schuart began asking questions most frequently while one-by-one, the other men shook her hand and moved on about their business. When the news reporters felt satisfied they had what they needed, they, too, excused themselves. Fisher motioned for Ernie Moross to come closer. With Brown and Allison nearby, he began his personal welcome.

"Well, again, Miss Scott, we couldn't be more delighted to have you with us. You are truly a trailblazer by every meaning of the word. This is our Contest Director, Ernest Moross. Ernie, how about giving Miss Scott a quick rundown of our card today and where we'd like her to be."

"I'd be delighted, Carl," Moross began. "We have fourteen races on tap for this afternoon. Seven of them are the new national championship races that the Triple-A have started. The other seven are free-for-all races, a handicap, a touring car challenge where passengers are required. That's for the John Wilson Trophy. We also have Barney Oldfield in his magnificent Blitzen Benz, who will attempt a new American track record for the mile. The feature of the day is the fifty-mile Remy Brassard and Trophy, which is our final event. If it is convenient, we would like you to drive your Overland forty-two down the front stretch just before the Remy contest so our fans can see you. Everyone knows you are here."

Below them, the cars Wagner organized came to life. Scott raised her voice to be heard.

"I am at your disposal, gentlemen. You tell me when and where to meet you, and we will get on with it."

"Unless you have other plans, I'd like to take you and Will to lunch," Fisher suggested. "We have several refreshment stands, and there are tables and seating. It's a beautiful day."

Scott accepted the invitation as Brown nodded.

"I do have one question about the races, though," she said. "What is this business of national championship races? Are the winners crowned kings or something?"

Fisher hesitated and then responded. Moross and Allison seemed to lean forward with interest in what he was about to say.

"It's more for the manufacturers, so they have something special to say in their advertisements. To tell you the truth, I think it is more to clamp down on the barnstormers like Oldfield. They want to elevate the Triple-A races to something superior to the pumpkin fair horse tracks. A lot of them are fixed, Oldfield has that Kerscher fella always finishing second to him. They make sure it's real close, and they go plenty fast."

Scott let go of a belly laugh. She was loud enough; others on the floor turned their heads toward her.

"I would like to see some of those pumpkin fair races. Maybe I can find some in towns out West."

"Talk to Oldfield at the end of the day," Moross said. "Knowing Barney, he may ask you to race with him."

On the track, Wagner waved the checkered flag for Bragg and his Fiat. He had just run down Kerscher on the final lap.

(Indianapolis Motor Speedway, May 30, 1910)

Carl Fisher bellowed deep from his gut, his diaphragm projecting his voice over the racers finishing the national championship for stock cars with engines of two-hundred-thirty-one to three-hundred cubic inches. Beside him, Jim Allison leaned his left ear closer to take it in as the twin yellow Marmons of first, Joe Dawson, and second, Ray Harroun dashed past them.

"Oldfield's next with that big Benz. He's going to get that mile track record!"

Allison nodded, and Fisher knew that he was not telling his partner anything he did not know. Still, Fisher's enthusiasm for the Speedway laying claim to the American track mile speed record could not be contained. It was exhilarating to shout, almost a relief, really, to holler out his desire to someone he was certain wanted that record nearly as much as he did.

"Look at those flags," Allison said, pointing at the colors of several nations fluttering above the grandstand. "They're buffeting around as much as if Wagner was waving them. That's going to make for a pretty exciting ride for old Barney."

Fisher did not want to think about it. He waved at the air as if he could swat away the wind to clear the way for Oldfield. The two men lifted their binoculars from their chests and dialed in an image of the Blitzen Benz parked by the pit wall further north up the straightaway. Fisher noted that Ernie Moross, hands in pockets, was observing Oldfield's mechanics, George and Jimmy Hill, as they scampered around the humongous German machine, apparently performing last-minute checks. The rotund Will Pickens had sauntered to Moross's side, gesturing at the car.

Finally, Oldfield vaulted aboard, and after pulling his goggles over his eyes, he began to fiddle with levers. One of the Hill boys vigorously yanked the crank at the front of the ominous machine, and the mammoth engine howled. Fisher heard it from a quarter of a mile away. Pivoting to Triple-A official Frank Trego at the Warner electric timing apparatus, he shouted, "Look sharp. This is it. This is the American mile track record!"

The barking engine grew louder as Oldfield picked up speed and passed the men of the judges' stand. Peter Paul Willis scurried to where Fisher and Allison stood, looking eager for something to write about.

"Records sell newspapers," he announced.

Fisher heard the man but concentrated on the image in his binoculars until Oldfield disappeared around the first turn.

"Carl, so what's the deal here? Barney picks up a full head of steam down the back-stretch and then trips the timing wire in the north end short chute. Then he trips another wire as he reaches the mile point coming out of turn one, right? There's a kilometer timing wire, too, right?"

"You got it, Willis, now let me concentrate."

Every head in the judges' stand craned in the direction of turn four. All the vantage points along the open-air window sills were occupied. Silence gripped the usually chattering men. Oldfield's big pearl Benz, with its giant brass beak bouncing a retina-bruising glare, emerged from turn four and leaped in bounds as it hurtled down the main straight and past the judges' stand. On down the track, it soared, and Fisher knew he had tripped the mile timing wire. He hustled to Trego's side, demanding a read of the time.

Looking sheepish, Trego shook his head in the negative. Sam Butler had sauntered beside him and peered over his shoulder.

"Malfunction," he said, deadpan and expressionless.

Fisher's exasperation overwhelmed him.

"Jesus Christ on a bicycle! What in the Hell are you doing? What are you people, some kind of chicken shit outfit? You can't work a goddamn timer?"

"Calm down, Carl," Butler said. "These things happen. These newfangled electric devices are pretty finicky. We'll just have to get Barney to do it again."

Fisher knew if he lingered, he would say something there would be no way to take back. He pivoted and immediately stumbled into Allison, who had silently followed him to the timer's desk. Butler appeared thoughtful and then shouted at the switchboard operator next to Trego.

"Connect me to the phone station down near Oldfield's men."

The man nodded and moving with alacrity, connected the judges' stand phone. Fisher felt blood rush to his cheeks and brow. Removing a handkerchief from his breast pocket, he dabbed at beads of sweat that had emerged from his pores. Butler took the phone receiver into his hand. He had Oldfield on the phone and began explaining the do-over. Noticing this, Fisher stormed to Butler.

"Give me my goddamn phone."

Butler, apparently flummoxed, forfeited the receiver. He remained at Fisher's side, glaring at him.

"Barney, I'm sorry you have to go through this bullshit. I don't know what these clowns are doing up here, but we'll fix it. When can you get back on the track?"

Satisfied with Oldfield's reaction, Fisher hung up the receiver. He felt the weight of Butler's scowl but had lost interest in shouting. He wanted to get on with the second try.

"Fisher, you have no right to speak to me or my men like you did. I think an apology is in order."

"Carl Fisher doesn't apologize to anybody. You can get your feathers all ruffled, but it's up to you to get over your bruised feelings."

Returning to the window, Fisher found another man had taken his spot. He tapped the interloper on the shoulder and instructed him to stand aside. Again, he peered through his binoculars to get a good gander at the goings-on around the Blitzen Benz. Within minutes, the lustrous pearl white machine growled and barked as it shot past them to set up the run. Fisher welcomed Willis and Heinie Schuart to his side after shooing off some Triple-A men. He wanted the newspapermen to be able to take everything in.

Less than a minute later, Oldfield again rounded turn four with a full head of steam. He soared down the front stretch to elicit all manner of applause, wails, and yelps from some sixty thousand witnesses. In a flash, he was past and obviously at the last tripwire at turn one. Fisher pivoted to look at Trego.

"Well? Jesus Christ on a bicycle, tell me you got his time on that run!"

"He just ran a new American track record for the kilometer at twenty-one and forty-five hundredths of a second. That's nearly two seconds faster than his record at Playa Del Rey."

"Kilometer? Jesus Christ on a bicycle! What about the goddamn mile?"

"No record there. Oldfield's about a second slower than Playa Del Rey on the mile."

Fisher abruptly bolted for the stairs, taking them two at a time to surge into a full northward jog. The grand Benz grew larger as he ran, but, panting, he slowed to walk off the distance at a still determined pace. Upon Oldfield, he beckoned him with his arms as he caught his breath.

"Jesus, Carl, you okay?" Oldfield said. "A little run too much for you? It wasn't that long ago you could run backward faster than most men could run forward."

"Never mind me. What's with the car? Why didn't you bust the mile record?"

"I need another shot at it, Carl. It's that damn wind. I'm getting blown around out there like a fucking kite," Oldfield said, pointing near the kilometer marker. "The grandstands block the wind a bit on the stretch, and it's a Hell of a lot tamer when I'm pointed straight. If this straightaway was longer, you would be handing me my bonus. The problem is turning into that first corner with nothing protecting me from the gusts. Give me another shot at it, Carl. I'm working up to it. I say we wait until later in the day and hope the atmosphere settles down."

Fisher felt deflated, but he sure as Hell would not be deterred. Going out right away did not make sense. The conditions would be the same. He nodded.

"Let me talk with some of my men and figure out where to work you in on the card. We still have eight races to run, and you're in two of them. I'll have Moross come down and let you know the plan."

Fisher pivoted in the direction of the judges' stand and began to march toward the wood structure. His active mind could not resist spinning around and shouting to Oldfield, who, with the Hills, had commenced to pushing his prized Benz to the garages.

"Hey, Barney. I need that record. It's important to the Speedway."

"We'll get it done, Carl. You just hang that bag of cash off the wall at the mile marker, and I'll grab it on the way by."

(Indianapolis Motor Speedway, May 30, 1910)

George Hill jabbed his left index finger into Barney Oldfield's right shoulder and flailed his right arm at something behind them as they soared down the backstretch of the Indianapolis Motor Speedway. Oldfield stole a quick glance over his shoulder as a freight train of blue National racers stormed toward his Knox racer. Oldfield had led the ten-mile national championship race for stock cars with engines of four-hundred-fifty-one to six-hundred cubic inches and had no intention of getting passed with a half lap to go.

In winning the five-mile national championship for the same class earlier in the day, he noticed that tucking in behind cars helped him pick up the pace and pass them. The first car broke the wind resistance so he could pick up speed and pass. The Speedway was full of exciting new experiences.

In a gentle, agile adjustment, Oldfield steered up on the bricks to squeeze the hurtling threesome of Howdy Wilcox, Tom Kincaid, and Johnny Aitken closer to the wall entering turn three. The inexperienced Wilcox, leading the other two, lifted his foot but tried to steer down behind the big Knox, and Oldfield knew what he would try to do next. The four cars rocketed into and out of turn three.

Oldfield, by taking the lane he knew Wilcox wanted, had unsettled him and the other two Nationals immediately behind. The threat was that the trio of blue cars would gather themselves up and take a run at him as they charged to Wagner's checkered flag. The Nationals were back in a squadron alignment at the head of the home stretch and steadily crept closer to the Knox's tail.

Within a hundred yards of the finish line, Wilcox pulled wide in an attempt to shoot past Oldfield. His teammates dutifully hung close from behind. The indigo machine appeared in the corner of Oldfield's eye, but Wilcox was out of time. Wagner's checkered flag unfurled, and simultaneously Oldfield's left arm shot into the air. The Knox and the three Nationals curtailed their breakneck pace but still moved briskly around the expansive brick oval. Drivers and mechanics saluted one another in their measured pace and continued on around until they could see their pits. As they slowed, all the commotion and clamor from the grandstands became evident.

Oldfield sailed past his pit. He progressed to a cluster of officials at a platform in front of the white-and-green-trim judges' stand. Relaxing pressure on the throttle entirely, he coasted to a speed where his brakes could halt his car. Sam Butler approached, clutching a gold-plated medal with red, white, and blue silk ribbon. Carl Fisher shadowed Butler, but Oldfield surmised it was not his latest national championship victory he wanted to discuss. Atop the platform, Ernie Moross clutched his megaphone.

"Ladies and gentlemen, I present to you Mr. Barney Oldfield, undisputed Triple-A national champion for stock cars of four-hundred-fifty-one to six-hundred cubic inch displacement. For the second time today, Barney has captured a national championship race!"

With that, Sam Butler thrust his hand forward for a shake and then draped the gold medal over Oldfield's head and about his neck. The Triple-A official greeted Hill as well. Oldfield inserted his right hand into his overalls pocket and extracted the medal he had been awarded earlier that afternoon, also hanging it at his collar. He sprung up to stand on his seat, his medals clinking together, with his hands above his head. Spitting out his worn-out cigar, he shouted, "You know me, I'm Barney Oldfield."

His words earned their intended effect as he stirred up another roaring ovation from lookers-on. Newspapermen and photographers encircled him now. Feeding on the attention, Oldfield beamed a considerable, face-stretching smile. Brimming with confident enthusiasm, he egged them on to ask him something. Heinie Schuart, with Ed Spooner behind him snapping his shutter, began to fire questions.

"Those are nice medals, Barney. Do you have a place to show them off?"

"Yeah, I can hang these trinkets around my neck. They could be bigger, though."

Oldfield glanced at Butler; he never met a Triple-A man he wouldn't sink a needle into. Butler emitted a strained laugh, but Oldfield knew that the executive wanted him to shut up, but was at a loss for the words to put the barnstorming driver in his place.

Peter Paul Willis chimed into the exchange.

"You've had a great weekend, Barney. Three race wins and two national championships. Are you going to get that mile record?"

Oldfield pointed upward at the flags, which were flitting about every bit as much as before.

"See those flags? It's going to take every bit of skill I have to keep that big Benz pointed in the right direction in the face of those wind gusts. Daytona was a piece of cake compared to trying to turn at great speed. It may not look like much to you, but just you try sitting in my seat at better than a hundred miles an hour. That's a gale."

Willis and Schuart busily scribbled on their pads, asking more questions about holding off the Nationals. Will Pickens emerged beside Hill and shoved a cigar at the driver. Not missing a beat, Oldfield clamped it between two fingers and instantly chomped it in his teeth.

"Tell us more about the winds," Willis insisted. "What does that mean? Do you think you can bust that record?"

Oldfield contorted his face into a sardonic grin. Imagining what he must look like, he failed to contain a burst of laughter.

"Think? Good God, man, don't you read your own articles? I'm America's Speed King!"

"Barney, over here. Give me your Speed King face," shouted photographer George Bretzman.

Oldfield responded with comical and exaggerated contortions. Finally, he gave the photographer a break. After Oldfield was satisfied that he had given the newspapermen enough time, he excused himself, motioning for the Hills and Pickens to push his Knox to the garages. Fisher darted to fall into step with him with Moross directly behind.

"Barney, give me the straight dope," Fisher said. "Does that wind have you spooked?"

"I've been through a lot to get to today, Carl. I was juicing those reporters up a bit; they like that. The fact is, I think I can do it. You get that bag of cash-filled up for me because I am going to give it all she's got. I want this as bad as you do."

Fisher slapped the driver on his back and wished him good luck. Moross continued at Oldfield's side.

"Your boss is a little bit on edge. If he gets any ideas of talking to me before my run, tell him I said stay away. I need to concentrate. Tell him I'll talk all he wants afterward."

"Sure, Barney. I can do that. Carl is on edge. Honestly, he's more concerned about the Speedway looking good than even the drivers. He was worried about Harroun after his wreck because if somebody gets killed, he could lose everything. That's all he's thinking about."

"I don't give a crap, Moross. That's his business. I'm focused on mine. Now I need you to leave me alone, too. I have things to think about."

Glancing at Will Pickens, who was keeping pace with the Hills in their efforts to push the Knox, Oldfield said, "Pickens, it's your job to keep everyone away from me. I don't want to talk to anyone until after I get another crack at that record. I'm only speaking to George and Jimmy. Got it?"

(Indianapolis Motor Speedway, May 30, 1910)

Blanche Scott halted her stark-white Overland 42 in the middle of the front stretch of the Indianapolis Motor Speedway and yanked its brake lever. From the judges' stand, Carl Fisher, standing with wife Jane, trained his binoculars past the female daredevil and into the stands. Both men and women were applauding this specimen of unleashed womanhood – and he liked that. She was good for the show. Like Oldfield, Scott stood atop her car as if she were conducting an orchestra. The salvos continued, and Fisher hoped she would drive off before they abated. Scott settled back into her seat and cranking her steering wheel, performed a sharp left turn to cut a path perpendicular to the track, and back to the judges' stand.

Jim Allison and Frank Wheeler joined Fisher at the judges' stand window. Appearing again on the trackside platform, Ernie Moross announced with flair the next event, Barney Oldfield's assault on the American track record. Allison caught eyes with Fisher and nodded.

"This is it, gentlemen," Fisher said. "We've had one Hell of a successful weekend, but we need this record. We need Oldfield to do good by us. We'll do good by him."

Not a day had gone by since his December time trials and Lewis Strang's failure to set the American track mile record that Fisher did not feel like punching a wall. It meant everything to have that mile record. It said a lot about a race track to own that, and it pissed him off to think that tracks of boards or dirt could claim to be faster than his modern Speedway. Again, he studied Oldfield through his binoculars.

In the pits, Oldfield traced his fingers over his Blitzen Benz and even spoke to the machine as George and Jimmy Hill ran final checks on the tightness of wheel hubs and other nuts and bolts. Will Pickens was good on his word to keep people away from his driver. Schuart had approached for a final word, and Pickens' imposing mass of six feet, three inches, and two-hundred-seventy pounds intercepted him. Pushing that bulk aside was not an option, there would be no talking to the Speed King until after his work was done.

Even Fred Wagner could draw no response. Oldfield saw him in his peripheral vision and gave the slightest of nods to Jimmy Hill, who darted to the flagman starter with alacrity. He only just allowed his ears to capture a murmur as he visually inspected his imposing machine. Unfolding the cowling, Oldfield gently tugged at wires, hoses, and the fuel line. He squatted beside each wheel hub and peered behind them to the brakes, to axles, and steering knuckle.

At the last wheel, he fished in the right pocket of his overalls to extract a crumpled piece of paper his mother had given him after the St. Louis accident six years prior. On it, she had recorded a prayer in cursive. He kneeled and cupped the folded, yellowing paper – smudged with oily grime collected over the years – in his right hand because he did not want anyone to see what he was doing.

"Let me live, oh Mighty Master,
Such a life as men should know,
Tasting triumph and disaster,
Joy, and not too much of woes
Let me run the goblet over,
Let me fight and love and laugh,
And when I am beneath the clover
Let this be my epitaph:

Here lies one who took his chances,
In the busy world of men,
Battled luck and circumstances,

Fought and fell and fought again;
Won sometimes, but did no crowing,
Lost sometimes but did not wail,
Took his beating, but kept going
Never let his courage fail.

He was fallible and human,
Therefore, loved and understood,
Both his fellow men and women,
Whether good or not so good,
Kept his spirit undiminished,
Never laid down on a friend,
Played the game until it was finished,
Lived a sportsman to the end."

Oldfield felt a mild smile creep across his lips as he thought of his mother. His mind spilled out a memory of riding his bike over the railroad tracks near her house. All of it was gone in an instant as he envisioned himself back on the bricks at high speed. Turn one was the trick. If he lifted his foot, the record would be lost. Intuition spoke to him, placing a bet he could hold his big machine to the track long enough to trip the timing wire – and lay claim to that mile record. He could see himself do it.

Burrowing his eyes into the bricks where his left knee and right foot supported his body like pillars, Oldfield found an intense feeling of being absolutely present in the moment. The gritty, tiny particles of loosened cement seemed perfectly in place resting on the red-brown blocks. He brushed them with his gloved hand, the grains scattered to arrive at new, perfectly-in-place positions. A looming presence from behind drew him back. Still, he refused to hear the buzzing din from the grandstand, and he averted his eyes from those infernal, incessantly flapping flags that told a threatening story of currents gone awry.

"Whenever you're ready, Barney," came George Hill's pleasant, familiar voice.

Standing, Oldfield, clenched his teeth harder into his cheroot and nodded to his mechanic. No one would ride with him on the timed run. No need for the weight, no need for anyone to look back, no need for another life teetering on the knife's edge. Wagner gently gestured with his flag, and then said, "Take your time, Barney. Everyone is ready when you are."

From the judges' stand, Fisher studied the Speed King through his binoculars.

"What the Hell is he doing down there, praying, for Christ's sake?" Fisher asked.

"I'm not a praying man," said Wheeler. "But I sure as hell would have a talk with the Almighty if I had the gumption to charge into that southwest turn at better than a hundred miles an hour."

"There's no better man to give us what we need than Barney Oldfield," Fisher replied.

"He's got the experience, he's got the guts, the skill, and the most powerful car in the world. But what he really loves is attention and money. Go take a look at those telegraph operators on the first floor. They're tapping out stories the newspapermen are writing right here, including the Associated Press. We have sixty thousand people on our grounds, but that's just a fraction of the number following what we're doing here worldwide through telegraph wires and newspapers."

Oldfield slid into his seat at the wheel of the Blitzen Benz. With George Hill at the crank, he adjusted the spark lever, and the giant engine barked out its husky, healthy growl. The car was a beast, and Oldfield thrilled at manhandling it.

A signal to Wagner that he was ready and the starter's red flag flashed. Oldfield edged the mighty racer into gear, and it began to roll. Picking up his pace, he moved briskly past the judges' stand and Ernie Moross on the trackside platform hollering into his megaphone. Oldfield rapidly accelerated through turn one and the south-end short chute. By the time he was through turn two, his foot was to the floor and only just lifting to enter turn three. Not wanting to lose too much pace, he finessed his wheel to get through the northeast corner smoothly, and then apply the power just before the timing wire near the exit of turn four.

Fisher, Allison, Wheeler, and everyone fixed on the approaching pearl car with its brass bird-like beak. Trained on the Benz through his binoculars, Fisher heard the precision of the German engine's guttural rhythm as it approached his station.

Through the seat of his pants, Oldfield felt the steady clip of his tires over the edge of each brick he put behind him. Winds assaulted the Benz broadside as if a giant hand might brush it aside by several feet. It was no time to ease up, but turn one looked like a dead end as he hurtled toward it. He could not see around it but knew in detail what was there. In an instant, he was at his moment of truth. He twisted the white-taped wheel to slide through and round off the corner.

"Oh shit! It looks like he's losing control," shouted Wheeler as he observed Oldfield's deliberate slide.

In rounding off the corner, Oldfield eased his pace by scrubbing off speed with his gliding drift instead of lifting his right foot. Beyond the jaws of turn one, the Benz straightened with its driver pressing the accelerator as hard as if he was attempting to shove it through the floorboard. As he tripped the timing wire, Oldfield knew he had delivered as perfect a drive as any man could – and if it wasn't good enough, it wasn't worth taking another shot. Not today.

"He did it!" shouted Frank Trego at the timer. "Thirty-five and sixty-three hundredths of a second. That's better than half a second faster than his record at Playa Del Rey."

Uproarious cheers emanated from the judges' stand and, in the ensuing minutes, extended as a wave throughout the grandstand as Moross's barkers exclaimed the news. Fisher was outside himself with whoops, hoots, and squawks. He, Allison, and Wheeler were the first to shake one another's hands, all shrieking out their howls. Even Sam Butler was applauding and cheering, as was everyone around them – all the Triple-A men, all the newspapermen, as well as Blanche Scott and Jane Fisher – the only two women among the group. Scanning a speed chart nailed to one of the platform's support beams, Fisher searched for the speed associated with the mile time. It was nearly off the chart!

"Jesus Christ on a bicycle! Oldfield just ran the mile at better than one hundred and one miles per hour."

Oldfield raced down the backstretch, maintaining much of his breakneck pace. His gut told him he had busted the old mark, but he couldn't stand not knowing. He took the remaining two turns at a measured gait, especially at the exit of turn four, where he slowed to allow his brakes to be effective. Without hearing a word, Oldfield found his answer through the racous cheers in the grandstand. The Hill brothers were jumping up and down, and men tossed their hats. Even that fat ass Will Pickens appeared to have mustered an instant of daylight between his boots and the bricks.

Bringing the Benz to a halt at the platform in front of the judges' stand, he waved at Ernie Moross, who gave him a thumbs-up as he continued with his carnival barker routine. Fisher charged to his side with Allison, Wheeler, and a gaggle of newspapermen. George Bretzman and Ed Spooner stationed their tripods in front of the Benz, apparently waiting on a still moment to catch an image. Oldfield motioned for Moross to come near, and when the Contest Director did so, he grabbed his megaphone, rose in his seat, and yelled, "You know me, I'm Barney Oldfield!"

The Speedway founders each clasped their hands with the Speed King, shouting above the epicenter of the pandemonium to heap on the praise and inform him he had eclipsed one hundred and one miles per hour. Fisher repeated a fevered pronouncement, "Fastest racecourse in the world," to no one and everyone.

"Barney, you looked to have a close call entering turn one," said Peter Paul Willis. "What was going on?"

"I about shit my pants, but do you want something you can print?"

Everyone about him howled laughter.

"Okay, here goes," Oldfield resumed. "The track was undoubtedly several seconds slow under the wind conditions. Naturally, I'm greatly pleased to have lowered the record, but I believe I can still do better. I never saw the Brooklands track, but I do not believe there is a faster course in the world than the Indianapolis Motor Speedway, and I will not be satisfied until I have placed the world's record to the credit of an American. I hope to get another chance on the Indianapolis track under good conditions, and if I do, look for a big reduction in the time for the mile."

Led by Fisher, all the men applauded, with many shouting, "Hear! Hear!"

"Did I get it right, Carl?" Oldfield asked with a hearty chuckle.

"Barney, you damn sure got it right. You got everything right today."

(Indianapolis Motor Speedway, May 31, 1910)

As the days had been for nearly a week, it was another beautiful day in Indiana. As Carl Fisher took in the view of glorious sunshine and blue sky, the only clouds he saw came from the smoke that emanated from the tip of his La Corona. From his spot on the finish line of the Indianapolis Motor Speedway, the vitrified surface of the straightaway leading to turn one unfolded before him. Glancing down at his handmade, custom tan Italian shoes, he instinctively checked on the presence of a bulging oxblood leather satchel.

"Carl!" boomed the voice of Barney Oldfield.

Waving in acknowledgment, Fisher thanked the driver for meeting him as agreed in his call to his room at the downtown Claypool Hotel. This was the way to greet a champion, Fisher thought. This was the way to greet a man who had buckled down and delivered the goods.

"Welcome, Speed King!" Fisher began. "You are always welcome to the fastest Speedway in the world."

"You outdid yourself with this place, Carl. You really built something extraordinary."

"Barney, it could be said you had a hand in constructing this facility. I've always said you carried track racing on your back for years. When so many people back East were trying to kill it, you gave it life."

"Yeah, and it almost killed me a few times. It took a lot of other men down."

Both men fell silent for a moment, as if, without speaking a word, they were paying tribute to people they had both known, but were no longer among the living. In their quiet pause, the distant sounds of laborers clearing the grounds, tearing down exhibit tents, and cleaning the track's forty-one buildings became evident. Race crews could be heard at work, organizing their equipment and hitching cars to teams of horses to tow to the rail siding at the south end of the track. Oldfield stationed his boxcar there, and it was where the Hills cranked their pulleys to haul his Darracq and Blitzen Benz on board. Oldfield had also told them he wanted to find room for the gold-plated Overland he intended to present to Bess.

"Aren't you going to ask me what's in the satchel?" Fisher asked.

"It better be my money," Oldfield said with a wink.

Carl bent his knees only slightly, tilted his back, and stretched his right hand down to the leather handle. Handing it to Oldfield, he waited as the driver slung the leather strap over his shoulder and across his chest. The men shook hands as Oldfield patted the cowhide container.

"Feel heavy enough, Barney? There's a little extra in there. Consider it a gratuity. You earned it. Are you headed out to the Dead Horse Hill Climb? Newby's men and a lot of the other fellas are pointed in that direction."

"Nope. I'm headed out to the track in Kansas City. I go to the highest bidder, Carl, you know that. The promoters in Kansas tell me they can rustle up a big crowd to pay good money to get a gander at America's Speed King in his Blitzen Benz. What's next for you, Carl?"

"Lots!" Fisher exclaimed. "We have the biggest Aeroplane airshow coming up in just a couple of weeks, and a few weeks after that, another big Triple-A race meet around the Fourth of July."

Oldfield studied Fisher, and then his eyes swept over the enormity of the Speedway. Thinking of the little tracks with ridiculous thin wood railings and their muddy surfaces mixed with horse shit, the wonder of a modern speedway paved with millions of bricks and dozens of white and green buildings positioned throughout the grounds hardly seemed real. But there it was, looking all the more magnificent in the sun's golden coating.

"I mean beyond that, Carl. This place is big. It feels like it should be the home of something huge. Something nobody has dreamed of before."

Carl removed his spent cigar from between his lips and tossed it onto a brick before pulverizing it with a twist of his foot. He winked at Oldfield.

"I feel a hen coming on, Barney. I feel a hen coming on."

Author's Notes

The real-life characters in my book are listed below. Some make cameo appearances or are otherwise simply mentioned, while others have more substantive roles. With this, I want to underscore that this is a fact-based historical novel. There are no fictional characters aside from very minor figures used as devices to move through scenes.

Primary characters are Barney Oldfield (America's first grassroots racing star), Carl Fisher (the leading founder of the Indianapolis Motor Speedway), Ernie Moross (promoter), and Tom Cooper (Oldfield's closest friend).

Some of the following make more frequent appearances in the story than others. I organized them by their profession or role in society. You can search my free racing history Website, www.firstsuperspeedway.com, for additional information about many of these individuals.

Fisher's founding partners at the Indianapolis Motor Speedway: Arthur C. Newby, James Allison, and Frank Wheeler.

Other Fisher associates: Earle Fisher, Margaret Collier, Park Taliaferro Andrews, Lemon Trotter, Margaret Collier, Frank Moore, Rolla Fisher, Stoughton "Stoat" Fletcher, William Galloway.

Race drivers: Ray Harroun, Charles Schmidt, Dan Wurgis, Jules Sincholle, Gerard Papillion, Earl Kiser, Frank Day, Maurice Bernin, Bernard Shanley, Sam Stevens, Frank La Roche, Ed Hausman, J. Walter Christie, Charles Wridgeway, Alonzo Webb, Webb Jay, George Arents, Paul Sartori, Al Campbell, Fernand Gabriel, Herb Lytle, Albert Clement, George Heath, Wilhelm Werner, Frank Kulick, Louis Chevrolet, Charlie Basle, Leon Thery, Tom Kincaid, Howdy Wilcox, Johnny Aitken, Charlie Burnham, William "Billy" Bourque, Charlie Soules, Montague Roberts, George Robertson, Bert Dingley, Bob Burman, George DeWitt, Fred "Jap" Clemens, Charlie Merz, Carl Wright, Len Zengel, Ralph DePalma, Adolph Monson, Fred Ellis, Al Dennison, W.E. Wright, Ralph Mulford, Eddie Hearne, Tobin DeHymel, Charlie Burnham, Dan Wurgis, Victor Hemery, Walter Donnelly, Newell Motsinger, "Farmer" Bill Endicott, Hughie Hughes, David Bruce-Brown, Leigh Lynch, Bruce Keen, Charlie Merz, Claude Kellum, Caleb Bragg, Don Herr, Frank Fox, Frank Gelnaw, Arthur Chevrolet, George Clark, William Tousey, Leigh Lynch, Joe Dawson, Louis Schwitzer, Ben Kerscher, Hugh Harding, John Stickney, John Ryall.

Mechanics: Andy Anderson, Harold Rigby, Carl Mensel, George Hill, Jimmy Hill, Cliff Litterall, Joe Betts, Herb Lyne, Bill Healy, Harry Holcomb, Claude Kellum.

AAA race officials: Lewis Speare, Fred Wagner, Peter Prunty, Robert Lee Morrell, Sam Butler, Dave Beecroft, Charles Root, Art Pardington, Frank Trego, Charles Gillette, Frank Hower, George Cox, William Gotshall (ACA), David Hennen Morris (ACA).

Motorcycle racers: Ray Seymour, Stanley Kellogg, Ed Lingenfelder, Fred Huyck, Albert Gibney, Paul Koutowski, Jake DeRosier, J.F. Torney.

Motorcycle officials: Charles Wyatt, Harry Dipple, Earle Ovington.

Journalists: Peter Paul "P.P." Willis, C. E. "Heinie" Schuart, Harry Deupree, John Gerrie, Roland Mellett, Betty Blythe.

Photographers: George Bretzman, Ed Spooner, George Grantham Bain, Richard LeSesne.

Vanderbilt family: William K. Vanderbilt, Jr., Elsie French Vanderbilt, Alfred Vanderbilt, Virginia Vanderbilt, Alva Belmont, Consuelo Vanderbilt.

Winton Motor Carriage Company executives & family members: Alexander Winton, Helen Fea Winton, Charles Shanks, Elizbeth Shanks, John Jack, Percy Owen.

Sports figures beyond motor racing: World Champion Boxer Bob Fitzsimmons, World Champion Boxer Jim Jefferies, Eddie Bald (Bicycle racing champion), Sam Berger (Jeffries sparring partner), World Champion Boxer Jack Johnson.

Prest-O-Lite employees: Percy Avery, Frank Sweet, Claude Hess, John Lucky, Elmer Jessup, John Van Garder, Doc Ketterhenry (Pharmacist across the street).

Indiana government officials: Indiana Governor Thomas Marshall, Indianapolis Mayor Charles Bookwalter, Lieutenant Governor Frank J. Hall, Indianapolis Coroner John Blackwell, Charlie Coots (Indianapolis Fire Chief), Robert Metzger (Indianapolis Police Chief) John Weaver (Indianapolis police officer), Indianapolis Police Sergeant Metcalf, John Merz (Indianapolis police officer).

Balloonists: George Bumbaugh, John Berry, Paul McCullough, Alan Hawley, Charles Glidden, A. Holland Forbes, Burgess the farmer (assisted Fisher in landing his balloon in Tennesee).

Auto industry executives: Henry Ford, Harlan Whipple (Stearns), Colonel Albert Pope (Pope-Toledo), Cliff Myers (Diamond Tires), Frank Maney (Energine Gasoline), Guy Wall (National Motor Vehicle Company), George Dickson (National Motor Vehicle Company), Howard Marmon (Nordyke & Marmon), George Weidley (Premier), William "Billy" Durant (Buick), R.H. Losey (Indianapolis Buick dealer), Will Brown (Overland), Frank Matheson (Matheson Automobile Company), Harry Stutz (Ideal Motor Company), George Schebler (Wheeler-Schebler Carburetor Company), Charles Warner (inventor of the Warren electric timer), Frank Remy (Remy Magneto Company), Perry Remy (Remy Magneto Company), Charles Jeffery (G&J Tire Company), George Crane (Knox Automobile Company), Lou Mooers (Peerless).

Aristocrats: Gould Brokaw, Howard Gould, Jay Santos-Dumont, Clarence Gray Dinsmore, John Jacob Astor, Major Charles Miller, Augustus Post.

Promoters: William J. Morgan, William Hickman Pickens, Al Reeves, Ad Miller, "Diamond" Jim Brady, Jesse Froelich (Manager, New York Benz Import Company), Asa Candler (Coca-Cola founder), Hugh Donald "Huge Deal" McIntosh (Boxing promoter and race car owner), Jack Prince (Board track constructor).

Others: Admiral George Dewey, Jeanne Spaulding (aka Louise Alexander, stage actress & wife of Lewis Strang), "Red Hot" John (Food vendor and Oldfield friend), Dr. Burton Parker (Oldfield friend), Virginia Vernon (Tom Cooper girlfriend), Helen Lovett (Tom

Cooper friend).

Indianapolis Motor Speedway medical staff: Ola Slaughter (Nurse), Dr. Maxwell, Dr. Weyerbacher, and Dr. Fred Meyer, Henry Lawrence (Claypool Hotel manager), Ned Broadwell (Rainmaker), John Newby (Art Newby's father).

The following women are also mentioned in my preamble. Jane Watts Fisher (Carl's wife), opera singer Gertrude Hassler (his girlfriend), Bess Oldfield (Barney's wife), Helen Fea Winton (Alexander Winton's daughter), Betty Blythe (Indianapolis Star journalist, aka Marie Chomel), Blanche Scott (aviator and all-around daredevil), Sarah Oldfield (Barney's mother), and Carrie Coey (the first woman to ascend over the Indianapolis Motor Speedway in a balloon).

Throughout my life, I have consumed a vast quantity of information about auto racing and its history. Below is a list of books that informed my opinions, expanded my knowledge, and proved particularly relevant to this effort.

"Barney Oldfield, the Life and Times of America's Legendary Speed King," by William Nolan. "The Pacesetter, the Untold Story of Carl G. Fisher," by Jerry Fisher. "James Allison, a Biography of the Engine Manufacturer and Indianapolis 500 Cofounder," Sigur Whitaker. "Famous but Forgotten, the Story of Alexander Winton, Automotive Pioneer, and Industrialist," by Thomas Saal and Bernard Golias. "Saga of the Roaring Road," by Fred Wagner. "Fabulous Hoosier," by Jane Watts Fisher. "Indy: Racing Before the 500, the Untold Story of the Brickyard," by D. Bruce Scott.

My work to assist Howard Kroplick in preparing his book, "The Vanderbilt Cup Races of Long Island," provided an excellent education for me. I enjoyed it as our work progressed, but I did not fully appreciate how valuable it was for me to be a part of that project. I am grateful to Howard for the experience.